The Right Bride

Also by Jennifer Ryan

THE HUNTED SERIES
Saved by the Rancher
Lucky Like Us

The Right Bride

Book Three: The Hunted Series

JENNIFER RYAN

AVONIMPULSE
An Imprint of HarperCollinsPublishers

EPub Edition MAY 2013 ISBN: 9780062271341

Print Edition ISBN: 9780062271358

12

Acknowledgments

I can't tell you how exciting it is to have the third book in "The Hunted" series published. The stories may be mine, but the road to publication and my dream job includes help from friends.

Lucia Macro, my amazing editor, there are no words to tell you how much I appreciate everything you do. Your faith in me and my work is always encouraging. I love working with you.

Meeting my agent, Eric Ruben, was anything but conventional. It isn't often an editor calls an agent on your behalf and tells him he needs to sign you. Thank you Sue Grimshaw for everything. Most of all, thank you Eric for all your hard work and taking this ride with me.

Shout out for my writer friends. Whether it's a critique, plotting the next storyline, flushing out the holes in a story, or sitting around drooling over my next book cover, you guys are always there for me. My Rogue writer's group, especially Marina Adair, Hannah Jayne, Julie Bardard, and Lea Taddonio, to name a few, and my friend and critique partner, Jaclyn Di Bona. Thank you for sharing your time, your knowledge, and your never-ending encouragement. Marina, thanks for being my cheerleader and screaming on the phone with me. I love you guys.

Chapter One

SHELLY SWIPED THE lip gloss wand across her lips, rolled them in and out to smooth out the color, and grinned at herself in the mirror, satisfied with the results. She pushed up her boobs, exposing just enough flesh to draw a man's attention—and keep it—but still not look too obvious.

"Perfect. He'll love it."

Ah, Cameron Shaw. Rich and powerful, sexy as hell, and kind in a way that made it easy to get what she wanted. Exactly the kind of husband she always dreamed about marrying.

Shelly grew up in a nice, middle-class family. Ordinary. She desperately wanted to be anything but ordinary.

She'd grown up a plump youngster and a fat teenager. At fifteen, she resorted to bingeing and purging and starved herself thin. Skinny and beautiful, boys took notice. You can get a guy to do just about anything when you offer them hot sex. By the time she graduated high school, she'd transformed herself into the most popular girl in the class.

Destined to live a glamorous life in a big house with servants and fancy cars and clothes, meeting Cameron in the restaurant had been a coup. Executives and wealthy businessmen frequented the upscale restaurant. She'd gone fishing and landed her perfect catch. Now she needed to hold on and reel in a marriage proposal.

Chapter Two

NIGHT FELL OUTSIDE Cameron's thirty-sixth floor office window. Tired, he'd spent all day in meetings. As president of Merrick International, long hours were the norm and sleepless nights were a frequent occurrence.

The sky darkened and beckoned the stars to come to life. If he were out on the water and away from the glow of the city lights, he'd see them better, twinkling in all their brilliant glory.

He couldn't remember the last time he took out the sailboat. He'd promised Emma he'd take her fishing. Every time he planned to go, something came up at work. More and more often, he put her off in favor of some deal or problem that couldn't wait. He needed to realign his priorities. His daughter deserved better.

He stared at the picture of his golden girl. Emma was five now and the image of her mother. Long, wavy, golden hair and deep blue eyes, she always looked at him with such love. He remembered Caroline looking at him the same way.

They'd been so happy when they discovered Caroline was pregnant. In the beginning, things had been so sweet. They'd lay awake at night talking about whether it would be a boy or a girl, what they'd name their child, and what they thought he or she would grow up to be.

He never thought he'd watch his daughter grow up without Caroline beside him.

The pregnancy took a turn in the sixth month when Caroline began having contractions. They gave her medication to stop them and put her on bed rest for the rest of the pregnancy.

One night he'd come home to find her pale and hurting. He rushed her to the hospital. Her blood pressure spiked and the contractions started again. No amount of medication could stop them. Two hours later, when the contractions were really bad, the doctor came in to tell him Caroline's body was failing. Her liver and kidneys were shutting down.

Caroline was a wreck. He still heard her pleading for him to save the baby. She delivered their daughter six weeks early, and Caroline suffered a massive stroke and died without ever holding their daughter.

Cameron picked up the photograph and traced his daughter's face, the past haunting his thoughts. He spent three weeks in the neonatal intensive care unit grieving for his wife and begging his daughter to live. Week four had been a turning point. He felt she'd spent three weeks grieving the loss of her mother and decided to live for her father. She began eating on her own and gained weight quickly. Ten days later, Cameron finally took his daughter home. From then on, it had been the two of them.

Almost a year ago, he decided enough was enough. Emma needed a mother. He'd dated several women since Caroline's death. More so, he took a few women to bed and felt no emotional connection to any of them. They provided a physical release. Nothing more than empty encounters between two consenting adults. Perhaps that's what made him feel emptier each time. He didn't want to examine it too closely. It hurt too much, this loneliness.

He didn't know if he was capable of giving anything more than his body to any woman anymore. It hurt too much to have his heart ripped out of his chest when Caroline died. He figured there was literally nothing left of it.

The women knew it, understood it, and took what they could get from him. No shortage of women who wanted to be seen with him, sleep with him, enjoy the money he had, and casually slip away when the time came. The problem with that was none of them would make a good mother to Emma.

He hadn't lost his head over a woman since Caroline until a month ago. He'd had a hard day and ended up right here, sitting in his office looking out at the night and thinking about Caroline and how much he missed her. He'd drowned himself in her memory and what it felt like to be her husband and to love her and be loved.

He'd gone downstairs to Decadence to have dinner alone at his reserved table. When he'd entered the restaurant, he'd seen a woman at the bar who reminded him so much of Caroline that he almost believed it was her. He struck up a conversation, and they'd ended up going at it on the sofa in his office. It had been the one and only time he'd lost his head that way.

When it was over and he'd realized what he'd done, he apologized to the woman and offered to drive her home. She'd made things easy and asked him to dinner.

So began his relationship with the blond beauty, Shelly Ramsey. They'd been seeing each other regularly for a month. He took her to several charity benefits and social functions he attended for business purposes. So far, they enjoyed each other's company.

He scheduled dinner with Shelly and Emma downstairs at Decadence and awaited his daughter's arrival. He stared at the picture of Emma again and wondered if it was too soon to introduce her to a woman he was seeing.

He thought about Shelly. Nice, well spoken, and beautiful, if not too made up at times. Caroline often made jokes about herself to make others feel comfortable around her. Shelly didn't have a sense of humor about herself. She took things too personally.

The more Cameron thought about Shelly, the more he realized his interest in her ran more to her resemblance of Caroline. The longer he spent with her, the more he realized her looks weren't enough to keep him interested.

Always nice to him, but not necessarily to others. That was a problem for Cameron. At every business function they attended, Caroline went out of her way to befriend everyone. She was a warm fire on a cold night. Everyone wanted to gather around and feel her warmth. He missed that about her. He'd bask in the praise and compliments about what a wonderful woman he'd snagged. They'd tell him how lucky he was and how they thought she was great. He hadn't needed anyone to tell him he was lucky. He knew it.

So far, Shelly hadn't shown that side of herself. If she even had it in her. He sometimes suspected some sort of hidden agenda.

Cameron sighed and put the picture of his daughter back on the corner of his desk and considered himself a royal jackass. Yeah, the sex was good, but he spent the whole time pretending Shelly was his wife. After the first time, he hadn't lost his head quite so completely. In fact, now he could take it or leave it. He chalked Shelly up to supreme stupidity and a deep longing for his dead wife.

He wished he'd realized Shelly was just a substitute for Caroline before he'd agreed to introduce her to his daughter. Emma would arrive any second, and he couldn't cancel now.

He continued to stare out the window at the ocean in the far distance. A row of lights appeared very small on the water. A ship, lights lining the mast. He imagined a sailboat and wished he were aboard right now.

MARTI STARED OUT across the water and sighed. She loved the ocean, the sound, the smell, the solitude, and most of all, the sheer size of it. You could lose yourself out here on the wide-open sea. She had for the past year, and now it was time to find herself back on land.

The saltwater spray swept up from the bow and misted her face. Her last day on the ship; tomorrow she arrived in nearby San Francisco.

She'd seen the world from the ocean and from port to port. She'd explored every wonderful place she'd ever dreamed of visiting: England, Ireland, France, Greece, Italy, Egypt, Fiji, Brazil, Chile, Australia, Japan, China. Everywhere her heart desired, she'd gone and explored.

Some people dreamed of a trip around the world and never did because they couldn't afford to, or just didn't take the time. Three hundred and sixty-five days at sea. On day three hundred and sixty-six, she'd dock in San Francisco, sign the estate papers at the lawyer's office, and make a life on dry land—alone. Her heart ached over the loss of her grandmother, and soon the sea.

She'd rather not go back to the city, but the year was up and she'd fulfilled her grandmother's last wishes. How could she refuse such a wonderful request? But she couldn't spend the rest of her life sailing from port to port. She wanted to, but needed to get back to her life. Actually, she had to start her life. She was ready to stay in one place for a while and make some friends.

"Marti, we've dropped sail and anchored for the night. The fog's rolling in and we should get settled. What time do you want to get underway and drop anchor in the bay in the morning?"

"Let's not make it early," she said over her shoulder to her trusted captain. "How about eleven? I can watch the sun come up and spend a quiet morning with you and the crew. It'll be our last breakfast together for a while."

"You look sad. It's been quite an adventure, wouldn't you say?"

Captain Finn understood her reluctance to leave the ship and begin an unfamiliar life.

"A grand adventure. I'm going to miss it as much as you salty dogs."

"I think we can call you a salty dog after a year of sailing. You handle this ship as well as anyone. You make a great mate."

"I learned from the best." She smiled to let him know how much she appreciated him for treating her like a part of the crew and not keeping some sort of boundary between them because she was technically the boss. "How long until dinner?"

"A few minutes. We're set up on the back deck."

"Perfect. We'll watch the fog roll in and play our last poker game."

"Will the men keep their money for shore leave?"

"They may just leave with a bonus tonight." She winked and he laughed.

An experienced card sharp, she'd make sure all the men left with her money.

Captain Finn caught her looking longingly at the water. "She'll still be here come tomorrow night when you're tucked into some hotel room. Stay aboard."

"I have things to do. I need to find a place to live on dry land. If I stay on the ship, I'll only want to sail away again."

"I understand and know just how you feel." He belonged to the sea and she was cut from the same cloth. "The ocean, she calls to you, but you have to find your way now that Sofia is gone. She gave you a gift, Marti. She would be proud to see you embraced it with your whole heart. I've never seen anyone take to the open water like you, or enjoy the adventure of exploring a new land with such enthusiasm. She understood your spirit."

"Yes. She did. She left me in good hands too. You and the crew have been wonderful to me. I couldn't have gotten through the first few weeks without your kindness."

"Kindness was easy to give to someone like you. You earned my respect, and that of the crew, when you insisted on becoming a sailor. Your Uncle Anthony doesn't deserve either kindness or respect from you. Remember that tomorrow and all the days after that. He'll come after you. He wants what Sofia gave you."

"Did he call?"

"This morning. We told him you went diving and couldn't be reached." He gave her one of his lopsided smiles.

"You tell him that every time he calls."

"It's been true a time or two." Captain Finn's mouth tilted up in an unapologetic grin.

"Thank you, Captain Finn, for everything."

"I loved your grandmother. I've taken her all over the world and watched her create some of her masterpieces. And now I've had the pleasure to take you around the world and watch you do the same in your own way."

Marti thought fondly of her grandmother, the world-famous painter. Her paintings hung in galleries and museums all over the world. She'd taught Marti how to paint from the time she was old enough to hold a brush. A smile touched her mouth at the sweet memories. How she'd loved painting with her grandmother.

Marti was an accomplished artist in her own right, but the public wouldn't know it. She'd never shown one of her paintings to anyone. To her grandmother's frustration, Marti painted for herself. Truth be told, she was scared to death to let anyone see her paintings and compare them to her grandmother's masterpieces.

Marti kept her talents on an anonymous level, writing and illustrating her own series of children's books. She wrote the series under a pen name. No one except her publisher knew the author was the granddaughter of one of the greatest painters in the world. Marti hoped she'd get to keep the secret. A hope she knew wouldn't come true. No secret stayed hidden forever.

"I only wish she could have made this journey with you," the captain said.

"I've wished the same since we left. She watched over us. I know she did." Marti gazed up at the darkening sky, the stars beginning to wink and twinkle to life.

Captain Finn walked back across the deck behind her.

Tomorrow would be a new beginning and facing it alone scared her. Instead of looking out at the ocean and the fog about to envelope them, she turned to the land and the city by the bay. San Francisco was lit up in the distance. She stared at those lights and wondered what all those people were doing right then. Working in their offices, going out for a night on the town, spending an evening with someone they loved, their family and friends. Maybe they were lonely like her and wishing to have something more in their lives.

Tomorrow she'd become a part of that world. Tonight, she belonged to the sea.

She stared out across the water to one of the tall buildings reaching up to the stars. For the first time, she felt as if something, or someone, was drawing her back.

CAMERON WAITED FOR his daughter to arrive, dreading the evening ahead. He watched the ship on the water, drawn to it like a beacon.

Chapter Three

"DADDY, DADDY, JIMMY let me put the window up and down in the car and have a soda while we drove here."

Jimmy walked in behind his little munchkin and put his hands on his hips and glared down at her. "You weren't supposed to tell."

"You didn't say not to." Emma beamed the big man a smile and threw her arms around his leg and gazed up at him. "It was so cool. I pretended I was a movie star."

She struck a pose and Jimmy and Cameron both laughed.

"How's my golden girl today?" Cameron turned his thoughts away from the sailboat out his window and the lost dreams of his beloved wife.

"I'm hungry. Can we go see Aunt Elizabeth now? Maybe she'll let me make something in the kitchen."

Aunt Elizabeth was married to his boss's brother-in-law. Cameron had become close with Jenna when she took over as CEO of Merrick International several years ago and made him president. Emma was just a baby. He and Emma had moved into a penthouse next door to Jenna and her husband, Jack.

Jack's brother, Sam, lived with Jenna and Jack at the time and they all spent many evenings together, especially after Jenna gave birth to her twin sons. Emma and the boys were close. They were all like one big happy family now. Emma thought of all of them as her aunts and uncles and cousins.

After marrying Sam, Elizabeth opened her restaurant on the first floor of the Merrick International building. Elizabeth was like a little sister who nagged him to eat right and "Don't forget dessert". He loved her like a sister and loved her more for treating Emma like her own.

Emma especially loved playing with Elizabeth and Sam's daughter, Grace. Emma thought the baby was as close to a little sister as she'd ever have. He wanted a mother, a complete family for Emma, but realized she had a close family of sorts.

"Aunt Elizabeth is expecting you and mentioned something about brownies tonight."

"Really?" Emma bounced up and down on her toes, her hands held in front of her like a prayer. "She'll let me make the brownies?"

"You'll have to eat all your dinner. But yes, you get to make the brownies."

"Awesome." Emma ran and jumped into his lap. She gave him a hug and a kiss on the cheek.

"I wondered how long I'd have to wait for you to give your old man some love."

"You aren't old." She stared at his face. "Not really. You're just tired. You should take a nap."

"A nap, huh. You think it will make me look younger?"

"No, I think it will make you not be grumpy."

Jimmy smiled. "She's got you there. Um, your guest is downstairs and she isn't happy about waiting. Elizabeth said you better come down or she's going to put Super Glue in her martini to shut her up."

Cameron frowned over his daughter's head. Why the hell was Shelly downstairs drinking when she was having dinner with him and Emma?

"Emma, remember I told you we're having dinner with my friend?"

"Yes." She dragged out the word with melodramatic exasperation, like only a five-year-old (or teenager) could do. "You told me last night and two times this morning. I'm five, not three. I can remember what you said."

Cameron held back the laugh. His shoulders shook with the effort.

"Of course you can, sweetheart. I want you on your very best behavior. Shelly has been looking forward to meeting you and . . ."

And he didn't want to introduce them, but couldn't get out of it now. He'd just have to do it and see how Emma responded. He'd cooled toward Shelly, but maybe she'd redeem herself and show an interest in Emma.

Maybe one day he'd stop looking for Caroline in every woman he met.

He let his thoughts run away. Back to the past, and here and now, where every woman was dull and flat and never sparked anything more than a quick flash. This meeting had better turn out well. He didn't want to disappoint his daughter or upset her in any way.

He wasn't sure what her expectations might be in meeting a woman he dated. She might think it meant more than it did. His fault. He'd spent last night and this morning telling Emma all about Shelly and her many good qualities.

He might have embellished a bit and told a few white lies. Again, he felt like a supreme jackass.

Irritable, he clipped out, "Let's go."

"Maybe we should go home, so you can take a nap. You're grumpier than normal."

He scooped up his daughter and headed for the elevator.

"I'm just hungry. Maybe I'll have you for an appetizer." He lifted her, pressed his mouth to her belly and blew on her stomach to make her laugh. Just being with her made him feel lighter and overshadowed his dark thoughts.

Chapter Four

"AUNT ELIZABETH, I want to make the brownies now." Emma tugged on her skirt.

Elizabeth stood beside the table of one of her most prominent guests. The restaurant was popular with the well-to-do, executives, and the office workers in and around the Merrick International building. Elizabeth had a very popular—and often very overrun—bakery several blocks away. Brides-to-be stalked her in hopes of having her make their wedding cakes.

Cameron was like a brother. She loved Emma as much as her own daughter, Grace. Since Emma didn't have a mother, she and Jenna often took over some of the more motherly duties, like baking with the child and sharing girl talk. Elizabeth often wished Cameron would find a nice woman to settle down with so that Emma would have a mother.

Until that day, Elizabeth and Jenna were surrogate

mothers. They couldn't be happier to fill the position until Cameron found someone to share his life with, someone who also loved Emma the way they all did.

Elizabeth looked down at the little girl with the grown-up eyes and the wisdom of an eighty-year-old trapped in a five-year-old's body.

"Emma, I'd like to introduce you to Mr. and Mrs. Stanford."

Emma turned to the two older people at the table. She held tight to Elizabeth's hand and said, "Hello. I'm pleased to meet you."

"Pleased to meet you too." Mrs. Stanford smiled warmly.

"You should have the chicken and pasta Florentine with garlic and butter sauce. It's my favorite. Aunt Elizabeth makes the best dessert. You should have some pie with ice cream. I haven't made the brownies yet, but maybe they'll be done before it's time for your dessert."

Mr. and Mrs. Stanford turned to Elizabeth. "We'll have Emma's recommendation."

Emma beamed a smile. "I'm supposed to eat dinner with my daddy and his friend, but she's boring. She's only being nice to him because he's the president. I think you should be nice to people no matter what, don't you?"

The couple smiled at the little girl with the insight of an adult. "Yes, dear. It shouldn't matter if he's president."

Elizabeth explained, "Her father is the president of Merrick."

The couple nodded their understanding.

Elizabeth smiled at her guests in a silent thank you for humoring the little girl. "Dinner will be out soon. Enjoy your meal."

She led Emma toward the kitchen. "You handled that like a master hostess. I might hire you."

Emma beamed. "I like it here."

"I like having you here. Let's stop at your dad's table and get his order before we make the brownies. Everything is ready in the back."

"The lady keeps touching Daddy and smiling at him, but she doesn't do it like you touch Uncle Sam. Do you know what I mean?"

"Yes, honey. I know what you mean."

Emma knew what love looked like between a man and a woman. She'd watched her and Sam together and Jenna and Jack together. It spoke volumes she didn't see those kinds of feelings between Cameron and Shelly.

Sharp, nothing got past Emma. Elizabeth had often admired the little girl's ability to sum up a person upon meeting them.

Elizabeth might have to talk to Cameron about Shelly and Emma's reaction to her. Cameron should know his daughter had Shelly's number. Elizabeth hoped Cameron had it too.

"Daddy, I found Aunt Elizabeth and I got to be a hostess."

"Darlin', I'm speaking with your father. It's not polite to interrupt," Shelly insisted meeting Cameron's daughter. She wanted to make a good impression. Cameron seemed so devoted to the little girl, so Shelly figured if she showed an interest in her too, he'd keep his interest in her.

She might have miscalculated, thinking Emma would stay out of the way and be quiet. Instead, she'd been rude and tried to dominate her father's attention. Shelly wasn't going to play second fiddle to a five-year-old.

Cameron heard the reprimand for his daughter's interruption. She didn't raise her voice, even sounded like a mother teaching her child a lesson, but still something bothered him. He let it slide and scooped Emma onto his lap and kissed her cheek.

"Hi, Elizabeth."

"I'm taking Emma in the back to make brownies. What would you like for dinner? Your usual, Cameron?"

"Sounds great."

"I'll have the filet and lobster dinner." Shelly cocked her head to one side and asked, "Are you sure you should take Emma into the kitchen? She could get into a lot of trouble back there. It's a lot of work keeping your eye on kids. At least that's what I'm told."

Not the kind of work Shelly was interested in performing. Elizabeth imagined the only work Shelly performed happened on her back, conniving to extract money from whatever male was on top of her at the time.

Shelly ordered the most expensive items on the menu and took little interest in Emma, except to criticize her. Elizabeth felt sorry for Cameron. He had the worst taste in women or, more accurately, he chose women who didn't make him feel anything besides lust. Shelly was the worst possible choice for him.

Cameron had gone too long without being loved. Elizabeth wondered if he remembered what it felt like to have someone love you above all else. Sure he had Emma, but it wasn't the same as being loved by a partner. She sighed and felt sorry for him. He had everything going for him, and yet he hadn't found someone who saw beyond the trappings of his life to the man who loved his daughter and wanted to be loved by a woman. Maybe the right person would show up before Shelly sunk in her claws and made Cameron's life worse.

She looked at Shelly and remembered her comment about Emma being in the kitchen. She'd just bet Shelly was happy to have Cameron to herself and Emma out of the way, no matter what she said to the contrary.

"Emma will be just fine with me. I'll get your dinners ready. How about some fresh drinks? Another martini, Shelly? Ice tea, Cameron?"

"That would be lovely. It's been such a trying day." Shelly did her best to look overwhelmed. Elizabeth held back the roll of her eyes at the melodramatic tone.

Elizabeth made a show of looking at Shelly's empty martini glass and back at Cameron. Shelly already finished two martinis; the next would be her third in an hour. "I'm sure it has been. I'll have your drinks sent over. Emma and I will be in the kitchen if you need us."

Alone again, Shelly confronted Cameron. "You seem close to her. She's very beautiful. Every time we come in here she treats you . . . special."

Shelly didn't want to say Elizabeth treated Cameron like they'd once shared a bed; maybe they still did, and that's why Elizabeth was so close to Cameron. She knew what he liked to eat. She talked to him like they had a history, and she treated Emma like she was her own daughter. Maybe they had a relationship and that's why Emma called her "Aunt".

"Elizabeth is like a sister to me. She's Jenna Turner's sister-in-law. Jenna and Elizabeth are married to twin brothers, Jack and Sam."

"Jenna the CEO. Wow." She scanned the expensive and lavishly decorated restaurant. "It must be nice to have an in with the owner of the Merrick International building. Elizabeth didn't do too bad for herself marrying into the Turner family and the Merrick wealth."

Cameron took exception. Elizabeth worked hard and was a great restaurant owner. Her bakery alone was renowned. The fact that Shelly assumed Elizabeth would use her marriage to Sam to get something from Jenna just showed how shallow she really was.

Cameron had made a huge mistake. It kept getting thrown in his face what a jackass he'd been for a piece of ass who reminded him of Caroline. Maybe he was just as shallow as Shelly, since he'd obviously looked past her mind and used her solely for the purpose of a face and body that looked like his former wife's.

"Elizabeth is Judge Hamilton's daughter. She runs this business and Decadence Bakery because she likes to, and because she's good at it. She didn't need Jenna's help to start this restaurant. She already had the bakery. She did it as a favor to Jenna. It's part of my perks that I get to eat here whenever I want. A few of the other executives have a standing table too."

"Well, you do know some interesting, wealthy, and influential people. Never hurts to be friends with a judge's daughter. Not to mention the Hamilton fortune. Wow. I completely misjudged Elizabeth."

The misjudgment was in how wealthy and influential Elizabeth was and had nothing to do with how nice and kind she was. He ran his hand over the back of his neck and tried to work out some of the tension.

"Listen, Shelly, we need to talk."

Shelly didn't like Cameron's definite brush-off tone.

"Cameron, darling. This night hasn't turned out like you hoped. I want so much to spend time with your Emma. She's such a pretty and smart girl. Too bad she had her heart set on helping in the kitchen. I'm sure if we spend some time together, we'll be fast friends." Cameron gave her a skeptical look and she went on quickly, "How about dinner again tomorrow? She can't possibly get to know me in just one night. She probably sees me as a rival for your affections and doesn't want to give me a chance. Let's try again tomorrow and see how it goes."

Cameron didn't want to put his daughter through another dinner, but Shelly seemed so intent on getting to know Emma. He didn't know what to do. He rubbed his hand over the back of his neck again.

"Come to my place tonight. I'll wear the pink negligee you like so much. We'll have a wonderful evening together and it'll take the tension right out of your neck," she said and cocked her head, indicating his action.

He dropped his hand and grabbed his ice tea. He liked the pink negligee. It was exactly like one Caroline had worn for him. The color made her skin look like porcelain and her golden hair glow. The pink made her eyes look deeper blue, the blue of the greatest depths of the ocean.

Cameron thought about the sailboat he'd seen in the distance from his office window earlier and wished again to be onboard, putting out to sea.

"Fine, we'll have dinner again tomorrow. If I know Emma, she'll be in the kitchen through the rest of dinner."

"That's wonderful, darling." She brightened her words with excitement, even though she could care less about another dinner with the child. It was the man she wanted, and a proposal. The sooner the better.

"You know how important you are to me. I want a chance to show you Emma and I can be close."

She almost choked on the word. The only person she wanted close to her was Cameron. Well, Cameron and his bank account and big penthouse, and the lovely limo and driver, and all the other perks she'd have at her disposal when she became his wife. He was having second thoughts about their relationship. Even the sex had tapered off. They hadn't made love in over a week. She needed to keep him interested. He liked that damn negligee because it reminded him of his dead wife. She didn't care so much, as long as she ended up with the ring in the end.

She needed to come up with a plan, because if tomorrow night didn't go well, she'd lose her ticket to easy street, and that would not do.

Chapter Five

MARTI CONSIDERED THE rain fitting for her last morning onboard her beloved ship. She felt as gloomy as the day.

Captain Finn would see to it her packed bags arrived at the Four Seasons. She had her backpack ready with all the folders and papers she needed for her meeting with her grandmother's attorney. She didn't want to go to the meeting, but she didn't have a choice. She'd fulfilled her grandmother's last request, and now she'd have to sit through the reading of her will.

The terms of the will dictated Marti take the yearlong trip before the final settlement of the estate. Although her grandmother requested the trip be for one year, Marti could end the trip at any time for whatever reason. She designated the ports of call and stayed in any one place as long as she liked. Her grandmother simply asked she take a year to see the world. Marti did just that and saw everything she possibly could in that short time. Everywhere she wanted to visit, she went with an eager heart. Many times the ship had sat in dock for weeks while she traveled inland by train or plane. She had the experience of a lifetime. Exactly what her grandmother wanted for her only grandchild.

Marti understood the trip was to repay her for being virtually trapped in San Francisco with an ailing grandmother. She'd taken care of Sofia for five years, since the time she was seventeen. Her grandmother took ill and become very frail. She spent much of her time in bed due to a bad heart. Any strain could set off another attack and leave her in bed for months.

Raised privileged, they employed a maid and cook, but Marti had been taught from an early age that her grandparents expected her to learn to take care of herself.

Her grandfather had been a hard man. She learned to get around him and his cantankerous ways. In the end, he loved her without having to say he did. She knew she was loved, even when he was ranting about a paper she'd written for school, or a position she'd taken on an issue. He loved to discuss business and politics over dinner and, ornery kid that she was, she often took up the opposing side just to set him off. He knew it, she knew it, and they enjoyed the exchanges. Her grandmother often joined in—on Marti's side, of course—and the two of them would drive her grandfather nuts for an hour.

Her grandmother spent a great deal of her good days painting and teaching Marti to paint. They'd often set up their easels in the solarium and paint for hours.

She'd attended college through correspondence

courses. When her grandmother was well, she'd attended classes at the University of San Francisco and Stanford.

A promise fulfilled for her grandfather, she graduated with a double major in business management and finance. Not her first choice, even if she did have an aptitude for it. She'd finished it because her grandfather had wanted her to have a secure future.

Her grandmother had taken care of her art education and her grandfather her business education. She'd used what she'd learned from both and found an outlet for her varied skills.

She sat on the board of her grandfather's company along with her uncle. Often in direct opposition to her uncle's agenda. More often than not, when she really took a stand against a business decision, the board backed her and let her take the brunt of her uncle's displeasure. She didn't mind. She was usually right, and when she was wrong, the other board members let her know it and why. She'd learned a lot serving on the board. Many of her classmates had been jealous she had such a prominent position even before she graduated.

Her grandfather appointed her to the board upon his death. The board had approved her grandfather's appointment because of her inheritance of his shares in the company. Actually, she inherited half the shares and the other half went to her uncle. Together they held controlling interest.

Although her uncle inherited part of the company, he wasn't happy she controlled the rest of the estate. Sofia's paintings alone were worth millions, and Uncle Anthony wanted them. He'd sell them for easy cash when his penchant for gambling got out of hand.

The other assets were property and trusts and financial accounts her grandfather amassed over his seventy years on this earth. Her grandparents had left her in charge of everything, knowing their oldest son would either squander it away or mismanage it until nothing was left. The only thing he had control over was the company. Because he answered to the board, and the other executives did the majority of the work, her uncle sat back and collected his sizeable paycheck and did as he pleased.

Most of the time he just liked to make her life miserable, because he felt like she'd stolen his birthright. After all, she was just a woman. What did she know about running a company and managing an estate the size of the one her grandparents left behind?

She didn't care about the money. She cared that it allowed her to have nice things and the education she'd promised her grandfather. She had the money left to her by her parents. She didn't need to have her grandparents' estate too. In fulfilling their wishes, she'd managed to find her own way of making money that allowed her to dabble in the business world and use her artistic ability. She loved creating her books and getting them published. It was her way of honoring both her grandparents and her parents.

She stood on deck and surveyed all the boats in the harbor. Her ship was so large it had to remain anchored away from the docks. Captain Finn finished launching the zodiac and hollered for her to hurry up. She looked around the deck one last time and out to sea and silently said her goodbye.

She'd take short trips, but it wouldn't be the same as living on board and being out to sea for months. She promised herself she wouldn't let time slip away before she set sail again. She realized that was her grandmother's intention for the trip. Marti had let five years slip away. It was for a good reason, taking care of her grandmother, but life had gone on for others while hers stood still.

She wouldn't let it happen again. She had plans. Unfortunately, those plans couldn't begin until she met with the lawyers.

Chapter Six

MARTI MADE HER way past all the boats and down the branching docks. The rain pelted her head and shoulders, soaking through her overcoat and drenching her hair. Water slid down her neck from the hair plastered to her face. Not the day to forget her umbrella on the dining table and remember it halfway to shore when the sky opened up. Too late now.

She caught a glimpse of something down the long pier and turned to investigate the strange sight. Suspicious, she wondered what a man dressed in a suit was doing out in this storm.

Without a second thought, she walked down the pier and casually leaned her back against the railing while she stood next to the obviously distressed man. The wind sent sheets of rain down upon her head and against her back. She braced herself against the wind and looked up over her shoulder at the man standing on the second bar of the railing, leaning over into the wind.

"Nice day, don't you think? Personally, I love a good storm. The rain washes away the grime. Makes the day seem fresh. I'm Marti, by the way," she shouted over the storm to the old man.

In his seventies, pale and frail, his suit was expensive, like he worked in an executive office. A definite distinguished look about him, he reminded her of her grandfather with his air of superiority, strength, and wisdom. She sensed he also had a kind heart beneath the disillusioned look on his face and in his eyes.

"You shouldn't be out in the rain like this, young lady."

The reprimand surprised her, as did his no-nonsense tone.

"I don't suppose it's a good idea, but I do love a good storm. I just got back from a long trip and I have a meeting to get to, but I thought I'd join you. You look like a fellow storm enthusiast."

"I'm just ... Oh hell, I'm being stupid." With a deep frown, he continued to watch the wild, white-capped waves raging by. Despite the cold, a flush of color brightened his cheeks. "I don't know what I was thinking coming out here. I didn't really think anything through, to tell you the truth. Do you have any idea what it's like to have a family who only wants to get what you have? They have no respect for a man's life's work. They just want to take the things and the money and use it to make their lives better. They don't realize without being happy in the first place and on their own, the money and the things will only cause them more trouble."

He shook his head and stared out across the bay. "And who says I have to leave it to them. They think just because I'm sick they can come in and take over. I'm old. I'm not dead yet."

She smiled and held back a laugh at his disgruntled tirade. He climbed down from the railing and stood facing the water. She turned and put her arms up on the railing, matching him, hoping he continued to open up about his problems instead of solving them in the worst way.

"I have an idea of what you're talking about. My uncle would like nothing better than to turn my grandparents' estate into his personal money pool he can squander away in the hopes of becoming a happy person. Since he can't get his hands on it, he's made it his mission to make my life hell."

"Do you think I did something wrong in raising my son and daughter in a way they can't see past the money to find a life for themselves? They're obsessed with having things. The easier it is for them to have it, the more they want."

"I think it's the double-edged sword of being a part of a wealthy family," she agreed. "There are those who are selfish and can only want for more, and then there are the few who see wealth and privilege as a responsibility and a kind of challenge to keep what's been passed down. Those few want to put their mark on the family history and the world. For them, it isn't about the money."

"You're an interesting woman. I didn't think another living soul understood my circumstances. So, which are you?"

"Definitely one of the few. My grandmother said I was unique. In a world where I was surrounded by wealth and privilege, I was more concerned about people than possession. They raised me as they did my uncle and father. My father was like me, one of the few, and my uncle was one of the many, who believe being born privileged gives them the right to the wealth. Even if they've never worked for it or done anything more than be born, they think they're entitled.

"Sorry." She frowned and stared across the swelling waves and into nothing. "You caught me on a day when I have to face my uncle across a conference-room table and listen to the reading of my grandmother's will. I'll have to spend the rest of the afternoon listening to my uncle argue every point."

"She left everything to you, I take it."

"No. But it won't matter to my uncle. He believes just because he was born of her flesh, he should have it all. I'm just the granddaughter, after all. Even more heinous, I'm just a woman." Sarcasm dripped from every word, and she rolled her eyes. "In his mind, I've already gotten much more than I deserve from my parents' estate and from my grandfather."

"Have you gotten more than you deserve?" he asked, genuine interest in his tone.

She cocked her head and thought about it. "Hard to say. I have more than I'll ever spend." She shrugged and let her thoughts roll off her tongue. "I look at it in a different way. I got what I have because I don't have my parents. They were killed when I was three. I'd give it all back to have them. I got more because my grandfather died. I'd give it back to have that grumpy old man fight with me over dinner about the latest business coup or political race. Whatever my grandmother left me will never take the place of the hours I spent painting with her, or the intangible gifts she's given to me that can't be quantified."

He heard the words, but more importantly he heard the love. She loved her parents and her grandparents and he had no doubt what she was saying was true. She'd give it all back to have them with her again. His children probably couldn't, wouldn't say the same.

"You know, I came out here because the doctors all say I don't have much time left. The family has been up in arms and making life miserable. I thought I'd just go for a sail on my friend's boat and sleep with the fishes. It would serve them right to wonder what happened to me and have to wait for my body to wash up somewhere, if it ever did. The lawyers would tie up my estate for a long time if I did."

He looked out over the water again. "The storm kept me from one fate and brought me another. The captain I hired said he wouldn't take me out. Too dangerous. Can you imagine what I thought about that? It's too dangerous to sail an old man out to sea so he can kill himself.

"I figured the waves here at the pier were rough enough they'd either carry me out to sea, or I'd just drown right here in the harbor. You came along and made me think maybe I should rethink my troubles. You're an interesting woman, Marti. You're a woman I'd like to get to know better. Would you consider having dinner with an old man like me? I'll even argue with you about politics and business deals if it pleases you."

"Nothing would please me more, mister . . ."

"Knight, George Knight."

She smiled and leaned up on tiptoe and kissed his cheek. "We have a lot to talk about, Mr. Knight, for you are my grandfather's most worthy adversary. I'm Martina Fairchild, granddaughter to Sofia and Martin Fairchild, founder and once CEO of Fairchild Industries. How fares Knight Enterprises?"

Fate had a way of working in mysterious ways. He hadn't been able to sail on Cameron's boat, and none other than his old enemy's granddaughter had saved him. Granted he and Marty Fairchild were long-time business rivals and had spent a great deal of time and energy pretending to dislike one another. In actuality, they had been reluctant friends because they'd admired each other's determination and business prowess.

"Marti, you must call me George. Your grandfather told me stories about you from the time you were born. I saw you grow up through his eyes, and whenever I'd see you at a function. He was so proud of you. I think he talked about you more than he talked about your father or uncle combined."

"He was an amazing man. I think we argued strategy against Knight Enterprises over many a meal."

"You were named for him?"

She smiled. A funny story, one only appreciated fully by someone who knew her grandfather well. To say he was proud to have sired two boys was an understatement.

Ending up with a granddaughter instead of a grandson was unthinkable. Even more unthinkable, him raising that girl child.

The man born to a family of eight boys had no idea how to raise a girl. The thought never occurred to him that he'd ever have a daughter or granddaughter. And yet she, Marti, had become both to him.

"I was somewhat jokingly named after him. When he arrived at the hospital to see my mother after I was born, he came into the room and asked to see his grandson. It never occurred to him he'd be cursed with a granddaughter."

"He would think that, wouldn't he? He was a man among men. Everything about him was male, right down to his chauvinism."

George thought he had some old-fashioned values, but he thought children were a blessing, no matter what their gender.

Disappointing, when the blessing of children turned sour and they grew to be their own people. His children had proven it. Well, except for one. But he didn't even know George was his father.

"Yes, he was very much like that. My mother was very much a woman and she had learned not to let my grandfather get away with his cantankerous ways. I'm told my mother was very much like my grandmother, a woman who could stand on her own and go toe-to-toe with any man, including my grandfather."

She smiled warmly. It was nice to talk about her grandparents and parents with someone who had known them. "Anyway, my grandfather saw my mother holding a pink-blanketed bundle. He looked at my father and said, 'Well, that's a disappointment. What are we supposed to do with a girl?'

"My mother was tired and not about to stand for my grandfather's disappointment in the daughter she'd just brought into the world. She got out of bed with me in her arms and walked to my grandfather. She unceremoniously dumped me into his arms, wrapped in my pink blanket, and told him, 'This is your namesake, Martina Fairchild, and you are to take care of her until I get back.'

"My father and grandmother erupted into laughter. My mother marched into the bathroom to take a shower. My grandfather stood there, frowning, holding his namesake, a girl.

"He took it in stride, I'm told. He sat in a chair with me in his arms and began reading the financial page to me. My grandmother told me I promptly burped and went to sleep after my grandfather told me Fairchild Industries' stock was up two points. Apparently, I wasn't impressed.

"I'm just thankful my mother thought better than to name me Martin, as my grandfather expected of his first grandchild," she joked and rolled her eyes expressively.

George laughed so hard he held his sides and coughed. She patted his back and laughed with him.

"I haven't laughed like this in a long time. I can just imagine him holding you and wondering what to do with a little girl. You are good for me, Marti. Dinner tonight at seven?"

"Perfect. I have my meeting downtown, but I should make it by seven."

"Let's meet at Decadence in the Merrick International building. Do you know where it is?"

"I'll find it." She swept her hands from her head down her body. "I'll even dry off and be presentable when I arrive. Do you think the lawyers will mind my appearance?" She combed her fingers through her long, wet hair, feeling like a wet rag.

"For as much money as they charge, they should offer to buy you a new dress just to keep your business."

He walked her to the parking lot, her arm entwined with his. She worried about his shivers and hoped he went straight home and got warm.

She smiled at the Bentley, complete with driver, waiting nearby.

"You had your driver bring you here so you could throw yourself into the sea?"

"I hate traffic." He gave her a lopsided grin and shrugged. Humor danced in his now bright eyes, letting her know the despair of moments ago had passed.

"I didn't really have a plan beyond my initial thought it was time to end it all and let the others fight it out. I have a better idea of what to do now, thanks to you. I'll take some time and make the appropriate decisions. I think your grandfather would say I was a man who fought for every inch I gained. Over the last several years, my family has worn me down to the point where I just didn't care what happened to my estate. I think I'd rather go out the man your grandfather and you remember."

"Will you be all right? I hate to leave you if you're still considering doing something supremely stupid."

"Supremely stupid." His lopsided grin turned to a contemplative frown. "I guess you're right. I'm fine now, thanks to you. Promise you'll come to dinner."

"It's a promise. If I'm a few minutes late, I hope you'll wait for me. My uncle can sometimes be long-winded."

"Dinner is more than seven hours away."

"I'll use it as an excuse to get out of there," she said, exasperated. "How long can he talk without having dinner? Right?"

George smiled, feeling lighter and younger than he had in years. He thought about some of the things he knew about her from Marty's stories. Something stuck out.

"Your grandfather once told me you were extremely private. He said you prefer to keep things to yourself."

Marti smiled. Her grandfather's way of saying his granddaughter didn't like to advertise she was heir to the Fairchild empire. Too many people held preconceived ideas when they heard someone belonged to a wealthy family. Her grandmother was a famous artist. When they found out she was her granddaughter, they automatically made assumptions about whether she painted or had artistic ability. She'd rather people looked at her for who she was, and not what they thought she was based on her family ties.

"I'd prefer it if you just thought of me as Marti. I'm sure you'd agree, when you add on a family name like Fairchild or Knight, people automatically have a picture of who they think you are. I like to be myself."

"Your grandmother was right about you, you're unique. Most people, my children and family included, would use the name to their advantage. Like you, I prefer to earn respect and friendship on my own merits."

She gave him a firm nod. "I'll see you tonight at seven. Decadence at the Merrick International building," she repeated to help her remember.

"Can I drop you somewhere?"

"I'll be fine, but thank you."

She waited while George drove away before heading for the street and hailing a cab. Soaking wet and cold, she didn't have time to go to the Four Seasons and change. Already fifteen minutes late for her meeting, she didn't care. George Knight was still alive.

Chapter Seven

CAMERON SAT IN his office looking out the window at the night sky and the ocean beyond. The ship from the night before had disappeared. He felt as lonely and desolate as the ocean looked without the ship.

He had to meet Shelly and Emma downstairs for dinner again. Emma never said much about Shelly on the car ride home last night and it worried Cameron. She usually talked about the people she met.

He needed to put a stop to this fiasco, and soon.

With one last look toward the sea, he rose from his desk. Still no ship. He didn't understand why he longed to see the boat on the horizon, to know it was out there waiting for him.

MARTI WAS RUNNING late. Her uncle had indeed been long-winded and prepared to do battle over her grandmother's estate. To his frustration and increasing anger, Marti sat through the meeting quietly refusing to rise to the bait and argue with him. Her grandmother's will was straightforward and spelled out her wishes in her usual meticulous manner.

Uncle Anthony was given the large estate property in Marin and a cash settlement. He would continue at the company per her grandfather's previous wishes. Marti received the sailboat and a cash settlement. Of course, there were stocks and bonds and trusts to be split between them and all kinds of other small treasures.

The icing on the cake went to Marti. To her uncle's angry protests, Marti received all of her grandmother's paintings. She and the lawyers would manage the pieces displayed around the world in museums and galleries, but she would also receive the entire private collection. Hundreds of paintings were stored in a special climate-controlled warehouse. Marti would be in charge of her grandmother's legacy.

She grabbed a dress from her suitcase. Not entirely wrinkled, made of a good fabric, with a little steam it would look great. She turned on the shower in the elegant bathroom and hung the dress so it would catch the steam.

No time for her to actually take a shower. Her hair hung limp past her shoulders after her stint standing in the storm talking to George. She thought about the man and smiled. She'd missed having an elder for company.

She used the dryer to fluff her hair. She pulled the sides away from her face, clipped them, and let the rest fall down her back. She'd been at sea for a year and her hair had grown out considerably. She took a critical look at herself in the mirror. Her hair, usually a rich brown, now showed streaks of gold from the sun. The color made her tanned skin and soft green eyes glow with warmth. Five feet seven and lean, maybe a little too thin. Climbing rigging and working on the boat had made her strong. Not to mention her long swims in the ocean waves. She had a nice figure. Round in all the right places, though no one would call her voluptuous—more softly feminine.

She brushed on a soft pink blush and checked her makeup one final time. Subtle, natural. Not bad.

She took one last glance. "That's as good as it gets," she said to her image in the mirror.

She took the royal blue wrap-dress down from the wall hook, shook it out, and put it on. She slid her feet into the black sling-back pumps, grabbed her purse, and ran out the door to catch a cab.

If she were lucky, she'd only be a few minutes late.

DINNER STARTED OUT well enough. Shelly was attentive and interested in Emma and her day at school. Shelly and Emma went over the menu and all of Emma's favorites. In the end, Shelly agreed to let Emma order for her. Shelly seemed pleased by the selection and gushed over Emma's choice.

Maybe Cameron had judged the situation too harshly last night. Maybe Shelly and Emma needed time to get to know each other. As for his relationship with Shelly, he liked her. She was pleasant to be around most of the time. When they were alone together, she always tried to please him in some way. In bed, she was everything a man wanted.

He wasn't in love with her, harbored no real feelings of affection, but that wasn't what he wanted. He wanted a good mother for Emma and a friend and lover for him. It was all he was capable of giving, and he couldn't ask for more from someone else. Maybe his previous misgivings about Shelly were just his apprehension to being married to someone who wasn't Caroline.

"Emma, don't use your fingers when you eat. Use your fork."

Shelly tried to hold onto her temper and her patience. She wasn't used to being around small children and Emma was a nonstop dynamo. She interfered when Shelly tried to engage Cameron in a personal conversation. Emma constantly tried to keep Cameron's focus on her and wouldn't let Shelly have a moment's peace and quiet. The girl was a chatterbox.

She looked across the table at Cameron. His focus remained on Emma. He paid more attention to the little girl than to her. She'd have to figure out a way to gain his focus.

"We should take a trip. Something short. I know what a busy man you are, but it would be nice to get away for a few days."

"Let's go fishing, Daddy. You keep saying we'll go out on the boat, but we never do." Emma continued making a volcano out of her mashed potatoes. She saw Shelly's unhappy face out of the corner of her eye and didn't care. She didn't like Shelly. She'd be nice because her dad always told her to be nice, but she didn't have to like Shelly in her mind. She poured gravy into the top of her mashed potato volcano and pictured herself sticking out her tongue and smiled.

"What a great idea, Emma. I was thinking about taking out the boat just yesterday. Shelly, do you like to fish?"

No. Absolutely not. You're rich, why can't we go to a resort in the Bahamas? "I'd love to go out on your boat. It sounds lovely." *Lovely, my ass.*

Cameron smiled. This was turning around nicely. A trip on the boat, Shelly and Emma spending time together, and he'd fulfill his fishing promise to Emma.

Out on the water, he could clear his mind. That had the most appeal of all. He spent too much time in an office building and not enough time having fun with Emma.

Emma stood on her chair, grabbed Shelly's shoulder to balance herself, and put her arms out to her aunt. "Aunt Elizabeth, we're going fishing."

"Emma. You got gravy and potatoes all over my new dress. You've ruined it."

Emma looked down at the dress and shrugged. "I'm sorry. I didn't mean to."

"Yeah, right. I told you to use your fork. You didn't listen, and now look what you've done." Shelly stood, threw her napkin down, glared at Emma with a deep frown, and stalked off to the lady's room.

"I didn't mean it, Daddy. I swear."

"I know you didn't. It was an accident."

"It sure was, honey." Elizabeth scooped her up. "Let's go into the kitchen and get cleaned up." Elizabeth smiled down at Emma's plate. "Nice volcano."

"Thanks. Can I make dessert?"

"Sure you can. I have some pastries we need to dust with powdered sugar. Want to help?"

"Yes. Yes." Emma took off to the kitchen, leaving Elizabeth to follow.

"Your girlfriend needs to learn a thing or two about children." She left the table to trail after Emma.

Cameron rubbed the hard knot at the back of his neck, digging in his fingertips. Things had been going so well, or so he thought. He was beginning to think Shelly was a good actress, but dismissed the thought just as quickly as it formed.

Surprised, Elizabeth reappeared at the table a moment later.

"Is Emma giving you trouble in the kitchen?"

"Even if Emma wrecked the joint, I wouldn't bat an eyelash. I just talked to one of my servers who came out of the women's restroom. This isn't the first time someone has mentioned this to me. Normally, I wouldn't say anything, but Emma is involved, and so I'm sticking my nose into your business."

Elizabeth took a deep breath to calm herself. "I don't want you bringing that woman here anymore. If she wants to eat and throw up a perfectly good meal, she can do it somewhere else."

"What are you talking about? Is Shelly ill?"

"Only because she made herself sick. This is the third

time someone has mentioned it to me. One of those times it was a customer. I can't have people thinking I'm poisoning my customers."

"Why the hell would she do that to herself?"

"Let me give you some insight into that woman. She orders the most expensive meals on the menu at your expense, she drinks martinis like they're water, and she isn't a nice person. She gets up a few minutes after eating and goes to the restroom where she purges herself of all the food and martinis she's had so she can keep that skinny figure of hers."

She waited for her words to sink in before continuing. "It's common enough among women who want to keep their weight off and have an unhealthy attitude about food and weight. I'll bet she was a fat kid or teen and figures the only thing she has to offer a man like you is her body. She certainly isn't smart enough to engage your mind."

She looked past Cameron before he said anything and greeted their friend, "Hello, George. This is an unexpected surprise. I saw your name on the guest list tonight and wondered if you'd truly join us yourself."

George frowned. "Has my family used my name to get in here?"

"Maybe once or twice. They're always welcome, of course, but they seem to like using your name to ensure a seat. I always get my hopes up you'll be coming." She winked.

"They'll get what's coming to them soon enough. Tonight, though, I have a very special guest with me."

"Where is this special guest?" Elizabeth asked, her eyes scanning the restaurant.

"She'll be along soon. She said she might be a few minutes late."

He looked at Cameron and frowned. "What's the matter with you, son? You look downright distressed."

"His guest turned out to be not so special." Elizabeth stuck her tongue out at him when he glared at her.

Cameron turned his attention to his dearest friend. He held his hand out to shake with George. He'd think about Elizabeth's remarks later. "How are you, George? You look better today than the last few times I've seen you."

"That, my boy, is thanks to Marti."

"Whatever the cause, you look great. Emma is in the kitchen making pastries or something. She'd love to see you. I hope you don't mind if I bring her by your table when your guest arrives."

"Not at all. In fact, here she comes."

Chapter Eight

"THE LITTLE BITCH ruined my dress." Shelly scrubbed at her sleeve and tried to clean the mashed potatoes and gravy out.

"God, my throat hurts. I'll be fat as a cow if I keep eating out all the time."

Pale, even her anger didn't add color back into her gaunt cheeks after she'd thrown up her dinner. She hated to end a perfectly good meal this way, but with all the rich foods and decadent desserts, along with the booze, she couldn't afford all the extra calories. Still, she couldn't keep this up and wished she could stop. She wanted to stop, but the compulsion overtook her good sense. Too many times she promised herself it was the last time.

She set aside her concerns and focused on her immediate frustration. "When I get my hands on her, I'll ring her neck. Two hundred dollars spent to impress a man who's more interested in the little mess maker than me.

Damn the little bitch," she said under her breath and continued to scrub the stain.

Marti heard the woman getting sick in the stall across from hers. She'd thought the woman was ill, now she reevaluated her assumption. The woman had some obvious problems, ranting at herself in the mirror and throwing up her dinner so she wouldn't gain any weight. Marti thought better to eat less and enjoy it than throw it up. But to each his own.

She flushed the toilet, thankful she no longer had to pee. She'd forgotten all about it after the meeting with the lawyers and her marathon getting-dressed session. She left the hotel without doing her business. When she finally relaxed in the cab on the way to the restaurant, she realized she still had to go and had forgotten all about it. She hated when that happened. She hated to keep George waiting, but better to get her business out of the way rather than say, "Hi. I've got to pee, back in a minute."

She exited the stall. The other woman's eyes went wide with surprise. Obviously, she'd thought she'd been alone after the server left. Marti washed her hands and ignored her. She left feeling sorry for whoever she confronted over the ruined dress.

She spotted George talking to some people and headed for him. "George, I'm so sorry I'm late." She turned toward the people he was speaking to before she arrived. "Hello."

"Cameron, Elizabeth, this is Marti." He left out her last name, remembering their conversation earlier in the day. Cameron's face went from distressed to intrigued in a flash. Interesting. Handsome, her stomach fluttered with nerves, but she smiled even though he didn't.

"I'm pleased to meet you both," Marti said and shook their hands. His was rough and warm.

A little girl barreled out of the kitchen's swinging doors and skipped toward them. She looked so cute dressed in a dark green jumper and covered in white powder. She had it everywhere from the top of her golden head and all down her dress.

The woman from the bathroom rushed toward the girl looking fit to kill and calling to her. Marti stepped away from the table, her instinct to protect kicked into gear.

"You come here, right now." Far enough from the table, none of the others heard her nasty tone. The woman quickened her pace toward the little girl. The girl sensed trouble and ran toward Marti.

"You come here right now, you little . . ."

"Don't you dare finish that sentence." Marti scooped up the little girl into her arms and glared over her shoulder at the irate woman.

Everyone behind her went silent. Marti took two steps back with the girl, who had a choke hold around her neck. Marti ran her hand over her golden hair and down her back. "It's okay, Sugar Bug. You're fine now. I have you."

She glared at the other woman. Cameron stood from the table and moved in beside her.

"Shelly, what the hell do you think you're doing?"

"I'm sorry. She ruined my dress, and I just lost my head. I didn't mean any harm, but the child needs discipline."

"If *my* daughter needs anything, I'll be the one to give it to her. Now sit down. You're making a scene. It's just a dress, for God's sake. I'll buy you a new one," he said under his breath. She brushed past him. Her intentional rub against his chest with her breasts wasn't lost on him. He inwardly cringed the moment she touched him, and he didn't know why. She was a beautiful woman by any standard, but the blatant flirtation at this moment didn't seem appropriate.

Although they stood in a private area of the restaurant, people stared through the archway and listened to the commotion.

Cameron looked at his daughter and Marti holding her so lovingly. He'd just met the woman, but he felt like he knew her, recognized her in some way. He had a hard time fighting the strange pull toward her. Especially when he saw his daughter in her arms, locked around her with absolute trust.

Emma sat back, hands on Marti's shoulders, and asked, "How come you called me 'Sugar Bug?'"

"Because you, little one, are covered from head to toe in sugar. I thought the name was appropriate and sweet, like you. I won't call you it if you don't want me to."

"I like it. It's nice. That's my dad."

"I just met him. I'm Marti."

"Hi, Marti. I'm Emma. Emma Shaw. My dad is president."

"He's president of the Sugar Bugs." Marti smiled hugely, mischief lighting her eyes.

Emma giggled. "No. He's president of this building."

Marti looked appropriately astonished. "Wow. President of a whole building. Now that is impressive. I don't have such a fancy job as president. I've been a pirate for the last year."

"Really? Awesome."

"Totally awesome. Sometime I'll tell you all about it."

Marti wiped the tears drying on the child's cheeks. She leaned in and whispered into her ear. The little girl laughed uproariously.

Emma turned to her father. "What do you call a witch who casts spells with sand?"

"I don't know, sweetheart."

"A sand witch." Emma smiled and laughed again at the joke. She turned back to Marti and wrapped her arms around her neck. "You're nice."

Marti closed her eyes and hugged the girl tight. "You're nice too, Sugar Bug."

Emma called over her shoulder, "Hi, Knight."

Marti turned to see George looking at the little girl with pure worship. "Hello, Princess. How are you?"

"I'm better now."

"Yes, I can see that." He saw a lot more. Like the way Cameron watched Marti like a man who'd just discovered water in the desert.

Emma's reaction to Marti was unusual. She was affectionate to Elizabeth and Jenna, but she was downright attached to Marti. Cameron had never seen her take to anyone so fast.

Emma wouldn't let go of Marti and Marti looked pleased to have his daughter in her arms, dirty or not. She didn't look like she'd put her down willingly.

"What's the matter, Shelly? Dinner didn't come up quite so easily tonight?" Elizabeth asked.

Shelly frowned, looked from Elizabeth to Cameron and knew just what they were both thinking. She had to cover her tracks and get back in Cameron's good graces. When she glanced at Emma in the woman's arms, she had the most brilliant idea. She'd seen the way Cameron looked at the woman, and she wasn't about to give up without a fight.

She turned to Elizabeth. "Is this how you treat all of your pregnant guests?" She locked eyes with Cameron, unable to hide her triumphant grin.

Brilliant, simply brilliant, she thought. "I didn't want to tell you like this, but she's making accusations. I won't have you thinking the worst of me. Isn't it wonderful, darling?"

Stunned at first, Elizabeth recovered. She looked pointedly at the martini glass, at Cameron, and back to Shelly. "Pregnant. Me too." She smoothed her hand over her stomach. She'd actually given birth to her daughter, Grace, five months ago. "Darn, I'm not."

She glared at Shelly and called her a liar. "Saying it doesn't make it true."

The woman had a lot of nerve saying she was pregnant and belting back martinis two days in a row. Elizabeth was furious.

Cameron's faced changed from stunned back to distressed again. He ran his hand over the back of his neck and found himself at a loss for words. His daughter was right there in the thick of this mess. He was not having a good night. After tonight, he'd lost any chance of ever getting a "Parent of the Year" award.

If he thought himself a supreme jackass before, tonight he'd earned the crown.

Chapter Nine

MARTI LOOKED AT the empty martini glass in front of
Shelly and the look of horror on Cameron's face. She
didn't like the fact that he'd put this woman in his daughter's life, but it wasn't her child, or her life. None of her
business.

"Cameron, may I speak with you a moment?" She
cocked her head to indicate he follow her a few steps away
from the group.

Cameron followed, because she held his daughter and
Emma held tight with no indication of letting her go any
time soon. Marti didn't mind at all.

"Listen, you need a few minutes alone with her to
work out . . . whatever. George appears to be a friend of
yours."

"He's Daddy's friend."

"He's like a grandfather to Emma," Cameron confirmed.

"Great. Then you won't mind letting her come and sit with us for a while. It'll give you time to work out this mess."

"Mess? She's pregnant, drinking, and yelling at my kid," he said irritably under his breath. "What makes you think this is a mess?" Cameron snapped at the woman who'd rescued his daughter and made him want to kiss her until he couldn't breathe.

He rubbed his hand over his neck again, knowing she didn't deserve his anger.

Marti sighed. She hated to get involved, but a child needed to be considered, and the man standing in front of her looked like he'd been swept under by a huge wave.

She felt for him. He needed a friend, and for Emma she'd stick her nose in his business.

"Look, I know you're upset. You have every reason to be. I don't have any business giving you advice or butting in, but for this little Sugar Bug I'm going to break my own rules and get involved."

She took a breath and leaned into Cameron and lowered her voice. Emma held her tight around the neck and settled into her arms. "I was in the bathroom with her earlier. She didn't know I was there. Let's just say I got an earful about her feelings toward . . ." She nodded in Emma's direction.

"That woman, in addition to not being fit to be a mother, has no desire to be a mother to this little girl, or any child. I don't believe she's pregnant, but you'll have to confirm it yourself."

She imagined what it must be like for him. He looked

like a man trying hard to struggle out of a riptide, only to find himself drowning.

"Take it from someone who wants to be a mother more than anything: even if she is pregnant, she doesn't want the baby. She doesn't have it in her to be a mother.

"You're obviously an important and wealthy man." She looked at the little girl and covered her ear with her hand and whispered, "Don't let her make a jackass out of you. She's a liar and"—she looked at the girl again—"worse. She'll ruin this little girl if you let her."

Why did it piss him off to hear her echo his thoughts back at him. He was a jackass. He knew he was a jackass. He didn't need her telling him too.

Don't shoot the messenger. How many times had he told himself that in business? Make sure you aim at the person who deserves to be targeted.

Marti hadn't done anything but tell him what he already knew and suspected. She'd heard Shelly saying something in the bathroom to make her believe Shelly was a liar—and worse, bad for his daughter.

He'd already figured it out himself when she'd yelled at Emma and went after her. No one spoke to his daughter that way. He didn't care who they were, or what they said about being pregnant with his baby.

He rubbed the back of his neck. God, this woman was getting under his skin. The longer he watched her hugging and loving on his daughter, the more endearing she became. If he didn't know better, he'd think Emma belonged to her.

Two dinners and Shelly hadn't managed to get one

tenth as close to Emma as Marti had by simply picking her up, giving her a pet name, and telling her a joke. A silly, stupid joke, but it had done the trick with Emma. Her smile returned and the innocence of childhood filled her eyes again. He owed Marti for that and more.

"Listen, I know you mean well and you have my daughter's best interests at heart. I'm holding on to my temper and my sanity by a thread tonight. I appreciate what you did by stepping in and rescuing Emma. If nothing else, you made her feel better. I would appreciate it if you let Emma join you and Knight, while I try to wade through the muck my life is mired under."

He rubbed at the back of his neck again. He wanted to say more. He wanted to keep her near and drink up all the good feelings inside him, watching her holding his daughter. He didn't get the choice. Elizabeth came over to help with Emma.

"Marti, please, join George at your table. I'll take Emma."

Emma grabbed on tighter to Marti. "No. I'm going to sit with Marti and Knight."

Cameron rubbed his hand from the top of his daughter's head and down her back. "You promise to be a good girl."

"I promise. Marti is nice."

"You're nice too, Sugar Bug. What were you making in the kitchen?"

"Pastries."

"Yum." Marti said with enthusiasm. "Elizabeth, Sugar Bug and I will have a pastry. Tonight, I'll have dinner backwards. Dessert first, and then the main course."

"You can't. Daddy never lets me have dessert first."

"Well, I heard you already had mashed potatoes and gravy. Sounds like you already ate dinner. I, on the other hand, have the ultimate reason for having dessert first."

Marti really did get an earful in the bathroom. Damn. Shelly must have really let her true feelings show.

"What's the reason?" Emma asked, very interested.

"I grew up into an adult and can do whatever I want. When you grow up, you can have dessert first."

"No fair. I thought it would be something I could use to get dessert first."

"You can use it. You just have to grow up first. And the only way to do that is . . ." Marti waited to see if the little girl finished the sentence.

"Eat my dinner first," Emma said with a dramatic roll of her eyes.

"You, Sugar Bug, are a smart girl. Let's eat. I'm starving, and poor George is waiting for us."

Marti took Emma to the nearby table and plopped her into a seat. She brushed Emma's hair over her ear and smiled down at her. Emma's smile notched up a few megawatts, making Cameron feel lighter.

"Too bad you didn't meet her before the martini-swilling, bulimic, child-hating monster waiting at your table with a look of triumph and disgust that defies the human expression."

"Rub it in, why don't you." Cameron put his arm around Elizabeth, needing her support.

"If she is pregnant, don't marry her and make a bad situation worse. Sue her for custody once the baby is born. You shouldn't have any problem getting a judge to see things your way. If she isn't pregnant, and I don't think she is, dump her and get Marti's number from Knight. Emma loves her already."

"She does, doesn't she?" Not hard to miss the instant connection and bond his daughter had with Marti.

"Yes, and it should tell you something. Emma hasn't had a single thing to say about Shelly. She doesn't like her.

"Did you see Emma, Cameron? She ran right to Marti. She bypassed you and me and went right for Marti's outstretched arms. There's something special there. You saw it when she held Emma."

"I did see it. Now tell me how to get out of this mess I'm in."

"You made the mess, you're going to have to clean it up. I'm still trying to get past the fact you slept with her. I thought you had better taste."

"She looks like Caroline," he said simply, knowing Elizabeth would understand. "Right up until she opens her mouth. I got caught up in my own twisted fantasy and things turned to shit." He squeezed Elizabeth to his side. A good friend. Whatever he said to her, she wouldn't hold it against him or throw it back in his face.

"Oh, Cameron. I had no idea. Caroline must have been a beautiful woman. Shelly is. But you're right, it's ruined when she opens her mouth."

Elizabeth looked back at Marti and Emma. "On the other hand, Marti is gorgeous and she's nice. I'd kill to have her hair color, all those shades of brown with streaks of gold. Did you see the color of her eyes? They remind me of Jenna's. A soft jade green."

If he closed his eyes, he pictured her in full detail. The fact that he couldn't remember what Shelly looked like in his mind at the moment hit him right in the gut.

"She's beautiful, all right."

Pulled in one direction, he went in the other, back to his table.

Chapter Ten

"How about another martini?" Elizabeth asked as she passed their table, getting in one more dig about her lying about being pregnant.

No self-respecting expectant mother would swill martinis night after night, Cameron thought. Shelly ignored the question. Nothing she said would overshadow her drinking multiple martinis over the last two days in his company.

Instead of answering Elizabeth, she turned her attention on him, went on the defensive, and lashed out. "Finished wagging your tongue over George's mistress?"

Direct hit. He rolled the idea around in his mind, never expecting the outrageous statement. He refused to believe Marti was George's mistress. He was in his seventies. She couldn't be more than twenty-five, tops. Hell, she was too young for him, and he was only thirty-two.

"Let's talk about this so-called pregnancy. You can't

really think I'd believe you're pregnant. I used protection every time we were together."

"Every time?" She raised an eyebrow and cocked her head. The knowing grin made him think hard.

He used protection, but she remembered the first time he'd been out of control with wanting her and he hadn't used anything. On the pill since sophomore year of high school, she'd just gone along, swept up by his enthusiasm and need for her. The office of the president of Merrick International had been a powerful aphrodisiac. How many million-dollar business deals were made in his office?

It hit Cameron like a sledgehammer over the head. The first night. He'd lost his head thinking Shelly was Caroline. Hungry for Caroline, he didn't think to be cautious or careful with Shelly, and now he was going to be a father again with a woman he didn't want around his daughter.

"What do you want, Shelly?"

She looked at him expectantly. "I want to be with you. We're having a baby. I thought you'd be happy about it. You love Emma so much, and you're a devoted father to her. You will be to our baby too."

"First you'll take a pregnancy test and prove you're pregnant. Once done, and it's positive, we can talk about the rest."

He pinned her with his gaze. "And just so we understand each other about what I expect if you are carrying my child, you will not drink alcohol. You will take care of yourself and my baby. Are we clear?"

Shelly got the message loud and clear. *My* baby, indeed. She was going to get a marriage proposal and everything she'd ever wanted out of this baby. *Their* baby.

"Absolutely, darling. I wasn't drinking to hurt the baby. I didn't even truly figure out I'm pregnant until tonight." She smiled at him and put her hand over his on the table. "You can't really think I'm so terrible I'd put *our* baby in jeopardy."

"Fine. Get the pregnancy test done. We'll figure out the rest once there's confirmation. I'll pay for all the medical expenses."

"Darling, surely you and I will be married. With a baby on the way, a man of your position and status would surely want to marry the mother of your child. You can't possibly think to let this child be born out of wedlock. What would my parents say?" She tried to put the proper distress into her voice and hoped he heard her upset and worry.

"What would people you work and do business with think of such a thing?" Pushy, but she wanted to lay the groundwork. The sooner they were married, the better. The sooner she'd enjoy the benefits of being Mrs. Cameron Shaw.

"Like I said, we'll talk about all that once the test comes back."

"I'll make an appointment as soon as I can get one. Won't Emma be so happy to be a big sister?"

Just the right kind of statement Cameron would expect from a woman interested in being with him and having a family. Why didn't it ring true?

Cameron didn't know what to tell Emma. What do you say to a five-year-old when you screw up and ruin your life—and hers in the process?

He was supposed to be her role model, someone she could look up to. He'd let himself down, he'd let Caroline down, and, worst of all, he'd let her down. He'd screwed himself and Emma over a piece of ass who reminded him of a woman he'd never get over. Well, he'd tried to accept her death and not having her in his and Emma's life anymore. Still, he'd never stop missing her.

Maybe it wasn't her he wanted, but what they'd had together. They'd been close, in love, the best of friends, and so much more. They'd laughed and loved together. They'd grown together and been there for each other. He wanted the same now. Too late, and to his detriment—and Emma's, he'd realized in the end—Shelly was just the image of Caroline. It wasn't what he wanted. He wanted so much more.

The moment he realized his mistake, decided he wanted the relationship and companionship he'd shared with Caroline, who should pop into his head: Marti.

The entire time he'd sat with Shelly, across the room, his daughter laughed and giggled and had a great time with George and Marti. Emma hadn't acted like that at dinner with him and Shelly. She wasn't this animated when they had dinner with Knight twice a month. It was Marti who made the difference and brightened Emma's world. The sound of her laughter rolled over him and renewed his resolve to spend more time with her.

"Let's go fishing this weekend. Saturday. You have three days to get to the doctor and verify you're pregnant. We'll go fishing on my boat with Emma. If you're pregnant."

If I'm pregnant. You'll see. "Sounds wonderful, darling. You know, it's been a long day. I think it's time to go home." She pretended to yawn to prove her point. She wanted to get away from his scrutinizing glare. He wasn't happy, and even more suspicious about her being pregnant. She'd have to be careful what she did and said from now on. Besides, she needed time to think this new part of her plan through.

"I remember Caroline could barely keep her eyes open some days when she was pregnant."

He remembered so many things about her pregnancy. How he'd lay next to her in bed with his hand on her growing belly. She was green most mornings for the first three and half months. Right when she woke up, she'd dash into the bathroom and he'd find her lying on the rug. She was so happy after a week of waking up without ending up on the bathroom floor. The end of the pregnancy hadn't been a picnic for her, but she was never down or wishing she weren't pregnant. She'd often tell him there was nothing like knowing a little person was living inside of her.

Shelly watched the emotions play over Cameron's face. She almost felt guilty. He'd lost his wife after she'd delivered Emma. She didn't know the exact story, but Cameron's face said it all. It hadn't been a happy ending and Shelly could admit it was too bad. Cameron was a nice guy who didn't deserve to have his wife die while bringing their child into the world.

Shelly could make Cameron happy and be a good wife. She wasn't into the whole baby and mother thing, but she could certainly make a good impression at a dinner party and keep him happy in the bedroom.

Those were the kinds of things she was good at, or at least tried hard to be. She wasn't invited to many business parties. The only ones she'd attended had been over the past month with Cameron. He seemed pleased with her at the end of the night. Though he'd never really said, they always ended up in bed.

More often than not, she got the feeling he liked her more for the way she looked, or rather her resemblance to his dead wife. They'd used each other for their own purposes.

She decided she'd take the next couple of weeks and really try to please him in every way. She'd get him to notice her. And while she did, she'd drive home her point. Getting married was the best idea.

"I am tired. It's been one of those days. George and his date would probably like to enjoy their meal in peace. He certainly didn't bring her here to babysit Emma. They probably had a romantic evening in mind."

"I think you have the wrong idea about George and Marti."

"I don't know. These May-December romances have become quite the in thing lately. George is a wealthy man with power and influence. Very appealing to a young woman."

"A lot like me and you, huh. Not so much the age thing. You're, what, thirty-one? The part about my being wealthy and powerful sure fits your idea of the perfect man. Appealing, as you said. You even liked Elizabeth a little more when you found out she was a Hamilton and married to Jenna's brother-in-law."

He had her attention. She couldn't allow him to think she was only after his bank account. She liked him too. She wasn't Marti, going after a man old enough to be her grandfather. At least Cameron was young and had a body any woman would fantasize about having pressed against her. His dark hair set off his amazing, silvery blue eyes. The contrast made him even more strikingly handsome.

"Darling, you have me all wrong. I didn't pursue you. You wanted me. If I remember correctly, you couldn't wait to have me. You just took me right upstairs and had me in your office on the sofa. I had no idea you were the president of Merrick."

She had known, but she wasn't going to tell him. She'd spent many nights at the bar trying to land an executive. She'd done her homework and knew who liked to hang out at the upscale restaurant. The bartender was a wealth of information when tipped well. She'd tipped very well.

Cameron had his doubts. Everyone knew the crowd in Decadence consisted of wealthy businesspeople from around San Francisco, and particularly Merrick International.

"Right, it had nothing to do with the fact that when I

told you my name, you wrapped yourself around me like I was a warm blanket on a winter night in Alaska. You were all too willing to go upstairs."

His behavior, and especially hers, gnawed at him. He dined at Decadence almost every day, and he never picked up women there. Too many people knew him. He was the head of the company and supposed to set an example, not generate gossip.

Shelly's argument for them getting married held a lot of weight and made him cringe. He just might have to do it to make things right, which meant he'd doom himself and Emma to a horrible marriage with no other end but disaster.

This was some kind of living hell. He didn't want to sign on the dotted line and make it official. No one said he had to, but his conscience nagged. He'd grown up without a father. Emma was growing up without her mother. He and Caroline and Emma were supposed to be the family he always wanted and Emma deserved.

Could he make that family work with Shelly? Maybe? With a baby on the way, he couldn't say absolutely no. For the children, shouldn't he at least try?

"Let's get out of here. I'll meet you at the car after I get Emma. We'll drive you home."

"Why don't I stay with you tonight?"

"I don't bring women home with me. I have Emma to think about."

"Darling, eventually you need to tell her we have a relationship and we're expecting a baby brother or sister for her."

"I'm sure she heard your announcement to the restaurant. I need time to explain things to Emma in my own way. She's just a little girl. For her whole life, it's only been the two of us. I will deal with Emma my way, in my own time. You will not interfere with my daughter."

"Fine. I'll stay out of it. You can't put it, or me, off forever."

He knew that all too well, but it was early in the pregnancy, which meant he had time. They needed it to come to terms and figure out a way to make this work.

"I'm not putting you off. Once you provide the proof you're pregnant, we'll negotiate."

"Negotiate. You're so romantic, darling." The sarcastic tone grated on his nerves.

He grabbed her wrist to stop her from leaving the table. "Let's get one thing straight. Even if you are pregnant, I am not in love with you, and I'm not about to fall in love with you. This relationship wasn't headed there in the first place. We enjoy each other in bed, it's pretty much all we enjoy about each other. *If* you're pregnant, we'll negotiate the terms of the pregnancy and what we're going to do once the baby is born."

"You are sucking all the fun out of this. I thought you'd be pleased. I guess I was wrong. Let's just go."

"*If* you're carrying my child, I will be pleased. I'll be a good father and provide for you and the child. Like I said, we'll negotiate."

Cameron hated to think of this situation as some kind of business deal. He needed time to think about all his options. Marriage was the sensible thing. He wanted his baby to have a mother and a father.

"I'll get Emma and see you at the car."

Any way he looked at it, this had disaster written all over it. Ever the optimist, he hoped to turn this into an opportunity to have the family he'd dreamed of with Caroline.

Chapter Eleven

"Ah, Dad, I'm not ready to go home yet. Marti is going to teach me how to play soccer with a quarter on the table."

Cameron's gaze shifted to Marti. A quarter sat on the tabletop in front of her. She put her hand over it, never taking her eyes from him.

"I have no idea what she's talking about. We were sitting here using our very best manners. Honest."

Cameron smiled and laughed. "I'll bet you were. My daughter laughing and giggling over the restaurant noise proves it."

"Sit down and join us, son. We've had dessert and dinner. I believe the salad is coming out next. And then the bread and appetizer." George smiled, appearing to enjoy the evening's events as much as Emma.

"You're sure having a great time, Knight."

"Who wouldn't when they spend an evening with two beautiful women?"

Cameron thought about the comments Shelly made and her implying Marti was George's mistress. He studied them sitting at the table together. George was on one side with Emma across from him and Marti beside Emma. Not an intimate way for the group to sit. He would have sat next to Marti, or as close to her as possible. They might brush legs under the table, or hold hands on top. Marti looked like she was more interested in Emma than a romantic evening with George.

"How did the two of you meet?" He tried to sound casual, but George caught something in his tone and his eyes narrowed a fraction.

"Marti saved my life today. To thank her, I invited her to dinner."

George would be grateful to Marti for the rest of his days. Unfortunately, those days were numbered. He heard it ticking down even now. Tonight he'd make Marti an offer and hope she agreed to be a part of his plan. Cameron would be a big part of the plan too. Maybe George could fix this mess Cameron had gotten himself into with Shelly and give him the life he deserved. The life he should have had all along.

"Oh, George. That's a little dramatic. The only thing I saved you from is catching a cold. You still might after we stood talking in the rain for half an hour."

"What did everyone say when you walked into your meeting drenched?"

"The lawyers remained silent, of course, but my uncle asked if I swam to shore."

"Swam to shore?" Cameron had sailing and fishing on

his mind and wondered why anyone would think Marti would swim ashore. From where?

"I met George at the harbor. I'd just gotten back from a trip."

"Where did you go?" Cameron asked.

"Everywhere," she said and smiled mischievously. "I was fulfilling a promise. It's a long story."

"You always keep your promises?" Unsure why he asked, her answer seemed infinitely important.

"Yes," she said emphatically. "I never make a promise I don't keep. It's one of my rules."

"Like not sticking your nose in people's business?"

"Yes. I only did it because you looked like you needed the help. Sometimes when you're in the situation you can't see it objectively. I hope I didn't make things worse for you. I never meant to harm you."

"Slow down, Marti. You didn't do anything wrong, and thanks for sticking your nose in. I owe you for Emma. I don't think I've heard her laugh as much as she has tonight in a long time."

"She's an amazing girl. Aren't you, Sugar Bug?" Marti poked Emma in the ribs and made her laugh.

"Come on, sweetheart. Jimmy and Shelly are waiting for us."

"I don't want to go home yet."

"You have school tomorrow and two late nights is more than enough for one week. It's home, books, and bed for you."

"What college do you go to, Sugar Bug?"

"I'm not in college. I'm in kindergarten."

"Could have fooled me, Sugar Bug. You are so smart."

"If I went to college, I could have dessert first all the time."

Marti laughed and so did Cameron. "Touché, Sugar Bug. Like I said, you are very smart."

"I hate to see you leave when you seem to want to stay," Knight began and went on quickly before Cameron corrected him. He needed to leave and get Shelly home. Okay, maybe he wanted to stay.

"Come to dinner this Friday," George went on. "I have something extremely important to discuss with you."

"We'll be there." Cameron looked to George for some answer in his face for his serious tone. He didn't get one.

"I'm only going if Marti will be there," Emma said and crossed her arms over her chest, trying to look like she meant business.

"Are you busy Friday night, Marti?" George hoped she'd be staying at the house before Friday.

"I have a few things planned, but for you, Sugar Bug, I'll make time. Are you sure you don't mind, George? If you have business to discuss with Cameron . . ."

"Nonsense. I want you there. Emma and Cameron want you there. We'll see you and Emma Friday night, Cameron."

"We look forward to it," he said and scooped up his daughter.

Emma turned back to Marti. "Will you teach me how to play soccer with a quarter on Friday?"

"Absolutely. We will use all of our best table manners during dinner. After, I'll kick your butt at quarter soccer."

"No way. I'm going to kick your butt."

"You're on, Sugar Bug. We'll begin the tournament Friday night."

Emma beamed when Marti handed her the quarter. Cameron hugged his daughter to his chest and looked over her at Marti. "Thank you for watching over my daughter."

Marti saw the love he had for his little girl reflected in his eyes and the sincerity in his voice. He loved her very much, appreciated that Marti saw how special Emma was, as special as he believed her to be.

"It was my pleasure." She spoke with as much sincerity as she felt, hoping to give the moment the depth of emotion it deserved.

Cameron nodded to her and George and turned to take his daughter home.

"YOU'RE AN AMAZING woman, Marti. I invited you to dinner tonight for two reasons. One is to thank you for today. You opened my eyes to what I need to do in my life to make things right. Two, I hope you'll humor an old man and an old family friend and hear me out. I have a request, and I hope you'll accept."

"George, of course I'll listen. There's no need to thank me for today. You needed someone to talk to. I was happy to be that person and get reacquainted with you after all these years. That's thanks enough for me. Besides, you saved me from dinner alone in my hotel room."

"Hotel room? You aren't staying at your grandparents' estate?"

"No, the estate was left to my uncle. As you can imagine, he and I don't get along well. I'll have to move my things out over the next few weeks, since the estate has been settled."

"Is that what your meeting today was about, finalizing the estate?"

"Yes."

She spent the next half hour telling him about her grandmother's request and how the estate sat in limbo until her return from her trip. Because he had a similar estate situation with his fortune and family, he understood all too well what she faced against her uncle.

They traded stories about her grandfather and caught up on current events with Knight Enterprises and Fairchild Industries.

Marti possessed a depth of knowledge that astounded George. Business-savvy and fair-minded, she added a great sense of humor to those qualities and others he found fascinating. She spoke of her grandfather with kindness and reverence. She understood his cantankerous attitude and found the love in his less-than-traditional ways of raising a girl.

He asked her about her plans for the immediate future, surprised to learn about her work and how she kept it private. He felt honored she trusted him with her secret. Besides finishing a few projects she was working on and finding a place to live, she didn't have a lot of business going on at any one time. She managed her time well and made sure she had time to do her work.

"I told you earlier, I have a request."

He hated to turn the tone from lighthearted storytelling to solemn and serious, but he needed her help.

"What is it George? Is everything all right?"

"No. I've learned from my doctors I have a terminal brain tumor. They can't operate and it's growing rapidly. Pretty soon, within weeks, I'll be dead."

"Oh, George, I'm so sorry. Is that why you were down at the harbor today?"

"Part of the reason. My family knows my days are numbered and the vultures are circling. They want to pick apart my life's work and get what they think they deserve. Today you reminded me I have control over what I leave behind. The story you told me about your grandparents' estate confirms my belief. I've been lax in dealing with my family. I called for a meeting with my lawyers tomorrow. I'll make the necessary changes to ensure things are handled the way I want after my death."

"Of course, George. You have control over what happens. That's the lesson. You don't have to let them destroy what you've built. Just because they're your children and family doesn't mean they should get it all."

She paused for a moment. "You do realize, whatever you decide to do, it will cause trouble among your family members. It's been only my uncle and I, and we've had trouble from day one. I'm telling you this so you know what it will be like for your family when you're gone. If they're like my uncle, they'll fight over the estate. It won't be pretty, especially if they don't get what they expect."

"That's the part that bothers me the most. They expect to take over and take it all. They're going to be surprised."

George turned thoughtful and decided to go ahead with his plan.

"I want to ask you for something. It's big, and I'll understand if you say no."

"What is it? I can see it's very important to you."

"Yes, very important. I'd like you to spend my last days with me. It would only be for a few weeks." He held up his hand to stop her from interrupting. "I want you to move into my home. I have several rooms for you to choose from. All of them are empty, and even if one of my children or family members moved in, it wouldn't be the same as having someone near who cares about me, for me. You aren't after anything. You've made me feel young and vibrant again. I like your company and you appear to like mine. Most young people don't have the time to give to an old man like me. You're different. You don't see my age. I'd really like to spend my last days with someone like you."

"Oh, George. Are you sure you wouldn't rather be with your children?"

"I'm sure they'll come by now and again to see if I've kicked the bucket and they can collect. They'll probably even resent you being there, but I want to spend my final days with you.

"I won't impose on your work or anything. It would be nice to have meals and talk in the evening with you. A companion. No one should die alone. I'm sure you'd agree there are lots of ways a person can be alone, even in a crowd of people. I don't want to be alone.

"It's a selfish request. You've already been there for

your grandfather and grandmother in their final days. It can't be easy to see a loved one die. I may not rank as a loved one, but I hope you'll grant an old man's last request."

She couldn't fight the tears. Indeed, she couldn't deny him his last request. It wasn't such a hardship for her to live with him, share his meals, have conversations, and be there for a man her grandfather had admired for much of his life. Her grandfather would have appreciated and been proud of her gesture.

"I'll move in with you, George. You were my grandfather's oldest and, although he'd never cop to it, his dearest friend. You did corporate battle and admired each other for your skills. We'll be the best of friends to the end."

She picked up her wine glass, which, like Emma's, was filled with fruit punch, and lifted it to George's. They toasted their bargain.

"To old friendships and new ones."

Chapter Twelve

CAMERON WAITED ON pins and needles in his office. He stared out the window lost in thought until the door opened behind him. Shelly entered, her image reflected in the glass, but he found himself staring at the ocean thinking about another woman entirely. Marti hadn't been far from his mind since he'd met her at the restaurant. Emma asked about her constantly. She wanted to see Marti again and had asked him to call her over and over. Even if he thought he should, he didn't know how to reach her. He didn't even know her last name. He wasn't about to call George to find out. Cameron had no business asking about Marti, even under the guise of Emma wanting to talk to her and see her again. Five-year-olds didn't call grown women for a play date. Cameron wanted an entirely different kind of play date with her. The only thing keeping him from calling George every two minutes was the dinner invitation he extended for tonight.

He'd get to see her again. Emma also reminded him multiple times over the last three days Marti would be there. Like he wasn't just as anxious to see her again. He hadn't felt this way about anyone since he chased every pretty girl in sight in high school.

God, three days. It felt like three months since he'd seen Marti.

He wished it had been three months since he'd seen Shelly. He rubbed at the back of his neck and turned around to face the woman who claimed she was having his baby.

Please, don't be pregnant.

"Darling, you look tired. Having a bad day?"

"I've got a lot on my mind. What did the doctor say?"

"Exactly what I told you, I'm pregnant."

"Do you have the lab results?" He put his hand out, waiting.

"What lab results? I pee in a cup. They tested it. It's positive. That's all. They didn't give me anything. I have an appointment in a month for a checkup. She said she'd see me once a month until I get close to my due date."

Caroline went through the same schedule of visits. Most of them, just routine checkups, she'd gone to alone. He'd gone to the appointment for the ultrasound and many others toward the end when she'd gotten sick.

"I told you I wanted confirmation."

"I just gave it to you." She dug in her purse and pulled out a slip of paper. "See, I went. This is the parking ticket from the hospital parking lot. Other than this, I don't have anything. Except"—she pulled out some brochures from her purse—"the doctor gave me these to review."

He scanned the parking ticket and array of brochures on breastfeeding and pregnancy and guessed she was telling the truth. Not exactly a lab report, but the best he'd probably get. Testing for pregnancy was so easy these days. You didn't have to draw blood for lab results.

"The doctor did take blood to check for any underlying health problems. Once those come back, I'll give them to you," she said offhand, but her anxious tone told him how much she wanted to prove to him she was pregnant.

"I want to see the report as soon as you receive it."

"The lab should send the report to the doctor early next week."

Damn. He'd hoped for a negative result. Butterflies fluttered in his stomach, and he knew for the first time he was happy about having another baby. Already a single dad, he could do it again: two A.M. -feedings, diapers, and crying, not a problem. Emma would love to have a sibling.

He thought about what he should tell her and decided only the truth would do.

"So, darling, we need to make wedding arrangements. You look pleased about the baby. We'll be married and the baby will arrive. We'll be a family. It'll be lovely."

So will all that money.

The penthouse, making love with him every night, access to his accounts and the limo. She would never have to type another letter or answer another phone for her stupid boss. Instead of taking orders, she'd be the one giving them.

Married. A baby. Cameron thought about his life and the lives of his children. The baby deserved a father and a mother. Did it mean he had to marry the baby's mother?

God, what a mess.

He'd wished every day of his life his father had been there. His mother said it was his father's choice to remain anonymous. She'd never told him his name. She'd made his father a promise, and when and if he was ready, he'd make himself known.

Cameron spent a lot of his youth angry she refused to tell him, but in the end it didn't matter. He had his mother, and knowing the name of his father wouldn't make the man appear and want to be his dad. It took Cameron a long time to get to that realization. Still, deep down, when he unearthed the hurt and anger, he still wanted to know his father. He wanted to know why his father didn't want him.

George had been in his life as far back as he could remember. Friends with his mother, he took an interest in him from the beginning. He made sure Cameron went to the best schools and received a full scholarship from George's company, Knight Enterprises.

Deeply grateful to Knight for being there for him all these years, he had been the father he'd never had. He'd attended every ball game, birthday, and graduation.

Even though Knight had been there for him over the years, Cameron had always wished for his father instead.

He couldn't do the same to his child. Deep down he

had some old-fashioned ways. He'd even asked Caroline's parents for their daughter's hand in marriage. Caroline found his old-fashioned ideas sweet, charming even.

It all came down to one thing: he believed his child should have two full-time parents. Emma needed a mother and he wished Caroline had been there for the last five years. This was his chance to give her a mother and the new baby a real family. Shelly was far from the ideal candidate. He only hoped becoming a mother to their baby changed her.

No one was born with a manual, telling them how to be a parent. It was a learning process. He knew that better than anyone. He'd come home from the hospital with a baby and made his share of mistakes the first few weeks alone with her.

All he had left was hope. Hope things worked out, hope he wasn't making the mistake of a lifetime, and hope he didn't ruin Emma's life and the life of his unborn baby in the process.

"We'll be married in six weeks. I'll make the arrangements. We'll have a quiet ceremony at the penthouse. You can have your family and a few friends if you'd like, but I'd like to keep things small and intimate."

"But darling, I thought we'd have a big fantastic wedding and invite your business associates and friends. We'll have a beautiful ceremony and a big reception." They'd receive a ton of gifts, and she'd have the wedding of the century. The San Francisco society pages would be filled with pictures of their wedding and people would clamor to get an invitation. Lavish and decadent, she pictured the whole affair in her mind, excitement zipping through her system, energizing every nerve.

"You're pregnant, I don't love you, you don't love me, and a big wedding would take time to plan and set up. We're having a baby. Not something I want to advertise and throw in people's faces months from now when my pregnant fiancé waddles down the aisle. Six weeks, take it or leave it.

"Oh, I'll have my lawyer draw up the prenup. Sign it, or we'll call the whole thing off."

"You can't be serious."

"I'm a wealthy man. I need to protect my assets and Emma's inheritance. If this thing goes sour, you'll be given a generous settlement."

"Darling, can't you try to have a better attitude? I realize your feelings for me don't run deep. We have our baby to think about," she said to reiterate her point, despite her fury over the prenup. Even if she signed it, it didn't mean she couldn't enjoy Cameron's money while they were married. "We can't be at odds all the time. Surely we can be civil, and hopefully more to each other. Over time, I believe we'll be close. We're great in bed. We just have to transfer that mutual pleasure to our everyday lives." That's it. She'd make him want to stay married to her.

She said all the right things sometimes. And sometimes she didn't.

Cameron needed to stop being so hostile toward her. He was upset about the situation. She wanted them to get along for the child's sake, if nothing else. He could do it. He'd start now.

"Come with me to pick up Emma from school. We'll give her the good news. We'll go fishing tomorrow like we planned and it will be one more opportunity for all of us to spend time together."

Oh, God, fishing.

Not her idea of fun, but time alone with Cameron might give her an opportunity to ask him about getting some money before the wedding to take care of a few things. What was one fishing trip in the scheme of things? She'd play the devoted fiancé for six weeks. Then she'd have everything she ever wanted.

"Sounds wonderful. I bet Emma will be pleased to find out she'll have a sister or brother soon."

"And a mother. I expect you to treat her like she's your own daughter. I won't have her upset or feeling left out. She and I are a package deal. You need to understand that going in."

"Of course I understand. Emma is a darling little girl. We got off to a rocky start. I haven't been feeling like myself. It's probably just the hormones. I promise you, darling, we'll be the best of friends. I'll be patient with her."

Cameron wanted to groan. It all sounded sincere. He hoped it was. If Emma got hurt because of him, he'd never forgive himself.

"Great. Let's get going. We'll tell her about the baby and wedding, then we'll bring you back here for your car. I'm taking Emma to Knight's for dinner."

"We aren't going as a family?" Okay, that might have been over the top, but she wanted to go to dinner and see inside the gorgeous mansion. It was just the kind of grand house she wanted to buy after she married Cameron. If she went to dinner with Cameron tonight, she could take a look around and get some ideas.

"Knight wants to talk to me about something important. He made it sound personal. I'd like to bring you, but it wouldn't be appropriate. I'd like some time alone with him."

He didn't want to take her. He wanted to talk to Knight, spill his guts, and get some advice. He'd help him put things into perspective. At this point, he feared he had no other options than the path he'd chosen. He hoped George could help him sort out this mess.

There was that word again. Hope. That's all he had left of his life. Well, he'd always have Emma. The brightest light in his life.

His mind conjured a perfect picture of Marti. He didn't want to analyze why he couldn't stop thinking about her. She hadn't been far from his mind since he'd met her and now he was engaged to another woman.

He rubbed at the back of his neck and thought he'd never get the knots out of it.

"Don't forget, I want those lab results. Until I see them, I'd appreciate it if you wouldn't mention the engagement or the baby to anyone. Like you pointed out, I have business contacts and associates. I'll make a formal announcement in some way that doesn't shock and surprise people when everything is confirmed."

"Sure, darling. Whatever you think is best. I'll have the results for you Monday or Tuesday of next week."

Time enough to take one of her old lab reports, scan it into her computer, "doctor" it, and present Cameron with a positive result.

So long as the ceremony was completed and she was Mrs. Cameron Shaw, she didn't care if he didn't tell anyone. All she needed was his name and access to his friends, his lifestyle, and all his money.

Chapter Thirteen

"I DON'T CARE what you say, she is not my mother. She never will be. I hate her." Emma was not pleased to hear about his impending marriage to Shelly and made sure he knew it, at the top of her lungs.

"I'm sitting right here. You don't have to yell."

"Can't we keep the baby? She can come and see it if she wants." Emma crossed her arms over her chest and glared across the limo at him.

Interesting the way his daughter had put her statement. *She can come see it if she wants. If she wants.*

Even Emma didn't believe Shelly wanted to be a mother.

Marti told him Shelly didn't want the baby. Was it true? Shelly appeared pleased, even excited when they told Emma after school.

"Emma, I think it's best if the baby has a mommy and a daddy together."

"Why? I don't have a mother. I have you. I don't need a mother. Not her. She doesn't like me, not really," she said sadly.

"She does like you. We'll spend more time together, the three of us, before the wedding. Tomorrow we're all going fishing on the boat. It'll be fun, don't you think?"

"For you and me. Shelly probably hates to fish. She just wants to be alone with you, so she can touch you and kiss you."

Cameron stifled a chuckle. He was beginning to think his daughter didn't want to share him. Not liking Shelly might not be the case. Maybe she didn't want any woman in Cameron's life. Two seconds later, she proved him wrong.

"Why can't you marry Marti? She's nice—she's like the other kid's moms."

"What do you mean?"

"She hugs me real tight like it matters. The other kid's moms drop them off at school and hug them goodbye. That's how Marti hugs. She tells me stories and jokes and tickles me. She tells me I'm smart, and she lets me talk to her. She listens to me. She likes being with me. I can tell she does. Shelly isn't any of those things." Emma crossed her arms over her chest, stared at a point across the car, and pouted.

Cameron rubbed at the back of his neck. He tried to be both mom and dad to Emma, but realized he wasn't enough for her. She might say she doesn't want a mother, but she's jealous of those kids at school who have moms who hug them like they mean it. Shelly didn't even come close to her description, and Cameron feared she never would. Emma wasn't her daughter, and he didn't think Shelly would ever see her as one.

He hoped she would. Man, that word was overused in his mind. How many people entered into a marriage with hope being the predominant feeling? Where were the love and devotion and the holding each other like you mean it? They wouldn't have anything of the sort at his wedding to Shelly. Maybe she was right, and they would grow into more.

"Shelly wants to be those things to you. We want to make a real family for you and the baby." He didn't know if he was trying to reassure his daughter or himself. Probably both.

Emma yelled, "I don't want Shelly to be my mother," and jumped out of the car and ran up the steps of Knight's house. She went straight through the front door like she owned the place.

Cameron stepped out, only to be met by Jimmy, his driver, friend, and Emma's after-school companion.

"She's right, you know. Shelly is never going to be the mother Emma deserves. No mother is better than Shelly as a mother. I know you don't want to hear this, especially from me, but you're making a huge mistake. You're an admirable man, and I know you want to make things right for the baby Shelly might be carrying. Marrying Shelly isn't the right thing. Not in this case."

"Why is everyone ganging up on me not to marry Shelly? She's pregnant with my baby. In most cases, people would demand I marry her."

"Maybe because we all see what you don't. She's using you. What's worse is she's using the baby to get to you."

Cameron rubbed at the back of his neck and contemplated the pile of shit building at his feet, reaching his knees. His daughter was angry with him, he was marrying a woman he didn't love, and he was going to be a father again.

He walked into the house without another word. He hoped he'd get to see Marti tonight and get her out of his head. Shelly made things worse today. He knew without question, Marti would make everything better. A sad realization, considering the situation he found himself in.

Chapter Fourteen

"HI, KNIGHT. IT's good to see you." Cameron made his way into the large living room. Emma sat on the sofa with her arms crossed over her chest and a tear running down her face.

"What did you do to my princess to make her so unhappy?"

"I'm getting married. Shelly is pregnant." Best to just spit it out.

"Are you sure?"

"About getting married? It's the right thing to do."

"I mean, Shelly *is* pregnant."

"She went to the doctor today and had it confirmed."

"Did she bring you documentation?"

"There really isn't any. They did the pregnancy test and it came back positive. It's a relatively simple process."

"So you took her word for it?" George shook his head in disapproval.

"I believe her, if that's what you mean." At least, he thought he believed her. "She had a blood test to check for any underlying health problems. The report is due back early next week, which should also confirm the pregnancy." Maybe there'd been a mistake. One could only hope.

No, he needed to face reality and his future with Shelly.

"I guess congratulations are in order. We'll have champagne tonight."

"Marti isn't here." Emma's small voice came out so filled with misery the words didn't quite come out.

"What, sweetheart?" He took the seat next to her and put his hand on her leg, hoping to comfort her.

"Marti isn't here. She had a meeting in the city and won't be back until after dinner, or maybe later." Emma sniffled, a single tear slid down her cheek.

"She had a few things to take care of, Princess, she'll be home later."

"Home?" Cameron asked, completely taken by surprise.

"She moved in two days ago."

Interesting development. How did this happen? "How exactly do you know Marti? You never really said the other night."

"She's the granddaughter of a very old business associate. Her grandfather and I were business rivals. Her grandmother passed last year and her uncle received the house as part of the estate settlement. Marti just got back from a trip and had no place to go. She was staying at a hotel. For reasons you and I will talk about later, I asked her to stay here for a while. I had all her things moved in upstairs.

"Don't worry, Princess, she said she wouldn't miss seeing you for the world. She promised she'd be here. She'll be a little late. That's all."

"So what do you want to talk to me about?" George's fatigue showed in every line of his face and the droop in his shoulders. Each time he saw George lately he looked a little more worn.

"We'll talk about it later," he said and indicated Emma with a quick glance in her direction. "Let's go in to dinner. The sooner we eat, the sooner Marti will be here."

The last he said for Emma's benefit, but George gave him a knowing look when his excitement at seeing Marti must have shown on his face. Cameron didn't say a word. Acknowledging his growing feelings for Marti would only lead to more trouble. He was in enough of that already.

MARTI SPENT THE entire day putting out one fire or another. Her uncle tried to coerce her into surrendering some of her grandmother's paintings still in her grandparents', now her uncle's, house. She had to lay down the law and demand, in no uncertain terms, the paintings be delivered to the warehouse.

Her publisher asked her to deliver the last two books in her series a week earlier than previously agreed. She still had several sketches and watercolors to finish. She faced some very long nights.

She had to buy a car and start looking for a place to live after George passed away. She hated to think about his death, but she had to be practical. Once he was gone, she'd need her own house. She sighed and put her troubles out of her mind. The cab continued to wind up the long drive to George's beautiful mansion.

She loved the home. The outside was stone, the façade reminiscent of a castle. Just right for a Knight. She smiled at George's sense of whimsy. The climbing roses and lush green ivy scaled the walls. She loved all the flowers and found herself a special corner in the back of the house, a small private garden with a lovely carved bench. She sat there yesterday sketching for her latest book.

Tired, she'd love nothing better than to crawl into bed. Not going to happen. A limo sat out front, Cameron and Emma arrived for dinner with George. She'd promised the evening to Emma and hated keeping her waiting.

She paid the cab driver and walked across the driveway in front of the limo. The driver waited inside, listening to the radio. He waved. Her heel caught in a crack and she took a nosedive to the ground, scraping her knee and hurting her palms as they slammed into the pavement to catch her fall. Before she stood, a strong arm wrapped around her middle and hoisted her up.

"Are you okay, ma'am?"

She dusted her hands down her dress and answered, "Just a scrape. Thank you for helping me. I'm Marti." She held out her hand to shake.

He took her hand and immediately liked her for not dismissing him as simply the hired help.

"Emma was right about you. You are nice. I'm Jimmy. I drive for Cameron and Emma. I'm also her companion after school."

"Companion. I like that. A much more appropriate term for someone who takes care of another. It's nice to meet you, Jimmy. I don't mean to rush off, but I promised Emma I'd be here and I'm late. I'm sure I've disappointed her already. I hate to make her wait any longer. Can I bring you a cup of coffee or something to eat?"

Stunned, he opened his mouth and closed it again. He found his tongue and answered, "No, ma'am, nothing. I'm just fine. Thank you for asking."

"Please call me Marti. Let me know if you need anything. Excuse me. I have to go see Emma."

"You have a nice evening. I hope I have the pleasure of seeing you again."

"Thank you, Jimmy. It's been a long day. It's nice to meet someone so nice."

"Indeed it is," he said and thought of how nice it was to meet her. Cameron had really screwed up. He should marry Marti, not that bitch Shelly.

Marti ran into the house and went straight to the living room and came up short in front of the small group. Cameron and George were talking and Emma sat next to her father with a very sad look on her face.

"Sugar Bug, why the long face?"

"Marti. You came home." Emma jumped up and ran to her and threw her arms around her hips.

"Of course, Sugar Bug. I told you'd I be here. Let me tell you, I moved heaven and earth to get here." She scooped up Emma and hugged her. She smelled of sunshine and green beans.

"Hello, George." She leaned down with Emma in her arms and kissed George on the cheek. "How is everything?"

"Just fine. How did your meetings go?"

"My uncle thinks I'll go back on my word to my grandmother and the others think I can move mountains with my little finger. It was an exhausting day." She hugged Emma closer. "I'm much better now though.

"Hi, Cameron. I see you moved mountains today as well." He looked tired and worn out. She wanted to run her fingers through his dark hair and kiss his forehead and make things all better for him. Instead she shook his hand and tried to ignore the charge of electricity shooting from their joined hands and up her arm. Their eyes met and something passed between them. She let go and the connection grew faint, but she still felt the pull.

"It's nice to see you, Marti. You've saved me again tonight by moving your own mountains and coming to see Emma. She's talked of nothing but you for three days."

"Goodness. You must have been tired of me before I even got here."

Cameron couldn't help but smile. She had a great sense of humor and even laughed at herself. Just like Caroline. Marti didn't look like Caroline in any way. He had to admit Marti was more beautiful. Even better, she had the same easy charm.

"On the contrary. I find you to be the bright spot in my dismal day. Seeing you hug my daughter has given me the first smile of the day."

"Daddy is going to marry Shelly. They're having a baby and I don't want her to be my mother." Emma burst into tears and buried her face in Marti's neck.

Emma's anguish brought tears to her own eyes and she found herself crying with the child. "You did have a big day," she said to Cameron.

She gained control of herself, choking back the tears and blinking them away. She held Emma close and rubbed her back to soothe her.

"Sugar Bug, don't cry. It'll be all right." She sat on the couch next to Cameron and smiled when he ran a hand over Emma's head and back and leaned in and kissed her on the head.

"Baby girl, Daddy will always take care of you. I promise."

"I don't want Shelly to be my mother. I want a mother like the other kid's moms."

Cameron knew what she wanted. She was right where she wanted to be. He didn't know what to say, or how to make things better. Sitting beside Marti was where he wanted to be too.

"What do you mean a mother like the other kid's moms?" Marti didn't understand. Shelly would be her mom when she married Cameron. She tried not to think too hard about why it bothered her so much. She chalked it up to Shelly not wanting to be a mother and using Cameron. What bothered her most was the whole thing upset Emma.

"I want a mother who is nice and makes me laugh and hugs me like she means it." She looked up at Marti and said, "I want you to be my mom." She buried her face in Marti's neck and cried harder.

"Oh, Sugar Bug. That is the nicest thing anyone has ever said to me." She hugged Emma tighter and stroked her hair. She turned to Cameron, whose silvery blue eyes held such deep sadness. He looked to be at a total loss for what to do.

"Sugar Bug, listen to me. Your dad asked Shelly to marry him, not me." Marti should have known the smart little girl would pick out the words she wanted to hear.

Emma turned to her father. "Ask her."

The sadness turned to hope in Cameron's eyes. He opened his mouth and nothing came out. She tried to ignore the feelings bubbling inside of her that he actually might have wanted to ask her. Ridiculous. They just met.

Marti let out a nervous laugh. She couldn't help herself. Ah, to have a five-year-old's logic. To fix her problem, Emma had decided to trade the mom she didn't want for one she did.

"Sugar Bug, I'm not laughing at you. It strikes me funny you summed up the solution to your problem by swapping women for your dad. Unfortunately, it isn't going to happen. Your dad chose Shelly, and she's having his baby."

Cameron wondered if Marti realized the way she explained things to Emma it sounded like she wanted to be considered in the running to be his wife. She made it sound like he'd chosen Shelly over her. In this scenario, there was no choice. Marti was the winner, hands down. He frowned over his own analysis of the situation. What did it say he'd rather marry a woman he'd only just met over the woman he'd been seeing for only a month and was pregnant with his baby?

"Let me tell you about when I was a little girl. When I was three, my mom and dad both died in a car accident. I grew up without them. I wished all the time for my mom and dad to come back. Of course, they couldn't."

"My mom died when she had me."

"That's terrible, Sugar Bug. I bet you miss her."

"I don't remember her, or know her."

"I don't remember my parents either. My grandparents raised me. That's how I met George years ago. He and my grandfather were businessmen. They fought many corporate battles."

"Knight tells me stories about fighting dragons."

"I bet one of those dragons was my grandfather," she said and winked at George.

"Marti's grandfather was the biggest, meanest dragon who ever lived. He was also the most worthy adversary." George smiled at Emma and Marti. He liked seeing them together sitting next to Cameron. They looked like a family.

"When I was little and first lived with my grandparents, my grandfather was very hard to get along with. He didn't know how to be a dad to a little girl. After a while, he learned by spending time with me. He used to read the financial and business news to me. It was so boring, I'd fall right to sleep. After some time, I liked having him read to me and I would ask questions. He would sit on my bed and tell me all about corporate takeovers and how to buy and sell stock. Pretty soon he let me sit on his lap in his office while he went over his work papers. I would help him make decisions and we would spend hours together."

"He liked spending time with you because you liked doing what he liked."

"You are so smart, Emma. Exactly. We found something we could do together and the other things became easier. He didn't mind taking me shopping for school clothes or out for ice cream because we always had something to talk about, business and finance. From there, we found other things we had in common."

"What does this have to do with Shelly being my mother?"

"Well, Miss Smarty Pants, you're just too smart for me. You know I'm leading up to something, don't you?"

"Daddy sometimes takes forever to get to the point, too."

Marti glanced at Cameron with a smirk. "You've raised a remarkable woman. She can't be five."

"She's eighty in a five-year-old body."

"If only it were true for us all. Wisdom is gained too late for some." She hoped Cameron would wise up to Shelly before it was too late.

"My point, Sugar Bug, is that my grandfather didn't know how to be a father to me. He learned by finding something we had in common and building on it. Give Shelly a chance to find something in common with you and you can build on that. She might turn out to be the kind of mom the other kid's moms are."

The last sentence was wrong on more than one level. The structure was wrong, but so was the part about Shelly being the kind of mom Emma wanted. Probably would never happen. Her grandfather wanted to connect with her. Shelly had no desire to connect with Emma. Perhaps Emma giving Shelly a chance would help. That's all anyone can do.

"See, sweetheart, it's like I told you. Just give Shelly a chance. We'll spend some time together and the two of you can find things you have in common." Cameron hoped.

"I don't like business. You bore me enough with business stuff when you talk on the phone all the time," she said and rolled her eyes.

"Maybe Shelly will like fishing and sailing as much as you do." Cameron hoped to find something the two of them had in common.

"You like to sail, Sugar Bug?"

"Yes. We're going tomorrow on Daddy's boat."

Marti turned to Cameron. "What kind of boat?"

"A sailboat. Nothing fancy, just a thirty-two-foot Catalina."

"Just," she said with admiration. "I love sailing."

"Tell Emma about your grandmother's request and

what she gave you." George thought it would be a good lesson to Emma about keeping a promise and it would show Cameron the kind of woman Marti was.

"Well, as you know I was raised by my grandparents. My grandfather was in business, like George, and my grandmother was a painter. My grandfather died when I was sixteen and my grandmother became ill and was sick and weak for several years. I took care of her. I wasn't able to go anywhere in her final years, and so I attended college from home. Sometimes I went to the University of San Francisco and Stanford when she was feeling well. That wasn't very often. Anyway, my grandmother wanted me to see the world, but I couldn't even leave the house for more than a few hours for fear she would take a fall or become ill. When she died, she had a final request. She made me promise to go and see all the places I ever dreamed of seeing. Then she gave me something so I could."

"What did she give you?" Emma sat up on Marti's lap, intent on listening to her tell the story.

"She gave me *The World*."

"Huh? The planet?"

Marti laughed. "No, Sugar Bug. She gave me a sailboat. It's named *The World*.

"For the last year, I played pirate and fulfilled her last request. I spent exactly one year sailing around the world. I gave her my promise, and three days ago I arrived home on day three hundred and sixty-six of my trip. When I met you in the restaurant, I'd just come from signing the final papers for my grandmother's estate."

"So cool. I have some books where the girl, Tina, goes around the world. They're my favorite."

"They are?" Marti held back a prideful smile. She knew the books. In fact, she'd written them. It pleased her Emma knew the stories and liked them. She'd never actually met a little girl who liked her stories.

"She makes me read one every night at bedtime," Cameron confirmed.

"Where did you go? Maybe you've been to some of the places we read about in the *Tina's Travels* books."

"I've been to all kinds of places: Italy, Greece, Egypt, France, England, Ireland, and just about everywhere around South America and more. I've spent days and weeks at sea and I've spent days and weeks in ports around the world. My grandmother wanted to give me the world, and she did in more ways than one."

"What an amazing story, Marti." Cameron was jealous of Marti's trip. He'd love to sail around the world with Emma.

"My grandmother was an amazing woman."

"What kind of sailboat is it?"

"If you want to see it, and you don't mind my intruding, we'll take it out tomorrow. I've missed the ocean these last few days and would love to spend a few hours out on the ship."

"Ship implies a lot more than a sailboat for recreational use."

"It's a hundred and seventy-eight-foot custom-built ship. My grandmother bought it at auction because it reminded her of pirates on the high seas. She was very whimsical at times."

Like her granddaughter. Cameron wanted to see the ship. He loved being on the ocean.

He already had plans to spend time with Shelly to go fishing. What did it matter if they did it on his boat or Marti's ship?

"Wanna go for a ride?" she teased him. She didn't know why she wanted to put a smile on his face, but she liked seeing him happy. "You know you do. I can see it written all over your face. How about you, George? Want to go sailing?"

"Not me. I'll let you young ones go and have fun. My son and daughter are coming tomorrow for a visit and to make some arrangements." George nodded at Marti for her understanding.

Cameron couldn't resist. "I'm in. I've got to see this. Sam and Jack will be so jealous."

"Bring them along. As many as you like. There's plenty of room for whomever you want to bring."

"You can't be serious."

"Sugar Bug, do I look serious?"

"No. You look determined."

"Close enough. Want to be a pirate tomorrow with me?"

"Yes." The brilliant smile died on her face and turned into a sad frown. "I can't be a princess anymore, so I guess I'll be a pirate."

"Why can't you be a princess? You're my princess." George leaned forward to pat her on the knee.

"Shelly said if the baby is a girl, I won't be Daddy's

princess anymore. She said the new baby would be the princess."

"Sweetheart, I don't think that's what she meant. You will always be my princess." Cameron didn't like seeing his daughter's feelings hurt, or knowing Shelly had been careless with her words.

Upset by this new development, Marti drew a deep breath. "Sugar Bug, you are making me work really hard tonight for a smile. George, I assume you still need to speak with Cameron."

"Yes, I'd like some time alone with him."

"Okay. Give me five minutes, and then I'll take Sugar Bug here for dessert."

"You didn't even have dinner," Cameron pointed out. She'd missed the meal and spent the last ten minutes trying to make his daughter feel better.

His gaze fell to her gorgeous legs and he sucked in a quick breath, surprised to see blood on her knee. "You're bleeding. What happened?"

"I fell on the driveway. Your nice friend Jimmy helped me up. It's nothing." She stood with Emma and set her in her father's lap. "Be back in a minute, Sugar Bug. I have a surprise you'll never forget. I hope.

"George, the things you showed me yesterday downstairs. May I use some of them? I promise to put them back tonight."

"Be my guest. Whatever you need."

"Thank you. Would it be all right to ask Gregory to make something for Emma and me? I hate to impose if he's finished for the night. Oh, never mind, I can do it myself."

"No. Ask Gregory for whatever you need. I have to say, I'm intrigued."

"Just wait and see." She held her wicked grin, letting her plans form in her mind, and winked at Emma and headed for the kitchen. She had a terrific idea to make Emma smile again.

Chapter Fifteen

MARTI MADE ALL the arrangements with Gregory and rushed upstairs to change and grab what she needed for Emma.

She loved the rooms he'd assigned her. She told him about her work and her hobby of painting, and he'd accommodated her for her stay.

George gave her the blue room. Cream-colored walls were the backdrop to her beautiful antique four-poster bed with a soft, sky-blue silk coverlet. The midnight rug beneath the bed was so thick her toes sank into it. Every day, at George's request, the staff freshened the vases of lovely garden roses and wildflowers. They graced the long dresser, the little table in front of the windows where she sat reading reports each night and looking up at the stars, and each side of the bed. When she woke each morning, it was to the glorious smell of roses and lilacs.

Her clothes filled the walk-in closet. One gown in particular caught her eye. Perfect for her purpose tonight.

Dressed, her excitement building, she ran downstairs and opened the vault. George made a point to show her how to open it, so when he died she could retrieve the contents for his family.

They spent a lot of time yesterday going over things in the house. He wanted her to know about the antiques and furnishings. She thought it was nice his home reflected him. He had a real appreciation for the things he'd collected over the years.

She pulled what she needed out of the vault and made a quick pit stop in front of the hall mirror to put the final touch on her outfit. She took a last look in the mirror and decided she did indeed look like a princess. Now to transform Emma.

Marti glided into the room and Cameron completely lost his train of thought. His mouth hung open in midsentence. His gut tightened and his heart stopped.

She looked like a queen in her gold dress. The skirt was full and billowed as she walked. The top was strapless and fitted like a corset. A band of golden beads went across the top of her breasts. She looked magnificent. Around her head and over her forehead she wore what was normally a necklace. Tonight it was a crown of diamonds and emeralds. A very expensive piece he recognized as belonging to George's dead wife.

Marti carried another necklace, a ruby and diamond choker. The wrap for her dress draped over her arm, and she carried a small bag.

"Are you guys okay?"

George recovered first. "You look like a queen, my dear."

Cameron remained struck silent.

"Not a queen, Knight, a princess." She made a deep curtsy and stood. "Princess Marti at your service. Princess Emma, stand and I shall transform you into your true self."

Emma jumped up from her spot next to her dad on the couch. She stood in front of Marti, while she wrapped the long golden shawl around her and secured it with a ruby and diamond pin on her shoulder.

"It's so sparkly," she beamed, a huge smile on her face.

Marti pulled her hair up, tied it in a knot on the back of her head, and secured it with a clip. She crowned her with the ruby and diamond necklace. For the finishing touches, Marti put some pink blush and eye shadow on her. She kissed her and transferred her own lipstick to Emma. Emma smacked her lips together. She spun on her toes to her dad.

"How do I look, Daddy?"

"You look like what you are, sweetheart, my princess."

Cameron swallowed hard. His throat ached with emotion. He couldn't help it. She looked beautiful. He couldn't believe Marti would go through so much trouble for one little girl, a little girl who wasn't even hers. What a shame Emma wasn't Marti's.

He fought the choked up feeling rising in the back of his throat. He looked up at the radiant smile on Marti's face as she looked down at his little girl. A golden goddess, the both of them.

This is what his daughter wanted. A woman to see her as special. Who didn't want to be looked at like Marti looked at Emma? He may not be able to give Emma the mother she wanted, but she had Marti tonight. Maybe it would be enough for a lifetime. Having Marti once would never be enough for him. He hoped it would be enough for Emma. It might be all she ever had of being loved by a mother figure like her.

"Come with me, Princess Emma. Your royal tea party awaits."

"I don't like tea," Emma said and scrunched her face in disgust and disappointment.

"Good thing we're having chocolate shakes."

"Yum." Emma jumped and spun around in her princess costume.

"Yum is right." She took Emma's hand. Before she passed George, she bent down and kissed his cheek. "Be gentle. He's already had a hard day."

Chapter Sixteen

SHE AND EMMA sat cross-legged *on* the dining room table drinking milkshakes out of the finest china teacups Marti had ever seen. They used a silver water pitcher to pour their "tea." A china plate overflowed with cookies. The sugar bowl was filled with cherries they dipped in the chocolate shakes and popped into their mouths.

Emma thought the tea party was so much fun. It did Marti's heart good to see the girl so happy. They talked about her school. Marti told her some funny stories about sailing around the world and about her childhood. At every opportunity, Marti tried to reiterate Emma was special, and no matter what happened with her father, she would be okay.

They toasted each other with teacups. Cameron entered the dining room to the clink of china. What a picture they made. Sitting opposite each other on top of the long table, a pretty tea set and a plate of cookies sat between them. Emma looked so pleased. No doubt the tea party was a huge hit.

The two of them glowed under the crystal chandelier, spilling light over the sparkling jewels and the gold of Marti's gown and Emma's wrap. His little princess had a chocolate mustache and jelly from the cookies on her hands.

They made such an amazing picture. Two beauties having a tea party on top of a grand table in a grand room. He would have never thought to do something so amazing and imaginative for his daughter. Marti not only thought of it, she'd put the whole tea party together in a matter of minutes.

Their joined laughter had rolled over him, filled his aching heart, even in the face of learning his oldest and dearest friend was dying. George meant so much, had been a huge influence in his life. He filled a gap in his life Cameron hadn't realized healed a bit more with each gesture George made toward him. Every game he attended, every encouraging word, every opportunity provided by George had filled the gaping hole in his heart. Losing George would be a profound loss for him and Emma.

Looking at Marti now, Cameron realized he owed George for her too. He'd brought Marti into his life and Emma's and in a matter of days she'd made a huge impact on both of them.

Cameron wanted her. He realized his life was going to be less than whole without her in it. He felt the loss of her, even though he'd never had her.

"You two make a pretty picture," he said from the entryway.

Marti turned toward Cameron and her heart ached. Seeing the sadness and anguish in his crystal blue eyes made her want to take away all the hurt, but she couldn't, and that hurt her too. His life was in so much turmoil, yet when his gaze fell on Emma's smiling face, the sadness softened to a love so deep she felt it from him too.

"I left my digital camera on the sideboard. Would you take our picture?"

He found the camera, turned it on, and snapped the photo. He couldn't remember ever seeing his daughter smile so big or look so happy. He didn't need the photo to remember this moment. He'd never forget it, or Marti.

"How was the tea party?"

"It was awesome, Daddy. Do you want a cup of chocolate tea?"

"No thanks. Um, sweetheart, Knight wants to talk to you for a few minutes. He wants to tell you a story before we go home."

"Okay."

She stood on the table. About to throw her arms around Marti, her father yelled, "No. You're covered in chocolate and jelly cookie. You'll ruin Marti's dress."

"It's all right. It's just a dress. You can buy me a new one," she mimicked his words to Shelly from the other night. "Actually, I can have it dry cleaned. I'd rather have the hug than the dress."

Emma hugged her and jumped off the table carrying the napkin Marti handed her.

"This looks like some tea party. Milkshakes in tea cups, very imaginative."

"Last night it was fruit punch in wine glasses, today milkshakes in silver water pitchers and tea cups. She brings out the child in me." Marti smiled for Cameron and hoped he'd smile back. He didn't.

Cameron was having a hard time dealing with the events unfolding in his life. He'd confirmed Shelly's pregnancy, gotten engaged, told his daughter about the baby and the upcoming wedding, and gotten a less than enthusiastic response. He'd come to dinner, a chance to relax and enjoy an evening with an old friend, only to find out George was dying. The lost look on his face didn't surprise her.

She scooted off the table and walked the few steps to him. She wrapped her arms around his broad shoulders and held him with her head on his chest.

For a moment he just stood there. He'd never forget the smell of her hair, the contours of her body pressed to his, the way she fit him to perfection. The longer he stood there, the tighter she held on. Giving in to need, finally, he put his arms around her and held her close. He'd been afraid to touch her, fearing he'd never let her go.

"Emma was right, you hug like you mean it."

"Why do it if you don't mean it."

She had a point. He lifted her, pressed his cheek to hers as she rested her chin on his shoulders. On her tiptoes, he wrapped her up closer, tighter.

"It's going to be okay, Cameron."

He took her in. Her scent intoxicated him, her heat

seeped into his soul, the feel of her so right in his arms. "Do you promise?"

"I don't make promises I can't keep. I'll tell you this though: things have a way of working out in the end. You've had a long day. Why don't you take Emma home and get some rest."

She pulled away and stood back. It felt too good, too right, to be in his arms. Dangerous to think and feel these things. He was engaged to another woman. No matter who the woman, or her deceit, Marti wouldn't put herself in jeopardy of falling for a man she couldn't have. A man who'd bound himself to another woman by, possibly, a child and a promise.

If she was honest, she was already falling for him, and it broke her heart to see him hurting.

"I'll see you both tomorrow. Meet me at the harbor at eight."

"We'll pick you up."

"It wouldn't exactly be on your way. I'll get there just fine. How many people are coming? I know you're bringing Emma and Shelly, but you mentioned some friends."

"Jack and Sam, maybe a few more."

"No problem. We'll have a great time. I don't know many people in the city, since I've been gone for a while. I was pretty isolated before, taking care of my grandmother. It'll be nice to meet some new people."

He looked at her all dressed up, looking like a princess, and couldn't imagine her isolated or lonely. Her expression said she had been for a long time. He'd see if

Elizabeth and Jenna would come along tomorrow. They had the kids, but maybe they could work something out.

"I'll see you tomorrow." He put his hands on her bare shoulders. Big mistake. Her skin felt as soft as he expected and he wanted more, but held back the impulse to let his hands roam over all that creamy skin.

He towered over her by several inches. The heat from her skin flowed up his hands and arms, straight to his heart. "Thank you for what you did for Emma tonight. It seems every time I see you, I owe you for more and more."

"You don't owe me anything. I got to spend time with Emma. It's thanks enough for me."

He believed her, and it made her all the more special to him. She didn't need anything in return for her kindness and friendship.

He cupped her beautiful face and lightly traced her cheek with his thumbs. She stilled in his hands and stopped breathing. He leaned in and kissed her on the forehead.

Overwhelmed with regret and fighting a need like nothing he'd ever felt, he turned and fled the room to get Emma and take her home. If he didn't get away from Marti, he'd throw her down and make love to her like he'd been dreaming about doing for days.

Chapter Seventeen

SHE SAT ON the railing by the docks waiting for Cameron and everyone to arrive. The sun warmed her shoulders and head. The group walked toward her through the parking lot. Cameron carried a life vest for Emma, telling her she couldn't go on the boat unless she put it on and kept it on. Emma did not want to wear the life vest and protested vehemently.

Shelly wore white shorts, a pink tank top, and underneath the thin covering a hot-pink string bikini showed through. The bikini barely covered her, nothing but a few strategically placed triangle swatches. Cameron and the other two men were getting an eyeful. Easy enough to see what Cameron saw in the woman. She had a great body. Too bad when she opened her mouth she spoiled all the beauty.

The two men with Cameron must be Jack and Sam, Marti assumed. Identical twins, right down to the way they walked. One wore a red polo shirt and the other a dark blue T-shirt. Both men wore cutoff jeans and boat shoes. They would do well on the ship. If they hit rough water, Shelly was going to have a hard time on those heels.

Cameron was dressed much like the other two men. Khaki shorts, a black T-shirt, and boat shoes. Emma had on a sundress and water shoes. She wouldn't slip on the deck and she was pretty well covered from the bright sun. Cameron carried a large bag, towels poking out the top. It probably held other necessary items for Emma. His daughter's well-being was his top priority. Marti liked him for it.

Shelly's mesh bag held her straw sunhat, several magazines, and a bottle of tanning oil.

This is going to be fun.

"You have to wear the life vest." Exasperation filled Cameron's voice.

"You know, we can leave you with the driver." Shelly snapped out. The way she said it grated on Marti's nerves.

They all stopped in front of her, looking eager to leave. To break the tension, Marti went with a joke.

"Cameron, really, you shouldn't have. I mean, you said you owed me, but twins? Wow. I know they say men have fantasies about twins. I have to say, I'm warming up to the idea."

Both Sam and Jack cracked up with laughter.

Shelly ruined it. "They're married, honey, to wealthy women. Hands off."

Marti looked directly at Cameron and frowned. "Now that's just downright mean. You bring me twins and they're married. To wealthy women no less," she said sarcastically.

Cameron smiled. "This is Sam, he's married to Elizabeth from the restaurant."

Cameron indicated the man in the red shirt. She shook his hand.

"Damn, he's married to a wealthy woman, and she's beautiful and can cook. Now how am I supposed to lure him away from her? You're just mean, Cameron."

"I like her," Sam said with a broad smile. "Elizabeth said you were great. She was right, as usual."

"Sure, rub it in. She's smart too. And she bakes. Who can compete with that?"

Sam cracked up again.

Even Cameron laughed. He couldn't help himself. She sounded downright disgusted he'd brought Sam and she couldn't have him.

He recovered enough to introduce his other friend.

"This is Jack. He's married to Jenna, my boss. They're like brothers to me and uncles to Emma."

"Let me guess, she's beautiful in addition to being wealthy. What else is she?"

"A wonderful mother and can turn the meanest stallion into a puppy dog. She's also the love of my life."

She looked sad. "Well, damn. You didn't hear that, Sugar Bug."

She held out her hand and smiled at Jack. "It's nice to meet you both. Now, take off your shirts, and I'll see if I can tell you apart without them."

She smiled and rubbed her hands together mischievously. They were both gorgeously well-built men. She'd like nothing better than to see them half naked, but most of all she couldn't help but continue with the joke and seeing Cameron smile.

"Elizabeth was right, you really screwed up, Cam. Do you think Elizabeth would kill me for keeping her?" Sam put his arm around Marti and squeezed. He also took note of the killer look he got from Cameron.

"I guarantee it," Cameron said. Elizabeth was right. He had screwed up, and now he was paying for it, painfully. Jack and Sam would make sure he knew it too.

Sam began the fun and games at his expense. "Maybe we should introduce her to my partner, Tyler. I think they'd hit it off. What do you think, Cam?"

"I think you should mind your own business," Cameron said irritably. He didn't want to see Marti with Tyler, or any other man. He rubbed the back of his neck and looked at Marti's smiling face.

Marti figured she'd change the subject.

"Shelly, we were never introduced. I'm Marti. It's nice to meet you." She shook Shelly's hand and hoped the show of goodwill loosened her up.

It didn't. Shelly shot daggers from her eyes at Marti.

"Well, Sugar Bug, looks like everyone is paired up. You're all mine, I guess."

Shelly leaned in and whispered, "Don't forget it, honey."

So much for goodwill. She scooped up Emma and gave her a hug. As usual, the girl held her tight like she didn't want to let go.

Marti put Emma down and looked at her very seriously. "Ready to go?"

"Oh, yes. Where's the boat?"

Marti turned and pointed way out in the harbor where her anchored ship bobbed on the waves. Too big to tie at the dock, she left her black zodiac tied up a few feet away. They'd take it to the ship.

"No way. It's a pirate ship." Emma's eyes went wide with excitement.

Everyone held the same stunned expression and started talking at once, telling her what a great ship, they couldn't wait to go aboard. She looked down at Emma.

"Ready to be a pirate?"

"Yep."

"Great. Pirates who don't know how to swim and are five years old wear life vests at all times. Even on the ship, you have to keep it on. If you don't wear it, we can't go. Pirate ship rules."

Marti waited for the little girl to decide. It only took a second. Cameron put the vest on her, silently mouthed thank you to Marti, and they all boarded the zodiac and Marti took them to the ship.

"Okay, Cameron, Sam, Jack, we'll head toward the Farallon Islands. Let's see if we can catch some salmon."

She brought out the fishing poles and got a lot of *oohs and aahs* over the equipment. The ship was fully stocked, the equipment top of the line.

Shelly had taken note of everything on the ship, from the leather sectional and antique furnishings to the lavishly decorated cabins below. She didn't have much to say about the stainless steel appliances in the galley, but she did take note of the elaborately stocked bar.

Impressed with the crew onboard, she had a good time ordering them to get her a drink, or move a chair on deck for her.

Pissed off, Marti put up with it for Emma's sake. She'd probably have to give the crew a bonus for putting up with the snob.

She set Emma up with a fishing rod and made her stand next to Cameron. She was safe enough, but accidents happened and Marti didn't want to take any chances with her.

They had a successful morning fishing. All the men pulled in a fair number of salmon. The fish were on ice and Marti had just put out lunch for everyone on the front deck. She made Emma a turkey sandwich, some fruit salad, and chips. Shelly insisted on taking her meal at the table below deck, so Cameron went down to eat with her.

It was a wonderful lunch with everyone talking and having a good time. She liked Jack and Sam. They were warm and kind. Even Captain Finn enjoyed the men's company, and most especially Emma. He relished telling her a number of very tall pirate tales. They all listened and laughed. Emma was having a grand time.

"Sugar Bug, you stay with your uncles and Captain Finn. I'm going to see if your dad and Shelly would like some more lunch."

"I'll come with you, Marti. I need a word."

Marti noted the concern in Captain Finn's voice. "All right."

They went below deck. Shelly and Cameron were not in the main living space. One of the cabin doors was closed and she frowned.

"What did you need?"

Sound carried on the ship, and he didn't want anyone overhearing what he had to say. He'd watched her and the people she'd brought onboard. One thing was clear. She had a thing for Cameron, and although he'd brought the wench with him, he clearly wanted Marti.

He watched Marti when she wasn't looking, and she did the same to Cameron. He'd overheard the wench say she was having Cameron's baby and they were getting married. It bothered him, because he'd watched her to make sure she didn't make any more rude comments or snide remarks to Marti. Every word out of her mouth pissed him off more.

He put his hands on Marti's shoulders, pulled her to him, and whispered in her ear. She immediately put her hands on his arms to keep herself steady on the moving ship.

"That wench who came onboard with Cameron has been drinking. She's half-crocked between the vodka-cranberry juice and too much sun."

Marti studied Captain Finn and saw the serious look in his eyes. "You're sure?"

"Oh, yes. I'm sure."

"She swore to Cameron she's pregnant."

"I doubt it. If she is, she should be drowned. I've

caught her three times sneaking down here to add vodka to her juice."

He was still holding her and whispering in her ear when the door creaked open behind them.

Marti turned her head, eyes connecting with Cameron's. Shirtless, guilt written all over his face, he slipped out of the cabin.

Shelly called, "Come back, darling," in a sultry tone that made her heart shatter.

"Thank you, Captain."

She let go of him and faced off with Cameron, her heart bleeding. "I see I didn't have to come down and see if you needed anything. Shelly already made sure to take care of you."

She shouldn't feel hurt or betrayed, but she did. She also knew it showed all over her face. "I'll just go back up and make sure Emma is okay."

Cameron stood there and Marti disappeared up the steps onto the deck. Nothing for him to say or do to change things, not matter how much he wanted to. He didn't belong to her. She'd never be his.

He rubbed his hand over the back of his neck and wondered how he managed to dig himself deeper and deeper into his own personal pile of shit.

He would never forget the pain on Marti's face when he walked out of the cabin. He didn't think he was capable of making someone hurt the way he'd seen Marti hurting when she saw him come out the door.

Hell, he'd spent the entire morning hard and throbbing, watching Marti in her bikini top and cutoff jean shorts helping Emma fish. She'd joked with everyone, been the perfect hostess, and kept the conversation moving from one topic to the next, engaging everyone. Thanks to her, everyone was having the time of their lives. She even included Shelly whenever possible.

Shelly didn't make it easy. She was too busy cataloguing everything expensive on the ship, or making rude comments about Marti personally. It made him angry, but Marti let it roll right off her back.

And just how did he repay her for a great day out on her ship? He disappeared with Shelly, who tried at every turn to spoil Marti's day, in a cabin on her ship. In the end, all her overzealous pawing and groping did was make him desperate to get away from her. He couldn't do it. He couldn't sleep with her. Not when Marti was the only woman he wanted. Going into that room with Shelly, well, he'd crossed the line. He might as well have slapped Marti. No matter how hard he tried, he couldn't hide the fact he didn't want Shelly. Not the way he wanted her. She wanted him too, and he'd thrown it in her face she couldn't have him. Worse, he hadn't corrected her assumption he'd been doing the nasty with Shelly.

Why should he feel so guilty? He was engaged to Shelly. He could sleep with her if he wanted. It shouldn't matter what Marti thought. Except it did matter. It mattered more than he wanted to admit, because he'd made a commitment and a promise, and he owed it to his children to give them the life they deserved.

He sat on the couch and looked out the window at the

sea. He didn't pay attention to Shelly coming out of the cabin on less than steady legs. He sat brooding and wishing to go back in time and not walk into the restaurant and see Shelly who looked like Caroline. He wished to erase her and start with the day he'd met Marti, only this time he would be alone when George introduced them.

Chapter Eighteen

MARTI FLEW UP the steps and out onto the deck. Jack and Sam saw the look on her face before she took control of her wild emotions. She sat with them at the table and plastered on a fake smile.

"Everything all right with Cameron?" Jack asked.

"I'm sure Shelly took good care of him." She shook her head and waved her hand to brush away her rude statement. "How about a poker game?"

Jack and Sam exchanged identical concerned looks.

Sam sighed and shook his head in disgust. Cameron was an idiot if he couldn't see how much Marti loved him and how good the two of them could be together. Sam thought about his own wife and how lucky he was to have her. He hoped Cameron fixed things in his life before it got worse. Sam had a sinking feeling it was going to get a lot worse before it got any better.

"Let's play. I warn you, though, I cheat," Sam confessed.

"You're an FBI agent. You can't cheat."

"I'm an undercover agent. I'm paid to lie and cheat." He gave her a cocky grin and winked.

He got a half smile in return and thought it better than nothing. She'd recover in a little while and be back to her old self.

Emma sat with her Uncle Jack and helped him play. They were losing badly, but Emma thought the game was a lot of fun. Before long, Marti was laughing and joking again.

"I want to go fish."

Marti set her cards on the table facedown so Sam couldn't see them. Poor Emma. Everyone had caught a fish but her. She was too little to use one of the big poles her dad and uncles used to catch the big fish.

"I'll take you in back, honey." Shelly came up the steps and swayed, but caught herself with a hand on the railing. "Oopsy."

Marti didn't want to let her go, but Shelly walked off and Emma followed. Marti, Jack, and Sam continued their card game. Two of Marti's crew walked forward from the back deck. Whenever Shelly was on deck, her crew disappeared. Captain Finn stood at the bow watching the sea. She liked to stand up there and do the same thing. It had a calming effect on her.

Emma had only been gone for a few minutes when Shelly sauntered up to the table where they were playing poker. Marti hadn't noticed Cameron come up on deck. Alarms went off in her head.

"Where's Emma?"

"Oh, I gave her one of those poles and got her set up. She's fishing. She's fine."

Marti jumped up and ran for the back of the boat. She passed Shelly and yelled, "You stupid, drunken bitch!"

By the time she reached the back deck, Emma was becoming just a speck of bright orange in the water. She rang the hanging bell and yelled, "Man overboard! Come about, Captain!"

She dove off the back of the ship, landing hard in the water due to the height.

Her head crested the water. She dragged in a deep breath and swam hard and fast to get to Emma.

Cameron came up the steps in time to see Marti rush by toward the back of the ship. She rang the bell and yelled to the captain to come about. To his horror, she dove off the back of the ship, a good twenty-foot fall into the water.

He rushed to the railing. Horror and dread filled him when he saw Marti swimming toward his daughter, nothing but orange life vest floating in the far distance. The ship turned quickly and at a steep angle. Everyone held on and tried to keep an eye on Marti and Emma, not wanting to lose track of either of them in the choppy waves.

He never took his eyes from them. Marti grabbed Emma. Relief washed over him seeing Emma safe in her arms.

Fear gripped Marti's heart like a vice. "Emma, open your eyes."

Emma didn't respond. The edge of her lips turned

blue in the fifty-four degree water. Marti saw blood in the water and did her best to lift Emma up and out of the water to see where she was hurt. A long gash across her palm bled profusely. Cut by the fishing line.

"I lost the fishing pole. He got away." Emma's bottom lip wobbled and turned into a deep frown.

"It's okay, sweetheart. We'll get a new pole, and we'll catch a hundred fish."

Marti took her hand and held it up out of the water. She kicked her legs hard to keep them both from going under as the waves bobbed and pushed them around. Her legs burned with exertion, but she had to keep them afloat and Emma's hand out of the water.

She pictured what happened, furious Shelly had left her alone. The little girl had snagged a fish and been pulled overboard by its weight and tug. She tried to hold on to the pole, and the line sliced open her palm.

She wanted to kill Shelly. Emma could have been killed. She wasn't in good shape right now. Marti needed to get her out of the water and warm.

She checked for the direction of the ship. They'd made the turn. Captain Finn would be there soon to scoop them up. One of her crew threw the rope ladder over the edge. No time to stop the ship and launch the zodiac. She'd have to grab on and hold tight to the rope ladder until they grabbed Emma.

Marti wanted to panic. The little girl's teeth chattered. Marti felt the cold sapping her own energy. She struggled more and more to keep their heads above the crashing waves. Without a wet suit, she'd freeze and drown in no time at all, especially trying to tread water and hold on to Emma.

Blood and the open sea were not a good mix, especially near the shark-infested waters surrounding the Farallon Islands. Marti was concerned every shark in a fifty-mile radius had caught the scent of blood in the water. She and Emma were sitting ducks.

Chapter Nineteen

"WE HAVE TO launch the zodiac," Cameron yelled at the captain, even as a crewmember threw the rope ladder over the side.

"We don't have time. The water is freezing. We have to get them out quickly. Marti has practiced this. She'll make it."

They approached Marti and Emma. They'd never slow down fast enough. As the ship drew closer, the crew dropped the sails, slowing the ship with a lurch before they smoothed out again.

Marti swam, getting in position to grab the rope ladder and waiting as the front of the ship passed her by. She put her arm up and held tight to Emma. It wouldn't do any good for her to grab the rope only to lose Emma. The water might drag her under the ship, maybe even both of them.

She grabbed the rope, hooking her arm through it.

She cracked her head against the side of the ship and fought the force of the water pushing on her as one of her crew took Emma from her arms, flipped her over his shoulder, and carried her up the ladder.

Marti used all her strength to drag herself out of the rushing cascade of water against the ship's hull with just her arms and finally got her feet on the last rung. Adrenaline gave her the strength to pull herself up and out of such a force. Once she had a foothold, she stepped up the ladder rather well, but fell exhaustedly over the side onto the deck at everyone's feet.

She coughed up seawater and rolled onto her side. So cold, she didn't feel Jack and Sam's hands on her trying to cover her with a blanket and dry her off.

Cameron kneeled next to Emma. He pulled her life vest off and patted her down with a thick towel. She shook violently, her lips and face still blue.

Disgusted, Marti saw Shelly standing back, looking at Emma and Cameron as if she didn't know why everyone was making a fuss.

Marti dragged herself up to her feet to a great many protests from Sam, Jack, and her crew, and grabbed Emma out from under Cameron's hands.

"Marti, wait. Let me get her dry," Cameron called after her.

She ran down the steps and headed for her cabin at the bow of the boat. She ran through the door and into the small bathroom. She grabbed a towel off the hanger and wrapped it around Emma's hand and pressed it to her chest. She turned on the shower with warm water, stood in the stall, her back to the wall, and slid down to the floor with Emma in her arms. She held her tight. The warm water poured over them, heat sinking through their skin and back into their bones. She shook so violently, it took her a few minutes to notice everyone standing in the open stall door.

"Captain, take us back. Call an ambulance. I want them waiting at the dock. Emma is hurt."

"Hurt?" Cameron asked, concern filling his voice and eyes as he bent and ran a big hand down Emma's wet hair, checking her out with a quick scan from head to toe.

Unable to see her injury pressed against her breast, Marti explained, "Her hand is cut."

"There's no need for an ambulance for a cut. We'll just put a bandage on it. I mean, really. What is the problem? She went for a little swim. Once she warms up, she'll be fine."

Shelly hoped she'd be fine, or Cameron was going to blame her. The little girl should have been more careful.

"Get that stupid bitch out of my sight." Marti held and rocked Emma in her arms.

"Come on, baby. Wake up for me, Sugar Bug. Wake up, baby." Marti kept rocking and rubbing her hands up and down Emma's back. Her little face remained tinged blue. She didn't wake up. The fear overwhelmed her and sent tears down her cheeks.

"Why didn't you wait for us to lower the boat? She would have been fine. She had a life vest on. She wouldn't sink."

"I swear to God, I'm going to kill you. Emma is bleeding."

"So? It's just a little cut, a little blood. She's fine."

"There are sharks in the water, you idiot."

"Sharks? You're kidding," Shelly said, disbelieving.

"Either get her out of here, or Emma or no Emma, I'm going to throw that bitch overboard." She shook violently now from the cold and pure fury.

Sam recognized the effects of the adrenaline coursing through Marti. She was a mother lion protecting her cub from a predator. He had no doubt Marti would leave Emma in the warm water and attack Shelly. He grabbed Shelly by the arm and pushed her out the door and into the main living area.

"Why don't you have another drink, sit down, and shut up? You aren't helping matters. You were supposed to watch her, the little girl who is going to be your stepdaughter. Don't you have any feelings at all for that innocent child?"

"Really, you're all making a big deal out of nothing. She got a little wet. She'll be fine. Sharks, my ass. Marti is just making a scene to get Cameron's attention."

Sam tried valiantly to hold onto his temper. "Shelly, this is the California coast. The Farallon Islands are famous for their great white sharks. This is their hunting ground. Marti and Emma are lucky they didn't get attacked. Now shut up and sit, or I'll throw you overboard myself."

Sam's words penetrated the depths of Cameron's mind, sinking into his heart. Finally hitting him, he understood what Marti had done. Not only had she jumped overboard to save his daughter, but she'd jumped into shark-infested waters without thinking twice.

He pulled his shirt off over his head, moved Marti forward, sat behind her, and put his arms around both she and Emma. Like hugging an ice cube, they both shivered against him. He hoped his body heat would help warm them faster. He rubbed his hands up and down Marti's arms. Her bottom nestled against his groin and the feel of her this close and tucked up against him sent a shaft of heat racing through his system. His chest pressed to her ice-cold back, but the feel of her skin to skin sent his mind on a journey to Dirty Town. He'd fantasized about having her this close. She shifted, pressing against his hard cock. To his surprise, she snuggled closer and he wrapped his arms around her and held her tight. He brushed the damp hair from her face and leaned his face to hers. She sighed and settled against him.

Emma's shaking subsided and the color began to bloom back into her face, but Marti still shook violently. Her teeth chattered so badly, it was a wonder she didn't chip a tooth. "I'm not very happy with you right now."

Cameron put his chin on her shoulder. "I know. I'm not happy with myself either. I'm on the top of my own shit list."

He held her to his chest tighter and squeezed the two of them to him. Jack didn't give him any privacy, standing and watching them. Sam came back in too. He didn't care. His whole world was sitting in his arms.

"Don't ever scare me like that again."

Cameron's warmth sank into her. The water helped, but nothing compared to the warmth of a person's body heat. Cameron this close created another kind of heat. His hard shaft pressed against her bottom.

"You're warm," she said to the side of his face. His big hand moved up her arm, over her shoulder, and up her neck to cover the side of her head and hold her close.

"You're like an ice cube." He held her tighter to his chest. The shaking subsided.

Emma stirred and mumbled something. She glanced down and Emma's eyes fluttered. She didn't open them but lay against Marti's chest and burrowed in closer.

Marti leaned back against Cameron and caught the smell of Shelly's perfume on him.

She remembered him walking out of the cabin after leaving her in bed and leaned away. She tried to stand up with Emma, but he stopped her.

"What's wrong?"

She turned her head to him. "You smell like her," she accused.

He held her tight. "I know it looked bad, but I didn't sleep with her. I'm sorry I'm hurting you. I'm hurting too," he said and leaned his head to hers.

"It's not the same when she has everything I want. You'll all be a family, and I'll still be alone. I won't have Emma, and I won't have you."

She didn't let him hold her down this time. She stood and turned to get out of the stall and saw the blood all over her chest. "Jack, quick, grab a washcloth behind you."

He did and rushed to her. He pulled the blood-soaked towel away from Emma's hand and pressed the clean, dry cloth over the hideous cut.

Cameron felt the blood drain from his face. He stood, took Emma from Marti, and set her on the floor outside the bathroom, where he kept an eye on Marti.

Jack used the washcloth to apply pressure to Emma's hand and stopped the bleeding. The cut was deep, and Emma had lost a lot of blood. Now the bleeding stopped, it looked better.

Emma started to wake up. He took off her wet dress and bathing suit. Cameron grabbed a dry towel and used it to dry her off and warm her.

"There's a T-shirt in the top drawer. Grab one for her. Get her warm." Marti stood under the hot water, trying to get warm herself. She could barely move her arms. In the end, Sam grabbed another washcloth and used it to wash the blood off her chest. Quite intimate, since all she wore was a bikini top.

Cameron wanted to skin Sam alive for touching Marti, even if it was only to help her.

His daughter needed his help. She was the only thing keeping him from going to Marti. She looked ready to pass out. He had no idea how she was still awake. Her legs still shook. Dark circles under her eyes marred her translucent skin.

Sam grabbed a towel and turned off the water. He helped Marti up and over the ledge and onto the floor. She stood swaying while he dried her with care. He walked her into the bedroom and waited while she took out another T-shirt and pair of sweatpants.

She stood with her back to Sam and the others and took off her bikini top, pulling the T-shirt on over her head. She tried to undo her wet shorts, but couldn't get her numb fingers to work. Worse, the material was plastered to her skin.

She glanced over her shoulder and found Sam ready to catch her if she fell. "It's your lucky day. I can't get these off. My hands are shaking and numb. The button won't go through the swollen material easily."

Giving her a cocky grin, he moved closer and drawled, "No problem, darlin'. Come here."

When he stood close, she whispered, "I don't have anything on under these shorts."

"It is my lucky day," he teased back. He put his body between her and Jack and Cameron. Unable to see anything, they were busy with Emma anyway. He undid the button and zipper. Before he pulled them off, he caught her eye and tried to make her smile by saying, "Promise not to tell my wife? I have a gun, and she just might use it on me."

Just what she needed to ease the tension and let out her held breath. She thought it funny he joked just this morning, wondering if Elizabeth would mind him having an affair with her. And here he was undressing her.

"I won't tell her, I promise. She won't let me eat in her restaurant again. That would be a tragedy in my book."

"Mine too."

He pulled her shorts off and helped her step into the sweatpants. He tied them off at the waist without another word. Quick and easy.

Cameron's eyes bore into his back the whole time, but

he didn't so much as turn around to acknowledge him. Let him sweat and be angry. He'd brought Shelly into his daughter's life and look what happened. The woman couldn't be trusted with a child. Cameron would be better off taking the baby away from her than letting her raise it, or Emma.

"What happened?" Sam watched Marti carefully. Exhausted, she slumped and sat on the edge of the bed. He tried to dry her thick hair with a towel. She looked angry as a wet cat.

"You were there. Shelly left her alone. She gave her one of the big poles and"—she smiled slightly—"Emma caught a fish. It pulled her right over the rail. The line cut her hand because her reflex was to hold on rather than let go. When I got to her in the water, she was bleeding and I thought every shark in the area was going to come hunting. I tried to hold her out of the water. Near impossible without a life vest of my own."

Marti trembled and the fear washed through her again. "If I'd have missed the rope, I don't know what would have happened. She couldn't stay in the water, and I was running out of energy."

She stood, the fear in her replaced with cold fury, and headed for the door. "I'm going to kill her."

Jack grabbed her around the waist and hauled her back up against him. "Calm down, Marti. Let's take care of Emma first. You can do whatever you want to Shelly. Once the adrenaline wears off, you'll have your head screwed on straight again, and you'll decide to kill Cameron instead. I'll hold him down for you." Jack smiled and glared at Cameron. This whole mess might have ended in death—either Emma's, or Marti's, or both.

"He's second on my list."

"That's my girl," Jack said and gave her a squeeze. She was all right in his book.

He let her go. She literally fell to her knees beside Emma. She pulled the little girl into her arms and held her tight. He didn't think they'd get Emma away from Marti any time soon.

Chapter Twenty

CAMERON RODE IN the ambulance with Marti and Emma. Marti refused to be separated from her. He knew just how she felt.

He'd held Emma's hand during the short trip and watched her wake up a little and look from him to Marti and smile softly. She knew she was safe.

Sam and Jack followed in the limo with Shelly. Cameron could care less at the moment whether Shelly dropped off the face of the earth. His daughter and Marti could have been killed because of her. Everything sank in, and his mind played out every horrible scenario ending with Emma, or Marti, or both of them dead.

Emma had been checked out, stitched up, and given the all clear. They were keeping her overnight for observation. She was still wearing Marti's white T-shirt. She looked so cute with the shirt down to her calves.

Marti was exhausted after the long day. Cameron

stepped out of the room to talk to Emma's doctor and change out of his wet clothes into the dry ones Jimmy brought back for him. He found Marti asleep in bed with her arms around Emma. He wished the bed was large enough for him to crawl in with them.

In the end, he'd sat in the chair behind Marti's back, leaned against the bed, and fell asleep with his arm over both the girls and his head resting on Marti's lower back and side.

Sam and Elizabeth walked into the room early in the morning. They wanted to check on Emma, but never expected to find Marti asleep with her, and Cameron sleeping on Marti with his arm around both of them.

Sam exchanged a look with his wife.

"They look like a family," Elizabeth whispered.

"Daddy? Daddy?" Emma's words came out scratchy, probably from the salt water.

Elizabeth came forward and touched Emma's head. "Hey, sweetheart. Your dad is sleeping. What's wrong?"

"Hey," Cameron said by way of a greeting.

"Hey, yourself." Elizabeth let her irritation show in the glare she shot him.

She loved Emma and wasn't happy when Sam told her what happened, thanks to Shelly.

"Make Marti move. She's heavy." Emma pushed on Marti's shoulder.

Marti's head kind of rolled, but she didn't seem to notice or make a sound. In fact, she didn't acknowledge the nudge at all.

"Sweetheart, let Marti sleep. She's probably still exhausted after yesterday." Cameron removed his arm from over them and took hold of Marti's shoulder to pull her off Emma. Emma moved away, but Marti didn't so much as twitch.

Little devils danced up Sam's spine. He leaned over Emma and pulled up one of Marti's eyelids. He ran his fingers over Marti's head and found a huge bump on the back hidden by her bloodstained hair. She never said she was hurt.

"Elizabeth, go get a doctor. Quick."

Cameron stood and glanced over Marti to see her pale face. "What's wrong?"

"Probably a concussion. She won't wake up." Sam shook her and patted her cheek to see if she'd respond. "Marti, darlin', wake up. Marti."

Elizabeth and a doctor rushed into the room. Sam picked up Emma and carried her to a chair by the window.

"Stay put, Emma. Marti needs some help. Okay?"

"Is she going to be all right?" Emma tried to see Marti around her uncle.

"The doctor will take good care of her."

Elizabeth came over and sat Emma on her lap.

Cameron stood next to the doctor, who examined Marti. He pushed a button on the bed and a nurse ran in immediately.

"Get a gurney. We need to take her up for a CAT scan right away. We'll take her to ICU after we get the scan."

"What do you mean, ICU?" Cameron's heart raced as panic stole every rational thought out of his head. This couldn't be happening. She'd saved Emma. She was fine.

She couldn't be hurt. He took her hand and rubbed his fingers over her warm skin.

"Marti, sweetheart, please wake up," he begged.

"She's in a coma. Didn't anyone know she was hurt?"

"No, we were so worried about Emma, no one asked Marti if she was okay. She seemed fine. She never complained about anything. She just wanted to be with Emma." Cameron looked at Marti lying statue-still in the bed. This couldn't be happening. He brushed his fingertips gently over her pale cheek.

Sam knew what happened. "The adrenaline kept her going. She was so worried about getting Emma to the hospital and making sure she was okay, she didn't realize she was hurt bad enough to need medical help."

"She fell asleep with a concussion and fell into a coma. We'll see how bad the concussion is and give her some medication to bring down the swelling in her brain.

"Are you her husband?" The doctor turned to Cameron.

"No, I'm not," he said, disappointed. He remembered what she'd said in the shower.

She has everything I want. You'll all be a family, and I'll be alone again. I won't have Emma, and I won't have you.

Elizabeth and Sam's eyes fell on him, but he couldn't answer their unspoken concern.

Cameron rubbed his hand over the back of his neck and watched them lift Marti's limp body onto the gurney and take her away.

"Are any of you family?"

"No," Cameron answered again. "She has an uncle. I know someone I can call and find out his information."

He grabbed the doctor's arm before he went after Marti. "Listen, my name is Cameron Shaw. I run the Emma Shaw Charitable Foundation. We donate a lot of money to this hospital and the neonatal unit. Contact the administrator of the hospital. They'll verify it. I want Marti to have anything she needs. I'll pay for it."

"What's her last name?" the doctor asked and pulled out his pen to take down the information.

Cameron stared at the doctor at a complete loss. He had no idea what her last name was, or what her uncle's name was, or anything. He only knew she was the most important person in his life besides Emma. He needed her.

"I'll go call George," he said and left the room to find a phone. He couldn't use his cell in the hospital.

The doctor left the room and Elizabeth stayed with Emma.

"Is she going to die like my mommy did?"

"I don't think so, sweetheart. She bumped her head really bad and she needs to rest. The doctor will give her some medicine to make her feel better." Elizabeth held Emma to her chest and kissed her head.

"If she dies, it will be all my fault, again." Emma buried her head in Elizabeth's neck and cried.

Sam took off after Cameron. He couldn't listen to Emma blame herself for what happened. They all knew who was at fault.

He found Cameron in the waiting room on the phone with George. Apparently, he didn't like what he was hearing. He hung up and rubbed the back of his neck. Sam hadn't seen him do it this much since he and Jenna were in the middle of a particularly difficult corporate buyout.

"George is contacting her uncle. He said he doubted he'd come down here. They don't get along and have recently had some problems. George is coming down to see her. He said not to worry, he'd take care of everything. As if I can't?"

"You're doing a bang-up job so far. Let's recap, shall we? You meet Shelly, sleep with her because she reminds you of your dead wife—I can't blame you, she's a knockout right up until she opens her mouth. She claims she's pregnant and you believe her, even though we all think she's lying. You make the situation worse by asking her to marry you when we both know you don't want to marry her. Hell, she knows you don't want to marry her, but she's using the baby to make sure she gets her ticket to easy street and the brass ring to boot, or rather gold or platinum in this case. You meet a really great woman like Marti and you want her, and she wants you. She's great with Emma and goes out of her way for your daughter.

"Then she invites you onto her outstanding ship and you show her your appreciation by fucking around with Shelly below deck and Marti finds out. That ship, in case you've forgotten, is Marti's only home. You should have seen her face when she came back up on deck. You devastated her. You threw it right in her face you'd rather be with Shelly than her."

Cameron tried to interrupt but Sam wouldn't let him. He pushed him up against the wall and made him listen.

"Shelly spent the day being rude to Marti, cataloguing the value of everything on her ship, and stumbling around drunk. She ordered around Marti's crew like they were her own personal slaves. She was supposed to be watching Emma, and instead left her alone on a boat. No one with half a brain would leave a five-year-old alone on the deck of a sailboat with a fishing pole.

"After Marti got Emma back on the ship, Shelly completely dismissed the danger Emma and Marti were in and didn't offer one bit of help.

"Marti, on the other hand, dove into shark-infested waters and saved your daughter's life. She didn't so much as think about her own well-being, but made sure Emma was taken care of at the hospital before she finally collapsed from a concussion and exhaustion.

"Thanks to your fiancé, you almost lost your daughter yesterday. You just might lose Marti today.

"Your daughter is in there with Elizabeth right now and asked her if Marti was going to die, and said if she did, it would be all her fault—again. Like the death of her own mother.

"Now, you're like a brother to me, so I feel I owe you the same thing I would give Jack. You are fucking up your life, and you're taking your daughter down with you. Fix this. Fix it fast before you lose everything."

Cameron was writhing. "Don't you think I know all of this and have berated myself every second? I saw Marti's face when I came out of the room after leaving Shelly. I didn't sleep with her, but I may as well have for all the hurt it caused Marti. I heard her voice when she was in the shower and told me she wants Emma and me. Don't you think it tore me apart to hear her say those words and know she wants us both? I know no one believes Shelly, but she went to the doctor. She is pregnant. Marrying her is the only option. I have more than just the baby to think about. I'm the president of a company, and I have to uphold a moral standard."

"Bullshit. Jenna would never have you marry her to make sure Merrick didn't lose profits. When Jack fills her in on what's been going on, she's going to ream your ass, and you know it."

He did know it. He didn't need another person telling him he was an idiot. Shelly didn't stay with them at the hospital. She claimed she was tired from the pregnancy and couldn't be expected to sleep in a chair when she was pregnant.

Happy to be rid of her, all he'd wanted to do was hold Marti and Emma while they slept.

His mind came up with any excuse it could conjure for Shelly's behavior. Because things couldn't be this bad. They just couldn't. "The rocking ship made her unsteady on her feet. That's all. I tried to get her to lie down and things got out of hand, but I reined it in. She was not drunk."

"Sure. She's pregnant, and she's not a lush. I must be crazy. We all must be crazy. Except for you."

Sam walked away and left Cameron to think about what he'd said. Maybe he'd come up with the right answer this time, instead of inventing excuses.

Chapter Twenty-One

MARTI BARELY GOT her eyes open before the pounding in her head beat twice as fast as her heart. The light struck her in the eyes and straight through to her brain like lightning.

Jack sat in the chair, reading a magazine next to the bed.

"Hi, Jack." Her voice came out weak and soft.

"Hey, welcome back to the living."

She held up her hand over her eyes to block out the light. Jack closed the drapes and shut off the overhead light above her head. She cautiously opened her eyes again and winced with pain.

"Do you want me to get the doctor?"

"Is someone sick?"

"You are, sweetheart. You had one hell of a concussion. You scared the hell out of everyone." He picked up the phone by the bed and made a call. "She's awake." He hung up without saying anything else.

She didn't care who he called, she just wanted the splitting headache to go away.

"So how'd you know I was Jack and not Sam?"

"No gun. Then again, I'm not positive. Maybe you are Sam. Take off your shirt, and I'll reconsider." She gave him a half smile and rubbed at her forehead.

Jack cracked up laughing.

"I'm Jack. You've got your sense of humor to go with a nasty bump on the back of your head."

"At least I got something. Cameron brought me twins, and I couldn't even keep them." She smiled, but it died on her lips when everything that happened came back into focus in her mind. "How's Emma?"

"She's hanging in there. She thought she killed you and it was her fault."

"It was that bitch's fault. She's going to wish she killed me." Marti winced. The sound of her own voice hurt.

"I think Cameron wishes he could kill her. She's still claiming she's pregnant. And I mean adamantly. She's been trying to play caring stepmother to Emma, but Emma isn't having any of it."

"I hope Cameron didn't leave her alone with Emma again."

"Nope. Cameron tries to avoid her at all costs. She placed an announcement in the newspaper about their engagement. He's getting nonstop congratulations calls. He stopped answering his phone because he can't stand to be congratulated once more on a marriage he doesn't want. Shelly is doing everything she can to make it happen."

"Wait. How long have I been here?"

"Going on four days. Cameron has been going nuts. He spends every night here with you, and one of us takes a shift during the day. He makes sure someone is here with you all the time."

"You drew the short straw today?"

"Not really. We all volunteered. Even Jenna sat with you. She can't wait to actually talk to you when you can answer her."

"I'd like to meet her too. Did someone call George? I've been staying with him."

"Cameron talked to him. George contacted your uncle. Your uncle contacted the hospital and gave them your information and you've been treated like royalty ever since."

Marti was surprised her uncle had helped. The last time she'd seen him, he'd been furious with her. They weren't close, but it was nice to know he'd come through for her.

"I don't feel like royalty. I feel like someone dropped an anvil on my brain."

"It'll pass soon. So tell me, Marti, who are you? Everyone around here jumps every time your heart monitor increases a beat."

She loved the intrigued look on Jack's face. She didn't answer his question, but gave him a reasonable explanation. "My uncle has a way of getting what he wants, when he wants it. He must have put on quite a show for whomever he talked to. He has a certain way about him. I'm sure you know people like that."

The door flew open and Cameron rushed in with Emma in his arms.

"See, sweetheart, she's just fine." Cameron set Emma on the bed next to Marti and leaned over and kissed her forehead. Relief like he'd never felt washed over him. "I'm so happy to see you."

Marti wanted to cry. She loved this man and he was going to marry someone else. She wanted to grab him and hold onto him and beg him not to marry Shelly.

She couldn't bring herself to do it, so she grabbed Emma and pulled her down to her and held her close. She kissed the little girl on the cheek and wiped away her tears.

"It's all right, Sugar Bug. I'm just fine. I was just sleepy after that long swim in the ocean."

"The doctor said you knocked your noggin and it made you sleep like Sleeping Beauty."

"Well, the doctor would know." Marti appreciated the doctor's attempt to make things easier for Emma.

"I made Daddy kiss you, but you didn't wake up like Sleeping Beauty. He said he wasn't your Prince Charming." Emma frowned.

He's Shelly's. Marti wanted to cry.

Cameron rubbed the back of his neck. She wouldn't even look at him, and he knew what she was thinking. He wasn't her Prince Charming because he was a stupid idiot, and he was marrying Shelly.

He had kissed her. It had been the sweetest torture to kiss her, even if she was unconscious. He'd touched her every chance he got and watched her for long hours while she slept.

He dreamed about sleeping with her and waking up every morning to her face. He wanted to be able to touch her and kiss her whenever he wanted.

"Sugar Bug, I want to talk to you about something."

"Am I in trouble because you got hurt?"

"No. No, Sugar Bug. You are not in trouble. You didn't do anything wrong. Do you understand me? This is not your fault. I just banged my head on the boat. It was an accident. Okay?"

"Okay. Daddy said it wasn't my fault, but I thought it was because you had to jump off the boat and get me. I lost the fishing pole, too."

"I don't care about the fishing pole."

"Shelly said it was really expensive and I would have to buy you a new one."

Marti glared at Cameron. He winced and rubbed the back of his neck.

"I don't care about the fishing pole getting lost. I care about you. I love you, sweetheart, and I would jump off my boat a million times to make sure you were safe."

"You would? Even with the sharks?"

Marti glared at Cameron again. "Let me guess, Shelly. She took a bad situation and used it to scare a little girl."

"She said you were an idiot for jumping in the water with the sharks." Emma's lips trembled and tears filled her eyes.

"Did she now? Well you know what? I don't want to talk about Shelly anymore."

She didn't want to think about Cameron kissing and touching that woman, and she didn't want to think about him marrying her. She didn't want to think about any of those things, and yet they were circling her cloudy, heart-banging mind. Tears threatened and she needed to move onto something else, or cry right there in front of everyone.

"Tell me what you've been doing for the last couple of days, Sugar Bug."

"Daddy let me have dessert before dinner when I came home from the hospital. I was real sad we had to leave you here, and you didn't have anyone to be with you. You don't have a mom or dad, and your grandparents are gone too. No one came to see you but us. Captain Finn gave Daddy your cell phone, but no one called you."

Leave it to a five-year-old to spell it out as plain as day. She didn't have anyone in her life, no family, no friends, no one to come and see her in the hospital. No one had called her cell phone because everything had been solved with the lawyers and her uncle knew she was in the hospital. He'd done what he could, and that was fine. Her editor gave her a week to submit her work. She wasn't expecting any calls and she hadn't gotten any. Who would call? The closest people she had in her life were Cameron, Emma, and his friends.

Unable to stop the tide, the tears fell. Jack and Cameron saw her crying, but she didn't care. Her head hurt. Most of all, her heart hurt. The special people she wanted in her life were Cameron and Emma and she couldn't have them.

Cameron was stunned by Emma's insight. He hadn't realized just how alone Marti was. He carried her phone with him for three days, hoping someone would call and he could tell them about her, or perhaps get some information about her.

She could have died, and the only person they notified was an uncle, who couldn't be bothered to come and see his niece.

He remembered again what she'd said to him in the shower.

She has everything I want. You'll all be a family, and I'll be alone again. I won't have Emma, and I won't have you.

The people she wanted in her life, who cared about whether or not she lived or died, would never be hers. When he married Shelly, he wouldn't be able to see Marti. Once George passed away, Marti wouldn't live at his home and Cameron would lose touch with her. She'd live her own life, find someone to love, get married, have a family, and be happy with someone else, someone who wasn't him and Emma.

He rubbed the back of his neck and hung his head.

Jack decided to save Marti, since Cameron seemed lost in thought. "Emma, how about you and I give your dad a minute with Marti? She's got a killer headache and should probably get some sleep. I'll buy you a candy bar at the vending machine."

"Any kind I want?" Emma asked and stood on the bed to jump into her Uncle Jack's arms.

"Absolutely."

Cameron nodded his thanks to Jack and waited for them to leave the room before he approached Marti.

Chapter Twenty-Two

CAMERON SAT NEXT to the bed in the chair Jack vacated and waited for Marti to turn and face him. It took a minute, but she finally did. The tears had stopped, but her damp cheeks mocked him with how much he'd hurt her. His gut tightened and his heart tore painfully in two.

"I thought I'd lost you. You scared the hell out of me, sweetheart." He took her hand from the bed and held it and savored the warm feel of her skin against his. He thanked God he could still hold her hand, and he hadn't lost her forever. The bruises on her arm where she'd grabbed the rope to haul Emma and herself back onto the boat were black and blue. He gently traced them with his fingertips. She probably hurt everywhere from using so much effort to save his daughter.

"Which part scared you? When I jumped off the ship to save your daughter after Shelly left her alone? When I had to let a ship come barreling toward me and grab a rope or risk Emma and I being pulled under the ship? When I told you I want you and Emma to be mine? I'm sure that's pretty scary for a guy," she said sarcastically. "Or maybe it was when I apparently fell asleep for four days?"

"All of those things, except the part where you told me you want Emma and me. That part just . . ."

"Just what? Made you feel sorry for me. Poor Marti has no one in her life. She wants a man who is engaged to marry someone else because of a lie."

"It isn't a lie. She gave me the test results on Monday."

He'd stared at the form for hours and the damning word spelled out in black and white: POSITIVE.

"She's having my baby and I can't turn my back on them. And I don't feel sorry for you. It breaks my heart to know I'm hurting you. I feel the same way about you, and there's nothing I can do about it."

"There's a big difference between not being able to do something and not being willing to do something."

She held on to his hand. He pressed it to his cheek and leaned his head into her palm. The pain etched in the lines on his forehead and dark circles under his eyes told her how much he'd suffered the last few days. It helped ease the ache in her heart, but only one thing could make it go away. The one thing he refused to give her. She'd tried to give him every reason to see the lies Shelly told him and choose her.

With a deep breath, she put everything on the line and gave him the only truth that meant everything. "Cameron, please, I—"

Love you, died on the tip of her tongue. Shelly glided into the room.

"Darling, there you are. You can't keep me waiting in the car forever, you know. If we don't leave now, we'll be late for our appointment at the bakery to pick out our wedding cake."

Cameron released Marti, the pain in her eyes too much to bear. He loved this woman and every time he turned around he put that look on her face and broke her heart. It killed him.

"Oh, hi, Marti. I hope you're feeling better."

She really didn't, but she'd say it to score points with Cameron. She didn't like seeing him holding Marti's hand and looking at her that way. He wanted Marti, but so long as she had the baby, she would keep Cameron. Once they were married, she'd have everything.

Marti choked back the tirade bubbling inside of her, ready to explode in a torrent of scathing words. She didn't turn around to even acknowledge the bitch. Cameron had come to see her and brought Shelly with him. Her heart shattered even more.

"Get out, Cameron," she whispered, barely able to get the words she didn't want to say out.

"Marti, I . . ."

"Goodbye." *How could one word hurt so much?*

"I'll come back and see you later."

"Don't bother. I'm fine now. I'm sure they'll let me go home soon."

"We need to talk."

"There's nothing to say. Leave a few pieces. Please."

He knew exactly what she meant. Leave a few pieces of her heart. He'd broken it enough. How much more damage did he expect her to endure because he couldn't let her go.

"Marti, I . . ."

"Go pick out your wedding cake. That says it all, doesn't it?"

"Yes, darling. Let's go. Marti, I'm sure, would like her privacy so she can rest."

Marti couldn't let Shelly leave without a warning. She didn't turn around, but the tone of her voice said it all. "Shelly, if I find out you hurt Emma in any way, it will be the last thing you ever do."

Shelly gaped at Marti's back. "Emma is a lovely girl. We're going to get along just fine. Cameron, let's go."

Marti stared out the window, shutting him out. Cameron walked around the bed to follow Shelly out the door. He trailed his fingertips over Marti's feet, not wanting to leave without one last touch. About to close the door behind him, he heard her sobbing. He would have gone back to her, but Emma and Jack were there, and he didn't want to make things worse by having Shelly make a scene if he went back to Marti and didn't leave to get the cake with her. He couldn't let Emma know Marti was crying because of him either.

He closed the door softly and leaned back against it for a moment with his eyes closed, every painful sob tearing him to shreds.

"Want me to just punch you? It might take your mind off the other pain," Jack whispered so only Cameron heard.

Jack couldn't imagine what it was like to love one woman and plan to marry another.

"I'd rather you get Sam to just shoot me. I'm afraid I'll feel this way for the rest of my life."

"If you marry her, it will only get worse. Imagine what you'll feel like when you hear Marti is marrying another man."

"Thanks, you just put the bow on my present."

"Speaking of presents. What should I get you for a wedding gift? Cyanide?"

"I couldn't leave Emma behind," he said self-mockingly.

"I meant for you to use on Shelly after the baby arrives."

"Do you believe there's a baby?" He kept an eye on Emma and Shelly standing together just down the hall, waiting for him by the elevator. He didn't want either of them to overhear.

"It doesn't matter what I believe. It only matters what Shelly can prove. Seems to me she hasn't actually done that."

"She gave me the lab report confirming it."

"Anything can be faked. Ask Sam. It'll be months before she starts showing. You'd be wise to wait until there's an actual baby bump or you see an ultrasound before you actually do get her pregnant."

"I already thought of that. I haven't slept with her since she told me she's pregnant."

"You mean since you met Marti. Doesn't that tell you something?" Jack glared. "Even you don't believe Shelly one hundred percent. I think you're a great dad and it would please you to no end to have another baby. Don't lose the woman you love because you want a baby and not his mother."

Jack decided to change the subject. Cameron had heard nothing but the same arguments against Shelly from him and everyone else over the last four days. None of them had gotten through to him.

"I'll take Marti to George's. The doctor's going to release her tomorrow morning. He said she'd be fine with some rest and medication."

"I wanted to take her home."

"Home? Where? To the ship, to George's, to your place? Where is home for Marti, who has no family or friends to come and see her in the hospital? We've all been here for her, but we're new friends and she hasn't learned to rely on us yet. You, on the other hand, she wants to build a life with and you're going off to buy a wedding cake with your bride-to-be. I'd like to take her home myself and adopt her into the Turner family. Between Jenna, Sam, and Elizabeth, plus all the kids, we could be her family."

"Are you going to keep rubbing salt in the wound? You're as bad as Sam. He read me the riot act the other day."

"We've decided to remind you of what an idiot you are and point out all your flaws until the day you marry Shelly. On that day, we'll throw up our hands in defeat and pray the only person who gets hurt is you, and not Emma. I'm afraid it's too late for Marti. You've already decimated her."

Jack poked a finger into Cameron's chest. "You asked

if I was going to keep rubbing salt in the wound, don't do that to Marti. She's taken enough from you."

"I can't let her go."

"You don't have a choice, brother." Jack put his hand on Cameron's shoulder and shoved him away from the door and toward his waiting fiancé.

"Happy cake shopping." Jack went in to see Marti. Cameron had made his choice and it didn't look like any amount of arguing would change his mind.

Stubborn, single-minded idiot.

Chapter Twenty-Three

JACK BROUGHT HER back to George's almost two weeks ago. She thought it would be the end of seeing Cameron. She would miss Emma, but confusing the child by allowing her to think there was any chance she'd be the mother she wanted was wrong. Shelly was going to be her mother, the end.

If only that was the end of the story, Marti thought sadly. Instead, Cameron found all kinds of ways for her to be with Emma, and therefore with him in most cases. He made it seem like he needed her help with Emma, but he was using it as an excuse to see her. She knew and went along with it anyway because she was as hungry to see him as he was to see her. She saw it in the way he looked at her, in the way his deep voice filled with emotion when he called to ask her for a favor. It's for Emma, he'd say. Every time, Marti went along with it, only to feel her heart break a little more each time she saw Cameron, so close and always out of her reach.

He'd come to dinner with George almost every other day. She knew he wanted to spend as much time with George as possible.

George's health steadily deteriorated and his son and daughter came by the house often, though not as much as Cameron and Emma. George's son made her uncle look like a saint. He constantly made snide comments about her being George's mistress and using him to get his money. Whenever they were at the house, she usually disappeared upstairs to the room she'd turned into her studio.

Since she couldn't sleep for thinking about Cameron and Emma, she spent many hours working late into the night fulfilling her publisher's request for the books she'd promised to finish. Her grandmother would be happy to know she was painting again. She'd completed several canvases and two more books for her publisher. She was ahead in work and had enjoyed the creative outlet.

Her back ached from standing at the easel for several hours when her cell phone rang. Who would call her after two in the morning?

"Hello."

"You don't sound like you're sleeping."

"Cameron?"

"Yeah, it's me. Why aren't you asleep?"

"I'm working."

"Working?"

"Contrary to the fact that you think I'm at your beck and call, I do have a job."

"I never really thought about it. You're always there when I need you."

"I've noticed. Why are you calling me so late?"

"I need your help."

"Nothing new there," she said resigned, because she wouldn't say no. She couldn't. She wondered what a therapist would say about her sadistic behavior. Self-torture was not a good thing.

"What's up?"

"Emma is sick, and I'm in Japan. Jimmy has been with her all day, but now he's not feeling too hot, and he needs someone to relieve him. Emma's upset and crying. She can't sleep. She wants me home, but I can't get there anytime soon. I'm in a bind. If she can't have me, she wants you."

"Why don't you call Shelly and have her go and be with Emma?"

She already knew why. He didn't trust Shelly with Emma and Emma didn't want Shelly with her. She wanted him to admit it.

"You know why, and it sucks, and I suck, this whole thing sucks. I'm in Japan until Wednesday afternoon at the earliest. Can you please go and take care of Emma? I'd ask Elizabeth, but she has her daughter, and I don't want them getting sick. Jack and Jenna went back to Colorado a week ago, so I only have you."

I only have you. Indeed.

"I'm holding onto my temper, Cameron. Choose your words more carefully."

He knew what she meant. He had her doing everything he asked for him and he gave her nothing but grief in return.

"One of these days, I'll figure out a way to make things right with you. I promise you that. Right now, I need you." *I need you in so many ways.*

"The only way to make this right is for you to let me go. Let me go, Cameron. I just can't bear to watch you with her anymore."

"I can't. Please don't ask me to. You're my every thought, my every hope, and my every dream. Seeing you and watching you with Emma is all I can ever have. It's the only thing that makes this whole damn mess bearable. I can't give that up. I can't give you up."

"It's all you choose to have with me," she said, letting some of her anger out.

"This is the same conversation we've had before. I can't abandon the baby. I've watched Emma grow up without her mother. She never even saw Emma, she was so out of it during the delivery. She only lasted a few moments after Emma came into the world. I grew up without a father. I had George, but it isn't the same. I want this baby to have a mother and a father, and I have a chance to make it happen."

The baby would have a mother and a father without Cameron marrying Shelly. She knew it and he knew it, but he refused to budge on the issue. He wanted his baby to have everything Emma didn't. Without love between Shelly and Cameron, the baby still wouldn't have what Cameron dreamed, and the baby and Emma would be the ones to pay the highest price.

She let the subject drop. She couldn't convince him to be with her. If she kept after him, she'd just sound desperate and pathetic.

"Call Jimmy. Tell him I'll be there in about thirty minutes."

He let the change of subject pass. No point talking about it anymore. He wouldn't abandon his baby to a life of being shuffled back and forth between parents. He'd make a real home for Shelly, Emma, the baby, and him, starting on the day he married her. On that day, he'd give up Marti. Until then, he would take every opportunity to spend time with her. Hopefully, he'd gather enough memories of her to last him a lifetime. He only hoped Emma would understand when Marti was gone. He didn't want to hurt Emma, but he couldn't marry Shelly and keep Marti in his life. He knew that now.

His chest went tight and he couldn't breathe through the raw ache.

"What were you working on? What do you do for a living?"

"Cameron, it's after two in the morning, I have to get to the city to be with Emma, and you want to play twenty questions with me about my job? Go work, go sleep, go do whatever you're supposed to be doing, besides bugging me."

"I like it when you're grumpy. You sound so disgruntled. It's cute. I also noticed you hate answering questions about yourself."

"I just don't see the point. In little more than three weeks, you'll have yourself a wife and it won't matter who I am or ever was to you."

"That's not true, Marti." Anger filled his voice. How

could she think she meant so little to him? "It matters. It matters now, and it will matter then."

"I'll see you Wednesday when you get back. If Jimmy isn't feeling well, tell him I'll stay with Emma until you get home."

"He'll appreciate it. Thank you. I know I have no right to call and ask you for anything. I've done it a hundred times over the last two weeks just so I'd have an excuse to see you. I don't deserve you."

"Sometimes I feel the same way about you."

The sarcasm wasn't lost on him. He laughed. It was ironic. He didn't deserve to have someone as special as Marti in his life. Someone he kept taking and taking from. She didn't deserve to be treated the way he treated her. He knew it, but couldn't help himself.

"I'll see you Wednesday." More softly, he added, "I miss you."

Marti hung up, but was reluctant to release the phone. Just like she was reluctant to release Cameron. She was holding onto him as hard as he was holding on to her.

Chapter Twenty-Four

LIVING IN CAMERON'S home without him there was strange. She'd spent all day Monday begging Emma to drink some broth to settle her stomach. By Monday night, the little girl was finally feeling well enough to sleep without waking several times during the night. Marti had slept little Sunday or Monday herself.

The doorbell to the penthouse rang and she set her morning coffee down on the marble countertop.

She didn't know who to expect, but Shelly certainly wasn't high on her list.

"What the hell are you doing in my fiancé's house?"

Here to cause trouble, of course Shelly knew Cameron was out of town. The bitch wanted to mark her territory.

"I'd invite you in, but Emma is sick. We wouldn't want you and *the baby* to get sick too," she said and looked pointedly at Shelly's flat stomach. "How far along are you?"

"It's very early in the pregnancy. That's why Cameron and I are getting married so fast. He wants me to be thin and beautiful on our wedding day."

"I'm sure that's his first concern about your wedding."

She blocked the door, refusing to allow Shelly in. Spiteful, but something small to repay her for all the unkind things she'd said and done to her.

"Let me in."

"No. Cameron isn't home, Emma is sick, and I don't want to talk to you."

Shelly was losing her patience. She wanted to get into the penthouse while Cameron was away, a perfect opportunity to look around alone and decide what changes she might want to make, how she'd like to redecorate. She also wanted to see all the lovely, expensive things Cameron had in the house.

"I'm Cameron's fiancé. If I want to come into his house, I can."

"If he wanted you here when he wasn't, he'd have given you a key."

"Things have happened so quickly for us, he overlooked it. He didn't want Emma to be confused by my coming and going."

"Cameron has good sense when it comes to his daughter. Like I said, she's sick and needs to have quiet so she can rest. Cameron will be home tomorrow night. I'm sure you already knew, however."

"Of course I did."

"What are you doing here now, when he told you he didn't want you coming and going and confusing

Emma?" She used her sweetest voice to irritate Shelly even more.

Marti got a sweet sort of satisfaction watching the woman steam outside the penthouse door. She was sure at any moment her head would explode. Her ears went red with rage.

"I want to come in and look around before we hold the ceremony in a few weeks. I need to make sure there's enough room for everyone."

Marti couldn't help herself. She glanced over her shoulder at the huge living area and decided a hundred guests would fit comfortably.

"They'll be plenty of room," she said.

About to close the door in Shelly's face, she took a determined step toward her and braced her hand flat on the door.

Down the hall, another door opened and a beautiful brunette woman came out and walked down the hall. Two twin little blonde heads peaked out the door before Jack grabbed them.

"Hi, Jack."

"Hi, Marti." He scooped up his little boys and took them back inside.

The amazing Jenna Turner was about to make her introduction. Marti heard a lot about her from Jack, Sam, and Cameron while they were on the ship and over the last few weeks.

"Marti, I'm desperate," Jenna said and looked Shelly up and down, making it clear she didn't approve. "Could I borrow a cup of sugar?"

Marti choked back a laugh, didn't so much as crack a smile. "I'm sure you know where Cameron keeps it. Please, help yourself."

When Jenna reached the door, she passed Shelly without so much as a hello and stepped past Marti into the penthouse.

"If you'll excuse me, I have company." Marti closed the door on Shelly's gaping face.

Marti assumed Shelly knew just who the woman was who entered the penthouse. Shelly couldn't make a scene in front of Cameron's boss and she knew it.

Ah, revenge is very sweet.

Marti turned from the door. Jenna sat in the chair in the living room facing her. She looked regal with the bank of windows behind her.

"She's probably pissed you know where the sugar is and have been inside Cameron's house and she hasn't."

"I have no idea where the sugar is, but I have been in here a lot. My boys love to play with Emma. We often swap play dates when one or the other has another appointment or engagement. I'm Jenna, by the way. Jack's wife."

"I know. I'm Marti. It's nice to finally meet you. Thank you for coming over to rescue me. I think she was ready to shove me out of the way to get in here."

Marti sat on the sofa nearest Jenna and smiled.

"I find it interesting Cameron had you come to stay with Emma and not Shelly."

"Tell me about it. I love that little girl, but sometimes I want to ring her father's neck."

"We're all feeling the same way lately. I understand why he doesn't want to trust Shelly with Emma after what happened on the ship. It makes me wonder what he's going to do once he marries her."

"I don't know. At that point, I won't have the ability to protect her. The only reason I've stayed involved this long is because of Emma."

"The only reason?" Jenna saw exactly what Jack meant. Marti was beautiful and had a good heart. She'd heard the exchange in the hallway with Shelly and thought poor Marti had put up with a lot over the last few weeks.

"No, not the only reason. I'm sure Jack told you I'm in love with Cameron, and he's in love with me." She shrugged and got more comfortable on the sofa. Jenna was easy to talk to, and she needed to talk to someone about this mess.

"I've tried to convince him, the rest of you have, Shelly is using him. He's convinced he has to marry her for the baby's sake.

"I think letting him go would be easier if I truly believed there's a baby. And if he cared deeply for Shelly. If I knew for sure she'd be a good mother to Emma and the baby."

"That's a lot of ifs," Jenna said. "Shelly is manipulative and deceitful. She'll do everything she can to make sure this wedding happens."

"Cameron is just as determined to see it through."

"You know about Emma's mother? She died having Emma."

"I know. Cameron harbors a lot of guilt. He thinks

he can alleviate the guilt over losing his wife and leaving Emma motherless by giving the new baby both a mother and father and providing Emma with a mother at the same time. Shelly is no kind of mother at all, and it makes me angry. It breaks my heart to think in a few weeks, I'll have to leave Emma to Shelly's care. I won't have a choice then."

"None of us will. Jack, Elizabeth, Sam, and I will all have to accept Shelly as Cameron's wife.

"I can only tell you the rest of us will do our best to watch over Emma. I wonder what will happen if he marries her and finds out later that she isn't pregnant."

"I've wondered the same thing. I can only say it'll be his problem. We've all tried to tell him."

Marti didn't want to talk about it anymore. "Cameron said you and Jack went back to Colorado."

"We did. We go back and forth between here and the ranch. I came back because I promised Cameron I'd take over the charity benefit he sets up every year. It's the night before 'the wedding' and he doesn't have time to plan both. I need to line up some artwork to display and an auction. The auction is the easy part, Cameron collects things from all over the world all year for the auction.

"I've contacted several museums and private collectors to see if I can borrow some art. I wanted to find an artist who is well known and will draw a large crowd, but also has a set of paintings themed around children."

"Why children?"

"The benefit is for his foundation. He raises money for the neonatal unit at the hospital where Emma was born.

She was premature, and they saved her life. He's had a benefit every year since, and donates all the proceeds to the hospital. The foundation is called the Emma Shaw Foundation."

"Wow. Very admirable."

"Yes, and just one more reason he won't give up on the baby Shelly is carrying. If she's carrying."

"Have you had any luck at all getting some art?"

"Lots of people want us to display their work. It's just, this is a big event in San Francisco, and I'd like to have something spectacular, something that will draw a huge crowd. You know, the kind of crowd with lots of money to donate. Cameron works so hard and travels so much, he can only do this once a year. Whatever he raises now will have to be enough, until he can do it again next year. The hospital would like to update some of their older equipment and hire two more full-time doctors. If we can raise enough money, they can do those things and more. Whatever is left over, Cameron rolls over to the children's cancer ward."

"You'll find what you're looking for soon." Marti would make sure of it.

If Jenna wanted a famous artist with a set of canvases depicting a child theme, she knew just who to call. She'd contact the curator of her grandmother's art collection and have him call Jenna.

"I hope you don't mind being here with Emma. It's kind of my fault. I sent Cameron to Japan. Obviously, I didn't know Emma would get sick. I thought a few days away to clear his head would do him some good."

"It probably won't change his mind. I don't mind staying with Emma. She's still asleep, but she's feeling better. I'll keep her home from school again tomorrow, but she should be right as rain by Thursday."

"Good. I need Cameron working on a land development deal on Thursday."

"Are you building something here in the city?"

"No, we found a piece of land over by San Pedro. We want to develop it, but the landowners don't want to sell. I'm hoping Cameron will change their minds."

"What kind of development?"

"It's part of our neighborhood restoration project. We take on one each year. We have a client willing to put up a grocery store and provide a loan to a neighborhood businessman or partners to own and operate the store. There will be some smaller shops in the complex and the same offer will be made to locals if they want to use the low interest loan to set up shop."

"Sounds wonderful. You know, a lot of communities are desperate for something like that in their neighborhoods. It also gives the local community members the chance to own their own businesses and remain in the community and help support local growth and community involvement."

"Exactly. I try to give back as much as possible. I'm sorry. This must bore you. I'm in charity mode, and I have enough ideas for this development project to do five more."

"Maybe you'll get the chance." Marti knew of a piece of land in a local community Fairchild Industries planned to develop years ago, but they got turned down on the building plans by the city because they'd wanted to build offices. The city building commission might approve a plan like Jenna's. Maybe Fairchild Industries could team up with Merrick International for the project.

Her uncle was always telling her to get more involved in the business. Here was her chance. She bet she could get the board to agree. As it stood now, the land was just sitting there, unused. This way they could put the land to good use and provide jobs and opportunities to locals.

"I lost you for a minute. What were you thinking about?"

"Sometimes things work out for the best when you meet the right person."

"I don't think you're talking about you and Cameron."

"That's one thing that won't work out and will only end bloody for me. I already know and I've accepted it. I'm here for Emma. I have a few surprises for her before I have to say goodbye."

"Does it have to be goodbye?"

"Not forever, but I can't stay and watch him marry her and be with her. I just can't, not even for Emma. She'll have to learn to accept Shelly in some way."

"She told Elizabeth and me that she wants you to be her mother. When she sees Cameron marry Shelly it will hit her you'll never be her mother and it will hurt her to the core."

Marti couldn't speak. She had nothing to say. She just nodded her agreement.

"Well, I'm off. Jack is waiting and I have to see if anyone has called about the art I need."

"I bet you'll get a call by the end of the day. It'll all work out. I promise."

Jenna gave her an odd look. "I like your optimism. Time is running out. I really want this to be perfect."

"It will be."

Chapter Twenty-Five

SHELLY SLAMMED HER apartment door, furious she'd been dismissed by that bitch Marti.

Who the hell does she think she is?

She tossed her purse on the sofa and grabbed the ringing phone off the side table, hoping it was Cameron. Disappointed by the number showing on caller ID, she answered, despite wanting to throw the phone against the wall.

"Hello, Mom."

"Shelly Bean."

God, she hated that nickname.

"How are you?" her mother asked, her voice gratingly cheerful.

Pissed. Furious. Frustrated, she admitted. Things with Cameron weren't going as planned and she needed to put things back on track and quick. "Fine," she answered her mother. "What's up?"

"Well, your father's diabetes is acting up and he needs a new blood pressure medicine."

"He needs to lose fifty pounds," Shelly snapped.

"It's not as easy for him as it's been for you," her mother scolded. "He tries the best he can to stick to the doctor's diet restrictions."

Easy. If her mother only knew what she went through to stay thin and pretty. How much it hurt. How frustrating it was to throw up a perfectly good meal because she was unable to stop herself.

"Sorry, Mom. How is he?"

"Getting by. Still, Shelly Bean, things are tight. I've had to put off some bills and sell a few things to make ends meet. Your father missed some work and cut back on his hours."

"How much do you need?" It cost her mother's pride dearly to call and ask, so Shelly tried to ease her guilt with the offer.

"A couple hundred would tide us over. Your father can retire in a couple years. We're thinking of selling the house and downsizing. The monthly bills and property taxes are more than we can manage with our medical expenses."

"Well, don't make any changes yet. I'll send you the money you need now. Pretty soon, I'll be able to help more." With Cameron's millions at her disposal, her parents would never need to worry about money again.

"You will? Does this have to do with the new man you're seeing? How's his little girl?"

"She's fine." Shelly hated to admit she'd made a huge

mistake on the boat trip. Not until she arrived at the hospital with them and the doctor explained the seriousness of the cut and hypothermia Emma suffered did she really understand. Emma could have died and Cameron would have been devastated to lose her. He'd lost his wife. Her manipulation prompted the marriage proposal that wasn't a proposal at all, but a way for Cameron to make things right.

He'd be disappointed when he discovered there is no baby, but she vowed from then on she'd do everything in her power to show him they could be good together. Maybe she'd made some mistakes in her attempt to keep him, but she'd make things right.

She'd signed the prenup without a word of protest to the terms. Not that she could complain. True to Cameron's generous nature, he'd been generous in the settlement if they divorced. She'd never have to work a day in her life as his wife, or as his ex.

"Is everything okay with you and Cameron?"

"We've hit a rough spot, but I'm hoping to make things up to him as soon as he returns from a business trip."

"You know what Gammy always said, 'You catch more flies with honey.'"

Shelly smiled, remembering her grandmother fondly. "As you would say, I've been showing a bit too much vinegar."

"You always had a single-minded determination to get the things you wanted. Sometimes, honey, you forget other people have feelings too. If you push too hard, you just might push him away."

When she didn't say anything, her mother went on, "We are so proud of you. Your father and I want you to be happy in whatever you choose in your life. If he's the one, it'll all work out."

Was Cameron the one? She liked him. He had everything she'd always wanted to find in a man and husband. Her mother married her father for love when they had next to nothing. They'd been married over thirty years and still loved each other, despite spending their lives just getting by.

Shelly wanted a different kind of life. She wanted more than getting by and asking her kid to help her out now and again. Shelly knew that life and wanted better. She wanted one lavish and beautiful and free of worry. She never wanted to have to think about pinching pennies, clipping coupons, and having garage sales to scrimp together enough money to pay for medication and food.

Shelly didn't subscribe to her mother's notion that things simply worked out if they were meant to be. No, sometimes you had to make things happen. Still, she'd gone after Cameron without considering the sensitive, honorable man behind the wealthy, strong, determined businessman she'd originally pegged him for. His determination to marry her stemmed from his need to provide his children with a stable family. Marti might be a distraction for him right now, but in the end, he wanted his children to have a mother and a father. If she wanted the man—and everything that came with him—she needed to remember she'd already played her ace and won the pot. She didn't need to push anymore. All she had to do was step into the role of wife and mother. Be the woman he wanted and he'd have no reason to call off the wedding. She could do that. Maybe she'd made a few mistakes, but nothing she couldn't smooth over with a gentler hand.

"Shelly?"

"Sorry, Mom. I drifted off. Listen, everything is fine here. Cameron is away on a business trip and I'm just missing him."

"Time apart can make the coming home that much sweeter."

Most of the time she thought her mother needed a reality check. Today, Shelly appreciated her mother's optimism.

"I'll send the money. Tell Dad I said hi. We'll talk soon."

Shelly hung up with a new determination to do what she originally set out to do. Like she told Cameron, they may not love each other now, but they could build a relationship based on friendship. The tension between them would ease, and they'd settle into marriage and a life together.

Chapter Twenty-Six

CAMERON HAD PUSHED up all his meetings and flown all night to get home. He didn't like being away from Emma when she was sick. Even with Marti there, he'd worried about his little girl.

When he came into the penthouse, he figured everyone was asleep. Past midnight, the house was quiet and dark.

He dropped his bags in the entryway and headed for Emma's room. He snuck in, only to find an empty bed. The sheets were rumpled and her butterfly nightlight shined a soft glow over a cup of water on the nightstand beside the bed and her favorite *Tina's Travels* books spread out on the blankets and floor.

Maybe Marti took her to George's. He'd come all this way and almost a day early and they weren't even home.

Disappointed, he walked into the master bedroom

and saw the sweetest sight he'd ever see. Marti and Emma slept curled up in his big bed together.

He didn't think about what he was doing or what the consequences might be. He stripped off his rumpled suit, put on a pair of pajama bottoms, and crawled into bed behind Marti. She had Emma wrapped in her arms and her back to him. He curled up behind her and held them both to his chest.

He buried his face in her hair and when he smelled her fresh, clean scent, he sighed and fell into a deep, contented sleep.

MARTI WOKE UP and noticed four things: light shown through the slit in the drapes, Emma wasn't in bed with her, Cameron was on top of her kissing her, and he was naked. His hard cock pressed against her thigh. Not a dream. Reality. Cameron was here with her, kissing her. He slipped off her nightshirt, ran his hand down her stomach to her panties and pulled them down her legs. He came back to her and continued loving her awake with soft openmouthed kisses across her belly and up to her neck.

"Cameron." Was that her breathless voice? He'd never touched her or kissed her like this. One stolen kiss here or there when he came to see George, but nothing as deep and passionate as this.

He kissed her neck and collarbone and his fingers combed into her hair, holding her head still. His entire body pressed down the length of hers. She loved the feel of his weight on her.

Giving in to temptation and need, she threw her arms around him and held him to her. She ran her hands down the smooth line of his back and dug her nails in when he licked her earlobe and sucked it gently.

"Emma woke up and saw us all sleeping together. You know what she said? Can I have some cereal? That's it. She's in there watching a cartoon movie and eating breakfast. She thought it was the most normal thing in the world to wake up in bed with both our arms around her."

"You've been here all night." He trailed kisses down her neck and over the swell of her breast, and she sighed with sheer pleasure.

"I got in a little past midnight and found you two in bed. I couldn't help myself. I crawled in with both of you and held the world in my arms all night."

He moved up and took her mouth. He'd wanted to kiss her, really kiss her, for so long he couldn't think straight half the time.

He kissed her soft and gentle, traced her bottom lip with the tip of his tongue, and when the tip of his hard throbbing erection pushed against her and she gasped he thrust his tongue into her mouth and slid it over hers. She sighed and moaned deep in her throat and grabbed the muscles of his back and pulled him to her more.

She spread her thighs, so he fit between them more easily, and she ran her feet up the outside of his legs.

She loved the way he felt. He was so strong and male. His legs were hairy and tickled her feet. She stroked her feet up and down them, bringing his erection to her entrance and away with each push and pull of her legs up and down his.

She moved her hands up and over his chest, on to his strong shoulders and into his rich, dark hair. She held his mouth to hers and matched each stroke and slide of his tongue with hers.

He released her mouth and she pulled his hair in protest until he took her nipple into his mouth and suckled and circled the tight, aching bud with his tongue. Then, instead of pulling his hair, she moaned and pulled his head to her asking for more.

He loved how she responded to every touch, every lick, every kiss and caress. She was embers in a fire and he was the wind flaring them to life. Her flames licked at him in turn with each stroke of her tongue on his neck, every little nip and bite she took, and every press of her hips to him, seeking for him to ease the fire and make it flare at the same time.

He lapped, licked, stroked her breast with his tongue, suckled, and she writhed beneath him. He wanted to bury himself in her fast and hard. With a supreme act of will, he slowed himself down, savored every contour of her body and the taste of her skin.

He moved his hand down over her ribs and stomach and found paradise. When he found her slick and wet, he groaned deep in his throat and took her mouth. He slid his finger inside her tight sheath and stroked until her passion spilled over his fingers.

She was on fire, burning only for him. She was being consumed by him. His finger inside her matched each stroke of his tongue over hers. She felt like she was being tightly wound around him, and just when she thought she couldn't take it any longer, he thrust two fingers into her and she exploded into a million sparks, flying in the wind to heaven. His thumb circled the soft little bundle of nerves and kept those sparks flying out. Heat built in her core and expanded out over her body.

She pressed her hips up, searching for him to end the torment once again.

He took her bottom lip gently in his teeth and bit softly until she opened her eyes. "I need you, Marti. I want to be a part of you if only for a moment, this moment, for however long it lasts. Say yes."

"Yes, Cameron, my love. I need you too."

He pushed deep inside her in one strong thrust. Her hips came up to meet his, and she took him deep inside herself. The world spun away and all he felt, all he knew, was Marti. He pulled out slowly and loved the sweet tight feel of her around him. He thrust deep again. Her nails raked down his back and over his ass and pulled him to her deeper.

She loved the feel of him inside her. Full and complete, for every stroke out, she met him when he came back to her with as much passion and pleasure as he gave to her.

He kissed her neck and nipped at her shoulder, keeping their pace slow and sultry. He loved every moan and sigh he drew from her. Her legs moved up over his hips, and he thrust into her hard. She called his name and groaned for him, only for him.

He moved his hand over her breast and squeezed her

firm roundness. He plucked at her nipple with his thumb and finger and she arched up to him for more.

He moved his hand under her hip, pulled her up tight against him, and increased the pace. Her moans came fast, ripples of contractions ran through her.

He took her mouth and drove his tongue deep inside, tasting everything and stealing her breath. He thrust again and again.

She pushed up to him, harder and faster until finally she called his name and threw her head back and held him to her. When she settled back into the bed, he thrust once more deep, groaned, and spilled himself inside of her.

Completely spent and satisfied, he let everything else go and just settled into being with Marti. Her hands rubbed up and down his back, soothing him. He wrapped his arms around her and rolled onto his side, keeping himself locked deep inside her. He didn't want to let her go. Not yet. He never wanted to let this moment pass.

She lay limp and lax as a rubber band. Her whole body pressed down the length of him. He was warm and held her so tightly, not a centimeter of space separated them.

She felt protected and surrounded by his heat and strength, like nothing could touch her.

For the first time in her life, she knew what it meant to belong to another, truly belong to them. She was Cameron's for this moment, for a lifetime. She'd never love another like she loved him.

Her breath whispered over his skin and her arm draped over his side, her fingertips stroking his back.

She nuzzled into his chest and used her arm to hold him tightly to her.

He'd never felt so wanted and needed more so than he did in this moment. Even with Caroline, his emotions hadn't been this strong, his need this possessing. He had to have her.

He grew rigid inside her, and she moaned. He tilted her head up to take her mouth, kiss her so tenderly it brought tears to her eyes. They spilled down her cheeks, and he kissed them away.

He draped her leg over his hip and moved slowly, pressing his hips to hers and pulled her to him. He stroked his hand up and down her thigh and over her hip, moving inside of her. She felt so good. He couldn't stop touching her.

He moved his hand and caressed it up her side and over the top of her breast. Her hard nipples pressed against his chest and he moved back and rubbed his palm over the peaked tip. She moaned and pressed her breast into his palm.

Slow and gentle, he brushed his fingertips around the fullness and up over her shoulder. With a soft caress down her spine and over her hip, he cupped her bottom, squeezed the firm globe in his palm, and pressed her closer. He thrust deep and slowly retreated.

He kissed her softly, nibbling at the line of her jaw and over her earlobe. He whispered sweet words in her ear about how beautiful she was, how soft she was, how much she pleased him.

He moved his hand between them and found the

soft, slick nub and slowly rubbed the pad of his finger in circles around and over it. She tightened around him in response to the soft caress. She called to him to jump over the edge and sail the wild sea of stars. Again, she shattered in his arms, and this time she took him with her.

Every aftershock and contraction of her body shot through him, milking everything he had to give. He held her tight and pressed his lips to her forehead.

At a complete loss after making love to her, he had nothing left inside him to put into words.

He didn't want the moment to pass because this was all they had, but it had to end. With a supreme act of will, he withdrew from her and rolled onto his back. Completely empty inside, he stared at the ceiling.

Chapter Twenty-Seven

SHE TRACED THE outline of his body from his shoulder, over his chest, dented abs, and down his hip and thigh.

"You are beautiful."

"I think I'm the one who's supposed to say that." He turned his head and stared at her lying beside him, right where he wanted her to stay forever.

Lying on her side, her breasts full and round with pink nipples still hard and begging for his mouth. She had a flat stomach, her hips slightly flared from her tiny waist. Her long, strong legs were lean and tan. She had great legs. He remembered what it felt like to be buried inside her and have those legs wrapped around him. He'd never forget a moment of their time together.

"You did tell me how beautiful you think I am."

"Not just me, any man with eyes."

Since she was lying on his arm, he cocked his elbow and ran his fingers through her hair. Soft and silky, a rich brown with strands of gold woven in between from the sun. He thought of how it looked spread on his pillow when he looked down on her.

He needed to get out of bed. If he didn't, he'd make love to her all day, and he couldn't. Not because of his sated body, he had obligations and promises to keep.

He couldn't keep Marti. Their moment was up. His heart broke into a thousand shards. With his heart full of reluctance and sadness, he pulled his arm free and sat on the edge of the bed with his back to her. Eyes locked on his feet, he mourned the loss of her.

"I have to check on Emma. Come and have cereal with us and watch cartoons."

She didn't know what to say. It was like a light switch turned off in Cameron. His back to her, he stared at the floor.

They'd made love just a minute ago. She thought everything had changed between them. Now she wasn't so sure.

He stood abruptly, pulled on a worn pair of jeans and a black T-shirt. He didn't even turn back to her before walking out the bedroom door.

CAMERON FOUND EMMA on the couch watching TV. Engrossed in the show, she didn't notice him come out of the bedroom and sit in the chair beside her.

"Feeling better, sweetheart?"

"Oh, hi, Dad. Lots better. Marti took care of me."

"She always takes good care of you."

"You look sad, Daddy. What's wrong?"

"I want something, and I can't have it because I was bad, and now I have to suffer the consequences." And he was suffering. More so now he'd made love to Marti and knew exactly what he'd be missing the rest of his life.

"You always tell me I have to fix whatever I did wrong. Say I'm sorry. Otherwise, you don't let me have ice cream for dessert."

Marti was better than ice cream. He'd never get to have her again. Not just after dinner. Never.

All of a sudden, forever seemed like a very long time.

"Emma, I want to talk to you about something. Marti is going away. She won't see you all the time like she does now."

"She already told me. She has to get back to work. She told me once you get married, she won't be able to see me, because I'll have a mother, and you won't need her."

He wouldn't need her. What a crock of shit. He'd need her the rest of his life. He needed her last night. He needed her two minutes ago. He needed her right now.

"She promised if I ever need her, she'd be there for me. She doesn't make promises she can't keep, so I know she means it."

He was rubbing the back of his neck when she came out of the room. She'd pulled her hair up into a ponytail and dressed in a tight pair of dark jeans and a blue blouse that buttoned down the front. His gaze fell to the V of her shirt and the enticing swell of her breasts.

Immediately responding, he shifted in the chair to accommodate his aroused body.

He noted the small suitcase she carried and dropped in the entryway by his own bags. This was it. The end.

Marti wasn't sure what Cameron's mood meant. She didn't like this wall he'd built between them. She hoped he was just worried about talking to Shelly, since their making love had changed everything.

"Sugar Bug, come here and let me check you out this morning."

Emma presented herself to Marti and stood in front of her for inspection.

Marti leaned down and kissed the little girl's forehead. No sign of fever. She whispered she loved her into her right ear and the left. Emma nodded each time. Her ears were clear and didn't hurt anymore.

"Open up."

Emma opened her mouth and Marti checked her throat. No redness. She tickled Emma and made her squeal with laughter.

"All better. No fever, no earache, no sore throat. Your lungs are in perfect working order." She scooped Emma up and plopped her down on Cameron's lap. "Cameron, I present one healthy daughter to you."

Emma laughed and squealed as he continued to tickle her. He didn't hear the knock at the door. When he looked up, Shelly stood in the entryway beside Marti. Again, that devastated look filled her face. He saw it every time he threw it in her face he and Shelly were together.

He'd just made love to one woman, and the other he didn't want to ever touch again.

He looked at Shelly now and realized the resemblance to Caroline was just that, a resemblance. Never enough for him to mistake one for the other. His own mind overlaid Caroline's image onto Shelly. Why he did that, he wasn't sure anymore.

"Cameron, darling, you're home."

"What are you doing here, Shelly?" He hadn't told her he was back. They had an agreement about her not coming to the penthouse until after they were married. He didn't want to confuse Emma. That's what he told himself. Truthfully, he'd never brought any woman to the penthouse. This was his and Emma's place together. Now he'd not only had Marti stay over, he'd made love to her in his bed.

He needed to find someplace else to live when he married Shelly. He couldn't bring her here and spoil his memories. She was already doing that by showing up unannounced.

"I heard Emma is sick, and I came to check on her." She turned on Marti. "You can go now. Cameron is home to take care of his daughter. Your services are no longer required."

The words were spoken in such a normal tone, Marti didn't get it at first. A second later it hit her. She was being dismissed like the hired help.

Her gaze found Cameron's. He sat staring at them both and never said a word. He didn't defend her or tell Shelly to have some respect for a family friend. Nothing.

"I'll just get my shoes."

His eyes were drawn to her bare feet under the hem of

her jeans. Her toes were painted a soft pink. He'd remember that, too, when he was missing her.

He should ask Shelly to leave, or at least get her to apologize to Marti for the blatant dismissal. Unable to speak, the woman he wanted was leaving, and the one he didn't want was staying.

Marti was tying her tennis shoes when Cameron walked into the bedroom. "Marti, I want to thank you."

"You're welcome. I guess now that Shelly is here she can scratch your next itch."

Stunned, he couldn't believe her words.

"I'm not thanking you for making love with me," he said under his breath, so no one heard them.

"Well, that's almost as rude as you allowing *your fiancé* to dismiss me like some servant. What are you going to do, Cameron, sleep with her tonight in this bed where we made love not even an hour ago?"

"No. No one has slept in that bed, except Emma and me. I'll burn the goddamn thing before I let another woman into that bed."

She stood and faced him. "The other woman is your fiancé. I want to hear you say it."

"What?"

"After this morning, everything you said, making love to me, you're still going to marry her. I want to hear you say the words."

No matter how determined she was to hear him say it, he didn't want to do that to her. He'd hurt her so much already. He didn't want to do it again. Not after what they'd shared.

She waited, not willing to give in, let what they'd shared be enough. One day, one time with her would never be enough. He didn't want to have to tell her it didn't matter, he'd chosen another. It didn't matter if the person he'd truly chosen wasn't really Shelly.

"I'm going to marry her." The words held little conviction, but he bolstered his resolve by adding, "She's carrying my child."

What if I'm carrying your child?

She shook her head sadly. It hadn't even crossed his mind. For him, the moment they'd shared was over. Nothing but a memory now, they would carry with them as they led their separate lives. It hit her hard, bit into her soul, and tore her to shreds. No matter what she said or did, he'd never change his mind.

"I wonder what you'll do after you marry her and discover she isn't pregnant after all? Maybe she'll lie and tell you she lost the baby. Maybe she'll tell you the truth, finally—there never was a baby."

"If that happens, I'll leave her and come after you."

"You can't, because you already lost me."

"I don't want to lose you."

"You know, you never had me, because she's been standing between us this whole time. I made a mistake this morning thinking you'd come to me because you changed your mind. When you said you wanted a moment, you didn't mean a lifetime of moments. You just wanted the time it took to have one good memory. Something you can pull out and look at when you're lonely and missing me. She's ruined so many things between us.

She's even ruined this," she said and threw her arms up over the bed. "All ruined over a lie."

"It's not a lie. She's pregnant with my baby."

"You want so much to believe she's carrying your baby. I even understand why you want to believe it. The thought of your baby is a wonderful idea, but you've completely lost all reason about everything else, including me. I can't be second anymore. I'm willing to be second to Emma, but not to her."

She pressed her fingertips to her mouth to hold back the sob, bit her lip, and tasted him. "I've made some promises to Emma. I'll keep them. I won't go back on my word to her. As for you, don't call and ask me to do things for you because you want to see me. It ends now. You'll see me when I come to fulfill my promises to Emma, but I want you to keep your distance. Be with Shelly if she's your choice. Maybe you can train her how to be a good mother to Emma."

"Marti, please, don't leave like this."

"You've left me no choice. I have no pieces left. You've taken them all."

She'd asked him before to leave her a few of the broken pieces of her heart. A heart he'd broken by not choosing her time and time again. This was the final piece. He'd made love to her, admitted to her how much he needed and wanted her, and he'd still chosen Shelly.

She turned to the bed and ran her hand over the covers, still rumpled and pushed down by their lovemaking. She took a moment and closed her eyes and remembered how they were in bed together. She remembered how she'd felt close to him, connected, whole. They'd become one in that bed. Now an ocean stood between them. An ocean named Shelly.

She turned from the bed with tears rolling down her cheeks. She headed out of the bedroom door wiping her tears away and left Cameron at her back.

He walked down the hall and winced when he heard Shelly and Marti's final exchange.

"All done with Cameron?" Shelly asked with a frown and her arms crossed under her breasts.

"He's all yours," Marti shot back and slammed the front door behind her.

He pushed back the pain and felt his heart turn to ice. He'd never love anyone the way he loved her.

Shelly smiled with what could only be described as triumph. A switch happened inside him and he faced his future with all the resignation of facing a firing squad. Everything in him wanted to go after Marti.

Shelly dropped her arms and smoothed her blouse over her flat stomach. A gesture Caroline made often when her belly was round with their child. He reminded himself that his children needed him. They deserved a family and he'd do everything in his power to give them the family he always wanted for himself and them.

Chapter Twenty-Eight

MARTI SPENT THE next ten days with George. His health deteriorated and his personal physician visited the house more and more often.

She spent every possible moment with him. He liked sitting in the private garden and telling her stories. The tumor was robbing him of his memory. He often repeated himself and forgot things he'd told her. Some of his stories seemed to meld together.

She didn't mind. She enjoyed his company. Being with him distracted her from thinking about Cameron. The pain and hurt lived inside of her, but she tried to hide it so George's final days were happy and unspoiled.

They were having breakfast on the back patio when his son arrived with the family lawyer. She didn't like the looks of this, but George was having a good day so far and she hoped he was up to the meeting. He'd had several meetings with the lawyer the first days she'd lived in the house. She hoped nothing was wrong.

"Father, Mr. Spencer and I have come to speak with you about the changes you made to your will several weeks ago."

"There's nothing to discuss. I'm sure Mr. Spencer has set up everything I asked him to do. The will is finished and to my exact specification. Is that not the case, Mr. Spencer?"

"It is, sir. Your son contacted me last night with concerns about your new will and has asked to see a copy. I've told him you wish for the contents to remain sealed until the time of your passing, sir."

"Those are my instructions. Walter, there is nothing you need to be aware of prior to my death. What's mine is mine. I can do with it as I please."

"No, Father. You have a brain tumor, and I believe you've been unduly influenced by your mistress whore."

George's face turned a dark red. Marti feared the stress might trigger a stroke or heart attack.

Without a word, she pushed her chair back and rose to leave. George grabbed her hand and held it. A light tug prompted her to sit again. The other gentlemen joined them at the table. Now she knew why he wanted her there. To make sure his son didn't try to make him do something he didn't want to do. He'd said often she gave him strength and renewed his convictions. He needed her to stand against his son, who was only after one thing: as much of his father's estate as he could get his hands on.

"Marti is no such thing. She is a friend and like a

daughter to me. More so than you've been a son these last several months. Your judgment and genuine concern are clouded by your greed. You and your sister don't come here to see about my welfare. You're checking to see how long it'll be before I kick the bucket, and I'm tired of it. I asked Marti to stay with me because she's here to be with me. She cares about my well-being."

"I'm sure she cares about your well-being," Walter said, dripping sarcasm. He knew just what Marti was taking care of and it wasn't his father's health. She was trying to get him to leave everything to her, if she hadn't already. He wanted to see the will.

"You know, Father, when you changed the will you were in your final weeks of illness. Whatever you've changed, I can have a judge fix based on your inability to think rationally with a tumor growing rapidly in your brain."

George just smiled at his son. He couldn't believe he'd raised such a selfish, self-centered man.

"You can try, but it will only be a waste of time. I had two well-respected physicians declare me mentally competent and lucid hours prior to the changes I made to the will. In addition, the changes I made were to include family members, not exclude them. You have nothing to worry about. I've taken care of your sister and you," he said cryptically, for it could mean a number of things.

He'd let Walter stew on it.

"What do you mean, you've added family members? Who? Some of the distant cousins?"

"My decisions are final. The document will remain sealed until my passing. Everything will be distributed forthwith. You'll receive your inheritance within a matter of days. That's all you need to know."

One of the servants stepped out on the patio to announce a delivery for Marti.

George's face lit with excitement. Marti, on the other hand, had no idea what the delivery could be. She hadn't ordered anything and her publisher couldn't have gotten the new books done so quickly.

"Walter, excuse us. I have a surprise for Marti. Come along, dear."

She helped him to his feet. His motor skills had been failing quickly. A wheelchair waited in the house, but George didn't want to use it until it was absolutely necessary.

She walked with him to the front door, supporting him around the waist. He had his arm around her and held her tight. To anyone looking on, it appeared they were walking arm in arm. The feel of him in her arms leaning on her made it clear. He was losing his battle with the tumor. His physician had told her it was a matter of days now, not weeks.

Once he was gone, she'd leave this house and be on her own again. She needed to make her own plans for the future. The task seemed daunting, especially since she'd set her heart on a life with Cameron and Emma. She didn't want to consider anything else, because everything else was simply existing, not living.

Cameron and Emma came over twice the last few days to have dinner with George. Cameron brought Shelly both times. Both times Marti excused herself after dinner and took Emma up to her room where they spent time alone together. He'd been nice and friendly. They'd kept what little conversation they shared to everyday things, Emma, and George, but she caught the heated looks and longing in his eyes whenever she let herself look directly at his face.

He and Shelly looked and acted like they'd come to some agreement on their relationship. Closer, more comfortable in each other's company, Cameron paid attention to her with an attentiveness that proved his intention to make a life with her. Shelly was friendly to Emma and didn't dismiss the little girl every time she talked. She'd actually heard Shelly engage the little girl in conversation several times. They were becoming a family. Marti was happy for them, but knew it was just another reason to make her own plans.

She never thought she'd have to say goodbye to so many after returning home from her trip.

Over the next two weeks, she needed to say goodbye to George upon his passing, and goodbye to Emma and Cameron before his wedding to Shelly. She'd say goodbye to Jenna, Jack, Sam, and Elizabeth after the charity benefit for Cameron's foundation.

She'd already taken care of the artwork for Jenna. Jenna didn't know it was her doing, but it was taken care of just the same. She'd had her assistant at Fairchild Industries contact Cameron about the property and working on a development idea. Those plans were in the works.

She had a few gifts to finish up before she left for good. It didn't matter if she stayed in the city or left on her ship. Able to work anywhere, she liked it that way.

She would forever be tied to Cameron, but she needed her freedom. Maybe another trip on her ship was just the ticket. Someplace exotic, warm, nothing like San Francisco and the memories she'd made here.

She opened the front door and stepped out onto the entryway with George at her side. A man wearing a suit handed her a set of keys.

"Miss Fairchild, I presume. These are for you."

She took the keys and looked behind the man at the brand new convertible Jaguar parked on the circular driveway. Black with tinted windows, it gleamed in the morning sun. She'd been looking at brochures with George, trying to decide which car she'd like to buy. She'd never had a car of her own and wanted something wonderful for her first big purchase. This was the car she'd picked out. Speed and beauty combined into the most perfect automobile. She loved it.

"George, no. You didn't."

"It's the one you wanted. I called the dealership and had it delivered. It's yours."

"No. You can't. It's too expensive."

"It certainly is," Walter said and stepped out the door. "Dad, you can't be serious. You bought your *friend* a car."

"Walter, shut up. I can do as I please."

He turned to Marti. "It pleases me to buy this for you. I hope you like it and enjoy it. Think of me every time you're behind the wheel."

"Oh, George. I will. I will always remember you. I'll remember our long talks and poker games. I'll forget you owe me twenty-five fifty, by the way," she said and winked at him. "I'll remember the day I met you, again, on the docks at the harbor, and how we stood in the pouring rain. I'll remember everything we talked about and the reasons for my being here. Because of you I met Emma and Cameron, and for a little while, I was happier than I've ever been in my life. My grandmother gave me *The World*; you gave me a little piece of heaven. I'll remember it all. I'll remember you."

In the end, a life came down to the people you leave behind and their memory of you.

George held her close. She understood his inner desire to be remembered by someone who loved him for who he was and not what he had.

"I'm leaving." Walter's angry voice intruded on her moment with George. "Just remember, Marti, no judge will uphold his will if he's left it all to his mistress. I'll keep you in court for the rest of your days."

"Just leave. I don't want anything from George except his friendship, and I've already got it. You and I have nothing to fight over."

The attorney thanked George for his time, assured him everything was in order, and left with Walter.

She took her new car for a spin with George. They took some back roads and listened to the purr of the engine as she put the car through its paces around every turn. George had the time of his life, told her he hadn't felt like this since he was a teen, driving his first car.

She was glad to give him one more fun day. It was the last one they would share. His health took a turn for the worse the next morning.

Chapter Twenty-Nine

CAMERON SAT BACK in the limo listening to Shelly talk on her cell phone with some girlfriend of hers. He'd never get used to her itemizing and calculating the cost of everything they'd gotten for the wedding or ordered for the ceremony. In fact, she did it all the time with everything. She was obsessed with how expensive something was, and the more expensive, the better.

Things had changed since he watched Marti walk out the door of his penthouse two weeks ago. He'd made a concerted effort to get to know Shelly better and make her a part of his life. He'd even taken her to dinner at George's. He knew it was just another stab in the back to Marti, but he couldn't help it. He had to make things right with Shelly, which meant accepting her as part of his life.

He had to let Marti go. He thought he was doing a good job of changing things between them to more of a friendly acquaintance. He told himself the lie that they were only friends; every second of every day he spent thinking about her and the time they'd spent together making love.

He watched Shelly closely over the last two weeks. The more he accepted her, the more she settled down and took a real interest in Emma. Pleasant to be around, she remained appropriate at all his business dinners and at George's. She never said anything snide or contrary to Marti. In fact, she ignored her unless absolutely necessary to speak to her.

Emma began to like Shelly. She chatted with her and they'd even sat and watched a movie together the other night.

While Shelly seemed to be doing better with Emma, she was a long way from being a mother to her. He felt like he'd lost two mothers for Emma, Caroline, and Marti.

He figured if things had improved this much in two weeks, over a lifetime things could change considerably. He'd accept her as a wife and companion and Emma would find a way to see her as a mother. Maybe just a friend.

He hadn't made love to Shelly since Marti left the penthouse weeks ago. He told her he wanted to wait until after they were married. She'd thought it an old-fashioned idea, and at the same time accepted it saying she'd been having some cramping due to the pregnancy and her changing body and the doctor told her to take it easy.

He was concerned about the cramping and told her so. She said it was normal and not to worry, she'd take good care of his baby.

He'd pampered her ever since, making sure she stayed off her feet and rested. He asked her to quit her job, which she protested because she had expenses, so he'd paid off all her bills. Nothing was more important than her health and that of his baby. He'd do anything and everything to prevent a repeat of Caroline's devastating fate.

They would move in together at the penthouse the night of the wedding ceremony. Elizabeth had agreed to keep Emma for the night and he'd had a new bed delivered to the house. Neither Emma nor Shelly said a word when the men arrived to deliver it. He'd simply said a new wife deserved a new bed. He'd even let Shelly go with him to pick out new sheets, pillows, and blankets. Nothing remained of his morning with Marti, except the perfectly clear details in his mind.

He rubbed the back of his neck. He was tired. He felt like he was working three jobs. Things at Merrick had become even more hectic, and he'd gotten a call from Fairchild Industries to work on a development deal on some property they owned. It was a great opportunity and would build community ties. A great project, one they requested he work personally on with Fairchild Industries. He'd been working to put together the proposal for the building and finances.

His mind veered back to Marti. He wondered if she'd be there tonight. Every time they went to see George, he wondered if this would be the day George said she was gone. He wondered if she left, would he ever see her again. What would he do when that day finally came?

Please, God, let her be there. I just want to look at her. I just want to be near her.

"Darling, did you hear me?"

"What? No. I was thinking about a land deal I'm putting together." It was partly true.

"We're almost there. What did George say he wanted to talk to us about?"

"He didn't. He probably wants to give us a wedding gift or something. He's getting worse each day and I'm sure he just wants to make sure he congratulates us on the wedding and the baby while he has the chance."

George hadn't been specific and Cameron wondered why he'd sounded so persistent about their coming tonight. He didn't want to think about George and his failing health. "You went to the doctor's today, didn't you?"

"Yes, of course."

"What did the doctor say?"

"Everything is fine. Normal. Nothing to report."

She smiled for him and patted Emma's knee beside her. Everything changed the day Marti left Cameron's penthouse. He paid attention to her and talked to her more about his job and life. He included her in his business dinners and invited her to George's with him. If he sometimes got a strange, almost sad look in his eyes, she ignored it and tried to make him smile. Emma broke through those solemn moments better than she did, and that was okay too. Things between them were good, settled, and the wedding plans were moving forward.

Even Marti's presence at George's didn't deter Cameron, or make him any less interested in her. She didn't know what happened between the two of them. She didn't care, so long as she had the ring on her finger and Cameron's last name on her bank accounts.

Only one problem. She needed to figure out how to explain not being pregnant when, no matter what she did, Cameron refused to sleep with her before the wedding. Options limited, she'd have to fake a miscarriage. She'd make a show of how upset it made her that he'd only married her for the baby and now that it was gone he didn't want her. A good guy, that truth would shame him into staying with her. She hated knowing the baby kept him with her, but she wanted the life she'd have with him and one day, given time to get to know her better, he'd want to stay with her.

"You never said: did they give you the baby's due date? I'll want to mark it on the calendar at work. I can take some vacation time at the end of the pregnancy and after the baby is born."

"He said the baby will be here near the end of December. Won't that be a lovely Christmas gift for us all? Right, Emma?"

"Sure," she said absently.

No matter how hard she tried, the little bugger remained polite but distant. She played along, which suited Shelly fine. Marti might have found the key to gaining Emma's devotion, but Shelly accepted she didn't have the instinct or inclination to be anything more in Emma's life than her father's wife.

"I thought you said your doctor was a woman?"

"She is."

"Why did you say, 'he', before?"

"Hormones. They shut off my brain. All the preparations for the wedding and the dinner engagements you have for business plus with George. It's just so much." She tried to sound exhausted as all pregnant women were in their first trimester. She wasn't exhausted. She loved all the attention and dinner parties. She'd met people she'd never hoped to associate with, rich people.

"What is the due date? I want to know."

"December twenty-seventh." Actually, the date was her old boyfriend's birthday and the first date to pop into her head. It would do.

Cameron turned skeptical. He knew a little bit about babies having had one already and gone through the process with Caroline. He'd read books and gone to her appointments both in the beginning of the pregnancy and in the end. He thought about the night he'd met and slept with Shelly and mentally went through the calendar he kept in his head. He calculated forty weeks' gestation for the pregnancy. She was close, but something was off.

They arrived at George's and the matter of the due date nagged at the back of his mind.

George waited for them in the dining room, looking wan and pale. Cameron took his seat after seating Shelly and Emma, immediately noticing the absence of a place setting for Marti. She hadn't joined them or come to say hello.

She had to be there, somewhere. The Jag George told

him he'd bought for her sat outside in the driveway. His heart raced at the thought of seeing her. Then again, maybe she left the car with George and sailed away on her ship. He wondered if he should ask about her. Thankfully, Emma saved him the trouble.

"Where's Marti?"

"She's upstairs. I asked her to allow us dinner together alone tonight. I want to talk to all of you in private."

"Why? She wouldn't tell anyone. She's good at keeping secrets. She taught me how. The trick is not to tell."

Everyone laughed at Emma's serious tone.

Cameron wondered just what secrets Marti was keeping. When he thought about her and tried to picture her during the day and what she might be doing, he often drew a blank. He had no idea what she did for a living, if she went into an office, what she liked to do in her free time (except play with Emma), or anything else. The things he knew about her were from the time they had spent together. He figured she knew more about him than he knew about her. She'd asked him a hundred questions over the last weeks. Every time the conversation turned to her, she evaded answering anything personal. He barely knew more than a few facts. Her parents died in a car crash, her grandparents raised her, and to fulfill a promise to her grandmother, she'd sailed the world for a year.

He wished he knew everything about her. He wished they had no secrets.

He would have to settle for learning all of Shelly's secrets, even if he didn't really care what they were.

"Marti wouldn't tell my secrets. I've told her a great

many over the last week. It's just, I want to give something to your dad and I haven't told Marti about it yet."

George took a sip of water. Tired, the shaking in his leg had become pronounced over the last day and a half. His legs had failed him. Soon the rest of his body would as well. The doctor had been feeding him medication like it was candy. He feared his days had turned to hours. He needed to settle things with Cameron.

"George, what do you want to give me? Something for the wedding, or the baby?"

Cameron didn't like the way George looked tonight. His skin turned a sickly grey. He shook and trembled uncontrollably. His speech was slow and slurred. He understood him fine, but it wasn't the same baritone voice he'd always heard.

"You know I think of Emma as my very own granddaughter and you as my son. I've raised you from afar. Your mother was a wonderful woman, and she would have been proud to see you grow to such a fine man and the president of a company like Merrick International. She'd have been proud of her granddaughter."

"I regret she died the year before Emma was born. I would have liked her to see her grandchildren. She'd have been a devoted and loving grandmother."

"Indeed she would have. This thing I want to give you is just a thing really, but in order to give it to you I require a promise in return. Well, a few actually, but you can still have the thing with just the one promise. You're an honorable man, and if you give me your word, I'll accept it and die knowing you'll keep it."

"Whatever the promise, it's yours. You know I'd do anything for you, George. Without your generosity and mentoring all these years, I wouldn't be half the man I am today. You're the father I always wanted."

George took that into his heart, let it heal old wounds. "Sometimes that's all a person needs when they don't have the parent they want, even if it is just for a short while." He looked at Emma and back to Cameron. "I wish we could have many more years together, and I would see your children come into this world and grow up to be like Emma. A beautiful, smart, funny, and kind girl," he said to Emma.

"Cameron, the promise I ask is this. The thing I'm going to give you will only be half yours. The other half will be given to someone else and you will own it together.

"The promise I request, you must never sell your half, not even to the person who owns the other half. You will own it together for the rest of your lives. Upon your death, your half will go to Emma, as she is your firstborn child. The other person will leave their half to their first-born child. This will become the legacy I want to leave."

"Okay, I agree. I promise you George, I'll never sell it even to them. Have they agreed to this promise as well?"

"Not yet. I haven't told them. If they don't, I will leave the entire thing to you, and then Emma, and then her first child, etcetera."

He smiled at Emma. "Agreed, Princess?"

"Yes, Knight. I will leave it to my child."

"That's my princess."

"What is it, George, I'm dying to know." Shelly found

the whole promise and gift to be too intriguing to keep her mouth shut.

"Are you sure, Cameron? This is big. It's very important to me you understand the promise must be kept. The item I'm giving to you will transfer to your ownership prior to your getting married. In fact, within days."

"I understand what you're saying." He knew exactly what George was telling him. Ownership of whatever it was would occur before his marriage to Shelly. If they divorced, she'd have no claim to it.

"The thing I am giving to you, well half anyway, is this house and the property it sits on. The contents of the house will go to the person who owns the other half. Many things will be distributed to my children at that person's discretion."

"George, you're giving me the house. Why? What about your children?"

"It's my house and this is what I want. Emma should have a backyard to play in. It's dark now, but I've had a playhouse and play yard set up in the back for her already."

He took Emma's hand. "You have swings and a slide. The playhouse was Marti's idea. It's a pirate ship with all kinds of toys. One day, if you have a brother or sister, you can play pirate with them. Marti made sure it had everything a little girl needed to play pretend."

"Oh my gosh, Knight. My very own pirate ship, swings, and a slide. It's all for me?"

"Yes, Princess. It's all for you."

"She'll still be able to attend her school," he said to

Cameron. "When she's bigger, a bus will pick her up and take her.

"The penthouse is nice, but I want you and your family to have a home. This is a home without a family. It's time to fill it with love and laughter again. I want that family to be yours, Cameron."

Cameron didn't know what to say. "Will the other owner be one of your children?"

"No. The house is split into two sections, as you know. It's large enough for two families. The east wing will be yours. You'll have the master suite and two additional rooms, one of which will be Emma's, of course.

"The west wing will be for the other owner. You'll share the common space down here."

"George, it's too much. This house and the property are worth a fortune. Your children aren't going to be happy about this."

"It isn't their house. It's mine. They will be well taken care of after I'm dead. Don't worry about them. They're greedy monsters who only come to see if I'm dead and find out when they can collect.

"Unfortunately, they've been causing some problems for Marti. I regret she was put in this position, and I'm going to make things worse for her after my death."

"What kind of problems are they causing Marti?" Cameron had given her enough pain and grief. She didn't need George's family harming her too.

"Stupid things really. They believe she's influencing me. And, well, they think she's going to inherit it all because she's my mistress."

"What's a mistress?" Emma asked, searching all their faces.

Everyone ignored Emma's question.

Cameron looked fit to kill at the thought of Marti being George's mistress. She couldn't be. He'd made it seem like she was, but it couldn't be true. George was dying; he couldn't possibly be sleeping with Marti.

"Cameron, you look like you swallowed a lemon. For God's sake, boy, Walter is just trying to find an excuse to cause trouble and make sure the will goes in his favor. The Jag really annoyed him."

"It was a lovely gift you gave Marti. I'm sure she deserved it." Shelly was sure she had earned every penny the Jag cost. On her knees, no doubt. She wasn't buying it Marti lived with the old man because they were old family friends. No way. Marti was in it for as much as she could get.

"It was a gift for someone who understands the value of being true to your word and not expecting something because of who you know, or who you were born to. She's unique in a way that surprises me more each day."

He smiled thinking of Marti. She'd been a true friend. He regretted things were going to get very difficult for her soon. He hoped his carefully laid plans would make everything work out in the end.

"Now, I think my next request will please Shelly. I know you are planning a small ceremony at the penthouse. I'd like you to have the ceremony here at your new home. I know it's a lot to ask you to contact everyone and change the address, but it would really please me to know the wedding was held here."

"Oh, George, what a lovely idea. Cameron, what do you think? We could let everyone know about the change in location without any trouble at all. It's just a few phone calls. That's all. The house and gardens are so lovely. We'll start our marriage right here at our new home."

Cameron didn't care. He just wanted to give his children a family. "It's fine with me. The location doesn't matter. I think it's a great idea."

"Perfect," said George.

"Now, for my second request. I'd like for all of you to move into the house the day after my death. I've already set up the movers and a few other small surprises. It will give you a few days to settle in before the wedding. I'd like your word, Cameron. The day after my death. It's important. I don't want the house to be empty after I'm gone."

"But George, we're talking about a week. You'll still be here for the wedding."

Cameron didn't want to think of George dying before the wedding, or any time soon. He wanted to hope he'd make it longer.

His hope was for George and himself, because as long as George was alive, Marti was in his house. She wouldn't go back on her promise to him. She wouldn't.

George shook his head. He didn't want to say any more about his death in front of Emma. She looked sad already, disappointed with Marti's absence at dinner this evening.

"It's what I want. Indulge an old man with a promise, Cameron, for my last request. This house will be yours and then Emma's. I want to know you are here and the house isn't empty for even a day."

"I for one think it's sentimental and wonderful. The house has meant so much to you and you want to know a real family is living here. Cameron, you can't say no."

Shelly couldn't wait. She'd love to move into the big, castle-like mansion. She'd have it all tied up with a bow, her very own castle with her rich prince. What more could a girl ask for?

"Yes, you see. Even Shelly is excited. She can move in with you before the wedding. Not all the rooms are furnished in the east wing. I'm sure one of the rooms in the west wing will suit Shelly until after the ceremony."

"Perfect," she beamed. Whatever it took to solidify her place with Cameron.

So what if she had to stay in the guest room. In a matter of days, she'd be in the master suite with Cameron. The rest of her life would be spent living here with servants and she'd have luncheons and dinner parties. It was going to be grand.

"Emma, what do you think? Would you like to move in here? You were very small when we moved into the penthouse. It's the only home you've ever known. This will mean a lot of changes for you." Cameron wouldn't make the promise without Emma's consent.

"Will we get to go back and see Aunt Elizabeth and everyone else? I don't want to move if I don't get to see them."

"Yes, honey. I'll keep the penthouse, and we'll stay there sometimes. You'll see everyone as often as you like.

I still work for Aunt Jenna and Aunt Elizabeth feeds me every day. We'll still have them all in our lives. I promise you. You won't lose them too."

He meant in addition to her home, but what he really thought was she'd still have them after Marti was gone.

Her eyes reflected her understanding. She was already missing Marti.

"It's settled. You'll move in and be married here."

"Agreed," said Cameron. "So long as the other owner doesn't object. This is going to be difficult to figure out until I know who the other owner is and if we'll be able to live under the same roof. I need to know Emma and the baby will like this person and get along with them."

"You have no worries there. I have a feeling it will all work out in the end. I know you very well, Cameron. I wouldn't have arranged this if I thought it wasn't good for you and Emma. Nothing is more important to me than the two of you. No offense, Shelly. They've been in my life a long time."

"No problem, George. I know how special you are to them as well." She did know, and the old man could leave her out of his good thoughts, so long as she got the house, the prince, and the wealth.

"So, as long as we're agreed, there's a surprise for Emma upstairs."

"Really? For me?"

"Yes. Cameron, I have your promises to all we've discussed?"

"Yes." Cameron couldn't deny George after everything he'd done for him. He wouldn't have the life he had now without him. He wouldn't have met Marti without George. It appeared George was making sure his life from then on would be taken care of as well.

"Okay, since everyone is finished eating, Cameron, would you take Emma upstairs to Marti? She's the one who put the surprise together for Emma. She's been working on it for me for two days straight. The girl has barely slept.

"Anyway, if she isn't in her room, knock on the other door. Emma knows which one. She spends every waking moment with me or in her rooms working.

"Cameron, you'll want to see Emma's surprise. It's quite extraordinary. More than I hoped it would be, or asked of Marti.

"Shelly, if you don't mind, I'd like to speak to you while they go up. It'll only take a few minutes, a chance for us to get to know each other a little better."

"I'd like that, George. You've been so generous. I'll see Emma's surprise in a little while."

She would too. She wanted to know what the great Marti had been up to for two days, so George could surprise Emma. She bet whatever it was, it was expensive.

Chapter Thirty

THE KNOCK AT the door dragged her out of her head and work. She took off her smock and studied the canvas and the pictures she used as a reference. She had to admit it was a good likeness. A few more hours of work and she'd have it finished.

"Is that you, Sugar Bug?" Marti stretched her back before covering the canvas.

"Yes. Daddy, too."

"I'll be right there." She went through the connecting door into her bedroom. She kept the door in the hallway locked, so no one came in that way. She liked her privacy and didn't want Cameron to see the project she was working on for him.

She stepped out into the hallway from her bedroom and stared down the hall at Emma. She held out her arms and said, "Come here, Sugar Bug. Oh, how I've missed you."

Emma ran to her. Marti scooped her up and hugged her fiercely.

"You saw me a couple of days ago."

"Way too long to go without you. How's school?"

"Fine. I can write my letters in lower case now."

"Excellent. Pretty soon you'll be able to write me letters."

"Are you going somewhere?" Cameron couldn't help but ask. He needed to know where she was always. He wondered if she'd be willing to check in with him once a week and tell him what she was doing and where she was. Irrational, but he wanted to know at any time he could find her.

"Eventually," was all she said. "How are you, Cameron?"

"Fine. Just fine." He wasn't fine without her. He'd never be fine again.

"You look tired, Marti." They were heading down the hall toward the east wing. He didn't know where she was taking them. "George said you've been up the last two nights finishing Emma's surprise."

"I have been. Wait till you see it, Sugar Bug. I hope you like it. George had some men come and build something for you. It's wonderful."

"I can't wait to see it."

Marti walked ahead of him. She lost her balance and almost dropped Emma. The hallway seemed to sway. Cameron grabbed her from behind, his big, warm hands clamped on her waist.

"Are you okay?" He held her hips and took the small step to her, pressing his body to hers. His throbbing cock pressed into the cleft of her bottom. She felt so good snug against his aching body. It had been too long since he'd felt her against him, since he'd touched her.

Disappointment lanced through him when she stepped away and continued onto the next door.

"I'm fine. Just tired. I haven't been feeling well. It's nothing. Probably just a touch of whatever Emma had."

She made it to the door and put Emma down. When she stood back up the hallway swayed again. Cameron's arms came around her and he pulled her back to his chest again. God, he felt good.

He leaned down and whispered into her ear. "What's the matter with you, sweetheart?"

"Nothing. I'm fine," she said over her shoulder. He was too close. If she turned just an inch, her mouth would brush his. She wanted to kiss him, but knew it would only lead to more pain.

"You're pale and dizzy. You're not just tired. Are you ill?"

"Don't worry about me. Worry about your *pregnant fiancé*. I can take care of myself."

She knew exactly what was wrong. Her period was a week late and she was pregnant with Cameron's baby. At least she was ninety-nine percent sure. She'd bought a pregnancy test kit, several actually, and was going to take it, but she was afraid it would say yes. Hell, she was afraid it would say no. She was getting used to the idea. That's all.

What would it matter anyway? He'd chosen Shelly time and again. Shelly was supposedly pregnant with his baby. He repeatedly said he wanted to make a life with her.

He hadn't even considered he might have gotten her pregnant too. It's not like she'd been prepared to make love to him. She'd woken up to him on top of her and she loved him so much she couldn't resist him. She'd wanted him and damn the consequences.

The consequence was the sweetest gift. The one thing from Cameron she'd take with her when she left.

"I am worried about you. Please, if there's something you need, let me help."

"I don't need help. I need some sleep. I'm just fine on my own."

He released her and rubbed the back of his neck. She was pushing him away and he hated it.

"Okay, Sugar Bug. Are you ready for the best surprise ever?"

"Are you dying? George is dying. My mother died. Is that why everyone is telling me you're leaving?"

Marti kneeled in front of Emma and took her shoulders in her hands. "You know I would never lie to you. I am not dying. I'm just fine. Do you believe me?"

Emma nodded yes.

"A lot of changes are happening in your life. Knight is dying and there is nothing we can do to make him better. It's a part of life, people sometimes get sick and die."

"Like my mom and Knight?"

"Yes, like them. I promise you, when it's time for me to leave, I will make sure you can always reach me. I may not be with you here, but you'll always be able to call me."

"You promise," she said, wanting it so badly.

"I promise you." She kissed her on the forehead to seal the bargain. "Now, how about your surprise?"

Emma nodded and turned to the door.

"Cameron, cover her eyes."

Cameron put his hand over Emma's eyes and glanced at her questioningly.

"You're going to love this. Even I'm nervous, and I'm the one who did it. Are you peeking, Emma?"

"No. Daddy has big hands."

"Yes, he does." Marti remembered every place on her body those big hands had touched and caressed. She didn't look at him. She couldn't. Her whole body echoed with the remembered sensation of their one morning together.

The blush rising up her neck and face told him what she was thinking. He was remembering too. The feel of Marti's skin, the soft fullness of her breasts in his palms, the hot, wet, slick core of her sliding over his hard cock. Oh yes, he remembered it all.

She opened the door and stepped inside, grabbing her camera, which she'd left on and ready inside the room.

She glanced at Cameron, saw the surprise and shock on his face. He scanned the room and turned to her.

"You did this?" Choked up, all his emotions lodged in his throat. The room was spectacular. He couldn't believe she'd done all this in two days.

Smiling, she told herself it didn't matter what Cameron thought. It only mattered what Emma thought. But it did matter what Cameron thought. It mattered a lot.

She put the camera up to her eye. "Okay, Emma. You can look."

As Cameron removed his hand and Emma stood stunned with a huge smile on her face, Marti snapped the picture to remember the moment.

"Oh my God. It's a princess's room. Just like in the medieval books you read to me. It's just like the room in *Tina's Travels* where she goes to England and visits the castles."

"This is Princess Emma's room." She indicated with a sweep of her hand, drawing Emma's attention to the wall behind her.

Princess Emma was hand-painted above the door, along with a vine of climbing roses trailing down the sides of the heavy wood doorframe. The entire room looked like stone block walls. Throughout the room, trailing vines of ivy and climbing roses in shades of pink.

Everywhere you looked on the walls there was something to discover. A bird and nest tucked in the vine and a fairy sitting on a toadstool. Dragonflies and butterflies fluttered among the flowers. A crowned frog hid in a hollowed-out tree stump.

The windows had roller shades. When pulled down, they looked like forests beyond a stone wall. Gauzy pink drapes would flow in the wind when the windows were open.

The hardwood floors bloomed with roses and pansies in pink and lavender carpet cutouts.

The dark wood armoire with double doors hid a TV and DVD player with every movie Emma liked. A wooden chest sat at the foot of the bed. Inside Marti had stashed costumes for Emma to dress up and have tea parties, or be a pirate, or princess, or whatever she dreamed up. A matching dresser stood against one wall with oil lamps converted to electric lights. A matching pair on either side of the bed sat on the marble topped nightstands.

The queen-size bed was the most spectacular piece in the room. A wooden box frame surrounded the bed with four posts supporting a top piece. Draped from all sides and tied back, white flowing gauze drapes completed the elegant look.

The spectacular part was when you laid on the bed, you looked up into the box above the bed and it appeared you were looking at the night sky. Marti had spent hours painting the top of the bed. She wanted it to be just right.

A special surprise waited in the night sky too. On a cloud brightly reflected in the moon's rays, Emma's mother gazed down. While Emma slept, her mother would watch over her from heaven.

She waited to see Emma's reaction to the room. The little girl stood silent next to her father staring. Tears ran down her face.

"You don't like it after all. I can change it if you want something else, maybe a jungle, or a forest? No theme at all. You want a grown-up room."

She looked at Cameron and he shrugged.

"It's just what I imagined. You asked me once what my favorite things were about the pictures in the books. There were lots of different pictures and I liked different things from them all, but none of them was exactly right. This is exactly right."

Marti stood speechless and filled with pride. Her eyes glassed over. Leave it to a five-year-old to tell you the truth and knock you to your knees.

Emma wiped her tears and ran to the toy chest and threw it open. She hollered about all the costumes. She ran to the windows and pushed the shades up and looked out at the garden below. She chattered and touched the designs on all the walls.

Energy and enthusiasm poured from Emma and filled Marti's heart with joy.

"Emma, the two empty spots on the wall are where we'll hang some paintings. They aren't ready yet, but I left the spaces ready for them," she pointed to the two spots and the hooks on the wall. She would give the paintings to Emma and Cameron at the benefit. "Come here. Up on the bed."

Emma used the step stool to get up on the high bed. She bounced up the steps and landed on her knees on the mattress. She'd look like a dwarf when she slept in the bed. Marti wished she'd be there to watch the little girl grow up and fit in the queen-size bed.

Marti lay down next to her, and Emma oohed over the sky.

"Cameron, would you turn off the light for a minute?"

Cameron hit the switch and walked over to the bed to see what held their attention. When he came close, he looked under the ledge and saw the inside of the bed lit up with stars. They'd been painted with glow-in-the-dark paint, and around the outside of the painting were little white Christmas lights.

"Emma, when I sail, this is the sky I see. When I'm on my ship and you're in your bed, we'll see the same night sky. Your sky has something very special. Look up on that cloud, the one closest to the moon. Who do you see?"

"Mommy," she squealed.

"That's right, Sugar Bug. Your mommy will watch over you every night. She does anyway, but now you can look up and see her. When you're sad or lonely, you can talk to her. She'll always be here for you."

Cameron's hand lay on her thigh, he squeezed, letting her know in a small way how much this meant to him.

"Someone signed their name up there. *M. Fairchild*," Emma pointed.

"You have good eyes. She's the artist who painted this for you. She thinks you're a very special girl."

Marti signed the mural in the corner using dark blue paint only a few shades lighter than the night sky.

Before either of them said anything about the artist's name, she rolled off the bed and almost fell again. The room spun and settled when Cameron grabbed her. Again. Unsettled, tired to the bone, and feeling very sad, she gave in and leaned her forehead to his chest. God, he smelled good and felt even better. His big hands held her hips and pulled her close. His breath swept through her hair a second before he kissed her on the top of her head.

"Marti, let me take you to bed."

She leaned back. Their gazes met, and she glared at him.

"I meant because you're falling down tired. Literally."

"Well, I hope it's what you meant, darling," Shelly said from the door, turning on the lights.

Marti stepped away from Cameron, away from where she most wanted to be, in his arms.

"Wow. Nice work, Marti. Must have taken you quite a while to oversee all this. Whoever the artist is, they do great work. Maybe we can hire them to do the baby's room."

Marti couldn't listen to any more. She didn't want this moment ruined too. She'd made this room for the daughter she'd never have, Emma. She wouldn't listen to Shelly talk about her doing a room for her and Cameron's baby. The only baby room she was going to do was for her baby, her baby with Cameron.

She went over to the bed and leaned over Emma and whispered into her ear, "I love you, Sugar Bug. *I* made this room for you. This room will always be your special place. I love you so very much."

Tears rolled down her cheeks and she didn't care. She walked out of the room without saying a word of goodbye to Shelly or Cameron. She went down the long hall and into her room.

She fell down on her bed completely exhausted with her feet hanging off the end. She sucked in a deep breath, hoping the extra air would push the hurt out of her chest. No such luck.

Cameron and Emma came in a few minutes later, saw her sprawled on the bed, and looked at each other.

"She's sleeping, Daddy. We should leave her alone."

"Why don't you kiss her goodnight? We'll thank her for doing the room another time."

Emma went over to the bed and kissed Marti on the cheek. "I love you too," she whispered.

Emma gasped when Marti scooped her up onto the bed. Marti held the little girl to her and let the rest of her tears fall. Emma patted her face with her little hand.

"It's okay to cry," she whispered.

Cameron took off her shoes and rubbed his hand over her ankle and foot. She pulled her feet away.

"Please, Cameron, take her home. I can't take anymore."

Cameron picked up Emma and kissed her cheek. "Emma, wait downstairs for me. Marti is very tired, and she's already missing you."

"I miss her too."

"I know you do, sweetheart. Go. I'll be there in a minute."

He waited for her to leave the room and kneeled beside the bed and looked at Marti sobbing. He'd done this to her. Whatever the reason for all the tears, he knew they were his fault.

He brushed her hair away from her wet cheek. "Sweetheart, tell me what's wrong."

"I'm tired and it all just overwhelmed me. I can't bear to let her go."

He leaned over and kissed a tear from her cheek. "Then you know how I feel about letting you go."

"Don't kiss me. Don't touch me. It hurts too much," she sobbed. "Go. Leave."

"I can't leave you like this."

"Shelly is waiting for you. Your daughter is waiting for you. Go be with your family. I'm just someone who had a moment with you. Our moment has passed."

"I live in that moment every minute of every day. Never forget that, my love."

She sobbed harder. If he cared so much, loved her so much, why wasn't he marrying her?

She thought about telling him about the baby and decided it wouldn't change anything. She was so tired. Her heart hurt and she just couldn't listen to him tell her one more time he was marrying Shelly because of their baby. She couldn't bear to hear him say his baby with her would come second, just like she had every time he'd chosen Shelly over her.

The door closed, Cameron left, and she continued to cry herself to sleep. Maybe tomorrow would be a better day.

Cameron leaned against the door, listening to the sound of Marti sobbing. It washed over him in a wave of pain. The pressure in his chest grew so tight, if he took too deep of a breath, he'd explode.

He turned to go back inside. He couldn't leave her like this.

"Darling, it's time to go home," Shelly called from the stairs.

Cameron laid his palm on the door and dropped his head. Eyes closed, he silently said the words he had no right to say to her.

I love you.

He left with his family, hoping Marti had somehow heard him and it healed some of the hurt he'd caused. Nothing would, but maybe one day thoughts of him and their time together wouldn't make her cry.

Chapter Thirty-One

THE NEXT DAY turned out to be the beginning of the end. She woke up feeling sick. She knew it was the pregnancy and decided it was time to confirm what she already knew. She had three different boxed tests in her bathroom. She took one, read the directions, peed on the stick, and waited all of ten seconds to see the test reveal she was in fact pregnant. The test said it took up to three minutes, but apparently it didn't need that long to tell her what she needed to know. She didn't need the other tests to be sure. She was pregnant with Cameron's baby.

She promptly threw up, sat on the floor, and cried. Overwhelmingly happy and sad at the same time, she lost Cameron and gained the child she'd always wanted. She dreamed of having a family of her own. She couldn't have it all, but she'd at least have a child to make it easier to bear losing Cameron and Emma.

Once she pulled herself together and dressed, she

stepped out of her room only to see the physician running up the stairs and racing to George's room. She ran after him.

"What's wrong?"

"It's begun. He's on a downward spiral. He woke up this morning and he can't move his legs. The night nurse called me."

"How long does he have?"

"It's hard to tell. He can still speak, though it's slurred. He's breathing on his own and he's awake. We'll watch him today and see how things go. I'll stay for the duration. I'll make him as comfortable as possible."

"I'll stay with him. Have you called his son and daughter?"

"Not yet."

"I'll make the calls first and come back in to sit with him."

She made the calls to George's children. To her dismay, they both said they had busy days and would get there when they could. Their cold and callous attitude made her sick. No wonder she'd found him on the dock almost two months ago. Her promise to him meant even more now. She was all he had.

She called Cameron at the penthouse, hoping to catch him there. Surprisingly, Shelly answered.

"Shelly, this is Marti. I need to speak with Cameron."

"He's busy getting Emma ready to go."

"It's important. Will you have him call me right away? It's urgent. George is dying." She had a feeling Shelly didn't want to give Cameron the message. She didn't know what else to do.

"I'll give him the message when I see him. Goodbye."

Marti stared at the dead phone in her hand and frowned. She left it on the table and shelved her own anger and frustration to go to the man who needed her.

She entered George's room, dismayed to see how pale and gaunt he looked. In just a few days, he'd deteriorated to a shell of his former self. She went to the bed and sat beside him and took his hand.

She'd sat by her grandmother's deathbed and been there for her death. A difficult task, but one she wouldn't abandon. George was her friend, and she wouldn't let him die alone.

"Tell me, Marti, are you in love with Cameron? I know there's something special between you, but there are also obstacles. Tell me, despite everything he's put you through, you love him."

"I do, George. I love him with my whole heart and I believe he loves me in the same way."

"He's marrying her because she says she's pregnant. I don't believe she is, and neither do you."

"No, I don't. I've tried to talk to Cameron, but he's adamant about giving his baby a mother and a father. He wants Emma to have a mother."

"And what about your baby?"

She gasped. "How did you know?"

"I know everything that goes on in my house. You've been looking ill the last several mornings, but by afternoon you glow. It's been nice to see. My wife looked and acted the same when she was pregnant. Somehow, I always knew before she did. Will you tell Cameron?"

"Not yet. I don't think it will make a difference. He's supposed to marry her next Friday. I wanted him to choose me because he loves me, not because I tell him I'm carrying his child. I want to know this thing between us is more than just an obligation, the way he's treating his impending marriage to Shelly. He makes it seem like he really wants to be with me, and he has no choice but to marry her because of the baby."

"And you think if she really is pregnant, he doesn't need to marry her in order to be a good father to the baby."

"Yes. He doesn't see it that way."

"You understand, part of the reason he's so adamant about marrying Shelly is because he grew up without his father."

"Yes, and Emma and Caroline are the other reason. I understand, but marrying Shelly won't guarantee a happy life for those kids. In fact, it will probably make things worse. Children know when their parents don't love each other. Without a solid relationship between the parents, the children will suffer in some way. I don't want to see Emma hurt. Or the baby, if there is one.

"I want him to marry me. If Shelly is pregnant, I'd never ask him to give up the baby or be less than the father he is to Emma to the new baby. I want him to see he has options. I guess I want the world," she said and shrugged.

"Your grandmother gave it to you in a way. I wish I could give it to you now. Things will be difficult for you when I'm gone. I have something to ask of you. I won't ask you for a promise, but I hope you'll consider it a favor.

If you can, you'll do it. It's something you may not be able to do for me, and I'll understand if you try and can't finish."

"I don't understand. What is it you want me to do?"

His mind ran in circles. "I should have started by saying there's something I need you to tell Cameron. He has to understand. I think he'll only understand if you tell him. You have a way of seeing things for what they are and not what we think they are."

"I'll tell him. What is it?"

"He's my son."

"Of course he is. You've been like a father to him since he was born."

"No. He truly is my son. I had an affair with his mother when my wife and I separated for a short time. My wife and I reconciled later and I found out Cameron's mother was pregnant. She wanted him. I wanted him, and I wanted to be with my wife. We had a great love despite some problems at the time in our marriage. Cameron's mother was a good woman. She wasn't in love with me, nor I with her. We made an agreement. She wanted to raise Cameron. I already had two children, so I agreed, so long as I could stay in his life. My wife was agreeable to the arrangement. When Cameron was born, I became the perfect weekend father, so to speak. I love that boy. I've been there for every significant and everyday event in his life. I had a better relationship with him than I did with my own kids, because he didn't know I was his father. He talked and confided in me because I was a mentor and a friend to him. He could count on me.

"His mother insisted I never tell him I was his father. I've kept my promise, even after her death. But when I die, I want him to know he did have a father. Me. I may not have been there every day of his life, but I think I did a fine job raising him. Of all my children, I am the most proud of him. You tell him that."

"I will tell him. I'll tell him all of it."

She knew why George wanted Cameron to know, now. He was in the same situation George faced years ago. He'd gotten a woman pregnant and wanted to be a father to the child, despite other circumstances. He'd been a father to Cameron, and been a good father without being there every day or marrying Cameron's mother. Cameron could do the same with Shelly, if he wanted, and the baby would grow up just fine. Cameron had.

"See, I knew you'd understand. Cameron is a fine man. I had a hand in his raising. Being married isn't what makes you a good father. Being a good father when you're with your child, no matter how little time you share, is what makes the difference. Look at you and Emma. She's a better girl and will be a better woman for knowing you, even if you leave tomorrow. You've left your mark on her heart. I hope I've done the same for Cameron."

Marti thought about it and had to agree. She'd shown Emma what having a mother is like. Emma would carry that with her the rest of her life. She might grow up and have children of her own and use what she'd learned from Marti to mother her own children.

"Yes, she'll be hurt when I'm gone, but at least we had a little bit of time together. If Shelly is a terrible mother to her, at least she knows I loved her with my whole heart. I'll still see her when Cameron comes to see his baby, but it won't be the same as being with her every day."

"You'll do your best, which leads me to my request. Once you've told Cameron my story, I ask you stay here for two months and watch over Emma."

He patted her hand when she tried to protest. "Hear me out. You know I left the house to Cameron. That's why I had you do the room. It's beautiful, by the way. Emma loved it."

"Yes, she did." Marti gave him a sentimental smile. She'd remember Emma's reaction for the rest of her life.

"They don't know you're the artist."

Not a question, so she didn't respond.

"You should tell them. You have an extraordinary gift, and Cameron has no idea of the kind of woman you are. He'd need a lifetime to discover them all. This is the joy of marriage. But you should tell him who you really are, and you're carrying his baby."

"Is that your request? You want me to tell him I'm a Fairchild, and I'm pregnant."

"No. You once told me simply saying your family name comes with too many preconceptions. I want you to tell him who you are. You're an author, an accomplished painter and artist, you're a remarkable businesswoman who works on special projects for Fairchild Industries and sits on their board of directors. He knows you're kind and generous and a great mother. Tell him the rest. Tell him just how much he'll be missing by not knowing all of you. You are a unique and wonderful woman. You are one of the most special people I've ever known. I'm proud to know my grandchild will be the son or daughter of Martina Fairchild the woman."

"Oh, George." Tears ran down her face. "I will tell my child his grandfather was a great man who understood giving your word meant something, and hard work and earning your way meant more than being handed everything. I'll tell him both his grandfathers were great businessmen, and at one time they were the fiercest of warriors across a conference table."

"I know you will. You're a woman of great honor. That's why I know you'll do the right thing and tell Cameron when the time is right."

"Yes, when the time is right."

"So, he's getting the house in a few days, and he's agreed to move in immediately. He and Shelly are going to be married here. My request is you stay for two months. Cameron won't ask you to leave, I've made sure of it. I know I'm asking a lot, but once Shelly has the ring on her finger, I'm afraid things will change. She'll have what she wanted and won't be so nice. I'm afraid for Emma."

"You think she's nice?" She joked about it, but she had the same fears. Once Shelly was married to Cameron and had access to his money, she'd be the person everyone knew her to be, a conniving bitch. She'd make Cameron's and Emma's lives hell before she'd give up any of it.

"I think she'll reveal there isn't a baby, and she'll spend Cameron's money like it's water. She won't let him go easily because he's her meal ticket to the country club set."

"Like I said, you see things for what they are. I tried to buy her off last night and stop all this madness. She wouldn't bite because she's after everything she can get."

"What did you do?"

"I offered to pay her a million dollars to admit she isn't pregnant and go away."

"What did she say?" Marti hoped she said something incriminating.

"She said a million wasn't enough. Marriage to Cameron would give her access to much more, and she'd have the rich and powerful husband she always wanted. He'll take her places a million dollars won't.

"I could have offered her more. For her, it isn't just the money, though the money is only a fraction of an inch behind what Cameron offers. She wants the whole lifestyle. She'll be invited to parties and luncheons, have respect because she's his wife. She wants that more than the money."

He had a surprising revelation. "Wait till she finds out you're the rich and powerful woman she wants to be. I'd give anything to see her face when she finds out who you really are. I bet it'll be priceless." George wheezed and coughed until he could barely catch his breath. She wiped his mouth. He settled back and took slow shallow breaths to calm himself.

Marti didn't care if Shelly found out she was a Fairchild. She could choke on it for all she cared. Her only concern was for Cameron and Emma.

"So your request is I stay for the two months so I can watch out for Emma when this whole thing turns sour.

Do you know what you're asking, both of us under the same roof with Cameron between us? It's a disaster waiting to happen, and more hurt than I'm willing to take on, even for Emma. I love him. I can't watch him take her to bed each night, or kiss her good morning over breakfast. Don't ask it of me."

"I'm asking you to watch out for my granddaughter and my son. If I had the time, I'd do this myself. I won't be here in the morning. I've accepted it, and I'm asking. I know I don't have the right to ask this of you and everything I'll be asking of you when I'm gone, but you're all I have. I know you'll do your best. I'm not asking for a promise because I know that won't leave you an out if things don't work out, and you'll feel obligated to see it through even if it destroys you. I'm asking you to try."

"I've already tried to fix this. He won't listen."

"Things will change when I'm gone and you'll have a chance to make him see."

He didn't know how to convince her without telling her everything. She'd learn everything from the reading of the will.

"I've left you something in my will. Actually, it's half of something. I'd like a promise, a true promise from you. I want you to promise you'll keep this thing I give to you. You can't sell it, not even to the person who owns the other half. When you pass, you'll leave your half to your child, Cameron's child. Will you promise?"

"Yes, George, I promise. I won't sell it. I'll pass it down to your grandchild."

He closed his eyes. The pain grew too much to bear.

His vision blurred long ago and now he only saw shades of grey and shadows. He wished to see her face one last time.

"George, you're tired. Rest now. We'll talk about it later."

"I don't have a later, Marti. I only have right now."

Pain clouded his eyes. He held his body rigid. His breathing became labored. He was right, he knew, there wasn't much time.

"George, my gallant Knight, I will try, for you. I'll stay as long as I think I can make a difference. I've already promised Emma she will always be able to contact me, even if I leave. I'll try, George. Do you hear me? I'll try." She grasped his hand, held it to her chest over her aching heart.

The doctor came to the bed and checked George's breathing and heart rate. "He's unconscious. It probably won't be long now. We've agreed on a means to make him comfortable until the end. I'll give him medication to help with the pain and allow him to slip away. I'll be with him the whole time, miss. You don't have to stay."

The doctor was trying to make things easy for her. She'd never abandon George.

"I'm staying."

Chapter Thirty-Two

"NOT HIS MISTRESS, my ass. Look at you all curled up with the old man. If he left it all to you, I swear I'll kill you myself."

Marti came awake with a start and gulped a few deep breaths to stave off the nausea. Walter stood at the end of the bed, glaring daggers.

What a terrible night. George lingered in a state of pain. Wakeful at times, though not lucid. Other times he slept peacefully. By the time the sun's dim rays broke the night, he was wracked with gasping breaths and periods of complete quiet where she thought he'd finally passed. In the end, the doctor gave him a final dose of morphine and George slipped away while she held him.

She checked the clock. The doctor had gone to call Walter and his sister not twenty minutes ago. She must have dozed off after telling George her final goodbye.

"Walter, your father passed away a few minutes ago. I'm so sorry for your loss."

She got up from the bed and grabbed the sheet the doctor used to cover George and pulled it over his head. She put her hand to his hair and closed her eyes. Tears poured down her cheeks.

"I'll miss you, George."

"Isn't this just sweet. They'll be here shortly to take his body to the funeral home. We'll have the service this evening."

"Tonight. He just passed away minutes ago. You want to have the service tonight?"

"His orders. The man loved to give orders. His funeral and the reading of the will are to take place immediately. We can't have the reading of the will until after the service. I expect you will pack your things and move out of the house tonight. Unless you'd like to stay on and provide your services to me. I have to say, the old man had great taste in women. You are one fine piece of ass."

She left the room without a word and her head held high. She couldn't be in the same room with him any longer.

She went into her room and straight to the bathroom opened another one of the pregnancy test boxes and peed on the stick. The test read positive again and she laughed and cried. Proof positive, life went on. Irrational, she knew, to take another test when she knew the answer. She just wanted an affirmation. Where there was death, so too was there life. George was gone, but his grandchild lay tucked safely under her heart.

She went to the service that evening and listened to Walter's eulogy. Cold and unfeeling, it lacked anything truly intimate and personal. Though the rest of the ceremony George planned was lovely. She feared George would have hated the whole thing. It was just a way for his children to save face in front of the people who attended. Walter was busy talking business with most of the guests. She'd left before the end.

Cameron, Shelly, and Emma had all attended. She didn't know if he finally got her message, or if he'd heard from someone else. He hadn't spoken to her, but sat quietly devastated next to Shelly. She managed to say hello to Emma and give the little girl a hug before she left.

No one would be coming to the house after the service, except for family and those indicated in the will. The lawyer was already in the library going over the papers before everyone arrived. She walked past the double doors without acknowledging the lawyer and went upstairs to lie down. She'd eaten to keep up her strength for the baby, but the pregnancy was draining her energy and she'd been up all night. She felt terrible inside and out.

The noise downstairs woke her. It sounded like quite a crowd had gathered. She splashed cool water on her face and left her room. The family, along with Cameron, Shelly, and Emma had arrived for the reading of the will. She didn't want to intrude, or see anyone. She continued down the hall to the east wing and went into George's room.

The room had been transformed to her exact specifications. She hated to think of Cameron in the newly decorated room with Shelly on their wedding night, but George insisted she work with the interior decorator he'd hired to breathe new life into the outdated room. The scent of fresh paint lingered in the air, but the cream walls brightened the room. The navy blue velvet drapes lent opulence to the elegant space. The bed had been stripped and a new mattress, still in the plastic, sat atop the four-poster antique bed. The blue, white, and turquoise silk brocade cover and new white sheets sat stacked on the antique dresser. Once on the bed, they'd set the tone in the room of quite elegance and tranquility.

"Dad thought of everything. He even had a new mattress delivered today. Just perfect for you and me to begin our own business arrangement, don't you think, Marti?"

"So you won't sleep on the same bed as your father, but you'd sleep with his mistress. Is that it, Walter?"

He liked the acid tone of her voice and the defiant stance she took. She'd be a challenge. "You're a beautiful woman. Exactly the kind of woman I like. You've got those long legs and tight ass. You're breasts are full, and I'll just bet they taste like peaches and cream. I love your hair. I'd like to wrap it around my hand and wrist and yank your head back until you cry out in pleasure and pain."

He advanced on her. She needed to get out of there. Things had turned bad quickly. The look in Walter's eyes told her he wasn't going to take no for an answer any longer. He'd been making passes and sleazy comments to her for weeks. Now that George was gone, he considered her part of his inheritance.

"You're wrong about me, Walter. I am not, and never was, your father's mistress. He was a friend of my grandfather's. He's known me since I was a child. You know that."

"He wanted us to think that. He'd had affairs before. He had one with a woman when he and my mother were separated, when I was young. I'll just bet there were others."

"You're wrong. He loved your mother. He strayed while they were separated, but he went back to her."

"So what? We're talking about you and me now."

He advanced on her again. Only a few steps away, she tried again to make him stop. "If you touch me, I swear I'll scream this house down."

"Who would care if I touched a whore like you?"

"I would," Cameron said from the door, "and she's not a whore. You should have some respect for the only person who cried for your father. She's one of the few who truly grieves for him."

"What is that supposed to mean? You don't think I'm upset about my father's passing?"

"I think you can't wait to hear the reading of the will. You don't have to wait any longer. The lawyer is ready. Go downstairs."

It wasn't a request.

Walter's eyes darted from him to her. "Pack your bags. You're out of here tonight."

"No, she's not."

"This is my house, and what I say goes."

Cameron continued to glare. Tomorrow, he owned

half the house. Marti could stay as long as she wanted. Tonight he'd find out who owned the other half and tomorrow he and Emma would move in, with Shelly in the west wing. He wasn't sure Marti would stay with Shelly there, but Emma wanted Marti to stay until the wedding. He'd try to convince her.

"We'll just see about that, won't we?" Cameron said defiantly.

"What do you mean?"

"Let's go listen to the reading of the will."

Walter glared at Marti and left the room, giving Cameron a wide berth.

"Are you okay?" Marti looked worse today than the last time he'd seen her.

"I'm fine. Just tired. I was up all night with George."

"Same story, different day. You told me the same thing last time. I didn't buy it then, and I don't buy it now. Why didn't you call me?"

She looked shocked. "I left a message with your assistant this morning and you never called me back."

"I got the message from my assistant, but all it said was call Marti. I didn't think it was important."

She looked at him like he was a stranger.

"I left a message with Shelly, telling you it was urgent and George was dying. She said you were helping Emma get dressed. She knew it was important. I guess that message wasn't important either, because it was just me calling," she said, letting her anger and hurt show.

Shelly did tell him she called, even if she didn't say why, which pissed him off, but she'd asked him not to call and encourage her. Shelly insisted Marti was just making a last-ditch effort to hold onto him and cause problems between them when they'd finally found solid footing for their relationship. Shelly convinced him Marti was jealous and trying to destroy the family they were trying to build for their children.

At the time, she made a good case. It sounded so convincing and true. He'd committed to his new life with Shelly. Despite his need to hear Marti's voice, he didn't return her call, never thinking she'd called about George. Stupid. He should have known better.

Now, seeing Marti again, he saw the truth. Marti wasn't petty, or the jealous type.

He would forever regret not calling Marti back and being there with George.

"Shelly never said anything about George."

"Not surprising. She didn't want you calling me."

"Do you blame her? We're getting married, and she knows there was something between us."

"Was? Was. I see," she said miserably. "Fine. You didn't call me back, so I sat here alone with George all night. I was here when he took his final breath. I was the one here when he needed his family. You couldn't be bothered to return my call."

"Dammit, Marti. That's not fair. I'm trying to be with Shelly. I'm trying to let you go. It's killing me, but I'm trying."

"Last night had nothing to do with our non-relationship. It had to do with the man who raised you your whole life dying, and you weren't here. You weren't here for him, or me."

"That's just it. I want to be with you, and I can't."

"No. You won't," she said and tried to leave.

He stopped her. They couldn't have this conversation again. Nothing would change what was and what was going to be.

"The lawyer wants to see you downstairs. You've been invited to listen to the reading of the will."

"I don't want to."

"You don't have a choice. George left you something and everyone listed in the will has to be present."

He took her arm and led her to the library, all the way downstairs without letting her go. Before they entered the room, he released her, but wished he didn't have to. He just wanted to touch her.

Chapter Thirty-Three

"WHAT IS SHE doing in here?" Both Walter and his sister, Claire, said in unison.

"I was invited." She sat in the only chair left for her in front of a TV brought in for the will.

The lawyer turned on the TV and George's image appeared in the paused video. She thought it fitting a boom of thunder exploded and rain poured outside. The rain threatened all day and she welcomed it now. She'd met George again during a storm. Fitting she should say goodbye with the rain pouring down outside.

"Hello, Marti," George said from the TV.

She stared up at his image and whispered, "Hello, George."

"I wanted to take a minute to thank you for what you did for me the day I met you on the dock. You saved my life—in more ways than one."

"What is he talking about, you saved his life?"

She ignored Walter and listened to George.

"You reminded me we are all unique, and nothing is ever given to us freely, except love and friendship. I love you, Marti, my friend."

"I love you too, George," she whispered.

"You told me not to allow my family to dictate my life and my death. We talked about how being born into a family fortune didn't mean you were entitled to something you never worked to contribute to the family's name and honor.

"You understand this, Marti. You've grown up to be a fine woman on your own, who has made your own way in this world. You took what you were given, both tangible and intangible, from your grandparents, and you've enriched your family's honor and name. Your grandparents had you to do that for them, and I have Cameron. Please Marti. Take Cameron aside and tell him the truth.

"I want to tell you I'm sorry, Marti, for what is about to happen. I'm afraid in order to try to make things right, I may hurt you very badly in the end. If it all works out, I know you'll be truly happy, and my grandchildren will have an amazing mother in you."

She felt Cameron's eyes bore into her back, but she refused to turn and face him.

"Emma, my darling princess. I love you. Don't be sad for me. I, like you, got to have Marti in my life for a short while and it has made all the difference. You will always be my princess and I shall always be your Knight."

Emma slipped up beside Marti and laid her head on

her shoulder. Marti reached up and held her head to her cheek.

The lawyer turned off the TV. "Marti, if you please. Everyone else, we'll continue in a few moments. Marti and Cameron need to have a private conversation."

"Wait a minute. What does it matter what she has to tell Cameron for my father?" Walter asked.

Marti had enough.

"Walter, you'll sit there and shut up for as long as it takes me to speak to Cameron," she snapped. "Are you so eager and greedy you can't allow George to have his final requests seen through the way he wanted?"

"Why the hell should I listen to you?"

"Because you asked why it matters what I have to say. I'll tell you. It matters a lot. I'm about to change all of your lives." Marti turned her back on Walter and faced Cameron. "If you'll please join me in the other room, I'll tell you what George wished he could have told you himself."

"Please keep an eye on Emma. I'll be back in a moment," Cameron said to Shelly.

"Of course, darling. Don't be long." She couldn't wait to hear what the old goat had left to Cameron. What was the big secret?

Chapter Thirty-Four

MARTI THOUGHT ABOUT what to say, how she was going to say it, and what Cameron would do once he knew.

George asked her to tell him the truth. She thought fleetingly about telling him the whole truth, who she really is, that she was pregnant with his child, and that Knight was his father. Marti followed Cameron out of the room.

Cameron sat on the sofa while Marti paced back and forth in front of the white marble fireplace.

"Marti, just say it. What did George want you to tell me?"

In the end, she decided to tell him about George and see where things went from there. Maybe he would understand what George was trying to tell him, besides the obvious.

He's a smart man. He'll figure it out.

"George had one great love in his life, his wife. He loved her very much."

"Yes, I know. They were married for forty years. She passed away a week after their fortieth anniversary."

"Yes. They had Walter and Claire. They raised them with love and gave them everything in the world two children could ever want. They went to the best schools, they had every new toy, cars when they could drive, money to spend, and anything else their hearts desired. They were rich and gave them everything a mother and father ever dreamed for their children."

"Yes. They had all the best things."

"Yes, things. Things they grew up to expect and demand and feel entitled to."

Cameron followed along. "George often said he didn't know where he'd gone wrong with them. I think he spoiled them until they felt like they didn't deserve anything less."

"That's exactly what George and I talked about. He and his wife loved them. They had a mother and a father and still George felt like he failed them in some way. In the end, having two parents who loved them didn't make them into good people."

He sat back and rubbed the back of his neck. "I don't want to make this about you, me, and Shelly."

"It's interesting you say that. George told me the truth about you last night. It was one of the last things he was able to tell me."

Cameron rubbed the back of his neck again. George had wanted to tell him something and he hadn't been there to hear his final words. "What did he want to tell me?"

"He said I have a way of seeing things as they are, and not as I want to see them. Do you understand?"

"Yeah, you see the truth of things, even if it isn't what you want to see."

"I hope you will see the truth of what I'm going to tell you, and not what you want the truth to be."

"What is it?"

"What do you remember about your father?"

"He was never there when I needed him," Cameron replied without missing a beat.

"Not the way to start, then," she said and drew her finger over her ear, tucking her hair behind it. She paced a few more steps, Cameron's eyes following her every move.

"George loved his wife . . ."

"We've established this," Cameron said impatiently.

"Shut up and listen. I'm telling the story, and you'll just sit there and listen to it. I'm trying to fulfill a dying man's last requests. I gave my word. Let me do it," she said, a trace of desperation in her voice.

This was difficult for her. She knew something about him and found it difficult to explain and make him understand George's position and actions.

"I'm sorry, sweetheart. George indicated he'd asked a lot of you and you might be hurt by his requests. Tell me your way."

She took a deep breath and sat on the coffee table between his knees in front of him. She met his gaze and pressed on.

"About thirty-four years ago George and his wife

had some trouble in their marriage and they separated. During this time, George met a woman and had a brief affair with her. They liked each other's company and had a few things in common, but they weren't in love with each other. George and his wife reconciled and the other woman was happy to see George back with the woman he loved. She knew he belonged with his wife, and he knew the woman was better off without him. He learned a few weeks later the woman was pregnant."

Cameron's face went completely blank, his eyes bore into her, but she didn't think he really saw her.

"She told him she was pregnant and wanted to have the baby. She didn't want to tell the child who his father is. She wanted to raise the child on her own. She was adamant.

"He agreed, but insisted the child be a part of his life in another way. She agreed." He didn't respond. "George Knight is your father, Cameron. Your mother made him swear never to tell you."

She paused and let him take in the news. "He kept his promise even after her death because it was her wish. He kept his promise until his death. Now that he's gone, he wanted you to know.

"Although you never knew your father's name, you had a father in every way that matters. He may not have been married to your mother, but he was there for you your whole life. Not every day, but when it mattered most. When you needed him, he was there.

"His wife knew, of course, and you were always welcome in their home. They treated you like a son because that's who you were to them.

"You are the man you are today because you are very much your father's son. He asked me to tell you, he may not have been there for you every day, but he thought he did a fine job raising you. He wanted you to know of all his children, he was the most proud of you."

Tears rolled down his cheeks. He didn't care, it was just Marti. With her, he could be himself. She'd grown up without her parents, knew how important this was to him. He considered George the father he always wanted. And now, come to find out, he was his father. Cameron was a Knight. It was unbelievable.

Marti took out the paper she had in her back pocket and held it out to Cameron.

"Your birth certificate doesn't list Knight as your father. This is the only piece of paper Knight had where your mother acknowledges you as his son. She sent him the note the day you were born. He wanted you to have it."

Cameron opened the paper. Yellowed and creased, well-worn, as if someone had opened and closed it over and over again through the years. Faint watermarks marred the paper as well. When he opened the paper, he dropped it to the floor and put his head in his hands and wept quietly.

The note read:

My dearest Knight,
Our son was born today. He is a fine Knight. I've named him Cameron Thomas Shaw. He is waiting to meet his father.
All my love, Amelia.

The watermarks were his father's tears. He'd wept when he got the news.

"Your mother was very fond of Knight. They just weren't meant to be together. You were named after your father and grandfather. George's middle name is Thomas and his father's first name was Thomas. You are a Knight and Emma was his princess. She's the only grandchild he ever saw born."

She put her hands on top of Cameron's head and just sat there with him.

He looked up and her hands dropped away. "His wife was always nice to me. She treated me like one of her kids."

"She was your stepmother. She understood your time with George was important. She didn't want you to feel like you weren't welcome. You always were. This was your home."

"So this is why George said you might get hurt. He wanted me to understand I've put myself in the same position he faced with my mother. His situation was a little different because he was married when I was conceived, but basically similar."

He shook his head. "I can marry you and still be a father to my child with Shelly, and you'll be the perfect stepmother, like his wife was to me. Or I can marry Shelly and hurt you. It seems I'm always hurting you."

"He just wanted you to know he was your father. He loved you and was extremely proud of you. He wanted to give you one final fatherly lesson.

"You can be a good father to a child even if you aren't

there every day. You just have to make sure you're there for the important things, and they know you love them.

"He was a good father to you. It made all the difference in your life knowing Knight loved you. You know that."

"I don't need you telling me what I know about Knight and how I grew up and what I think about family and having a father who is there for you. I know," he yelled. "Why can't you just let it be? I'm not going to abandon my child. I'm going to be there every day. He'll never wonder where I am because I'll always be there. I'm not going to change my mind."

She understood the anger, felt his pain. She knew what it was like to miss parents, wish they were there for you every minute of every day. She had her grandparents, but still, somehow, it wasn't enough. Cameron had George, but it wasn't enough. Not to a child.

Cameron made this decision from his child's point of view.

Resigned to her heartbreak, she couldn't keep asking—or what amounted to begging—at this point. She would if she thought it would make a difference. No matter what she said or did, he still chose a life with Shelly over one with her. She understood that now. It wasn't Shelly he wanted, but the life he'd never had with his mother and father. Even George being his father didn't change anything.

Telling him about their baby wouldn't either.

"I have to go back in and tell your brother and sister who you are. Come back when you're ready."

"What was he doing at the docks? He mentioned you saved his life once."

She sighed. She didn't want to tell him about the day at the docks. His expression, the way he waited, told her he wouldn't let her get away without telling the story.

"The day I returned from my yearlong trip, I saw a man at the end of the dock standing on the railing in the pouring rain. I went over to him and said, 'Nice day, don't you think? Personally, I love a good storm.'"

"He was going to throw himself into the sea?"

"No. He was just having a bad day. He told his children he was dying and instead of being compassionate, they wanted to know when and how much they were getting. I told him about my uncle and my relationship with him. We bonded. I realized who he is, and he and my grandfather were old friends. He remembered me as a child. Instead of doing something foolish, he asked me to dinner, where I met you and Emma for the first time."

"So you're telling me if you hadn't been on that dock, I wouldn't have met you, *and* I might never have known Knight is my father?"

"Things happen for a reason. My life wouldn't be what it is now either. I wouldn't have met you and Emma, maybe Shelly wouldn't have lied and told you she's pregnant, and Knight might have been foolish enough to jump," she said and shrugged.

If she hadn't met George, she wouldn't be pregnant with Cameron's baby now.

He didn't say anything about her calling Shelly a liar

again. She let it go. Why keep fighting it. All it did was make her sad.

He studied Marti's face, saw the toll this was taking on her in her pale skin and tired eyes. Overwhelmed by the urge to take her to bed, wrap her in his arms, and let her sleep. Instead, he reined in the impulse, curled his hands into fists on his thighs, and reminded himself she wasn't his to touch. Not anymore. He had Shelly. His daughter and baby would have a full-time mother and father.

Chapter Thirty-Five

THEY RETURNED TO George's study and Cameron sat next to Shelly again. Marti walked to the front where the lawyer waited. Walter and several other family members made comments about making them all wait. She wanted to tell them all to go to hell, then she could go upstairs and sleep.

She addressed the lawyer, "I've done what George requested. You don't need me any longer. I'll let you speak with the family alone." She turned to leave, but the lawyer stopped her.

"Marti, George has asked you stay until the end. The will contains items which pertain to you specifically."

She nodded and sat back and crossed her arms over her stomach. The nausea was back. She hoped she wouldn't have to dash out of the room to throw up.

The lawyer went over the provisions in the will. He read the items and cash amounts allocated to the house staff and all of the distant relatives. Once complete, he asked everyone but the immediate family and Marti remain.

Marti didn't pay close attention. She lost herself in the pouring rain outside the window. Emma came over and sat on her lap. She rested her head against Marti's shoulder and watched the rain with her. It was so nice to hold the little girl in her arms. She imagined someday this would be her child with Cameron.

"I love you, Sugar Bug," she whispered into her ear.

"I love you too."

"Marti, did you hear me?" the lawyer asked.

"What? No. What did you say?"

"I'm going to read what has been left to everyone in this room. I will end with you and Cameron."

"Okay. Fine," she said distracted. She didn't really care. She was holding the most important thing. She had Emma in her arms and a baby in her belly.

"I leave to my daughter, Claire," the lawyer began, "the sum of ten million dollars and twenty-five percent of my shares in Knight Enterprises. To my son, Walter . . ."

Walter shifted to the edge of his seat, ecstatic. If his sister only got ten million and twenty-five percent of the shares, he got the rest. He was richer than rich. He sat back smiling, smug with the knowledge he'd gotten the bulk of the estate and his sister had been screwed. He always knew he was the favorite son.

"I leave the sum of ten million dollars and twenty-five percent of my shares in Knight Enterprises."

"This can't be right. What about the rest? Millions,

the house and furnishings, the jewelry, and the other fifty percent of the company shares? He better not have left it to that whore." Walter screamed the words, stood, and pointed a finger at Marti.

Marti covered Emma's ears so she couldn't hear Walter shouting and calling her names, but it was too late. Emma curled up in her arms.

Cameron didn't care where the rest went. He had more than he could ever spend on his own. He hoped maybe Knight left something special for Emma.

"Walter, I assure you the will is sound. If you'll give me the chance, I'll finish and you'll know who George allocated the rest to."

"By all means, let's see what my crazy father did with the rest."

"To my son, Cameron, I leave fifty percent of my shares in Knight Enterprises."

"Wait a minute. Cameron is not his son." Walter stood and braced his hands on the back of the chair in front of him.

Marti didn't give Cameron a chance to answer. "Yes, he is."

"I am, Walter. Knight was my father. Knight asked Marti to tell me outside. He kept the secret all these years."

"It's not true. He was married to my mother for forty years."

"Knight was Daddy's dad?" Emma looked up at Marty.

"Yes, Sugar Bug. Knight was your grandpa."

Tears rolled down Emma's round cheeks.

Cameron watched his daughter in Marti's arms. He wanted to go to her, but knew she was where she wanted to be.

"He was separated from her for a short time and had a brief affair with my mother. They agreed not to tell me who my father was, so long as he could be in my life. Your mother agreed and welcomed me here. I didn't know Knight was my father until tonight."

"I want a DNA test. This can't be true."

The lawyer took out a folder with some lab reports. "Your father thought you might feel that way and had the tests run. Cameron is his son and Emma is his grand-daughter."

Cameron looked surprised. "How did he run the tests?"

"He took a swab from Emma and stole your hairbrush on one of your overnight visits."

"Knight had a man use a funny swab to tickle the inside of my cheek. It was a secret, but I guess everyone knows now," she said to Marti.

"I guess they do," she replied.

"Let's continue. Let's see, fifty percent to Cameron, oh yes, here we are. Cameron, you will also receive the sum of fifty million dollars."

Shelly gasped and covered her mouth.

Stunned, Cameron tried to wrap his head around everything. "Why would he do this?" He'd left Cameron more than he'd left his other two children. Why?

"The money is in other stocks, bonds, cash, and assets. In addition, you are to receive one half interest in this home and property. I'm told George already spoke to you of the promise you were to make about the house."

Cameron nodded his agreement.

"Good. Miss Emma Shaw, you are to receive a share in the sum of fifty million dollars. Upon your eighteenth and twenty-first birthdays, you will receive portions of your share. The number of children Cameron produces will determine the shares. I understand there is one child on the way. At this time, Emma would receive half. If Cameron fathers another child, the shares will be split three ways, and so on." He glanced at Marti, though she kept her face blank.

"This can't be. The bulk of the estate goes to Cameron and his children." Walter's face turned red with outrage.

Claire remained silent, a soft content smile on her face. Cameron hadn't spent a lot of time with her growing up, but he assumed the ten million plus what the shares were worth would last her through her lifetime and then some. She seemed happy to take what George left her and let Walter rant about the rest. Cameron remembered this same dynamic from when they were kids playing together. Walter always had to have his way and Claire let him.

Cameron was floored. He'd left it all to him and his children.

"Marti, you made a promise to George," the attorney continued.

"Yes. Well, one promise and I told him I'd try on several other things."

The lawyer smiled. "You don't make promises lightly."

"Nope," she answered, ready to get this whole thing over and done.

"George left the contents of the house to you. You may wish to designate items to whomever you choose, such as Walter and Claire, if there are items of sentimental value to them. George indicated they took most of what they wanted when they moved out years ago. He told me to remind you the contents of the safe belong to you. Since you changed the combination with him, you are the only one who has access to the contents."

Marti sat stunned. The safe. George had her change the combination and memorize it because his mind was failing him and he didn't want to have the safe destroyed after his death in order to get it open. She hadn't bought the story, not really. All he had to do was provide the safe combo to his lawyer. Now she knew. He wanted her to have what was in the safe. He knew she'd do the right thing. She thought of a particular story George had told her. She set Emma on her feet and stood.

"If you'll all excuse me a moment. George would like something from the safe given now." Marti left and over-heard Walter protesting and calling her names. Cameron warned him in no uncertain terms to watch his mouth; there was a child in the room. Shelly told Cameron she couldn't believe they'd gotten fifty million dollars.

She came back into the room several minutes later carrying a large velvet box. Emma sat on Cameron's lap holding onto his arm. She kneeled in front of the little girl and showed her the box.

"When George asked me to do your room upstairs, he

told me it was my job to remind you every chance I can that you are his princess. You will always be his princess. I know now he didn't want me to just remind you with the room, but to make sure you always feel like a princess. What's in this box holds a very special memory for you and I. I cherish this memory we share. I will take it with me wherever I go."

"I don't want you to go."

"I know you don't, Sugar Bug." She leaned up and kissed the girl. Unshed tears shimmered in her eyes. Leaving this child would be the hardest thing she ever did.

"Knight gave this to his wife on their twentieth wedding anniversary with a note telling her he wished for twenty more. He and his wife were married for forty years. He got his wish. He told me he believes this is special. I think he would have wanted you to have it. You, his one and only granddaughter, his princess." She opened the box and showed Emma the diamond and ruby necklace Marti had crowned her with for their milkshake tea party.

Shelly gasped when she saw the necklace. The rubies were the size of grapes and clusters of diamonds surrounded them. It was a necklace fit for a queen, and probably cost a king's ransom.

"It's gorgeous," Shelly said and leaned forward to get a better look.

"This is yours, Emma. Every time you wear it, I want you to remember you are a princess and your grandfather was a Knight."

"You can't just give away my mother's jewelry. It belongs to me and Claire."

"Walter, your father left the contents of the house and safe to her. She can do with them as she pleases. Your father had faith in her to do the right thing. If there's something you want, ask her."

"I want the contents of the safe," he demanded.

Marti closed the box and kissed Emma. She took the box and held it to her chest.

"Can we have another tea party?"

"Soon, I promise," Marti said and stood.

"You mean it when you promise, so I know we'll have our tea party."

Marti smiled at the little girl. "You know me so well."

She turned on Walter. "As for you, Walter, you don't know me at all. I'll forget the name-calling and the outbursts, but don't push me. I'd just as soon burn the contents of this house than hand them over to you just because your last name is Knight and you think you're entitled. Your father spent weeks telling me stories about everything in this house, particularly the contents of the safe. At the time, I thought it was just a dying man reliving his life by telling stories to a friend who would listen. They were wonderful stories, and I will remember them always. I will remember your father and his wishes. If you want something from the house, let me know, and I'll decide if it's what George would have wanted."

"You'll decide. You. Who the hell are you?"

"Wouldn't you like to know? You'd be surprised. For the purposes of George's estate, I'm the person he trusted to see to his last wishes. I'm the person he trusted to keep their word. I told him I'd try. Don't push me. I don't like to go back on my word. If you make me, I'll be really angry."

"Let's finish the will," the lawyer interrupted before Walter continued with his tirade. He removed two envelopes from his briefcase.

"George knew you very well, Marti. He left these for you. He said one would make you laugh and the other will make you angry. He said to tell you not to be angry, he wanted you to have it, so take it and deal with it." He smiled at her. "Those were his words," he laughed. "He knew you wanted your privacy, so the contents are for you only."

He handed the envelopes over and she opened the first, immediately angered by the contents. She read the note inside and said, "Dammit, George. I love you too." She closed the envelope containing a check for twenty million dollars.

She opened the other envelope and looked inside. Several bills and two quarters were tucked inside. She pulled out the money, crushed it in her hand, and held it to her chest while she laughed and cried.

"What the hell did he leave you?" Shelly asked, her eyes locked on the bills crushed in her hand. Let her think it was all George left her. While Marti was thrilled with her winnings, Shelly was salivating, could barely sit still in her chair since she'd learned of Cameron's inheritance.

"It's not your business, but fifty-seven dollars and fifty cents," she said and continued laughing.

"Why are you laughing? Surprised he didn't leave you millions?" Walter looked smug.

"It's the money your father owed me from our poker game."

She wiped her eyes and stood to leave. She assumed they were done. The lawyer asked her to sit again.

"There's something else, Marti. You made a promise to George."

"The thing he doesn't want me to sell? I won't sell the contents of the house."

"That wasn't what he didn't want you to sell."

Cameron looked at the lawyer. "He didn't."

The lawyer smiled. He'd expected this. "He did. Marti, your promise was the same as Cameron's. You own one half ownership in the house and property. Neither of you can sell your half to anyone else, or to each other. Your half will be passed down to your firstborn child and to his. Emma, in his case."

"No," she said, disbelieving. "He never said it was the house. I can't own the house with Cameron."

"You do. As of today, you two own this house together and will leave it to Emma and your child upon your death."

"George, no. You can't do this to me."

"He told me to tell you, it is his last request. Your grandmother gave you the world. He's giving you a home."

"No." She stood and ran out the French door and out into the garden. The rain poured down and covered the tears running down her face.

Chapter Thirty-Six

CAMERON FOUND HER on a flat bench in a hidden part of the garden. She sat alone, face tilted up to view the dark clouds as the rain pelted her face and body. Beautiful in her black dress, her arms stretched out behind her, supporting her as she gazed up at the sky. Hard and throbbing, he scanned her body, outlined by the wet dress.

He walked over to her, ignoring the rain, focused on Marti. Her grief so palpable, he felt it to his own soul.

He came to her, picked her up, and sat her on his lap and held her. Just held her to him with his arms locked tightly around her.

She lay against him and accepted his comfort. "How could he do this to me?"

"I don't know what he was thinking. He didn't tell me you were the other owner. It's a big house. We'll work it out."

"He asked me to try, but he never told me about this.

How am I going to try when he makes it impossible?" She cried harder.

Cameron held her tighter. He couldn't stand to see her so upset. He kissed her hair and the flowery scent filled his senses. He kissed her temple and her cheek and tasted her tears and the rain. He couldn't stop himself. He wanted her so bad, and she was in his arms. He wanted to take away her pain and show her nothing but pleasure. Touching her, being with her like this, felt so good, so right. He didn't want to feel this sadness and grief anymore. He only wanted the desire, passion, closeness, love, only she made him feel.

He took her mouth and kissed her. When she opened her mouth to him, welcomed him in, he lost all conscious thought to reality. He lost himself in her. He didn't notice the rain or remember Emma was inside the house with Shelly. He kissed Marti and pushed his tongue into her mouth and slid it over hers, savoring her taste and texture. Something inside him tilted back to right and he felt lighter, unburdened.

He lay her down on the wide bench and held her and kissed her. He kissed her neck and her hands moved under his suit jacket and over his back.

She held him to her, and he kissed her neck and down the V of her dress to her cleavage. The tips of his fingers explored the exposed flesh.

He undid the buttons down the front of her dress, and each new patch of skin he uncovered, he laid a trail of kisses. He spread the dress wide to her sides and looked down at her tanned skin and the black lace bra and panties covering what he wanted most right now. Rain pelted her skin and made it glisten. So beautiful. He leaned over her and kissed the swell of her breasts. They seemed larger, fuller. They spilled over the top of her bra, and he licked and traced the line of lace. She gasped and dug her fingers into his wet hair. He undid the front clasp and pushed the barrier out of his way. Her nipples were hard, beckoning his mouth. He took one breast in his hand and the other in his mouth and she arched off the bench and offered herself to him with a soft sigh.

She moaned his name and loved the feel of his tongue on her nipple and the soft pull as he sucked. She covered his hand on her other breast and squeezed. Her breasts were swollen and extremely sensitive with the pregnancy. The more Cameron kissed and sucked the more heat spread through her system.

One of his strong hands moved down her stomach and traced the outside of her hip before returning to her lace panties. He pulled them down her legs, tossed them to the sodden ground, before his hand came back to her heated center. Without warning, he thrust his finger deep inside her. She exploded and pressed her hips up to his cupped hand. His mouth devoured her breast. Relentless, he suckled her breast and used his finger to drive her back up the crest. Each time she came close to release, he slowed down and took her back up. His thumb found the bundle of nerves vibrating to life and rubbed over the slick sensitive flesh, sparking another wave of heat to wash over her. She moaned and pulled his hair, holding his head to her breast, begging for more.

Her release building, he undid his pants and came down on top of her, his mouth taking her in a devouring kiss. He used his legs to spread her thighs wide and thrust into her hard and fast to the hilt. He had to have her, all of her. He buried himself deep, felt her heat surround him. Tight, hot, wet, she fit him so perfectly.

She burned for him. The rain poured down on them, but all she felt was his warmth and fire. The flames spread out from her center where she was joined with Cameron and burned and consumed. She pressed her hips up to him as he came down on her again and again.

Completely lost in her, he kissed her cheek, her ear and neck, and took her mouth with his and smoothed his tongue over hers to the pace of their hips moving together. She tightened around him, and he gave himself over to her. She shattered in his arms with a soft cry and moan. He surrendered his own release and spilled himself into her fire.

When his mind cleared and his brain started thinking of things other than possessing her, he gazed down at her. Eyes closed, the rain came down and drop-by-drop slid over her beautiful face. Her hands rested on his chest as he held himself above her on his elbows.

"Oh, God. What the hell am I doing?"

He pressed his forehead to hers. He couldn't believe he'd made love to her. He wanted her all day, every day, but he'd made a commitment to Shelly. What the hell was he doing?

He hadn't even taken off his clothes. He'd opened her dress, tore off her panties, unzipped his pants and taken her right there in the garden on a bench. It was pouring rain, for God's sake. Her silky, soft skin puckered with goose bumps. She shivered with the cold. The rain soaked her, and her skin glistened in the moonlight. She was beautiful and he was an idiot.

You are a supreme jackass. You love her. Why do you treat her so badly?

He got off her and redid his pants. He grabbed the lapels of his jacket and shook out the wet material uselessly. He rubbed the back of his neck.

Marti sat up and pulled her dress closed to cover herself. He didn't know what to say, how to explain or say how sorry he was for doing this to her, so he went with mundane details. "I promised Knight I would move into the house the day after his death. We'll be here tomorrow."

"You will?" Surprised and happy, she smiled. He and Emma would be moving into the house. They'd all be together.

Tell him. Tell him you're pregnant. Now is your chance.

"Yeah. George told me we have the east wing and you have the west wing. Since the other spare room in the east wing isn't furnished, Shelly will stay in the west wing until the wedding. I hope that's okay. We'll hold the wedding here on Saturday."

Shocked, the smile died on her face and everything inside her froze. He just made love to her and he was talking about moving in with Emma and Shelly and marrying her here at the house. She'd almost told him the truth.

One minute he made her feel like the most precious

gift in the world and the next he made her feel like the biggest idiot ever born.

"Wait. You're moving in with Shelly. You're getting married here—on Saturday."

"Yes."

She dropped her hands to her sides. Her dress fell open down the front unnoticed. She gripped the edge of the bench and held tight, because if she didn't, she'd explode into a million tiny pieces of pain. "You just made love to me. You grabbed me and practically ripped off my clothes to have me. We shared something beautiful, powerful, and wonderful, and you're telling me you're still marrying her."

He rubbed the back of his neck. He'd put that hurt look on her face again.

"The last time you made love to me, you turned your back on me and chose her. Now you make love to me again and you still choose her. I love you, Cameron. Doesn't it mean anything to you?" she yelled over the rain.

"It means everything to me," he yelled back.

"No, it doesn't because time and again you choose her over me."

"I have to give my family what I think they need, a father and a mother."

"You have other options. George has shown you, you have other options. I love Emma. I'd be the very best mother I can to her."

"This is what I want," he said angrily.

The blow from those words sent her back a step, knocked her on her mental ass. She stood and faced him determinedly. "I'll be gone before the end of the week."

"You don't have to leave. This is your home. It's what George wanted you to have."

"I told him I'd try. I'd try for Emma. I said I would stay here and watch over her for two months. I won't be here and watch you marry that lying, gold-digging bitch. I won't stay here and watch you make the second biggest mistake of your life. I'll come back and watch over Emma like George wanted, but you make it so damn hard for me to keep my word. I'd rather you take a knife and stab me in the back, it would hurt a lot less than you shredding my heart every time I see you." She turned to walk away.

"What was my first mistake?" He thought she'd say not choosing her. He was wrong. So very wrong. Marti never thought about herself first. Should have been his first clue as to who she really was, the kind of person she really was.

She didn't turn around to face him, just said, "Continuing to blame yourself for Caroline's death. It wasn't your fault."

She turned back. His shoulders sagged. He did what he always did when he was stressed out and frustrated, he rubbed the back of his neck. She smiled. She'd seen him do it often. She hoped one day she wouldn't see him do it quite so much. She wouldn't be here to see it. She had to put an end to this.

"George asked me to watch over Emma because he knows the minute you say your vows and the ring is on Shelly's hand, she'll turn on you and Emma and make your lives a living hell.

"I'd give you and Emma so much, and you turn your

back on me and the love I offer to you, freely, no strings attached. No more, Cameron. I can't do this anymore. It hurts too much to have you choose her over me, to have you put me last, to have you not even consider life with me as a possibility.

"She lied, Cameron."

"She's pregnant."

With a shake of her head and a very heavy heart, she gave up. "I can't take you making love to me like I'm your whole world, only to watch you turn your back on me when we're done. Let me go. Say the words, Cameron, and let me go."

"I can't." He wanted her to be happy. He wanted to be the one to make her happy. He couldn't say the words. Nothing could make him say those words. Not when everything inside him wanted to hold onto her.

"Then you leave me no choice." She walked away, up the back steps, leading into the west wing of the house.

He didn't know exactly what she meant, except that he'd lost her forever. He sat on the bench, rain pouring over him, his hands on his knees and his head down between his shoulders, and wondered how he'd screwed up his life so badly he'd made the woman he loved hate him.

Chapter Thirty-Seven

MARTI STAYED IN her room. Cameron, Emma, and Shelly moved into the house on Sunday. Since the house had everything they would need and Cameron was keeping the penthouse, it was simply a matter of bringing in suitcases and a few boxes of personal belongings.

They moved around the house, but Marti couldn't bring herself to even go out to see Emma and welcome her home. She watched Emma running in the garden and playing on her new play yard. Cameron pushed her on the swing and chased her around the huge back lawn.

Shelly complained about everything, annoying her the most. She didn't like the room across the hall on Marti's side of the house. Must be too far from the master bedroom and Cameron's bed.

Marti wanted nothing more than to kick her out. Petty and childish, but it's what she wanted to do.

Satisfaction came when Shelly discovered the bedroom bed and bath hadn't been made up for a guest: no sheets or towels in the room, or fresh flowers like in Marti's. Shelly practically screamed down the house calling for the maid. Marti had given the staff a few days off. The maid, the cook, and the gardener had all been given time off to grieve for their former employer.

Cameron knocked on her door several times. She didn't answer. He'd finally resorted to sending Emma. She hated to ignore the little girl, so she'd simply told Emma she'd see her later. Emma left feeling rejected and Marti felt terrible for hurting her, but she needed time.

She'd only gone downstairs to get something to eat when she knew everyone was somewhere else in the house, or outside.

She'd stayed in her office-slash-studio working for hours and well into the night, until she was so exhausted she fell into bed and slept like the dead. When she was in her studio, she thought she heard someone outside the door. She wondered if it had been Cameron, but dismissed it as an old house settling.

Morning came quickly and so did the nausea greeting her each new day. She'd accepted it as part of being pregnant. Although she didn't like it, it was kind of good to wake up each morning and be reminded she was going to have a baby. She'd rather her body told her in a different way. Soon it would. Her belly swelled, making her pants fit tighter around her waist.

She went down to Emma's room and peeked inside. Emma was just waking up. She helped her dress and brushed and braided her hair down the back of her head.

They went downstairs together. Still early, no one was in the kitchen. She began making Emma and her breakfast. She handed Emma some silverware and asked her to set up the table on the back patio.

Shelly came in, but Marti ignored her.

"Where's the cook?"

"Gregory has the day off, along with the rest of the staff."

Shelly frowned, showing her displeasure. Again, Marti ignored her.

"Well, it's nice you're making breakfast for everyone. You could have been more hospitable yesterday when we moved in."

"You have a roof over your head. Be thankful for small favors."

Marti continued making breakfast and sat out three plates. Jimmy came into the kitchen and she served him up a plate of pancakes and eggs with fresh fruit salad.

"Thanks, Miss Marti. I sure appreciate it. It's hard being a bachelor. A good home-cooked meal is hard to come by."

Marti gave Jimmy a warm smile. "Emma is on the back patio. Please, join us."

"I'll see you outside." He took his plate and walked by Shelly with a good morning glare Marti appreciated.

"I like my eggs over easy."

Marti didn't say a word. She dished up two more plates for she and Emma, shut off the stove, and walked out the back door with the two plates.

Shelly huffed in outrage. It only made Marti smile more.

Cameron came in dressed for work and glanced at Shelly sitting at the table looking peeved. *What now?* "What's the matter?"

"Her. You know what she did? She gave the staff the day off. She made breakfast for Emma and Jimmy and herself and not for me. She's so rude. Who's going to make me breakfast?"

Cameron didn't know what to say. Shelly couldn't actually expect Marti to make her breakfast.

"I guess you'll have to make your own. I need to get to the office in a few minutes," he said and poured a cup of coffee.

"You aren't going to pour me a cup?"

"No. It's not good for the baby. Have some orange juice."

Marti walked in and passed him and poured a cup of coffee for Jimmy and got two glasses of orange juice for her and Emma.

"I've been wondering what was in the envelope you got from George that made you mad. It's interesting he'd give you something just to upset you," Shelly said.

"Keep wondering. It's none of your business."

"Just because you own half this house . . ."

"And all the contents in it," Marti interrupted.

"Doesn't give you the right to be rude," Shelly finished.

"You're right. I do it just to piss you off. I'd recommend you remember I own every piece of furniture, every rug, every picture, every plate, cup, spoon, fork, everything. It's all mine. Move one thing without my permission and you'll regret it. I'm sure you've already spent half the morning cataloguing how much everything in your room costs. Just remember, it's all mine," she said with a touch of sarcastic whimsy.

"How can you afford to pay the staff and the taxes and the upkeep of this house? You can't possibly expect Cameron and I to pay for everything."

"Cameron and I will work it out, since I know you aren't bringing fifty million dollars to the wedding. You know, when he divorces you after he discovers you're nothing but a lying bitch, you aren't entitled to anything he has before the wedding. Not the money, not the house, nothing," she smiled and started for the door.

"Marti."

"Cameron," she shot back, knowing he didn't want her calling his fiancé a liar to her face, but she didn't care and kept walking.

Cameron didn't want to get in the middle of Shelly and Marti, but she'd given him the perfect opening to talk about the expenses for the house. "Wait, we do need to talk about this situation with the house. I'll pay the expenses for the house and staff, but we need to talk about the living arrangements."

"You know, it's amazing how little you know about me. I guess now you'll never know. I will pay half the expenses for the staff and everything else required for the house. As for the living situation, the west wing is mine. I expect whether I'm here or not, you'll respect the boundary. As for the contents of the house, I'm serious, not a single candlestick gets moved without my permission."

"You can't possibly afford to pay the expenses on the

house and property. A place this size costs a fortune to upkeep."

"How do you know I can't afford it? Tell me what you know about me. Am I rich? Poor? Middle class? What do I do for a living? How much money do I make? Here's an easier one: what's my last name? If you know the answer to even one of those questions, you have the answer you need."

Those questions were just a few of the things he didn't know about her.

"Well, Cameron? Who is she?" Shelly asked.

The woman I love. The woman I don't know nearly enough about because I've been too selfish to ask and taking everything I could from her. I know she's kind and doesn't give her word unless she means it. I know she loves me. I don't know who she is, and yet I know everything I need to know about her to fall head over heels in love with her.

I know she loves Emma like a mother should love her daughter.

"Cameron?" Shelly asked.

"She's right. I don't know any of those things about her. Not even her last name."

"You won't get any of those answers either. At least not from me."

Surprised, Shelly knew they were attracted to each other and had been dancing around the situation since that night at the restaurant. Still, the hurt and pain in Cameron's eyes at not knowing the answers to Marti's questions surprised her. Did he feel that deeply for Marti?

If so, that could be a real problem, especially this close to the wedding.

"I don't know how we'll live in this house together. What was George thinking when he gave half the house to each of you?" she asked.

Both Cameron and Marti knew what he was thinking: they'd work things out and be together.

"I'll call you a taxi anytime you're ready to leave," Marti said sweetly.

"I'm pregnant and engaged to Cameron."

"Sure you are, sweetie. Cameron's the only one who believes that crap."

"Marti, what's gotten into you?" he asked, noticing she still looked pale and a little green this morning.

"You, the other night."

He winced at her words.

"What's that supposed to mean?" Shelly darted glances from her to Cameron.

"Figure it out," Marti said and walked out the door.

"What did she mean, Cameron?"

"We had an argument the other night. Leave it alone, Shelly."

Shelly didn't want to leave it alone. Marti had sunk her claws into Cameron and refused to let him go. Well, she knew the best way to lure him away from another woman, get him in her bed and he'd forget all about that bitch. Hopefully, she'd get him so worked up again, he'd forget the whole condom thing and she'd get pregnant for real.

Emma ran in the back door and Jimmy followed, carrying their empty plates.

"Marti is speaking alien. It's so cool."

"She's speaking French, munchkin." Jimmy dropped their plates in the dishwasher. "Ready to go, boss. We gotta get this little one to school."

"Yeah. Why is she speaking French?" He couldn't help but ask.

"She received a call, said it was for work. Why?"

"No reason." Every reason.

Why was she doing business in French? Who did she know in France? Is that where she'd go when she left at the end of the week? He'd been up all night thinking about her leaving and remembering making love to her in the pouring rain. He'd gone to her room late last night. The lights shown under the door. He wondered what she was working on that kept her up so late. Question after question, and now she'd said she wouldn't answer any of them for him. She'd remain a mystery and everything he *didn't* know about her would haunt him the rest of his life. Everything he *did* know about her would haunt him. She would haunt him.

Chapter Thirty-Eight

COMPLETELY DRAINED AFTER her first morning at home with Cameron, Shelly, and Emma. She handled several business calls, went into her office at Fairchild Industries to exchange the paperwork she'd finished for the paperwork she needed to complete. She shot off several emails on the Fairchild/Merrick land deal and ended her afternoon in the city at her publisher's office. The two new books were going to press. The publisher had gotten the advanced copies Marti requested. She had them gift wrapped along with another surprise for Emma.

She had almost everything in place for her to leave at first light on Saturday. Cameron would be married in the afternoon, and she'd be long gone.

The Decadence restaurant lunch crowd must have thinned out at this late hour. She took a seat at the bar and gulped down a glass of water. Elizabeth came out of the kitchen with a huge smile on her face.

"I told the staff to tell me if you came in. I called Jenna upstairs, she's on her way down."

"Um, why?"

"Because we haven't seen you in quite a while and we were wondering how things are going. Cameron is a bear. Jenna threatened to fire him if he keeps yelling at people and drifting off into space half the day. His assistant is about ready to poison him. Lucky for him, he eats here every day."

"Lucky for him is right. I, on the other hand, plan on killing him the first chance I get and think I can get away with it. Your husband's an FBI agent. Maybe he can give me some pointers on how to kill someone and not get caught."

Elizabeth laughed. "That bad, huh. We heard about him and Shelly moving in with you. That really sucks."

"You don't know the half of it. She catalogues the value of everything in the house. 'Oh my, just look at this vase. Hand painted in Venice, it must be worth a thousand dollars,'" she mimicked Shelly's annoying voice.

"You're kidding. Sam mentioned when she was on your sailboat she did the same thing."

"Yes, very annoying."

"I can imagine. We all know she's after Cameron for his money. Now that George left him a fortune, well, I can imagine she's thinking she can sleep on a fourteen-karat gold bed."

"How about we just dump a molten load over her head and put her in the garden?"

"She'd scare away all the birds." Elizabeth put a hand

on Marti's shoulder. "Are you okay? Don't take this the wrong way, but you don't look so hot."

"It's been a long couple of weeks." She picked up the bag at her feet and handed it to Elizabeth. "I brought this in because I need a favor. It's important, and I'd rather Cameron not know about it."

"Okay. What is it?"

"It's the dress I had made for Emma for the benefit on Friday night."

"Which you'll be going to, right?" Jenna asked from behind them.

"I promised Emma I would be there, and I will. How's it going by the way?"

"Are you kidding? The day I talked to you I got a call from the curator for the Fairchild Collection. They're lending me eight paintings to display. Plus a member of the Fairchild family is giving Emma a painting as a gift, since the foundation exists because of her. I got a call from the publisher of the *Tina's Travels* books and they're donating two hundred books all signed by the author. We've got so many people coming to see the paintings, I had to ask the hotel to give us the largest ballroom. Once word got out the author of the books is attending, I got more calls asking if children could attend. I still don't know if we'll have enough room for everyone, but at two hundred dollars a plate and the auction, I don't care."

Marti's spirits lifted. "Wonderful. So it all worked out."

"Worked out. We'll probably raise more money this year than any other year. It's funny you said I'd probably get a call by the end of the day, and I did." Jenna's last words were laced with suspicion.

"Things have a way of working out."

"You said that too."

"What can I get you to eat, Marti?" Elizabeth wanted to get some food into her. She looked exhausted and, well, ill.

"I have the biggest craving for some apple pie. Please tell me you have some," she pleaded.

"I have a fresh baked one in back. I'll get you a big piece. How about you, Jenna?"

"I'd love it."

"Put some chocolate sauce and whip cream on mine." Marti needed something sweet. She smiled at herself when she realized she was having her first craving.

"What are you smiling about?" Jenna asked, suspicion laced in her words.

"Things have a way of working out in the end. I may not have Cameron, but I did get something out of the last two months."

"Emma?" Jenna knew how close she was to the little girl. If she could make Cameron marry Marti, she would. They'd all tried and tried to make Cameron see reason, but he just wouldn't budge. She'd even threatened to fire him if he didn't marry Marti. He told her to go ahead.

"Emma. God, I will miss that little girl when I leave."

"You're leaving?" both Elizabeth and Jenna asked in unison.

Marti grabbed her plate and dug into the aromatic pie. Baked apples and cinnamon. The scent made her mouth water. At the first bite, she moaned with pleasure. She looked over the ledge of the bar and grabbed the bowl of olives. She dipped one in the whip cream and ate it. *God, that's good.*

"You are so weird." Jenna shared a look with Elizabeth.

"I'm hungry. Oh, Elizabeth, I forgot to tell you something about the dress for Emma. Please make sure she wears her necklace from George? She'll want to wear it like a crown."

"Okay. I'll tell Jimmy to bring it when he drops her off at the penthouse after school."

"Perfect," she said around a huge bite of pie and whip cream.

"How are things going between you and Cameron? I know he's miserable. Frankly, you don't look much better."

Jenna suspected the strange food combo meant Marti was pregnant.

"Things went from unbearable to downright devastating the other night. Then, he moved his fiancé into my house and she asked me to make her eggs this morning. Over easy, I believe she requested."

"You didn't make her eggs," Elizabeth said.

"No, I did not. Instead, I was a complete bitch to her and implied Cameron and I had slept together the other night."

"What did she say? Did she ask Cameron if you guys slept together?"

"I doubt it. She's too stupid to figure out what I meant.

Correction, she doesn't care to figure it out because Cameron is worth too much money for her to care if he slept with me."

"Do you think she's pregnant?" *Are you pregnant*, is what Elizabeth wanted to ask.

"I think it's more likely Cameron is pregnant than Shelly. He won't listen, though. After everything I've said to him, what he learned about George being his father, and everything else, he still won't believe she's lying and only after him for his money. It doesn't matter to him I love him. He chooses her each and every time I make a case for him to be with me."

She stabbed at the pie with her fork with each word. "I feel like the more I show him he has a choice, the more pathetic and desperate I look. He made love to me the other night, and in the next breath he tells me he's holding the wedding at the house, my house, and he and Shelly are moving in the next day."

Marti sighed deeply. "Thanks, guys. I'm so happy I got all of that off my chest. I feel so much better." The sarcasm didn't fool them. She took another big bite of pie. "I feel like crap," she said around the bite.

"Chew your food, for God's sake. I've never seen anyone eat pie so fast," Jenna teased.

"So he loves you, wants you, and turns around and is a complete asshole to you."

"Thanks for summing things up for me, Elizabeth."

"Speaking of the asshole, here he comes," Jenna said.

Cameron saw all of them the minute he came through the door. He'd been in a bad mood all day. He'd left thinking of all the questions she'd asked him to answer about her and he couldn't answer one. Her last name was at the top of his list of things he wanted to know.

Besides the questions, he couldn't get the memory of making love to her in the rain out of his head. His body acted like he was a testosterone-strung-out teenager, keeping him in a perpetual state of arousal.

He walked right up to her, spun her seat at the bar around to face him, and leaned over her and took her mouth with his. He held her face in his hands and wouldn't let her turn away. He kissed her hard and insistent until she opened her mouth to him. He rubbed his tongue over hers, tasted apple pie and chocolate on her lips. He didn't stop until he knew she was kissing him back with all the ardor he gave to her. When he pulled away, he looked her right in the eye and asked, "What's your last name?"

She went from stunned silence to spitting mad and shoved him away and stood. "You can't do this to me. You can't kiss me like that, come home tonight, kiss her hello, and think it doesn't hurt me.

"Tell me, Cameron, will you kiss me like that now and sleep with your fiancé tonight? Do my feelings mean so little to you, you think it doesn't matter how you treat me, so long as you get what you want? Did you ever once consider my feelings before you did any of this?"

She didn't wait for a reply. She grabbed her purse and ran out of the restaurant crying.

"You're an asshole," Elizabeth and Jenna said.

"Thanks. I didn't know that already." He sat in the

chair Marti fled and rubbed his hand over his face and neck, digging his fingers into the tense muscles. "Do either of you know her last name?"

"We wouldn't tell you if we did," Jenna said.

"That's what I thought."

"You're an idiot. She loves you and you treat her like some cheap piece of ass. Shelly is a cheap piece of ass and you ask her to marry you. Tell me, what the hell is wrong with you?"

"Shelly is pregnant."

"And you love Marti," Jenna said. "Finish Marti's pie."

He looked at her plate. Less than half of a piece left, it had chocolate sauce, ice cream, and whip cream on top. Olives on the side?

"What's with the chocolate sauce and olives?"

"I think she was having a craving."

"That's just gross," he said and pushed the plate away.

"You're an idiot." Jenna walked away with that parting shot.

Elizabeth left and went back into the kitchen, carrying a package.

Cameron was left sitting there alone, brooding.

Chapter Thirty-Nine

CAMERON ARRIVED HOME and found Shelly having a fit because the staff wouldn't be back until tomorrow. She wanted to get the house in order for the wedding, but Marti stepped in and told her she couldn't move any of the furniture. He pointed out she shouldn't be doing anything like moving furniture when she was pregnant. He'd never forget the look on her face, almost like she'd forgotten.

He made everyone dinner, disappointed Marti didn't come down to join them. He made enough for all of them, but as he was cleaning up the kitchen, she came in long enough to grab a bottle of water, banana, and a spinach, chicken, and berry salad, and go back up to her rooms.

The whole time she was in the kitchen, she spoke on the phone in Italian. Maybe it was Italian. It sounded like Italian. He wondered how many languages she spoke and how and why she'd learned them all. He wondered if she was talking to a friend or doing business. He still had no idea what it was she did for a living. Hell, the woman didn't even speak English when it was a business call.

He spent the evening avoiding Shelly and doing homework and playing with Emma. Shelly went on and on about the plans for the wedding. She talked about the flowers, the caterers, the tables and chairs she'd ordered to be set up on the back lawn. He didn't care about any of it.

When he thought about Marti, he was hard as stone. When he thought about Shelly, his rock-hard cock turned into a limp noodle. He wondered if he'd spend his marriage thinking about Marti in order to make love to Shelly. He wondered if he'd ever be able to make love to her.

After putting Emma to bed, he went to Shelly's room to talk to her. The minute he'd stepped through the door, she complained her back ached from the pregnancy and would he rub it for her. He'd have a lot more nights like this once she rounded with the pregnancy. She claimed a headache and refused to engage in more than a few words, despite his best efforts to talk to her about their future.

She tried to seduce him, but the more she tried, the less interest he could muster. Eventually he grabbed her hands, stilled them, and pulled her next to him on the bed. He covered with a lie, telling her he hadn't slept well since George's death and he was exhausted.

How many lies would he have to tell over the coming years?

Marti, and his thoughts about her, were the reason he

hadn't slept, not George. After he'd made love to her in the rain and she'd left telling him he'd left her no choice, he'd stayed up wondering what she meant. She planned to leave, which made it even harder to sleep. He was afraid he'd wake up and she'd be gone.

He woke up in Shelly's bed, the woman he didn't want snoring at his side. Disgusted with himself, he rubbed his hand over his tense neck. He was supposed to be happy about marrying her. He wasn't supposed to be thinking about another woman, or wanting another woman. A man in his prime with a beautiful woman in his bed, he should have been able to make love to her hard and fast and long.

He rolled off the bed. His jeans weren't even buttoned and he didn't have his shirt on. He glanced at the clock. After one in the morning, he didn't want Emma to find him in Shelly's room. After the wedding, he'd explain to her a wife and husband slept together, but not until then. He didn't know why he was putting it off, he just was.

He walked out of Shelly's door and ran smack into Marti in the hall.

"Well, I guess I don't have to ask what you're doing up." She looked at his unbuttoned jeans and the shirt in his hands. "Well, I guess you aren't up anymore. I'm sure Shelly took care of it for you." She couldn't help it. She was angry. He was on her side of the house and sleeping with Shelly right across the hall from her rooms.

"I wasn't doing anything. If you want to know the truth, I couldn't."

"Sure. It's one in the morning and you're half naked

and sneaking out of her room because you didn't sleep with her. I'm not blind, or stupid."

"I did not sleep with her." Frustrated, he dropped his head and stared at the floor and her pretty bare feet. "What are you doing up anyway?"

"Working. Why do you even care?"

"I care about you. You're working every night and into the morning. You're pale and you look ill. You don't take care of yourself. You hardly ate anything tonight. And what the hell where you doing eating pie and olives for lunch? That's not a proper meal, or even a good one," he said and made a face of disgust over her choice of lunch foods.

"Like I said, why do you care?"

He pushed her up against the wall and held her there with his body. "I care, dammit. Don't you think I wish and hope everyday for you? Don't you think I'd rather it was you who is pregnant, rather than Shelly?"

"Wish granted." She planted both hands on his hard, bare chest and shoved him away. She tried to move on to the stairs and head for the kitchen for something to eat, but he stopped her.

"What do you mean, 'wish granted'?"

"You want me to be pregnant and not Shelly. I am, and I'll bet everything I have she's not."

"You aren't pregnant. You're lying. You just don't want me to marry her."

She threw up her hands. "Are you kidding me? Why is it you take her side over me every time and on everything? She tells you she's pregnant and you believe her. I tell you I'm pregnant and you call me a liar."

She grabbed his hand and marched him straight through her bedroom into her bathroom. "You want proof. Fine."

She opened the drawer and pulled out one of the pregnancy tests. She pulled down her pants, sat on the toilet, and peed on the stick.

"Marti, for God's sake. This is ridiculous."

She capped the stick, put it on the counter, wiped, and flushed the toilet. She pulled up her pants, faced him, glaring.

She took out the other three tests she'd already taken over the last few days and held them up to him.

"Sometimes we need to be reminded good things can happen, even when we're in the worst of circumstances."

She put the first test down on the counter.

"Sometimes we need to be reminded even when there is death, life brings us hope."

She put another test on the counter.

"Sometimes we need to be reminded when someone makes us feel like we're worthless, another can make us feel like a god."

She put the test on the counter. She pointed to the test she'd just taken.

"Sometimes we are reminded people are willing to tell the truth and back it up, no matter what the cost."

He stared at all the tests. They all had two lines indicating she was pregnant. Beyond stunned, he had no words. He'd called her a liar to her face.

He'd put that hurt look on her face again.

"Don't worry, Cameron. She was pregnant first, so

you just go ahead and marry her. Your child with her will have the full time father it deserves. My baby will be just fine having a part-time dad, because he'll have a mother who wants him and loves him. Shelly doesn't want to be a mother. You know it, and I know it."

She took a steadying breath. "You wanted me to prove I'm pregnant and I have. I wouldn't lie to you. I thought you'd know that much about me. Now, I see just how little you really do know about me, and it makes me sad. How can you love me when you don't even know me? The answer is you don't."

She put her last pregnancy test box on the counter.

"Why don't you make her prove it? In all this time, you never once thought to make her take a test you can pick up at the drugstore."

She turned and left the room, grabbing her purse from her bed and left the house.

Cameron, rooted to the floor, stood in the bathroom staring at all the pregnancy tests when he heard her car engine rev up and she drove away. Her words echoed in his mind. She thought he didn't love her. He'd called her a liar. She didn't want him to marry her. She thought she came second because Shelly had gotten pregnant first.

She doesn't think I love her.

It kept ringing in his mind. *She doesn't think I love her.*

She was gone and he didn't know if she'd be back. He didn't even know where she would go. He didn't know how he'd find her.

She was having his baby and he didn't know her last name.

Chapter Forty

JENNA MARCHED INTO Cameron's office to demand some answers for why the president of the company had canceled all his appointments, wasn't taking any calls, and had essentially locked himself in his office. She wanted to yell, but when she saw him, she couldn't. The devastated look on his face and the desolation in his eyes stopped her cold.

"Cameron? What happened?"

"She's pregnant."

"Yes, I know."

"Not Shelly, Marti."

"Yes, I know."

He waited for her to explain.

"Who eats apple pie with chocolate sauce, whip cream, and olives? You're an idiot."

"That's what you and Elizabeth meant yesterday. It was right in front of my face, and I didn't even see it."

"Shelly has been right in front of your face, is she pregnant?"

"She swears she is. She showed me the lab report."

Jenna waved away that last statement. "Those things can be faked."

"She goes to the appointments. She says all the right things." He rubbed the back of his neck.

"Marti obviously told you she's pregnant and you believed her."

"I called her a liar, told her she was only saying it so I wouldn't marry Shelly, and pretty much made her feel like crap."

"Nice. So what made you change your mind and believe her?"

"She actually took me into the bathroom and peed on a pregnancy test right in front of me. It was positive. She handed me another test kit and dared me to make Shelly prove it."

"God, I like her. You're an idiot."

"Thanks, again."

"So, did you make Shelly take the test this morning?"

"No, I was too busy getting Emma ready for school and worrying about whether I'd ever see Marti again. After she took the test, she walked out the front door and drove away. She never came back. I don't know where she is, if she'll be back, and the worst part, I don't even know her last name, so how can I even begin to try to find her?"

"You know, you should concentrate on what you do know about her and less on what you don't."

"Is this another lesson where you already know something and I turn out to be the idiot?"

"Yes, it is." Jenna had a pretty good idea who Marti was. She couldn't be certain, but since she'd met Marti, Merrick had gotten a new deal with Fairchild Industries for a building contract and someone from the Fairchild family was allowing them to use Sofia Fairchild's paintings for the charity benefit. Jenna had spoken to Marti about both things and she'd promised it would work out. It had.

"You know there's one thing I know about Marti for sure. If she makes a promise she keeps it."

"Another thing I'm supposed to be an idiot about?"

"Apparently," she said and sighed. Cameron really needed to clear his head and think straight if he was ever going to figure out what was real and what was a lie. He was so busy seeing what he thought was true, instead of seeing things as they are.

"Why is it you're so reluctant to make Shelly prove she's pregnant? You take her word for it over Marti's. They say love makes us blind. Perhaps you love Shelly and you don't want to find out she's lying. Or maybe you love Marti, and that's why you can't see her for who she really is. Either way, you're an idiot."

"You already told me that."

"It bears repeating. Believe it and move forward. You're stuck in the same place you were two months ago. You believe Shelly. You don't believe Marti. What's wrong with that picture?"

She watched him trying to sort it all out in his mind.

It was like watching a hamster running on a wheel, using a lot of energy to get nowhere.

"Go home and sort out your life. Until you do, you're no good to me."

"Are you kicking me out of my office?"

"I'm kicking you out of my building. Go home. Figure out fact from fiction, and do it quickly. Doomsday is Saturday."

"I'm getting married Saturday."

"And who will you marry? Shelly because she might be pregnant, or Marti, who we know for sure is pregnant and the woman you truly love."

Cameron winced and rubbed the back of his neck. "You know, you've been a very busy boy. Maybe you'll have two babies just a month or so apart."

The thought he'd have two babies within a month took a minute to sink in. He looked at Jenna and shook his head to clear it.

"You really need to look at this situation with clear eyes. You're so adamant about marrying Shelly to be a father to her baby, but you love Marti. Now Marti is pregnant and you might be having two babies, or more likely only one, Marti's."

"How did my life get so complicated?" he complained. Luckily, Jenna didn't answer his rhetorical question. He'd fucked up his own life by being irresponsible.

"I want to be with Marti. Her and I raising our baby and Emma together would be a dream come true. The thing is, I already promised to marry Shelly. What kind of person does that make me if I go back on my word and make Shelly raise our child on her own and I'm only the weekend dad?"

"Sue for custody. Shelly isn't interested in anything more than your money and the lifestyle she wants to live. You can afford to give her that and make her go away. Again, that's if she's pregnant."

He considered his options and only one appealed to him. Marti and a life with her and his children.

Jenna broke into his thoughts again. "Figure out all the variables and make the best decision based on the facts, Cameron. Facts are how we make good business decisions for the company. You're making decisions based on past guilt and anger that Knight didn't tell you he's your father. Go home. Make Shelly take that test. Fix your problems."

He didn't know what to do. Everything swirled around in his head and nothing was settled. He thought about what he knew for sure. Marti was pregnant and she loved him. He loved Marti. Emma loved Marti. Shelly may or may not be pregnant. He didn't know for sure. She hadn't handed him a pregnancy test she'd taken in front of him.

No other choice, he certainly wasn't getting any work done, he needed to go home and find out if Shelly was pregnant and put an end to all the chaos in his life.

Chapter Forty-One

MARTI WALKED IN the front door and heard the commotion upstairs.

"Give it back," Emma screamed.

"You have to share," Shelly yelled back.

Marti took the stairs two at a time, topped them, and wondered if she was at some warped elementary school fight. Shelly sidestepped in circles with Emma jumping up trying to grab the ruby and diamond necklace out of her upraised hand.

"That doesn't belong to you," Marti snapped.

Marti took a menacing step forward and Shelly started explaining quickly, "I want to wear it for my wedding, and the little brat won't even let me borrow it, so I can try it on with my dress."

"I'll only tell you once, give it back to her. The necklace was her inheritance from her grandfather."

"She got millions. It's just a necklace. She needs to learn how to share."

"Give it back to her," Marti said emphatically.

"No. I'm going to be her stepmother and she needs to learn to respect me and do as I say."

Marti refused to listen to another childish word. She grabbed the necklace and held her hand out to give it to Emma. With a frustrated growl, Shelly lunged for her, planted her hands on her shoulders, and shoved her backwards down the stairs.

She hit her shoulder, tumbled, and wrenched her knee. The pain from her shoulder shot up her neck, and her knee felt like it exploded with a pop.

Emma screamed. Shelly dragged her away from the stairs, pushed her into her room, and bent over her.

"If you say one word about what happened, I'll make sure you never see your father again. Not one word," she said and pointed her finger in Emma's face.

Emma ran and hid under her bed. She held the necklace clutched in her fist and cried, thinking only one thing: Marti was dead and it was all her fault.

Shelly needed to do some damage control. She hadn't meant to push Marti down the stairs. She just wanted her to butt out. It was worth a fortune and would look so great around her neck in all the wedding pictures.

She grabbed the phone and called Cameron. "Cameron," she said breathlessly. "You have to come home quick."

"What's the matter? I'm almost there. Are you okay? Is it Emma?"

"No. Marti's gone crazy. She tried to shove me down the stairs. She said she didn't want me to have your baby and she was going to make sure I didn't. You have to come home," she sobbed out.

"Are you okay? Is the baby okay?"

"Yes, I managed to fight her off, but I'm not feeling well. Help me, Cameron."

"I'm not far from the house. I'll be there in a minute."

He shouted to Jimmy, even though he'd probably overheard everything. "Jimmy, you have to hurry. Marti tried to throw Shelly down the stairs."

"That doesn't sound like something Marti would do." Jimmy put his foot on the gas and hurried to the house.

A fight between Marti and Shelly couldn't be good, no matter what the circumstances.

"Hurry. Shelly said she isn't feeling well. I hope nothing happened to the baby."

They pulled into the driveway and Cameron flew out of the car. He ran into the house. Marti sat on the stairs, leaning against the wall.

"Cameron." Marti barely got that much out, she was in so much pain.

"What the hell did you do?"

"I . . ."

"I have to check on Shelly. She called me and told me what you did," he accused. "How could you?" He ran up the stairs past her.

"Cameron, please," she called after him.

"I don't have time for you, Marti." He cleared the last of the stairs and raced to Shelly's room.

Jimmy came in and heard and saw everything. Cameron left Marti sitting there on the stairs. One look at her told him she was in bad shape. "Marti, are you okay?"

"No. Hospital." She couldn't move. Every little move hurt.

"What happened?"

"She pushed me down the stairs," Marti whispered. She couldn't take a full breath, her back hurt so badly. She had no idea how she'd managed to get up to a sitting position.

"Where do you hurt?"

"Everywhere. My back is hurt and my knee. I think it exploded. I'm pregnant," she sobbed. "I can't lose my baby."

"Are you having any cramps?"

"I can't tell. The pain in my back is terrible."

"I have to get you to the car to get you to the hospital."

"Just pick me up, but keep my leg straight. It hurts to try to bend it."

He put his arms around her, lifted, and she stifled a scream of pain.

"I'm sorry," Jimmy said and rushed her out the door.

Jimmy put her into her car and threw her purse in the back seat. He got in the driver's seat, peeled out of the driveway, and raced to the hospital.

Cameron stood in the bedroom doorway, heard the car leave, and felt torn. He shouldn't have spoken to Marti that way, but fear for his child overrode his common sense. He hated that she'd left and wanted to go after her, but Shelly needed him and he needed to be sure his baby was okay.

He lowered himself to sit on the bed. She cried softly into her pillow. Her back to him, he rubbed her lower back and told her it would be okay.

"Tell me what happened." He tried to console her, praying she didn't lose the baby.

"She attacked me. She doesn't want me to have our baby. She tried to throw me down the stairs, but I moved away, and she fell instead. She tried to kill our baby."

"She fell down the stairs?" Cameron's heart stopped. He froze in shock. He'd been in such a hurry to get to Shelly, make sure his baby was okay, he hadn't realized Marti might be hurt. Oh God, their baby.

"Yes. I got out of the way before she pushed me down. I couldn't let her hurt our baby. Oh, Cameron, she's so jealous you're marrying me. She tried to hurt us. Our poor baby," she sobbed.

She was laying it on thick, but she needed to go for broke. She'd gotten up the night before and heard everything Marti said to Cameron. Marti was pregnant, and she dared Cameron to make her take a pregnancy test. Only a matter of time before he demanded she do it. Now she had him thinking Marti tried to hurt her. He wouldn't forgive her for trying to hurt his baby. She only had to get to Saturday and through the wedding. Nothing else would matter. She'd be Mrs. Shaw and there would be nothing anyone could do about it, baby or no baby.

He saw Marti sitting on the stairs. She wanted to say something to him. He didn't know she'd fallen. She must have been all right to have peeled out of the driveway the way she did. Still, he pulled out his cell and called her. Voicemail.

Frustrated, he rubbed the back of his neck and let out a frustrated breath. Unable to reach Marti, he focused on the woman beside him. He ran his hand over her hair and down her arm. "Can I get you anything? Maybe we should go to the emergency room and make sure everything is all right with the baby."

"No, darling. I just need to rest. I'm feeling better and the shock is wearing off. All this stress can't be good for the baby." She took his hand and held tight. Her eyes found his and he read the desperation. "She can't live here with us, Cameron. It just won't work. What if she tries to hurt me and the baby again?"

"She won't. I won't let that happen."

"Lie down with me. When you're with me, I feel safe. I'll be able to rest and that will be best for the baby."

Unable to deny her such a simple thing, he lay down on the bed behind her and pulled her to his chest and held her. She needed to remain calm. Stress during pregnancy could be detrimental to her health and the baby's.

His mind wandered to Marti as it always did.

Where is she? Are she and the baby okay?

He had a fleeting thought of Marti falling down the stairs, but he forgot it the moment Shelly moaned and complained about not feeling well. He held her tighter and hoped his baby was safe.

Chapter Forty-Two

MARTI WAS LYING in the hospital bed in agonizing pain. She'd dislocated her shoulder, severely bruised her back, and twisted her knee quite badly.

Her leg was in a brace suspended above the bed keeping it straight. The throbbing through her leg kept pace with her heartbeat. Her whole body tensed, wound tight as a spring just waiting to be let go. She held herself rigid, trying to fight the pain. The medication they were giving her didn't even touch it.

The doctor did an ultrasound and checked on the baby, reassuring her he was safe and sound. She was so relieved by the news she'd cried and watched the monitor and her baby's heartbeat with such wonder.

Because of the trauma of the fall and the pain she was in, she spotted blood. The doctor told her it was okay and nothing to be concerned about, yet. She'd have to wait and see, hope the minimal bleeding stopped and she didn't develop any cramping.

She spent the very early morning concentrating on breathing normally and deeply and trying to relax her body. It was a supreme act of will to relax her muscles and not fight the pain. She was also fighting the horrible pain in her heart after Cameron dismissed her completely when he came home.

Jimmy had told her about the call from Shelly and she was even more despondent. He'd believed Shelly. He actually thought she'd try to hurt Shelly and her imaginary baby.

Sometime in the night she'd become numb to the pain in her heart and soul over Cameron's betrayal and began concentrating on keeping the pain in her body under control.

"Marti, can we come in?" Sam stood in the doorway with Elizabeth behind him. Jenna and Jack were with them.

"Yes," Marti said and tried desperately not to move.

They all came in and Marti lay as still as stone.

"Jimmy called this morning and told us what happened." Sam came to her bedside and took her hand. The moment he raised it, she went completely white and squealed in pain. He dropped her hand.

"Don't move anything. Too much pain." She closed her eyes and tears ran down her face.

"Oh, Marti. What happened?" Elizabeth wanted to cry for her. She looked like death.

"Shelly. Emma. Tried to take necklace," she said breathlessly. "Pushed me down the stairs."

"Shelly pushed you down the stairs because of Emma's

necklace. Shelly tried to take Emma's necklace?" Jack was surprised. He knew the woman was obsessed with all things expensive, but to take a little girl's necklace was low.

"They were arguing at the top of the stairs. Shelly was holding the necklace up over her head and yelling at Emma."

"Take it easy, Marti. You don't have to talk if it hurts too much," Sam said and wiped a tear away.

She wanted to tell someone. She needed someone to believe her. "I told her to give it back to Emma. She wouldn't and I grabbed it. She shoved me down the stairs backwards. I dislocated my shoulder and twisted my knee."

"Where the hell was Cameron? I sent him home early," Jenna said, outraged. "How could he let this happen?"

"He came in after I went down the stairs. I tried to tell him, but he ignored me and went to her."

"Jimmy told us he left you on the stairs and why."

"He always chooses her." She closed her eyes and waited for the nausea to pass and to get control over the pain again. She took several slow breaths.

"Marti, what did the doctor say about the baby?" Jenna asked, concerned.

"You know." She hadn't told anyone but Cameron. He must have told one or all of them. Maybe he was happy about the baby. If he was, maybe they had a chance to work things out.

"Elizabeth and I knew when you ate your bizarre lunch the other day. Cameron confirmed it yesterday. Nice job proving it to him. Pretty direct."

"Cameron doesn't give me the benefit of the doubt. She lies and he believes her without a doubt."

"We all think he's an idiot."

"The baby is fine, so far." She glanced from Sam to Jack with her eyes only. She'd already learned turning her head wasn't an option. She hated to talk about woman things with them there, but what the hell. These four were the only friends she had and they cared about her.

"I've been spotting a little blood, but the doctor thinks it will stop if I rest. There haven't been any cramps, so far." She looked at Jenna and Elizabeth and tried to smile. "I got to see the ultrasound of the baby. I saw his heart beating."

"There you go. You concentrate on that. The baby is going to be just fine."

"I hope so. I couldn't bear to lose my baby. Would one of you stay with me for a while today?"

Sam knew she didn't have anyone and Cameron couldn't be counted on. They'd already called him this morning and told him to meet them at the hospital. He had no idea Marti was hurt. He hadn't taken the time to find out before going to Shelly. "One of us will stay with you for as long as you need us."

"Thank you, Sam. I hate to be a baby about it, but I don't want to be alone. Too much time to think."

"I know what you mean. Thinking is overrated. It's too bad they can't just knock you out."

"The medication they gave me doesn't work, and it's the best they have without risking the baby's health."

"You must be in terrible pain," Elizabeth said. She and

Jenna had been through a lot. They'd at least had the benefit of good drugs.

"It only hurts when I breathe or move." She smiled and cringed at the same time.

"Believe it or not, it's hard to keep still. Isn't it?" Sam knew just what she was going through. He'd been shot in the back. His bulletproof vest had saved him, but his muscles had gone into spasm. Even the slightest twitch twisted the muscles into massive pain.

"Yes. Every little shift sends shockwaves of pain through me."

They all sat with her for a while and talked amongst themselves when she quieted.

"You need to check on Emma and make sure she's all right."

"Don't worry, Marti, we'll do everything possible to make sure she's taken care of and Shelly gets what she deserves. We'll set Cameron straight," Sam promised.

"Give it up. He went too far when he left me on the stairs."

"You don't mean that," Jenna said.

"I can't do it anymore. How many times does he have to prove he intends to marry her, no matter what."

"What about the baby?" Elizabeth asked. "Now that he knows you're pregnant, he'll change his mind."

"He hasn't yet. I don't think he ever will. Not after yesterday."

CAMERON EXITED THE elevator on a tear. Sam called and told him to meet him at Marti's hospital room. He gave him the room number and nothing else. He hadn't even said how bad she was hurt. Jimmy arrived in Marti's car just as he was leaving the house. Without a word, and giving him the silent treatment all the way, he'd switched cars and drove him to the hospital.

Worse than anything, Cameron felt worse than guilty he didn't even know she was hurt in the first place.

Steps away from the door, he overheard the doctor outside her room saying, "... she lost it." Those words tore his heart to shreds.

Marti lost the baby. His baby.

He'd spent the night consoling Shelly, lying in bed with her. She was completely traumatized by Marti's attack.

Now, to find out Marti hurt herself in the fall and lost his baby because of her jealousy over Shelly. It was too much to bear.

He may have just found out about the baby, but he'd wanted it more than anything because it was a piece of Marti too and their love.

Consumed with anger and hurt, he burst into her room. Jack, Sam, Elizabeth, and Jenna sat around Marti's bed.

Pale, completely still, her leg hung suspended by a sling encased in a brace. A brace strapped around her middle held her arm across her chest.

"Nice of you to show up. A day late if you ask me, but I'm glad you finally made it to see the woman you supposedly love." Sam couldn't take it any longer. Watching Marti fight the pain for the last half hour had taken its toll on him and everyone else.

Cameron came over to the bed and glared down at Marti. She looked terrible, and he thought she deserved it for killing his baby.

"You just couldn't leave it alone. You had to go after Shelly. You were so jealous, you tried to throw her down the stairs and instead you fell and killed my baby with you. I'll never forgive you for this."

Stunned, she couldn't respond. She'd expected him to think she'd tried to hurt Shelly, but why would he think she'd lost the baby?

Everyone in the room remained stunned and silent. No one could believe Cameron would treat Marti like this.

He didn't ask if she was okay. It hurt more than she thought possible that he didn't care.

"Don't you have anything to say?" he yelled, the anger visibly growing the longer she laid there, not moving or saying anything.

"I guess you know everything." She tried to make her voice sound strong, but something in it caught his attention. Hurt? Pain? Anger? Too far gone himself, he'd sort it out later.

"That's it. You're not even going to apologize for killing my baby and trying to hurt Shelly."

"You are the stupidest smart person I know. Get out."

He just stood there glaring at her. What did she mean he was the stupidest smart person? She wasn't making sense.

"Get out," she screamed and closed her eyes and held her breath until the pain passed.

"Breathe through it, Marti." Sam stood beside her, stroked his fingers down her arm. "If you breathe through it, it helps." She took a few shallow breaths and started to relax. "That a girl."

"What's wrong with you?"

"It's too late for you to ask that question," Sam said and stood in front of Cameron with his chest out and his hands on his hips. "Jack, how about we walk Cameron to his car?"

"Excellent idea, and long overdue."

"Play nice, boys," Jenna warned.

Both brothers answered as only twins could, in unison. "No."

They walked forward, backing Cameron out the door. He got the hint and turned to the elevator doors.

"What's the matter with you two? She tried to kill Shelly and the baby. She killed my baby."

"We heard you already. Marti is right, you're stupid," Jack said and turned to Sam. "I can't wait until we get downstairs." He punched Cameron in the gut.

Cameron doubled over from the blow. About to ask why Jack hit him, he never got the words out before Sam grabbed his shoulder, hauled him back up to standing, and punched him in the jaw. Seeing stars, his face hurt like hell. He couldn't catch his breath.

The elevator doors opened and Sam shoved Cameron in and pushed the button for the parking garage.

"Go home to Shelly. Nobody wants you here. Stay away from Marti." Sam stood back and let the elevator doors close on a bewildered Cameron.

"Think he'll figure things out before he gets to the garage?"

"No. He's too upset and angry. He's so focused on what he thinks is the truth he can't see what's right in front of him. He's going to marry Shelly and we're going to let him. He deserves that bitch. I hope it costs him a fortune to get rid of her."

"What about Marti? I hate to see her get hurt in all this."

"Too late. She's done everything she can to make Cameron see the truth. He blew it."

"That's an understatement. How could he choose anyone over an amazing woman like her?"

"We got lucky with Jenna and Elizabeth. Too bad we aren't triplets. I'd love to have her in the Turner family. If my partner Tyler wasn't so wrapped up in Morgan, I'd introduce him to her." Sam slapped his brother on the back. "Nice gut shot. I think I saw his feet come off the ground."

"I should have hit him in the nuts. Put a stop to all this baby business for good."

Sam and Jack walked back into Marti's room laughing.

Chapter Forty-Three

THEY TRIED TO console Marti after Cameron's visit. A distinguished gentleman interrupted and walked into her room carrying a large box. Another man followed with another large box.

"Martina, I've brought what you requested. I hope you're feeling better this morning."

"Hello, Uncle Anthony."

Her uncle set the box on the floor by the bed and stood to greet her company.

"Uncle Anthony, these are the Turners, Jenna and Jack, and Elizabeth and Sam. Jenna is head of Merrick International.

"You guys, this is my uncle, Anthony Fairchild of Fairchild Industries."

Jenna gasped. "I knew it. The deal with Fairchild Industries is because of you."

"Martina is in charge of special projects at the company. The project with Merrick is completely her doing." Anthony looked around the room at everyone. "It's nice to meet all of you. Martina speaks highly of you. I'm glad to see she has some friends in her life. She spends far too much time alone."

"Martina Fairchild," Jenna said. "Your grandmother was Sofia Fairchild, the artist."

Marti smiled. Anthony stood taller. They both loved Sofia and had common ground between them, because of her.

"I am the granddaughter of Sofia and Martin Fairchild. My father was Frederick Fairchild."

"The writer." Elizabeth exclaimed. "He was brilliant."

Anthony looked stoic. "He was a great man and taken from us far too early in life. He had a great many stories left to tell. Martina is very much like her father. Perhaps it's why we clash so often."

"You're not so bad, Uncle. I'm just too much of a free spirit for you." She looked at the others. "Uncle Anthony is a lot like my grandfather. He'd like to see me spend my life in an office building. I prefer a little more freedom."

"Martina, you're rich. That doesn't mean you have to be eccentric too."

"To you, eccentric is anyone who doesn't work in an office sixty hours a week. I have a job. I have three, actually." She may not spend her life in an office, but she also didn't spend her free time gambling like her uncle. It was his vice, and one that sometimes cost him dearly.

"Yes, I know. You're great at all of them, and I don't

give you enough credit. I'm difficult and ornery. I can't help it, and you put up with me because I'm family."

"I put up with you because I love you, and I find you a challenge."

"How's my great-nephew?"

"Just like grandfather, won't even consider the baby might be a girl."

"I'm still not sure you're all girl. You do business like a man."

"Of which you and grandfather will forever be proud."

"Damn right."

"The baby is doing just fine."

"Perfect. Fairchilds are strong stock. We don't go down without a fight." He kissed her on the head in a rare gesture of affection. "I'll see you Friday at the benefit. Let me know if you need anything else. Do you need me to come back for the books?"

"No, I'll give them to Jenna and Jack to take with them."

"I have a meeting. I'll try to come and see you again tonight."

She didn't want to know if the meeting was business or a card game. She was just happy they were on good terms. Today, anyway. "Thank you, Uncle."

"We've been at odds for too long. You're the only family I have. I'll try to be more flexible."

"I'd like that."

He turned to leave, but glanced back. "You're the richest woman in the state, couldn't they give you a better room?"

"I'm fine right here." She rolled her eyes at her uncle's back, the door closing between them.

"I can't believe you're Martina Fairchild," Jenna said with wonder.

"Oh, there's more. It's time I told you all exactly who I am. Open up the boxes."

Jenna pulled out one of the *Tina's Travels* books. "Why do you have these books?"

"Because the author promised she'd sign all of them for the benefit." She smiled and waited for them to figure it out. She didn't wait long.

"Oh my God. You're Tina Fair, the author." Jenna was even more stunned.

Everyone looked at Marti and waited for her to explain.

"I am Martina Fairchild, Tina Fair, and just plain Marti. I'm the granddaughter of a famous artist, daughter of a famous writer, granddaughter to a corporate mogul, and the niece to a grumpy bear of an uncle, who runs the corporate empire.

"I'm a children's book author, a painter, a corporate mogul, a sailor, and so much more. I don't give out my last name because as soon as I do people make all kinds of assumptions about me. They don't take the time to get to know me past the part about my being rich.

"It's the same for you, Jenna. If you introduce yourself as Jenna Merrick Turner, people know you own Merrick International and they automatically start cataloguing all the things they think they know about you. Elizabeth, I understand you're a Hamilton. I'm sure people have heard that name and assumed a great many things based on your family history.

"Fairchild is just a name. It isn't who I am, unless you get to know me and understand my place in the family. Then you can decide if you like me for who I am, and not based on my last name or how much money I have."

"Was your uncle kidding about you being the richest woman in the state?" Jack was impressed because he thought Jenna was rich. The Fairchilds were in a class of their own.

"He would know. Everything is about dollars and cents for my uncle. It's part of the reason he and I don't see eye to eye. I don't put a dollar value on everything."

"And Cameron has no idea who you are?" Elizabeth thought it amazing Cameron could be involved with Marti all this time and never discover who she really is.

"He thinks I'm Marti. Killer of his baby, jealous of his fiancé, a great mother figure for Emma, lover, liar, and all kinds of things he thinks he knows. The hardest part about all this isn't that he doesn't know my last name, or even what I do for a living. He doesn't even believe the things he's seen me do, or the things I've said to him. I painted Emma's room. He knows George asked me to do it, he thought it was spectacular, but he didn't even assume I'd done it personally. He thinks I stayed up for two days straight watching someone else work.

"He doesn't see what is right in front of him. I told him I was pregnant, and he called me a liar. She tells him and he believes her without a doubt. I just can't get over that.

"I don't know what else I can do to make him see me for who I am. I guess he'll find out on Friday at the benefit. I'm afraid when he finds out I'm a Fairchild, only then will he change his opinion about me because of my name and wealth."

"You think he'll only listen to you because you're a Fairchild." Jenna knew just how Marti felt. Sometimes she couldn't get people to listen to her, but when they found out she was the CEO of Merrick, they all of a sudden wanted her opinion.

"I think it will make a difference and it shouldn't. I'd rather he love me and believes me because I'm Marti, not because I'm Martina Fairchild and all it implies."

Chapter Forty-Four

CAMERON SPENT THREE days brooding since leaving the hospital with a sore gut and a bruised jaw. He'd locked himself in his office and worked like a demon, ignoring all the problems in his personal life. In the quiet evening alone in his office, he gave in to the grief eating at him and mourned his lost baby with Marti.

Emma refused to talk to him. She was quiet and stayed close to Jimmy.

Shelly continued to rest and claim the trauma of being attacked was too much to bear. She stayed in her room and ordered the staff around like she was queen of the manor.

He let her. He didn't want to deal with her, or Emma, or anything besides the pounding in his head and heart, telling him he'd lost his baby and Marti.

He'd never recover from losing the baby he wanted more than life itself and the woman and the life they might have had.

He hadn't gone back to the hospital to see her. He couldn't. When he finally called to check on her, he didn't know her last name and he'd forgotten the room number. He had no idea if she was okay, or where she was now. It was like she'd dropped off the face of the earth, or had simply been a dream.

He was the most concerned about Emma. She wasn't eating well, never smiled anymore, and every time he asked if she was okay, she ran to her room and slammed the door.

He and Shelly were just arriving at the hotel for the benefit when he saw Elizabeth, Sam, and Emma get out of their own limo and walk into the hotel lobby. Emma looked beautiful in a gold gown. He wondered if Elizabeth bought her a new dress, because it wasn't the dress he'd left for her to wear. She wore her necklace on her head. He thought of George and his wish for Emma to always feel like a princess. Cameron hadn't made her feel that way in too long and he regretted it.

"What's the matter?"

Shelly avoided being alone with Cameron. She was afraid he'd ask her about the incident with Marti again, or he'd ask her to prove she was pregnant. She'd made it this far and the wedding was tomorrow.

Marti hadn't come home and she had no idea what happened to her since going down the stairs. She didn't care, so long as she was gone.

Cameron worried her. He seemed sad and lonely and something else she couldn't really pin down. He worked till all hours in the library and barely ate a thing. Probably missing Marti. She'd help him get over it, once they were married and she had him all to herself.

"I just saw Emma. She looks beautiful. Just like her mother. She won't talk to me anymore. She stays in her room and watches movies. She isn't the same."

"Since Marti left, right? Isn't that what you mean? She tried to hurt me and our baby, and you and Emma are just waiting around for her to come back and try again."

"I doubt she's in any shape to do anything. Last I saw her, she was in the hospital with her leg in a sling."

"Serves her right for trying to hurt us," she said and put her hand on her stomach. Cameron had been so sweet about the baby lately. He came home from work today and wrapped his arms around her from behind and put his hand over her stomach. She thought the gesture sweet, and for a moment even wished she was pregnant. The thought was immediately replaced with how fat she'd get. It would take her months to lose the weight.

Cameron caught the gesture of her putting her hand on her stomach and he was stricken with how he'd never see Marti do the same thing. Their baby was gone.

He stepped out of the limo and escorted her into the lobby. When they reached the doors leading into the ballroom, he stopped short, surprised. The benefit usually got a lot of press, but this was something else. Reporters and photographers were everywhere with flashes going off and people clamoring for interviews with Jenna.

Jenna made an announcement to the press. "I promise all of you Miss Fairchild will be in attendance tonight.

She won't answer questions. There will be a photo opportunity when she presents the gift to Miss Emma Shaw."

"What about Tina Fair? We understand a lot of children attended tonight to see her."

"She will be here and has an announcement and a gift for Miss Shaw. If you'll excuse me, Cameron Shaw has arrived and we need to get inside."

She turned from the press and headed for the doors to the ballroom with Cameron beside her.

"Ready to go in?" Jenna asked.

"Are you actually speaking to me again?"

"I've made an exception for tonight. This is going to be an enlightening evening for you. Shall we?"

"Hello, Jenna, your dress is lovely. You look spectacular."

Jenna didn't respond to Shelly. She thought Shelly looked tacky in a black skintight gown with a deep V-neck, leaving her boobs barely covered. Her blond hair was so teased and fluffy, Jenna thought she might be hiding a bird's nest inside.

"I hope you have your speech ready to welcome everyone and thank them for coming tonight," she said to Cameron.

"You never said I was speaking tonight. I don't even know half of what you've got planned. Who is Miss Fairchild? Why are there so many children here? How did you get all these people to attend? I see at least twice as many people as we normally have."

"You're an idiot. We have nearly three times as many people. They're all here to see the Sofia Fairchild collection and Tina Fair, the author of the *Tina's Travels* books Emma loves so much."

"She does love those books. I read them to her all the time. How did you get the author to come tonight?"

"She fell in love with Emma and had her publisher contact me to set things up. Miss Fairchild asked the curator of Sofia Fairchild's paintings to contact me and provide eight paintings by the master artist. They're all of her granddaughter when she was little. The series is called Martina."

"I can't wait to see them."

"Wait till you see Miss Fairchild herself and Tina Fair."

"Fairchild? The same Fairchild as Fairchild Industries?"

"One and the same. Miss Fairchild is in charge of special projects at Fairchild Industries. She's the one you hear on the conference calls between our team and hers."

"Great, we can do some business while she's here and get to know each other before the project really takes off."

"Oh, you already know her," Jenna said under her breath.

Cameron didn't hear her.

"I can't believe I get to meet a Fairchild tonight. She's wealthy beyond belief." Shelly squeezed Cameron's arm and smiled hugely.

"I understand she's the richest woman in the state." Jenna smiled at the statement Anthony Fairchild had once made about Marti. Shelly could appreciate a statement like that.

"You're kidding."

"Her uncle claims she is, and he should know. He runs Fairchild Industries. You've met Anthony Fairchild, haven't you Cameron?"

"Several times. The man is impossible to get along with. All he thinks about is money."

"So Miss Fairchild tells me."

They arrived at the table. Cameron helped Shelly into her seat next to Sam's partner, Tyler, of all people.

"Nice to see you." Tyler extended his hand and Cameron shook it.

"Long time no see," Cameron responded. "This is Shelly."

"I have heard a lot about you," Tyler said, no smile or welcome in his voice.

Shelly beamed him a smile, but at the cool reception she leaned back in her seat and gave him a confused look.

"I've been working undercover. I heard I missed one hell of a fishing trip. You've been busy, I hear," Tyler prompted.

Cameron didn't want to talk about the fishing trip or his life the past few months. "What brings you here tonight?"

This wasn't exactly Tyler's scene, or affordable on his cop's salary. Not that Cameron thought he shouldn't be here, but the sly smiles on Jack and Sam's faces told him something was up.

"Charity. For children. I'm in. Don't worry, I paid my two hundred bucks. I love kids. Besides, Sam promised to introduce me to Marti. I've heard so much about her, I feel like I know her already."

Cameron glared across the table at Sam, a silent warning not to set Tyler and Marti up together. The last thing he wanted was one of his friends dating the woman he loved.

"I thought you were hunting down Morgan," Cameron tossed out to rile Tyler about his psychic ghost.

"Yeah, well, she doesn't want to be caught. Tonight, it's all about the kids and Marti." Tyler shared a knowing look with Sam and Jack, one Cameron wished he understood.

One of the organizers brought Jenna a microphone, ending all conversation. Since Cameron wasn't in the loop about tonight's events, she made the opening announcement.

Jenna tapped her spoon to her water glass. Once the crowd quieted and shifted their focus to Jenna, she began. "Ladies and gentlemen, thank you for coming tonight. We are pleased to have you here with us to raise money for a very worthy cause. The Emma Shaw Foundation supports the children's hospital's neonatal unit where Emma was born more than five years ago.

"As a special treat, we have Emma's favorite author, Tina Fair, with us tonight. We also have a collection of Sofia Fairchild's masterful paintings on display, which depict her granddaughter, Martina, as a young girl. Martina will be here tonight to present a special gift to Emma.

"Before we start tonight's activities, please enjoy your meal. Thank you for coming, and most of all thank you for your generous donations."

Everyone clapped and Jenna took her seat at the table reserved for the Turner and Shaw families.

Cameron tore his mind from thoughts of Marti and Tyler together and glanced across the table at his daughter sitting next to Elizabeth. She held Elizabeth's hand and stared at Shelly with such fear, Cameron's gut tightened. He needed to find out what had Emma so spooked.

She looked beautiful in her golden gown with her ruby and diamond necklace crown. He thought about the night Marti and Emma had their tea party on top of the dining room table.

"Elizabeth, the dress you bought Emma is beautiful. Emma, did you pick it out?"

Emma sat silently watching Shelly. Elizabeth squeezed her hand. She still didn't answer him.

Elizabeth stepped in. "Marti had the dress made for her. She asked that Emma wear it tonight with her necklace crown."

Cameron didn't know what to say. A waiter placed his dinner plate in front of him, but even the smell of prime rib and mashed potatoes didn't entice his appetite. He'd lost it the second he discovered he'd lost his baby with Marti.

"Cameron, why is everyone ignoring us?" Shelly was finally sitting at the table with all the important people and no one even acknowledged her.

"They're all mad at me. It's nothing. Don't worry about it."

Jenna thought she might see how big of a hole Shelly

could dig herself into. "Shelly, it was terrible to hear Marti attacked you. I hope you and the baby are all right."

"We're just fine. Cameron has been wonderful taking care of us."

"I'm sure he has. There's nothing more important to him than the baby *you* are carrying."

Cameron caught the wording and glared at Jenna. Completely untrue, his baby with Marti was a dream come true, and devastatingly a reality that would never be. He missed his baby, even though they'd never met. The grief hit him hard again and his throat clogged. He wondered where Marti was. Was she all right? After he'd lost his mind and yelled at her in the hospital, did she hate him?

"He's so excited about the baby," Shelly's cheerful voice broke into his dismal thoughts.

"When exactly is the baby due?" Jenna asked.

"Um, December seventeenth."

Funny, she'd told him December twenty-seventh. An alarm went off in his head, making him listen more carefully to the exchange.

"Just before Christmas. What a nice gift," Jenna added.

"I told Cameron the same thing."

"I can't believe Marti fell while trying to push you. It must have been horrible to see her fall face first down the stairs."

"It was terrible. She pushed me, I moved, and she fell forward."

"Wow. I'm surprised she didn't break an arm or something."

"Cameron said she hurt her leg. She deserves a lot worse for trying to hurt me and the baby."

"Well, no wonder Emma's been so upset. Seeing Marti attack you must have been awful. I'll bet you must have been a big help in consoling her."

Cameron sat straight up in his chair and leaned forward on his elbows. "Emma wasn't there. She was in her room."

"No, she wasn't," Jenna replied.

Well, this was news to him. After what happened, he'd tried to talk to Emma, but she froze up and refused to speak about it. Now he knew why. "Emma, sweetheart, did you see what happened?"

Emma crawled up on her Uncle Sam's lap and hid her face in his chest.

"It's all right, baby girl. No one is upset with you. You don't have to talk about it." Sam put his arms around Emma and held her tight. "Your dad thinks he knows everything."

"What's that supposed to mean?" Cameron had enough of everyone telling him what he did and didn't know. The problem was, he didn't know what he knew. Everything was mixed up and the only thing that mattered was he'd lost his baby with Marti. He'd lost her too.

"You already know what happened. Shelly told you, so that's it, right? I mean, you marched right into Marti's hospital room and told her what went down. It must be true," Sam finished.

Jack got in on the act now. "That's right. I've never seen anyone sum up what happened so succinctly without ever asking for both sides of the story. It's too bad Sam and Tyler can't lock up every suspect by simply having someone say, 'He did it.' All that evidence and finding out the truth is highly overrated. It's better to accuse people and find them guilty without determining the facts."

"What the hell are you all talking about?" Angry and even more confused, Cameron tried to read between the lines, but came up with nothing as usual. Emma still hid her face in Sam's chest. She wouldn't even look at him.

"Did you ever find out her last name?" Elizabeth asked.

Cameron squirmed. One simple question. It haunted him because he still didn't know.

"No. Why? Did you?"

"Yes. After you left her uncle came to visit her. It was quite enlightening. We found out all kinds of wonderful things about her."

"So, what's her last name? What did you find out?"

Jenna joined back in on the fun. "You know what's the most interesting thing about finding out who she is? The fact that she never actually hid it. It was right there for all of us to see, especially you, Cameron. It was right there in front of you the whole time, and you missed it every time she showed you who she is."

Cameron remained confused and angry. He worried about Emma.

Jack got back in the fun at his expense. "She told us she never actually came out with her last name because if she did, we'd only know her because of it. Once we knew, she was right, in a way. It's really impressive and hard to get past the name and everything you know about the name in order to get down to the person she really is. I, for one, am glad I got to know her as Marti. Imagine all we would have missed if we'd gotten caught up in her name."

"What is her last name?" Shelly asked, but everyone ignored her again.

"You know, her uncle calls her eccentric because she works three jobs and hardly ever goes into an office. She likes her freedom and can work wherever she is. It's amazing the amount of work she's accomplished in such a short amount of time. Hell, she got Emma's room done in two days."

"Emma's room is amazing. She must have had a dozen people in there getting it done." Cameron thought of Marti every time he went into Emma's room. She'd made her dream come true.

"Did you ask her how she did Emma's room?"

"Well, no. I didn't. It was so amazing, and . . ." Cameron remembered she'd been exhausted and Shelly had come in and spoiled things. "She was exhausted and went to bed."

"You must have thanked her profusely. I mean it's not every day you get the granddaughter of such a famous artist to do your daughter's bedroom."

"Are you talking about the person who painted the room? The mural on top of the bed was signed by M. Fairchild," he said and sat back and looked up at the ceiling. "She had Sofia Fairchild's granddaughter paint the room," Cameron realized.

"You're an idiot. You come so close, and then you blow

it," Sam said, disgusted. He really thought Jenna had led him right to the truth.

Dinner was cleared away and people were starting to mill around. The curtain for the paintings was closed and people were moving in that direction, waiting for the display to be revealed.

Sam's cell phone vibrated, and he looked at the caller ID. "I believe this call is for you, Emma." He handed her the phone.

"Hello."

"Hello, Sugar Bug."

"Marti." Emma sat up on her uncle's lap.

"I'm coming to see you tonight, just like I promised."

"You always keep your promise. I knew you'd be here tonight."

"That's right, Sugar Bug. Uncle Sam is going to come and get me. I'll meet you by the paintings. You stay with Aunt Jenna. Okay?"

"Okay. I'll see you by the paintings."

She handed the phone back to Uncle Sam, jumped off his lap, and took Aunt Jenna's hand.

"Jack and Tyler are going to make sure you behave yourself," Sam warned. "You're in for the shock of your life. Everything you know about Marti is about to be blown to shreds. She tried to show you who she is as a person. Now you've left her no choice but to show you who she is to the world. That hurts her more than anything you've already done to her. You've accused her of a lot of things. None of them were true. You're an idiot, and she's about to prove that to you too."

Sam left the table and went to a side entrance and waited for Jenna and Emma to make their way to the curtain by the paintings.

The curtain opened and everyone in the room saw the display, a set of paintings depicting a child from the age of about three until about twelve. The little girl had dark, wavy brown hair and the greenest eyes. Each painting showed the girl in different poses and scenes.

Cameron thought the little girl looked familiar. Very familiar. A shiver danced up his spine, but before he could really put his finger on it, Jack leaned over and said, "You wanted to know who Marti is, watch Sam at the door. You're about to get your answer."

Chapter Forty-Five

JENNA PICKED UP Emma and put her on a chair next to a covered painting. Jenna stood next to her with a microphone. Emma didn't like all the people watching her, but Marti was coming soon and she'd stay with her.

"Ladies and gentleman. As you can see, the paintings we have here tonight are the wonderful creation of world famous artist Sofia Fairchild. The paintings are of her granddaughter, Martina Fairchild. The series was named simply, 'Martina.'

"As promised, her granddaughter is here with us tonight to present Emma with a special gift. She was taught to paint by her grandmother from the time she was three when she came to live with her grandparents after her parents' death."

Cameron sat back, reeling. This was Marti's story. "Oh my God, Marti is Martina Fairchild." Cameron had no idea. It was right in front of him the whole time. She'd done

Emma's room and even signed her name. Everyone had given him hint upon hint and he just didn't put it together.

"Welcome to the party. It's about time you showed up," Jack said snidely.

"I can't believe I've been living with the richest woman in the state," Shelly said, surprised. "She seemed like such a normal, ordinary person."

"Because you thought she was just Marti. Now you know she's a Fairchild, so you look at her in a completely different way. She's rich and powerful and has the world at her fingertips, and that's all you see."

Jenna's introduction continued. "Although she is an accomplished painter in her own right, she's never before shown any of her paintings like this.

"The world knows her artwork in the form of children's books she writes and creates the artwork for under the pen name Tina Fair.

"You see, Martina Fairchild is Tina Fair, author of the children's books *Tina's Travels*, which she wrote while fulfilling her grandmother's final request.

"She spent a year traveling the world by sailboat, or 'pirate ship', as Emma would say, and writing children's books, so all children would know what it's like to be in a foreign land.

"In addition to the personally autographed books she's donated tonight, she has two special edition books to present to Emma.

"Without further ado, I'd like you all to welcome Miss Martina Fairchild, aka Tina Fair, and to those of us who call her friend, Marti."

Sam opened the side door and Marti stepped into the room and took his arm. Still in a lot of pain, but she'd promised Emma she would come, and she wasn't about to let her down.

Sam took her arm, supporting her as she walked. The brace helped her knee, but it wasn't enough. The doctors wanted her on crutches, but she wanted to walk in the room tonight. She wanted to make Emma proud.

Sam leaned into her and whispered in her ear. "Did the doctor numb you up?"

"She gave me several shots in the knee and in my shoulder. I can't feel either. If you let me fall on my face, I'll have to steal your gun and shoot you." She squeezed his arm tighter for support.

She trembled next to him. "No need to worry. I won't let you fall. You look like a queen."

"Thank you. Emma and I dressed up like this one night and had a tea party."

Marti wore her gold gown. The shawl she'd used to wrap Emma in was draped around her back and shoulders hiding the bruises. Atop her head, she wore the diamond and emerald necklace.

They made it to where Jenna stood next to Emma, who was on a chair. Marti stood in front of Emma for a moment and they were face-to-face. She didn't even acknowledge the applause from the crowd behind her.

"Hello, Sugar Bug. I promised I'd come tonight and nothing would keep me from seeing you. Are you surprised?"

"You wrote the books Aunt Jenna said."

"Yes, I did. I have some special gifts for you."

Marti gave Jenna the go-ahead and Sam helped her take her place on the other side of the covered painting beside Emma.

Jenna waited for everyone to stop clapping for Marti's entrance. The press snapped multiple pictures. They waited for everything to settle down.

Cameron watched closely. He'd seen Marti say something to Emma and she'd smiled. He hadn't seen that smile in a few days. He wanted to see Emma smiling again like she used to. Sam helped Marti take her place. He didn't like the way Sam held her in such an intimate way around the waist and close to his side. If he didn't know Sam, he'd think they were a couple.

"Why the hell is Sam holding onto her like that? Elizabeth is going to kill him."

Elizabeth stood off to the side of Jenna watching the proceedings. She smiled and clapped along with everyone else. She saw Sam. Why wasn't she upset?

Jack enjoyed watching Cameron squirm. He'd been assigned to make sure Cameron didn't make a scene by trying to approach Marti during the benefit. They didn't want him to accost her like he'd done in the hospital.

"Sam is making sure she doesn't fall. She's not supposed to be here, but she made a promise and she's keeping it. She should be in bed lying down and resting. The doctor had to shoot her up full of drugs to numb her knee and the muscles in her shoulder. She's been in excruciating pain. It's amazing what she'll put herself through to keep a promise."

"Why the hell doesn't the doctor just give her some pain pills?"

"I wonder," Jack said and rolled his eyes.

"Wait till you see this," Tyler chimed in. "I snuck a peek earlier. You're about to see something amazing. Seriously, I can't wait to meet her."

Cameron glared and held back the fist he wanted to plant in Tyler's face.

Jenna continued with her announcement. "Martina has never shown one of her own paintings. As a gift for Emma, she painted a very special piece. It commemorates a very special evening in which Emma and Marti had a milkshake tea party. Emma, if you'll do the honors, unwrap your gift."

Emma pulled off the cover from the large painting, nearly as big as her. When she saw the painting, she squealed, "It's our tea party!"

Marti smiled at the little girl and tried to ignore the flashbulbs going off from all the photographers.

"Yes it is, sweetheart. Now you'll always remember our special night."

The press went wild over the painting. It showed Marti and Emma sitting on top of a dining room table under a brightly lit crystal chandelier. On the table with them were an elaborate tea set and a plate of cookies. The two looked like princesses in their gold dresses and jeweled crowns. They appeared in the painting as they did tonight.

"Everyone, Martina has another surprise for Emma." Jenna took the two books being held by the security guard behind her.

"Martina has written two new books, which won't be available to the public for several months. The books feature Emma."

Jenna had Emma hold the books in front of her for the press to snap more photos.

Shelly couldn't believe all the attention Marti was getting. This was Cameron's charity benefit and he was just sitting there watching. No one paid any attention to them. Jenna had taken over and turned the whole event into a worship-Marti fest.

"I can't believe Jenna is letting Marti push her books here tonight."

Jack wasn't going to let Shelly get away with being rude. "If you'd shut up, you'll see this has nothing to do with publicity for Marti and everything to do with Emma and this charity benefit."

"Martina has two advanced copies of the books available for all of you to bid on in the auction. The special edition books will be a limited release. Emma has the first copies, and copies two and three will be in the auction."

A cheer went up from the children and many of the parents.

Jenna was going to take the books back from Emma, but she wouldn't let them go. Jenna anticipated her desire to hold onto them and signaled the guard to stay with Emma.

"Martina has also brought along autographed books from the *Tina's Travels* series for all of the children here tonight."

Jenna waited for all the kids to stop cheering again.

"She's also donated five hundred copies to the Emma Shaw Foundation to be given to the children's hospital."

Everyone applauded and Sam helped Marti over to where many of the children waited. She stood talking with them and handing out books to each child with a smile and special word to each of them.

Emma jumped off the chair and ran to Elizabeth with her books. Elizabeth brought Emma back to the table where Cameron sat with Shelly looking perplexed.

"Daddy, look. She put me in the books."

Emma stood next to her father and showed him the covers.

Cameron read the title, "*Tina and Emma's Pirate Adventure.*" The cover showed a picture of Marti's ship with Marti and Emma standing on deck. The other book's title was *Tina and Emma's Princess Party.* The book cover showed Marti and Emma sitting atop a table having a tea party. The pictures of Marti weren't an exact likeness, but more a likeness of her as a child Emma's age. Cameron was surprised, and so very happy for Emma. Marti was an amazing artist and author. He'd read all of her books to Emma and he enjoyed all of the stories himself. It was a pleasure to go on an adventure in the *Tina's Travels* books with Emma each night.

"Those books are very special, Emma. Marti loves you very much. Isn't it amazing, you're in a book?"

"It's so cool."

"It sure is, Emma. May I see the books?" Shelly asked.

"No. You can't have my things." Emma ran to Jack and hid behind him.

Jack grabbed Emma and sat her on his lap. He held her in his arms. "It's all right, sweetheart. You don't have to let her see them. They belong to you and you can do whatever you want with them."

"She needs to learn how to share," Shelly said.

"You take things that aren't yours." Emma buried her head in Jack's tuxedo jacket.

"Emma, honey, what's the matter with you? Shelly won't take the books. She just wants to see them."

Emma didn't answer. She looked at her aunt instead. "Aunt Elizabeth, can I stay with you tonight?"

"Sure, sweetie. I'll take you home with me and Uncle Sam can read your books to you and Grace, if she's still awake when we get home."

Cameron looked at Elizabeth. "The wedding is tomorrow. I want her at home with me."

"She doesn't want to go home with you. I'm taking her home with me." Elizabeth didn't care what Cameron said. After what Emma had told them about Shelly and her threatening Emma if she told Cameron what happened with Marti, she wasn't about to let Emma be alone with Shelly. If Cameron was smart, he'd fix things with Marti and get rid of Shelly by tomorrow.

Chapter Forty-Six

CAMERON SAT AND watched Marti for an hour. She talked to all the children and everyone else who came up to her. The entire time, Sam stood beside her, holding onto her. No one seemed to notice he was holding her up. Cameron watched closely, noticing as time went on Sam took up more and more of her weight, until Elizabeth brought her a stool.

He wanted to get close to her, talk to her. The constant crowd around her kept him away and he didn't think he'd ever get the chance. He had no idea what he'd say, but the one thing he knew for sure, she'd been right. He had no idea who she really is.

"Emma, would you like to show me your painting. I'd really like to see it up close."

Emma jumped off Jack's lap and came to him.

Shelly stood to go with them, but Tyler grabbed her shoulder and pushed her back into her seat.

"Hey."

"Sit down. Let Emma have some time with her dad. This is her night," Tyler said.

"I'm going to be Cameron's wife tomorrow. I'll be going to events like this with him in the future. I want to be by his side."

"You want everyone to see you by his side. If I were you, I'd be worried about whether the wedding is actually going to happen. Marti has another surprise for Cameron tonight, and it just might change everything," Jack warned.

Cameron studied the painting, amazed at how well she'd captured the moment in such detail. Emma looked so real in the painting he felt as if he could lean over and kiss her. The same was true of Marti. The table was set exactly as it had been that night. He remembered taking a picture for Marti and realized she'd wanted it to paint the painting.

Every painting had a brass plaque on the frame. They all said: MARTINA BY SOFIA FAIRCHILD.

Emma's painting's plaque read:

MARTINA AND EMMA
"PRINCESS PARTY"
ARTIST: MARTINA FAIRCHILD
OWNER: EMMA SHAW

He picked up Emma and turned to go over to see Marti, but she was gone. He looked around and found Sam, alone, heading back his way from the side doors.

"Mr. Shaw? Do you know who I am?"

Cameron turned to the older gentleman and remembered him. "You're Anthony Fairchild. Marti's uncle."

"She asked me to give you this." Anthony handed over an envelope Martina had entrusted to him.

"You must be Emma. I've heard a lot about you over the last few days. Martina loves you very much. You are an amazing little girl. I owe you a big thank you."

"How come?" Emma asked, a soft smile on her pretty face.

"Until today, Martina has never shown anyone one of her paintings. She used to paint with my mother, but she never showed them to anyone. She's as great as my mother ever was, and it shows. Thank you. Because of you, I finally got to see one of my niece's masterpieces.

"You know, Cameron, she doesn't do anything to draw attention to herself. She hides the Fairchild name as often as she can because she believes she should stand on her own merits. It used to make me angry. Now I see she brings honor to the Fairchild name because she doesn't use it to get what she wants.

"My mother used to say she was unique. I thought it was just a grandmother doting on her granddaughter. I was wrong. Martina is one in infinity.

"You had her for a moment, but you lost her because you didn't believe in her. I almost made the same mistake.

"Now, instead of looking at her and only seeing the Fairchild name, I see her for the woman she is. You saw her for the woman she is and that wasn't enough for you. It's not often a man gives up such a treasure. I'm sure it won't be long before another man discovers what a prize she truly is." He paused before adding, "Have a nice evening.

"Emma, it was a true pleasure to meet you. Marti was right. You are a princess. If that painting didn't belong to you, I'd buy it, whatever the cost."

Emma smiled hugely. "I'm going to hang it in my princess room."

"Excellent idea. Marti told me she painted it for you. You're a very lucky girl."

Chapter Forty-Seven

CAMERON SAT AT their table, staring at the envelope from Marti afraid to open it.

"Just open it, Cameron. It's not going to bite you," Jenna teased, though it didn't hold a lot of amusement.

"What's in the envelope? Who gave it to you?" Shelly asked, confused as ever by everyone's odd behavior.

Emma went back to giving him the silent treatment, watching Shelly like a hawk from Sam's lap.

"It's from Marti." Cameron held the envelope, stared at his name scrawled in Marti's flowing script, unable to make himself open it. He didn't want it to be goodbye, anything but that. He'd been hard on her in the hospital. He hadn't slept much since. All he thought about was their baby. He didn't even know if Marti had been upset by the loss. She looked okay tonight. She was in public though, so he couldn't tell if she was in pain or grieving for their child. Worse, he didn't know if she wasn't grieving their child.

That wasn't the worst. He hadn't even talked to her about it. He'd yelled at her. She loved him. She must have been devastated to lose their baby, and he hadn't been there for her, hadn't sought his own comfort in her arms over their shared loss.

He felt like his brain was in some kind of whirlwind with his thoughts spinning around. He didn't know what was right or wrong.

Everyone kept telling him to see Marti for who she was. She would be devastated if she lost the baby. He knew that for sure. He needed to get to her and talk to her. If she was feeling as bad as he was, she needed him as much as he needed her.

He knows her. She loves him and Emma. She keeps her promises, never lies. He put her through hell by choosing to be with Shelly because of the baby, and not because he loved Shelly over Marti.

He wanted the baby. He didn't want Shelly. He wanted Marti.

"Who cares what she has to say. She tried to hurt me. Tomorrow, when we're married, she won't be able to come between us ever again. She'll realize you belong to me."

Cameron winced. The only people he belonged to, heart and soul, were Emma and Marti. The only thing he wanted from Shelly was his baby, if there was a baby. He wasn't so sure anymore, he hadn't been for a while, but hated to admit to such a colossal mistake. Pride be damned, he needed some straight answers.

He looked around the table at his friends, who he considered his family. Emma called them aunt and uncle.

They told it like it is. They'd kicked him out of Marti's hospital room and Sam and Jack had punched him. They considered him their brother, and yet they'd taken Marti's side after the whole stairs incident. Why would they side with her over him?

"Okay. Enough of all this crap. Tell me what you know, and I keep missing."

"You're an idiot," Jenna said.

"You're stupid," Jack said.

"You're an asshole," Sam said while he covered Emma's ears.

Elizabeth offered up something less irritating. "You're engaged to the wrong person."

That was the only thing that made sense to him. Yeah, he was being an idiot and stupid for not sorting this mess out sooner. He could even admit he'd been an asshole to them and to Marti. He'd finally had enough. He wanted his life back in order. He wanted his daughter to smile again. He wanted to stop living with this all-encompassing grief over losing George and his baby in a matter of weeks. He couldn't think straight anymore.

"Tell me the truth."

"We just did," Sam said and smiled. "You want the truth about Marti? We'll tell you, even though you already know. Shelly's confused you over the last two months by feeding you lies. You believed the lies and refused to accept the truth. The truth is simple. Marti loves you. She isn't a liar.

"It's also interesting to note Shelly claims Marti fell forward down the stairs. She doesn't have a single mark on the front of her, but her back looks like a set of stairs hit her."

"Those are the marks on her back. You pulled down her wrap when her back was to me, so I'd see the bruises across her shoulders." They were the perfect image of where she must have hit the stair ledge when she'd fallen.

"I made sure you saw her back. You were so busy telling her what you thought you knew in the hospital, you never even asked her what happened. You weren't even concerned about her well-being. You left her in the hospital hurting and thinking you don't love her, when she hasn't done anything wrong. You left her on the goddamn stairs," Sam snapped. "Open the damn envelope. If you don't sort this out now, I'll pound it into you with my fists."

"This is outrageous," Shelly complained. "I'm carrying Cameron's baby. We're getting married tomorrow. She tried to kill me to stop me from marrying you."

Sam glared, his eyes cold as steel. "Wrong on all counts."

Cameron studied Sam and considered everything he'd said. He wouldn't do this just to hurt him. He meant what he said. They all felt the way Sam did. How could he have been so wrong about everything?

He opened the envelope and pulled out the note.

Cameron,
      You know my last name. You know what I do for a living. You know I love you and Emma. I never lied

to you. I never tried to hurt Shelly. I was protecting
Emma.

I didn't lose our baby.

Now, you know everything.

You told me the morning we first made love, you'd
spent the night holding the world in your arms. I
took a piece of that world with me, and I'll forever
be grateful. If I couldn't have you, at least, I have our
child. The proof you need is in the envelope.

I'll always love you.

Marti, Martina, Tina

Whoever it is you think I am, because you don't
seem to know me.

He pulled out the pregnancy test from inside the
envelope. She'd written today's date on it. The test was
positive.

The relief he felt holding the positive test in his hands
might have felled him if he'd been standing up. Their baby
was still alive, tucked in his mother's belly safe and sound.
He held the test in his hands and closed his eyes and savored the moment of pure joy and overwhelming relief.

"She didn't lose the baby," Cameron said it out loud.
He needed to hear it to believe it. His wish come true.

"No," Sam confirmed. "We don't know what you overheard, but she didn't lose the baby. It was touch and go
the first day, but the doctor gave her and the baby the all
clear. She was at a complete loss when you came into the
room yelling at her."

Sam narrowed his gaze on Shelly. "You look disappointed. Funny, you don't look surprised to hear Mari is pregnant with Cameron's baby."

Shelly was smart enough to remain silent. She didn't want to give anything away. She was holding on to Cameron by a thread. She just needed to get to tomorrow and the ceremony.

Emma looked up at her uncle. "Marti is having a baby too?"

"Not too, sweetheart. She's the only one. At least, the only one willing to prove it. Again. And again. And again." Sam held Emma tightly to his chest.

"I'm not going to sit here and take this. Cameron, you can't let them talk to me this way. I'm going to be your wife."

Cameron didn't answer her. He kept staring at the test in his hand and reading the note from Marti.

He knew her. He knew he knew her. She was right; he was the stupidest smart person. He had all the answers in business and with other people, but he'd screwed it all up with Marti. He swore he'd fix it all.

"Cameron, aren't you going to set your friends straight?"

"I think they already know the score and I've come to the game late."

"What the hell does that mean?"

He didn't answer her. "How long do I have?" he asked the table at large.

"She's not stupid. You have time. A lifetime if you're smart."

Sam and everyone breathed a collective sigh of relief.

He held onto the test and the note, tucking them into his coat pocket next to his heart for safe keeping. The auction began and the books were up first. He watched them both go to families with children and for over ten thousand apiece. Several other items sold well. Cameron was impressed with how much money they were raising for the foundation.

A painting came up for auction and the sound of clapping drew Cameron's attention. He looked up at the painting and saw that it was of Marti's ship on a calm sea with the moon high above and the stars shining bright. Marti stood on deck facing the moon with her dark hair and white gown blowing in a soft wind. He couldn't see her face, but there was no mistaking the woman he loved.

"Daddy, I want the painting," Emma said, excited.

"I want the painting too," he replied and raised his hand at the next bid.

The bidding went back and forth and around the table. Jack, Jenna, Elizabeth, and Sam were all making sure he paid big for the painting and the things he'd done to Marti. Petty revenge, but he deserved it. They finally relented and he got the painting for an astronomical three hundred thousand dollars. He'd have paid any price to get it regardless of the fact the money was going to the foundation.

Shelly sat beside him fuming over everyone clamoring to get the painting. As the night went on and Cameron continued to ignore her, she got even angrier. He didn't care. Not anymore. Trying to do the right thing blinded him to the truth. He'd never let that happen again. He had a lot of making up to do, but he held fast to the promise in Marti's note. *I'll always love you.* All he needed to know to get her back. As long as they shared this kind of love, they could overcome anything, even his temporary insanity.

Chapter Forty-Eight

He spent the night alone in his room making plans, deciding what to do and how he was going to do it.

Emma stayed with Elizabeth and Sam. He went into her empty room in the early morning, dawn breaking the new day, and looked at the room Marti had painted for Emma. Truly spectacular. The fact that she'd done all of it, every detailed wall, was an amazing feat. She was a world-class artist.

He lay down on Emma's bed and looked up at the starry sky she'd painted and the image of Emma's mother looking down on him.

His heart and soul became quiet and he stared at her image. Silently, his heart spoke to her, telling her he was sorry she'd died. He told her about Emma and how well she was growing up. He remembered stories about Emma and told Caroline how sorry he was she missed the chance to see their little girl grow. He told Caroline about Marti and how he'd screwed things up so terribly he might have lost the mother he knew Caroline would have wished for Emma. He promised to make things right and their daughter would smile again.

He lay there for a long time cleansing his soul. He'd spent so much time being angry at Caroline for dying, leaving him and Emma, he hadn't grieved her properly. He hadn't put all his hopes and wishes for them aside. He did now and felt a weight lift as he lay there on his daughter's bed.

He went down the hall to confront Shelly. Before he got to her room, he went into Marti's. It smelled like her. Fresh. Flowery. Inviting and calming. Whenever he smelled her, something deep inside him sighed and relaxed.

The empty, perfectly made bed reminded him how she'd collapsed in exhaustion the night she'd shown Emma her new room. Pregnant then, it explained her dizziness and fatigue. She hadn't said anything. He'd made it next to impossible for her to tell him.

Hairbrush and lipstick and a bottle of perfume sat atop her dresser. He picked it up. French. He wondered if she'd gotten it on her world trip. He opened a drawer and found her nightgowns. He didn't even know what she wore to bed. Silk. They would probably skim her thighs. Some had lace, others plainer. All of them would look great on her, and she'd look great when he took them off her.

He opened the door, connecting the other room, the room she'd been working in the night she'd told him she was pregnant. She'd been hurt the next day on the stairs, and he'd left her alone in the hospital.

He rubbed the back of his neck and wondered how he'd ever make this up to her. She could have lost their baby. She must have been so scared and all he'd done was yell at her. She'd understand, know he was just upset because he'd thought she'd lost the baby.

He took a deep breath and glanced around her workroom. A simple desk with a laptop computer. She had a phone and fax machine set up. What amazed him were all the folders and files on the desk. It looked like she had more work than he did. He had no idea what everything was, but he saw her organized and efficient methods. Everything appeared to be in its place.

She'd spent so much time with he and Emma. He had no idea how many late nights she must have put in, allowing her the time to spend with them. She never told Emma she didn't have time for something. She always made the time.

Two easels were set up by the windows and a long table with tubes and jars of paint. Brushes and sponges and all kinds of tools he didn't recognize stood in jars and lay about the workspace. He stepped around the easels and looked at the paintings she'd been working on.

The first painting caught him by surprise. The garden bench they'd made love on in the rain. The painting captured her sadness. The garden and the night were all done in grays and dark blues. The moon peeked through the gloomy clouds highlighting the bench and the sparkle of the rain. The bench appeared lonely and isolated, cast in shadow, in the center of the lush garden, rain pouring down. The life and vibrancy of the garden had been sucked away by the loneliness and emptiness of the bench.

He felt ill. He'd ruined that night and left her feeling this way.

The other painting had a cloth draped over it, a piece of paper attached with his name scrawled in Marti's script.

He opened the folded sheet.

I thought you might find your way in here. This painting is for you, my love. It's your wish come true, at least on canvas. It's the best I could do to give you a memory to heal your pain.
Love, Marti

He pulled the cloth back from the painting and took a step back, stunned.

The painting showed Caroline holding Emma as a baby. He had no idea how she had done the painting. He looked around on the table of paints and saw some photos from Emma's baby book. Marti must have used them to make the painting.

Caroline held Emma, her beautiful face turned down to Emma's. Caroline wore a white gown and her hair spilled over her shoulder like a curtain behind baby Emma. As you looked out from the center, the painting blurred into white clouds or mist. Like a scene from a dream.

She'd given him his greatest wish. He'd always wanted

to see Caroline holding her baby. It was something she'd never gotten to do, but Marti had created the moment so perfectly he imagined this was exactly what they would have looked like together.

She'd helped him heal by giving his daughter her mother to watch over her while she slept. He'd used the mural to let go of his pain. She'd furthered his healing by giving him his greatest wish.

It was his turn to heal some of the hurt he'd caused her.

He took the painting of Caroline and Emma and went down the hall to Emma's room. The "Princess Party" painting already hung on the wall where Marti had left a space when she'd done the room. He hung the picture of Caroline and Emma on the other hook. Marti had thought of everything.

Everyone walked into Emma's room and found Cameron staring at the paintings in their spots on the wall. Sam, Elizabeth, Jack, Jenna, and Emma all stared up at the paintings with him.

"Oh, Cameron. They're perfect."

"They're Emma's mothers," he said and glanced down at his daughter. "She painted you your mothers. Marti is the mother you want, isn't she?"

"Oh, yes. I want that more than anything, Daddy."

"I'm going to do everything I can to make it come true for you and me. I'm sorry I didn't make it happen sooner."

Emma ran to her father and jumped into his arms and hugged him tight. "It's all right. Marti said it would all work out."

"She did?"

"Yes. She always tells the truth."

"Yes, she does."

Shelly came into the room. Her gaze went to the paintings. "It's not a very good likeness of me. How does she know what the baby will look like?"

Everyone had been calling *him* stupid. "The painting is of Emma and her mother, Caroline."

"Oh. Why is everyone here so early? No one is dressed for the wedding. Oh my God, Cameron, you can't see me today, not until the wedding." Shelly turned and started for the door.

Cameron handed Emma over to her Uncle Jack.

"Everyone, will you excuse us?" He grabbed Shelly's arm and led her down the hall and into Marti's bathroom.

"What the hell, Cameron? Why are we in here?"

Cameron opened the drawer where Marti had pulled out the pregnancy test kits and found one left. He took it out and put it on the counter.

"You have only one choice. Take the test and prove you're pregnant. Right now. Either way there isn't going to be a wedding. Take the test, now, and if you're pregnant we'll settle on custody arrangements and payment. If you aren't, you can leave here and I never want to hear from you again. Refuse to take the test, and I'll take you to court and make you take the test. If it's positive, I'll sue you for full custody and I'll win. If it's false, I'll sue you for fraud and make sure you pay me back every dime I gave you to pay off your bills."

"Cameron, I already told you I saw the doctor and they did the test. I'm pregnant. We're supposed to get married today."

"No wedding, Shelly. Not today. Never. I've spent the last two months hurting the woman I love because you claim you're pregnant and all I wanted to do was give my children a whole family. Now prove it. You aren't leaving this bathroom without peeing on the stick."

"I will do no such thing."

"Yes, you will, because it's the difference between leaving here on your own, or leaving here in a police car. I've already contacted my lawyer. If you don't pee on the stick, I'll proceed with fraud charges, and since you benefited financially from the fraud, you will be charged and prosecuted to the fullest extent of the law."

"It'll be in all the papers if you do that." Shelly tried to make him change his mind. "You and Merrick don't want that kind of publicity."

"Pee on the stick, or I'll be the first one to call the newspapers. You won't get out of this house without the press following you everywhere and waiting to find out the results of the test. You'll have exactly what you want, all the attention focused on you. You won't have the money though. I'll never marry you. No millions for you. No mansion for you. You won't be the queen of the castle. Two princesses already live here, and that suits me just fine. I don't need a witch spoiling things anymore."

She'd never heard him like this. So far, she'd been able to talk her way out of things and get him to take her side. He wasn't buying it this time, and she had nothing left to bluff with.

"Fine. You win. I'm not pregnant. I never was. I'm on the pill. How's it feel to be played for a fool?"

"Feels like shit. I almost lost my friends, my daughter is upset, and I've treated the woman I love more than my own life like crap for two months when all she's done is love me and Emma. All because you lied. Pee on the stick."

"I told you, I'm not pregnant."

"You could be lying and come back after me later for child support for some other fool's baby. You aren't leaving until you prove it one way or another. Pee on the goddamn stick," he shouted.

He planted his feet, stood with his arms crossed, waiting for her to comply with his demand. Humiliating her wasn't his goal, he didn't care about her feelings at this point. Time to get rid of the trash and go after Marti.

She peed on the stick, knowing this was the end. She wouldn't get what she wanted. "You know, I quit my job. I don't have any money. I've already given notice on my apartment. I have to have everything cleared out by the end of the month."

"You should have thought of that before you lied."

"You could at least give me a little something to get by until I can get a job and a new place."

He took the pregnancy test and watched the windows. The results were negative and the test confirmed with one line it had worked. He glared at her with pure hatred surging through his chest and mind.

"Had the test been positive, I would have paid you a king's ransom to get the baby from you. You aren't fit to be a mother. It's negative and you won't see a dime."

Sam waited behind Cameron. "You should have taken

the million George offered you before he died. Now you've got nothing. As it should be, if you ask me."

Cameron had no idea George made the offer to Shelly. It must have been the night he'd asked him to take Emma up to see her surprise room with Marti. He wasn't surprised by George's gesture. He was always trying to protect Cameron. He was a good father, Cameron realized, not for the first time. It felt good to think of him that way.

"You really screwed that one up," he said to Shelly. "I guess the fifty million I got from his death must have looked real tempting. It must really burn you I'd give it all to Marti if she'd take me back."

"She doesn't need it. She's rich."

"She doesn't care about it, because for her, life isn't about the money. It's about being honest. She truly wants to be a mother to my children, and I thank God she's the one having my baby and not you. I'd have never let you keep the baby."

They all walked out of the bathroom and Cameron grabbed Shelly's arm and propelled her into her own room. He didn't want her in Marti's space anymore.

"You have five minutes to pack your stuff."

"Cameron, why are you being so mean?"

"I spent the night Marti was in the hospital consoling you over a baby who doesn't exist. She was lying in a hospital bed alone, terrified she'd lose our baby. There's no end to the number of things I've done wrong, but that one thing will haunt me the rest of my life. I wasn't there for her when she needed me most."

"You left her on the stairs after Shelly shoved her down them."

Cameron turned on Sam. "Is that what really happened? Shelly pushed her down the stairs?"

"No, I didn't." Shelly didn't want Sam arresting her for pushing Marti, and Cameron was mad enough to make him do it.

Emma stopped in her tracks in the center of the hallway and shouted, "Yes, she did. She stole my necklace from my room and yelled at me and wouldn't give it back. Marti came up the stairs and told her to give it back. She wouldn't. Marti took it, and Shelly pushed her down the stairs. Marti fell and hit her back and fell over backward. I thought she was dead." Emma's bottom lip trembled and tears filled her eyes. "Shelly said if I told, I'd never see you again, Daddy. I hid under my bed and cried." She cried harder now.

Cameron scooped up his daughter and held her close. He turned on Shelly.

"You stole a little girl's necklace and you pushed Marti down the stairs, knowing she was pregnant."

"I couldn't let her ruin everything."

He had never wanted to hit someone so much in his life. Her being a woman barely kept the reins on his control. "Your five minutes is running out."

"Cameron, the jeweler is here," Jenna announced from behind everyone.

"The jeweler. You got me a ring, finally?" Shelly's eyes lit up.

"No. Funny, I never got around to getting you a ring.

Then I just didn't want to. I had my assistant call everyone this morning and cancel the wedding, including your parents, who were surprised to find out you were getting married. I guess you figured you better make sure it happened before you told them. She canceled the flowers and the food and everything else. My next call was to Harrison Jewelers. I asked them to bring over a selection of their most expensive and unique engagement rings."

"Harrison's is the most exclusive jeweler in town. You have to have an appointment to get into the back room to see the best pieces," Shelly rambled.

"Yes, or you have to be really rich, like me, and they'll bring the goods to you." He gave her a snide smile. He hoped she realized just how much she was losing. He was a nice enough guy to pay her off and make her go away. She'd gone too far, and even his need to be nice didn't exceed his need to get her out of his and Marti's house with nothing.

"Emma, want to pick out a nice ring for Marti with me."

"I hate you, Cameron," Shelly shrieked and stomped her foot.

"The feeling is mutual. Pack your bag. If I was you, I'd be real careful about what I take. Marti won't be happy if she finds something of hers missing."

"I think we should get Marti a really sparkly ring," Emma said with a huge grin.

"Great idea. Sam, please see Shelly out. Shoot her if she takes more than five minutes."

Sam leaned against the door, cocked his elbow, and watched his watch and Shelly.

Cameron took Emma downstairs and sat in the living room with her. Several trays of diamond rings lay spread on the coffee table before them. He made sure to hold up the largest of them when Shelly came down the stairs. Drawn to the huge diamond, she frowned, her face heating with rage. Cameron felt a little satisfaction. Sam saw to it she was taken home in the cab waiting outside.

"I like this one the best. It sparkles the most," Emma said and held up a ring.

Mr. Harrison smiled his agreement. "A fine choice, my dear. It does indeed sparkle the most." He turned to Cameron. "It's the most expensive piece I brought. Your daughter has excellent taste. It's a round, brilliant cut diamond. Six carats and set in platinum. It would pair nicely with this diamond eternity band for the wedding ring. If the lady likes the sparkle, you can't beat the two together. For spectacular, you could use two eternity bands and place the solitaire in between."

He showed them how it would look and put the rings on Emma's small finger.

She held it up, admiring them. They caught the light, the many diamonds twinkled.

"It's like rain dancing in the moonlight," Emma smiled and made the light dance some more.

That's all Cameron needed to hear. He thought the rings looked great. He couldn't have picked a better set for Marti. Emma helping him would make Marti happy.

"We'll take all three."

"Don't you want to know the price?"

"It doesn't matter, that's the one she wants and I want. Marti will love it."

"Yes, she will," Elizabeth said. She and Jenna had sat with their children watching Cameron and Emma picking the rings. It was so sweet to watch the little girl with her dad getting a ring for a mom she always wanted.

Cameron paid the man and escorted him to the door, along with the two security guards who came with him.

He turned to everyone waiting in the living room. Only one thing left to do. Beg them to tell him where Marti is.

"Listen you guys, I know I've been a complete jackass. I'm sorry I didn't listen to you all sooner, and I'm even more sorry I hurt Marti and made Emma miserable. I hope you'll all forgive me."

Sam wanted to prolong the agony for Cameron a little longer. "We thought we'd take all the kids to the zoo today. It's beautiful out and Emma said she'd like to go."

"I like the zoo. They have monkeys." She and Jenna's twins sat on the floor at Jack's feet.

"Do you want to join us, Cameron?" Jenna smiled and looked mischievous.

Jack wanted in on things himself. "How about we take Emma? She can stay the night with us and we'll bring her back in the morning."

Everyone got up to leave. Elizabeth carried Emma's overnight bag.

"You look tired, Cameron. You should go upstairs and get some rest. A nice nap will do you good."

"Wait a minute. Aren't you going to tell me where she is?"

"Elizabeth already told you what you should do. I think you should take her advice." Sam grabbed Cameron in a huge bear hug and slapped him on the back. He picked up his sleeping daughter in her car seat and headed out the door.

"Me too." Jack gave Cameron another bear hug, slapped him on the back, and left with his twin sons holding his hands.

Jenna kissed him on the cheek and Emma hugged him tight and kissed him goodbye.

Elizabeth was the last to leave and before she walked out the door she kissed his cheek and said, "Make things right, Cameron. She's been through enough. She loves you enough to forgive you and make it easy on you. She's upstairs waiting for you. Jack carried her up while you were in with Shelly. We all love you and we'll see you tomorrow when we bring Emma home."

"Don't make it early. I plan on sleeping in," he said and ran up the stairs two at a time before the front door closed behind Elizabeth.

Chapter Forty-Nine

CAMERON STOPPED IN the double doorway and stared at the beautiful woman asleep on his bed. Wearing a white sundress, she looked like an angel sleeping on the blue and white bed cover. On her side, her dark hair spread back from her face and over the pillow. The outline of the brace on her knee keeping it straight showed through her dress. Her arm lay across her belly, strapped into the brace around her waist keeping her shoulder in place. He walked to the side of the bed at her back and saw the bruises on her shoulder the dress didn't cover. He hung his head, eyes on the floor, mind locked on the past, wondering how he could be such a fool.

Sensing his presence, she tried to turn to him, but whimpered in her sleep when she hit her bruised shoulder on the bed. She turned her back again and made a sound of displeasure. He stepped around the bed and sat beside her. They'd both been through too many sleepless nights over the last week. Pale skin, dark circles beneath her eyes, she needed her rest, but he needed to talk to her and make things right. This mess had gone on far too long. His fault completely. His to make right.

He traced his finger along the curve of her cheek and over her ear, tucking her hair back from her beautiful face. With a soft touch, he swept his fingertips along her hurt shoulder and down her arm. He rested his palm on her hip and squeezed gently.

He'd missed her. Everything inside him ached to hold her and kiss her and promise her . . . everything and anything.

First he owed her an apology. Then he'd beg, because no matter what, he wasn't letting her leave this bed without agreeing to put him out of his misery and marry him.

He leaned down and kissed her forehead. Her eyes fluttered open and stared up at him. He looked down into her soft green eyes, far too serious and weary for his liking.

"Did you get that woman out of my house?"

"Yes, sweetheart. I did. I'm so sorry for everything that's happened over the last two months."

"You should be."

"I am. God, Marti, I'm so damn sorry." He squeezed her hip and made her gasp. "You're in pain. Do you need something? How can I help you?"

"Stop. I'm fine. My back goes into spasm. The muscles are sore. The doctor said it'll get better."

"What about the baby?" He moved his hand down to her belly and covered his child.

She placed her hand over his. "Our baby is just fine. There's no more spotting."

"You were bleeding," he said, frightened. She'd been through so much without him. He kissed her forehead. "Oh, sweetheart, I'm so sorry I didn't come to you in the hospital and take care of you. I'm sorry I didn't listen to you when you were on the stairs. I'm sorry for everything. I'm so damn sorry."

"I don't want to do this."

The finality in her voice and blank face scared him even more.

Please God, don't let her want to leave me. I can't bear to lose her now and live without her.

"Do you love me?" Her soft voice sounded unusually shy.

Marti didn't like the scared and worried look on his face. She didn't want to listen to him tell her he was sorry. She knew he was. Most of what happened was because of his guilt over Caroline's death and his need to be a good father. Who could blame him for that? She had a lot more compassion for him because she knew what it was like to wish for a mother and father. He wanted the best for his baby. Knowing that, she forgave the rest. She loved him and wanted him and was ready to move on to being happy with him.

"I love you so much. More than anything. I want to spend my life with you and raise Emma and our baby and as many more babies as you'll give me," he said. "I want to wake up with you every morning and have your face be the last thing I see at night. I want to learn everything about you. I'm pretty sure it's going to take the rest of our lives, because you're an amazing woman, and every day I learn something new about you. I want to marry you and have you adopt Emma as your own. I want her to have the mother she's always wanted. And that's you, Marti." He slipped off the bed and knelt on one knee beside her. "Martina Fairchild, please marry me, because I can't live without you." He slid the rings onto her finger and kissed them in place. "Please say yes."

Her eyes filled with tears, and her gaze locked on the three rings.

"Emma helped me pick them out. I knew they were perfect when she said they looked like rain in the moonlight."

"They're beautiful." She laid her hand on his chest and admired the diamonds twinkling on her finger.

"I'll never forget making love to you in the rain. I saw the painting and it was like a punch in the gut seeing the lonely bench in the moonlight with the rain pouring down. I don't want you to remember it that way. Somehow, some way, I will make everything up to you, sweetheart. I want to make a thousand happy memories with you."

"That's all I ever wanted. You're all I ever wanted. You and Emma and our baby."

"You have to believe me. After everything that's happened, you have to know I always wanted you. I didn't want to turn my back on you, but I wanted to give my children what I never had, a whole family. I thought I owed them that after what happened to Caroline.

"You are the most amazing mother to Emma. I would have been the same kind of father to the baby. I can't tell you how relieved I am we'll never have to deal with Shelly again. I have the proof. I'll show you she isn't pregnant."

"I don't need the proof."

"No, you already knew she lied about the pregnancy."

"I don't need the proof because I trust you."

"And I didn't trust you," he said and lay his forehead to hers.

"I don't believe that." She brushed her lips to his in a soft sweet sweep of her mouth over his. "I think you wanted to do the right thing, and you got caught up in trying to be there for the baby and trying to hold onto me too. You thought you couldn't have both, so like a good father you chose the baby. I understand. That's why I came back today. I could have sailed away with our baby and let go of an amazing dream to punish you for everything that's happened. I'd rather have the dream. I'd rather have you and a life with Emma and our baby."

"I'll give you the world if you say you'll marry me."

"You already know I'll marry you. But if you need to hear me say the words. Yes, I'll marry you. Anywhere. Anytime. I already have the world."

"Your ship." He looked up at the amazing painting of Marti standing on the bow of her ship looking up at the moon and stars he'd hung above the fireplace last night. From the bed, he'd stared at the painting all night wishing for her.

"No. You."

Wish granted. He smiled, happier than he'd ever felt in his life. Everything was going to be all right now. Actually, it was perfect.

He kissed her gently and ran his hand over her face, mapping her beautiful features. Her green eyes watched him, and in those eyes, he saw the world, his world.

Give in to your impulses . . .
Read on for a sneak peek at a brand-new
e-book original tale of romance from Avon Books.
Available now wherever e-books are sold.

ALL OR NOTHING
A Trust No One Novel
By Dixie Lee Brown

An Excerpt from

ALL OR NOTHING
A Trust No One Novel

by Dixie Lee Brown

Debut author Dixie Lee Brown launches
her *Trust No One* series with this tale of
a hunted woman and the one man who
can save her life . . . if she'll let him.

"Trust me. This is the safest way."

Everything required trust with Joe. So, did she trust him? If she ever got back on the ground, she might be able to answer that question. Cara looked over the edge of the platform. *There's no way!*

"Take your time. Go when you're ready . . . unless you want me to give you a little push."

"You wouldn't dare!" She wrapped her arms around the pole.

"You really don't trust me, do you?" He laughed.

"I was starting to, before you said the word 'push.' "

"There's hope then? If I choose my words more carefully?"

"Maybe . . . if I ever get down from here."

"Let's sit for a minute. Things will look different from that perspective." He sat, dangling his long legs over the side. Cara positioned herself beside him, her hands nervously flexing on the rope that joined her to the zip line.

"Jumping doesn't seem any more reasonable from here." Too bad, since sitting close enough to rub shoulders with him made her nearly as uncomfortable as the stupid zip line.

"We'll just hang out and talk for a while then. That okay?" He gripped the edge of the platform and leaned forward, turning to look at her.

"The last time we talked, it ended badly."

"Now we know which subjects to stay away from."

"Yeah, anything to do with either of our private lives."

"I think it was your ex-husband and my desire to protect you from him that got us crossways with each other."

Cara glanced sideways at him. He was looking at her. Their eyes met. The strangest emotions coursed through her. Somehow, it didn't sound so bad when he said it like that. Who didn't want a knight in shining armor? She was afraid for Joe, but he sounded so confident that he could protect her, and himself, she almost believed it. Recognizing the danger in that, she tore her eyes away from his.

"We're making progress. You didn't rip into me that time." A grin came through in his voice.

"It doesn't do any good to try talking sense into you." She wanted to sound serious, but her heart was no longer in it. She forced her mind back to the task at hand, considering the likelihood that she'd ever be able to *zip* off this ledge. What was the worst that could happen? The cable could break, and she'd plummet thirty feet to the ground. End all of her problems. More likely, it would be a gradual descent, with the jump from the platform the only really exciting part. She could do this.

"We've got unfinished business, you know. We might as well take care of it while we're sitting here."

"What's that?"

"I almost had you talked into dinner that night we met."

"You weren't even close."

"I think you were as intrigued with the idea as I was." He grinned. "I also think we stood a good chance of ending the evening with a kiss."

"That's a stretch. You're making the same mistake you made that night. Going from confident to arrogant in about two seconds flat. There was no chance in hell you were going to get a kiss." Cara smiled at his wounded look.

"Will my chances ever improve?" His eyes met hers again.

She'd forgotten what a good-looking guy he was. The same mesmerizing pull she'd experienced the night she met him overcame her better judgment now. For a moment she wondered what it would feel like, his lips on hers, his arms holding her close, while they lost themselves in each other.

Cara drew herself up short. Was she completely crazy? She was barely free from one dangerous man. Why would she get involved with another? There was an attraction between them she couldn't deny, but nothing could ever come of it.

"Maybe." The word slipped out, almost on its own.

Spectacles

Spectacles

SUE PERKINS

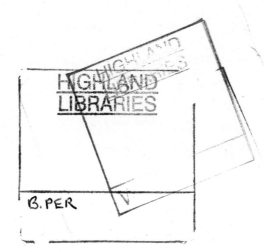

MICHAEL JOSEPH
an imprint of
PENGUIN BOOKS

MICHAEL JOSEPH

UK | USA | Canada | Ireland | Australia
India | New Zealand | South Africa

Michael Joseph is part of the Penguin Random House group of companies
whose addresses can be found at global.penguinrandomhouse.com

First published 2015

003

Text and images copyright © Sue Perkins, 2015

The moral right of the author has been asserted

Set in Dante MT Std 12/14.75 pt
Typeset by Palimpsest Book Production Limited, Falkirk, Stirlingshire
Printed in Great Britain by Clays Ltd, St Ives plc

A CIP catalogue record for this book is available from the British Library

ISBN: 978–1–405–91854–1

10% of the royalties of this book go to The Serpentarium on the Isle of Skye.

For Scarlett Jukes

Heron   A reasonable effort.

The cruel beaked menace
Savage and ruthless, evil
Terror of all fish

S Perkins

(B-)

Contents

Contents

Most of this book is true.

I have, however, changed a few names to protect the innocent, and the odd location too. I've skewed some details for comic effect, swapped timelines and generally embellished and embroidered some of the duller moments in my past. I have sometimes created punchlines where real life failed to provide them, and occasionally invented characters wholesale. I have amplified my more positive characteristics in an effort to make you like me. I have hidden the worst of my flaws in an effort to make you like me. I may at one point have pretended to have been an Olympic fencing champion.

Other than that, as I say – I've told it like it is.

Preface

I've always wanted to be a writer; since I first felt the precarious wobble of a book in my hand, since I first heard the phrase 'Once upon a time', since I first realized that fairies, wizards and seafarers could transport you from the endless grey of 1970s south London. I was a prolific child. By the age of seven, I had produced several anthologies of poems about God, death and aquatic birds. I was prolific right up to the point I received a B- for a haiku I'd written about a heron. The uninitiated can be so unkind.

As an adult I started writing articles, reviews and glib little pieces for glossy magazines. I'd hide away in my room on the days I wasn't on set and continue work on *Ra'anui and the Enchanted Otter*, the intense, magic-realist novel set in Tahiti I'd been working on for the best part of a decade. By the time it neared completion, it was clear that there was never going to be an appetite for it and that the book world had changed beyond recognition. Almost to prove that point, I had a meeting in the autumn of 2010 with a well-known publishing house to discuss the possibility of writing something. I'd been invited to a swanky restaurant in St Martin's Lane. I arrived late, as always, in full wet-weather gear to find a semicircle of unspeakably beautiful people sat at the table waiting for me.

'Hi, I'm Tamara,' said the immaculate blonde to my left, proffering a manicured hand. 'I'm head of talent acquisitions.'

I leant forward to greet her. Dried mud cascaded from my sleeve into the *amuse-bouche*. 'Sorry, I've been walking the dog on the heath.'

'I'm Sarah-Jane,' said the immaculate blonde to my right. 'I'm the publishing director.'

'Nice to meet you. Ooh, I wouldn't hug me – I'm a little damp around the edges.'

'Hi, I'm Dorcas,' said the immaculate blonde dead ahead of me. 'I'm the managing director.'

'Hello – oops!' I said, as a roll of poo bags unfurled from my coat pocket.

It wasn't the best first impression I'd ever made. I sat down and panic-nibbled on some artisanal micro-loaves.

'So, Sue . . .' said one of the immaculate blondes, staring at me as if I were a monkey smearing itself with excrement at the zoo. 'What would you like to write?'

It was the question I had been waiting all my life to answer. Twenty-five minutes later I finished speaking, having evoked, in minute detail, my proposed epic:

'. . . so Ra'anui finally tames the beast with his uncle's amulet and marries Puatea. It's essentially a meditation on climate change.'

There followed a long pause during which I awkwardly pushed some 'textures of artichoke' around my plate.

'Well . . .' said one immaculate blonde, breaking the silence, '. . . that's great!'

'Really, really great,' chimed the second.

'Great!' said the third.

This was going so well. All three had said 'great'. In a row! Then came the stinger.

Blonde 1:   Now, you see, what *we'd* like you to write . . .
Me: Oh . . .
Blonde 2:   No, hear us out . . .
Blonde 1:   We've looked at what generates mass sales – you know,

what really works piled up at Tesco and Asda. And we've developed a formula . . .

Blonde 2:   *[blurting]* Death is really hot right now . . .

Blonde 3:   And pets . . .

Blonde 1:   So either of those would make a great starting point.

By now I thought we were all having a laugh, that I was among friends. We'd ordered *sharing plates* for goodness' sake. I'd dug my fork into Blonde 1's sweet anchovies. Blonde 2 had tried my avocado tian. I mean, we were *mates*. In that spirit of fun I joined in.

Me: *[grinning]* Well, what about combining the two?

Blonde 1:   *[intrigued]* What? Death *and* pets?

Me: Yes, why not? *[Carrying on]* A kind of *Lovely Bones* meets *Lassie*.

Blonde 3:   *[squealing]* Amazing! Amazing!

Me: We could call it . . . *Angel Dog.*

Blonde 3:   Oh my God – *Angel Dog*!

Me: The dog dies, doesn't go straight to heaven – ends up in some kind of canine purgatory, depending on how deeply Catholic you want to get – and ends up guarding his owners from the plane of the undead. *Angel Dog.*

Blonde 1:   *Angel Dog* . . .

Blonde 2:   Wow. *Angel Dog.*

Blonde 3:   I love it. I love it!

I roared with laughter. Roared. It took me nearly a minute to realize no one else was roaring with me. The penny finally dropped – they were being serious.

Well, I'm sorry, but this book isn't *Angel Dog*. There is a dog in it, later on, although she was far from an angel, as you shall see. I doubt this book will ever disappear in huge numbers from supermarket shelves, or that shoppers will scuffle over the last discounted copy in a frenzied Black Friday riot. But neither is it the Polynesian pan-generational epic I pitched all those years ago. It's something in the middle. Mid-range. Comfy. The sort of book that turns up to a meeting covered in mud and shit having not changed into something more appropriate.

Something a little more me.

It's October 2014. My family are gathered together at my parents' house in west Cornwall. Rain relentlessly spanks the windows. There is the grumble of a distant tractor. My dad, brother and sister are bunched up together on the sofa watching a marginal American sport on a marginal subscription channel. Mum is perched on the armrest, jabbing at her iPad with a stiff finger, ET-style, muttering 'Well, I never!' in a loop.

It's at this moment I decide to tell them about the memoir. It's important to do so, I think, because memories are prismatic. I have my recollections, but they may well be totally different from those of my family. I want to see if I can integrate our perspectives so we can all be happy with the end result.

Me:	Hey, everybody, listen – I'm writing a book.
David:	What?
Me:	I'm writing a book.

Mum:	What kind of a book?
Me:	Well, sort of an autobiography.
All:	Oh God . . .
Dad:	Who's it about?
Mum:	Bert!
Me:	Hilarious, Dad.
Michelle:	Do I have to be in it?
Me:	Well, yes. You've been in my life for thirty-eight years, so you feature pretty heavily . . .
David:	Don't you mention that incident with the honeydew. I was just a teenager . . .
Michelle:	Can't you just say you've only got one sibling?
Me:	Not really. It'd just be weird.
David:	I'm serious – it was just experimental.
Dad:	What kind of book is it?
Me:	Dad, I've just told you. It's a memoir.
Dad:	Who the bloody hell wants to read that?
Mum:	Bert! [*To me*] Will there be swearing in it?
Me:	I don't know. Maybe.
Mum:	I don't think you should swear in it. People will realize you're not classy.
Michelle:	Surely you could just not mention me?
Mum:	Will we come across as mental?
Dad:	You are mental!
Mum:	BERT!
Me:	I don't know. How do you want to come across?
Michelle:	I don't want to be in it.
Dad:	I'd like to be taller. Like, really, really tall. Can I be six foot five?
David:	Can I be incredibly handsome and not a Lego nerd?
Me:	All right . . .
David:	I want every girl to fancy me. Can you do that?

Mum: Will there be swearing?

Me: I said I don't know!

Mum: Well, I'd like it to be clean. I don't mind what you say, but keep it clean.

Dad: [*to the telly*] Hit it, you little shit! Oh for Christ's sake.

Mum: Bert!

And so, with that in mind – taking into consideration their thoughts and wishes – I started writing the memoir my family and I had agreed upon.

ONE

Croydon

Chapter One

My first memory of Dad was him approaching my cot. I must have been around two years old at the most. I remember this towering figure coming towards me, blocking out the light as he bent forward to pick me up. We're not known for being especially tall in our family, but Dad was the exception. He stood at just over six foot five high – a magnificent oak of a man – born, as he was, from countless generations that never got beyond thin and weedy saplings.

'Hello, pumpkin,' he whispered, gathering me tightly to his chest, before standing back upright and knocking his head, hard, on the light fitting.

'Goodness gracious me, that was painful!' he said, and then carried me down the stairs for breakfast.

I was three when my brother, David, came along – and from the get-go we realized he was headed on a single-track road marked ADONIS. Wherever we went, pensioners, young mums and kids alike would peer into his pram and exclaim, 'What a stunning boy! I've never seen a child like it! He's an angel!'

He was born cool and grew up cooler. While children his age played with Scalextric and Lego, David would be programming computers and dabbling in abstract painting. Girls worshipped him, of course, but he'd only known what it was to be beautiful, so he took it in his stride. At the age of nine he was signed to a modelling agency, after being spotted at the local shopping centre, and by the time he hit puberty he had become the face of a well-known luxury goods brand.

By sixteen, David had queues of women following him – meaning, unlike his peers, he had no need whatsoever to masturbate into large round fruit while fantasizing about the opposite sex. Sexual opportunities afforded themselves at every turn. His popularity with women was so overwhelming that it even affected our family time. I have to admit it was hard growing up alongside him – alongside such perfection – and I would go through phases of resentment. Why does *he* get all the girls? Why did *he* get the beautiful genes and not me?

Mum had always wanted another baby, but she was so busy with her high-flying job as obergruppenadviser at Deutsche Bank that it never happened. Sometimes, when we'd get together as a four, and Dad and David were larking around, she'd wistfully remark in my ear, 'Wouldn't it be nice if I'd had another girl – you know, so we could outgun the boys . . .'

Sometimes I too longed for a sister, but it was never to be. What would she have been like? Would she have been as poor at relationships as I was? I doubt it. Would she have had the same issues with eye bags, anxiety and sugar addiction? Of course not. She would have been a younger, better and brighter version of me. And then, as I thought of her, I was glad she wasn't real. Because having a sister as amazing as that would have been *seriously* infuriating.

I remember clearly the day David introduced us to his first serious girlfriend after years of playing the field. It was Christmas Eve. Dad was tending to the logs on the fire as the doorbell rang.

'Mind your head, Bert!' shouted Mum.

Too late. Dad stood back, and there was a loud crack as his skull made contact with the ceiling.

'Gosh! That hurt!' he exclaimed. 'If only I wasn't so ruddy tall all the time!'

He went to the door. Standing there was David with wife-to-be Lynne on his arm. They made the perfect couple. They had matching luggage and everything.

'Finally, another daughter!' cried Mum, one eye on dinner, the other on the progress of her global equity derivatives. 'Come on – give me a hand with these giblets!'

I watched as Dad and David sat down together. Each cast a shadow over the other. A marginal sport was playing on a marginal subscription channel.

'Gosh, I do wish this fellow would make a better job of scoring!' bellowed Dad, and we all laughed. The fire crackled and the room pulsed with warmth. I looked over at my family and . . . and . . .

. . . and I thought, *This is ridiculous*. Honestly. Let's just say it as it is. Dad, you're a little bit squat. David, you still like Lego and you're a forty-two-year-old father of two, and, Michelle, sorry, but you *do* exist and you're a part of this mental, mental family. Deal with it. Oh, and people swear, so – and I mean this in the nicest possible way, Mum – fuck you. I'm doing this book my way.

The Museum of Me

When I began writing this book, I went home to see if my mum had kept some of my old stuff. What I found was that she hadn't kept some of it. She had kept *all of it* – every bus ticket, stub, programme, letter, postcard and picture, every school report, essay, poem and painting – all filed. From the moment I was born to the moment I was able to have the confidence to turn round and say, 'Why is our house full of all this shit?'

It's fair to say, Mum's 'collecting' (hoarding) has become a problem. She's probably only one back copy of the *National Trust Magazine* away from being the subject of a Channel 4 documentary. Every trip home I try to help out by bringing a skip with me. I'm best friends with the regional managers of at least four civic amenity sites, and I can separate paper, plastic and glass quicker than anyone I know.

We realized things had got out of control when, whilst helping her with a recent house move, we discovered that she had washed, and packed, over a hundred margarine cartons and taken them with her.

Me: [*eating a Müller Light*] Mum, why do you need these?
Mum: To put things in.
Me: What things?
Mum: Just, you know . . . *things*.
Me: Do you think collecting tubs to put things in might be encouraging you to collect yet more things to put in them?

Mum: No. Yes. Maybe. [*Pause*] Have you finished with that yoghurt carton?

And so there is this museum – a museum of me. It's not a museum I'd pay to enter. Or one with artefacts of any interest – not even, in many cases, to the very person to whom they relate. The exhibits aren't pretty. They aren't even exhibited; they lie in countless large plastic tubs, stacked four feet high. Endless boxes full of bone-dry papers that hurt my fingers almost as much as they hurt my heart to go through. Because it is painful – it has been painful – to go back and see in such forensic detail and with such unimaginable clarity the person I was, trying to become the person I wanted to be.

Sometimes we don't want to be tethered to yesterday. It's nicer to forget. Maybe the gaps in our memory are there for a reason, evolutionary perhaps, to give us the space to grow, to get away from childishness or childish things. Or maybe it's so we have the chance to invent, or at least include, some magic in our yesterdays. Surely the consolation of getting older, of moving away from youth, is that we can shape our past to our fantasies. So, even if the present isn't going the way we want it, we can stand back and remember our earlier selves as exciting and funny and daring.

I don't have that luxury. I have it all laid out in front of me. No magic. No mystery. No possibility that I was ever fun or dynamic. The mundanity of me writ large in endless lever-arch files and black bin bags.

Sometimes, when searching, I have come across things which cut deep. An innocuous cardboard box with 'I love you' scribbled on it in the carefree scrawl of an old boyfriend. A sorry note from a little girl to her parents, a little girl who hadn't yet done anything to be sorry for. There were so many sorry notes in fact that nowadays, in arguments, when I'm being intractable and defensive, I wonder if I didn't use up all my apologies as a kid, leaving me nothing left to use in adulthood.

I started going through everything a few months ago in preparation for writing this. I became my own curator. I picked key pieces that I could display in this Museum of Me, arranged them and put them in a bag for safekeeping. The rest I stuffed into bin liners ready for recycling.

'Are these bags to go?' shouted my mum from the top of the stairs.

'Yep,' I shouted, idly, back.

Two days later my bag of treasures was no longer there.

It didn't take me long to realize that my mum had misunderstood me and taken the wrong bag. She had left countless sheaves of junk* and dumped the gems. If that doesn't sum up my family, I don't know what does. Good intentions – annoying outcomes.

Even though I hadn't seen any of it for nearly forty years, it felt like a bereavement – like something had been taken from me. It was good stuff. Funny stuff. Meaningful. I felt emotional and wobbly.

Mum, on discovering what she'd done, cried for two hours non-stop. 'I've ruined everything,' she bawled.

Me: No, you haven't. Besides, there's loads of other stuff. I can turn my attention to the remaining forty-two boxes . . .

Mum: I have! It's ruined! The book is ruined!

Me: No, it's not. I'm just going to have to . . . well, I'm now going to have to actually *write* it.

---

* Including a bad drawing of a wizard, a poem about corn on the cob and a series of pressed flowers Copydexed to pink cardboard.

In truth, she'd done me a favour. A memoir, after all, is as much about what you don't shine the light on as what you do. It's about judicious choices and edited picks. With that much primary and secondary source material, it would feel more like I was writing a biography than an autobiography. A biography of a shy person with limited social skills who collected pebbles and wrote bad poems and, bewilderingly, was obsessed with wearing kilts. That person was documented in so much detail, it didn't feel like me any more. I've outgrown me. I keep on outgrowing me.

Onwards . . .

If Mum makes herself feel safe by hoarding things, then Dad gets his sense of security from shedding them. For Mum the endless documents and pictures she keeps are like keys, keys which unlock emotional memories in extreme and dizzying detail. Dad's idea of hell is an emotional memory – for him life needs to be stripped bare of anything and everything extraneous. Dad experiences life through the prism of one thing – DATA.

Data is safe. Data does not lie. Data can be controlled. And that's why the world of patterns, information and numbers is the world my dad is happiest in.

Dad is basically the Matrix in human form. Every morning he wakes up, notes and logs the time of his waking, the atmospheric pressure on his barometer and the rainfall radar as indicated on the Met Office's website. Whereas I might be captivated by the skeins of pink in the heavens at dusk, he will be looking at his watch to check the exact moment the sun leaves the horizon. Whereas I'll be entranced by the sight of a wood-pecker boring into the ash tree in the garden, he'll be counting the exact number of pecks per minute.

It's not that Dad is emotionless. Quite the opposite. He is overwhelmed by emotion. He feels *too* much. And the thought of being overcome by sensation is so frightening that structures need to be put in place to stem and control the flow.

Ever since I was a child, I've watched Dad codify his surroundings, obsessing over numbers and patterns, using stats and facts as a way of self-soothing. Nailing his life down to a series of fixed points gives him a sense of calm. It's perhaps inevitable that his eldest responded by being rule averse, disinterested in boundaries and perpetually chaotic.

Since he first learned to write, Dad has kept a diary. He prefers a five-year diary as he doesn't need a great deal of space for his entries, which are, in essence, factual one-liners about events, climactic conditions and his children's height. When he turned seventy-five, he collected the data from the assembled diaries and boiled it all down into one single Mega-Journal. Finally, his life has been reduced to a series of clear, simple stats: 30 degrees, David born, Gerbil died, got cancer.

But more of that later.

I don't say all this to judge him; I say it (and he'd love this) as a matter of *fact*. I love him whatever. We all have our peccadilloes. But the saddest thing is it doesn't matter whether I say that I love him or not as he will never read this book. Why? Well, certainly not because he's unsupportive. I can't think of anyone who has allowed me to be myself more. No. The fact is, reading this would make him uncomfortable. Squeamish even. He doesn't know how I'm going to tell the story, how many surprises the pages might contain. There would be too much emotion, too many twists and turns; the journey would make him anxious. He prefers Science Fiction. He likes his stories comfortably displaced to another galaxy.*

So there you have it. My parents. I grew up with the Hoarder Indoors and Rain Man.

* To my great surprise and delight he has read this. His comment? Good, but a few spaceships would have livened it up no end.

When Two Became One

My parents met in Brockley, south London, on 4 June 1966 at a party organized by my mum's school friend Christine Cavanagh. It's at this point I'll let the lovebirds take over and tell their own story, romantic and heart-warming as it is. This is taken, verbatim, from a recording made of them in the summer of last year.

I have asked my parents to recall the night they met. Mum tilts her head upwards, picking tiny sensory jewels from the black sky of memory. Dad has stomped into the study and fetched his diary.

Dad: Why have I got 'poaching' written in my diary?

Mum: *Pochin*. Pochin was Christine's maiden name.

Dad: Oh, right. [*Spends the next minute fastidiously cancelling and amending the entry*]

Mum: Your dad arrived on a motorbike. He was very memorable. He was wearing an orange Bri-Nylon shirt and very tight synthetic slacks.

Silence.

Me: What was Mum wearing, Dad?

Dad: Clothes. And a very heavy fringe . . .

Mum: Well, it was actually a hairpiece. Trouble was, I was laughing so much –

Dad: [*muttering*] Drunk.

Mum:	– that it fell forward and got stuck there, low on my forehead, for the rest of the evening.
Dad:	What's the name of that character from *Planet of the Apes*?
Mum:	Anyhow, your father came over to chat –
Dad:	Cornelius. That's who she looked like.
Mum:	He came over and his opening line was 'Hello, I'm a misogynist.'
Me:	What?
Mum:	'Hello, I'm a misogynist.'

Dad roars with laughter.

Me:	Was that your chat-up line?
Dad:	Yep.
Me:	What, always?
Dad:	Yep.
Me:	And how often was it successful?
Dad:	Never.
Me:	Ever think of changing it?
Dad:	Nope.

Mum then embarks on an epic monologue, during which Dad closes his eyes and drifts off. After fifteen minutes of listening, I feel like I have drunk liquid morphine and every cell in my body is shutting down. I am now cutting to the end of her tangential mutterings to spare you, Dear Reader, the pain of the whole thing. Although I might release it as a download for people suffering from insomnia.

Mum:	Anyway, his shirt was vile, and it created static when we danced . . . then we sat and had a chat and things went on from there . . . and then he got up and said, 'Well I have to leave, my mum will have done breakfast.'

I am suddenly alert again. Something in that last sentence hinted at potential gossip and/or excitement.

Me: What? Why? Why did he say that? Was it morning when he left?

Mum: No. His mum used to put his breakfast out the night before. And he needed to get back for it.

Me: Right . . .

Dad: [*looking in his diary and suddenly bellowing*] Seventh of October 1967!

Mum: We got married, and we had our honeymoon in Majorca at the Hotel Bahia Club in Paguera.

A profound and awkward silence as they remember.

Me: So . . . Did you enjoy it?

Long pause.

Dad: It was certainly the best honeymoon I've had.

Opening Night

I was born on 22 September the following year at East Dulwich General Hospital – ironically in the same ward that my father ended up in fifteen years later after another one of his 'accidents'.*

Me: Was I premature?
Mum: Yes, you were a week early.
Dad: I'm still not ready for you.
Mum: You were very little and thin but very beautiful.
Dad: You were a red mess.
Mum: And then a yellow mess.
Dad: Jaundice.
Mum: And that awful acne . . .
Dad: Waxy head, that's what I remember.
Mum: You fed every three hours.
Dad: She still does – have you seen the size of her?
Mum: We had to get your weight up to five pounds before you could leave the hospital.

A slight pause for Mum to catch her breath.

Dad: [*reading*] One foot five inches.
Me: What?

* Dad is notoriously clumsy. Notable accidents include: falling out of the loft head first, severing his finger on a ham tin lid and leaping backwards into a greenhouse while playing catch.

Dad: That's how tall you were when you were born.

Me: What? You measured me? You measured me when I was born?

Dad: No, the hospital measured you. I didn't want to go anywhere near you.

At this point Dad buries his head in his stats book and produces a graph of my height and weight from birth right up to the age of twenty-two. At twenty-two I obviously found the strength to tell him that grown women don't tend to stand against an architrave and have their parents draw a pencil line above their heads. Again, he had nothing emotional or personal written down about that time, merely raw data. I'd been stripped to my essentials. Rationalized. Rendered. Made Statistic.

I understand it now – after all these years of raging I get it. The more he could associate me with mere facts, the more reassuringly distant I became. The less he had to engage with the idea of me being a living, breathing human being that he loved – that he might have to see hurt or ill or heartbroken. I wanted to say to him – I've always wanted to say to him – *There's nothing you can do, Dad. That's what life is. You can't just cherry-pick the nice bits and block your ears to the painful bits. Plus, in insulating yourself against the bad stuff, you miss so much of the good stuff. Don't you see?*

Mum had fallen suspiciously quiet. I always think something is seriously wrong if she goes without speaking for longer than thirty seconds.

Finally she punctured the silence. 'I think I've still got it.'
'What?'
'My diary from when you were born.'
What? You've got a diary as well. Oh God . . .
'I'll go hunt for it.'

'Mum, it's OK, really . . .'

She disappeared for some time. There was a scraping of boxes on the upstairs floor, then she reappeared brandishing a yellowing piece of paper.

It's rare that I'm lost for words, but this was one of those occasions. It turned out that my mum is *so* good at cataloguing, she even managed to keep an hour-by-hour account OF HER OWN LABOUR. You don't see that very often on *One Born Every Minute*.

The maternity unit of a busy London hospital. A fixed-rig camera looks down on a woman in the advanced stages of labour. There is the sound of medical equipment beeping.

Midwife: That's right, keep pushing!

The woman screams in agony.

Midwife: Come on, you can do it! Nearly there . . .
Woman: [*panting*] Please –
Midwife: Remember, push *down*.
Woman: Please, could you –
Midwife: Push *down*.
Woman: [*getting weaker*] Could you . . .
Husband: She's asking for something.
Woman: Please . . .

The husband goes over to her.

Woman: Please, my diary . . .
Husband: She needs her diary!

He rushes over to a bag in the corner of the delivery room and retrieves a small notebook. She lets out another bellow as the pain rises again. He hands the diary over; she opens it and starts writing furiously.

Midwife: I can see the head!
Woman: [*screaming*] What time is it?
Husband: It's 19.31.

She writes this down. Then screams again.

Midwife: Nearly there!
Woman: What's the name of this ward again?
Husband: Magenta Four.
Woman: Thanks.

She writes this down. One final, long wail of pain.

Midwife: There you are! You did it! It's a girl. It's a lovely little girl.
Woman: [*to husband, pen poised ready for the answer*] How would you describe the furnishings in here? Mustard? Taupe? Plain beige?

That's how stoical my mum is. A mere seven stone in weight, slap bang in the middle of labour pains, shoved in a cold bath and left there until nearly eight centimetres dilated – and she *still* manages to get in a diary entry. Screw you, Samuel Pepys, you lightweight. Try commentating on the Great Fire with a bowling ball pushing its way out your arse with just a little gas and air, and no man, woman or child to comfort you.

Here is Mum's entry.

21/9/69   6.00 pm mild backache
           10.30 pm bed but only
           slept till 2.00 pm Backache
           & tummy pains. Up again at
           30.0 & 4.00. Then back to bed

           4.45 - 8.00.
           Made tea for Mum. Then went
           into her bed. Bath.
           Got up for breakfast at 10.00
           went back to bed at 11.00 am.
           Got up for lunch at 1.00 approx
           But went back to bed at 2.00 —
           Pains more intense but not regular.
           2.30 Bilious attack
           3.30 ate orange
           4.00 Bilious attack
           Left to come up to London
           Arrived D.H.hospital 5.30 approx
           5.45 Waters broke while waiting
                in admissions

6.00 - 6.30 was palpated, shaved
+ had enema. Show of blood
— rush after enema. Frightened me.
Bath & then up to ward. Contraction
every 3 or 4 minutes.
Into Labour ward on F3.
Want to push (approx. 7.15)
Moved to Delivery room — can
push. Used gas & oxygen. All
very quick. Marvellous staff.
Baby born 7.50 pm 4 lbs 6½ozs
Stitches put in by Dr. Handler
about 8.45 pm. Then bed
bath & entered ward at 9.45
approx.

Detailed, isn't it? Except for the actual *baby* bit, you know, the *important* bit. That part, well – it's just 'Baby born.' Notice I don't even get an adjective. The staff do. The staff are 'marvellous'.

'Baby born.' Ha ha ha.

Imagine. I *lived* with that.

I still think my favourite bit is when she has a bilious attack at 2.30 p.m. and thinks the best thing to do is have an orange. My mum is allergic to oranges. Always has been, always will be. Yet she thought that moment, that specific moment, was the right one in which to play Russian roulette with her digestive system. Unsurprisingly she has another bilious attack an hour later.

Question, Mum. Would an anaphylactic decide to have a handful of cashews just before their baby was born?

No wonder my sister Michelle thought twice about being associated with us.

Kindergarten and Junior School

Here are the things I learned from playgroup:

- If you spend the whole of the lunch break cutting the heads off Barbie Dolls, you tend to be left alone by everyone for the rest of the afternoon.
- If you know Anthony, then you are part of the cool gang.
- If you are Anthony's girlfriend, YOU RULE THE WORLD.

Anthony owned that playgroup. So much so, he didn't even need a surname. Like all true leaders – Hannibal, Alexander the Great, Chico – a second, family name was superfluous.

The playgroup that Anthony presided over was brutal – feudal – like a toddler's version of *Game of Thrones*. Justice was swift and merciless. Get on the wrong side of Anthony and he would bite your face, drive a buggy into your knees or smash a Fisher-Price My First Medical Kit over your head. The day he did the latter was, coincidentally, the day I discovered irony.

I don't know why Anthony and I hit it off. Perhaps I was the much-needed moderate queen to his despotic king. Perhaps my pudding-bowl fringe screamed, 'I was put on this earth to be your henchman.' Perhaps he was just looking for someone happy to go around saying 'Sorry' after he'd battered and smacked his way around the group. I don't know. All I know is that he hated everyone else. But he loved me.

Anthony's modus operandi was to be the first to everything: every toy, every experience, every break-time snack. I remember the teachers once organized a tea party. A vast array of sandwiches and scones and cakes sat on a gingham tablecloth behind glass doors in a prescient sign of what awaited me in adulthood. No sooner had those glass doors opened than Anthony steamed in, elbowing everybody out of his way, whereupon he firmly pressed his dirty thumbs into every snack in sight. There wasn't an egg-and-cress bap without his DNA on it, nor a square of Nimble without his fingerprints embedded deep into the dough.

I looked on with a mixture of awe and dread. It was like watching a rogue Staffie cock his leg against the opulent *fruits de mer* display at Harrods Food Hall – half of me was appalled, the other half applauded the sheer, glorious chutzpah of it all.

Anthony's finest hour came when the playgroup's new slide arrived. We'd been promised this new toy for weeks, and there it was in all its magnificent wooden glory. His eyes burned as he saw it wheeled into place. I could hear the cogs of his brain whirring, trying to figure out how best to stamp his authority on his peers once and for all. The teachers moved the slide into its new home, and just as they stood back to admire their work Anthony launched himself at the steps for the inaugural descent. Before the teachers could so much as shout his name, he had made his way down the chute and was standing for applause at the bottom.

Immediately I knew something was wrong. Pure instinct. Like when a rabbit sits up, alert in a field, and knows it's being stalked. Something told me I didn't want to go down that slide any more, and so I let my friends jostle past me to the front of the queue. Sure enough a few seconds later there was a loud cry. We all crowded around the slide to find a poor girl called Melissa stranded midway down, legs akimbo, buttocks seemingly glued to the wood.

I shot a glance at Anthony. The front of his trousers was soaked through. He had wilfully, deliberately pissed himself all the way down the slide. One thing I did know: wet slide, no glide. Not so much a scorched earth as a damp chute policy. And very effective it was too. Nobody but Anthony ever went on it again.

I don't know what happened to Anthony. He disappeared from my life as forcefully as he'd arrived. Back then he was deemed a 'little character'; nowadays he'd go by the slightly longer label of 'attention deficit hyperactivity disordered, oppositionally defiant'. I imagine he's now either in a penthouse office at Canary Wharf running Europe's finances or drawing pictures with crayons using his feet in a rubber room somewhere in a secure facility. With Anthony it could have gone either way.

After playgroup, Mum and Dad decided to send me to the local Catholic school.

Dad: Ronnie Corbett's children were at that school with you.
Me: Is that pertinent?
Dad: No, it's name-dropping.

The school in question was a little convent outfit in Sanderstead, just where the concrete of Croydon met the manicured park life of Surrey suburb. There were trees and front lawns and everything felt neat and clean.

The most exciting thing that could possibly happen at our school (or indeed I imagine at *any* school) was someone cracking their head open on the playground. We'd heard about this – someone said, 'Nicholas fell and cracked his head open.' *Open*. We imagined a head split in two, with blood and brains spilling out of it, and sat around in gangs at break praying for it to happen until the sight of a wimple sent us rushing back to class.

The nuns were a terrifying bunch led by Head Horror Sister Mary Dorothy. Sister Mary was old-school strict with an old-school belief in right or wrong – and by old-school I mean MEDIEVAL. It was bad enough I was a brunette (mildly satanic) with short hair (sorcerer's overtones), but the crunch point came when she discovered I was also left-handed (aka the full Beelzebub). Every time I sat down to eat in the school hall I found myself surrounded by wimpled women telling me to swap my cutlery around. Nineteen seventies beefburgers were rigid offerings at the best of times, but try cutting into one with a weak right hand that has never used a knife before. My brain would hurt and my fingers ache, but every time I tried to swap the utensils back, the nuns would descend again until I became exhausted and confused and tearful.

I started getting skinny. I started resisting going to school of a morning and became paranoid at mealtimes, wondering why my parents didn't swoop on me when I picked up my knife and fork in my usual fashion. Finally, Mum managed to get the truth out of me. Dad went very quiet. You only ever worried about Dad when he went very quiet. The next day he went in and 'had a word' with Sister Mary Dorothy, which involved backing her against a wall and telling her to leave his daughter alone. Effectively, he went a bit Liam Neeson on her ass. It's easy to see why – ask my dad to splay his fingers, and two on each hand are battered out of shape courtesy of the ceaseless rectifying ministrations of the Brothers of Holy Joe's School for Boys in 1940s Beulah Hill.

The other thing the nuns loved to do was make you finish your food. Not because there were starving kids in the world – oh no, they didn't seem too concerned with all that. No, they simply wanted to see a five-year-old face down in cold tapioca or collapsed in a puddle of viscous, greasy gravy.

One day I got locked into a war of attrition with a starchy ball of Smash instant mashed potato, which had been delivered lovelessly from the clutches of an ice-cream scoop. It sat there, and so did I. Neither of us moved. Neither of us was going anywhere. Sister Mary Dorothy did her rounds of the hall, wordlessly peering at our plates and dismissing those lucky enough to have finished. I had not finished. As she walked by, I nonchalantly flicked a lump of potato off my fork, which landed, by accident rather than design, just feet in front of her.

She carried on, polished shoes clicking on the polished floor, until her toes hit the tattie slime.

The rest was pure poetry.

My classmates watched as the Bride of Christ skidded, feet outstretched, until the wall provided a brake. There was a crunching sound and then silence.

'Has she cracked her head open?' said Thomas, the kid next to me.

'Maybe.'

'I think she has. She's cracked her head! She's cracked her head!'

A ripple of excitement went down the table.

I quietly picked up my fork with my right hand and let a little smirk cross my face. If you're going to be treated like a devil, you might as well behave like one.

Lesson learned.

Pets

A girl in a psychedelic dress, sporting a pudding-bowl haircut, approaches her father. She looks like Damian from *The Omen*, if Damian were a girl and liked psychedelic dresses.* Her father is busy 'doing stamps'. No one in the family knows what 'doing stamps' means, but it seems to involve him spending a lot of time in the box room drinking whisky and sobbing.

Girl: Dad?
Dad: What is it?
Girl   Can I have a dog?
Dad: No.
Girl: Dad, pleeeeease.
Dad: I said no!
Girl: [*a single tear forming*] But why?
Dad: Because pets die and leave you despairing and alone. [*Pause*] Pets are pain, Susan.

There is a profound silence. The girl walks slowly away.

I was six years old.

Over a decade after I left home I discovered that my dad, as a boy, had owned a cat. He fed it raw fish every day, and it

* Don't believe that anyone could actually look like that? Turn to the next page.

slept on a rug at the foot of his bed every night. I don't know the name of the cat, because even seventy years on he finds it too sad to talk about. It is merely Cat. Nameless. Generic. All I know is that when Cat died, my dad never, ever got over it.

That's what pets were to him – unimaginable solace and unimaginable pain – in sparing us the latter, I guess it never crossed his mind he might have denied us the former.

I grew up in a nondescript road in a nondescript borough of London.

Croydon – twinned with Mordor.

It's less of a place, more of a punchline.

Croydon was like an airlock in the middle of the A23, a place neither one thing nor the other. It wasn't close enough to the city to feel like London proper, nor far enough away to feel like the bosom of green-belt Surrey. It was the poor relation of both town and country, mocked, maligned but with an enviable degree of office space. It was a place you went to get to somewhere else. It's all relative, of course. We'd come from Peckham, so it was paradise.

To give you an idea of what Croydon felt like . . . Every year there was a funfair on the Rotary Field. A sense of torpor hung in the air. The skinheads couldn't be arsed to spin the waltzer. Candy didn't floss. Bunting wouldn't flap in the breeze. Kids would risk injury standing under the swinging pirate ship in order to catch the coins as they dropped from upturned pockets. Every year we all queued religiously for the centrifuge ride. You know the one – it looks like a giant salad spinner in the sky. We queued and we queued and we queued. Why? Because word had got out that John Daniels' dad had detached his retina on that ride. That's the kind of place Croydon was in the 1980s. You joined a long queue of people waiting to spin themselves blind.

We lived on a wide road lined with silver birch trees, which held sway from my earliest memories right up to the time Michael Fish murdered them in 1987. A jumble of bungalows, 1930s semis and mid-century monstrosities lined the route like broken, wonky teeth. It must have all looked rather lovely once upon a time, when the suburbs were in bloom, but this was the 70s, and now concrete was king.

We moved there when I was barely nine months old, but I've seen photos of what our house looked like when my folks took possession of the keys. The outside was a dull cream, with coils of paint hanging from the bay windows like Hasidic curls. Green slate tiles, which resembled fish scales from a distance, decked the roof, and inside sagging ceilings held on to antique brass light fittings as if for dear life.

My parents set about getting rid of all that 'old stuff' as soon as possible – after all, it was the 1970s, and the phrase 'original features' was right up there with 'Baader-Meinhof Gang' and 'Vietnam War'. So out went all that junk and in came proper stuff – polystyrene ceiling tiles, neon strip lighting, endless miles of teak sideboards and a swirling Axminster carpet that gave you a window into what mild epilepsy might feel like.

Only one thing could make this concrete metropolis more perfect for a kid.

A dog.

Not even my dad's epic three-quarters-of-a-century grief was going to stop me in my mission to get a hound. So I wore my parents down with the most toxic weapon in my arsenal. My personality.

I tried again.

29 March 1976

A girl in a tartan kilt and thick tights with a pudding-bowl haircut approaches her mother. She looks like a Scottish version of Damian from *The Omen*.

Girl: Mum, can I have a dog?
Mum: No.

Girl: Mum, pleeeeeeease.

Mum: I said no.

Girl: [*plug of snot forming in nostril*] But why?

Mum: Because . . .

Girl: But why?

If my dad's reason for not having pets is that they will die and make you sad, then my mum's excuses are way more comprehensive . . .

Mum: Well, for starters, they're dirty. They're unpredictable. They transmit diseases. They can give you asthma, hives, ringworm, roundworm, heartworm, tapeworm –

I am going to stop her in her tracks because that list goes on and on. What you need to know about my mum right now is this: she is a weapons-grade catastrophizer.* That is to say, she's a professional mountain-maker when only a molehill is called for. Give her an inch, she'll panic about running the mile. OK, let's return to the list.

Mum: – hookworm, toxocariasis, campylobacter, Lyme disease, scabies . . . oh . . .

Here it comes – the Big One.

Mum: . . . and rabies.

---

* Me: Mum? How many catastrophizers does it take to change a lightbulb?

   Mum: Change it? Are you out of your mind, Susan? You need a qualified electrician to do that. Sandra Harvey tried that and she was in hospital for a week.

Yep, just to reinforce the point, she'd dropped the R-bomb. Anyone who was a child during the 1970s understands the knee-jerk horror created by the mere mention of rabies. We grew up watching endless public service announcements – the whole of my childhood in fact felt like one long cautionary tale voiced by Donald Pleasance dressed in a Grim Reaper outfit. Many of these 'Charlie Says' information films were specifically about the dangers of slathering wild dogs (usually from France, of course), which could, at any time, cross the Channel and bite us into insanity.

The rabies thing worked. It was a while until I asked about dogs again.

My mum actually liked dogs. When she was little, her parents had bought her a poodle called Tracy, who turned out to be the only hypo-allergenic thing to have come out of the 1960s. After Tracy shuffled off her many mortal coils, Mum's folks invested in a series of ever-larger beasts, culminating in Dusty and Clyde – two vast and menacing Alsatians that looked like they'd run straight from Berchtesgaden. I was four years old when I first clapped eyes on them and was fascinated by Dusty in particular, especially when she was feeding. There was something about her powerful jaws as she crunched through lamb bones that intrigued me. So I decided to take a closer look. One dinnertime, as her bowl was put down, I decided to saunter over and get a worm's-eye view of her mouth in motion.

As my mum entered the kitchen, she was greeted by the sight of her four-year-old daughter lying on the floor, back of her head in the dog bowl, with Dusty's vast teeth clamped either side of her face.

Mum: [*suddenly very quiet*] Susan, what are you doing?

Me: I can see inside!

Mum: There's a good girl, Dusty, good girl. [*Trying to prise the dog's jaws apart*]

Me: It's dark. And it smells weird. Where does the food go?

Mum: [*sound of growling*] Easy now, easy now.

Me: [*pressure in my head growing*] My ears feel bursty, Mummy.

A pop as my head is released. There is a moment of calm, followed by the time-honoured Ann Perkins battle cry.

Mum: Bert! Get the Dettol!

As far as my mum is concerned, there isn't a single situation that can't be cured by either a.) a bath in Dettol or b.) gargling with TCP. Her anxiety is constant. Oftentimes I'll come home and she will have left a message on the answerphone like this one, which is taken, verbatim, from a recording in 2011.

'Hi. Just to let you know that I've heard from Jean about a new Yardie scam in London. They flash their headlights at you, and if you flash yours back, they'll steal your car and kill you. Thought you should know. Oh, it's Mum, by the way.'

Recently, while visiting them in Cornwall, I chucked a handful of dog biscuits on the lawn for my pet hound to sniff out. Mum immediately starting fretting.

Mum: Will they sprout?

Me: What?

Mum: Only your father and I have spent ages on that grass.

Me: Mum, they're dog biscuits.

Mum: Yes, but will they sprout?

Me: Yes, Mum, they'll grow into kibble trees, with pelletized dog-food fruit that will drop onto your lawn all summer.

There is no situation, however banal, that my mum can't infuse with dread. To read about a promotional credit card offer is to have it completed, sent off, card received, maxed to the limit and thence be whisked to debtors' prison. During the anthrax scare of 2001 she opened all her mail wearing Marigolds. One day, on returning home to visit, I found her bent over the steps to the front door, daubing the edges with luminous white paint.

'What are you *doing*?'

'These steps are a trip hazard!' she replied.

'What? Suddenly? Since last week?'

'Yes. Your dad's not getting any younger, you know.'

'He's *fifty-five*!'

'Yes, he's fifty-five *now*,' she replied – and carried on painting.

And yet, for all her anxiety, she didn't see the threat that lurked just outside her home. Despite all the consternation about poisoned Royal Mail packages and credit card debt, my mum seemed oblivious to the fact that she and Dad had chosen to buy a house *right next to* an electricity substation – a brick bunker hung with daisy chains of barbed wire and stock-proof fencing. There was even a massive sign, replete with skull and crossbones that said:

WARNING!
KEEP OUT!

But no. She was so concerned with what was happening within a six-foot radius of herself, she never even noticed I was living my entire childhood within sight of a sign reading:

DANGER OF DEATH

And thank goodness, because what I discovered for myself is that when the DANGER OF DEATH is permanently on your doorstep, it takes an awful lot to freak you out from further afield. I was fearless.

Pinky and Perky

A couple of years later my parents relented and got us two gerbils. Even though I was not the sharpest tack in the box, I was aware that the furry sausages shitting in the cage in front of me were not the Dalmatians I had asked for. My mum christened them Pinky and Perky because apparently (as I was duly informed) Christopher and Reeve were not appropriate pet names.

Never owned gerbils? Want to know a little more? At this point I defer to world-renowned gerbil expert Susan Elizabeth Perkins, aged seven. I have asked for the author's permission in publishing these extracts . . .

WHAT IS A

GERBIL?

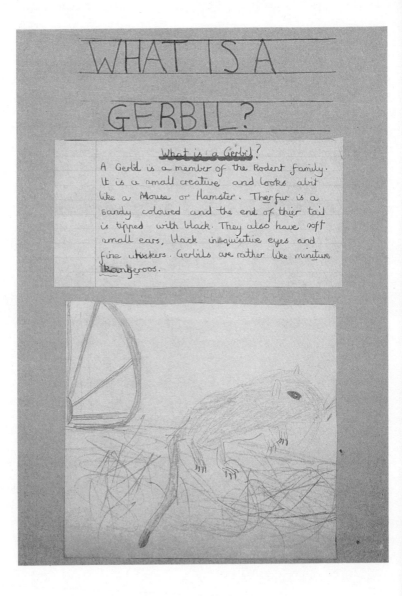

What is a Gerbil?

A Gerbil is a member of the Rodent family. It is a small creature and looks abit like a Mouse or Hamster. Their fur is a sandy coloured and the end of their tail is tipped with black. They also have soft small ears, black inquisitive eyes and fine whiskers. Gerbils are rather like miniture Kangeroos.

*BREEDING.

Baby Gerbils.

Baby Gerbils look more like pink sausages than Gerbils at all. When they are born they are hairless and blind. The usual number of Gerbils born is about 5 though the female can have 1-10 babies in a litter.

When the Gerbils are born the Mother is always alert. If someone came in she would dart to the nest to cover them. She also is very aware of what her babies are doing and if one strays out she will pick him up by the scruff of its neck and gently puts it back.

The babys open thier eyes in about 16-20 days and the fur starts to appear at about 10-12 days My Gerbils have had 27 children.

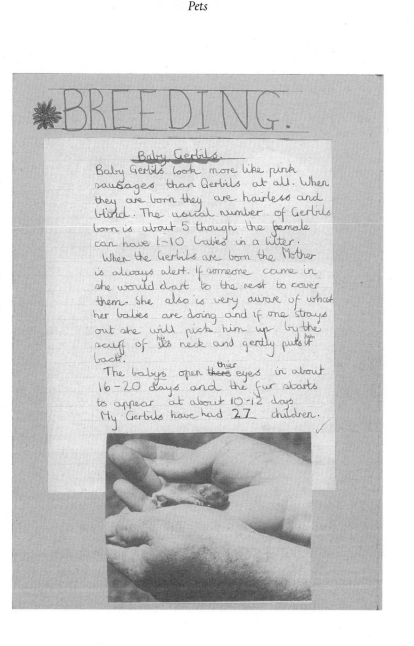

Now, my rule of thumb when it comes to choosing a pet is simply this: am I ever going to see it? In the case of the gerbils, the answer was clearly NO. Gerbils are nocturnal. And I, at the age of seven, was not. (Unless I'd been on a Robinson's orange squash binge, in which case this little soldier was going on a four-eyed 24/7 rampage.)

Our incompatible sleeping regimes meant I probably only spent about twenty minutes of quality time with our pets in just under four years. I say quality time; I mean grabbing them from their slumber and squeezing their back ends till their eyes bulged. The gerbils' main hobbies were eating a plastic wheel and defecating in a nest, both of which they appeared to excel at. I say 'appeared' – I have no idea, since everything they did was performed in the dead of night when I was out for the count.

In fact, the only time I ever saw my gerbil do anything, was when she ate one of her babies after my brother bombed down the stairs while giving a spectacularly rousing version of the *Batman* theme tune. This act of casual infanticide was the only thing I witnessed my pet doing in all the four years of its life. I was distraught. I was disturbed. But mainly I was confused.

Me: But why? Why did it do that?
Mum: Well, Susan, the mummy was protecting her babies.
Me: What? By EATING them?
Mum: [*leaden pause*] Yes.

I'm forty-five years old now, and I still can't see the logic in that. It's like worrying that your child might get bullied at school, so beating them to death to protect them.

They've got a lot to learn about motherly love, gerbils. Even now I can't listen to the opening strains of the *Batman* theme without thinking of that fat infanticidal mamma licking her lips in a now empty cage.

She may have been a slouch when it came to childcare, but Perky was certainly game in the procreation stakes. My mum had made it clear to Helen Banks' parents that she wanted two of the same sex. And yet, just a few months after taking receipt of them, in a miracle of same-sex breeding, six babies were born. And then another five. Then six again. Then seven.

Always one to turn tragedy into profit, I sold the babies to the local pet shop for sixty pence a pop. What began with a pair of nocturnal siblings, ended in a thriving cottage industry. Every month was like Christmas. I'd come down the stairs to find a writhing mass of pink four-legged sausages, like recently severed still-twitching fingers.

Once, a tiny baby escaped and made a bid for freedom behind the piano. We hunted high and low and finally had to assume it was dead. We lit a candle, said prayers – I may have even made a cross out of lollypop sticks. Those who say Catholicism can be easily sloughed off have never seen a seven-year-old give full burial rites to what basically amounts to a posh mouse. Two weeks later it turned up, alive and well, behind the sofa, where it had grown fat on a diet of discarded Marmite sandwiches and fluoride tablets. It was fat, feral and happy – with a set of gnashers more gleaming than Donny Osmond's. When I handed it over to the pet shop, I couldn't help but think they'd got a bargain.

My lack of interaction with them notwithstanding, when Pinky and Perky died in quick succession, I grieved like a drama-school Medea. Not only had I grown to love them, I had made a total of £23.40 out of them in a mere three years. Their death brought not only emotional pain, but my own personal credit crunch.

Dad knelt in the garden, Farah action slack stretched against beefy thigh, flicking the rigored corpses into an ice cream tub and thence into a hole in the garden.

'See, I told you,' he said, fixing his beady blue eyes on me. '*Pain.*'

Later the postman arrived and seemed to pay an awful lot of attention to Dad's frantic digging.

Mum: It was the time of the torso murders, so it looked very suspicious.

Me: What kind of torso could fit into a one-litre tub of Wall's non-dairy solids ice cream?

Mum: Oh, you'd be surprised. They can be very devious, these serial killers . . .

After Pinky and Perky we went through a period of what can only be described as pet surrogacy. Here are the creatures that passed through our doors.

Rollo the budgie

Dad was obsessed with Rollo the budgie and used to spend hours every day training him to say 'You bastard'. However, Rollo did not *want* to say 'You bastard' and therefore remained mute for the entire period of his stay. The next, and last, time Rollo came to stay with us, Dad renewed his efforts – staying up late into the night repeating the same phrase over and over and over again. Still nothing.

Rollo's owners came to collect him the next day. As his cage crossed the threshold, I heard Rollo mutter something. I couldn't be sure, but it sounded an awful lot like 'Thank fuck for that.'

Tasha/Kara

Kara, like her sister Tasha before her, was a Samoyed, a bright white husky as gormless as she was cute. And she was very, very cute. She belonged to our beloved family friends the Szilagyis, and we'd look after her when they went on their summer holidays. To say Kara shed fur was an understatement – she'd drop hairballs the size of fairground candyfloss wherever she went. Her finest hour came following a long walk after she had been put in the back of the car. Suddenly she caught sight of a squirrel and leaped straight through the back windscreen, leaving it in shards behind her. She didn't even feel it. Told you, gormless.

Unnamed hamster

I don't remember this creature's name – just his testicles. That's me for you. He arrived one autumn, and it became immediately clear the poor thing had a serious case of elephantiasis of the gonads. He looked like two beanbags attached to a pipe cleaner. We spent a few weeks watching him gamely lug his junk from one end of the lounge to the other, until his owners came back from a fortnight in Magaluf and our fun was over.

Polly the cat

Polly, or Pog as we called her, was our neighbours' cat – but as with most cats the concept of home was a movable feast. She used to occasionally pop round for some chicken and a cuddle, but she decided to come and live with us full time in the winter of 1999. She made her home on my dad's stomach as he lay sleeping on the downstairs couch. His insomnia had become increasingly bad, and he'd set up camp in the lounge so as not to disturb Mum.

Shortly after Pog started making pilgrimages to his tummy, he was diagnosed with colon cancer. There were operations which cut his already scarred belly into ribbons. Then there were the ridges of incisional hernias which followed. During this time Pog seemed to understand she shouldn't sleep *on* him, so lay beside him, purring like a pair of bagpipes cranking into life – a contented wheeze that was the soundtrack to his long road to recovery. After the hernias there were more ops. Radiotherapy. A year of chemo delivered through a Hickman line into his heart. She purred while his nails went black and fell out, while he bloated with steroids, as he crunched endless mints to get the metal taste from his mouth. She purred through the whole damn thing.

The Christmas after Dad got the all clear, Mum took a whopping seven-kilo turkey out of the chest freezer and stood it in a large bucket to defrost. We went out en masse to do some last-minute shopping and returned to find Pog in a state of some distress, dragging the bird around the floor, her fangs fused to the frozen meat. We didn't shout at her; Mum merely got out the electric carving knife, hacked off the entire breast that she'd punctured, popped it in the microwave and gave it to her to finish at her leisure.

A few weeks later Pog took herself off to die. We never got the chance to thank her, or to let her know that any one of us would have happily lain next to her, like she did with Dad, in her hour of need.

ᗒᗕ

I did finally got the dog I'd always wanted. At the age of thirty-one. It turns out that Dad was right – animals are pain.

But what a joyous, joyous pain.

Nineteen

Describing how sound recording equipment worked in the 1980s to a teenager today is like a *Homo habilis* explaining how he used to slap mammoths to death to the *Homo erectus* who has just invented the spear. Even as you describe the process, you feel as obsolete in the world as the technology you're describing.

Well, kids, in the olden days, if you wanted to listen to music and most importantly find out what was number one, you had to wait until Thursday nights and *Top of the Pops*. For those too young to remember, *Top of the Pops* was a documentary about a group of predatory paedophiles set against a backdrop of disco music and early electronica.

My brother received a Prince cassette deck for Christmas in 1985 and immediately set about taping every *TOTP* he could. To do this, you had to get your recorder, depress the Play and Record buttons together and hold the machine directly against the TV speaker for the duration of the programme. The main problem with this method was that not only did it record everything on the television, but everything that went on in the background too.

What strikes me, listening back to these tapes, is not the quality of the music, but the relentlessness of my family's pesterings, particularly my mother, who made a beeline for us any time *TOTP* was on. Partly out of interest, partly out of an instinctive feeling that there was something not quite right with the presenters.

Transcript of tape recording made 28 February 1985
featuring Paul Hardcastle's '19'

Narrator: In 1965 Vietnam seemed like just another foreign war. But it wasn't. It was different in many ways – and so were those who did the fighting. In World War II, the average age of the combat soldier was twenty-six.
             In Vietnam he was nineteen.
             In-in-in-in-in-in-in in Vietnam he was nineteen. [*Repeat*]

Mum: [*shouting from nearby room*] David!

Narrator: The shooting and fighting of the past two weeks continued today twenty-five miles west of Saigon.

Mum: David, are those your trousers in the bathroom?

Soldier: I really wasn't sure what was going on.

Narrator: Ni-ni-ni-ni-nineteen, ni-nineteen, ni-nineteen, nineteen.

David: Mum, shut up – I'm taping!

Narrator: In Vietnam the combat soldier typically served a twelve-month tour of duty, but was exposed to hostile fire almost every day.

Mum: Can you please come and pick your trousers off the bathroom floor?

Narrator: Ni-ni-ni-ni-ni-ni-ni-ni-ni-ni-ni-ni-ni-

Singers: Nineteen!

Narrator: Ni-ni-ni-ni-ni-ni-ni-ni-ni-ni-ni-ni-ni-

Singers: Nineteen!

Mum: They're a trip hazard, and you know what will happen if your dad gets his foot caught in them.

Narrator: Ni-ni-ni-ni-ni-ni-ni-ni-ni-ni-ni-ni-ni-

Singers: Nineteen!

Narrator: In Saigon a US military spokesman said today more than seven hundred enemy troops were killed last week in that sensitive border area. Throughout all of South Vietnam the enemy lost a total of 2,689 soldiers.

Mum:	He could put a toe into the gusset and fall. You know how clumsy he is.
Singers:	All those who remember the war They won't forget what they've seen Destruction of men in their prime Whose average was nineteen.
Mum:	David! Are you listening?
Singers:	De-de-de-de-de-de-de-de-destruction.
Mum:	This isn't a hotel.
Singers:	De-de-de-de-de-de-de-de-destruction.
Mum:	I'm not a chambermaid, you know. You're thirteen years old . . .
David:	Mum!
Narrator:	According to a Veterans' Administration study, half of the Vietnam combat veterans suffered from what psychiatrists call post-traumatic stress disorder. Many vets complain of alienation, rage or guilt. And some succumb to suicidal thoughts.
Mum:	You're big enough to bend down and pick up your own trousers, aren't you?
David:	Mum. SHUT UP!
Narrator:	Eight to ten years after coming home almost eight hundred thousand men are still fighting the Vietnam War.
Mum:	Don't you talk to me like that! You're not too old for a wallop, you know . . .
Singers:	De-de-de-de-de-de-de-destruction. De-de-de-de-de-de-de-destruction.
Mum:	I'm coming down. I'm leaving your trousers for you to deal with. Bert!
Narrator:	None of them received a hero's welcome.
Singers:	Ni-neteen.
Narrator:	Saigon Saigon Sa-Sa-Sa-Sa-Saigon Saigon.

Spectacles

Singers:	Ni-neteen.
Soldier:	I really wasn't sure what was going on. [*Repeat*]
Dad:	What now, Ann?
Mum:	There's a trip hazard in the bathroom! What on earth are you listening to, David?
Narrator:	Ni-ni-ni-ni-ni-ni-ni-ni-nineteen.
Mum:	Is there something wrong with the sound or does that man have a stammer?
Narrator:	Vietnam Sa-Sa-Saigon Vietnam Sa-Sa-Saigon.
Mum:	[*sound of heavy footsteps coming into the room*] And that's enough of that.

Tape ends.

Bitten

Everyone's first, and sometimes last, experience of acting is the school Nativity play. Remember the part you played? It's pretty easy to recall, isn't it, seeing as the cast of characters has remained unchanged for over two thousand years. Take a guess at what I played.

You: How about Mary and Joseph?

Me: Oh, don't be silly.

You: Little Baby Jesus?

Me: Per-lease.

You: The three shepherds around the manger?

Me: Nope, not even close.

You: [*getting exasperated*] The Three Kings who came from the east, bringing gold, frankincense and myrrh?

Me: Still wrong . . .

You: One of the angels?

Me: Now you're just taking the piss. Come on! There's only one character left . . . Yes?

You: Sorry, I've no idea.

Me: The fox! Yeah, you remember! The fox! You know, the fox. The fox at the Nativity? Come on, you must remember. Just to the left of the crib. The fox. You know – *the fox*.

Yes, that's who I played. A fox. I was the imaginary vermin that might have bitten the boy child Jesus and given him rabies *had I existed*. Though God only knows, had I been allowed to extend my role into biting the Saviour, I might just have done it, such was my frustration at the pitiful nature of my role.

A year later, after much jostling I graduated to fourth shepherd. Out of three. I didn't care; I got to wear a tea towel with a bit of old rope wrapped around it. I was living the dream.

Finally – after frantic lobbying bordering on stalking – I got the big one. An angel. Once again I rocked the Damian fringe, which made me look, in retrospect, less Right Hand of God and more Left Armpit of Satan.

It's no wonder I didn't get plum roles or perfect casting opportunities: I was freakishly pale and perpetually odd. Added to which, I was terribly shy with a mild stammer, and I couldn't look anyone in the eye. I know – fun, eh? Don't you want to invite the young me to *all* of your parties?!

So there I was, a weird conflicted kid, split down the middle, as riven as a floor tile. Desperate to be at the centre of it all but too afraid to do anything but loiter on the margins. A friend once described me as 'backing into the limelight', which is about the most accurate description of me I can imagine hearing.

At the edge of the school playing field, where grass met path, there was a run-down shed which went by the genteel description of 'the Pavilion'. The name conjures a village green – young men with oiled moustaches and pressed flannels endlessly rushing at one another, the soprano hurrahs of the assembled wives, the *chink* of bone china as the sun sets on Empire.

Our pavilion, however, amounted to a single cold room – no heating – with a desk at one end and a few chairs at the other.

At that desk, one day a week, sat Ms Carole Schroder, manicured and perfect, the sort of character you find in a Roald
Dahl novel – suspiciously prim at first but who turns out to
unexpectedly save the day.

I walked into that room a gibbering wreck. Week after
week I was encouraged to stand up and read out painful,
faltering renditions of Shakespeare, Wendy Cope and Pam
Ayres. I began to learn about breathing. Cadences. Intonation.
I began to relax. My voice became less staccato. I raised my
head and looked out at the world. A few years later I walked
out of that room able to speak clearly. Fluently. Finally, the
voice coming out of my mouth matched the chattering inside
my head.

Ms Schroder gave me the gift of speech.

And in doing so she created a monster.

In the early spring of 1983 the school production was
announced, something modest that would befit our tiny little
educational establishment in south London –

The Hobbit.

When J.R.R. Tolkien wrote his fantasy dystopian master-
piece, I believe he knew, deep down, in the back of his mind it
could only *truly* be realized by a gang of thirteen-year-olds. I
also feel *The Hobbit* was a particularly appropriate choice for
a single-sex girls' school, since there are just *so many* women's
parts in the book.

It became clear early on in rehearsals that we were all merely
pawns in a much larger game, namely fulfilling the hitherto

failed ambitions of a litany of English and drama teachers that had gone before us. Ambitious simply wasn't the word. Ridiculous, however, comes close.

Now I was able to speak properly, I had hoped for a starring role, a Gandalf or a Samwise Gamgee, but, as always, I ended up with something derisory – in this case third dwarf from the left. I was incandescent. This was, remember, WAY before Peter Dinklage as Tyrion Lannister made smaller folk sexy. In 1983 they were just, well, small.

I was Oin, brother of Gloin, distant cousin of Thorin Oakenshield (if you're interested). I had read the book and noted that they were northern dwarves, so gave my character a rich Yorkshire twang, based on a guy I'd seen birthing a calf in *All Creatures Great and Small*.

My line, and it was JUST ONE LINE, was:

'Never any sun.'

As parts go, it was pretty weak, though I fared better than my friend Sarah Ebenezer, who played a sheep. Now I don't especially remember sheep in Tolkien – though I'm sure some media student will have done a meta-critical study of ungulates in the Shire and will let me know otherwise. Having said that, I don't remember foxes in the Christmas story, and this casting came from the same imaginative source. Sarah's role, as the unnamed grass-muncher of the piece, was to wear a zero-visibility wire-mesh animal head festooned with cotton wool and make it through 'the forest' without shattering her coccyx. Crucially, she managed this for only two out of the three performances.

There were several problems with the show from the outset, not least my costume – a millefeuille of heavy woollens, with hessian pedal pushers that rode dangerously high up my dwarfish arse crack. Added to which my make-up made speaking virtually impossible. I say, make-up; it was essentially orange panstick and a beard.

Yes, a beard.

This was basically wire wool fashioned into Brian Blessed-style face-fuzz and glued to my chin with spirit gum. For those not used to spirit gum, let me illuminate – it's an industrial resinous adhesive with a high alcohol content. It's a solvent. My dwarf was about to become a glue sniffer.

So . . . to the show. My job was simply to say my line, then crouch down and hold a piece of cardboard battlement next to a load of other dwarves holding battlements. Together we formed a vast, yet ultimately recyclable, wall designed to withstand an orc invasion. And, indeed, the sight of a line of schoolgirls about to hit puberty would have been enough to repel *all* marauders.

Finally, after what seemed an age of crouching and listening to other people mumbling through facial hair, it was my turn. I was baking hot, mouth dry and cracked, and feeling woozy from the glue fumes. I got up to speak and immediately wanted to vomit.

'There's never any t'sun!' I roared in a broad, generically northern burr. Silence. The silence I now identify with so many of my subsequent performances.

I waited. Nothing. I waited a little longer. Sadly, it seemed the udders of appreciation were dry.

I sank back down behind the cardboard battlements and once again felt the thick material of my costume chafing my Middle Earth.

'What the massive fuck was that?' hissed my friend Karen Flanders – also in full beard.

'What do you mean?'

'You're increasing your part!'

'What are you talking about?'

'You're supposed to say, "Never any sun," said a goblin who may or may not have been Helen Renwick.

'You said, "*There's* never any sun,"' spat Karen.

'So *what*?!'

'That's a 25 per cent increase!'

'And what's your point?'

'Actually, that's a 33 per cent increase,' said a nearby elf, helpfully.

'SHUT UP!' yelled the hobbit to my left. 'And hold that battlement straight, you twats.'

'Don't call me a twat,' said Karen.

'You *are* a twat,' I ventured, cleverly.

And so it went on.

As the Battle of the Five Armies raged above us, a battle of our own was developing behind that cardboard wall, which was now shaking with a mixture of hysteria and righteous rage.

'Some of us are holding our fortifications still,' said a smug little dwarf further down the line.

'Good for you! GOOD FOR YOU!' I responded.

'Your wall is wobbly.'

'Well, so is your goatee!'

'At least it's not real, like yours,' said Karen, still fuming.

I can't remember who won that day, but we can safely say it was not a victory for theatre.

That production stayed with me for a very long time – or at least the beard did. It took nearly three weeks to remove it completely, despite the best ministrations of my mum. Her medicine cabinet had been stocked with weapons-grade exfoliants in preparation for its removal, but that glue was stubborn stuff. For weeks afterwards my jawline was mottled with reactive red lumps and residual grey wisps. I looked like a pensioner with PCOS. In the end Mum went back to basics.

'Bert! Get the Dettol!'

Subsequently, I have watched the Peter Jackson films. I liked them. Although for me they will never have the rich dramatic resonance, the dizzying emotional range of that glorious, definitive 1983 stage adaptation.

The next year at school we did *Finnegan's Wake*.*

After *The Hobbit* I graduated to something a little simpler – *Peer Gynt*, a five-act play in verse by Norwegian dramatist Henrik Ibsen. I played Peer's mum, Ase, an ageing peasant. If that wasn't already way beyond my range, this particular production was set, for reasons still unknown to me, in Northern Ireland. For three and a half hours the cast roared at one another like kids doing an impression of an adult doing an impression of the Reverend Ian Paisley.

My dad, under duress, came to the opening night and promptly fell asleep. Mum woke him every hour or so – 'to avoid him getting pressure sores' – whereupon he'd bellow, so the whole auditorium could hear, 'Bloody hell – is it *still going?*'

Some two hours into the play my character met her tragic end. My sister, eight at the time, was the only one of my family remotely moved by my death scene. As I extravagantly wheezed my way into the afterlife (screw you, Karen Flanders) Michelle shouted out from the audience, 'Daddy! Susan's dead!'

* This is a lie. We did Homer's *The Odyssey*.

Dad woke in an instant.

'Thank God. Does that mean we can we go now, Ann?'

I learned two things from this experience. Firstly, I wasn't cut out to be a proper actor. Secondly, when your co-star, a seventeen-year-old boy, says he wants to drive you to the woods for a walk, he doesn't really mean a *walk*.

Next on the list, after Tolkien and Ibsen, came Bizet's *Carmen*, a four-act tragic opera with full orchestra and vast cast. We didn't have a full orchestra; we had our brilliant music teacher Lora on an old out-of-tune piano. We didn't have a vast cast, so we joined forces with the neighbouring boys' school (who also didn't have an orchestra).

Of course, it didn't matter that there was no band. We weren't doing it for that. We were in the show because we were going to meet *boys*. Real, actual *boys*. Essentially this production was a 1980s Tinder, with arias.

The show was the passion project of a man called Roland, an unspeakably glamorous Italian teacher with olive skin and slicked-back hair. I imagine he wore pomade. Even though I have no idea what pomade was or is, it's exactly the type of unguent he would have smeared himself with. Rowland had all the zeal of Alec Guinness's character in *The Bridge on the River Kwai* – creating a doomed edifice to reflect his own inner glory, dragging a pack of disinterested kids with him. It didn't matter to Roland that none of us could really sing or play an instrument or speak French. It didn't matter. What mattered was that we gave it a go – and that was enough.

The boys and girls rehearsed separately for the first few weeks. We girls were mainly playing prostitutes, if memory serves – although we decided, tacitly, that we would play these prostitutes as kids who had Latin lessons, wore uniforms and were terrified of touching boys. I like to think it was a novel and refreshing take on the classic trope. If I thought *we* seemed uncomfortable, it was nothing in comparison to the lads. Instead of playing football, they found themselves being squeezed into gold bolero jackets, mouthing some homoerotic badinage about smuggling.

A fortnight before the show the two schools came together for rehearsals. The boys flooded into the school hall, and we gasped and giggled as their energies met ours. Lora thumped away at the piano, and Roland barked things in Italian, like 'Staccato' or 'Lento, lento'. We had no idea what he was talking about but were surfing a sea of hormones, so details like that didn't bother us.

And then *he* walked in. Late. Scruffy. Laughing.

Rob.

It was love at first sight – at least for me. Now I look back on it, he didn't so much as glance in my general direction, so it's fair to say Cupid didn't strike us with his arrow at the same time. Maybe the arrow went through me and clipped him a bit as it exited – collateral damage – so it took a while for him to notice I even existed. Who knows? Love is strange, and all you can do is go where it takes you with a modicum of grace and gratitude.

Rob was like Tom Cruise, only visible without an electron microscope. He had an unruly mop of black hair and stooped slightly, the way that tall men do when they are kind and self-aware enough to realize they are taking up too much space.

Our relationship proceeded like most other relationships do when you're that age. We met in car parks and drank cider. We sat for hours until our sciatics thrummed with cold, chatting and snogging. We broke up at parties after litres of Southern Comfort. We got back together after more Southern Comfort and woke together on floors, wrapped around each other, forgetting that there'd ever been a cross word. We dragged family and friends into dramas that burned themselves to nothing in a heartbeat. Yet it worked. It worked for over five years. I had no idea why.

In my last year of college we drifted apart into sharper versions of ourselves. Rob went away to Florida to work. I was supposed to go out and visit in the holidays, but the night before I was due to fly he called me and said he didn't want me there. He wouldn't say why. He sounded small. Far away. Much further than the 4,594 miles that lay between us.

I flew out anyway.

For the first night we were close. Intimate. The next day he seemed choked, like something invisible had him by the throat. On the third day he cried and then fell into a silence. On the fourth day he started talking. And talking. And talking.

It turned out that Rob was having a breakdown. It turned out that Rob thought he might be gay. It turned out that Rob had cheated on me.

The last time I truly recall us being together, as a couple at least, was in 1991, at our HIV test in a humid sexual health clinic in Florida. A video on the dangers of pubic lice was playing in the background, a monotonous voice-over laid on top of some crude animations of genital critters.

A big Southern mamma filed her nails and sang tunelessly into the hot, static air.

Take the ribbon from your hair
Shake it loose and let it fall.

I sat on the porch as the receptionist typed up my notes. *Tip tap, tip tap.* The sun cowered behind the low-rises in the distance. The cicadas began to own the night.

Time to grow up.

High Days and Holidays

As a child my summers were spent freewheeling the pavements on my bike or loitering on corners trying to master the art of blowing bubblegum. Occasionally, if I wanted an extra adrenalin rush, I'd mix it up a bit and opt for a spot of low-level shoplifting. I only ever worked the small-time con – I left the big stuff to the pros – in fact my thieving ambitions didn't ever stretch much beyond the odd Yorkie bar, Sherbet Dip Dab or packet of sugar cigarettes. But damn, I was good. Real slick. I had perfected what I believed to be a fail-safe, as well as highly original, technique. I would take my brother David to the newsagents with me. He was young and cute and therefore beyond reproach. I would make him wear his heavy-duty parka come rain or shine, and I would secrete the stolen items in his fur hood. Then we would walk out of the shop bold as brass.

David was basically a cocoa mule – a kind of Klepto-Kenny from South Park. It was the perfect scenario – my hands were clean, his hood was full. What on earth could go wrong?

On the way home I'd pick the chocolate bars out from the folds of fur lining and eat them. Occasionally, he'd hear me munching, look up at me sweetly and ask, 'Chocolate! Where did that come from?'

'It fell from the sky,' I'd answer, and break him off a chunk by way of a reward.

'I'm really, really hot, Suzy. Can I take my coat off now? Please?'

As so often happens in these situations, I became a victim of my own success. I got cocky. I pushed my luck, started playing with the big boys – family packs, large Toblerones and my ulti-mate nemesis, the Terry's Chocolate Orange. You see, unlike a Caramac or a Milky Way, a Chocolate Orange doesn't nestle discreetly in the fake fur of a parka hood. No. It sticks out like a sore orange. A sore Chocolate Orange.

In retrospect, I got a few things wrong. Firstly, and most importantly, it never occurred to me to actually *buy* anything in the shop. A kid in a sweet shop *not* buying sweets – I mean, *repeatedly not* buying sweets – was only ever going to arouse sus-picion.

One particular afternoon, as Klepto-Kenny and myself made our casual bid for freedom, the light was suddenly blot-ted out. Mr Wesson, the shopkeeper, was standing in the doorway, barring our exit.

'Now then, I think you might be leaving with some things you haven't paid for . . .'

It's in these testing moments you truly know what you're made of. It transpires I am made of the yellowest custard of cowardliness, with a slight back note of chicken.

'It's him!' I squealed, pointing at David. At that moment, as I stared at my brother accusingly, I realized just how much I had overdone it. His hood resembled a bulging Santa sack, stuffed full of confectionery. So much so that the weight of it was pulling the whole coat back, causing the fabric around his neck to choke him a little.

'What? What?' squeaked David, his larynx crushed by the weight of a dozen Bounties and a box of Milk Tray.

'Now let's have a look here then,' hissed Mr Wesson, delving into David's hood and producing fistfuls of contraband. David was visibly confused; on the one hand traumatized that a burly stranger was rootling around in his coat, on the other, relieved that his airways were now becoming clearer.

'Well, I have no idea how those got there,' I asserted, followed by an accusatory 'David, what have you *done?*'

David began to wail – one of those soundless wails, all cartoon tonsil wagging. Boulevards of green snot appeared under his nose.

I wondered how bad it could get. There would be a custodial sentence, of course, but for how long? Weeks? Months? A year? But Mr Wesson was way more vengeful than that. He did something far worse than call the police. He demanded I went home and told my mum – *my mum* – and that the three of us returned to the shop to see him.

I remember the slow plod home – David, silent save the odd pained gulp and viscous sniff. My mind was racing. How the hell could I get out of this one?

I let myself in and wandered upstairs. I could hear her in the bath.

Me: Mum . . .?

The occasional splosh. Faint humming.

Me: Mum . . .?
Mum: What is it?
Me: Mr Wesson wants to talk to you . . .
Mum: Why?
Me: It was an accident. You see, some sweets, *accidentally* –

Mum didn't hang around to hear the rest. She leaped out of the water like Glenn Close at the end of *Fatal Attraction*. There was a blur of wet dugs and blind rage as she launched towards me. Game over.

One thwacked arse, a trip back to Mr Wesson and a thousand public apologies later, I returned home. Then my mum told my dad. Another thwacked arse and a thousand apologies later, things calmed down.

That evening Mum was busy cooking dinner. The reassuring reek of fried onions and grilled cheese floated from under the kitchen door.

'Susan! Hang up your brother's coat and come and sit down for tea, please,' she shouted.

I bent over to pick up the anorak. As I stood upright, there was a rustle as a Twix, hitherto hidden undetected in a fold of the hood, worked its way loose and fell to the floor.

Revenge is sweet.

We didn't go abroad as kids. Abroad was a dangerous place, which my mum would often mutter about.

'Felicity went to Tenerife and came out in terrible hives after going in the pool.'

'Did you hear about Muriel? I don't think her stomach will ever be the same after that mussels incident in Majorca.'

My childhood holidays were brutal one-day affairs that invariably involved the pebbled beaches and sub-zero waters of 'summertime' Brighton as their endgame. Mum and Dad shared a loathing of traffic and a love of driving in the pitch black, so we would leave at the crack of dawn, around 5.30 a.m. There we'd be, deep in REM, when we were plucked from our beds and bundled into the car barely conscious. It was essentially a kidnap with a holiday twist.

'Dad . . .' I'd mumble, my mouth still furry with sleep, 'why's it so early?'

'We want to miss the traffic.'

'I've made sandwiches,' said Mum, by way of placation, brandishing a wonky Marmite doorstop.

Even at that young age there were two key points I wanted to raise. Sadly, I was always too shattered. Let me now, as an adult, make them . . .

Firstly – and this one's for you, Dad – we lived in *Croydon*. Croydon is a mere forty-three miles from Brighton. We didn't need to leave at 5.30 to get there in good time. Next up, Mum, this one's for you. My digestive system, it's fair to say, has evolved into a fairly robust beast. But no one, no one *on this planet* wants to eat Nimble bread slathered in yeast paste AT DAWN.

By 5.33 a.m. we'd be bundled into the back seat and Dad would start the Austin Princess, which would rumble into life just loudly enough to mask the screams of the neighbours it had by now woken from their slumbers. A strong petrol reek filled the car.

Dad: [*cheery*] We're off!
Mum: Bert! [*Screaming*] MIND THE SIDES!

Mum and Dad never had a lot of cash, but my God they were wizards on a budget. It's fair to say that for them the Age of Austerity began at birth and will only truly end once I've taken full responsibility for them in their dotage. Then it'll be the full Werther's Original all the way, guys. Mum was born into the culture of make do and mend and has never quite left it. Dad, for his part, was unnaturally good at saving, and so, between them, they would occasionally have enough funds to embark on

MAJOR WORKS.

Every few years or so Dad would announce that he was 'doing something to the house'. This filled us with terror. Dad's only contribution to the canon of interior design was to insist on bright swirly carpets everywhere. Ev-er-y-wh-ere – including up the side of the bath. Rad, eh? Eat your heart out, Kelly Hoppen.

When Mum and Dad embarked on

MAJOR WORKS

disaster was never far behind.

One year they decided to spend all their savings repainting the exterior of the house.

Mum: I want it white

Dad: White is boring

Mum: It's traditional!

Dad: I don't like traditional. I'm not traditional. I hate tradition!

So they decided to get some swatches. So far, so reasonable. Paint swatches, however, are notoriously misleading, due to the fact they are

- Printed facsimiles that don't always bear much relation to the actual colour you'll get from the tin.
- Usually about one centimetre long and three centimetres wide, so it's very hard to work out how a larger area might look.

What happens with 'normal' people is that they pick a couple of swatches, then buy a tester pot, then paint a largish section of wall so they can gauge how the colour works within the environment.

Not my parents.

Mum and Dad waited for a nice rainy day, just as dusk was falling, to look through the swatches. The perfect light, you'll agree, in which to make a large-scale paint decision.

Dad: [*giving a cursory glance, before returning to the football*] I like that one.

Mum: Oh, Bert! It's white!

Dad: No, it bloody isn't!

Mum: You said you didn't want white.

Dad: It isn't white!

Mum: Have a look at it!

Dad: You're bloody blind, woman! It's not white! It's white*ish* . . .

The clue was in the 'ish'. We should have known. Ish! You never trust an 'ish'. You don't go with an 'ish'. You don't let a sleeping 'ish' lie. This much I have learned.

So the masonry paint was bought, dozens upon dozens of litres of the stuff. No tester pots, no trial runs – they just flat-out went for it.

I remember coming home from school with Mum that afternoon. I remember turning the corner and being met by the sight of our house. Our nice, discreet little house was discreet no more. The formerly shy, shabby 1930s nonentity was suddenly and shockingly transformed into something you might find at Disney World, or in the grounds of a Victorian stately home whose owner had been driven to folly by the ravages of tertiary syphilis.

Even Mum stopped talking for a split second. As if on cue, Dad appeared from around the side of the house.

Dad: [*cheerily*] What do you think?
Mum: Oh, Bert! BERT!
Dad: What?
Mum: It's pink!
Dad: No, it bloody isn't!
Mum: Have a look at it!
Dad: It's not pink!
Mum: Yes, it is!
Dad: It isn't! It's pink*ish* . . .

Yes. As pinkish as blancmange. As pinkish as baby sick. Pink. Ish.

So, back to our 'holiday' to Brighton. We are in the car and my mum is screaming, 'Bert! MIND THE SIDES!'

Here is the thing. When Mum and Dad decided more
MAJOR WORKS
were needed, they opted to splash some cash on a garage. Our local builder Pat, as always, was on hand to help. Now Pat was a lovely man, but on the official cowboy scale he ranked somewhere between Billy the Kid and Buffalo Bill. He had many skills, but mathematics was not, it transpired, one of them.

In his build calculations Pat had made a key error. He made the garage too narrow at the front, and *even more narrow* at the rear. Once constructed, we discovered that the inside of the front half of the garage was just four centimetres wider than the total width of the car, but hey, that was roomy compared with the back.

'Shit. Want me to bin it and start again, Ann?' Pat had said blithely on discovering his mistake.

'Not at all, Pat,' said Mum, with a passive aggression I have, apparently, gone on to inherit.

Mum and Dad could have parked the car outside the house, on the roadside, but no. They had paid for that garage and they were damn well going to use it. Parking meant painstakingly edging the nose of the car inside, until the backs of the wing mirrors hit the entranceway. Only the bonnet was hidden from view, the rest of the car stuck out, proudly, arse to the elements.

In order to exit safely without scratching the paintwork, it would routinely take my dad a good two or three minutes from turning on the engine to finally hitting the road.

Back to our 'holiday'. It's 5.33 a.m.

Dad: We're off! [*Putting the gearstick into reverse*]

He edges out of the garage at roughly the speed of evolution.

Mum: [*shrieking*] You're clear on the left! Watch the wheels!
Dad: We're off! [*Again, as if trying to convince us*]
Mum: Bert! MIND THE SIDES!

5.36 a.m. The excitement of departure over, tiredness would hit me, whereupon I'd black out.

We would arrive in Brighton around 6 a.m.

Let me tell you, 6 a.m. wasn't the romantic time it is now, with people making artisan bread, taking Bikram yoga classes and sipping on their barista's best Chai latte. NO. This was the 1970s, and 6 a.m. was a brutal hour. Nothing was open, no one was out, and no fun whatsoever was to be had.

'Are we here?' I murmured.

'Is it morning yet?' whispered Michelle.

'Would anyone like a Marmite sandwich?' said Mum brightly,

holding aloft something brown and sweaty wrapped in cling film.

'What now?' moaned David, in and out of consciousness.

'We wait,' said Dad like some kind of Fair Isle-wearing ninja. And wait we did. We waited and we waited. Occasionally we'd drift off, only to be woken by a savoury waft as Mum unwound the cellophane to check on the mummified sarnies beneath. We waited for THREE HOURS until the shops opened. I say shops; it was actually only one shop we were interested in – the fudge shop.

Finally, nine o'clock would come and the fudge shop would open. We'd run in, buy a block of rum and raisin and rush out. Thirty seconds later it was all gone.

Then came the sugar rush.

As we hit peak hyperglycaemia, we'd get booted out of the car for some enforced 'fun'. This took the form of swimming. Brighton is famed for its sole-splitting pebbled beaches; what's perhaps less well known was the sheer volume of dog shit and used needles on them in the mid 70s. We'd pick our way through the obstacles, with the promise of the black sewage-streaked waters of the English Channel in front of us. Happy days.

'Help me, Mum. Please! I'm dying!' I'd say, shivering piti-fully on the shingle after my brief dip.

'Nonsense, it's refreshing,' said Dad, who hadn't set foot anywhere near the water.

'Sandwich?' said Mum, proffering a boomerang of bent dough with Stork margarine oozing from its sides.

It took me the best part of a decade to realize why we'd leave so early. It wasn't because Dad wanted the A23 to himself (and he's welcome to it), and it wasn't because they were wor-ried all the fudge from the fudge shop would get eaten if we didn't queue outside from six in the morning. No, Dad wanted to leave early so he could be home in time for 12.15 and *Grandstand*.

By the time midday struck we'd all be back home, comatose, with ripped feet and spiked insulin levels. Whereupon we'd pass out again until the sound of the vidiprinter and Dad's wailing (as Charlton Athletic got held to another no-score draw) echoed round the lounge.

By 5 p.m. we were awake again, somewhat bewildered, wondering if we'd made the whole thing up.

'You ready for tea?' said Mum. 'It's Marmite sandwiches . . .'

Old south Wales and the newsagent of doom

One year, we tried to have an actual holiday. You know, a *holiday* – where you go away for somewhere *longer than six hours*. Dad had decided it was high time we visited his favourite place in the whole world – Wales – specifically the Gower. So far, so glorious. But, because this is Dad we're talking about, this wasn't going to be your normal tourist pilgrimage to the gorgeous sands of Pobbles, Three Cliffs or Rhossili Bay. No. Dad wasn't interested in beaches or countryside or scenery or any of that nonsense. The only reason he was going, and by extension *we* were going, was because he wanted to find a newsagent.

'What do you mean, a newsagent? We've got one of those down the road,' shouted Mum, on learning of our destination.

'It's a special one. In the Gower.'

'Why on earth do you want to find that?' said Mum.

'I went there as a boy. I want to see if it's still there.'

'Was it a particularly *nice* newsagent?'

'Perfectly pleasant, thanks. Now I'm going to get the car out. I'll see you outside in ten minutes.'

And that was that.

Our accommodation was a static in a 1970s caravan park. For those unfamiliar with statics, they have all the worst aspects of caravanning without the one redeeming feature: mobility. I can remember the tang of chemical toilet, the endless grey concrete, but most of all I remember the rain. I have never known rain like it. It started raining the moment we arrived and it did not stop for one single second until we left. It was the sort of rain that ate at your bones. The sort of rain that turned the sky to slate, so that day was indistinguishable from night. It drummed relentlessly on the roof and hit the windows like hysterical toddler tears.

It rained so hard that my eardrums held the memory of it for weeks. You know when people have a leg removed yet still have a sense of it being there, post-amputation? A phantom limb? Well, I had the same sensation with the sound of rain. Even after the deluge the echo of it lingered faintly in my eardrums.

In these conditions the static caravan quickly went from what we had hoped it would be – an occasional base – to a full-time prison. Within hours of our incarceration, the five of us had descended into open warfare. We screamed and shouted and lashed out. After one particularly fraught exchange, Dad chased me in circles around the minute lounge area with a hair-brush, like a coiffeur Jack Nicholson in *The Shining*. Mum ended up having to pacify him with a lukewarm Fray Bentos pie.

After three days of breathing each other's stale air, we finally donned full waterproofs and headed out for our trip. The fury of the rain on the car roof meant that all conversations inside had to be bellowed at full volume.

Mum: WHERE IS THIS NEWSAGENT?
Dad: WHAT NEWSAGENT?

Mum: THE ONE YOU'VE DRAGGED US HERE TO SEE.

Dad: I TOLD YOU – IT'S IN THE GOWER.

Mum: BERT, THIS *IS* THE GOWER! THE GOWER IS SEV-
          ENTY SQUARE MILES! YOU'RE GOING TO HAVE TO
          BE MORE SPECIFIC!

Dad: WELL, I THINK WE SHOULD KEEP LOOKING – TRY
          SOME OTHER STREETS. I MAY HAVE GOT IT WRONG.

*We carry on. Mum lapses into silent fury. Dad circles the roads for hours,
slowing at every shop.*

Mum: [*barking, as dusk starts to fall*] DO YOU THINK IT MIGHT
          HAVE SHUT DOWN? IT WAS THE LATE 1940s LAST
          TIME YOU VISITED . . .

Dad: FINE. WE'LL STOP THEN. LET'S JUST PULL OVER
          AND GET THE KIDS SOME CRISPS.

We drive for another hour. It transpires every single newsagent in Wales is shut.

Dad: I WONDER IF THE CHIP SHOP I USED TO GO TO IS
          STILL HERE?

Not one of us replies.

◠◡◠

Sometime in my early teens my maternal grandparents decided
to move, like so many other nouveau riche, to the Costa del Sol.
I never really understood how they made their money, only that
they ran a car dealership in south London and that my granddad

was in the Masons. To my mind, the Masons was an organization so scary it ranked somewhere between Opus Dei and the Ku Klux Klan, where hooded men sat around and whispered about the Rotary club or how to influence the planning guy at the council.

I loved the idea of Granddad being in a secret society, especially since someone at school told me the Masonic induction ritual involved holding a compass in your right hand while dropping your trousers. Why I had no idea. Perhaps Masons were required to be able to find north in all situations, including when caught in flagrante. Anyway, if it is true, it's one in the eye for all those who say that men can't multi-task.

From looking at my granddad, you'd deduce one of two things: he was either a car salesman or a Caucasian Huggy Bear impersonator. He was permanently encased in sheepskin and always behind the wheel of a Mercedes. On Sunday he and Grandma would turn up for lunch in a brand-new car, straight off the forecourt. Next week a different one would get a spin. I am not one for cars, but even to this day I get a visceral thrill from seeing a vintage Benz – the bulky SEs, the pillar-less coupés and my favourite, the 1969 280SL in black with cognac interior. Strange how we fetishize our past. I couldn't give a monkey's about the car I drive, but the thought of that one . . .

My grandparents bought a flat several floors up in a white-washed high-rise in Torremolinos. Yes, my friends, they were living the expat dream. England had gone to the dogs, while Spain was a promised land of whitewashed high-rises, displaced bank robbers and knackered beach donkeys.

We visited just before my fourteenth birthday. It was my first time on a plane. It was the first time I'd seen the sun. I immediately went from Nosferatu to lobster, before peeling and turning Nosferatu again.

We lived off rugby-ball-shaped loaves of *pan rustico*, which would go from fresh to stale in twenty minutes. We drank Fanta through straws, which made it automatically 100 per cent more exotic than the same stuff we'd guzzled out of cans back home. At night we would wander in T-shirts along La Carihuela staring at the craftsmen and their stalls – a toothless man selling statues made from torn Coke cans, a hippy with amber eyes and skin like tobacco leaves, weaving strips of leather into bracelets. It was unbearably exciting, the bustle, the heat, the energy. What's not to love about a country where even the question marks fly in the face of convention¿

By the time I finished school I had travelled to London, to Edinburgh and to most of the fast-food outlets of the Costa del Sol. That was it. I was no different from my parents, whose sole lifetime excursion, excluding those I've mentioned, was a brief trip to Malaga. I'll let them take over.

Dad: We were on a bus.

Mum: It was heaving. Full. Rammed full of Spanish.

Dad: Who else was it going to be full of? We were in Spain . . .

Mum: I had you [Me]. You were ill.

Dad: She's always ill . . .

Mum: I think it was whooping cough.

Dad: It was a cold.

Mum: It was whooping cough. I did all the checks.

Dad: Anyway, I had David. And he suddenly started kicking off and screaming, so I thought I'd pick him up. I held him up in the air. Cut a long story short, he pissed in my face.

Me: Pissed in your face?

Dad: Yes.

Me: What? What, did he have no nappy on? Was he just a naked baby on a bus?

Mum: You have to remember, Susan, it was the 70s.

Me: Well, what happened after that?

Dad: Well, everyone stared at me. And I smelled. And then it dried. And then I think we went back home. Is that right, Ann?

Mum: [*very quietly*] Yes.

Their honeymoon they also recalled in loving detail.

Dad: [*getting down his dossier from the shelf and reading from it*] Seventh of October 1967, Paguera in Majorca.

Me: Thanks, Rain Man.

Mum: The Hotel Bahia Club. We still have the ashtray from it.

Me: Why?

Dad: Good question.

Mum: Because it hasn't broken yet.

I love that. That sums up my mum in one sentence. Why keep something? Because it isn't broken. Retain until destroyed. Cling on until obliteration. Never give up, never surrender. Ann Perkins is the veritable Buzz Lightyear of all things, including love. I often think to myself, *Why do they stay together, these two people – through thick and thin, through depression and anxiety, through sickness and health?* And there is the answer. Because, as stretched as it may be, it simply hasn't broken yet.

It was my relationship with Rob that really opened the doors to international travel. He was a man of the world, having been to Portugal and everything. A year before the sadness of that clinic in Florida we headed off for a holiday in Los Angeles.

Rob and I decided to visit all the theme parks we could while we were there. Perhaps subconsciously we wanted to do something innocent and childlike together in the midst of the increasingly grim realities of adulthood. It was a terrible idea. I'd had an overwhelming fear of roller coasters ever since John Daniels' dad detached his retina that time so anything more rigorous than a teacup and saucer ride is guaranteed to render me giddy with terror. As we approached the entrance to Six Flags Magic Mountain, I started to feel anxious.

Me: I hate rides, you know I hate rides . . .
Rob: This isn't a ride, I promise you.

We join a snaking queue of hopped-up adolescents, nervous and not sure what to expect. Sure enough, as we get nearer the entrance, I see the telltale health disclaimers.

Me: [*suspicious*] What's this ride called?
Rob: It's not a ride! Stop worrying!
Me: Yes, but what's it *called* . . .
Rob: ISN'T THIS FUN! [*He shouts in what I take to be an attempt to mask the screams coming from above*]
Me: Why does it say you have to declare if you have a heart condition?
Rob: Oh, you know Americans . . .

It was too late. No sooner had my eyes seen the legend FREE FALL than I was bundled by a joyless teen in a branded T-shirt into the cart. As we started to move, all became clear. Rob had got me there on a technicality. No, it wasn't a ride, it was a drop. A sheer drop. A high-speed zero-gravity drop to the centre of the earth. The bars clamped down on my knees, and up we went, up to more than a hundred feet.

'Isn't this fun?' screamed Rob again, quickly followed by 'Don't cry.'

Once we reached the top, the cage came to a violent halt. Then it moved forward a little. I could see the whole of North America laid out in front of me. There was a grinding of metal, a slight pause and then we were let loose.

You know those cartoons? Where the character suddenly drops, but leaves something of themselves behind? That's what happened with my stomach. As my body fell, my guts resolutely remained in the same place. They passed up my windpipe and seemed to hang in the breeze, until some complex bit of intestinal wiring forced them back down and inside again.

We ended up upside down, braking sharply, the roots of my hair stiff with fear.

'That was great!' roared Rob, quickly followed by, 'Susan, would you like me to call someone?'

The next day we went to Universal Studios, where it was agreed we'd do something more sedate. The ET ride seemed like a decent compromise. There was an element of roller-coaster elevation (albeit at 0.2 mph) for him, with a good dose of the sentimental and the infantile for yours truly. Now, the best thing – the *wonderful* thing – about the ET ride was that you got to say your name into a voice-recording machine as you went in, so that ET could say goodbye to you, personally, when you left.

So I said, 'WANKER.'

It really is impossible to overestimate how thrilled I was as I mounted that bike and slowly ascended to the bright moon above. Fibre-optic stars glittered in the black drape of night as the sound stage swelled with the luscious sounds of John Williams' strings. And, as I began my descent, there he was – ET, arm outstretched, finger lit.

As I glided past he murmured in that distinctive timbre, 'Goodbye . . . WANKER.'

There was a moment, just a moment, when I felt like the funniest person in the world. I was poleaxed with laughter, tears running down my face. And then I heard ET continuing, behind me:

'Goodbye, dickwad!'

'Goodbye, flange face!'

'Goodbye, numb nuts!'

That wizened foul-mouthed alien was spewing the most awful filth. It turns out I wasn't the only one who'd had that idea. Word had got out and now EVERYONE IN THE WORLD WAS DOING IT.

They've shut it down now – that ride – something to do with 'people abusing the system'. It's terrible, really. People are awful, truly awful. But, as ET would say, 'Fuck 'em.'

Nowadays I love nothing more than holidaying in the UK. I love the landscape, the people, even the weather, Nothing beats Sennen Cove in December, with the wind whipping at that empty curve of white sand. The Dales, shrouded in autumnal mist. Glencoe at dusk. I often stay in National Trust or Landmark Trust properties – mainly because they're beautiful, but also because I get to play my favourite game of all time, Spook the Tourist.

The beauty of this game is it requires only three things – a pen, the visitors' book and your imagination. The aim of the game is to unnerve the next guests as much as possible by detailing you've experienced ghosts or paranormal phenomena during your stay. If you're playing this game for the first time, here are a few sample suggestions, taken from entries I've made.

- Lovely comfy bed, gorgeous views – but what was scratching at the bedroom door all night long?!
- Great cottage, although I avoided the lounge. Had the feeling I was being watched in there!
- Came here for a long weekend with the rest of the investigative team. Can't believe we finally saw the infamous Grey Lady! With love from the Solihull Paranormal Society.
- Sorry for the breakages. We came down to see the plates flying off the dresser! PS Where are the cushions in the main bedroom from?

Enjoy!

TWO

Cambridge 1988–91

Go East

I was far from a model pupil at school – not badly behaved as such, just . . . well, *distracted*. Sadly, *distracted* looks an awful lot like *badly behaved* to members of the teaching profession.

I can be devastatingly obtuse when the mood takes me. I certainly wouldn't want me in my class. Recently I was handed a children's book called *All Dogs Have ADHD* by a friend of mine. It was an OK read – I got through most of it in twenty seconds to be honest. Sadly, I didn't get the chance to finish it as a squirrel caught my eye in a nearby tree. It was only then I realized it had been less of a reading suggestion and more of a diagnostic tool. Oops.

I'm an all-or-nothing student. I get As or Es, distinction or fails, firsts or thirds. If I'm interested in something, then I'm fanatically interested. If I'm not, then I'll make my excuses and leave, disrupt the lesson or try to make a large hat or makeshift cape out of any bits and bobs to hand.

Chemistry interested me right up to the point I was banned from setting anything else on fire. Biology interested me until they wanted me to toy with the insides of a dead frog. Arithmetic started well but hit a dead end once they got our art teacher, Mrs Samson, to stand in for our maths teacher for a term. Mrs Samson was, I believe, the first maths teacher to wear a smock, and certainly the first to do equations in watercolour. Crucially, she knew exactly as much about maths as the eight-year-olds she was teaching.

In our first lesson we examined the relationship between

fractions and decimals. In that lesson I learned that half of something equates to 0.05.

Yes, 0.05.

It all went downhill from there.

In my penultimate year at school a careers adviser from London came to visit us for the day. The idea was she'd briefly interview us about our likes and dislikes, then give tailor-made suggestions for our potential life journey. My classmates filed in one by one, and one by one she told them, in a bored monotone, that they'd make good secretaries. All of them. She told *every one* of the thirty people in my class that – except me.

She told *me* I should be a dentist.

When I said that I didn't want to be a dentist, and that I had almost zero interest in teeth, she gave me a long hard stare and scribbled something in her notebook. When her report came back, it said that I should maybe apply to a polytechnic to do a subject other than English.

That was the exact moment I decided to study English.

I've never really responded to peer pressure. What I do respond to, however, is someone categorically telling me I can't do something. I trill at the sound of a gauntlet going down. It feels like a dare. And I've *never* been able to resist a dare.

That night I vividly remember going home and asking:

Me: Mum, what's the best university?
Mum: [*carving a Viennetta*] I don't know. Ask your dad.

I wander into the lounge, where Dad is shouting at the Charlton Athletic result.

Me: Dad, what's the best university?

Dad: How would I know? One of the rowing ones, I guess. Cambridge? Yes, Cambridge, I think.

So that sealed it. That's where I was going to go. I was going to Cambridge to study English.

I have no idea why Cambridge took a punt on me and asked me for an interview. My O-level results had been average at best (As for the subjects I enjoyed, Cs for the subjects I didn't). I suspect my wonderful music teacher Lora stuck her neck out and gave me a decent reference. Either way, in the autumn of 1987 I received notice that I was to come to New Hall and be interviewed by the senior tutor.

There are three parts to getting into college: the interview, the offer, then getting the grades. I was now one third of the way there.

Or 0.03 of the way, if you prefer it in decimal.

That morning Dad woke me at first light and inched out the dun-coloured Peugeot so I could climb in.

'BERT! MIND THE SIDES!' shouted Mum from the front door, still in her nightie and slippers.

I'd barely slept but felt awake, skin prickling with excitement – the first flickering of my now constant colleague adrenalin, I guess. I'd never been east before. I'd never really been anywhere before – so I nestled back into the faux-suede seat and watched the landscape flattening to greet the rising sun.

Looking back, whether it's true or not, that day feels like one of the very few times as an adult that Dad and I spent any proper time together. He was ever-present in my childhood – waking us every morning before he went to work, returning in time for dinner at 6 p.m. sharp to share some jokes from his day. He bookended my life from the moment I had a conscious thought right up to the point I left home. The morning routine never varied in all that time. At 6.30 a.m. exactly there'd be his lumbering tread on the stairs and the clank of cups on metal tray. Slowly we'd stagger like zombies (in varying states of annoyance and doziness) into our parents' room. We'd sit on the carpet and I'd sip on cold milky tea each and every single morning until I was old enough to tell him I actually liked it strong with one sugar and just a splash of the white stuff.

Dad was particularly good when I was sick, which was often when I was little. There'd be the comforting sounds and smells of Mum busy in the kitchen, and then Dad would materialize out of nowhere, brandishing a bottle of Lucozade. I remember the rustle of gold cellophane, the dizzying fizz as it opened, that particular stinging sensation in my nostrils. Then he'd settle himself down on the side of the bed to deliver the next instalment of my favourite story, Sammy the Squirrel.

There wasn't much to Sammy, other than he appeared to live a relatively uneventful woodland life in a support group for alliterated animals. Other members of this group included Henry the Hedgehog, Richard the Rat and Deirdre the Deer – not forgetting their nemesis, Wicked Willie the Wolf.

I loved those stories as much as I loved him, although strangely they have left me with a pathological fear of chains of words with the same first consonant. These feelings will often overwhelm me, particularly in the refrigerated section of an M&S Food outlet. I can't tell you how incendiary I find those pre-packaged tropicals – Mango Madness, Fabulous Fruity Fingers, the Perfectly Pointless Pip-Riddled Pomegranates. It makes me want to commit a Motherfucking Murder Medley.

When we finally arrived at New Hall that October morning, I thought I'd just be an hour or two – a quick 'Hello, yes, I know I don't belong here, goodbye' – but it transpired I needed to do an interview, an exam, another interview and then an analysis of the exam. I'd never been so scared. Dad stood there, looking lost in his threadbare camel coat. What would he do in a place he didn't know – for a whole day? His answer was:

1. Locate the nearest tea room.
2. Analyse the height, depth and width of the scones on display at the counter.
3. Order the scones with the largest surface area.
4. Eat scones.
5. Leave the tea room, carefully counting the number of steps between there and the next available tea room.
6. Order scones at the next tea room.
7. Using a stopwatch count how long the scones take to arrive.

8. Eat the scones.
9. Pay for the scones while calculating how much they would cost in francs, Deutschmarks and pesetas.
10. Leave the tea room and head off in search of another tea room, keeping note of how many blue cars seen on the way.
11. Repeat from 1.

At 5.30 p.m. he came to pick me up, his arteries lined with clotted cream and his collar caked in scone dust. By that point my head was buzzing with the possibilities of a brave new world: Marxist dialectics, post-structuralism – a subsidized bar! We drove home in the rain, the earth rising to greet the setting sun. I knew something had changed – that I was about to let loose my family moorings and become my own person. I didn't think that exact thought, as such; I was just aware of that moment being tinged somewhat, that moment of being a kid, in the car, with her dad – and how goddam transitory and precious it all was.

On 5 January 1988 I found out I'd been offered a place, but it wasn't until a summer's morning six months later that I found out I'd actually got the grades I needed to get in. These were still the halcyon days of the Royal Mail – when something you sent arrived at its destination rather than boomeranging to a depot in an industrial estate on the A406. These were the days when you knew the name of your postman (Bill), and that Bill would be there at 8.20 every morning and 12.30 every afternoon.

The morning my exam results were due I leaped from my bed at dawn, crept downstairs and made a beeline for my parents' drinks cabinet. I instinctively knew this wasn't one of those moments when you could countenance being sober. My arm snaked past the dusty decanters and old sherry bottles to the very back, where I pulled out a neglected bottle of cheap whisky.

I loaded up a tumbler and sneaked back to bed. By the time Bill arrived at 8.20 on the dot, and the metallic snap of the letterbox rang through the house, I was properly, properly blotto.

I still remember opening that letter. I remember every second of it. I remember how small the envelope was, and how thin the paper inside – as if it had done everything it could to belie its own significance. I remember the black punch marks of the typewriter and the indented lines and curves that spelled my future. I remember the thump of my pulse in my neck.

It felt like my whole life was on that page.

I read its contents and breathed out. I noticed a peaty stink as I exhaled. I wandered into my parents' room. They were both in bed with the sheets up above their heads, waiting – as terrified as I was. I guess I knew, and they did too, that this wasn't just a certificate. It was a passport.

I remember saying my grades out loud, woozy with booze, and them leaping into the air like the Buckets in *Charlie and the Chocolate Factory*. There was a sudden blizzard of threadbare sheets and handmade quilts. It wasn't just my joy, it was our joy. It wasn't just me heading off, it was all of us – the Perkins and Smiths and beyond – the countless generations of car dealers, midwives, soldiers and charladies. Here we all go, onwards and upwards, until the next generation comes along and mercifully outdoes us all.

Finally I could start to make plans for the intervening year. But that was going to cost money, so I had to resort to the worst thing imaginable to any seventeen-year-old.

WORK.

I'd had a Saturday job since I was fourteen, chambermaiding at a family friend's hotel. It mainly involved hoovering architraves and cleaning toilets. I earned £7.50 for a morning shift, which I'd spaff on fags, vodka miniatures and pick 'n' mix sweets. Once, after cleaning a particularly unpleasant bog bowl, I realized the Arab gentleman responsible for the eruption was still in the room, dozing under a pile of blankets.

'You. You come here,' he growled exotically as I made to leave. I approached the blankets. His breath smelled of something I can, with hindsight, now identify as halloumi. He grabbed my hand and opened my fingers. 'You take this. For your trouble.' Christ, but his intensity was captivating.

Something heavy fell into my palm. We locked eyes for a moment. I headed for the door, but it wasn't until I was outside that I allowed myself to look at my booty.

A kilo of half-eaten pistachios.

It was then I realized the service industry was not for me.

In 1988 Sherratt and Hughes bookshop was a rare jewel in the brutal concrete coil that was the Whitgift Centre, Croydon. It was an independent outfit, struggling to avoid the clutches of increasingly expansive chainstores. Most importantly, and most memorably, you could smoke on the shop floor. Baby, you could smoke *all over it*.

Smoking was my hobby. It remains the only thing I have ever been really good at and truly committed to, so working there was my dream job. It was a dream job, with dream colleagues,* but with a business model doomed to failure as the dark shadows of corporate branding and mega-bucks bullshit loomed.

Every day I'd pitch up around 9.30 a.m. and sit at the till,

---

* One employee, Stephen, ran the Business Books section downstairs. We were all a little in awe and in love with him. He was older, in his early twenties, and a graduate. Impossibly cool. He introduced me to the short stories of a new writer called Ian McEwan, who he suspected would go on to great things. Stephen now runs one of the most august publishing houses in the world. I'm so proud one of us at least has gone on to do something decent with our lives.

puffing away like a bastard. There was no dress code and we were actively encouraged to read at our stations. I never once took my eyes off the page. I read and read. Then I smoked and read some more. This approach had its pros and cons. On the plus side, customers never felt pressurized by any of the staff and browsed at their leisure. On the down side, the store had one of the highest rates of shoplifting in the south-east. Apparently one bloke would come in every week, regular as clockwork, carrying a large empty cardboard box. He'd proceed to fill it to the brim with bestsellers, then walk out, bold as brass, with it over his head. We only found out a year later when we had CCTV installed. We hadn't even noticed.

Every Tuesday we'd open the shop late, and instead of serving customers spend that first hour telling each other what books we'd read. We'd take notes, get recommendations, widen our horizons. It meant that when someone asked us to suggest a damn good read, we were better equipped to answer them. See? I told you. *Terrible* business model. With that level of care and love it could *never* have worked.

My regular dealings with the general public meant I got an awful lot better at lateral thinking.

Shop doorbell goes. Customer enters.

Woman: Excuse me? Do you have *Tess of the Duracelles*?
Me: Absolutely, madam. [*Heads for Thomas Hardy's* Tess of the D'Urbervilles]

Shop doorbell goes again. Another customer enters.

Man: Do you have *Rogit the Dinosaur*?
Me: Rogit the dinosaur?

Man:	Yeah. I'd never heard of it. I think it's a kids' book.
Me:	[*thinks for a second*] Here you go. [*Hands over* Roget's Thesaurus]
Man:	Cool. [*Looks inside*] Where's the pictures?

After nine months there it was time to go on my travels. I'd earned enough cash to get me on a plane to New York and thence on an Amtrak train down the East Coast. I went with my wonderful friend Polly, who had friends in America. This was unbelievably rad. The furthest-flung friend I had was from Caterham.

It was the little things – chewing on a bagel in Grand Central Station, looking out from the top of the Empire State, seeing steam billow from the street vents. When you're young you don't care that you're chasing clichés. You're unfettered by embarrassment, the need to feel 'unique' or 'independent'. You just pick the lowest hanging fruit, and it tastes bloody great. We spent two days in Manhattan, too overwhelmed and jet-lagged to venture beyond Midtown. Before we knew it, it was time to get to Penn Station for our ongoing train.

We were only a few blocks into our walk when I experienced my first and, thankfully, only mugging. As a woman of the world (and my mother's daughter), this was one of four dangerous scenarios I'd been preparing myself for while in the States – alongside rodeo riding, gunslinging showdowns at High Noon and being held hostage by a family of inbred rural banjo players.

This turned out to be no ordinary mugging, however – this was America's Most Benign Mugging.

As we trundled our suitcases along Avenue of the Americas, we were joined by a tall guy with a salt-and-pepper beard and dark, tatty clothes, who ambled alongside us.

| Man: | Morning, ladies. Can I carry your suitcases? |

Me:	[*brusque*] No, thanks. We're fine.
Man:	Come on now . . .
Polly:	Really, we're OK.
Man:	Now, ladies, I think you should let me.
Me:	We can manage.
Man:	I said, I think you should let me, you know?
Polly:	Don't worry.
Man:	[*getting exasperated*] Girl, are you getting me?
Polly:	Not really.
Man:	I'd like to have your bags, please.
Me:	That's not necessary; we can carry them.
Man:	[*increasingly menacing*] Don't make me ask you again.
Polly:	You don't need to ask us again. We've said no . . .
Man:	Damn it, girl!
Me:	Really, we're just fine. They're on wheels.
Man:	Jesus. I'm gonna have to get old school with you . . .

And with that, he grabbed my shoulder bag and ran off.

I was left with a confusing set of emotions. On the one hand, I was relieved that we hadn't been the victims of America's Most *Violent* Mugging, on the other, curiously furious that he'd been so polite.

Me:	I mean, he *asked* for our bags. *Asked for them.* What's that about? It's confusing. He's being a gentleman and a thief at the same time. Talk about mixed messages.
Polly:	[*wisely*] Americans are weird.
Me:	I mean, if you're a criminal, just be a criminal. It's them and us. Perpetrator and victim. There should be a moral distance between the two.
Polly:	It's confusing.
Me:	Yes! He asked our *permission.* Like he was getting us to collude

with him. I feel dirty. I feel like I'm an accessory to my own crime . . .

Polly: Mmm. Can we get on the train now?

In reality, all the Gentleman Mugger got away with was a handful of traveller's cheques (good luck cashing them, even in the 1980s) and a selection of hand sanitizers provided by my mother.

'You'd better take them. I bet there's threadworm in the Big Apple, and you know how that's spread – from toilet seats to bums to hands to *your hand*. YOUR HAND!'

I like to think of him, the Gentleman Mugger, back at his underground lair, tipping out the contents of my shoulder bag and examining the booty before exclaiming wisely, 'The English are weird.'

Two months before my first term at college, my reading list arrived – on *headed notepaper*. Suddenly it was official. In celebration, I headed to the shops to buy the next best thing to books – chocolate, fags and whisky miniatures – none of which, I noted sadly, seemed to feature as course requirements. Dad volunteered to come with me, which I remember thinking was odd. Dad never went with me *anywhere*. We headed there in silence, bar the adhesive tug of our shoes on the hot summer pavement.

'Well done,' he finally said. 'Well done.'

'Thanks, Dad.'

He stopped and turned to me.

'One thing.' I could see that his eyes were brimming. 'Make sure you don't become posh, eh?'

New Hall

I didn't know what he meant until I arrived. You can't under-estimate what a shock it was for a girl born and swaddled in the concrete of south London to see something as truly beautiful as King's College, Clare Chapel or the Cam River wreathed in mist. How impossible it was to try to accept, even for a moment, that you might belong there. (I didn't. I don't. I won't.)

New Hall, as it was then (it now has a new name – Murray Edwards College, named jointly after the inventor of Murray Mints and Huw Edwards*), was rumoured to have been built according to the designs of a Swedish prison. Yes, Dear Reader, you heard correctly – a Swedish prison. Apparently, the specifi-cations were originally intended for a jail outside Stockholm, but the Swedes rejected them. I'm not sure why. Had they hoped for something a little more classical? Doric columns? Pediments? Balustrades? Or maybe something stucco? Mock Tudor? Perhaps I'm just being snotty in assuming that people would have stipulations for penitentiaries that involved any-thing more ornate than a.) very high walls and b.) A MASSIVE LOCKED DOOR.

Anyway, for whatever reason, the Swedes turned down the plans. Fair enough. It's the next stage that interests me. What on earth made someone then think, *OK, we're not going to use this design for a maximum security stronghold, so . . . let's use it for*

---

* This has not been fact-checked.

*a single-sex college in Cambridge! It's a directly transferable struc-
ture, after all. Both sets of needs are exactly the same, aren't they?
Aren't they? Anyway, the girls won't mind – they've only been allowed
to take degrees at the university since 1948. They're just delighted to
be there. Plus, worst-case scenario, if they do kick up a fuss, we can
just LOCK THE MASSIVE DOOR on them.*

To give you an idea of the look of the place, think brutish St
Paul's. Or concrete Taj Mahal. In modern architectural par-
lance you might get away with saying it had 'clean lines' – but
this was the late 1980s, and back then it was simply 'ugly as all
shit'. Long wide concrete boulevards stretched from the
entrance. A murky shallow pool ran parallel to the main walk-
way, decked with algae and pigeon shit – in the days before
Pigeon Shit was an aspirational paint colour.

The college's main claim to fame (other than being the only
guaranteed escape-proof structure in East Anglia) was that it
had a hydraulic canteen. I am not sure whether this particular
feature was part of the original Swedish schematics. Perhaps it
was a ploy to distract and entertain the inmates with an ascending buffet. We shall never know. Certainly, *Orange is the New
Black* would be a very different show had the Federal Department of Corrections had an ascending buffet. No one would
give a toss about stalky ol' Suzanne 'Crazy Eyes' Warren or the
evangelical mutterings of Tiffany 'Pennsatucky' Doggett;
everyone would just drop their makeshift weapons/dildos and
watch in awe as Galina 'Red' Reznikov mechanically rose from
the bowels of the refectory.

Dinner took the form of classic mass catering, but with a
few twists. Firstly, once weekly, there was Formal Hall, which
essentially meant same food, different outfits. New Hall prided
itself on being a more relaxed and informal college: larger state
school intake, less traditional in its outlook. Even so, every

Thursday we had to don long black gowns when we ate in a nod to wider university etiquette. It was all a little Harry Potter, but without the fun of the Sorting Hat after dessert.

The catering team were veritable spin doctors. Their primary skill lay in creating a deeply mediocre pile of food and then putting a lady's name on the end of it – think Chicken Barbara, Lamb Diane and Guinea Fowl Cynthia – as if somehow that addition would work a kind of culinary alchemy. That suddenly the viscous puddle of grey gravy cosseting even greyer meat would become interesting. Romantic, even. In reality, each and every plate that hit the table was a triumph of hope over experience.

I'd specified on my application form that I would prefer to share a room in my first year, thereby acknowledging I considered loneliness a fate far worse than the possibility of being hacked to death by a total stranger while sleeping. Although I had seen the college at my interview, I'd never actually visited the halls of residence. So it was a surprise when I first clapped eyes on my accommodation.

F18 was a split-level room, with steep open concrete treads leading to another room upstairs. At the foot of the treads there was a large glass window. Waiting. Inviting me to get drunk and fall through it. I smashed against it many a time, but with too little force to shatter the glass, although my friend Jamelia went one better and leaped clean through hers during a heated debate at a Black Causus meeting. Her brave political gesture became the stuff of legend – tempered only by the fact she lived on the ground floor and was therefore able to break her fall with a gentle forward roll.

Essentially, our digs were open plan – affording roughly the same level of privacy as a flannel wash in Paul Dacre's office. I arrived first, no room-mate in evidence, so decided to climb the treacherous stairs and make my nest in the mezzanine. In fact it was pointless worrying about where to put my stuff, because there would have been no boundary strong enough to keep out the woman I ended up sharing with. Enter the irrepressible

Shayla Clare Walmsley.

Shayla was unlike anyone I have ever met before or since. The term 'whirlwind' isn't wild or chaotic enough to describe the mass of raw energy she was fashioned from. Quixotic? Yes. Maverick? For sure. Welsh? Utterly.

Shayla was the first person I'd met in my life who was genuinely *different*, something other than the nice, monochromatic, lower-middle-class girls I knew from Croydon. Her otherness thrilled me to the point that ever since I met her, I've been looking for that shock of the new in everyone else I've encountered. She stormed in that afternoon, a corona of cigarette smoke over tangled red hair. Then, emerging from the fug, came a pair of Deirdre Barlow glasses and a syrup-thick Caerphilly burr.

'Who the fuck we go' ure?'

It turned out that Shayla had never met anyone from the south-east before and therefore had a few preconceptions. It was only when she asked whether I owned my own pony that I felt I needed to disabuse her of one or two of them. What started out as an awkward, self-conscious cultural exchange developed seamlessly into a unique and peculiar friendship. I say peculiar; it must have looked like abuse from the outside, she and I permanently slagging and jostling one other. Robust. Honest. No prisoners. And just bloody, bloody wonderful.

Shayla gave me two key things – firstly, a working knowledge of Spanish. She was a light sleeper and most nights would wake bellowing, '*¿Donde está, Eduardo?*' in a gruff and thoroughly convincing Andalusian. She had spent her year off riding horses in the Spanish hills. I'd worked in a bookshop in the Whitgift Centre. That sort of sums us both up, really.

Secondly, she loaned me some of her derring-do. Shayla threw herself at everything with an almost suicidal force. 'DO IT!' she would shout if I expressed the faintest interest in something – often accompanied by an impromptu grab or slap. 'DO IT! DO IT! DO IT!'

'I'm thinking of invading Nantwich.'

'DO IT!'

'I've always wondered what it might be like to milk a pig.'

'DO IT!'

'I'm thinking about forming a funk and soul collective with Eamonn Holmes.'

'DO IT!'

By the end of the first week of the first term Shayla had spent her entire grant (yes, we had them back then, children – as we basked on the sunny plains of state funding) on a box of contact lenses, a semi-permanent wave and a pair of stone-washed dungarees. This was back in the days when contact lenses needed to be hand-rinsed in a vat of chemicals and hung on a washing line to dry overnight.

Shayla had never had money before, and boy could she burn through it. Within seven days of starting college, all she had left to her name was a tenner.

That night, as we sat eating potatoes out of a can ('I spect you're used to caviar, love'), I expressed a mild interest in going to watch some comedy later at the Footlights Club Room.

'DO IT!' she said. 'Do a spot, an open spot!'

'What? No! Don't be silly.'

I could feel her fingers digging into my bicep.

'Ten quid. I'll give you ten quid. Go on! DO IT!'

By now she'd worked out I couldn't resist a dare.

'Go on. DO IT!'

So I did.

I loved her. I loved the bones of her.

Cambridge was also the place I met my brilliant beloveds, Nicola and Sarah. Nicola hailed from Essex and wore a full hunting outfit to her interview 'so they won't forget who I am'. (They didn't.) Sarah spent most of her undergraduate years in a pair of orange tie-dyed trousers bellowing, 'Who's got weed?' They're family, but without the burden of my genetic material. They're my rocks, my touchstones, my sounding boards. Together, we're proof that good things can come in triangles. Together, we're the unholy trinity of silly. Lucky me.

As for Shayla, we had a spat – over a boy. The three of us got close in our final year. It turned out that the boy liked me. It turned out she liked the boy. I bowed out, and they ended up dating for a while after we graduated, but the damage was done.

Stupid kids.

I saw her sporadically after we graduated. Well, twice. Twice in all those years, and yet not a week went by when I didn't think of her. There would always be something: a Welsh lilt, a raised, excitable voice, the impetus to do something wild and rash. It all reminded me of her. I'd go online and find hints of what she was up to: community work, teaching in Tower Hamlets, fostering big 'bad' Staffies. She could and would love the unlovable with a fire you couldn't put out. The more I heard about her good heart, following itself so clearly and purely, the more shame I felt about my rather tawdry and venal one.

I got the call last year as I was heading into the garden to hang out some washing. I vaguely recalled the voice at the end of the phone – as faint as all yesterdays. An old acquaintance from college seemed to be telling me that Shayla was dead. How very strange. If my brain didn't quite register it, then my body did. I lost my legs. I lost my legs and sat slumped on the floor, sobbing, with a wet bra slung over my shoulder and a tea towel hanging somewhere round the back of my head.

Oh Shayla. Oh Shayla, what have you gone and done now?

Shayla can't be dead. Not Shayla, with her lioness heart and flaming hair and bottle-top glasses. Not her, with that firm grip on my forearm, leading me off to try something daring and life-affirming. Who will push me now? Who will tell me to DO IT if not the Architect of Crazy herself?

A week after the news, and just before her funeral, I sat at my desk as I had often done over the years and tried once again to see if I could find her online. I typed in her name. In the blink of an eye I got 19,000 results. I looked through the first few pages, only to find the same out-of-date references and articles. Nothing I could have used to connect with her. I'd tried. I'd tried before – I'd sent emails into the ether – and nothing.

And then, halfway down the page, I saw it. Her Twitter account. She'd had a Twitter account. I clicked on it and up popped the face of my beautiful larger-than-life friend – head thrown back, mid-roar, as always. I could still hear that husky laugh in my ears. And then I saw, underneath her photo, two words:

FOLLOWS YOU

If I think about it too much, I cry. I cry because after all those years of silence she was one simple click away. She was only ever and always one click away.

I owe you, you infuriating, brilliant Caerphilly nightmare. I owe you always. Because if you gave me my first gig, then you also gave me the greatest gift that came with it:

Melanie Claire Sophie Giedroyc.

Melanie

I met Mel at that first open spot gig in the October of 1988. I had been at college less than a week. Here are a few basic things you need to know about her:

1. She is two years older than me.

Actually, that's it. That's all you need to know.

So where were we? Ah yes.

'DO IT,' said Shayla, when I told her I might, at some point, want to give performing a try. 'I'll give you a tenner if you do.'

DO IT. DO IT. DO IT.

And so I did.

That night I headed down to the Footlights, Cambridge's comedy club, with a few random jottings in my hand. The Footlights is one of the most talked about, and most shrouded in mystery, of all university societies. How do *you* picture it – if, indeed, you care to picture it at all? Perhaps you see it as a sort of light-entertainment wing of the Bullingdon Club, where men with red cheeks and even redder chinos bray at one another like coked-up donkeys.

Toff 1:   Hugo, is your pa still running *The Times*?

Toff 2:   Totally, but he's off to Deutsche Bank in the summer. Is yours still selling arms to Sierra Leone?

Toff 1:   God, yah. Now listen. Lollo and his chums are coming for sups at my rooms tonight. Fancy it? There'll be totty for sure. We're talking about some new thing called a dot.com start-up. You game, old chum?

Toff 2:   Yah, bloody yah.

The truth is way more prosaic. The Footlights Club was a tatty little room in the basement of the Cambridge Union. It had a dusty, beer-stained carpet and benches upholstered in fake leather ran along each side. These were invariably decked with a multitude of props – rubber chickens, Swedish-blonde wigs, moustaches and sombreros. All the important stuff. And there, at the back of the room, was the stage, a slightly raised dais onto which a spotlight was trained. Maybe two. A deep fug permeated everything, no matter what time of day you entered the room – a perma-stink of booze, fags, fun and shame, the key notes of any comedic perfume.

I cannot overstate what an unprepossessing space it was (and most likely still is). It didn't resonate with a sense of its own history. It didn't feel momentous or special. It was just another damp, stinking student hole. The posters on the walls, some from the 70s, were tatty and unframed, the black curtain hanging at the back of the stage as ripped as a witch's hem. But I loved that. It's not a museum – it doesn't look backwards. It's a clubroom. It's for the *now*. It's a dirty bustling hive of success, failure and silliness.

History is reality distilled, events boiled down to a manageable partisan narrative we can easily remember. The Cambridge Footlights history has been duly reduced to the select list of those who 'made it' (Cleese, Cook, Idle, etc.), whereas the real lifeblood of the club came from the vast numbers who went on to do proper jobs. Oftentimes those people were the funniest – the ones who went on to be vets or gynaecologists or chemical engineers. My business isn't, as I'm forced to admit daily, a meritocracy.

To be part of the Cambridge University arts scene, and the Footlights Society in particular, was a pure privilege. The *people* weren't particularly privileged; they were just nerds with good A-level results. The absolute privilege came from the ability to experiment. To do *anything* you wanted. Want to tour Europe in urine-coloured leggings with a same-sex production of *King Lear*? Here's the cash. Want to put on Lorca's *Blood Wedding*? In Spanish? Naked? Knock yourself out. Hell, if I had the power, I'd make every community, college and university arts society as well funded as the ones I was lucky enough to be part of as a student.

At night the place came alive, transformed from generically unpleasant basement to Britain's most exciting underground lair. And on one of those evenings, in the middle of October 1988, I walked down there, scrap of paper in hand, and took that single step onto the stage. It often still strikes me how small a distance it is, that walk from real to heightened – from normality to performance. One small step for a woman, one giant leap for your adrenal system. How quickly we can move from one part of ourselves into another. How performance formalizes that. How, if you're not mindful of the gap, it can split you in two.

I remember the singular glare of the spotlight, blocking out everything. I remember my ramblings being accompanied by the drunken burble of the crowd, sometimes listening, sometimes not. I remember I was wearing a hot, red lambswool jumper and that my neck starting itching furiously mid-routine.*

But most of all, I remember Mel.

She was standing at the back of the room at the end of the

---

* Because I'd not had the time, skill or indeed motivation to craft anything in advance, this 'routine' mainly consisted of wry observations about the journey from college to clubroom that I'd taken some thirty minutes beforehand. On the plus side, no one could say it wasn't fresh material.

show, a shock of white hair and wayward teeth. She wore pink DMs and ripped jeans and was gassing with a gaggle of students wearing what looked like pyjamas.

She sidled over to me and introduced herself like some post-punk Svengali, and we got chatting. I couldn't tell you what we chatted about. All I can tell you is that there was just a feeling – that most perfect of feelings – a slow, unfolding understanding that I had met a person that I would know for the rest of my life.

Mel and I didn't work together much at college – on account of her being *so much older than me*. In my second year (her third) she went off to Bologna and power-ate spaghetti for a year. In many ways this was training for what was to come in our later careers. While she was gone, I spent my days trying to bluff my way through Jacobean tragedy and Anglo-Saxon, Norse and Celtic (boy, is it hard to bullshit in Norse). I spent my nights in the Footlights basement. By the time I hit my final year and Mel returned, I pretty much lived in that comedy bunker and rarely saw daylight.

I ended up becoming president of the club, a presidency defined by the fact that on my watch we received sponsorship from a beer company. I still have no idea how that happened. I don't remember 'reaching out' to them, 'establishing core values' or 'cascading information with a view to establishing value-generating paradigms'. Plus, with my cropped hair, army boots and charity-shop clothes I looked more like an advert alerting people to the dangers of alcohol abuse, than an ambassador who could bring shiny new folk to the 'brand'.

All I remember was that a van turned up at the beginning of term and it was full, and I mean *full*, of lager. At the back of the van was a small fridge, which I put in my room, then filled. With lager. I don't remember anything much for the next six months. By Christmas I had split up with Rob and was drinking heavily – you know, being a *grown-up*. I'd wake up on floors and try to piece together how I'd got there. I collapsed in the street. I drank like a pro until I got a stomach ulcer, by which time I had scraped through graduation and left the pressure cooker of college, so no longer needed the grog to hide my insecurities.

Considering how slapdash, hare-brained and ham-fisted we are, my double act with Mel had an extremely formal beginning. Shortly after we graduated I received a brief handwritten letter in the post.

Dear Susan,
    Would you like to be in a double act with me?
Love Melanie

I believe I may have written back:

Dear Melanie,
    Yes I would.
Love Susan

And so that was that.

Auld Reekie

Do you remember the Blair–Brown summit that famously took place in that Italian restaurant in north London? The power-transitioning pact made over meatballs, gnocchi and *affogato*? Well, I like to think Mel and I got there first, when in 1993, at the food court in Victoria station, on plastic chairs nestled between the warring outlets of Singapore Sam's and Spud-U-Like, we shook hands on a plan to take our first show to Edinburgh.

Mel and I had left it rather late to sort a venue for the festival, so after the highs of the Spud-U-Like summit we were forced to confront a more realistic reality. Come February, most venues are already fully booked, but we managed to get our friend Hartley, who was running the C Venue on Princess Street, to give us his last available slot, which happened to be at

10.05 a.m.

Yes, that holy grail of comedic timeslots, the hour of the day that *every* self-respecting performer wants to make their mark on. I can't imagine why there wasn't more of a clamour for the

10.05 a.m.

slot, since that's universally acknowledged to be *the most* fun time of day. What you might not know, is that at

10.05 a.m.

your body and mind are at their most receptive to sixty minutes of surrealist, stream-of-consciousness sketches performed by total unknowns in an airless box overlooking a busy thoroughfare. And if *that* isn't enough to convince you, the other *amazing* thing about the

10.05 a.m.

slot, is that it's not the more conventional

10.00 a.m.

slot, which is when all the competing shows start.

What can I say? We were way ahead of the curve.

And so, for our first Edinburgh Festival together, an event world renowned for its bacchanalian excess and hedonistic splendour, we had the

10.05 a.m.

slot, meaning we had to get up at

8.00 a.m.

EIGHT A.M. Just as our peers were going to bed after a night on the tiles, we would be getting up and bracing ourselves for the long walk to Princess Street from our student digs.

Putting on a show isn't cheap, so we scraped together what we could and borrowed money from our families on the understanding we'd try to turn a profit. Part of our crowd-luring strategy focused on the name of the show, *The Naked Brunch*. Great, eh? Eh? What do you mean, it's shit? You're obviously missing the hilarious subtext. It's a play on both William S. Burrough's seminal drug-vignette novel and the time of day we were performing. Brilliant, isn't it? And in no way obscure/pretentious/doomed to failure.

I set off for this, our first Edinburgh Festival together, at around 8 p.m. one evening in August. I had a backpack and a large bin liner, which held my share of our vast array of props. Mum was having a dinner party, was elbow-deep in Marie Rose sauce and didn't even hear me say goodbye. I slipped out of the house. It felt exciting. I felt like Dick Whittington.

The plan was for me to take the direct train from Sanderstead to Victoria and meet Mel at the coach station. From there we'd get the all-night National Express to Scotland. It was a perfect plan, although if there was a flaw in it, that flaw would be called South East Trains.

I waited at the deserted platform for the 8.03 p.m. train. 8:03 p.m. came and went. No worries, I thought – I can still catch the 8.33 and be in plenty of time. 8.33 came and went. Still no train. Finally a bored adenoidal voice on the tannoy, 'South East Trains regrets to inform you that all trains have been cancelled due to a fault further up the line.' The whine of feedback. Then a deafening silence.

I went into a flat panic. *You can't do this*, I thought. *You can't have a fault on the line! Not now! Not today! I have to peddle my 'barely rehearsed'* form of sketch comedy at the Edinburgh Festival. I need to be there!*

I panicked. I didn't own a mobile, and the nearby payphone was so lacquered in acrid man-piss it had long since stopped working. There was only one thing to do. This was a bonafide crisis, so it followed I'd need someone who could embrace that crisis. I needed to get Ann Perkins – Mega-Mum – involved.

I left the station and walked home, fast. The bag of props

---

* This was our first genuine review. You can't fault it for factual accuracy.

rattled in time with my footsteps. There was the rhythmic squeak of a plastic chicken and the rustle of a nylon Swedish-blonde-fantasy wig. From a distance it looked like I'd murdered Britt Ekland and kept her hair as some form of trophy.

I arrived home just after 9.15 p.m. Mum was half-cut,* in a velour playsuit, breadcrumbing the hell out of some Icelandic prawns. Dad was exchanging blue jokes with his best mate Mick and his wife Eve.

'What's happened?' said Mum, one eye on me, the other on a meringue nest.

'There are no trains, Mum. They're all cancelled. I'm going to miss my coach. I'm going to miss the festival.' And I was so tired and so exasperated, I might just have had a little cry.

There were two ways Mum could have gone. She could have pointed out that the festival runs for a whole month and therefore I would hardly miss a thing. OR she could join me in making a mountain out of a molehill. My mum's whole life has been about waiting and preparing for catastrophe to come knocking. And here it was. An actual catastrophe. And she wasn't about to look that shit-horse in the mouth.

'Right,' she said with a steeliness which was thrilling, 'I'm taking you. Call Victoria and be ready to leave in the next few minutes.'

I dragged down the enormous phone directory from the shelf and thumbed through its pages. Finally I arrived at the Customer Services number for Victoria Coach Station and dialled. Minutes later, someone answered.

---

* She'd had two sips of sherry. This is enough to get my mum hammered. Once she had a full glass of Cointreau and couldn't get out of bed the next day. 'My head and my body hurt,' she wailed. 'Is it Lyme's disease?' We had to explain gently to her that it was a hangover.

Woman: Hello. Victoria.

Me: Hello, Victoria. I'm Sue. I need you to do me a massive
          favour. I'm due to meet a friend of mine around about
          now and I am late. Very late. I need you to get a message
          to her. Can you do that?

Woman: Mmm. I don't know. We'd have to put it out on the tan-
          noy. Is it an emergency?

I stared at the squeaky chicken in my bag. *Yes, of course!* I
wanted to scream. *I'm young! EVERYTHING is an emergency!*
'It's very important I get in touch with her,' I replied, moder-
ately but firmly. 'It's *urgent.*'

'OK,' she said. 'Who am I trying to contact?'

And then the full nightmare struck me. I was going to have
to spell Mel's surname out to her. Over the years I'd come to
realize that you have to set aside a good fifteen minutes to get
that properly through to someone. I looked at my watch. It
was 9.28 p.m.

'Mel,' I said desperately, hoping that would be sufficient.

'Mel who?' she replied.

DAMN!

Me: Won't 'Mel' do?

Woman: No, it won't. There might be lots of Mels. I'm afraid I'm
          going to need a surname.

I take a deep breath in preparation.

Me: Giedroyc.

Woman: [*slight pause*] Goodrich?

Me: Giedroyc.

Woman: Oh. Oh. OK. [*Another pause*] Say it again?

Me: [*slower this time*] Giedroyc.
Woman: And how do you spell that?

Trust me, that won't help, I think, but carry on nonetheless.

Me: G-I-E-D-R-O-Y-C.

I hear the endless scratch of her pen.

Woman: So that's Guy-ed-ro-ik?
Me: [*raising my voice in desperation*] It's pronounced Ged-roy-ch.
Woman: Gee-roy-cee.
Me: [*bellowing*] GED-ROY-CH.
Woman: Ged-royds?
Me: That'll do. Perfect. Thank you.

I gave her the message and put the phone down. It was now 9.31 p.m.

We ran down the front steps and hurled ourselves into the car. Then, of course, we had to negotiate the bloody garage.

'MIND THE SIDES!' shouted Mum. To herself.

It was now 9.35 p.m.

It's around nine miles from South Croydon to Victoria. I have never known anyone drive it in less than fifty minutes. Ann Perkins had just twenty-five.

'We're never going to make it. Everything's ruined,' I whined.

'Shut up,' she said. 'I'm concentrating.' We sat in silence. I imagined her dinner guests trying to make the best of their uncooked prawns and unfilled meringue nests and felt bad.

'Sorry, Mum.'

'Shut up.'

She gritted her teeth, the walnut of muscle in her cheek hardening. Ann was ready for business. She was heading for Victoria come what may. My heart was in my mouth as we sped through the leafy paradise of Thornton Heath and along the boulevards of Brixton.

Meanwhile, Mel had arrived on the bus station concourse and was waiting for me, oblivious to the drama taking place just a few miles south. She was loading her bin liner of props onto the coach when she heard the tannoy announcement.

You've never known true pain until you've heard a disincentivized transportation worker try to pronounce a Polish surname (before Poles were familiar visitors to our shores) over a public address system late at night. It was like someone firing vowels at a wall.

'Will Mel . . .

[*Her eyes taking it in*] 'Will Mel . . .

[*Plucking up courage*] 'Mel Gee . . .

[*Finally going for it*] 'Will Mel Gee-eye-ay-ee-dee-roo-ooo-eeck come to the information desk immediately.'

[*Pretty cocky now*] 'That's Miss Mel Gee-ee-der-ee-ooky-ck to the information desk.'

Finally, deducing that the only person on the concourse with a name even close to that being mangled was her, Mel approached the desk. The woman dutifully passed her a piece of paper with my succinct message on it. It read simply, 'HOLD THE COACH, Perks x'.

Back in south London, Mum was haring up the A23 in a trance state. It was as if fifty years of compliant behaviour was bubbling up inside her. Here was a woman whose entire life had consisted of behaving well, doing the right thing, doing what everyone else wanted. Here was a woman who could not and would not take it any more. *Screw you, authority! This is the real me. I've gone rogue!* I swear she ran a red light or two. She screeched into the coach station in what may or may not have been a handbrake turn. I kissed her on the cheek and flew out of the passenger door.

10.03 p.m.

Mel, meanwhile, was putting on one hell of a show, demonstrating pretty much all of the reasons she had been rejected from every drama school in Britain. She had assumed a starfish position in the doorway of the coach, effectively blocking it open, and was pretending to cry. The driver meanwhile was trying to close the pneumatic doors and get under way. I skidded across the concourse floor, heart in my mouth and yelled as I saw her. With that, I hurled myself, a squeaky chicken, Britt Ekland's hair and a load of miscellaneous junk into the bus, and the doors hissed shut behind us.

The coach was due to arrive at Edinburgh Waverley at 6 a.m. after an all-night potter up the M1. It transpired we were the only non-French-speaking people on the bus. Just Mel, myself and fifty-eight extremely shouty students from Paris. Our seats were in the shadow of the medicated toilet, which was continually in use – meaning that every time we tried to drift off, we'd be woken by a gust of something distinctly evocative of the second arrondissement.

Eight nostril-challenging hours later, we arrived.

There can be few less romantic starting points for any relationship than St Andrew's Square bus depot in Edinburgh, yet it was there I first fell in love with Scotland. Since then I've slept on the warm beaches of Arran in November, I've underwhelmed audiences from Cumbernauld to Aberdeen and back again, I've cried at the immaculate stillness of loch and mountain in Torridon, and I've tried skiing in Aviemore and lived to tell the tale. Scotland has been the crucible for my double act, the site of myriad memorable holidays and the settling point for my wanderlust brother, who married a girl from Perth and together created my brilliant wee nieces.

But it was the festival that started it all. I've spent every August since the age of fourteen at the foot of Edinburgh Castle, marching up and down the cobbles of the Royal Mile at festival time dressed as a milkmaid or bunny rabbit or zombie to advertise my latest hare-brained dramatic endeavour. It began when the Children's Music Theatre came to Croydon auditioning for their touring show. I managed to get a bit part and headed north for the summer with my oldest mate Gemma, who'd also bagged a role. It was the first time I'd been away from my parents. They saw it as a great artistic opportunity for their daughter; I saw it as a magical teenage sex workshop.

I went to the festival during my time at college too, taking part in execrable feminist reworkings and pretentious new writing. But it was that first show I did with Mel that truly sealed the city in my heart. The drunken ramblings on the cobbles of the Pleasance Courtyard. The late-night spicy haggis on the London Road. The thrill of seeing my peers Lee and Herring, Armstrong and Miller, the impeccable League of Gentlemen. My tribe, my new-found family. We lived on nothing but cold hot dogs and warm beer and the kindness of strangers chancing their hard-earned cash on our unique brand of utter silly. It's perhaps the closest I've ever been to truly, completely happy.

Our debut show at the Fringe, as I've already mentioned, was called *The Naked Brunch* – a little bit like a sketch show, a lot like being cornered by a couple of inmates from a psychiatric facility.

We got off the coach with everything we thought we needed: bags and bags of props, interminable voice-overs lovingly recorded to DAT, play-in music, costumes and publicity posters. What we didn't have, it turned out, was an end to the show. Somewhere along the line, due to laziness, forgetfulness or simple shame, we'd just not bothered to finish writing the thing.

The room we'd been assigned was a hot black sweat box on the top floor of the C Venue on Princess Street. It looked like somewhere you'd conduct an extraordinary rendition rather than pay to watch comedy. The heat was so extreme that later in the run, after numerous complaints, an enormous silver coil was put through the door to vent the steam and sweat. If it was hot at

10.05 a.m.

then I dread to think of the ambient temperature at 4 p.m. when the experimental troupe from Godalming began performing their production of *Equus*.

We treated the first show as a dress rehearsal. We hadn't meant to. It was just that no one turned up – and after all surely a performance is only a performance if there is someone there to watch it. Without that, it's just a thought experiment – or at best two nutters in a room shouting at each other in regional accents.

The second show was different. This time we had an audience, although 'audience' is a slightly grandiose term for a single person. This person came into the room wearing a large rucksack. Rather unusually, she didn't take it off as she sat down, and so sat perched forward at a forty-five-degree angle for the entirety of the show. At points during the performance she would take out a large street map of Edinburgh, which she would unfold and unfold and unfold until it covered almost her entire top half. Then, after examining it, she would fold and fold and fold it back into a neat concertina. At several points during the show I wondered if she'd perhaps mistaken the venue for Edinburgh Castle and found herself somewhat disappointed by the dimensions of the rooms.

The initial idea behind *The Naked Brunch* was to showcase sketch characters within an overriding narrative. This ended up being a rather shoddy conceit involving them all being trapped inside a computer game. The result was that it was meta without in any way being good. The characters included paramilitary Brown Owls, some Dutch VJs, a pair of US East Coast post-feminists and a couple of lovelorn Aussie PE teachers, who expressed their desire for one another exclusively through the medium of sport. That's one hell of a computer game, right there.

The problem was, the more we wrote, the bigger and more bizarre our characters became. And the bigger they became, the more constrictive and less credible the framework around them seemed. But, rather than ditching the whole thing and just delivering a simple sketch show, we persisted with the computer game theme, which petered out as the hour wore on. By the final sketch none of it, and I mean NONE OF IT, made any sense. So we did what so many young writers do when something isn't working. Nothing. We just left it and hoped the problem would go away all by itself.

It didn't.

Because there was no show-stopper ending, for some reason that has mercifully faded with time, we decided to end with our backs to the audience (singular) shining a torch on a croissant. Yep, shining a torch on a croissant. No dance numbers for us – no recapping, no show tunes – just a greasy baked semicircle caught in the thin beam of a cheap torch bought from Ali's Cave on the Lothian Road.

Don't ask me why. Even twenty-one years on. Don't ask me why.

When the show finally ground to a halt, the voice-over stopped and silence again prevailed, we burst through the fourth wall to have a chat with our lone punter.

Us: Hi!

Her: [*American*] Hi! [*Folding up her map again*]

Me: We're really sorry about that.

Her: About what?

Mel: The accent.

Her: What accent?

Me: The American accent . . . the American post-feminists.

Her: Oh. Really? American?

Mel: Yes. We're sorry.

Her: They were *Americans*?

Me: Yes.

Her: Oh. Oh, I didn't notice.

The run lasted for another three weeks.

Mel and I have been responsible for some truly disastrous performances over the years. Too many to mention. But let me give you my top four.

1. Stockton

In 1994/5 we embarked on a tour of small arts centres. If there was a tiny, dilapidated, endangered cultural space in the UK, we'd find it and half-fill it. One such space was in Stockton-on-Tees. Our manager, Ted, a fabulous pint-sized dynamo in double-denim, booked us in for a gig starting at 8 p.m. 'It'll be great,' he said. 'There's a do in there first and then a disco after, so there'll be a guaranteed crowd. It's all part of a package. It's going to be amazing. Amazing!'

When we arrived, bags of props in hand, we became aware of a group of women in the theatre, sat on chairs in a semicircle. There seemed to be an awful lot of crying and hugging.

Me: [*nervously*] What kind of 'do' is this?
Ted: Well . . . it's not so much a *do* . . . [*Suddenly sounding evasive*]
Mel: Why is everyone sobbing?
Ted: Well, the thing is . . .

Now I know we're in trouble – no sentence ends well that begins with 'The thing is . . .'

Ted: The thing is, it's not so much a 'do' as a support group.
Me: What do you mean 'support group'? What support group?

And then the truth emerged. We'd been booked to do our comedy show after a workshop for battered women organised by the charity Zero Tolerance. The audience was a mix of abused women and repentant, teary men. It couldn't get any worse.

It did.

Because after the support group, and just before we were due onstage, the organizers decided to put on a film. This hard-hitting documentary charted the emotional journeys of both perpetrators and victims of domestic abuse, and was punctuated by deep sobs emanating from the audience.

After a truly devastating thirty minutes, and just as a close-up of a bruised and swollen face faded into black, our cheesy 70s intro music began. As awkward emotional gear changes go, it was right up there with Phil and Holly on *This Morning* going from Syria to *Towie* and back again.

Mel: Shit! That's us!
Me: [*shouting to make myself heard over the keening*] Oh God . . .

And on we went, into the darkness. I never knew that bewilderment had a sound until that very moment. Now I know that it does.

After we finished the show (an hour-long affair that, it transpired, ran at only forty-three minutes without laughs) the disco began. No sooner had the smattering of applause died away than Gloria Gaynor's 'I Will Survive' kicked in, and the crying started again.

I ended up slow-dancing with a sixty-year-old woman from Macclesfield; Mel was locked into a deep sway with a former offender, and Ted, well Ted had been grabbed by a rather substantial woman and was now being rocked from side to side, his head trapped between her space-hopper breasts. We left him there, gently asphyxiating, as penance. He needed to know that when it came to being mis-sold a gig, we had zero tolerance.

2. Cambridge

Billed as a glorious homecoming by nobody except us, we returned to our old stomping ground, gigging at the Cambridge

University Playhouse as part of our tour in the autumn of 1995. In true Mel/Sue fashion, we had failed to book a lighting and sound operator for the show, hoping that local techie stalwart Liam would be available. I loved Liam – he was the stuff of legend. He was fuelled by two things: prawn cocktail crisps and an abject hatred of all performers. He also had the largest set of keys in East Anglia, which he hung from his belt, giving him his trademark limp. Liam huffed and eye-rolled his way through every piss-poor production I ever did at that theatre – and there were an awful lot of piss-poor productions – yet for some unknown reason he simply wasn't available when we came back that autumn.

At that time my brother was working as a manager of a foreign language school near Cambridge. The night before the gig he came over to visit, which set Mel thinking.

Mel: Maybe David could do the lights?

Me: David? What, my *brother*, David?

Mel: Yes. Why not?

Me: Have you actually met him?

Mel: Well of course I have . . .

Me: Then why are you even *asking*? He is the only person on the planet who is as technologically illiterate as I am.

Mel: He'll be fine. Plus I've always had a slight crush on him.

Me: He won't be fine. He's mildly dyspraxic and easily distracted, with a healthy dose of 'couldn't give a shit' thrown in for good measure.

Mel: I think it'll be hilarious. He doesn't even have to do much. Come on. It'll be fun!

The next night, the night of the performance, we received word from the front-of-house manager that the audience was seated and we were ready to go. Normally, when you get clearance, you make your way to the wings and get on with things as soon as possible, but our double act is a little different. It is *exactly* at that point, on the cusp of starting a show, that Mel's bowels swing into action.

Mel's GI tract is a source of wonderment to all those who know and love her. Or have sat on a bus near her. Or been in a room with her. Or a room after her. There is not one single event, emotion or situation that Mel's digestive system can't translate into instant and devastating flatus. And so, for decades, in those precious seconds before a performance – where you'd normally be riding the adrenalin rush, pacing, going through lines and focusing – I have had to endure the sights, sounds and aromas of Mel's malevolent wind. Or worse.

At the Edinburgh Festival of 1998 we took part in a gang show called *The Big Squeeze* with the brilliant Geraldine McNulty and our mega-mucker Emma Kennedy. Straight after our slot a friend, Penny, was performing her one-woman show at the venue. It was getting near the end of the run and we felt it was the comradely thing to do to stay on afterwards to cheer her on. As we were called backstage for our opening sketch, Mel, as always, heard the distant call of nature.

Mel:	[*whispering*] I need a wee . . .
Me:	Well why didn't you go thirty seconds ago? You remember thirty seconds ago? When we were downstairs? Next to a *toilet*.
Mel:	It's not my fault! It's like a Pavlovian reaction. I get stressed.

Emma approaches, wearily.

Emma:	Is it Mel?
Me:	Yes.
Emma:	Does she need the toilet again?
Me:	*Of course* she needs the toilet . . .

Emma rolls her eyes and walks on.

Front-of-House Manager:	[*emerging from the shadows*] That's clearance.
Mel:	But I'm busting!
Gerry:	[*desperately trying to focus on the performance ahead*] Well go downstairs, for goodness' sake!

Opening music starts.

Mel:	Oh God! There's no time!
Me:	Oh for goodness' sake, Miggins, go in the bucket!

I point over to the black bucket in the wings that has been there since the beginning of the run. A paintbrush sits in a thin puddle of liquid at the bottom. Mel looks at it in desperation then parks herself above it. We look away. The sound of a zip. A deluge. The zip again. Then we all run onstage to do the show. Ah, showbiz.

Once done, we collected up the costumes and props littered at the side of stage and plonked ourselves in the auditorium in preparation for our mate's solo show. This turned out to be a marvellously involved affair with multiple characters and complex plots. We were lost in it – lost in it almost to the point of sleep – when suddenly Penny started talking in an Irish accent, transforming into the character of a raging fire-and-brimstone priest. There was a lot of vengeful Old Testament babbling and shouting at us, which roused us from unconsciousness. The character reached fever pitch, cursing us as sinners and telling us we needed to be bathed in the holy water of Christ the Redeemer. Whereupon she left the stage and reappeared a moment later . . .

. . . with the bucket.

Emma, Mel and myself sat suddenly upright, rigid with fear. Like animals on the plains who know instinctively that danger is coming.

Penny dipped the paintbrush into the bucket, then flung the liquid at the audience. The spray flew to the left and right of us. The audience laughed. 'Don't laugh!' I wanted to shout. 'You're being drenched in piss!' But I was stopped in my tracks by a frenzy of droplets raining down on my head. Mel refused to look, burying her face in her palms as the wee kept on coming and coming and coming.

That was the last time I went to an experimental theatre show. You don't get that with Shakespeare.

Anyhow, I've digressed. We're back in Cambridge, 1995, and my brother was in charge of operating the show. We'd been told to get to the wings and stand by, so we duly headed backstage and waited. And waited.

Finally, the intro music and voice-over began. Then stopped, abruptly. Then started again, this time at a deafening volume. We waited for the lights to dim in the auditorium. They didn't.

Mel: [*bellowing over the din*] Is that us? Should we just go on?
Me: I guess so . . .

The intro music suddenly stops. There is an all-encompassing silence.

Mel: [*pushing me forward, hissing*] Go on! Now! Now!

The moment we stepped onstage a strange thing happened: the house lights increased in intensity, thus illuminating the audience further, and the spotlights went down, thus plunging Mel and me into darkness. We were now in total silence and total blackout. It was a devastating comedic double whammy.

I looked up to the lighting booth and saw David staring at the script and shaking his head. It's not the sort of thing that inspires you to begin an eclectic offbeat hour of character comedy.

'I told you,' I hissed as another random piece of music exploded on the PA. 'He's a technological fucking *idiot* . . .'

A spotlight came on, stage left. *Finally!* We walked towards it. The moment we started to feel the heat of it, it flicked off again, only to reappear on the other side of the stage. So we turned around and walked across. The same thing happened. We began chasing visibility.

For the next hour we went on a voyage of audio-visual discovery. Sometimes we'd get a high-decibel burst of incongruous sound effect – a lion roaring, a juicy fart, some cicadas in the bush. Sometimes we would be squashed into a pinprick of light at the very back of the stage, desperate to be seen for at least a small percentage of the show. However, in the final ten minutes David appeared to find his mojo, opting for what became his signature lighting state – Guantanamo Bay. He decided to put every single light at his disposal on full – backstage, audience, side lights, spotlights – you name it. There was even a glitter ball going full pelt. He had also decided to alleviate some of the tension by stripping to the waist and donning a large Robin Hood hat that had obviously been lying around the booth.

The *Cambridge Evening News* review of that night said it all: '. . . it's hard to comment on the quality of the show, as the multiple technical failures rather overwhelmed proceedings. In fact, in all my decades as a theatre critic it's hard to bring to mind a more woeful display from a lighting and sound operator than the one witnessed last night.'

But hey, remember, ALL publicity is good publicity. Yes?

3. Brighton

The old Komedia in Brighton's Kemptown was one of my favourite venues ever – not least because its founders Colin, Marina and David were pretty much the only people who ever wanted to book us. It was like all great theatres – bijou and friendly, well loved by the locals, with good grub and a bit of jazz at the weekends.

It was 1996, and we were touring our third show, *Women in Uniform*. By now we had established a small (see also: negligible) posse of people who'd regularly turn out to see us – mainly sex workers, ex-offenders and those wrestling with their sexuality. Oh, and a man called Perv, who ran a nightclub nearby. I remember going to the Zap Bar with him one evening, and Mel had no idea it was gay night. At the end of the evening she merely said, 'It's nice that the women here are so *friendly*, isn't it?' I long for that naivety. Just for a second.

So, it's the opening night of a week-long run at the venue. We are in the dressing room getting ready when we suddenly get the all-clear to head to stage. This news, albeit entirely expected, causes Mel's digestive system, once again, to start firing on all cylinders.

'Sorry, mate, I'm desperate . . .'

Her limbic system has gone into high alert. This is fight-or-flight time. She needs to run, and in order to do that most effectively, she needs to get rid of anything extraneous that might inhibit her movement. And what she decides to get rid of is her microphone receiver pack. She summarily drops it into my hands and dashes for the toilet.

There's just one problem. The microphone equipment comes in two parts: firstly, the receiver, which I am now holding, and secondly, the microphone itself, which Mel is wearing on her lapel. Crucially, the two parts are connected by a metre-long cable. This expensive umbilical can't be disconnected at speed without risking damage, which means only one thing.

Where Mel goes, I go also.

I find myself standing next to her in a cramped bog, palms up, holding the receiver like it's the Holy Grail. She perches below making low moaning sounds. It begins like a distant rumble, like thunder. The hairs on my arm stand to attention. Then comes the noise. Like a thousand tins of beans being hurled against a wall. Then the toxic gust. I feel like Karen Silkwood: contaminated, angry, compelled to seek legal advice.

'Cheers, chum,' says Mel once the horror is over. 'Ooh, let me take that,' retrieving the receiver from my grasp and clipping it back on her belt. I say nothing.

Mel did the greatest gig of her life that night. She was light and springy and refreshed. I spent that hour dry-retching and trying to get enough oxygen in my lungs to say my lines.

As part of my rider,* we now have separate dressing rooms.

---

* This also includes five new-born puppies, a Clairol Foot Spa and a wheelie bin full of Reese's Pieces.

4. Leighton Buzzard

And so it came to pass, in the Year of Our Lord 1996, that we visited the Bedfordshire town of Leighton Buzzard. Sadly, it transpired that the residents were far from ready for our unique brand of poorly thought-out 'fun'. The venue we had been booked into was the council-run Library Theatre, which appeared on first impression to consist of an awful lot of library and not a lot of actual theatre.

There was a smattering of people in the audience, all of whom seemed furious before we'd even started. Well, if they were furious then, I don't have a descriptor for the hostile vibes we were getting a mere five minutes into proceedings. There is a profound telepathy at work in all close relationships – a short-hand, if you will. A flicker of the eyelid, a tilt or cock of the head, and you're both on the same page. Mel and I have that telepathy. As the atmosphere became increasingly toxic, we shot each other a glance. A glance that said, *Let's get this over with as quickly as possible.*

If we couldn't make them laugh, we could certainly get them home before they turned violent.

We increased the speed of our delivery, making snap cuts, overlapping one another's lines. We did not pause, because pausing is for laughter, and why wait for something that will never arrive? Under normal conditions our show ran for just over an hour. In Leighton Buzzard it lasted exactly thirty-six minutes, beating our previous record (Stockton-on-Tees) by a full seven minutes. We didn't bother coming back onstage for a bow; instead we used the closing music to cover the sound of our exit from the stage door. We sprinted for the station. Sprinted. Mercifully there was a London-bound train waiting on the platform as we arrived. As we hopped on, and the doors closed behind us, we saw a gang of young men running towards the carriage. To this day I have no idea whether they were members of our audience desperate to take us to the Old Mill and burn us or just regular Joes on a night out. But we've never gone back, just in case.

THREE

London

The Trouble with London

The essayist and lexicographer Dr Samuel Johnson famously once said, 'When a man is tired of London, he is tired of life.'

Well, Samuel, when a *woman* is tired of London, she usually tries to get away for the weekend – you know, get some perspective. She doesn't tend to think of it as a precursor for ending her existence. My advice would be: stop being so absolutist in your thinking. Think about changing it up. Failing that, some of the modern SSRIs are really very good.

I returned to London after college just as I was beginning my double act with Mel. I didn't have a bean and so made like Blanche duBois and depended on the kindness of strangers. I stayed, briefly, with Nicola's then boyfriend Seth, whose parents had a flat in a posh stucco square near Earl's Court. It was the model of elegance from the outside, but empty on the inside – 'all fur coat and no knickers' as my nan liked to say, just before they arrested her for soliciting.

Seth was a wiry, febrile genius who wanted to be a poet and ended up a venture capitalist. Life as Tennyson, it turns out, was a shrub short of the full hedge fund. Having said that, I wanted to be a novelist but was working on a direct sales marketing manual for Kleeneze. So much for *my* integrity.

Seth and I smoked, talked shit and ate fancy burgers from a place called Hollywood down the road. *Classy.* We listened to Radiohead and The The, read e e cummings and didn't use capitals for a year (which was both tough and compromising, since I was working as a copywriter at the time). We cried at

Anne Sexton and Louis MacNeice and Pablo Neruda and felt part of a tribe. Although had that tribe found out that we were living in a half-million-pound flat in the Sloane heartlands it might have been time for our membership to be rescinded. I slept on a sofa bed in a lounge with no furniture save a chicken-mesh sculpture of a woman who appeared to be giving the Hitler salute. I have no idea why she was there or how Seth, a devout Jew of Ashkenazi hue, felt about her. But there she stood, eight feet high, her outstretched arm suggesting a lazy *Lebensraum* in the vague direction of Fulham.

I loved Seth. He was an emotional soul. Once he took a bread knife and carved up his entire book collection. I thought that was kind of arty. Then he took a lighter and set fire to his eyebrows. I thought that was the right time to move out.

For the next few years I lived with Sarah and Nicola. We were the Three Graces in reverse – uncouth, grotty and lazy. Shortly after my stay at Seth's, his parents sold the Earl's Court flat and bought a disused office space at the end of a leafy cul-de-sac in Hampstead, north London. While they waited for planning permission to come through for their minimalist dream home, they kindly asked if we wanted to live there and keep the place occupied.

I had never, in all my life, seen such a beautiful part of town – a pristine village within the city. It had cobbled streets, and early-Victorian cottages with handmade dimpled-glass windows that moved like water when the sun caught them. Every front garden seemed to burst with flowers, and every house was studded with blue plaques that boasted of Constable, Blake and the like.

I'd never seen a plaque in Croydon, not one – I'm not sure the sort of thing that happens in Croydon would merit the attentions of English Heritage.

CAPTAIN SENSIBLE URINATED ON THIS CORNER
DIZZEE RASCAL STOPPED HERE TO ASK FOR DIRECTIONS
ADELE GOT WOLF-WHISTLED BY A ROOFER HERE

Our accommodation was basic, at best. In truth, our existence trod an extremely fine line between squatting and tenancy. The building itself was a frail white prefab with weeds growing through the concrete steps and looked at odds with the neighbouring mansions, with their exfoliated brickwork and Farrow & Ball facelifts.

Next door lived a man who owned an entire mobile phone network, in a house so tall we spent the first summer listening to the soundtrack of his lift being installed. He spent *his* first summer listening to a bunch of stoners rowing about Tory education policies and how best to fire flaming clods of horse shit at the Rt Hon. Michael Howard.

His daughter once knocked on our door and asked for a cardigan.

'I'd get my own, but I can't go back in the house,' she said.

'Why?' we asked, ignoring the look of horror on her face as she stared in at our accommodation.

'Oh,' she replied nonchalantly, 'it's on fire.'

It's on fire. That's the thing about the super-rich. Nothing, not even a domestic fireball, bothers them. Not even an inferno can dent their sense of entitlement.

I was unemployed, but hey, I had things to do. For starters, every other week Sarah and I would stroll down to the dole office on Finchley Road. Plus, since our building had no heating, much of our day was spent trying to get warm – like the Ancients did. Sarah devised an excellent thermal preservation technique whereby every morning we'd put our duvets on the floor, lie horizontally across them, then wrap ourselves up like albino sausage rolls. Finally, we'd stagger upright and take it in turns to run gaffer tape around each other to secure the wadding tight.

The whole day was spent like a game in *Jeux Sans Frontières*, hopping from one room to the next like giant Tampax, yelling, 'Who's got my lighter?'

We had no money for internal decoration, so we glued bits of newspaper to the wall like wallpaper – the Underclass Range from Cole and Son, Benefit Seekers by Osborne and Little. I say we had no money, we had a five-pound note, which was lovingly stuck to the wall. This was a special five-pound note – sacred no less – as it had been sent by Jilly Cooper to Nicola in response to a begging letter for money to fund her RADA tuition fees. We loved Jilly so much, we kept the fiver there in honour of her and her kindness, and there was never any privation, nor desperation deep or profound enough to incite any one of us to touch it.

There were no white goods in the flat, so every other day we would make something lovingly referred to as 'pants soup'. We'd gather our collective stash of underwear and dirty clothing, run a bath, chuck it all in with some cheap soda crystals and stir the resultant broth with a stick. Then we'd drain the bath, refill it a little to rinse, then hang the sodden items on a rail above the bath to drain. The soda had the same effect as Agent Orange – for the next twelve months I was puffy, red and horrendously, horrendously itchy.

I met a girl. Emma. She was a trainee lawyer who was a grown-up by day (she could cite precedents and article numbers and everything) and a total toddler by night. I know what you're thinking – *But Sue, you must have been inundated with women, what with you living in a squat with no washing facilities or heating* – well you'd be wrong. You'd be amazed how many girls are put off by the fact that a) you live inside a duvet and b) everything underneath that duvet is unwashed.

We met and seemed to bypass the normal parameters of friendship. There was no *Maybe let's meet next month for a coffee* or any of those boundaries. We met the next day, and very shortly afterwards, maybe even the day after that, we met again. Then we started meeting *every single day*, often sitting next to one another at my computer to play a Star Trek video game. This involved staring at a seemingly endless black screen and moving your mouse up and down, left and right in a vain attempt to find a Klingon. We never found a Klingon. It was forever dark in space. Although I did find that we were now sitting so close to one another that our legs were touching.

I became restless. I didn't sleep much at night and would catnap during the day. I stopped being interested in things. I sat daydreaming, waiting for Spock o'clock. Something felt wrong. Very wrong. I phoned my sister.

Me:	Gel, there's something wrong with me. I don't feel right. I can't sleep and I feel sick to my stomach. I just sit around . . .
Michelle:	Can I just stop you there?
Me:	Is it irritable bowel syndrome?
Michelle:	It's worse.
Me:	Oh God.
Michelle:	Yep.
Me:	Oh God. I'm in love, aren't I?
Michelle:	I am rather sorry to say, yes. Yes, you are.

Out and About

Every gay person in the world has an idealized notion of their coming-out in their head – a fantasy version which eases the anxiety about the inevitable horror to come. This was mine.

Mum is running her hands along the smooth clean lines of her kitchen, wondering if her obsession with minimalism isn't creating a rather austere living space. I come in just as she turns her attentions to the sofa.

Me: Mum, there's something you should know.

Mum: What is it, angel?

Me: I've been wanting to tell you for a while but couldn't find the right time.

Mum: [*plumping cushions*] Well, I think now is the perfect time. Sit! Can I get you a herbal tea?

Me: No, I'm fine.

Mum: Thank God. I don't have any mugs anyway. I got rid of them. You know I can't stand extraneous crockery. Anyway, go on.

Me: Well, the thing is . . . I'm gay, Mum.

A pause. Mum gets up wordlessly and walks to the window.

Me: Did you hear me, Mum? I'm gay.

Mum: [*muttering to herself*] Oh God.

Me: Mum?

Mum: Oh God, no . . .

Suddenly her legs seem to give way, and she collapses, grabbing at the damask curtains as she slides to the floor.

Mum: No! Not my little princess. Not my Susan. Oh God, I'm in shock. I'm going into shock. I can't believe it! I can't . . . I can't cope!

I walk over and offer her my hand.

Me: It is a shock?

Mum: It's a massive shock. I cannot think of anyone in the entire world less likely to be gay than you. You're so . . . un-gay.

Me: I know. Come on, Mum, please stop crying. Try and put into words your knee-jerk prejudices about something that is essentially nothing to do with you – merely a matter of personal choice that, due to bewildering social convention, I'm forced to share with blood relatives.

Mum: [*taking my hand, pulling herself up and resting against the sofa*] I guess, my initial worry is that now you're a lesbian –

Me: Yes . . .

Mum: – you'll have to spend the rest of your life in a fleece.

Me: We only wear fleeces 50 per cent of the time these days, Mum. Get with the programme. And there are so many advantages to me being a lesbian: I can perv over men without them noticing, and dress like a teenager well into my forties. Plus, you'll always be able to rely on me having spare wet-weather gear, should you need it.

Mum: But I assume, because you're such a maverick, that you will forgo the time-honoured lesbian obsession with cats?

Me: Yes. Yes, I will. Cats leave me cold. I shall have dogs. Many, many dogs.

Mum: You're so unique.

Me: I know, Mum. I know.

Mum: [*drying her tears*] You've totally changed my views on sexuality and gender politics. I'm going to tell everyone I know in the Croydon area, while making sure I credit you utterly and exclusively with this incredible transformation. Thank you.

Me: You're welcome.

Mum: I'm so proud of you, my darling.

Me: Don't be silly. I'm just glad I've had such a powerful and positive impact on your life. Now go! Go tell everyone what you've learned here today.

Mum: I shall.

Me: And you'll credit me – remember?

Mum: Of course. I love you so much.

Me: I love you too. Now c'mon – get outta here. You're embarrassing me.

This is how it actually went.

Me: [*on phone, strained voice*] Mum. Can I come home tomorrow?

Mum: Yes. Why? Are you all right?

Me: Yes. I just . . . I just want to talk to you about something.

Mum: [*matter of factly while eating what sounds like toast*] Is it about you being gay?

Long, long pause.

Me: Yes, it might be that.

Mum: [*still munching*] *Is* it that?

Another long pause.

Me: It might be.

Mum: Fine. Well, just whenever you like. No rush. Lots of love, darling.

Click of the receiver.

And that's why I do what I do. You've got to get your drama somewhere, haven't you?

Our next gaff was a flat on the fourth floor of a mansion block in Abbey Road. By now Emma had moved in. In the basement of this block lived John, the night porter, a waxy-faced man with bad teeth who looked like the sort of thing Gunther von Hagens had had a crack at plasticizing. John was a weapons-grade bore who originally hailed from Sligo. Every night when we returned home we'd run the gauntlet from the front door to the rickety cage lift, desperate to avoid his hypnotic honeyed vowels. His chat ammo of choice? The life and works of seventeenth-century herbalist Nicholas Culpeper. It didn't matter what ailment you had, John would let you know, in painstaking detail, using his approximation of a Jacobean voice, what old Nicholas would have done. (This invariably involved boiling onions . . .)

Most nights, our arrival home went as follows.

Open front door, clasp keys tightly to avoid jangling. Run to lift and press button. The cabling sparks into life and the cage slowly descends. Suddenly there is the sound of heavy footsteps ascending from the basement and the noise of a key turning in a lock.

Me: Shit . . . shit! [*Frantically jabbing at the lift button*]

The basement door swings open. The smell of boiled onions fills the lobby.

John: Well, hello, Susan.
Me: Hello, John. I was just –
John: Is that the sound of mucus in your passages?
Me: No.
John: I think it is. A little thickening of the membrane. I can hear it in your voice.

The cage drops into view. Salvation is at hand.

Me: No, I think it's just because . . . Well, you know, it's late. I'm tired . . .
John: The damp. Do you feel it in the flesh, the bones or the ventricles?
Me: Really . . .
John: Try thistles in wine. Culpeper says they 'expel superfluous melancholy from the body and make a man as merry as a cricket'. Will you do that?
Me: Yes. Yes, John. Absolutely.
John: Well, you're a feckin' liar as you can't get thistles this time of year. Honestly. They're ruled by Saturn and Mars, you know. Saturn and Mars!

I rise in the iron cage, high above him, away from the smell of alliums and the sound of silly oldy-worldy babble, back to the safety of the flat and a double whisky.

The strange thing about John was that, for all his guff about late-medieval herbalism, he was a devout and unrepentant chain-smoker. I don't know what Nicholas Culpeper said about tobacco, but we've had a few more credible physicians since who assert that it isn't the healthiest. More worrying, however, was John's insistence on carrying his air rifle with him wherever he went. Whether he was investigating a drains blockage or coming to collect the service charge, his trusty firearm would come with him.

'It's for the squirrels,' he'd insist as I backed away from him in the small kitchen in which we both found ourselves.

One morning, after we'd had to call upon his services to inspect some suspect cracks in the ceiling, I noticed him gazing intently out of the window. None of my attempts to lure him back on message were successful; he merely stared resolutely out until, in a flash, he raised his gun and popped a tree rodent out of the sky.

'Got the little bastard.'

During an impromptu birthday party, one of the more rowdy guests redecorated an entire wall with Cabernet Sauvignon. We did our best to conceal things from John, sneaking off to buy a tin of fresh paint, only to get collared at the last minute.

We turn the front door key and rush to the lift, stabbing at the button. The reflex of cabling as the iron box lowers towards us. We will it on. The sound of heavy footsteps heading upwards from the basement. The door opens. The stench of boiled onions.

John: How are ya, girls?

Me: Good, really good.

John: I see one of yous got mail from the hospital. Are you all right?

Sarah: It's mine, John. It's for me.

John: May I ask what's wrong wit ya? Only –

Sarah: It's nothing. Just a check-up.

John: Private, eh? Or is it your privates? Venereal disease, maybe? Well for that Culpeper would be recommending a poultice of stewed leeks – or wild pansies. It's not always the safest, but do you happen to have mercury in the house?

Sarah: No, John. It's not venereal disease.

John: Mmm. Shame.

The lift finally descends to the ground floor. Free at last.

Whereas Sarah spent the year dodging questions about her genitals, Nicola spent hers staging a John-and-Yoko-style bed-in with a gorgeous boy called Barney. They holed up in the box room overlooking the Abbey Road studios, surfacing occasionally to eat anything beige that might be lying around – bread, pasta, jacket potatoes . . .

Whatever gets you through the night.

After completing our twelve-month tenancy, we escaped John but went from the frying pan into the fire. We decided to move further north, to Golders Green, renting a ramshackle Edwardian house that had remained untouched since its first paint job. Our landlady was an extraordinary character named Rhoda, an indomitable South African in her early nineties. Half the time I had the sneaking suspicion she was being played by Barry Humphries.

Rhoda had never lived in the house but had a fixation with it that none of us could understand. Occasionally we'd hear mutterings that her son had lived there and had died in one of the rooms, but whatever her reason, she had instilled in the building a sort of Havisham's-by-proxy. The place remained as it had done for decades, and no amount of cajoling would get her to spend a penny on refurbishment. There was a small conservatory which had the rare distinction of being colder inside than out. Adjoining it was a small toilet which had been designated 'spider loo' in the first week after Emma sighted a huntsman suspended over the cistern. We never used it after that.

It was a strange relationship we enjoyed with Rhoda, with complex and ever-shifting boundaries. Sometimes we would be her surrogate children, then her friends, then strictly her tenants. The problem was, you never quite knew at what point on that continuum you were currently positioned. At the beginning of every week we'd do her food shopping and bring it round to her house. At the end of every week, by way of thanks, we'd receive a parcel from Fortnum & Mason containing one pack of sausages and two packs of ginger thins. The contents never changed. She had obviously taken one look at us and thought, *What those girls need are pigs and biscuits. Pigs and biscuits!*

Rhoda would also hold random, infrequent 'happenings'. Our attendance was mandatory. Invariably we would be stuck next to an old colonel or someone who had invented radiotherapy, but we were young, stupid and cocky, so were impervious to their stories and achievements.

On one such occasion we arrived on Rhoda's doorstep to be greeted by a beautiful black waiter. He seemed not to have a name but was merely part of the shadowy force known as 'the staff'. It was going to be one of those evenings. Rhoda was an unapologetic racist who had spent her formative years with no context other than apartheid, which meant you oscillated between hating her and feeling rather sorry for her. To be honest, on these evenings I felt sorry for everyone – suspended as we were in the aspic of class, power and money.

Rhoda's entry to these parties was the stuff of legend. There would be the sound of brass and the rumble of machinery as she wobbled into view, descending – on her Stannah stairlift – in fuschia dress and red velvet turban, blowing like billy-o on a hunting horn. We'd applaud awkwardly. The problem was on this particular night the stairlift got stuck mid-descent, so we were forced to carry on clapping for several minutes while the unnamed beautiful-black-man carried her down.

Finally she reached us. She stood, gathered herself, pulled the back of her dress from out of her large cotton pants and ushered us into the dining room.

'We're having cold soup!' she exclaimed cheerily. 'I asked *them* to make it,' gesturing to the staff. 'I asked them to make it with avocado. Never seen that before, and I thought it could be fun!'

Three vast tureens were brought in. The lids were lifted. A cumulus of fruit flies flew out of each. Inside sat a lurid green broth with thick skin on top. From where I was sitting, it looked like Kermit cellulite.

Well, I thought, *that is fun.*

A deep and profound silence set in over the guests after the very first mouthful, which had the consistency of petroleum. It was as if we had reached a common consensus that our energies were best spent focusing on getting the pea-coloured potage down our throats rather than attempting conversation.

'Get down, Blackie!' bellowed Rhoda at a sable Labrador bolting towards the table. Though even the Labrador, a breed famed for its untrammelled appetite, baulked at the contents of the tureen once he'd clapped eyes on it. There's a reason people don't make soup out of avocados. And that reason was now making itself incredibly clear to my colon.

That particular night I had been sat opposite Rhoda, while Emma was at the other end of the table next to a twinkly-eyed Polish octogenarian. He had been referred to vaguely as a 'war hero' – in fact, he may have referenced himself as such. Either way, we were careful to show maximum respect. That's why it felt particularly gauche that Emma should choose to pull faces at me for the entirety of the meal.

'What's up with you?' I hissed across the table as dessert arrived, which appeared to be cold rice pudding with an unidentifiable drizzle on the top. 'Why are you gurning at me?' Emma and I had just broken up and we were finding the transition into friends a little fraught.

'Him!' hissed Emma back. 'The guy next to me! He's had his hand on my knee all night!'

'What, the war veteran?'

'Veteran sex pest more like. What should I do?'

'I don't know. Has he crossed The Maginot Line?'

'Oh, piss off, Sue.'

It's dilemmas like this one we really need to see in *Debrett's*. Humans are tribal. We work through complex systems of affiliation which ebb and flow in individual importance. I am a human being, a woman, a daughter, a sibling, an agnostic, a feminist and a gay. Which of these important tribes I choose to affiliate with the most at any one point in time changes. So, what to do? Rumble him? Denounce him as a groper to the assembled diners and be true to ourselves as women and feminists? Or let him, a flaccid pensioner, keep his hand resting on Emma's leg and take the broader, human perspective.

It was an infernally difficult decision. In the end Emma decided to respect his service to our country in time of conflict by allowing his palm to rest for another hour on her thigh.

'It's my way of saying thank you,' she whispered.

Lest we forget.

Let Them Eat Lunch

A month after Rhoda's dinner party, in the spring of 1997, our agent asked Mel and me if we'd be prepared to audition for a Channel 4 live daytime show called *Light Lunch*. We were, it's fair to say, less than enamoured by the prospect. The daytime landscape was arid in those days, acres of dry *Kilroy*-ish terrain with the occasional Ricki Lake oasis. We turned up to the casting in our best 'smart' outfits – which in retrospect made us look like a supermarket security guard and GPO worker respectively. Despite repeated attempts by the channel and the production company to hire proper professionals, Nicky Campbell OBE and the like, we somehow managed to slip though the audition, through the pilot and on to the actual television. Up to that moment our combined media experience had been:

- dressing in full bridal outfits (brief movie review, the *Little Picture Show*)
- dressing up as bearded Highland crofters (non-speaking roles, *French and Saunders*)
- dressing up as Elizabeth Bennett and Unnamed Georgian Woman (non-speaking roles, *French and Saunders*)
- dressing up as Noel and Liam Gallagher (non-speaking roles in a thankfully un-broadcast pilot)

You can see from this extensive CV that we were, in so many ways, the ideal candidates for an hour-long live daily show.

Live television is the apotheosis of multi-tasking. It's like patting your head and rubbing your stomach at the same time. Add to that a shit-eating grin and you're pretty much there. Anything can happen and everything does – and that chaotic unpredictability is what I have always loved best, perhaps because it's the medium that closest matches the pinball tangentialism in my head. Whether or not *Light Lunch* was the show that Channel 4 actually wanted, I don't know – but it was a place where banality walked hand in hand with eccentricity, and I will always love it for that. Sometimes we got it right (I'm thinking of the unlikely but sublime pairing of Michael Bolton and John Inman) and sometimes, well, sometimes we got it wrong . . .

Mel and I had been obsessed with Kate O'Mara since we were kids – not only for her performance as the Rani, a power-dressing Time Lord in *Doctor Who*, but also for her mesmerizing turn in the epoch-defyingly abysmal *Triangle*. For those too young to remember *Triangle*, let me set the scene. It revolved around a ferry making its three-point journey from Felixstowe to Gothenburg to Amsterdam and back. I know – all the sexy places. Based on US show *The Love Boat*, the British version eschewed sun and fun, and instead gave us a soap opera on the choppy black waters of the North Sea. In one of the more memorable sequences Kate is forced to lie on deck, topless, sunbathing, while a punishing easterly wind necrotizes her nipples. Do watch it online and share her pain. For that sequence alone she will always be the stuff of legend.

I first crossed paths with Kate when I was on the Footlights tour in 1989 and we happened to converge at the Drum Theatre, Plymouth. I was in the studio space, in a wig, shouting; she was in the main house doing *Blithe Spirit* or something classy along those lines. I'd occasionally see her at the stage door, surrounded by adoring flunkies, beautiful and imperious, sporting cheekbones you could grate Parmesan on.

Connecting these two theatres was a public address system that fed into each and every dressing room. For a nineteen-year-old, it was just too much temptation. As part of a dare (I cannot, as you now know, resist any dare) I sneaked into the stage manager's lair, commandeered the microphone and bellowed into it, 'Kate O'Mara's pants to the laundry. Kate O'Mara's pants to the laundry, please.'

And then again, for good measure, just so *every single room* in the building could catch it, 'Kate O'Mara's pants to the laundry. Kate O'Mara's pants to the laundry, please.'

Then I went back to our green room, got on with our little show and thought no more of it. Time passed. Everything got lost in its midst.

Years later Kate O'Mara accepted an invitation to be a guest on *Light Lunch* and duly appeared, with fellow *Dynasty* actress Stephanie Beacham, on the show on 8 May 1997. We wanted to show these grandes dames full respect, and, erroneously believing that imitation was the sincerest form of flattery, we came to set with me dressed as Krystal Carrington (bouffant platinum hair, long fake nails, litres of lipgloss) and Mel as Alexis Carrington Colby (sharp black suit, shoulder pads, statement fascinator). Kate and Stephanie came dressed

as normal human beings.

What started as something hilarious soon became one of the most painful interviews of my life. From the moment they came on set it became clear we had hugely misjudged the situation. It was, after all, like inviting Sir David Attenborough on and dressing up as a bonobo and a manatee respectively. The interview went from bad to worse when, in an ad break, Mel elected to ask Kate whether she remembered her pants being discussed on the tannoy system of a regional theatre nearly a decade previously. She didn't. But boy it must have been good for her to hear that story again.

By the time we came back live after the break, you could have not only cut the atmosphere with a knife, you could have portioned it up and served it to the assembled audience, who were now becoming aware there was 'a problem'. As the final question fell out of my mouth and languished in the ensuing silence I heard Stephanie mutter under her breath, 'You silly, silly girls.'

And do you know, she was absolutely right.

We were constantly putting our feet in it. When Patrick Duffy came on the show we sang an impromptu version of 'The Star-Spangled Banner' to welcome him and were most irked when he failed to stand to salute. It turns out we were actually singing *La Marseillaise*. Weeks later I found a woman wandering aimlessly around backstage and asked her if she wanted help in finding the audience seating. She was Susanne Vega. In the '*Star Wars* Reunion Special' Kenny Baker (R2D2) was accidentally dropped on the floor by our make-up supremo and mate 'Madame' JoJo. A *Robin's Nest* special, where we had finally learned our lesson and NOT dressed up, featured Tessa Wyatt and Richard O'Sullivan – neither of whom, it transpired, could remember a single bloody thing about the programme. And last but not least, my own personal favourite – the unholy alliance of Nookie Bear and Sooty. Yes, it was a puppet special. Aaah. Lovely puppets. Lovely, sweet, children's puppets. Lovely.

From the get-go it seemed that the personalities of Nookie and Sooty were not compatible. Or, perhaps more pertinently, the personalities of Roger de Courcey and Matthew Corbett were not compatible. Matthew was rolling with a benign kindergarten vibe, while Roger was going for something a little more late-night working men's club. The pair of them in combination was unsettling enough – and then we added the late Keith Harris and Orville to the mix.

The problems began when Nookie (Roger) picked on Sooty (Matthew), who brushed him off with characteristically silent insouciance. Then Nookie (Roger) picked on Orville (Keith), who bore it, literally, through gritted teeth. Desperate to calm an escalating situation, Sooty (Matthew) began gently stroking Nookie's (Roger's) arm, who responded by rolling his eyes and maniacally hissing, 'Go on, say something, Sooty.' Panicking, Orville (Keith) returned to his default mode, expressing a strong desire for flight. The painful hour ended with Nookie (Roger) hitting Sooty (Matthew). It was in essence Roger hitting Matthew, the puppet acting as a boxing glove with a face. In the post-Clarkson world we would have all got the sack as accessories to ABH, but this was 1998, so we simply tucked into a Summer Pudding and waited till the credits rolled.

In 1998, after 150 episodes, the show had reached its peak, before our tired capitulation led to *Light Lunch* becoming the less effective *Late Lunch*, and we walked away from it all in an optimistic, unfocused daze. The schedule of the show was such that real life had not only taken a back seat, it had ceased feeling like real life at all. We had become institutionalized, with little time for the important stuff happening outside the four walls of the studio – family, friends, relationships.

Over the last few years there had been occasional mentions of Dad feeling tired, but his mutterings were lost in the hullabaloo of work. There's always something, isn't there? Something bright and shiny to take your gaze from where it should be. Change is often glacial. It happens under your nose, but so incrementally your eyes can't detect its movement. Dad's was a slow puncture. And I didn't notice there was something wrong until he was nearly pancake-flat.

I knew that he'd gone to the doctor's. I knew that he needed a scan. Then he had the scan and the next thing I knew was that it was cancer. On 23 December 1998 we found out Dad had cancer.

I arrived home on Christmas Eve and rang the doorbell. I'd lost my keys nearly a decade before but couldn't bear to tell Mum, lest she run wild with visions of homicidal maniacs wading their way through our luxuriantly tufted hall carpet with a beady eye on her knick-knacks.

She opened the door. Dad shuffled towards me from behind her and promptly burst into tears.

My dad. *Crying.*

I'd only seen him cry once before, when I was six and decided to run away from home. It wasn't much of a bid for freedom – in truth I'd talked a big game ('I'm going and I'm never coming back!'), but I'd only made it as far as the privet hedge in the garden. I snuggled into the shrubbery and ate a packet of salt and vinegar Chipsticks while my parents frantically screamed my name. Once the packet was empty, I made my triumphant entrance, expecting a fanfare as the Prodigal returned. In fact I got a clip around the ear and a tear-stained lecture from my dad. Turns out those few minutes, when they really thought they'd lost me, were enough to reduce him to rubble.

Dad was admitted to Mayday Hospital as soon as the Christmas holidays were over, in early January 1999. I remember the reassuring list of West Indian hips as my favourite nurse walked through the ward with the drinks trolley. I remember the kindness of an Australian man called Craig Backway, who, with a name like that was always destined for a colo-rectal unit some-where in the world. But most of all I remember trying not to think *anything*, not for a *second*, because thinking would lead to feeling, and feeling would lead me to the pressing reality that I might actually lose my dad.

I moved on. Kept busy. I was practical. It turns out that in a crisis I am 100 per cent my mother's daughter. I can do it. I can do anything. Just don't ask me to stop. I cannot, not for a *second*, stop.

Every night after work I would head down to sunny Thorn-ton Heath and joke around with everyone on the ward. *Look at me – I'm the life and soul – look at how much fun I am!* I have never brought my work home with me, but there I was, taking that exhausting, inflated version of myself out of hours, bouncing cheerily around the beds until visiting time was up and I could give way to silence.

I'd come home and cook dinner with my sister, who was still living at home and bearing the brunt of it all. We'd serve acres of lasagne, steaming colanders of fusilli and cheap tomato sauce that tasted faintly of metal. There were buckets of tea. Then we would laboriously wash and dry the dishes. We had a dishwasher. No matter. We wanted the extra work. We wanted something to do. When I finally gave in to tiredness, I'd sleep until dawn. At 5 a.m. it was time to get in the car and head north of the river to work. And repeat.

And repeat.

Dad's ward was like every NHS ward you've ever been in. The blue plastic sheeting, the beige plastic furniture, the tiny plastic cupboard where you keep the one or two things that mark you out as an individual human being. There are pipes and tubes and alarms. Trolleys rattle with packaged meds and blood-pressure monitors. The toilet signs take your gaze with a luminous yellow ferocity.

It was a men-only ward. Strong men. Fathers. They had been the axis on which their children plotted their burgeoning lives. And here they all were – brought down, levelled, lying there in hastily bought pyjamas and kept awake by each other's coughs, moans and excretions. Welcome to the grim camaraderie of cancer.

One by one they left. A bed would fall empty and then be filled again. Sometimes you would dare to ask whether they had managed to walk out of the ward themselves, or whether they had been pushed, on a trolley, to the silent chill of the basement below.

Dad had several friends on that ward, but in particular he bonded with a man called John. John was a good man. A good family man – like my dad. And his wife, Marian, was a good woman – like my mum. And their kids were good kids – like we hope we're good kids. John and Dad got diagnosed together (both tumours, graded C for 'Christ that's bad'), went through serial, brutal operations together and the endless ensuing blood tests, CT scans and radiotherapy. They even clicked their morphine pumps together, through the dead of night, in wordless synchronicity.

We shared a destiny. Their family and our family. Together.

As part of a randomized trial Dad wore a Hickman line for twelve months which pumped chemo through a capillary into the right atrium of his heart. I can still see my parents' fridge now, full to bursting with fruit, vegetables and fluorouracil 5FU. John, on the other hand, received his chemo once every month at the hospital. Random. Random. Random.

John didn't make it.

Dad did.

Dad 'beat' cancer. His mate didn't. Isn't that the definition of a pyrrhic victory?

I hate that phrase – 'beat cancer'. Cancer isn't a war or a fight that you win or lose. It's bad luck. It's bad genes. It's bad timing. It's a postcode lottery. Call it what you will, just don't call it a fight. Doing so makes all those who don't make it weak. Or losers. I hate that.

Surviving cancer is hard. It returns you to your home a different person. It changes you, changes your world view. Sometimes it changes you for the better – you're more resolved to squeeze the juice out of your remaining years. That at least is the trope we most often see in books and films. But sometimes it returns you scooped out and hollow – resentful that you've worked yourself to the bone for nearly fifty years and that what was supposed to be the glorious era of retirement has been scarred by disease and incapacitation.

That's the dad who came home to us. Silent. Sad. Reduced.

Dad's an empirical soul. He needs to see proof – evidence. And if you can't see it – if you can't pick through the mesh of your insides and see your guts free of taint for yourself – then how can you truly believe or trust that it is gone?

So yes, Dad survived cancer. But trust me, he didn't 'beat' it.

Sadness grew up around him like ivy. This man, the vital father who had worked hard and played harder, now sat in his chair, exhausted, for the best part of a decade. And as his world narrowed, so did Mum's. The two of them handcuffed together. For better, for worse. In sickness and ill health.

And perhaps that's why I rush at everything now with such intensity – because I know that maybe, one day, all that is coming for me. Maybe. But until then . . .

All clear.

Go on.

All clear.

A Gram of Gorilla

As my thirtieth birthday loomed, Mel went very quiet – possibly remembering her own thirtieth *two long years* before.

I had my suspicions she was organizing a surprise party.

I've never been any good at entertaining. Perhaps it comes from my mother's catastrophizing gene – 'Well I wouldn't want to cater. My friend Jean knows someone who got Cushing's from a mushroom vol-au-vent' – or perhaps it comes from my father's over-empathetic gene – 'Don't ask them. They won't want the imposition of being asked.' Either way, I fear holding a party. What if the people I know from school don't get on with the people I know from college? What if the people from college don't get on with my work colleagues? What if *any* of those people find out I'm not really an Olympic fencing champion?

It's made, as it turns out, for a rather compartmentalized life. And that's annoying and self-defeating. Silly me. Anyhow, I digress.

So, the story I'd been given was this. I was told to come to our local for 7.30 p.m. for a quiet meal with Mel and my closest mates. As I walked up to the main doors I could hear a throng of people shouting.

'I told you to get here at 7.30!'

'Shut up, Dan!'

'*You* shut up!'

'Shh, you bunch of twats – she's coming!'

I approached the door, and, even though I could imagine what lay the other side, I still felt sick with apprehension. As I pushed through, the place erupted.

SURPRISE!

I'll tell you what *was* a surprise – the fact that my parents were there. Why? Because it turns out their ability to keep a secret is second to none. They didn't tell me about the surprise party when I phoned to say I would come and see them for lunch on my birthday. They didn't tell me after I drove – for *two hours* in the pouring rain – the fifteen miles home to Croydon. They didn't tell me as I sat opposite them eating a metre of vegetarian lasagne. And they certainly didn't tell me as I turned round and drove – for another *two hours* – all the way back to north London.

'Careful when you brake!' said Mum as I pulled away. 'The roads are treacherous! And remember what I told you about that Yardie scam. If someone flashes their lights at you, don't flash back, else they'll carjack you and leave you for dead in Norbury.'

And with that she stood on the front step and waved until I disappeared into the distance.

Bastards. They must have got in their car and followed me as soon as I was out of sight. And so there they were, as I opened the door to the pub in Kensal Rise that very same evening.

'Surprise!' they shouted alongside everyone else.

'You utter pricks!' I shouted back into my mum and dad's faces, somewhat ungenerously.

I spent the evening getting very drunk. There were a few speeches, some mild indiscretions, some gift-giving. But as the night wore on, things took a sinister turn. At around 11 p.m. I became aware of a rather shifty-looking guy loitering at the margins, talking to Mel.

'Who's he?' I asked Emma. 'Do we know him?'

'I dunno. I mean, he's probably no one,' said Emma, unconvincingly.

I felt the cold hand of fear clamp around my throat.

Out of the corner of my eye I saw the man pull out of a bag what appeared to be a large Marigold studded with pubes. Next came a full body suit, similarly hairy, and a large *Planet of the Apes* face mask. I watched as Mel gave him a surreptitious thumbs up, and he disappeared into the toilets. I tried to carry on my conversation but found myself staring at the door, transfixed, waiting for the inevitable to appear.

I didn't have to wait long. The music suddenly changed. Leery music. Sexy music. The crowd moved back into a semi-circle leaving me isolated. Finally, emerging from the bogs, a figure resembling a bargain-basement silverback approached. I remember seeing an ex-boyfriend pre-emptively covering his face with his hands and hearing the sound of our mate Gareth, head flipped back like a Pez dispenser, laughing that room-filling boom of his.

What followed was so deeply traumatizing all I remember is a patchwork of images – fragments that come and go in no particular order:

Firstly, the man in the pube-suit lumbered towards me, arms outstretched. As he did so, his face mask slipped so that he could no longer see through the eyeholes. The lack of visibility meant he became less Gorilla in the Mist, more Gorilla's Slightly Pissed. His fingers made their first point of contact with me just around my nipples, whereupon he ground to a sudden halt.

In an instant he was frantically stripping. There was nothing erotic about it – it was simply mask off, suit off, job done. In fairness he did take his time struggling with one of the rubber gloves, which gave the performance a faint air of burlesque mystique. Other than that, he dispensed with his clothes with all the urgency of a contaminated chemist shedding a biohazard suit.

The man now stood before me wearing nothing but a pair of leopard-skin micro-pants and a furry gauntlet.

In a flash he had pushed me down to the floor and stood over me, gyrating. The PA kicked into Tight Fit's version of 'The Lion Sleeps Tonight', and I could see, as I lay there prostrate, Mr Gorilla's pelvis thrusting to the beat, and his ball sack following a second later, in joyous syncopation.

'Oh dear . . . Oh dear . . . No, that's . . . Oh. Oh dear . . .' said Mel weakly from the sidelines.

Mr Gorilla decided to take it up a notch. Without warning he spun round, squatted down onto all fours and started doing press-ups – ON ME – his body facing the other direction from mine. As his groin battered my nose, I got the unmistakable tang of unwashed fur fabric and sweaty seam. I gagged a little and tried to block out the fact that all the people I loved in the world were not only watching this horror unfold, but may actually have had an active role in planning it.

Added to which, I could hear him, each time his face descended towards my groin, moaning a name, rhythmically in time with his thrusts. It was indistinguishable at first, but gradually grew clearer.

'Mel . . .

'Oh, Mel . . .

'Yeah, that's right, Mel.

'Mel. You love it, Mel.

'You love it, don't you, Mel. Oh yeah . . .'

Let me tell you, there is only one thing worse than being cock-slammed by a man with questionable hygiene wearing a single poorly made gorilla glove in front of your family and friends. That is when the man with questionable hygiene wearing that single poorly made gorilla glove happens to be orgasmically groaning the name of your best mate.

The booking was made under the name of Mel. He thought I was Mel. Hell, everyone, even a bloody gorilla, thinks I'm Mel.

The atmosphere in the room had now changed. The laughter and cheering had subsided, and now there was just an uncomfortable silence. This was slowly turning into a primate re-versioning of *The Accused*.

'He was only supposed to read a poem,' said Mel despairingly, her voice now a mere whisper.

Mr Gorilla jumped up and pulled my limp body from off the floor. *It's over*, I thought. *Finally, it's over.*

It wasn't. He proceeded to lean me up against a wall and dry-hump me.

During the next five minute ordeal, I remember Mel approaching Mr Gorilla, proffering his other glove and gently encouraging, nay *pleading* with him to put his clothes back on. She then held up the suit, which now looked like a massive used condom that had been rolled on by a million Labradors. But no, he carried on, oblivious, until the final track had finished.

All I can say is this. Mel, you are fifty in a few years' time. On that day I will find you – and I will be bringing Cheetah with me.

Births, Deaths, Marriages

Melanie Giedroyc, who is nearly two years older than I am, could have chosen any outfit she wanted to dress me in for her wedding, and boy, she really thought about it. *She's my maid of honour, after all*, she mused, *so I could legitimately put her in a peach meringue with puffball sleeves. Or something bias-cut, in ivory. She'd love that. Mmm . . . But what would cause maximum damage? What would cause maximum damage to Sue's already fragile psyche?*

She finally found the ideal sartorial weapon, in the form of a pair of acid-pink silk pyjamas with a Mao collar. It was November. I looked like a Chinese Jane from Rod, Jane and Freddy – but colder.

I turned up late to Mel's wedding, like I do to all weddings. You see, I have form when it comes to public splicings. I was so late for my friend Catherine Hood's nuptials that she was already at the door of the church when I arrived. As I wandered down the aisle, desperate to find a seat, the organist started 'Here Comes the Bride' – which caused quite a stir, I can tell you. 'Gosh, we didn't think it was *that* sort of marriage. Why on earth didn't she *say* . . .?'

I went one better for my brother's wedding. I nearly didn't turn up at all.

It took place in Perth in Scotland over a long and very drunken weekend. I arrived heartbroken and skinny (which is the best kind of heartbroken) and spent the night before the ceremony ruefully reflecting on yet another failed relationship. The next morning I saw my family for a full Scottish breakfast, after which we all went to our respective rooms to get ready. The plan was we'd rendezvous at 11 a.m. and the minibus would take us all from there. Simple. What could possibly go wrong?

OK, so I was a little late. Maybe five minutes – ten, tops. Quarter of an hour at the most. I may or may not have been watching a World Cup match, which might have gone to penalties. Plus I had to do my hair. I have the hair of a baby – fine and flyaway – and it takes tubs of goop to make it do anything or go anywhere. In the end I was forced to grease it into a shape thereafter rather unkindly known as the 'wonky cockerel'. I put on my suit, a rather flamboyant affair in a rich Lenten purple which with hindsight made me look like a Laurence Llewelyn-Bowen impersonator. Finally, after twenty minutes – max – I headed down to reception.

The hotel was silent. No one was there. Not in the entrance hall or the bar or the dining room. The panic was immediate. There is no way my anxious mother and equally anxious sister would not have been on time. They would, if they had been allowed, have camped out all night outside the church with sandwiches and a Thermos. I approached the woman on the front desk.

Me: Scuse me. Do you know whether the minibus for the wedding party has arrived?

Woman: Oh aye, that's away now.

Me: What do you mean away?

Woman: They've been away up the church – ooh – about ten minutes ago. Hang on – let me check . . .

Me: No, it's fine . . .

Woman: It's nae bother. I'll check for you.

She proceeds to ring each and every room. I desperately try to interject . . .

Me: Listen . . .

Woman: Och, I'm not getting an answer from your mum and
         dad.

Me: It's really OK.

Woman: Let me try your sister's room.

Me: Please.

Woman: It's ringing!

Five whole minutes pass as I watch this sweet, kindly woman help me. For a moment I long for the unhelpful churlishness of a London receptionist. If nothing else, impoliteness is a time-saver.

Woman: Nope. All gone!

Now I could have just *rung* my mum, but this was 2001. Mobile phones were the size of house bricks and the price of unicorns. I did own one, but as usual I hadn't bothered charging it.

You need to know this about me. In almost all situations I have no charge on my mobile phone, plus:

b. little or no idea of where I am

c. little or no cash

d. no credit card

e. an extremely, *extremely* limited well of personal
   resourcefulness

So, the facts were these. My brother, my beloved brother, was getting married in twenty minutes. My family had all left without me in the minibus provided. I had lost the invite months ago and had no idea which church they were getting married in. Desperate, I turned again to the kindly receptionist.

Me: Sorry, would you be able to call me a cab? As soon as possible?

Woman: Of course, dear. Let me ring my pal Sammy, up at the station. He's the best driver round this way.

Me: Thank you.

The phone rings. I hear a man answer.

Woman: Is that you, Sammy? Halloo, it's only Moira up the hill. How are you?

The man rumbles a response.

Woman: I'm very glad to hear it. Will you be wanting your tea again tonight, only it's no bother for me to fix it . . .

More rumbling.

Woman: I can do you soup and a roll?

Monosyllabic bark.

Woman: Will you be needing something more substantial?

Miscellaneous jibber-jabber.

Me: Seriously, I should be getting on . . .

Woman: How's Jacky? His hip still giving him bother? Ach, poor lamb . . .

I wonder how long it might take. How long my instant-gratification city-honed demanding personality can take. The answer is thirty seconds.

Me: [*shouting maniacally over her*] I need a cab now! Now! NOW!

Five minutes later a smiley-faced octogenarian with grey mutton chops pulls up at the hotel entrance.

Cabbie: Right, where can I take you?
Me: To a church. Any church. All the churches. NOW!

I had turned into everyone's worst nightmare of a Londoner. Rude, pushy and with wonky cockerel hair.

Perth has at least fourteen churches. I know because I visited them all, one after another. I had no idea which denomination the building I was supposed to be in was, so the cabbie and I did a whistle-stop tour of two Methodists, one Presbyterian, a Church of Scotland, Free Church of Scotland and the distinctly happy-clappy Evangelical Church of the Nazarene.

I had all but given up hope when suddenly a long, sleek black limo came into view. It was a fifty-fifty chance – either wedding or funeral cortège. I took that chance.

'Follow that car!' I bellowed at the minicab driver while secretly wondering whether, if I had indeed chosen wrongly, I could rock my purple Regency-fop look at a crematorium.

We followed the car until it came to a halt at yet another of Perth's churches. I held my breath to see whether a cadaver or my sister-in-law-to-be would emerge from the vehicle. I can still feel the relief as she got out – radiant, nervous and beautiful.

'STOP THE CAR,' I screamed, 'and have soup and a roll on me!' I shoved a twenty-quid note into the driver's lap.

I will always remember Lynne's face as I sprinted past her. The organ started up. *Not again*, I was thinking. *Don't go down the aisle to 'Here Comes the Bride' again.* I pelted through the church door and past the pews until I found my family, at the front. Michelle was sobbing. Dad was fiddling with the stopwatch setting on his wristwatch. Mum was rocking anxiously and threw her hands in the air as I dropped into the seat next to her.

Mum: Oh gosh, Susan! I'm so sorry – we forgot all about you!

Me: [*hissing*] There are only three of us! And one of us is busy getting married! So really you only had *two of us* to remember. You forgot about 50 per cent, 0.05 of your available children!

My sister carries on sobbing, clinging on to me like a taffeta barnacle.

Mum: [*wailing*] You're right! I'm a terrible mother!

Me: Oh Christ, here we go again . . .

Dad: [*bellowing*] What's going on with you?

Me: What do you mean?

Dad: Is that deliberate?

Me: Is what deliberate?

Dad: You. You look like Laurence Llewelyn-Bowen.

And then the bride walked up the aisle. I will never forget the face of my sister-in-law-to-be as she walked past our assembled family: two keening women, a man holding a digital watch timing how long it was taking her to get to the altar, and a tardy, dishelleved lesbian dressed like Beau

Brummell. It was a face that said, *Is it too late for me to pull out?*

Welcome. Welcome to Clan Perkins, love.

But back to Mel's wedding – Mel, who is nearly two years older than me. The groom was (and still is) a wonderful man called Ben, who is six foot five inches worth of utter magnificence. Their ceremony was a perfectly beautiful, simple affair at the local church, followed by a reception at the village hall. I don't think I'm breaking any confidences by revealing that Mel was four months pregnant when she walked down the aisle. As a result, she was having alterations to her dress every single week in the run-up to the actual day. Forty-eight hours before the event the seamstress finally gave up on any attempt at finesse and simply installed a couple of giant side panels which made room for last-minute expansion. Even so, on the morning of the ceremony the bridesmaids were frantically unpicking seams to make way for a little extra baby spread.

So, I was the maid of honour – a maid in psychedelic jim-jams thanks to Mel. This job carried with it responsibilities. (I know, have the people closest to me learned *nothing* by now? If there are responsibilities to be dished out, give them to *responsible people,* not the distracted moon child in the dirty glasses.)

My prescribed role was to give a speech celebrating the bride. After Gorillagate? I don't think so. Truthfully, it felt strange. Public speaking was something I did for work. I didn't want this to feel like work; I wanted it to be real and raw and heartfelt. So I decided not to prepare anything. When the time came, I got up, stood in front of the assembled crowd and

immediately realized I'd made a huge mistake.

As I began speaking, there was this sudden tightening in my throat. My breathing became shallow. *I must be going down with something*, I thought and carried on. The tightness persisted, moving deep into my chest.

I'd never actually been called upon to describe my relationship with Mel before; I'd only ever spoken about it in terms of what it *wasn't* . . .

Are you best friends? No.

Like sisters? No.

Twins? No.

Just work colleagues? No.

Are you lovers? GET OUT OF TOWN – THAT'S GROSS!

Yet here I was, finally, having to define it. Having to stand there and give my account of what she meant to me, this other strand of my double helix. The more I spoke, the more I started to connect with what I was really feeling.

Loss.

I know, I really am an A-grade arsehole. There I am, putting myself and my emotions in the centre of my mate's BIG DAY. I felt all the joy of the occasion, for sure, but it was accompanied by a profound sense of something being over. It felt like a death. I was a mourner, as well as a celebrant, at the wedding.

I was so overcome that I spent the next three hours clinging to the bride like a luminescent koala. So much so that in every photo it looks like it was Mel and I getting hitched. The three hours after that I spent clinging to the groom so it looked like Ben and I were getting hitched. As a result there's not one single photo of that day where the newly-weds are actually pic-tured *next to each other* – photo-bombed as they were by me, the Girl in the Pink Pyjamas.

When Mel went into labour I paced up and down my front room like a laboratory animal. Occasionally she was able to get word out from the hospital: she'd had a curry, she'd been induced, she'd been induced again. For three days she wan-dered the corridors of the hospital hooked to a drip, desperate for some cervical reaction. Something. Anything. Then everything went quiet.

Radio silence.

Those hours felt the longest of my life. We're never, ever not in touch. Finally the phone rang. There was a weak voice at the end of the phone – familiar but battered. An old friend. A new mother.

Breaking into a hospital is very hard to do. Trust me, that night I tried. I busted through fire doors and circumvented matrons; I even managed to make it as far as the inner sanctum of the maternity unit. Sadly, my progress ended there. There were even alarms going off. Bloody security. Storm in a teacup, I'm telling you. There really was no need for that armlock and all that shouting.

The next day I opted to go through more-official channels and turn up at visiting hours. I was shocked by how tired Mel looked. But radiant too. How could she manage that? How you could look ruined and complete at the same time?

Once mother and baby were back at home later that night, I

dropped round. We lay on the bed on a bedspread made by my mum for Mel's thirtieth. We'd lain there a million times – laughing and gossiping – but this time, instead of talking, we were silent, in a kind of awe at the little thing she had created. Mel bent her head forward and lightly touched her daughter's nose with her own, and I watched her watching her child.

She's done it, I thought, *this friend of mine. She's crossed the Rubicon. She's gone somewhere I can never go, somewhere beyond the reach of my understanding or experience. We've gone everywhere hand in hand together. But I can't go here. Not here. I can't go here with you and share it.* It was one of the most beautiful and painful experiences of my life, that hour on the bed with my darling mate and her hours-old child. I could feel that love, that transcendent love, but as if through glass. I could see it, but I couldn't get at it.

I think that night was perhaps the first time I had to contend with the painful reality of being a grown-up – that messy, unarticulated feelings stay with you for ever without finding resolution. You just live with this unnamed weird stuff. We all do. So I did what I'd seen proper grown-ups do – I swallowed it down, all of it, took a deep breath and moved on.

Over the ten years we had gigged together we had gone from performing to no one to performing to thousands and back, in 2003, to performing to just a few disinterested people again. Our final ever tour date was at the famous Haymarket Theatre in Leicester. There were fewer than a hundred people dotted around the stalls and circle. That night we said the words in the right order but there was no joy behind them. We simply couldn't inhabit the fun any more. There was no work on the horizon and there was no interest in us any more. We knew it was over. Our double act was done.

Until our own little cake-baby arrived some seven years later.

When it comes to Mel and me, I genuinely forget where her experiences end and mine begin. Writing this book, I was about to recount an anecdote from school involving a pair of pants and a discus, and then realized it wasn't my anecdote at all. It wasn't my life, but hers. Such is the hive mind, the collective consciousness we have become over the years.

Sometimes when we're drunk we'll try and articulate all that stuff – that awkward stuff that sits at the margins of love and friendship. But mainly we leave it alone, leave it all unsaid and carry on regardless in a thoroughly British fashion. What I do know is that this kinship will always remain. It is constant. It is a love that cannot be weathered, not by time, not by circumstance.

Nothing can alter it.

Unless, of course, UKIP get into power and has her sent back to Eastern Europe.

FOUR

Cornwall

The Ballad of Pickle and Parker, or How I Fell in Love

They say a dog is a man's best friend. Well, Nicola, Sarah, Emma, Mel, Neil, Gemma and Andy are my best friends, and what's more they don't shit on the carpet and whine outside my bedroom door for food at 5.30 a.m.*

It was all Emma's fault. She started it. She got a beagle called Poppy, and there was something so intoxicating about the constant exhaustion, commitment and inability to have a second to oneself that it made me want one of my own.

I'm nothing if not impulsive, so the following week my sister and I duly headed to the same breeder in Cheshire – a redoubtable woman called Janet, all flush-faced and tweedy. She was the sort of woman who displayed rosettes on the wall rather than family photos, and who just might have kept a Shetland pony in her living room. I suspect she would have found even a no-nonsense approach a little frilly for her tastes.

I had barely set foot through Janet's door when I was greeted with the now-familiar gust of wet dog and Dettol. Suddenly, out of nowhere, a miniature pinscher thundered towards me and began making breakfast of my trouser leg.

Janet: You all right?
Me: Yes, thank you.
Janet: Well shut t' bloody door then.

* OK, Mel did once, but it was a long time ago now.

Me: Oh yes, sorry.

She sizes me up for a few seconds while the dog yaps incessantly at my heels.

Janet: Will you BE QUIET, Jasper! [*To me*] See there, over t' way?

She motions across the street with her free hand, the other attempting to wrestle the dog's jaws from my ankle.

Me: Yes . . .

Janet: Little bastard over there, hangs himself from the beams every night, watching me.

Me: Really? Your neighbour . . . *hangs* himself?

Janet: Auto-erotic something. I don't know. Dirty bugger. I just shut me curtains. Out of sight and all that. Do what he likes then. I don't mind. Anyway, come and meet Prunella.

Me: Prunella?

Janet: The bitch. Now mind yourself down t' stairs – they've gone to shit.

I wander into a field behind the house, towards a large enclosure. I honestly have no clue what I'm looking for. I've never had a dog before, so the idea of looking for something more than just the standard four legs, tail and face, is totally new to me.

Janet: Right. Pups are only couple weeks old, so don't go near 'em. You can have a peak through int' kennel, but more than that and I'll give you what for.

I peer through the wooden slats and the effect is instant. My skin slackens, my eyes widen and what feels like the distillation of a million Disney films starts working simultaneously on my heartstrings. Even the usually pragmatic Michelle stands there for half an hour with her hand over her mouth, entranced.

Janet: They've all gone, been sold – bar t' little one. Runt. We've had to bottle-feed her, but she's right as rain now. You want me to put tha name down or what?

Me: Yes.

I speak without thinking. It's not a conscious response. All rationality has left the building. In fact, from that point on rationality never returns.

Janet: Right. Back in a month then. I'll show you t' door. I said MIND T' STEPS!

When I returned four weeks later I was once again led to the field outside, to the wooden hut where I'd first seen the litter.

I waited in silence with Janet, even though I had no idea what I was waiting for. It would have made for the most tedious episode of *Springwatch* ever recorded, that's for certain. Finally, after many minutes, a single pup emerged, stretching and yawning as she hit the daylight.

'Ooh, here she comes. She knows she's for you all right. Come here, girl.'

With one motion, she scooped up the dog, who was so small she fitted on her outstretched hand. She stayed there, surfing Janet's palm, legs wobbling to the sides and outsize ears flapping in the breeze, giving the horizon that bored thousand-mile stare that I would come to know and love.

'Right, here you are . . .'

Whereupon Janet transferred her into my hands, this little warm thing that smelled of milk and sawdust. Eight weeks old. 2.26 kilos.

The exact weight of love.

Janet, meanwhile, had taken a large pair of what looked like bolt cutters and was trimming the dog's nails as she wriggled in my arms. I had no idea what on earth to do next. It was a singularly odd sensation. I'd never been in love and not known what to do about it.

Me: What . . . what do I do?
Janet: Don't look at her, touch her, do owt for her – she's a dog – not a human. Be strict with the little bugger.

She turns to the dog.

Janet: Right you, don't give me that look. I'm glad to be shot of you. Needy, you were, terribly needy. Go on and piss off, and don't be a pain. Don't give her grief, like you're wont to. Go on.

As she turns away from us, I see a single silvery tear making its way down her cheek.

I put Pickle, as she was to be known, in the car, in a crate like I'd been told, and instantly knew I'd done wrong. She gave me a look – the sort of look that Damian gave his nanny in *The Omen* just before she hangs herself from the light fitting. I know now this was Pickle's first attempt at mind control. She became much more effective at it over the eleven years she allowed me to live with her. Within a minute I'd buckled. She was out of the crate and in my sister's arms, and from that moment on it didn't matter what grate or luggage rack or obstacle blocked her way – she would always find a way to barge through from the boot onto the passenger seat. That was *her* seat. *She* was the co-pilot.

Once home, I tried to give her boundaries – NO to the sofa, NO to the bed, NO to my entire dinner – but within a week of arriving at my house she merely had to flash me one of her celebrated withering looks before I'd be racing for the treats jar or rushing over to adjust the contours of her bedding for greater comfort. It wasn't just *mi casa su casa*. It was my bed your bed, my food your food, my life your life. I would go to sleep with her curled at my feet and would wake to find her head on the pillow next to mine, paw over my shoulder, staring at me intently. She was the only creature I've ever met that was as wilful, stubborn and downright odd as I am.

Pickle redefined contrary. She would have broken Cesar Millan in a heartbeat. If there was something a dog was supposed to do, she refrained from doing it. It wasn't that she overtly refused; she just found the request itself nonsensical. She didn't come back when called or run for balls or play with other dogs. Why on earth would you want to do *that*? She would just sniff things, wee on them, then run off in the opposite direction everyone else was heading in.

If she was bored (heaven forbid), she would systematically destroy anything and everything I was fond of. If I watched too much telly, she'd eat her way through the cables. Problem solved. If I headed for the door without her, she would eye up the CD rack, and one by one would crunch the plastic cases between her jaws. Let me tell you from experience – Led Zeppelin and PJ Harvey sound exactly the same once a six-month-old hound has been at them.

Now I had a dog, I had to do the one thing I had avoided all of my life – exercise. I began walking on Hampstead Heath every day, and for the first time I got it. I got how beautiful it all was, you know – *outside*. I grew to appreciate the subtle shifting of colours and textures as one season greeted another. I started to love the reddy slush of autumn, the reassuring suck of December mud, the white winter sun struggling for definition in the white winter sky. And then I'd look forward to the fat spring grass and the paths slowly turning to powder in the heat of whatever summer we had.

It was a love affair. A love affair between me and my dog. And then it became a love affair between me and my dog and the Great Outdoors. And then, just when I thought I couldn't feel any more goddam love, there came the biggest love of all.

And with her came another bloody beagle.

Parker.

I met Kate in the summer of 2003. We would occasionally bump into one other, and as we had friends in common we'd share the odd wander until our paths home diverged. That year there was an Indian summer, and I remember the sun stretching out across endless balmy evenings. The grass was high, and lovers, drunk on cheap fizzy plonk, rolled around on the margins of the meadows. By autumn we had started to arrange to meet, rather than relying on haphazardly finding one another. Once a week. Then twice. Then more. For an hour. Then two. Then more. By November we were walking four hours a day, seven days a week. Even the dogs were exhausted.

Something felt wrong. Very wrong. I phoned Michelle.

Me: Gel, there's something wrong with me. I don't feel right. I can't sleep and I feel sick to my stomach. I just sit around . . .

Michelle:	Can I stop you there?
Me:	Is it gout?
Michelle:	It's worse.
Me:	I'm in love, aren't I?
Michelle:	I am rather sorry to say, yes, you are.

Two weeks later Kate turned up at my door with a plastic bag containing a toothbrush and her purse, and Parker on a lead. Nothing more. It was all we needed. It was perfect.

Parker was a rather different beast to Pickle. Whereas Pickle was mercurial and charismatic, Parker was lumbering and distinctly on the spectrum. Added to which her breath was a cross between closing time at Billingsgate and the mother alien in *Aliens*. If she licked you, you had to wash it off pronto, lest it burn your skin to the bone. But I loved her from the outset.

We all just loved each other from the outset.

A Shock to the System

As you may have gathered by now, I'm not someone who understands halves, let alone how to do things by them. I probably wouldn't recognize a half if it came up and punched me, though I'd remember the punch itself as a bit, well, half-arsed.

In 2007 I started experiencing severe stabbing pains in the centre of my chest. I would become dizzy and then occasionally collapse. Once, after a gig in Darlington, I spent half an hour on all fours crawling down a hotel corridor trying to get to my room. In retrospect, this would probably be in the top three distressing half-hours on all fours I've had, and, trust me, that's a very long list. There would be days when I'd find it hard even to walk up a single flight of stairs without my head getting foggy and my legs giving way.

One morning after a really acute attack, I was panicked enough to head down to the A&E department of my local hospital. I was admitted to triage pretty sharpish and was duly weighed and measured before sitting down for a blood pressure test. There was a hiss of air as the armband deflated, whereupon the nurse looked quizzical.

Nurse: Are you all right?
Me: Well, no. Not really. That's why, you know, I've come here, you know, to a *hospital* . . .
Nurse: Mmm . . . [*A long and confused silence*] Are you an Olympic athlete by any chance?

I am going to pause for a brief while, just to illustrate how *ludicrous* that question was.

I loved school, mainly because I loved wearing a uniform. In uniform we were all the same, Stepford Kids in navy-blue pleats and nylon shirts. In uniform you couldn't tell who was cool, or whose parents had money, or who was hitting puberty first or last. But in gym kit – that was another story. There is nowhere to hide in an Aertex shirt and granny pants. Trust me, I tried. In PE we were exposed and vulnerable. And I hated it.

I knew from an early age I wasn't cut out for sport. I successfully managed the carb loading, so I was 50 per cent of the way there, but the bit after that, the running and jumping bit, just bored the tits off me. Added to which, I'm lazy. Oh, and weak.

My first memory of running was as a six-year-old at Catholic school playing kiss chase. I was finally collared under the vast statue of the Virgin Mary. Yes, my very first kiss took place under the baleful eye of the mother of Christ. Pathologize *that*, O therapists of London town . . .

In my teens, at a school sports day, I ran the 100 metres. I didn't finish it. You don't see that very often, do you – a runner stopping before the finishing line in a sprint race. Mind you, there were mitigating circumstances. Midway, I was overtaken by my friend Karen Flanders, who was under five feet tall and heavily asthmatic, and the sight of her wheezing next to and then past me made me wee a little. That's another reason I'm no good at physical activity – I have a singularly lame pelvic floor, and it's liable to give way, like old plasterboard, at any given minute.

Much of my antipathy towards sport stems from a genuine failure to understand the point of it. After all, time outside kicking things and throwing things takes you away from a song on the piano or a good book or film. Don't get me wrong – if you throw a ball at me, I will catch it. It's a reflex. I respond a little like Robert De Niro's character in *Awakenings*. Job done. But if you throw the ball and I have to *run* for it – well, as far as I'm concerned that means you've not thrown the ball accurately enough, so why should I reward your incompetence with a return? You're effectively asking me to patronize you, and hey, little lady, I won't do it.

I am as boundaried with all physical activities. I have rules. I *will* swim a little in the sea, as long as there is no one within five miles of the beach to catch sight of me in my cossie. As a result I have not swum since December 1976. As for swimming baths, forget it.

'Hi there, stranger! Mind if I join you in that Petri dish of piss and bacteria? And hey, why don't I strip down to my bra and pants so you can see what I look like with virtually no clothes on!'

I did once go horse riding, but I actually like my vagina so refused to do it again. However, if you're unhappy with your pudenda, why not hop on a pony and batter your genitals into a totally new shape! Plus, the relentless pounding motion provides its own anaesthesia so you won't feel a thing until it's too late!

My dad had been sporty in his youth – although (and this is crucial) not *talented* and sporty. He expended an awful lot of energy, but to no real avail. He was goalkeeper for his local football team as a lad, and his claim to fame was that he dislocated every single one of his fingers while diving to make a save. If only one of those precious fingers had touched the actual ball, he could have been a legend.

In his forties he took up golf because it was an excellent way, as he put it, 'to get away from all you women'. I remembered this, and so in my thirties, when keen to 'get away from all you women' I gave it a go. MISTAKE. It turns out that the golf course is like a living-history documentary, where men dress up in diamond-patterned jumpers and adopt the gender posturings of the 1970s.

I have set foot on links twice and both times have resulted in explosive arguments. The second time, I was following a friend around a course when some twonk in plus fours made a 'hilarious' comment about us having a hole in one, or some such. Needless to say, the red mist came down and I ended up chasing him in a golf buggy until I was overcome with laughter. It's amazing how quickly a high-tensile situation can be defused by a ride in an open-sided electric vehicle.

Throughout most of my adolescence until my mid-thirties, I evaluated all sporting activities according to how likely it was I'd be able to smoke while doing them. I first took up smoking when I was sixteen and was immediately in love with it. It remains one of the very few things I was ever any good at. For this reason, I was a huge fan of rounders. I would always be picked last for the team, and would march delightedly to the outfield. While everyone else slugged away with ball and bat in the centre of things, I'd spark up a Marlboro and find out what base my fellow fielders had got to at the weekend.

I am digressing. You get my point. *I don't do sport.* And so, with that in mind, let's return to the A&E department and the triage nurse's question.

Nurse: Are you an Olympic athlete by any chance?

I slowly survey my sprawling midriff.

Me: No. No, I'm not.
Nurse: You're sure you're not in training?

Me: Absolutely sure.

Nurse: Gosh. Well, in that case you're technically dead. I'm flummoxed. I've never seen a reading like that. Let me get someone . . .

Less than five minutes later I was wheeled into the resuscitation unit. By now I felt woozy and confused. Next to me lay a fifty-something man out for the count, getting his pinstriped suit cut from his body with a pair of surgical shears. There was the squirt of gel as lubricant was applied to the paddles followed by the mandatory holler of 'Stand clear!'

The patient spasmed for a second, then was still, then suddenly sat bolt upright.

'I'M AN ESTATE AGENT!' he bellowed, before collapsing back down again.

The estate agent was deemed drunk and given some IV fluids, but he remained an estate agent, for which, sadly, there is still no cure. I, however, proved a somewhat more mysterious case and so was kept in overnight for observation.

Kate arrived to find me rigged up to drips and nebulizers and lay in the bed with me until the staff finally chucked her out at around midnight.

The next morning when she phoned, I immediately knew something was wrong. I pushed her and pushed her to tell me what was up, and she finally gave way. She had come home from the hospital, put the dogs to bed and was just getting ready to go to sleep herself when there was an almighty crash at the front window. She ran to the front of the flat to find a man in motorbike leathers and full-face visor smashing his way through the lounge. His two accomplices were revving their scooters outside.

Kate didn't get to the end of the story before I was unclipping my oxygen monitors and peeling the electrodes from my chest. It didn't matter what the doctors wanted or what tests they had planned, I was going home. I arrived to find shards of window glass littering the flat. The dogs were still shaking from the ordeal. Kate was doing her best to appear stoical, but I could see the upset beneath.

I know what it is like to feel unsafe. I have been in a nasty relationship and know what it is like for the ground to feel unpredictable and volatile. All I wanted was to get her away. Perhaps to get me away too. To get us away.

What might you have done after a burglary? What pragmatic steps might you have taken? Fixed another lock on the door? Joined the Neighbourhood Watch?

We sold up and moved to a farm in Cornwall.

The Nuts End Up at the Bottom

The track to the house was long and unmade. A tombola of gravel churned against the underside of the car as we bumped along. The estate agent had told us to take a look ourselves – it was so far out of town that she couldn't be bothered to attend the viewing.

We had only got halfway down the track when I knew I wanted to live there. By the time the house itself came into view, I was phoning to make an offer. It was a futile gesture as that part of the world has never had, and will never have, mobile reception. In fact, in that part of the world it's widely believed that electricity comes in buckets from the Magic Well.

The ridge of the slate roof undulated like a wave and the guttering below clung to it for dear life. Inside it stank of damp, the staircase was rotten and most of the downstairs had been pine clad then painted in a deep-orange stain. No matter. I loved it. It wormed its way into my heart and it has never left. As the conveyancing rumbled on, I sat at my desk in London and made plans. Kate would paint, and I would . . . I would . . . well, I'd have a vegetable garden and keep chickens. I could make artisanal chutney! Bespoke jams! Unusual pestos!

It was going to be heaven.

The day we arrived the entire neighbourhood came to say hello, including several artists, a semi-professional water diviner and a white witch. I'm a fan of white witches. After telling me my aura was pink, she winked and said, 'You're in the right place. The South West is like a Christmas stocking –

all the nuts end up at the bottom.' And with those words of wisdom, she turned on her ruby slippers and left.

That afternoon, as a spectacular sea mist rolled in, we headed to the local shop to get firelighters. On returning we found a brace of partridge nailed to the front door, with a long trail of blood dripping down the paintwork. I remain unclear as to whether it was a neighbour's way of saying hello or the Cornish mafia's version of the horse's head in the bed.

I had imagined heaven, and indeed it was. It was heaven for exactly four days. Because the week I moved there the work phone started ringing again.

Music, Maestra, Please

As a child I believed that piano lessons, like everything else related to education and self-improvement, were to be endured. I knew what suffering was; after all I was brought up a Catholic. I'd read *Foxe's Book of Martyrs* and so knew how to accept my lot with a silent and resolute dignity. Playing the piano was simply something I 'should do' – another unexamined, unemotional achievement on the way to adulthood.

Once a week, every week, I would get out of the car, leather satchel flapping in the wind, and wander down the path to Mrs Green's house. The door would open, there would be a gust of boiled cabbage, and a kindly, frail old woman with a single Nanny McPhee tooth would usher me into her lounge. I'd sit at the piano, place my hands in the grooves of yellowed ivory, invent an ever-more elaborate illness which had impeded my practice that week, then inflict an hour's worth of broken scales, faltering arpeggios and syncopated Mozart on her. Poor, poor Mrs Green.

I passed all my grades by the time I was fourteen, due, quite frankly, to my teacher's persistence rather than any real talent on my part. And yet, despite those certificates, I couldn't do the one thing any decent musician would want to do – play a tune. Outside the rigours of the Associated Board syllabus, the three-minute exercises in technique to which I had become accustomed, I was utterly stuck.

Then along came Michiyo Onoue, beautiful, bright and talented – just the sort of lovely girl that other girls love to hate.

Aged just fifteen, she sat down at the rickety piano at school assembly – a spot previously ruled by me – and played Chopin's *Fantaisie-Impromptu*. Perfectly. Musically. It was as if she had exposed me for the faker I was. I never played the piano again. I never played anything again.

So, it's 2008. I am in Cornwall. The work phone is ringing.* I am deep in a raised bed, using a tape measure to make sure my borlotti bean seedlings are planted exactly twenty-five centimetres apart. I am nothing if not my father's daughter.

The job on offer was a show called *Maestro*, a music commission for BBC2 in which eight people compete to learn the basics of conducting an orchestra. I said no. My turning down interesting jobs on successful shows will become a motif, as you shall see.† Thankfully, my amazing friend/agent Debi Allen persuaded me to change my mind by repeatedly shouting 'You're wrong' at various hours of the day and night. A few weeks later I left Cornwall early one morning to begin filming.

I turned up in Britain's sexiest town – Watford – in what I now, with hindsight, see was a DISGUSTING shirt. There was a crowd assembling outside the concert hall, including my fellow contestants:

- King of the swing, the adorable Peter Snow

---

* I don't have a separate phone for work. Separate phones are for criminals, billionaires and Batman.
† And yet I readily agreed to be the voice of cluster-fuck omni-flop *Don't Scare the Hare*. I really am a proper cretin.

- Suave and sophisticated Katie Derham
- Evergreen beauty, actress and cake mogul Jane Asher
- Man-explosion Goldie
- Gentleman and clown extraordinaire Bradley Walsh
- Eternal Hutch David Soul
- Handsome cheese-botherer Alex James

Inside the hall there was the sound of the orchestra warming up: a wheeze of horns, the bubbling of clarinets, the knife-edge finessing of strings. It's a sound that immediately heightens my senses. It's a sound that says, *Something amazing is about to happen.*

We were each handed sheet music for a famous piece. The tunes were universally known, so it wasn't too onerous for those unfamiliar with scores. Five of us knew how to read music. The remaining three, who happened to be the professional musicians of the group, didn't. I got Johann Strauss's waltz, 'The Blue Danube' – you know, the one that's always on when you inadvertently come across Classic FM. It's a majestic piece of writing, but we've oversung and overplayed it into little more than a cliché. Now it sounds like something that might have been dreamed up to advertise a Kia Picanto.

We barely had a moment to collect our thoughts before we were herded one by one into the concert hall like Brahms to the slaughter. Peter was first. He had been given the tune from Prokofiev's *Romeo and Juliet*, more commonly known as 'Music for Lord Sugar to sack people to'. Bradley and I glued our ears to the door to listen. Surely the Human Swingometer would be a genius conductor, yet the noise within sounded less like star-crossed lovers and more like a fight in a squeezebox museum.

Then it was my turn. There was a suck from the weighted

door as I pushed it open, puncturing the seal on the assembled musicians inside. The orchestra. I'd never seen one up close. The nearest I'd been was the darkest reaches of the dress circle in the Fairfield Halls when Arthur Davison's Family Concerts came to Croydon when I was a kid. I remember an old man standing in a crucifix shape at the head of a bunch of monochromatic dervishes, all blowing, bowing and bashing the hell out of their instruments. It was exhilarating. *So* exhilarating that the combination of too much excitement and a face-full of ice lollies meant I was fast asleep within the first five minutes.

I walked over, past the violins, to the podium. It felt distinctly odd. Instead of following my instinct to face the audience, I had to stand with my arse towards them, staring instead at the semicircle of strangers below. It was then I got a sense of how truly out of my depth I was. I made a joke. It was lame. There was silence. After all, words aren't what turn musicians on.

The orchestra had been charged with following our beat exactly. Whatever moves we busted, whatever time we set, they would follow. I took a deep breath. My shoulders instantly rose to my cheeks with fear. *Come on! This is easy. It's just waving. I know the piece is in three, and I know how to beat three, so I'm laughing.*

The traditional way to beat three is to make a triangle shape, first going down from your head to your chest, then horizontally away from your body, then up to the original starting point around about your head. I put my hand down for the first beat. Some of the band started. Some followed a beat later. The musicians fell, one by one, like dominos, into a puddle of sound. If Les Dawson did strings, this was exactly the noise he would have made.

I was confused. *I'm making triangles*, I thought. *Why aren't they playing along to my triangles?* The orchestra appeared to be looking in my general direction, but just in case some of them had missed me, I started making larger, more emphatic, triangles. The sound dragged still further. *What's going on? WHY CAN'T YOU FOLLOW MY TRIANGLES?* I carried on. By now I looked like Bruce Willis in *Die Hard 2* when he's on the runway frantically waving at the doomed and rapidly descending plane.

After nearly three minutes of manic, incomprehensible semaphore, I was shattered. My face was red. My arm hurt. The piece didn't so much end as gradually disappear – with more of a whimper than a bang.

One by one we lined up to receive this punishment. Our embarrassments were nothing short of genius, a televisual *coup de grâce* – the death blow to those who believe that the conductor doesn't *do* anything. They patently do, because you can see me on screen *not doing it*.

Conductors are deeply enigmatic figures, their profession shrouded in mystery. 'What does a conductor do?' is the second most iterated question on the planet after 'What do lesbians do in bed?' (God forbid, I'd now be tasked with answering both.)

Although a few international conductors are venerated, most stick wavers are, at best, merely tolerated by the band. There's probably a maestro joke for every orchestra in the world, but the one I heard most often was:

Q: What's the difference between a bull and an orchestra?
A: With a bull, the horns are at the front and the shit up the back.

My personal favourite (when enquiring who is in charge of the baton for the night) was the fabulous line, 'Who's doing the carving?'

After the humiliation of Baton Camp, it was time to learn

what 'doing the carving' actually entailed. We spent the next few months studying and rehearsing at the Trinity Music College at Greenwich, a cluster of impeccable Regency buildings in south-east London. My mentor was the charming Jason Lai, who had the face of an angel and the terrifying intensity of Mussolini. That time, out of the sight of the camera, studying scores, developing my instinct, physicality and confidence, turned out to be one of the most profound periods of my life.

Everything I am about to say about my experiences as a conductor I say as a rank amateur. It may seem – especially if you, Dear Reader, are a professional musician – childish, naive or misguided. To you, the professional, I will most likely seem as much of an advert for musicianship as Maria Schneider is for butter. But this is what the experience felt like to inhabit, so forgive what are inevitable simplifications and gaps in my knowledge.

To make something as discernible as sound, you begin with silence. Silence is the essential canvas onto which everything else is laid. A piece starts and ends with silence, and into that calm, still space, before a single note is struck, the conductor must give what is known as the upbeat. This is the upward motion that announces that the first beat of the piece is coming. It is a signpost. It prepares. With it you are flagging your intent, you are gathering the energy of the group in order to unleash it upon the auditorium. The upbeat will carry messages about the tone, the feeling of the music and sometimes, although not always, its speed. I have seen some conductors give an upbeat as if they are gathering the air towards them like unruly children. Some simply waggle their fingers. Others expand their chests, raise their heads and violently push to the heavens. Each upbeat for each piece is different, and each conductor will give it in their own inimitable fashion.

(At this point, now I'm getting into this, I can't tell you *how much easier* it is to answer the question 'What do lesbians do in bed?')

In basic terms, your lead hand sets the speed, or tempo. It's responsible for 'distributing music on the axis of time' as the New York Philharmonic's Esa-Pekka Salonen rather beautifully describes it. More often than not, a conductor holds a baton in their lead hand (in my case the left, as I am left-handed) – a white pointy stick which amplifies your hand movements, making them easier to see from the back of the orchestra.

Your *other* hand is tasked with providing notes on expression and timbre. What is important? Which line do you want to shine in that moment? With what kind of sound? What colours and textures do you want to show? It's a kind of 'emotional ventriloquism', as Justin Davidson of *New York* magazine puts it. It's feeling by proxy. You calibrate the mood, then ask the musicians to physically create it for you.

You can tell a lot from the way someone holds their baton. (Oh, stop it.) It's a pretty good indication, I think, of how someone approaches power in general. Do you grab at it? Do you bully or do you cajole? Or does it bounce, all loose and fanciful? I've never felt very comfortable with a baton in my hand (I said *stop it*) perhaps because I feel, inherently, I don't deserve to brandish one. I'm much more comfortable with a pencil or a biro. Once I even used a toothbrush for a concert. However you hold it, I'm afraid I don't agree with the loaded notion of the maestro, i.e. the conductor as boss. For me, the conductor is the moderator of a million exciting artistic conversations happening simultaneously – a graphic equalizer, a sculptor of sound.

OK, now to the beat. The beat is always a downstroke. Place your hand in front of you, palm up. Then bring your lead hand down to clap it. Clap it rhythmically for a while. Then remove your bottom hand. When you create a beat for the orchestra, you are essentially replicating hitting a surface somewhere in front of you.

Of course, it's not just about the beat but about everything between it too, which would explain why, during my 'Blue Danube', the orchestra got progressively slower the larger my triangles became. The space between the beat got larger, and so the beat itself slowed down. Also, I was marking time with stiff, rigid lines, so the music sounded stiff and rigid too. If you flow, they flow. And if you manically score a giant Dairylea in the sky, then your 'Danube' will sound truly, truly shite.

The hardest thing about conducting is that you cannot wholeheartedly listen to the orchestra. You have to be a fraction ahead, leading the beat. If you get lost in the music they are making, you are already slowing down. You must be simultaneously in the now and the next, creating a feedback loop, a charmed circle, a beating heart with you at the centre of it.

That's the idea. The reality, as I discovered, proved to be somewhat harder.

The first live show on *Maestro* featured music from film and TV and I struck gold with *The Simpsons*. I loved it. It had a chaotic, wonky intensity with everyone, especially brass and percussion, at full tilt. I started to learn how to echo the textures of the piece with my physicality. This was hard, as I have very poor posture and don't love the way I look. I may have sloughed off a slight stammer, but hints of chronic shyness remain in my lolloping walk, dropped head and sloping shoulders. It took a team of mentors to get me to stand straight, and to look the orchestra in the eye. So much of the work of the conductor is in the eyes. You gaze at strangers with the intimacy of a lover, glare at them with the visceral hatred of a rival. It is not for the shy, it is not for the weak, it is certainly, as I was to discover, not for the emotionally closed.

Opera week arrived, and I was given the famous aria 'O mio babbino caro' from Puccini's *Gianni Schicchi* to carve to. It's a song that speaks of yearning and desire, as a daughter tells her father of her love for her boyfriend. It's searing, soaring, open-hearted stuff.

And I couldn't do it.

This was the first time I'd had to conduct slow music, and I immediately felt myself resisting. It made me uncomfortable – the delicacy, the poignancy, the messy emotional intrusion of it all. Quite simply it was asking something of me I didn't want to give.

Like many families, the Perkinses aren't given to grand displays of affection. We don't say, 'I love you.' We *think* it, but we don't *say* it. That sort of thing would be far too continental and embarrassing. Love, in my family, is generally assumed rather than iterated. *I wouldn't want to force it down your throat*, I can imagine my mum and dad saying, like it would be an unbearable burden they'd be saddling me with. My parents never heard it from their parents, so they weren't accustomed to saying it in return. You pass on what you get, don't you? The family baton of hopes and dreams and happiness and screwups. You pass it down the line like a relay across time and space.

I say 'I love you' all the time. I say it to partners* and friends. I write it on Post-it notes and scribble it on chalkboards. I sign

---

* One at a time. I am too tired to be polyamorous.

off emails with it and whisper it down the phone. I like saying it as often as I can. But in my family it remains resolutely unsaid. Which isn't to say that my folks didn't love me. I always felt loved. Always. I just didn't have it *confirmed* to me in the way you see in movies and on TV.

This is what you need to know. I am an appalling, appalling softie. But somehow, somewhere along the line, I've learned how to hide it. Hide that sentimentality and vulnerability. Control the emotions beneath. My dad does it using data. My mum does it by catastrophizing, so that reality always turns out better than her imaginings. I do it with words. Bluster. It fortifies me against the outside world.

Take away the words, and I am lost.

Music asks questions that your head will attempt to answer, but only your heart can truly understand. If you try to hide your heart, then you are not a musician. The one thing I had never given music, in all the years at Mrs Green's, hacking at the ivories, was my vulnerability. My passion. My soul – whatever *that* is. It's a big ask for a weirdo like me who has spent her life concealing her vulnerability with fake, polysyllabic bravado.

The final was between me and Goldie. I love Goldie. He's an explosive keg of raw energy and ideas. He's fun. He looked the part too, all handsome in his spanking tux.

It meant more than I thought it might to win – because, while it's utterly true to say that the experience itself was reward enough, the previous years had been so very dispiriting. I hadn't worked for as long as I could remember. I'd left the familiarity of London and the job I loved, but, more importantly, I'd lost every trace of self-belief. And that night, the night when the result came in, was the start of my rebuilding myself from scratch.

When I allowed myself to think about conducting in Hyde Park at the Last Night of the Proms, many images sprang to mind. None of them included a horde of menopausal women throwing knickers onto the stage, shouting 'We love you, Terry Wogan' while I drove my hands to the beat of 'Pomp and Circumstance'. There wasn't a lot of pomp, and as for the circumstance, well someone's large frilly camisole was now draped across my left foot.

While the Proms was a strange come-down from the show, the most extraordinary night of my life was gifted to me by conducting. Comic Relief took command of the Albert Hall one night in May 2011, in an effort to break the Guinness world record for the most kazoo players playing simultaneously. The place was packed. It was a fabulous bill – Julian Lloyd Webber, Nicola Benedetti, Tim Vine and the gorgeous BBC Concert Orchestra.

I had the honour of conducting two pieces with the band. Firstly, 'Mambo' from Leonard Bernstein's *West Side Story*. It's hard for a stolid northern European like me to conjure the spirit of Cuba. 'Mambo' is fast and vertical, with jagged offbeats, dizzying virtuoso brass and whirlwind percussion. There's a riot of bongos, timbales and cowbells. It is jumping. It screams life from the top of its lungs. If you want to see the Albert Hall being ripped apart by the sheer joyous force of it, then check out Gustavo Dudamel leading the Simon Bolivar Orchestra at the Proms on YouTube and prepare to SOAR, baby.

I wasn't particularly worried about 'Mambo'. It's frenetic and has its own momentum, as with *The Simpsons*. Most importantly, it asks nothing complicated from you emotionally; it merely requires the maximum amount of joy you can throw at it. If an amateur like me can just start it off right, then if things go off the rails, the tuned percussion will glue themselves to the beat so everyone can hang off them if needs be.

At the end of the night came my personal nemesis, Elgar's 'Nimrod'. It is one of those pieces often deemed hackneyed, and yet, when you hear it, I challenge you not to be flooded with sentiment. It's in our DNA that piece, whether we like it or not. It has an ancestral vibration that reaches out from the past and pulls you to it. It is for us what Barber's 'Adagio for Strings' is for the Americans, a wordless evocation of the soul of a nation.

Go on, get it down from your shelf if you have it. If not, download it now. I like Sir Colin Davis's version, but there are millions to choose from. Get it and put it on – loud. Let it wash over you, as each bar gradually increases in intensity. Like a clenched fist gently unfurling and then reaching for the heavens . . .

'Nimrod' is however an utter nightmare to conduct. On the page it looks relatively simple. It's in three – yes, that old chestnut – but such a *slow* three. With 'Nimrod' and other slow burners it isn't so much about what you do with the beat, it's what you do *between* it – how you sculpt the space within the notes so that it flows and builds to its ultimate crescendo. And Jesus, it's tiring. Try drawing your hand across your body in long, smooth lines for four minutes or so. It becomes agony after a while.

What I wasn't expecting, though, was how I'd *feel*. Nothing prepared me for that.

I put down a beat for the violins and watched as their bows skimmed across the strings. So far, so good. At bar three I turned to the violas, and they expanded the line with an incredible sweetness. And then it happened. A mere five or six bars in I started to lose myself in the music. Just a little at first. But then, slowly and inexorably, it began to eat me up. My hand started to droop. So much so I couldn't hold the baton. I dropped it on the stand and carried on with just my hands, fingers dragging as if hanging off a boat and dangling in the water beneath. The sound began to lag.

I wasn't leading. I wasn't following either. I was inside it, inside the guts of it, and I couldn't get out. My chest vibrated with the sound. My head flooded with a million sudden thoughts and feelings – snapshots, sounds, smells. My past. My family. Love and the loss that walks so closely behind it. My hand was now so heavy I could barely drag it across my body.

The music was either too big for me, or I was too small for it. Either way, I will never forget being so utterly overwhelmed. In that moment I understood something profound – that words would only distort should I choose them to describe it. I learned about performance, connection, intimacy, sadness. I learned about me. Every part of myself I tried to hide, it came looking for – ripping me open like a tin can.

All of which made for a bloody *terrible* 'Nimrod', so I'm sorry if you were listening.

The next day I obsessed about the fact that I'd had the opportunity of conducting one of the greatest pieces of music ever written in one of the greatest concert halls in the world, and I'd blown it. It was too slow. It was too leaden. All day long it hung over me – the shame, the shame of getting it wrong.

I arrived home the next night to have dinner with my parents. As usual, I hadn't told them I was doing a gig. After we'd eaten, I went into the kitchen to help Mum with the washing-up. Minutes passed with nothing but the squeak of dishcloth on glass as our soundtrack.

Then Mum piped up, 'I heard your concert on Radio 3 last night.'

'Really?' I had completely forgotten it had been a live broadcast. There was a pause. 'It was terrible. Sorry, Mum. It was too bloody slow.'

I reached for the tea towel in embarrassment. Mum turned to face me. 'No, Susan, it was yours. And it was perfect.'

There was that silence again.

I love you, I thought.

I thought but didn't say.

I love you.

Oh No, I Can't

By now I was travelling up and down the country so frequently I could recite the whole of the First Great Western London-to-Penzance timetable from memory. It was an utterly pointless skill to have, of course, since First Great Western rarely stuck to it. For them the timetable appeared to be more of a suggestion than a schedule. Still, the trains themselves were always a pleasant surprise when they arrived.

I was happy in Cornwall. I learned how to build a drystone wall (well, I watched Kate do it); I was twitching ('Look, there's a magpie! And another! And another!'), and I was growing heritage seed vegetables (I had some of the most bulbous 'Chioggia' in West Penwith). Then I'd leave my rural idyll, get on a train, and six hours later find myself spewed forth into the madness and filth of Paddington. At home I was quiet and still. At work I was manic and displaced. Slowly I became happy in neither state. The grass was always greener. I lived on the road, between here and there, in perpetual motion. Slowly my mind became as fragmented and split as my time.

After *Maestro* I started doing piecemeal bits of television. I dressed as an elf for an insert on *Countryfile*. I contributed to various talking-heads shows, *I Love The Eighties*, *Britain's Best Wasps*, *My Top Ten Favourite Lists* – that sort of thing. Then came the blink-and-you'll-miss-it *Never Mind the Full Stops*, a BBC4 panel show about grammar. That's right. Grammar. You know – colons, parentheses, ellipsis – the natural springboard for comedic badinage.

The show was hosted by Julian Fellowes before he was Mr Downton. Back then he was just Nice Posh Man in Salmon-Coloured Chinos. Julian was utterly convinced that I'd been one of the presenters on *Loose Women*. No matter how many times I tried to disabuse him of this notion, he resolutely clung to it.

Julian: And on the panel to my right we have . . .
Me: Sue.
Julian: Yes! Hello, Sue.
Me: Hello.
Julian: Now you did that show at lunchtime . . .
Me: *Light Lunch*.
Julian: *Loose Women*, that's right. There were a few of you – around a table. You'd talk about repatriating ethnic minorities and menstruation, that sort of thing . . .
Me: You're thinking of Jane McDonald . . .
Julian: No, definitely you. Anyway, lovely to have you on the show. Can you start by telling us what a demonstrative pronoun is?

Five minutes later.

Julian: That's right, David – one point to your team! The answer was indeed epanadiplosis. Now Sue, over to you . . . Now I don't suppose you get many of these on *Loose Women*, but what's a dangling modifier?

While taping one of these episodes I encountered the tele-visual legend that is Daisy Goodwin. Daisy has a Silicon Valley mainframe for a brain and an extraordinary capacity for fusing the clever and the populist. Some of the greatest shows of the last twenty years have had her manicured hands on them. A few months later she recommended me for a one-off gastronomic history documentary called *Edwardian Supersize Me*.

My co-presenter was the gorgeous choleric writer and columnist Giles Coren. I loved him from the get-go. I'd already had the honour of working with his dad, Alan, and his sister, Victoria, and meeting him merely proved there's no such thing as a mediocre Coren. There was a weird chemistry between me and Giles – an immediate closeness that sometimes veered towards the sibling and occasionally towards the sexual. I do believe we may have snogged under a table at some point during the seventeenth century. If so, then I was a very lucky Hanoverian.

The general gist of *Edwardian Supersizers* was that we dressed up in period costume and ate what posh people would eat in the early 1900s. Every day for ten days I scoffed over 5,000 calories. For breakfast there were mutton chops, devilled kidneys and eggs, followed by platters of game birds – widgeon, teal and snipe. For lunch I would stagger under the weight of roast beef and towering puddings. At dinner there would be endless bottles of plonk and the ferric tang of duck cooked in its own blood. I ate all of this while encased in an unyielding whalebone corset. My waist maintained its rigid twenty-one inches, but all that food had to go somewhere. By the end of each night a vast uni-tit of lard would form around my décolletage, on which I could rest my head as I became more and more hammered.

Supersizers ended up running for a couple of series, with a few spin-off shows thereafter. What started off as a history documentary soon became a drinking competition with a few Wiki facts thrown in. Giles truly channelled George IV and passed out in a grate after getting hitched to my Caroline of Brunswick. I collapsed in a French chateau dressed as Marie

Antoinette and had to be dragged down three flights of stairs by my ankles. Giles pissed in a bucket by his chair during a Samuel Pepys feast, and I fell face down into the lap of a respected historian and stayed there, snoring, while he told me about coffee-drinking in the Restoration period.

That show remains one of my favourite things, extemporaneous, unpredictable and new. The only thing I didn't like about it was the medical. For such a free-form show, it felt odd to have this heavy-handed formatting bookend. We were required to have blood tests at the beginning and end of every week to see whether or not our metabolisms had been affected by the onslaught of booze and offal we had subjected them to.

In Victorian week the show had more of a female slant. This was the era that saw the rise of anorexia, drug addiction (laudanum) and the early stirrings of feminism, after all. Giles was delighted that his arm was not required for pin-cushion services (he is prick-averse), so I gamely rolled up my sleeves alone. My blood was duly taken; I was whisked to west London and spent a week in a farthingale, retching over a sheep's head and drunkenly snogging a bunch of elderly contributors who'd only turned up to talk about turkey production in nineteenth-century Norfolk.

As Giles wrapped for the week, lucky bastard, I got sent to the clinic to discover how my body chemistry had shifted over the last seven days. The doctor, formerly upbeat and open, had seemed shifty during filming. We completed the shoot whereupon she asked if she could have a word in private. It turned out one of my readings was off. Like off-the-chart off. Prolactin. Bloody prolactin. You make it when you're stressed. If you're really stressed you can show readings of up to 23 or so. If you're pregnant (the hormone is produced during pregnancy) it can get up to nearly 400.

My reading was 3200.

I explained that I wasn't stressed. I explained that I wasn't pregnant.

Then she explained I had a brain tumour.

The littlest things freak me out – arriving late for a meeting, not having the right pen to hand, being mistaken for a *Loose Women* presenter. But when life gets properly hardcore, I have the strangest ability to relax. Maybe I enjoy the fact that finally, *finally* something is out of my control.

And so I was perfectly calm as I walked into the deserted nuclear medicine unit at my local hospital. Calm while they scanned my bones. Calmer still as the magnets clanged and clanked around my ears as my body lay strapped to a table. I was even calm, six weeks later, when the time came for me to see the consultant to get my results.

The best way to tell a woman she can't have children

Consultant:	Hi. Are you Susan?
Me:	Yes.
Consultant:	It's lovely to meet you. I'm Mr X and I'm the endocrinology consultant here. Now, do step inside and have a seat. OK, well, I imagine you have an awful lot of questions, and I'm happy to answer all of them as fully and comprehensively as I can. Let me tell you what we *do* know first of all. You OK?
Me:	Yes. Yes. It's just a little weird.
Consultant:	Of course. Hospitals are deeply scary places if you're not familiar with them. Try not to worry because you're in very safe hands. Now we have the results of your blood tests and scans. You have a micro-prolactinoma, which is a tumour of your

pituitary gland. Now the great news is that it is benign, and that it won't require surgery. The only issues that arise from this tumour are that you are more susceptible to osteoporosis and that it causes fertility issues . . .

Fade to black.

NOT *the best way to tell a woman she can't have children*

Consultant: Hi, right. Let's have a look at your scans. So, there's your pituitary there, right in the middle of your head. And see that lump? That's a tumour. Don't need to take it out; we can keep an eye on it by looking at your bloods and monitoring you regularly. Now, you married?

Me: No.

Consultant: Boyfriend?

Me: No. I'm gay.

Consultant: Oh, OK. Well that makes it easier. You're most likely infertile. You can't have kids.

Fade to black.

That's how I found out.

I was fine for about twenty minutes. Fine to rebook another appointment, head down the stairs to the exit and greet the late-spring sunshine. Fine to buy a grande latte from a tax-avoiding multinational and walk, sipping it, up the hill home. I was fine right up to the point my flat came into view, then I slumped down on my front step, shaking. I rang Kate.

'I don't know why I'm upset,' I sobbed. 'It's not like it was on my mind to have kids. I wasn't planning it. It wasn't on my horizon. It's just so brutal though – the reality that there's nothing more than me. I'm it. I'm the end of the line . . .'

She listened. Occasionally she interjected. But mainly she listened.

I cried myself hoarse till my eyes ran on empty. Then I hung up, opened the front door and let Pickle lick the tears from my face.

All Cats Are Grey

It's a summer's morning, 11 June 2008 to be precise, and I'm driving through wide, faceless south London streets. The radio is on, a phone-in show, and an adenoidal presenter with too much jolly in his genes is wittering down the microphone. It's the usual fare, a dollop of banality, a splash of whimsy and a heavy dose of censorious middle-aged morality.

'What would *you* do if you woke up and it was 2049?'

'Water – good thing or bad thing? Let us know. Call 0207 . . .'

'What *is* the point of cats? You know the number – 0207 . . .'

I am making the trip to see my grandmother, Granny Smith – who, like her fruit namesake, is crisp and bitter but a firm favourite nonetheless. She has just turned one hundred years old, and my entire family is congregating at her old people's home. This may or may not be the thing that finally pushes her over the edge.

The radio is still blaring: 'So our topic this morning – what's the most unusual thing you've done for love?'

I switch it off as I pull up outside the residential home – a loveless, anonymous red-brick on the edge of Kent.

Inside, there is the smell of overcooked greens and a million heavy exhalations. Snooker blares from the television. A dozen eyes gaze in a myopic haze in the general direction of the screen. In the distance I can hear the sound of a bewildered man refusing to take his meds.

I am met in the hall by a sprightly lady called Judy.

'You here to see Lil?'

'Yes,' I reply.

'She's a slouch that one – only a hundred. I did that last year. It's a breeze! I'll go see if I can root out the little darling.'

This is the first time I have heard my grandmother referred to as a 'little darling'. Granny Smith is a redoubtable bag of paper-thin skin full of bile and piss and grit, who has sloughed off war (twice), cancer (twice) and the death of her beloved husband Stan (once, obviously) to get to this point. Whatever she is, she is certainly *not* a little darling . . .

Judy bounces around the communal lounge like a new-born gazelle, enquiring about Grandma's whereabouts. I watch her dart here and there, sharp as a tack and bright as a button.

She returns.

'They've found her. They've wheeled her outside to get some air. Shall I show you through?'

Grandma is indeed outside, in the garden, where she sits surrounded by my family in her wheelchair. I am late. I am always late. She winks at me as I bend to kiss her, and as I do I breathe in the familiar top note of lily of the valley mixed with cheap carbolic, a scent that takes me back to a time and place before words came and got in the way of everything.

She looks older – it's only been a few months since I last saw her, but she looks older. From the side you can see the milky sheen of developing cataracts, and a wobble of goitrous chin that makes me grin. *That's coming for me one day*, I think, and then I stop grinning.

We crowd around her chair and have our photo taken. There's me, David, Lynne, Michelle and Mum. Gran is holding something and beaming proudly. It's a card from the Queen.

'What's this?' I say, staring at the cheap paper. 'Is that it?'

I'm genuinely shocked. Her Majesty's signature is photo-copied – the whole thing mass-produced and impersonal. It's a far cry from the romantic notions you have of the 'telegram'.

'Well that's not worth waiting a hundred years for,' I scoff, almost offended on her behalf.

But Grandma isn't laughing. Grandma isn't joining in. In fact she is totally silent.

And then I realize that this isn't just a card to her.

Grandma's father hailed from Leipzig, her mum from Moscow, and she was born (one of eight children) in Riga, Latvia. The family fled from the pogroms, and for a while her dad was interned in the Isle of Wight. During the war a Quaker couple took her and her sister on holiday to the seaside but, on finding out they had German blood, deliberately starved them. It scarred her for life and taught her to conceal her identity, her ethnicity. It was wrong to be foreign, it was wrong to be Ashkenazi. Right up until her death she would staunchly deny she was Jewish, though when drunk (which was most of the time, courtesy of Harvey's Bristol Cream) she would launch into snatches of Yiddish.

So it isn't just a card; it's so much more than that. For her, an immigrant, it is everything – validation, acceptance, authentication. It says, *I belong. I belong because the Queen, the head of state, says so. And here's the proof.*

Gran moved into the home in 1994, just after Granddad died, and it quickly became clear she wasn't built for communal living. Firstly she was a racist and secondly she was hard of hearing, which meant that every time she felt like giving her views on benefit claimants or Labour's 'open door' policy, she did so in the LOUDEST VOICE IMAGINABLE. She was that particular breed of immigrant who felt, with absolute conviction, that the UK government should have left the gates open just long enough for *her* to enter the country, and then shut and bolted them immediately behind her so that no one else could come in.

And I mean *no one* else. The best thing you could say about her attitude to foreigners was that she was an equal-opportunities hater, meaning no particular group was singled out more than the other. Having said that, there was something particularly painful about the way she described and referred to any nurses of colour.

'Get me the nurse,' she'd demand, annoyed, as I wheeled her around.

'Do you mean May?' I'd enquire.

'Is she the chocolate one?'

I'd remain silent for a while, gritting my teeth, remembering something from Sunday school way back, something about hating the sin, not the sinner.

'Grandma, she's from—'

'Milk chocolate? That one? No, not that one – the Bourne-ville one.'

As she carried on, yelling her way through the various cocoa-solid options, I would let loose my grip on her wheel-chair, and off she would drift, away from me. Sometimes, in these situations, the best way to get an errant pensioner to behave is to just roll them down a ramp into the sun room, where they can bake under the hermetically sealed uPVC windows until penitent.

Coming out to a grandparent is one of the most toe-curling, awful experiences of one's life. Having to shout one's sexual proclivities into the impaired ear of a nonagenarian surely ranks in anyone's list of top-ten worst moments. Now imagine that same pensioner is losing her memory . . .

Towards the end of her hundredth year Granny Smith started to become more and more forgetful. I'm reluctant to use the word dementia, as she could still recall with pinpoint accuracy the price of a pair of mules she bought in Colchester in 1968. But the past, and the people who inhabited it, was becoming increasingly hazy, blurred and vignetted by age. This meant that *every time* I saw her, I had to come out to her in a process I liked to call

GROUNDHOG GAY.

Every time I made the pilgrimage to her bedside, it was the same painful routine.

Me: Hi, Gran.

Gran: Oh hello. Who are you?

Me: I'm Susan, I'm your eldest grandchild.

Gran: Oh. [*Pause*] Are you married?

Me: No, Gran.

Gran: Why not?

Me: [*long sigh*] I'm gay.

Gran: Oh. Oh dear.

A month or so later I'm back. I enter the room and settle next to her chair.

Me: Hi, Gran.

Gran: Oh hello. Who are you?

Me: I'm Susan, I'm your eldest grandchild.

Gran: Oh. [*Pause*] Are you married?

Me: No, Gran.

Gran: Why not?

Me: [*long sigh*] I'm gay.
Gran: Oh. Oh dear.

The last time I saw Granny Smith was that day of her centenary. When the heat of the midday sun became too much I wheeled her back inside while my family went in search of a hundred candles for the cake. Her room was dark and embraced her with a silence you could almost touch. I went up to her and held her hand, a jumble of bones and rope veins wrapped in translucent skin.

Me: Hi, Gran.
Gran: Oh, hello. Who are you?
Me: I'm Susan, I'm your eldest grandchild.
Gran: Oh. [*Pause*] Are you married?

The silence grows heavy.

Me: Yes. Yes, I am. I'm married to a lovely man called . . . Simon.
         And we have . . . three kids. You remember?
Gran: Oh yes. Lovely. Well done.

I walked away from the home and got in the car, my face streaming with tears. I knew it was the last time I'd ever see her. I turned the key in the ignition and the radio blared once more. The phone-in was still running, and for the first time ever I wanted to ring in. I wanted to ring in and tell them about the most unusual thing I'd done for love.

One hundred-plus years on the planet, a million rich and varied life experiences, and the one, single thing that Grandma Smith chose to share with subsequent generations was this pearl of wisdom she gave my mum. When I was around sixteen, my mum duly shared it with me. Here goes.

All cats are grey.

Yes, that's it. That's what she gave us. No family heirlooms, no jewellery or photos. Just that phrase.

All cats are grey.

This pithy little saying originates from John Heywood's book of proverbs, published in 1546: 'When all candles be out, all cats be grey.'

From which we can deduce two things:

1. John is implying that, in the dark, physical appearance is irrelevant.
2. John obviously spoke in a thick West Country accent straight out of Central Casting. Think of him as a kind of sixteenth-century Jethro.

This saying is now generally attributed to Benjamin Franklin, who used it when arguing why one should not necessarily dismiss an older woman. In other words, they may not look like much, but they become more appealing a prospect in the pitch black. Charming.

Have you seen a picture of Benjamin Franklin? He looks like a Scotch egg in a wind tunnel. No wonder he was advocating a world where we should dismiss a person's physical attributes. You would need a written guarantee of zero light pollution before you laid a finger on him, and even then you'd need a promise of no kissing. And even then . . . well, there's still all your OTHER senses . . . You'd be able to taste and smell and touch him and . . . Oh no, he'd just feel like a blood-temperature landslide. Not for me, thanks.

What's even odder is that the man who reminded us that we all look the same when the lights are out spent most of his spare time trying to illuminate the skies with either electricity or his own invention, the lightning rod. That's one hell of a mixed message right there.

I often wonder why Grandma chose to hand down this particular phrase. Perhaps it was her polite way of saying, *You Perkinses are none of you lookers but, don't worry, in a power cut you'll really come in to your own.* Or was it just aimed at me? Was she saying, *Susan, always date in dim lighting*?

Of course, if I were *only* judged on physical appearance I would have never got very far, which isn't to say that looks aren't important. Visual attraction is the portal that leads to the really great stuff, like how people like their tea, whether they mind burned toast, what they think of Cy Twombly and Carol Ann Duffy and if can they stomach West End musicals.

All of which goes to say, *Grandma, that's great, but all you've done is confused Mum and then confused me and then confused Michelle. I think, on reflection, in terms of a legacy, we'd have preferred jewellery. Don't need the diamonds – the paste stuff would do. Whatever's in the bottom of your cupboards. Just a token. Thanks.*

The End of the Line

Pickle first had cancer at two years old, a hard lump that ulcerated as soon as the vet's needle touched it. It was a mast cell tumour; nothing much on the outside, malignant as hell on the inside. It was a vicious op – the wide margin of tissue they needed to cut away meant her skin was stretched as tight as a drum around her back, with thick steel stitches holding it all together at her chest.

That night was the first and last time I ever heard her cry.

'Keep her lead-walked for a fortnight; she'll want to rest,' said the nurse as Kate and I arrived to pick her up.

Two days later she slipped her collar on a walk and went hunting in the woods for an hour and a half. Impossible, impossible beast.

Less than a year later Pickle developed a limp. I took her to see the vet, Joshua, a brilliant man with a look of mild exasperation etched permanently on his forehead. I guess I would too, were I to spend my days listening to people with too much money asking whether Chianti the bichon frise needs her teeth whitening or Sally the Burmese needs leg warmers now the nights are drawing in.

Joshua felt round Pickle's back legs. Pickle endured it as per because she had already eyed up her prize – a jar of treats on the side cabinet. He then asked me to take her for a walk up and down the street so he could examine her gait. We pounded the pavement. Nothing. Much as I tried to get her to limp she seemed sound again – until the fourth lap, when her back left started failing again.

Josh: Ah, I see it. It's probably a strain.

Me: But what if it isn't?

Josh: [*a pause, then that exasperated face*] It *is* probably a strain.

Me: Shouldn't she have an X-ray?

Josh: I don't think that's necessary. Take her home and keep an eye on her. And then, if it persists and you're worried, bring her back and we can look into getting some diagnostic work done.

Me: I am. I am worried. I'm already worried . . .

There is a loud crash from inside the surgery. Pickle has finally claimed her biscuits. Joshua says nothing but raises his eyes to the heavens.

For the next two weeks I watched Pickle like a hawk. The limp would come and go, but it seemed to increase in severity each time. I phoned Mum. That was the worst thing I could have done.

Me: I've looked in the medical encyclopedia. It could be rickets. And . . . and do dogs get deep vein thrombosis?

After a month I returned to the surgery. A new jar of treats sat on the side.

Me: Josh, it's got worse.

Josh: Really? OK, well, let's have a look at her.

Pickle once again endured an examination and the endless walking outside. Nothing. In the end Josh agreed to perform an X-ray. I arrived at 4 p.m. to pick her up.

Me: How is she? What did it show?

Josh: It was inconclusive.

Me: What does that mean?

| Josh: | It could be a repetitive strain or cartilage issues or something not showing up on the slides. Just try not to worry. |
| Lindsay the nurse: | She'll be very tired. Just lead-walk her for a few days. |

There is a loud crash from inside the consulting room. Pickle, high on meds, has just found the new jar of treats.

Two weeks later and I was frantic. I headed back to the surgery.

Me:	[*wailing*] What else can we do?
Josh:	[*by now a broken man*] Well, there is a specific orthopaedic hospital near Bedford, but I really don't think–
Me:	Yes! Let's do that!

And so I drove Pickle to Hertfordshire for further examination. The team there kept her in overnight for observation (£400), and the next day she was taken, in a private human ambulance (£250), for an MRI at the neighbouring hospital (£400). After another overnight stay (£400) I picked her up and waited for Joshua to get the results. I was terrified. Finally, I got the call.

Josh:	OK, so I've got the results of all the MRIs and bone scans. And –
Me:	Oh God.
Josh:	I don't know how to say this . . .
Me:	Oh God.
Josh:	There's –
Me:	What?
Josh:	There's –
Me:	I can't live without her!

Josh: There's nothing wrong with her.

Me: Sorry?

Josh: Nothing. Not a thing.

Me: I don't understand.

Josh: I've reviewed everything and spoken to my colleagues at the hospital, and . . . well, the truth is –

Me: Oh no . . .

Josh: She's doing it for attention.

Me: What?

Josh: She wants your attention. That's why she's doing it.

Me: You mean . . . you mean she's *putting it on*?

Josh: Yes.

Me: You're telling me I've got a dog with Munchausen's?

Josh: Yes, if you put it like that.

Me: Three THOUSAND pounds, and she just wants my attention?

Josh: Yes.

There is a pause. In the background a fully operational Pickle is desperately launching herself in the direction of the treats jar. I march over to her until I loom large.

Me: You want my attention do you, little Pickle?

She sneezes on my foot, then looks up.

Me: WELL YOU'VE GOT IT NOW.

We didn't make it, Kate and I. Not in the end. My schedule, my stupidity, my thoughtlessness made an ex of her. We could have got through it. She could be sitting here as I write, shaking her tousled head at my silly puns and childish efforts to make you love me, but that's hindsight for you. I made the worst mistake of my life. And then she made the worst of hers. You see, it turns out that my capacity for total self-destruction was matched only by her own – compatible to the last.

We didn't speak for a while and got on with our lives, meeting new people and forging new paths. Her absence became the right side of bearable. Just. When Pickle was diagnosed with terminal cancer last year, I sat at my computer and emailed her. She had the right to say goodbye. I asked her if she would like to be there at the end. She replied that yes, she would.

And so we met on the Heath and walked together – all of us. Then we went back to my flat to prepare for the unthinkable.*

When Joshua had left with Pickle's body and all had fallen quiet, Kate and I sat beside one another on the sofa. We drank tumblers of whisky, hands shaking, in total shock that we'd just killed our little girl – that we had just lost part of our family. As we talked, I could feel our ties weakening, one by one, and realized that soon I would have nothing left to moor me to her. I would just be cast adrift on an ocean of memory and regret.

After a while Kate got up to leave, and I joined her, with Parker ambling behind, seemingly untroubled by the loss and in dire need of a piss. She walked round the block with me, arm linked in mine, the years forgotten.

Then she got in her car and left.

---

* Later that night I wrote a letter to my dog. It is here, at the end of this chapter, exactly as I wrote it.

◡◠

It turns out that I had been in SUCH shock during the euthanasia procedure that I had forgotten to fill out the requisite paperwork. So when I phoned the surgery a few weeks later to pick up Pickle's ashes there was a slightly awkward encounter with the receptionist.

Me: Hi. I'm just ringing to see when I can pick up my dog.
Woman: Ah. OK.
Me: Is there a problem?
Woman: Well . . . she's still with us.
Me: What do you mean – still with you?

An uncomfortable pause.

Woman: We've been . . . waiting on your instructions.

Finally, it dawned on me. She was in their fridge-freezer. She'd been in it for six weeks. I thought I'd sorted the cremation out but in reality hadn't handed over the correct forms or money or anything. I felt awful, truly awful, though I was momentarily cheered by a friend reminding me that Pickle had spent the majority of her life trying to get into fridges, and therefore it was fitting, in death, that she had finally got her wish.

I didn't pick up Pickle until 10 March, a warm spring day. The waiting room was empty. I had a lump in my throat, but tried to style it out and pass it off as typhoid.

It was the weight that got me – the sheer weight. I don't know. I thought that the ashes would be light, like grey candyfloss, that I would take the bag and swing it into the air, and she and I would go walking into the fresh spring morning together, united once more. No one tells you how heavy the urn is going to be or how much dust you'll have to spread. No one tells you how to deal with someone handing you something you adored in a carrier bag in front of a waiting room full of hacking cats and three-legged dogs. It's hard to be nonchalant in that situation. It's hard to pretend that being handed a plastic sack full of something you love is an everyday occurrence.

The urn weighed one kilogram. The exact weight of loss.

I'd like to say that we sprinkled the ashes together, Kate and I, in the fields of Cornwall a few months later – that our eyes locked in that moment, as the wind took the hard grey dust and spirited it away into the sky. And that all the pain of those awful yesterdays went with it, blown to nothing, leaving only the purest concentrate of love behind.

Wouldn't that have been wonderful? A perfect, full circle, the sort of thing writers write about.

And I guess I am a writer now, and I could write that – I could write the perfect ending. I'd love to, you know. More than anything, I'd love to.

But it didn't happen. Why would it? Life doesn't give you the neatly tied ends of a romcom. The world would be insufferably saccharine if it did, plus we're so contrary as a species, we'd only sit around longing for the tragedy and agony of unrequited love.

And yet, in all the loss, something of the family remains – Parker, our arthritic darling, now with blue discs for eyes and pegs for legs – and my beloved Heath, which holds the memories of yesterday in its boughs and meadows.

This is the tree where you first kissed me. Sometimes it is full of leaf and fills the sky, sometimes it is thin and stark, like it is now. This is the tumulus where we cried that final time. Here is the path where you first held my hand. Here is the wood we made our own. Here are the secret short cuts, the magnolia with one flower, the mournful benches, the familiar pooches. Here they all are.

We occasionally bump into each other, never arranged, always haphazard. And we walk a little, until our paths home diverge. Look at the emotional palindrome we have become.

And my feet marching this ground, day after day, tell the tale of

You and I, you and I, you and I, and trees and sky and always and for ever but

Gone.

A Letter to Pickle

My darling girl,

First, a confession: I had you killed. I planned it and everything; asked the vet round and a nurse in a green uniform with white piping – all with the express intention of ending your life. Yes, I know. I know you had no idea, because I had been practising for weeks how to keep it from you, and how – when that time came – I could stop my chest from bursting with the fear and horror and unbearable, unbearable pain of it all.

I sat there, in your kitchen (it was always your kitchen), numb, and filled in a form about what to do with your remains. I ticked boxes as you lay wheezing in your sleep on the bed next door. I made a series of informed, clinical decisions on the whys and wherefores of that beautiful, familiar body that had started to so badly let you down. Then, once the formalities were over, I came in and did what I've done so many days and nights over so many months and years. I lay behind you, left arm wrapped round your battle-scarred chest and whispered into your ear.

I love you.

So that was my secret. And I kept it from you until your ribs stopped their heaving and your legs went limp and your head fell as heavy as grief itself in my arms. Then, when I knew you were no longer listening, I let it out – that raging, raging river of loss. I cried until my skin felt burned and my ears grew tired from the sound of it all.

It wasn't pretty.

OK. Confession over.

Now what you also need to know is that this is NOT a eulogy. Quite frankly, Pickle, you don't deserve one, because, as you are well aware, your behaviour from birth, right up to the bitter end, was unequivocally terrible.

As a pup, you crunched every CD cover in the house for fun. You chewed through electrical cable and telephone wires. You ripped shoes and gobbled plastic. You dived into bins, rolled in shit and licked piss off of pavements. You ate my bedposts.

As an adult you graduated to raiding fridges and picnics, you stole ice cream from the mouths of infants, you jumped onto Christmas tables laden with pudding and cake and blithely walked through them all, inhaling everything in your wake.

You puked on everything decent I ever owned. You never came when called, never followed a path, never observed the Green Cross Code and only sat on command when you could see either a cube of cheese or chicken in my hand (organic, or free range at a push).

And last, but not least, you shat in my bed (yes, I know they were dry and discreet little shits, but they were still shits, you shit).

Here's another thing, while I'm at it. I'm angry. Why? Because you, madam, are a liar. You made me think you were OK. You allowed me to drop you off at our mate Scarlett's farm and leave you there for weeks while I went away working thinking that all was well. Yet it wasn't, was it? The cancer fire was already lit, sweeping through your body, laying waste to it while my back was turned.

I look back at photos sent to me while I was away from you, and I can see it now – that faint dimming of the eyes, the gentle slackening of muscle. The tiniest, tiniest changes in that cashmere fur of yours. It haunts me still. Had I been there, I would have noticed, would I not? Me, your anxious guardian and keeper of eleven and a half years.

I found out about the lump the day I landed. Scarlett rang me with the news as I boarded a train for Willesden Junction. The most momentous moments can come at the most banal. It had just appeared, out of nowhere, as surprising and fast as you, on your neck. You never did anything by halves, and there it was, the size of a lemon, wrapped round your lymph.

I took you home the next day, to Cornwall, the place that we love best, and you allowed me, for a while at least, to believe that nothing was wrong. We rose at sunset, in the light of those Disney-pink skies, and walked the ancient tracks together – before you got bored and veered off, full tilt, in search of the latest scent.

But your lies could only carry you so far before your body gave you away. I saw your chest starting to heave when you took a breath at night. Your bark became hoarse. You no longer tore around the house causing havoc. You were biddable (you were never biddable), you ate slowly (oh, don't be ridiculous).

Yet still, the denial. Forgive me for that. After all, we'd beaten it before, you and I. Twice. Even when the vet told me your lungs were hung with cancerous cobwebs and there was nothing more to be done, I went out and started doing. I sped to the health food store and returned with tinctures and unguents and capsules. And there you were having to eat your precious last dinners covered in the dusty yellow pall of turmeric and a slick of Omega 3s. So silly. So silly, in retrospect. I should have let you eat cake and biscuits and toast and porridge. But I thought I could save you. I really thought I could.

I didn't ever believe that something as alive as you could ever succumb to something as ordinary as death.

After all, how could you be sick when you ran and jumped and played, day after day after day?

And then, I got it. You were doing it all for me. You were dragging yourself into the light, every morning, for me. All of it. For me.

And as fierce and possessive as my love was, I couldn't let you do that any more.

Spectacles

You were eighty years old, by human reckoning. You were eighty years old and you still flew into the boot of the car without assistance (assistance is for old dogs, you didn't know how to be an old dog), you still strode the Heath with that graceful, lupine lope of yours. You skidded round corners, you sniffed and barked and hectored and lived to life's outer margins. On the day you died, you pottered for over an hour in the meadows with the sun on your back, without a care in the world. I am so very grateful for that.

When someone once took a punch at me, you leaped in the air and took it. When I discovered I couldn't have children, you let me use your neck as a hankie. You were my longest relationship, although I think any decent psychologist would have deemed us irredeemably co-dependent. You were the engine of my life, the metronome of my day. You set the pulse and everything and everyone moved to it. What a skill. I woke to your gentle scratch on the door (it wasn't gentle, it was horrific and you have destroyed every door in every house we have lived in – I am just trying to make you sound nice), and the last sound at night was the sound of you crawling under your blanket and giving that big, deep, satisfied sigh.

I have said I love you to many people over many years: friends, family, lovers. Some you liked, some you didn't. But my love for you was different. It filled those spaces that words can't reach.

You were the peg on which I hung all the baggage that couldn't be named. You were the pure, innocent joy of grass and sky and wind and sun. It was a love beyond the limits of patience and sense and commensuration. It was as nonsensical as it was boundless. You alchemist. You nightmare.

Thank you for walking alongside me* during the hardest,

---

* I say alongside, you're a beagle. More like 400 yards to the right. In a thicket.

weirdest, most extreme times of my life, and never loving me less for the poor choices I made and the ridiculous roads I took us down.

Thank you, little Pickle. I love you.

From the four-eyed one who shouted at you, held you, laughed at you, fed you and, for some reason utterly unbeknownst to you, put all your shit in bags.

X

Pickle Perkins
Born: 20-08-02
Skipped to next destination: 14-01-14

Back to Black

In the autumn of 2009, as I turned forty, my life as I knew it ended. I will never know to what extent I pushed it to change and to what extent I was simply a lemming senselessly trundling over that midlife-crisis cliff. I lost my love, my future and my bearings. Completely.

The house in Cornwall was a wreck. I could neither bear to live in it, nor get rid of it. I simply locked it up and left it – out of sight, out of mind. It became like a museum – the past, preserved in aspic. As each month went on, the place got danker. Blue mould blossomed on the sofas and crept up the walls. Thick boughs of cobwebs hung from the ceiling. I remember driving down, intending to spend the weekend there and clear everything out. I walked into the bedroom and saw Kate's book still on the bed, upturned, where she had left it. I burst into tears, walked out the door and drove straight back to London.

I rented a tiny one-bedroom flat on an alleyway down to the Hampstead Ponds. The flat itself was about as soulless a thing as I have ever encountered, but the beagles liked it, and therefore I made do.

It has such a stagnant feel, that passageway down to the water. The ponds reek of sadness. The fishermen sit there in the autumn and try to catch something other than rusty bikes and gym shoes. People stand by the water watching the ducks and wonder whether to throw bread, or themselves, into the murk. A very famous photograph of Nick Drake was taken right by the little side door that led to my garden. He is mid-lollop, back to the camera, his dog Gus alongside him. I was that close to the great man. I wondered if the sadness he felt and the sadness I felt were a contagion – a plague that ravaged the area. A sadness that not even our faithful hounds could alleviate.

Every mood should have a soundtrack, and this soundtrack's name was Brad. Brad was my next-door neighbour, who I was secretly fond of, but he kept even more antisocial hours than I did. At around 2 a.m. he would put on some deeply drearsome 1940s crooner, and the depressing waft would seep through the walls and up the chimney until dawn. I would hammer on his door until it stopped. I'd post expletive-strewn A4 rants through his letter box. Brad would reply on a postcard of Christopher Marlowe or the Earl of Rochester. He had style and class, that one. It seemed almost a shame to report someone of his *noblesse* to Camden Council for noise pollution.

Despite the posh postcode, it felt like an unsafe place. Occasionally I'd wake, and a burly fisherman would be in my garden trying to drag his rod out of the water beyond. I had another horrific break-in which still haunts me. After that, after the safety seal was broken, the energy changed, my luck ran out, and everything and everyone seemed to find the flat fair game. Including the local wildlife.

One night there was the sound of crashing and scuttling in the kitchen. I came out to look in a state of total panic. Pickle and Parker, characteristically, did nothing dogs are supposed to do and merely lay in their baskets, snoring. Minutes passed. Nothing. Not a sound. I was about to return to bed when I noticed something sticking out from beneath the fridge. That something turned out to be a tail. A foot-long tail that could only belong to

a rat. A dirty rat.

At which point, I did what any normal human lady would do.

I moved out.

Luckily, I had some friends over the road – Jenny and Ewan. She was a fabulous Welsh earth mother, he a slightly deranged but affable stoner. I rang their doorbell.

Jenny: Hey, love, you all right?
Me: No. I'm sorry. No.
Jenny: Jesus, you look as white as a sheet. Come in, come in!

I scuttle in, still shaking with shock.

Ewan: What is it? Do you need me to sort someone out?
Jenny: Ewan, stop being a prick.
Ewan: What?
Jenny: Come on, love. You tell us what it is. Come on, have a seat.
Ewan: Honestly, though, I'm not that pissed. I can go and sort them out.
Jenny: Ewan! Now what is it?
Me: There's a rat in my kitchen

You can imagine how the next five minutes panned out.

Me: There's a rat in my kitchen.
Jenny/Ewan: What are you gonna do?
Me: There's a rat in my kitchen.
Jenny/Ewan: What are you gonna do?
Me: I'm gonna fix that rat, that's what I'm going to do.

After we'd wrung the life out of that joke (and several minutes beyond), Jenny and I started making up the spare room. Ewan got busy rolling a forty-seven-paper spliff, whilst regaling us with his own personal rat stories.

Ewan: I'll go kill it if you want. I've done it before.

Jenny: Have you fuck. You've never killed a thing.

Ewan: Yep, I have. I've killed one. I have!

Me: How?

Ewan: I was round my mate's – on the lash – and I see it scuttling along the skirting. And I just reacted, quick as a flash . . .

Jenny: You're so spaced you can't react to shit.

Ewan: We had a massive ghetto blaster –

Jenny: Ewan! You can't call it that! Sue, can you call it that now?

Me: I don't think so. No.

Ewan: Massive thing – twin speakers, the lot. And I kicked it against the rat and it kind of pinned him against the wall so he was trapped. Then I grabbed a CD, threw it, and – BOOM – it decapitated him. Head clean off.

A pronounced pause.

Jenny: Ewan, you telling me the rat was killed by a flying CD?

Ewan: Yep.

Another silence.

Ewan: *Ballbreaker.* AC/DC. Love that album.

I moved out a week later.

It takes me substantially longer to learn life's lessons than most. I'm stubborn, I'm a creature of habit, and, for all that I'm addicted to experience, I dislike change. So what did I do? I stayed in the same area, and moved around the corner to yet another basement flat.

My first morning there I was woken by the doors bouncing on their hinges. Above me the ceiling vibrated so intensely that I thought it would cave in. It was rhythmic and heavy. I feared the worst. Sex slavers, porn makers, Grindr addicts . . .

I ran upstairs in my Union Jack onesie and pair of Crocs – because I'm classy like that and I like to make a good first impression. I expected to find an orgy going on – swingers in full swing – instead I was greeted by a breezy whip-thin German woman called Jolanda with a pronounced speech impediment.

Jolanda: Hello, I'm Jolanda.

Me: I'm Sue.

Jolanda: Are you calling about the noise?

Me: Yes, it's horrendous.

Jolanda: Oh. Well, I'm wee-bounding.

Me: Wee-bounding?

Jolanda: Yes. Wee-bounding.

Me: Wee-bounding. Right. Mmm. I'm sorry, forgive me – I've got no idea what that is.

Jolanda: You know. Wee-bounding. Like twampolining.

Me: Oh. *Wee*-bounding! I see!

Jolanda: It's gweat for the lymphatic system. You should twy it.

Me: Well, I might. It's just that the bouncing is . . . well, it's terrifying.

Jolanda: Should I wee-bound later?

Me: Yes, you do that.

Jolanda was true to her word, and the rebounding moved to around 10 a.m. for a week.

Week two, I was woken at 6 a.m. by the sound of something resembling the running of the Pamplona bulls. I put on my Crocs and ran upstairs. Then ran down again because I'd forgotten my onesie. I ran up for the second time, now clothed, and hammered on the door. Jolanda popped her head out of the window and greeted me joyfully.

Jolanda: Hi, Sue!
Me: Hi, Jolanda.
Jolanda: You're up early!
Me: Yes. Strange that.

Hostile pause.

Jolanda: I'm not wee-bounding, Sue.
Me: No. What *are* you doing?
Jolanda: Bikwam.
Me: Bikwam? I'm sorry, I've no idea what that is.
Jolanda: You know. Bikwam.
Me: Bikwam. Nope. Still no idea.
Jolanda: Bikwam yoga.
Me: Oh! Yes! I see!
Jolanda: Should I Bikwam later?
Me: Yes, perhaps sometime between the wee-bounding and the indoor Lacwosse.

I moved out four months later.

The Cock and the Car

I was wandering back from work one afternoon when I noticed my car had been vandalized. There were deep key marks down the length of one side, right down to the metal. It wasn't a posh car, just a dusty, knackered old Mark 4 Golf ('rides like a Thai prostitute!' – *Top Gear Magazine*) but I loved it. As I wandered around to the front, it became clear that the damage wasn't just limited to a cursory keying – this was full-on vandalism. There, on the bonnet of the car, scratched deep, was a cock.

A cock. I couldn't believe it. A cock. On *my car*. A lovingly drawn shaft and helmet scored for all time into my beloved jalopy.

I went inside. My younger girlfriend was sat, dressed like Cinderella's Buttons, listening to white noise with a lady yodelling on top. Young people, honestly.

'What's up, honey?' she called.

'It's my car. Someone's defaced my car. They've drawn a cock on it.'

'It's London, babe,' she said, breezily, swaying her head in time to the static.

Well, people might draw genitals on cars where you live, you crrrazy hipster, but here they don't, I thought but didn't say.

I was a pressure cooker for the next hour. A cock on my car. Why? How? Mainly *why*? I decided to call Emma. She used to be a lawyer, after all. She, at least, would be a voice of reason in all of this. After three failed attempts she finally answered.

Em: I told you not to call me again.

Me: Hilarious. Listen, you're not going to believe this. Some little shit has scratched a cock on my car!

I didn't get the opportunity to finish the story, as there followed ten minutes of raucous laughter and mockery, some of which was extremely unkind. Emma was patently going to be useless, so I put the phone down on her, mid-roar, and called Nicola.

Nic: What's up? You split up with someone again?

Me: No. Not yet.

Nic: Oh. So what's up?

Me: Well, someone's scratched a cock on my car.

Nic: What – keyed it?

Me: Yes.

Nic: Wow. Shit. [*Pause*] That's a hate crime.

Me: Is it?

Nic: Yep.

Me: Really?

Nic: Yep. Classic.

Me: *Classic?*

Nic: Yeah.

Me: Yes. Yes, it is, isn't it? That's what I thought. It's a classic hate crime.

Nic: You shouldn't let them get away with it. Call the police. I would. I think they have a unit for that sort of thing.

Me: Do they?

Nic: Expect so. That's abuse, plain and simple. It's homophobic abuse.

Nicola is an amazing actor and has played a lot of detectives in her time, so when she says something about law enforcement,

I believe her. In the same way I'd believe Martin Shaw if he talked about open-heart surgery, or Robert Powell if he disclosed what *really* happened at the Last Supper.

Buoyed by our conversation, I put the phone down and immediately called the nearest police station, who duly transferred me to the relevant unit. Within five seconds of calling and explaining my situation, I could hear a wheezing noise that may or may not have been laughter in the background. In my mind I chose to rebrand it as an asthma attack.

To the credit of the local crime team, a mere hour later a young man in uniform appeared, clutching a Moleskine, the notebook of Hemingway and trainee coppers.

Policeman: So . . . what's happened?
Me: My car has been the victim of a homophobic attack.
Policeman: Your car?
Me: Yes.
Policeman: OK. Is your car gay?
Me: No! I mean . . . I don't know – I haven't asked.
Policeman: Right . . .
Me: What I mean is that I'm gay and I've been targeted. There's a cock keyed on the bonnet. Look!

I gesture in the vague direction of the bell-end. The copper moves to the front of the car to study it more closely.

Me: See it?
Him: Yes.
Me: See the cock?!

There is a long pause. What's he playing at? *I think. Finally, he breaks the silence.*

Him:	The *cock*?
Me:	Yes.
Him:	Oh.
Me:	What?
Him:	Looks like a smiley face to me.

Everything goes very quiet. Silence except for the thumping of my pulse. I go around to join him.

Him:	Look. See? Two eyes and a smile.

As he said it the image in front of me transformed. Suddenly the shallow shaft wasn't a shaft at all – it was two downward strokes representing eyes. The helmet – that expansive semi-circle – wasn't a helmet but a broad, beaming grin. The vandal's scratches had gone from angry penis to Cheshire Cat in a heartbeat.

There was a long pause, finally punctuated by the police-man clearing his throat. I guess they learn that at Hendon – how to cut through awkward moments with a classic copper's cough.

Then horror dawned on me, the horror of what he must be thinking. Either it had been so long since I'd seen a cock that I no longer knew what one looked like (or at least couldn't dis-tinguish between one and a smiley face) OR I am so obsessed with cocks that I see them *everywhere*, even on the bonnets of cars. I'm like that character in *The Sixth Sense* – I see penises. ALL THE TIME.

We wandered down the street towards his panda car. I tried to make small talk. It failed. It was then we noticed that all the other cars had been defaced. They too had smiley faces and scarred sides. I hadn't been singled out. I hadn't been targeted.

There was no penis. There was no homophobic hate crime. In fact there was nothing but a lingering sense of humiliation that still makes itself felt every time I think back.

The Moleskine shut, the key turned in the panda's ignition and the policeman drove away. In a fit of humiliation and despair I scratched a pair of tits on my girlfriend's bike.

That's London for you.

Getting It Wrong

When you agree to take part in a panel show, you do so with the tacit understanding that there will be little or no prep required – that you can turn up an hour beforehand and 'riff' or 'banter' your way through it. This means that if and when you are goddam awful, you can defend yourself by saying that it was all spur-of-the-moment, off-the-cuff-type stuff. If that doesn't work, you can claim you were:

a. on new meds
b. experiencing a break-up
c. under the illusion you were appearing on *Question Time*, and the first you realized it was a panel show was when one of the male comics started talking about wanking.

Some shows, however, particularly those with more of a chat-show bent, require my least-favourite thing in the world – the Briefing Chat. A briefing chat is a prearranged phone call that you have completely forgotten about. It is so boring a thing, it disappears from the mind almost as soon as it has been mentioned. A briefing chat is usually scheduled for first thing in the morning, invariably after a night on the sauce, and because you have erased it from your memory is always a surprise. On the other end of the phone is an exhausted, underpaid researcher asking a series of complex and detailed questions you're ill equipped to answer at that ungodly hour. These questions had, of course, been emailed to you days before, but you studiously refused to engage with them.

The resultant interview is a cluster bomb of mistakes, apologies and knee-jerk decision-making.

Researcher:	What do you think about the rise of fascism?
Me:	[*wiping sleep from my eyes*] Not nice.
Researcher:	What is your favourite kind of horse?
Me:	A brown one.
Researcher:	Describe yourself in three words.
Me:	Tired. Sorry. [*Pause*] Did I say sorry? OK. Tired.
Researcher:	Do you like sausages?
Me:	No.
Researcher:	Shame. We were thinking of doing an item about sausages. Never mind. How about rivers? Like them?
Me:	Well . . .
Researcher:	What would you do if you had scissors for feet?
Me:	Oh . . . Errr . . .
Researcher:	Who would be your ideal dinner party guests? Name any sixteen from history.
Me:	Sixteen? Oh God, I don't think I have enough cutlery . . .
Researcher:	One last thing. We're going to end with a song. Do you mind dressing up as a wizard and joining in?

It was during one such briefing chat that I properly, properly shamed myself. I had been booked to appear on *The Matt Lucas Awards*, unsurprisingly presented by the lovely Matt Lucas. The rough premise of the show was that three guests would compete to win awards for 'Best' or 'Worst' in different categories.

'Soooooooooo . . .' said the researcher at the end of the

phone, with the elastic vowels of the truly bored, 'our first category is "Worst Holiday Destination".'

Fabulous! I had been waiting all my adult life for that question, and here it was, all teed up and ready to go.

'That's easy! Torremolinos! Next!'

I paused, expecting him to say 'Right answer!' and move on to the next question. (It's a known fact that Torremolinos is the definitive answer to 'Where is the worst place you've ever been?' no matter how extensively you've travelled.)

'Great!' said the researcher, in a tone that screamed *NOT GREAT*! 'Thing is . . . we want something a little more . . .'

But it's about ME! MY worst destination! Surely I am best, some would say uniquely, *placed to answer questions about my own likes and dislikes,* I screamed. Inside my head.

Me:	But Torremolinos really is hellish! Or at least, it was. I don't know what it's like now, but back then, in the early 80s, it was full of British Bulldog bars and lager louts and high-rises, and no one spoke Spanish. In fact, it was about as authentically Spanish as Nigel Farage in a Real Madrid strip enjoying a Pata Negra toastie . . .
Researcher:	Mmm . . . Thing is, we've got Richard Madeley on the show, and he's saying Benidorm, so we want something a little bit more . . .
Me:	Un-Spanish?
Researcher:	Yes.
Me:	So it can't be Spain?
Researcher:	We'd rather not.
Me:	I can't choose anything from Spain?
Researcher:	No.
Me:	Even if it was, genuinely, the most hellish place I've

	been.
Researcher:	No.
Me:	OK. [*Pause*] So the most hellish place I've been can't be the answer to the question 'Where's the most hellish place you've been?'
Researcher:	No.
Me:	I get it.
Reseacher:	Soooooooooo . . . anything else?

I froze. I didn't want to let on that I'd barely seen anything of the world. I cast my mind back to the pebbles and crosswinds of the South Coast, the Costa del Sol, the East Coast of America. Nothing much to play with there. But then I remembered a trip I'd made with Mel and her family to the Isle of Skye – that beautiful, craggy wilderness to the north-west of Glasgow. I got a couple of random pictures at first – a wild and windy day, rain scoring across the Cuillin, the igneous black peaks barely decipherable in the gloom – then, slowly, fragments of memory started to form around the snapshots.

We'd gone walking and got caught in the rain. We'd decided to find an indoor attraction. We'd taken Mel's niece and nephews to the Serpentarium . . .

The researcher was becoming impatient. 'Anything?'

I was being rushed. I panicked. I forced the jigsaw to piece itself together. Emotions came in to fill the cracks; sounds, smells, sensations.

'The Serpentarium on the Isle of Skye!' I blurted without thinking.

'OK, that sounds good . . .'

Before I continue, let me tell you, as honestly as I can, what I really remember of that day.

Mel, her brother and his kids, Emma and myself were staying with lovely Lady Claire McDonald at Kinloch Lodge, the family seat of the McDonald clan. We'd had warm scones and kippers for breakfast (note how my memory so perfectly records food) and browsed through the numerous oil paintings of previous McDonalds that hung on the wall. We'd particularly enjoyed the portrait of Lord Ronald McDonald although were sad he was without his trademark red wig and large yellow shoes. It was raining. A gale was blowing. We enquired as to what might be a fun thing to do with the kids if the weather stayed inclement, and Lady Claire recommended the nearby reptile sanctuary. So off we went.

Memories are slippery bastards – bring them into the light, handle them too often, they'll bend, change colour. Keep them in the dark and they'll slowly retreat to a place you can't find them. In truth, I could only recall the very basics of that trip:

- We approached an unprepossessing low-rise.
- A large sign outside proclaimed something along the lines of WELCOME TO THE MOST EXCITING EXPERIENCE ON EARTH. We took a photo of the two of us outside it.
- A kindly woman welcomed us in.
- Jan, Mel's nephew, was frightened of snakes, but the aforementioned kindly women got a wee albino corn snake out of his tank and let him hold it. At first Jan was loath to touch it, but slowly he became transfixed by how smooth it was, how strong. By the end he didn't want to leave, his phobia totally cured.
- We went back to Kinloch Lodge for high tea by the

roaring fire. I can remember the EXACT contents of
the tea, but I won't bore you with the details.

And that's it. That's the sum total of my real memories.
And so back to the briefing chat.

Me: The Serpentarium on the Isle of Skye!
Man: OK, that sounds good . . .

*I hear the sound of sticky biro on paper as the researcher jots down 'Serpen-
tarium'. I wonder if he spells it correctly, an indictment of both the skills
shortage in television and my own inveterate snobbishness. There is an
expectant pause.*

Man: So the Serpentarium is your worst holiday destination.

*So, just like that, my trip has been rebranded 'the world's worst'. Suddenly
it's become a fact.*

Man: Why was it hell? What was so hellish about it?

It was sealed. Now I had to find something negative, even if it
was barely there – blow it out of all proportion and bend it so
it was funny. Fill it with stuff that would make it entertaining.
Neatly tie off experiences with an exhilarating, upbeat flour-
ish. So my imagination set to work, rounding off the rough
edges, adding detail, quirks, shaping it into a perfect narrative.
To sell. To sell to the crowd, whoever they might be.
Which is what I did.
And so the yarn began. Into all those blank spaces little silly
details got poured. Into the silences went 'funny' dialogue.
That quiet, sweet visitor centre became a dark dungeon with

sticky walls. The bucket that had been in the corner became the snakes' repository. The snakes themselves were things of horror. On and on I went, like a dancing bear, until I felt the researcher was happy. And every adornment, whether big or small, went down as fact. FACT. How tragic that I'd rather invent an experience than admit the simple truth:

a. I hadn't had many *real* experiences.
b. I have a terrible memory for anything outside of comestibles.

And then I went one step further by going on national television and saying it all out loud, in public. And the more detail I threw in about how dreadful it was, the more people laughed, and the more people laughed, the more I embellished the detail.

Even as I did it, I felt something was wrong. It felt personal. It wasn't like I was slating Benidorm – a burned tract of land filled with drunk people (there, I have slated it) – this felt way too singular and personal a target.

But I did it. I complied. I did my bit. I made myself look good by making some strangers look worse. And then I got into a nice car and got whisked home.

For the next twenty-four hours I felt uncomfortable but wrote it off as general post-performance malaise. Then I returned to normal, went about my daily business – everything was fine. The show aired. I didn't see it because recording a television show then tuning in to watch it is like a dog returning to its own vomit. Plus, there's always this annoying speccy girl in my shows who irritates the living hell out of me.

About a week after airing I was checking my Twitter feed

when I noticed a message from a man who seemed hurt and angry. It's rare that a negative post has adverbs in it, so it stuck out from the usual crowd of trolls and click-baiters. I read on. The man, it transpired, was the son of the couple who owned the Serpentarium. Understandably, he wanted to know why, instead of all the corporate holiday behemoths out there, I had chosen to focus my limp comedic ire on his parents' tiny rescue centre.

Oh. Didn't I mention that bit? Yes, it's a wildlife sanctuary. It's a CHARITY. It's a NON-PROFIT ORGANIZATION.

I did what I always do when confronted by a calm, rational adult with a genuine point to make – I became a terrified, whiny child. I immediately followed him back so we could continue the conversation privately on direct message.

It became clear, pretty quickly, that my comments had had an impact on the island. Folk had rallied round the couple, who were well loved and respected. There was outrage that I could have picked so small and innocent a target. I think there might have even been an article or two in the local press.

I privately messaged their son who, even though protected by the anonymity of social media, opted to be a gentleman and was dignified throughout. Our exchange went something like this:

Me: I am so so so sorry. What would you like me to do?

Son: Why did you do it?

Me: I don't know. I really feel awful about it. What can I do to make it better?

Son: I don't know. That's up to you. Personally, I think you should call them.

Me: Oh.

*My worst nightmare is unfolding. I am going to actually have to take respon-
sibility. For myself. I carry on typing.*

Me: Would that . . . help?
Son: Well, it might. You should ring them.

Their number follows. The digits of doom. Then we say goodbye.

I sat on the number for a day, working up the courage to call.
Eventually I took a deep breath and dialled.

'Hello,' came a gentle voice at the other end. It was a voice I
remembered, the voice of the kindly woman who had cured
Jan of his snake phobia.

Me: Hello. My name is Sue.
Woman: Hello!
Me: Sue Perkins.
Woman: Oh.

There is squirmy moment during which my arse makes buttons.

Woman: Well, I am surprised to hear from you. We didn't think
           you'd ring.
Me: I am so, so sorry.
Woman: OK . . .
Me: Really, I am.
Woman: The thing is, we don't mind that you didn't like our Ser-
           pentarium, but we did mind that you implied we don't
           treat the snakes well. Because, well . . . the thing is, we
           love those snakes and we're the only hope they've got.
           There's no one else doing the work we're doing. And we
           don't get paid for it; we just do it because we want to help.

Another pause – just long enough for me to fully inhabit what a monumental twat I've been.

Me: I'm sorry – it just came out.

Her response is simple, measured.

Woman: Really? *Really?*

Of course it didn't just slip out. I chose to do it. Not because I wanted to hurt a lovely couple on the beautiful Isle of Skye, but because I was too lazy to commit to a better option. It wasn't anyone's fault but mine. Not the researcher or the producer or the programme or the BBC. It was me, just me. I did it.

I've done lots of things I shouldn't. I have behaved in loutish and cavalier ways. I have hurt those I loved. But there's something about that still, small voice I keep coming back to, that small, still voice that remains in my head every time I give an interview, or tell a story, or embellish an anecdote. That still, small voice that peeps through for a tiny moment, just to catch me before I fall – that makes me stop and think, *Who does it hurt? Why am I choosing that target? Can they fight back?* That still, small voice that simply says:

'Really?

'*Really?*'

The Power of Trance

At last, I'm happy again. The dust I kicked up around me aged forty is finally, finally settling. I have moved to a top-floor flat, so there is no zealous German above me performing esoteric crack-of-dawn exercises. There are no rats. No rogue fishermen. I do, however, live above the north London legend that is Sylv, a septuagenarian peroxide and perma-tanned powerhouse who spends nine months of the year in a boob tube.

Sylv's modus operandi is to greet you with a threat.

'I'm going to rip your fucking head off if you don't take them bins out . . . Morning, darling!'

'If you don't wipe your boots when you come in I'll carve off your ear 'oles and fucking post 'em to you. Now where you been? I've missed ya . . .'

I love Sylv. We keep an eye out for each other. I find her cheap antibiotics on the Internet and she power-hoses journalists off the top step. It's a perfect symbiotic relationship.

I am now with my new partner, Anna. There's that old adage: you don't know how long you've been contending with the gloom until someone turns the lights on. Well Anna didn't just turn the lights on; she brought several spotlights, a couple of flares and a glitter ball for good measure.

She has balls of steel, a heart of gold and a pancreas of pewter (though she's having an op for that). If you want to know what kind of a person she is, then consider that this is the woman who organized a full-on thirty-strong rounders match in the park, just so I, aged forty-five, could finally know what it's like to be picked for a team. I'll always love her for that.

Anna is not only excellent at her television job, she's also training to be a cognitive hypnotherapist. On the one hand, this is wonderful – I now have a first-hand resource when life is difficult. On the other, it's a total and utter nightmare. Now every time we have a row, I find myself put in a trance-like daze with my subconscious self being informed that it is a total and utter arsehole. A lot like my conscious self.

After one such row Anna suggested (see also: demanded) I might want to do some timeline regression, a process which involves going back to a difficult past event, amending it, then leaving it well and truly behind. I say she suggested; in truth, I no longer know whether I have anything approaching free will or if everything I do is being subliminally influenced (see also: demanded) by her. Maybe I've just become her mind-bitch.

I like hypnotherapy – it works for me. It helped me quit smoking, dulled my tinnitus and calmed my PTSD (gifted to me by that second break-in). These were, however, sessions conducted by qualified healthcare professionals in a dispassionate environment. It's an entirely different ball game when that professional is

a. your girlfriend
b. has an agenda
c. not yet a professional.

Much as Anna has the makings of an incredible practitioner, she is only halfway through her diploma. At the moment her technique consists of lots of swearing and flicking through manuals, the flow of the therapeutic process slightly jarred by the constant, exasperated, 'Oh wait, I haven't done that bit yet.'

Would you let a trainee hairdresser loose on your fringe? Maybe.

Would you let a hobbyist accountant loose on your VAT return? Possibly.

Would you let an unqualified hypnotherapist tinker with the darkest recesses of your mind after doing only half of the required reading? I did.

As part of her studies Anna needed a guinea pig to practise on. And apparently I was it. Our first few sessions together were something of a mixed bag, although they started well enough. It's fair to say Anna had mastered the art of getting me *into* a trance state, but was less confident about getting me *out* of one. In the first session Anna suggested (see also: demanded) that I should examine the feelings I still had for an ex and our excruciatingly painful break-up through a technique known as visual squash.

We settled down on the sofa – me lying prostrate, Anna sitting by my side. As I feel shattered most of the time, the induction bit was easy.

Anna: You are feeling sleeeeeepy . . .
Me: Yes, I am . . .
Anna: You are feeling nice and relaaaaaaxed . . .
Me: Why are you doing that weird voice?

It has suddenly become soft and silky. And more than a little bit posh.

Anna: Shuuuuut uuuuuup.

And off I went, down an imaginary flight of steps, each tread sending me deeper and deeper into trance.

I listened to her voice, felt my muscles relax and my bones

melt. My body felt like warm syrup in a drawstring bag. If you've not experienced it, the hypnotic state is hard to describe – in that moment you are both a particle and a wave, resisting and complying, acquiescing and questioning. A dance between the self you live with and know and the one behind the scenes, pulling the strings, that you don't.

Anna asked me to imagine the break-up as an object. Immediately I felt my left hand sag with the weight of a large spiky metal ball. She carried on talking. The weight in my arm grew more intense. She carried on talking. I could feel the prickles of the ball digging into my palm. She carried on talking.

And then she stopped.

Anna: Shit!
Me: [*struggling to speak*] What's going on?

I am still in a dream state but slowly become aware of the frantic flicking of pages in the background.

Anna: Oh God, I think I've done it wrong . . .

My consciousness scrambles to attention. I sit up, suddenly taut with anxiety, my eyes still closed.

Me: What do you mean 'done it wrong'?
Anna: I can't remember what you do after that.
Me: What are you talking about!? What . . . What am I going to do with this?! [*I moan, struggling to raise my leaden arm*]
Anna: I don't know. We haven't got to that bit yet.

The imaginary ball feels heavy and cold in my hand.

Me: Does that mean I am going to have to just carry her around
        with me?
Anna: For God's sake! Yes! Probably!

Since then I've been a weekly guinea pig. Every Sunday night
I've had sessions in metaphor therapy, positive and negative
hallucination, future pacing – all in an effort to stop me, and
these are Anna's words, from being a 'massive dick'. It got to
the stage where I became frightened of the sound of her key in
the lock. Until she hypnotized me out of that.

One particular Sunday night Anna came back, the familiar
textbook a little more thumbed and nearly completed. This
week, I was informed, it was time for the *Time Tunnel*.

I assumed the position.

Anna: Right, so what would you like to achieve?
Me: I'd like . . . Gosh, that's a big one. Well, I'd like to be more
        free. More creative. Confident. Socially adept. I'd like a
        house, if I'm honest. I like the flat, but I'd love a house. I'd
        like not to be blocked. I'd –
Anna: Right, Sue – do you want to pick just *one*?

[*It really is impossible to underestimate how annoying she finds me.*]

Me: OK. I'd like to be more creatively free.

We established that my life's timeline was above me, running
from left to right, like a zip wire. I'm a fairly visual person, so I
could see it clearly and it was easy to hop on board. Using this
zip wire I could scoot along to points in my past and look down
from a position of safety.

Spectacles

Anna: Right, Sue, if you'd like to travel back to a point in time when you feel you are being blocked.

There's a nagging itch in my big toe. I can't move to assuage it. I am too busy, too busy travelling down my own personal zip wire to the past.
    And I am there.

Anna: Where are you?
Me: I'm over my bedroom.
Anna: How old are you?
Me: I'm eight.
Anna: Who's in the bedroom with you?
Me: My mum.
Anna: OK, do you want to go down into the room . . .
Me: I'm in the room.
Anna: Right . . .
Me: She's SO annoying . . .

My hands move to my hips and my jaw juts out like a chicken. I am the very model of petulance.

Anna: And what are you talking about?
Me: I've done a project. On the Romans.
Anna: Right . . .
Me: I could do a project on anything I wanted. That's what the teacher said. So I've done it on Roman food. I've done a bunch of papier mâché grapes and a papier mâché dormouse.

There is the sound of a snigger. Both levels of my consciousness choose to ignore it.

Me: Mum's saying that it isn't right. That the perspective isn't right and that the dormouse is way too big.

Anna: OK, Sue, listen to my voice. Now let's try to turn the colour down on the scene . . .

Me: Shut up! I'm busy talking to my mum. I am SO angry. I can do a project on anything I want and I want to do it on Roman food and it doesn't matter that the dormouse is three times the size of a bunch of grapes because I have been told I can do anything I want . . .

Fifteen minutes later I am hoarse, arguing with a mother in a tight perm and pink jogging suit who hasn't existed for thirty-five years. Anna's interventions are now becoming desperate.

Anna: And now let's move upwards, can you do that?

Me: Yes.

Anna: OK then, let's go upwards – back to your safe place, and look down on the scene from above. Does that seem better?

Me: Yes.

Anna: [*palpable relief in her voice*] Thank God.

Me: Oh, hang on – no.

Anna: Christ! [*Now despair*] Do you want to go back down?

Me: Yes.

And I'm in my childhood bedroom again. Hands on hips, locked in an eternal battle of wills with Ann Perkins.

Me: It doesn't matter that the grapes are blue! I can do anything I want! I can do anything I want! The teacher said! The grapes could be orange or red or white . . .

Another ten minutes pass. I am exhausted and grow quiet. Anna leads me back onto the zip wire and I look down at myself and my mum. I feel calm. Resolved.

Anna: OK, now let's move along the years.

Me: Stop!

We've barely moved six months or so.

Anna: [*muttering*] Give me strength . . . What is it? How old are you?

Me: I'm eight and a half.

Anna: What's happened?

Me: I've done a project on drums. I can do anything I want, and I've chosen drums. She's saying the snare drum's too big . . .

We never did timeline regression again. Shortly after that Anna stopped using me as a guinea pig and started practising on her friend Lesley. Now she is fully qualified and will be the most amazing therapist. Even better, I no longer have to be the trial-and-error brain she practises on. These days, when we row, I don't have to spend hours in a trance state – I can just be like everyone else. I can storm off to the pub, have a drink and crawl back later full of regret.

But every so often I get the strangest feeling, like a ball of heavy metal in my left hand, weighing me down.

It's All Over the Front Page

I have 'issues' with driving.* When everyone else at school turned seventeen, they seemed to absorb the Highway Code through osmosis and instantly understand the multitasking of mirror, signal and manoeuvre. They'd sail through their parallel parks and three-point-turns and were, in a heartbeat, racing to exotic places like Woldingham, Westerham and West Wickham. *I want to go to West Wickham!* I'd think while sitting red-faced atop my rusty Chopper, chain-smoking and contemplating the slight incline home.

The only compensation for being a non-driver was that I could drink myself unconscious every night of the week and rely on my boyfriend Rob for transportation home. Rob owned a diarrhoea-coloured Datsun Cherry, the only vehicle on earth that could make the idea of walking preferable to a teenager. You'd hear it before you could see it. Hell, you could *smell* it before you could see it. His arrival was heralded by the roar of ripped clutch and the reek of a benzo-cloud of horror hydrocarbons.

'Yes, everyone!' I'd shout to bystanders. 'This is MY BOYFRIEND! He drives the car of a Latin-teaching MOT-failing sex offender! Deal with it!'

ᴗᴗ

* According to every DVLA examiner I came across 1986–99.

I am in denial about how many times I failed my driving test. It may be as few as three, it may be as many as six. I care not. It's like your A levels. Nobody asks you about the results until you're in court.

If the test had been purely academic, I'd have passed with flying colours. Annoyingly there's this practical section, where you actually have to get in a car. All my tests *started* well enough. I managed to get into the correct side of the vehicle, the side by the steering wheel, and turn the key in the ignition. But after that it all went downhill. As did I – usually during the hill-start portion of the exam. There would be the inevitable squelch of tyre against kerb, the nudge of bumper on bollard, the crack of examiner's head against windscreen – those tell-tale signs that my vehicular dreams were over and that once again I'd be getting the night bus home.

One reason for my consistent failure may have been my eye-sight. My right eye has the vision of a sparrowhawk; my left, however, is a mess. I had an accident as a kid, and it's now a short-sighted ball of jelly with peripheral double vision. I'm not sure if they do something as basic as this now, but the first part of the driving test used to be a bit like an eye exam. You had to read the number plate on the car in front of you, just so they could check you had eyes that worked. It's a fairly commonsensical starting point for a test in my opinion, but one I had to try and get around. I was in denial and too vain to get a pair of glasses, so my eyes had bewilderingly different depths of focus. In order to get a crisp image, I had to cup my left eye so that the sparrowhawk side of me could go about its business. However, it proved quite hard to do this without alerting the attention of the examiner. On my first test I overdid it and looked like a budget pirate. The sight of me, Cyclops, palm over one eye, did nothing to instil confidence in him. Next time I was more subtle – pretending I was scratching my eyebrow. The third I pretended to be winking at a passing builder while recording the plate details.

I finally passed my test at the age of twenty-nine and a bit. By which I mean thirty. Mel and I sat our exams in the same week, and it is still a bone of contention between us that I scored one mark higher than her in the written test. (I knew the depth of tread that tyres need, she didn't. It doesn't matter.*)

Just because I'm not *good* at driving, doesn't mean I don't *like* driving. My love of motoring stems from when I was seven years old. Our road was on a small incline, and our house sat at the very top. Our car, as you know, was always parked half-in and half-out of the garage, due to the construction issues outlined earlier. Having said that, even if the garage *had* been built to the correct dimensions, and the car *could* have fitted inside, I still believe Mum would have parked the car where she could see it. There are two possible explanations for this.

a. Mum adheres to the now outdated Copenhagen intepretation of quantum mechanics, which posits that an object exists in simultaneous states until observed. Thus, if the car was parked *inside* the garage, it could be both safe *and* stolen. By observing the car half-out of the garage, Mum can maintain the knowledge the car is safe.

b. Mum is nuts.

I'm digressing. So, I'm seven. My mum is taking my brother and me somewhere – judo, ballet or some combination of the two – but she has forgotten something and rushes back to

---

* It really, really does.

the house. I climb into the driver's seat. My brother climbs into the passenger seat next to me.

'We're going to do driving,' I say, leaning right into his face.

'OK,' he says, playing along as always.

I have been studying my parents for years. I know what to do. It takes all my strength, and both hands, to lift the hand-brake and let it fall again. But I manage. Slowly the wheels turn, gaining momentum as we reverse.

'We're doing driving,' I tell David.

'OK', he says, head pressed back into the seat.

I see Mum coming down the steps of the house. Then I see her seeing us. Her mouth widens into a scream. It all goes a bit slo-mo from there.

I still remember the thrill of it. The acceleration. The slow turn of the steering wheel. The bump as we crash into the neighbour's wall, the crumble of brick against metal until we finally come to a halt. The screaming. The terrible screaming. It's a series of sensations I've relived several times since then – although the thrill is somewhat lessened when you're the one who has to pay the bill.

So, at the tender age of twenty-nine, I was officially allowed on the roads. To celebrate the occasion I bought an ex-boy-friend's car – a turd-green Spanish ringer which he, for some reason, appeared very keen to get rid of.

The week after my test I thought I'd take my baby for a spin, so I hopped in and turned the key in the ignition. Radio 1 blared from the speakers so loudly I couldn't hear myself think. Perfect. I put the car into reverse, floored the clutch and pumped the accelerator. Nothing. I pumped again – couldn't hear a sausage. So I lifted the handbrake and put the pedal to the metal. Still nothing. Something must be wrong. I lifted the clutch a tad, and that was when it happened. The car lurched back with such force I was in danger of severing my head with my own jowls. I smashed into the car behind, then, panicking, removed both feet from the pedals and promptly stalled.

The car behind belonged to my wonderful mate Neil, who had heard the roar of an engine and the thump of heavy house music and come to take a look just in time to see a cloud of smoke billowing from my exhaust as I hurtled backwards at breakneck speed. I don't know exactly what happens when you reverse at full speed into a stationary car. But I do know how much it costs.

£1,200

Every year since then I have managed to put on a similarly cretinous display. I have reversed into fork-lift trucks, boulders and gates. For me the bumpers of a car exist solely to provide a handy first-hand indicator of just how close you are to an object.

But this year I excelled myself. I didn't just stick to *my* car.

Poo-etry in motion

One Friday night I planned to collect my surviving dog, Parker, from the farm where she stayed when I was working. The idea was then for Anna and myself to carry on and have a weekend away in the West Country. There was just one slight problem.

Me: Sweetie . . .
Anna: You never call me sweetie. What do you want?
Me: Can we take *your* car this weekend?
Anna: Why can't we take yours?
Me: It's in the garage getting serviced, and I can't be bothered to pick it up. Pleeeease . . .

Anna: [*loud and forceful exhalation*] I've just had it valeted. I love Parker, but she smells.

Me: No she doesn't!*

Anna: She really does . . .

Me: Listen, she'll be on her blanket buckled up on the back seat. You won't even know she's there . . .

We arrived at the farm and Parker seemed her usual self, namely emotionally disconnected and food-obsessed. I clipped her into her seat belt on the back seat and we all got under way.

Half an hour into the onward journey I became aware of the dog circling on the back seat and pulling on her lead. Then came a wave of heavy stink – gastric, fecal – all the smells you never want to smell in a confined space.

Anna: Your dog has just thrown up.

Me: [*instantly defensive*] Oh, FFS!

Anna: [*peering round*] It's all over her blanket.

Me: [*even more defensive*] Right. Right! Well I'll pull into the service station and sort it out then. Jesus!

Bridgwater Services

is my least favourite service station on the M5. It has an air of menace that not even the finest Greggs Baked Bean Lattice can alleviate. Whereas most service-area car parks are open to the air and spacious, this is cramped and concrete. The parking is free, as is the overpowering stench of piss that greets you upon leaving your vehicle.

* She does.

I pulled in, whipped Parker's puke-sodden blanket out of the car and popped it in a bin. Thankfully Anna's upholstery was untouched. Phew. I went off to grab us some sandwiches, which we ate in an uncomfortable silence in the front seat. I was a ticking time bomb of rage. I love my dog. I wanted Anna to love my dog. Why, therefore, had my dog decided to vomit in her car? Did she *want* Anna to hate her?

After wolfing down something that claimed to be a crayfish bap, we bickered about where to recycle the leftovers. I was a dick. The bicker quickly developed into a full-blown row – so full-blown that we didn't notice the dog panting in the back.

We got under way again and managed around ten or so miles before we noticed Parker's heavy breathing – gusts of stale stomach air pumping onto the back of our necks. Before long, that wave of sick/shit was back.

Anna: She's done it again.
Me: Fuck!

I turn round to see a bile-coated turd nestled into the seat, sticky brown liquid oozing into the fabric.

Anna: Keep your eyes on the road, Sue!
Me: Fuck's SAKE!
Anna: Just concentrate on driving!
Me: Jesus Christ, that bloody dog!
Anna: Is her arse supposed to be blue?

Taunton Deane Services

is a civilized bijou outlet – a series of dark low-rise buildings accessible through a cobbled entranceway lined with picnic benches for the discerning outdoors eater. By the time I pulled in, Parker was standing in her seat, a long thread of greenish saliva hanging from her mouth. I unclipped her and took her for a walk, whereupon she threw up again and shot out about a litre of sand-coloured diarrhoea. I cleaned her with a pack of moist fragranced toilet tissues while enjoying the chorus of 'Bake!' that greeted me from my fellow motorists. 'Yes! Bake!' I shouted back weakly, dabbing at my pet's weeping arsehole.

Half an hour later I returned to the car. Anna was listening to something on Radio 4, eyes closed, with all the windows open. I popped Parker on a fresh blanket, clipped her back into her seat belt and we headed off again.

Exeter Services

is, I think, out of all the services on the M5, my favourite. Not only is it large, with a children's play area, grassy knoll and multiple fast-food outlets, it also has a Ladbrokes, should you wish to place a bet on whether the A30 will be gridlocked all the way to Land's End. By the time we reached it the day was fading, and with it our hopes of making it down much further west. The back seat was coated in a toxic combination of poo and puke – pooke, if you will – and the footwell in front of it was swilling with gob. Anna had gone into shock and was now silent, trying to get her head around the fact her beloved car was being destroyed, slowly, from the inside out. It was the same routine as the other services: dog out, moist towelette, water if she wanted it, more shit/sick, moist towelette, 'Oi, isn't that Mel from *Bake Off*?' vomit, moist towelette, 'Oi, Mel, BAKE!' buckle her up and off.

It was pitch black by the time we neared Exeter. All plans had been abandoned. Anna was starting to get a headache from the smell and we both felt distinctly nauseous. We had rowed ourselves hoarse and now fell back into a tense silence.

It was then that Parker detonated.

Yes, detonated. I really don't have another word for it. She went off like a canine grenade. It was an eruption the like of which I have never seen before or since. Every pore in her body leaked something foul. It hit the windows, the driver's seat, the passenger seat – it sprayed every conceivable corner of the car.

Anna broke the silence.

Anna: I'm going to stay in a hotel. Drive me to a hotel.
Me: Please, don't do that. We'll go to our mate Michele's. She's nearby. She'll help.
Anna: Fine. Don't talk to me.
Me: OK.
Anna: I said don't talk to me.

I pulled over. I unbuckled the dog and let her pad around the pavement.

'On your marks, get set . . .' shouted a passing motorist.

'BAKE!' I hollered back, before turning once more to my sopping hound.

'Is there anywhere on or in this car – anywhere AT ALL – you haven't shat?' I screamed partly to the dog and partly to the heavens.

Almost as if in response, Parker turned a rheumy eye towards me and fired a cannon of liquid shit against the wheel arch. It went on and on and on – like something out of a *Little Britain* sketch. Then all went quiet again.

Suddenly I noticed that there were spots of blood all over the pavement, blood over the wheel, blood over the dog. I panicked. I popped her back in her seat and shut the door and drove off like a nutter in search of an emergency vet.

What I *didn't* do was buckle up the dog.

By now it was raining – driving, driving rain. Parker was retching in time to the windscreen wipers. I felt exhausted and teary, but I stayed focused. Just a few more miles until we reached our mate – I could drop Anna off, then get the dog to a vet.

The motorway was busy with all the erratic stop-and-start stuff you get with bad weather. We were going at around sixty miles an hour when Parker, fresh from another rectal sneeze, decided she had had enough. She was ill and upset and she wanted to sit with her mum.

So she did.

Unfettered by a seat belt, she clambered between the two front seats and thence made the attempt to get onto my lap. In doing so, she kicked the gearbox into sudden and shocking neutral. There was a roar, a loss of power, and I struggled to pull us over onto the hard shoulder amid the traffic.

The engine stalled. I tried the ignition. Nothing. Again. This time it turned over. I crawled the rest of the way – power steering ripped, the electrics erratic, the clutch – don't go there.

I don't know exactly what happens when your clutch burns out on a motorway, but I do know how much it costs.

£2,500 (and counting).

There was also £300 on valeting, though some days you can still catch the odd whiff in the air.

As for Parker, she had colitis. I don't know exactly what colitis is, but I do know how much it costs.

£1,200 for a weekend stay at the vet's on a drip. (She is now, thankfully, right as rain.)

And now, whenever we go anywhere, wherever we go – we take *my* car.

It's not only my poor eyesight and tendency towards the erratic which make my driving less than perfect. I also suffer from road rage. Outside a car I pride myself on being a reasonable, tolerant, empathetic human being. Inside one I am an animal. A vile, invective-spewing animal. I have been run off the road. I have stood, nose to nose, screaming at a fellow motorist in the middle of the A406. I am not proud of these things.

In a car I think I am Jason Statham – although, I mean, I don't put on the voice or anything weird like that.* In a car I become this totally focused tank of aggressive fervour. I'm a pedal-to-the-metal nut job. I'm a wheel-spinning high-revving hot-rodder. I steer with the palm of my hand and scream and shout at every single junction. I mean, I *really* think I am Jason Statham – although, I mean, I don't invent scenarios or anything weird like that.† I don't shout, 'I'm the Transporter! Get out of my way,

---

* I do.

† I do.

bitches – I've got to get a pint of skimmed milk from the garage before it closes!'

One day around about four years ago I was in the car heading to the supermarket. Actually, in truth, I don't remember where I was going or indeed if there was any urgency about the trip. It was broad daylight. The sun was shining. It was a bright day – a very, *very* bright day – the sheer, unforgiving brightness of it will become significant later.

The arterial roads near my flat are narrow and lined with Audis. Every day is German Automotive Superiority Day in Hampstead, north London. It was the school run and I'd had a nightmare getting out of my road; I could feel the veins in my neck twisting like rope with the tension. My face flushed. In front of me appeared hazard after hazard – parking lorries, darting kids, dogs off leads.

I started with a few generic 'piss offs', just to warm up, get my eye in. Then I proceeded to work through a couple of light-to-medium-grade slurs on parental legitimacy and IQ. The car in front of me failed to indicate – I let loose a smattering of what the 1970s British Board of Film Classification would deem 'sexual swear words'.

By the time I hit Downshire Hill, some three minutes from my flat, I was ready to kill. I pulled in to let a lorry pass. The driver didn't thank me. He got a middle finger and a 'Screw you, mate' for his trouble.

Then I saw it, a showroom-fresh spanking-new Mercedes – top of the range and glinting in the sun. Its bonnet buffed by a thousand lackeys. From where I sat, engine idling, it appeared to fill the entire width of the road – towering over me at the top of the hill while I waited like a supplicant in an old banger at the bottom.

It came upon me like an electrical storm, hard and fast – a

potent mix of class war and pure envy. I was the last in a long line of Perkinses doffing their caps to their Lords and Masters in a daisy chain of generational oppression, and I wasn't having it.

I wasn't having *any of it*.

This was one game of chicken I could afford to lose, I thought. So what if my car got scratched? It was scratched already. So what if it got written off? Its resale value was maybe a couple of hundred quid. Who cares?

I put the car into first and started up the hill. The Merc didn't tuck in. The obstruction was their side of the road but they didn't tuck in. I casually flicked some double digits and carried on. Second gear now, and still no sign of them backing down. I worked a combo of V-signs and F-bombs as I started to accelerate. They continued forward.

Just one more chance for them to pull in, just one more space – I was now leaning forward, my boiled face randomly spewing every epithet I'd ever heard, like a four-letter fruit machine.

You seismic shit-splat!

You cock-juggling thunder-quim!

You deliquescent dick-cheese!

But they don't take that chance. They're coming straight for me.

We were locked in. No backing down. We now had to try and pass one another on this bright, double-parked, German-lined street. I was slamming my fists on the wheel as our bonnets met . . . and then . . .

Then I pulled out a combination move I'd never tried before – double bird, single bird and multiple Vs. I followed this with a fast-cut series of mimes – gun to the head, noose around neck, machine gun spraying, grenade launching, howitzer firing –

and, just as our windows met, I slowly drew my finger across my neck as if slicing it, and said, 'You . . .

Both of our windows were open, nothing more than a cigarette paper's worth of space between us. And there, at the wheel, Esther Rantzen.

. . . cunt.'

The word dropped into her lap like a hot angry baby.

Esther's face was, for a second, the very model of bland acknowledgement. She was, after all, merely passing another vehicle, slowly, in a London street. She saw me and registered two things. First that it was me, someone she knows from the TV, and second that the person she knows from the TV was miming cutting her throat while uttering possibly the most offensive and certainly the most visceral word in the English language. Something crossed her face – her eyes flickered a little, as if reacting to an alarm sounding in the distance. Later, I thought. Later she would process what had happened. Later she would realize what I'd said and what I'd done.

My hand finished its action across my neck. It dropped to my knees like a stone.

'Hi, Esther!' I said, making the gear-change to jolly as our cars inched past. 'Hi!'

And then I was gone.*

---

* There is no punchline to this story. Sometimes life doesn't give you one. I'm as sorry as you are.

As I was finalizing the manuscript for this book, I was lent an entirely new perspective on cars, courtesy of the BBC show *Top Gear*. *Top Gear* isn't a show I've ever really watched. For starters it's about cars, so I'm only mildly interested from the get-go.

Anyway, somebody, somewhere made up a story that I was in line to be the new presenter of *Top Gear*. If you didn't already think that was a ridiculous idea, then hopefully the previous chapter has convinced you otherwise. Then the bookies got hold of the story and duly (even though it had no basis in truth) tipped me as favourite for the job. Suddenly, after years of peaceful existence on Twitter, my timeline was full of thick-necked white men in the twilight of their usefulness telling me that I should be dead. The general gist appeared to be, 'Man do car, woman do cake.' One tweeter even went as far as to say they'd like to see me set on fire.

I'd never join a club that would allow a person like me to become a member, said Woody Allen, paraphrasing Groucho Marx. Let me add to that. I'd never join a club that would like to see me burned to death, because that club sounds AWFUL.

So I took myself off social media for a bit.

Then the trolling story became front-page news. I said nothing. I just assumed that somebody, somewhere would say, 'Don't be silly, of course she isn't the next presenter. Have you seen her? She can barely stand up straight, let alone operate machinery.' But nobody did. So the more I appeared on the front pages, the more people thought I was indeed the next *Top Gear* presenter, and the more venom came my way. It became a Möbius strip of indignation.

Sometimes I comforted myself by having imaginary conversations with those journalists in my head.

Me: The thing is, this has all been rather upsetting.

Journo: IT'S DISGUSTING. IT'S PC GONE MAD. YOU'RE A WOMAN, FOR GOD'S SAKE.

Me: Yes. Yes I am.

Journo: ANOTHER EXAMPLE OF THE METROPOLITAN LIBERAL ELITE USING POSITIVE DISCRIMINATION.

Me: Listen . . .

Journo: YET MORE BED-WETTING PINKOS DRIVING A RADICAL LESBIAN LEFTIST AGENDA.

Me: The thing is –

Journo: WOMEN CAN'T EVEN DRIVE! EVERYBODY KNOWS THEY DON'T HAVE OPPOSABLE THUMBS!!

Me: Please . . .

Journo: COME ON, SHOW ME YOUR THUMBS! SHOW ME YOUR THUMBS!

A month later it all died down. Now all is quiet on my timeline again.

So . . .

I'm putting it out there. I'm the new presenter of *Songs of Praise*.

Come and get me.

I Am Become Cake,
the Destroyer of Midriffs

This is a photocopy of a project I did when I was a girl. I would like to start by addressing some comments to the teacher who marked it.

Dear Teacher,

Thank you so much for your feedback on my project. Here are some of my own notes, made some thirty-eight years after your markings.

Firstly – disappointed? Really? ARE YOU OUT OF YOUR MIND? My baker is making bread on a levitating bench!!!! How many of those do you see in catering situations? Plus, he/ she is doing so while wearing a hat larger than their own torso. Those are tough conditions in which to create the perfect crusty cob.

As for 'Pictures would improve your project' – well, Lady-Whose-Name-I-Can-No-Longer-Remember, you might want to take a look at all those funny things above your comments. Can you see them? They look suspiciously like pictures, don't they? They do to me.

Finally, on the 'interesting' front. You see that bird in the foreground? The picture of the bird? Well, it's not going 'cluck-cluck' is it? If it was, it would be a chicken. But no, this bird is going 'quack-quack' because it is a duck. I am using DUCK's eggs instead of common or garden HEN's eggs. That is one hell of an enriched dough going on there FYI, lady . . .

Anyhow, I do hope you are enjoying your retirement, which I have done a project on below. I'm sorry it doesn't include any pictures.

Yours,
Susan Perkins, aged 45

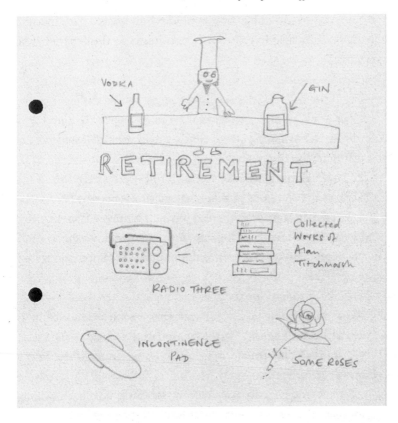

I was six years old when I did that project. We made bread at school, and I LIKED it. I liked it not only because it was messy, but messy in *the best possible way* – because you could actually eat the mess after you'd made it.

I certainly didn't need to do a project about cake to alert my senses to the thrill of sponge. I loved it. I loved it raw, I loved it cooked, I loved it warm, I loved it stale. I loved it so much that Granddad Smith used to trick me by holding out a teaspoon of pale brown goo for me to taste while Mum was baking, only for me to discover upon eating it that it wasn't cake mix at all, but pokey English mustard.

My earliest culinary experience was a batch of rock cakes I baked for my mum in the mid-1970s. The best thing one could say about those cakes was that they didn't breach the Trade Descriptions Act, resembling, as they did, something you might get hit with should you lose your way in an asteroid belt. I had made a schoolgirl error – forgivable only by the fact I was actually a schoolgirl at the time. I had made the mixture according to the recipe, baked it until golden, but then failed to let the cakes cool. Instead, I slung them, piping hot, into a tin and Sellotaped the sides in preparation for Mother's Day morning. I was thirty minutes and one wire rack short of perfection.

My mother welled with pride as she opened the tin – she's always been a fan of the home-made present. That pride lasted right up to the point her teeth started to fracture against the granite-like intensity of the bake.

I didn't need to be any good at baking, since Mum was such a good pragmatic cook – brought up on the commonsensical recipes of the late, great Marguerite Patten and Mary Berry (whatever happened to her?). Mum was, it's fair to say, a master of mass catering – vast tray bakes, bubbling batter puddings the size of double duvets and undulating sheets of lasagne without end. There were usually only the five of us sitting down to eat, but I think the huge volumes of food were pre-emptive, precautionary – in case a coach full of starving football supporters happened to break down right outside the house. In which case, she, Ann Perkins, was ready to serve a piping-hot linear metre of cannelloni directly into the chops of a needy centre forward.

There wasn't an awful lot of spare cash knocking about when we were little, so we often ate soya rather than beef mince, which was freeze-dried and packed into clear plastic bags. It was the colour of sadness and the texture of granola, but could be heated and cajoled back to half-life with tomatoes and stock. It was cheap – though I wouldn't go as far as to say cheerful. I ate so much of the stuff that I'm pretty confident I'm one of the most genetically modified presenters working in television today.

I haven't always been a big eater. I was underweight and sickly at birth, and remained that way until my late thirties when I discovered the Healing Power of Sponge. My indifference to food extended back to primary school during the reign of Sister Mary Dorothy and her right-handed harpies. When I was seven, I developed a full-blown eating disorder. Most food related problems stem from a deep-rooted psychological issue, although mine came courtesy of an unlikely source – *Buck Rogers in the 25th Century*. Remember *Buck Rogers*? Gil Gerard, as the eponymous hero – all teak bloat and enthusiasm, with Jack Palance as a scene-chewing space wacko heading up a nomad cult on Planet Vistula. (Vistula? You can get a cream for that. You're welcome.)

I loved *Buck Rogers*. I believed every word of it. But Buck lied.

Yes, Buck, you did indeed predict the rise of the onesie and the playsuit. And, by God, you looked dapper in both. But no, Buck, the world did not end in a nuclear catastrophe at the close of the 20th century leading to the founding of the Earth Defense Directorate. The worst thing that happened was that a few people got frightened about the millennium bug, stockpiled tins of beans and thought their computers might crash. Oh, and the Wall of Fire which was supposed to light the Thames on New Year's Eve 1999 was pretty shit. A Wall of Shit as it happens.

OK. So one particular episode of *Buck Rogers* – 'Planet of the Slave Girls' if you must know – featured a storyline in which the earth's fighter squadron became totally incapacitated after eating poisoned food. This led me to the totally natural conclusion that even though I a.) wasn't in an intergalactic fighter squadron, or b.) didn't routinely eat weird discs covered in toxins, I too was being poisoned.

Other things that *Buck Rogers* made me frightened of:

gay robots

acid-coated boomerangs

Roddy McDowell

So convinced was I that my food was contaminated, I started to hide cheese sandwiches, spat things into napkins, feigned illness – anything to stop solids entering my digestive tract at the meal table. I was skinny as it was, and after a week of self-imposed starvation it became clear my parents were going to have to stage an intervention. One day, as I sat down for my tea, lips pursed, I noticed my mum and dad staring at each other in an unusually intense manner. She kept nodding at him, as if to say, *Go on, Bert. Get on with it!*

So Bert/Dad got on with it. He leaped from his chair, held my nose and, as my mouth obligingly fell open, rammed the Captain's finest down my gullet. Yep, my dad force-fed me fish fingers, which incidentally is the most alliterative way you can be force-fed. Afterwards my mum said they both cried. 'It was an act of violence,' she said. I didn't say anything because I was still coughing up neon-orange grit and the odd gobbet of cod.

In retrospect, I'm just glad she's never asked me if I think that particular early trauma is one of the things that has made me gay. My mum is deeply cool about me being lady-homo but will sporadically try to link childhood events (where she perceives herself to be lacking in some way) to my sexuality in an attempt to rationalize it.

Mum: When I forgot to bring your jacket with me and you

nearly froze to death in Sainsbury's car park that time, do
you think that had anything to do with your sexuality?

Me: No, Mum.

Mum: When we refused to allow you to go on the school day-trip
to Calais and you had to sit with Karen Rosenberg all day
– who couldn't go because she was an observant Jew – did
that make you gay?

Me: No, Mum.

Anyhow, after Fishfingergate, I ate with gusto. I am in no
way condoning or celebrating force-feeding. I'm just saying
that it worked for me. And it may or may not have made me
gay.

Mum, I'm kidding. Look. See? I was fine. I even did a project
about it.

Sadly, I only got a C grade from my teacher, as there weren't any images of fish fingers in it.

As I hit double digits, Mum started entertaining in earnest. We three kids would sit on the stairs in height order, like myopic von Trapps, and peek through the wood-effect balustrade at the adults below. There would be the comforting peaty reek of Scotch and the rumble of banter, in the days before 'banter' was a euphemism for 'white male doing rape jokes'. These early dinner parties soon evolved into more lavish events – often themed and costumed – culminating in a series of vicars-and-tarts parties. These were all the rage back then, back when there was some form of moral divide between the two camps.

I am still in therapy over the sight of my dad dressed as a 'tart'. He looked like an east-European shot-putter wearing the pelt of Farah Fawcett. Occasionally he would ram a hand down his nylon blouse and adjust one of his balloon breasts, which would sag and pucker over the course of the evening until, around 2 a.m., he would put them out of their misery with the prick of a pin.

Finally, Mum was able to put the mass-catering skills she'd been honing for a decade into practice. Not only that, but she started experimenting with serving suggestions, presenting things in Kilner jars or atop scrubbed scallop shells she got from the fishmonger. She never served the actual scallops, of course – they would have ended up in the bin. Why? Because

'They're foreign muck.'

Dad's answer to anything that wasn't ice cream, sausages or chips was

'Not for me. It's foreign muck.'

Dad's gastronomic conservatism didn't stop Mum though –

she loved to push herself. The most exciting thing that ever happened was one of us bringing home a vegetarian. These were the days where vegetarian meals were just side dishes or listed on menus under 'Accompaniments'.

Mum: Are you saying we never gave you enough vegetables? Do you think that might have made you gay?

Me: No, Mum.

Once I'd left home and the 90s established themselves, the dinner parties faded out. I imagine it was because the kids had grown up and now the parents had to do the same. Either that or my dad's unconvincing and unrelenting transvestism had created a rift between him and his mates. After that, Mum and Dad opted for smaller affairs with only the closest of friends, the sort of friends comfortable with

    a. Dad pretending he had an enormous pair of breasts.
    b. Mum mainly serving food in seashells.

I remember that my dad's mate Mick would come round a lot. I loved him and his missus. He'd known Dad since they were kids, when they'd ripped around south-east London creating mayhem together. Mick would arrive and then the drinking would begin. And by God, could they drink – bottle after bottle after endless bottle. Sometime around 3 a.m. Mick would fall into the hedge in the front garden on the way to his car. He always drove. Right up to the time they banned him for life.

At the sound of grown man collapsing into hedgerow, we'd wake up.

Me: What's happened, Mum?

Mum: Your Uncle Mick has just had one of his dizzy spells. Now go back to bed.

I loved those two. Loved them for reasons I am only now starting to fully understand. I believe that Mick was the only person keeping the black dog of depression away from my dad after the cancer pecked at him, until even he retreated for a while and let it consume Dad at will.

Taking the Époisses

One such evening Eve, Mick's wife, brought round a large cheese. At the end of the meal the women duly unwrapped its cling-film shroud and, hey presto, the whole room smelt like instant arse.

Dad: Christ! What's that? It's awful.

Mick: It's making my nose bleed.

Mum: [*burying her nostrils in her sleeve*] I'll open a window.

There was no way we could eat it – for starters, it was impossible to get it within arm's length of your face without retching. Any proximity set the whole of your GI tract into spasm. But it couldn't stay in the room. It was a health hazard just sitting there, sweating. And so it got moved to the fridge. Out of sight, out of mind, but very much still in nasal passages.

Then, at the end of the evening came the fight about who should take it home.

Mick: I'm not having it in the fecking car.

Eve: I'm not having it in the fecking house!

Mick: And it was a present. A *present*. You can't return it. You can't look a gift cheese in the mouth, Bert.

So we were stuck with it. Stuck with the cheese of doom. God only knows what cheese it was, but after years of making food television my money's on an Époisses. The house was humming for weeks – imagine a boiler room densely packed with wet golden retrievers and you're not even close. The French might not have won a major war for over a hundred years but, I'm telling you, they have been stealth-attacking British households for decades with devastating efficiency.

Every time we opened the fridge, this gust swept over you, like a flatulent bison with giardia. It made my eyes water and my hair rise at the roots. My entire body would stiffen, every atom sending messages to my brain – *This smell? This smell ain't right . . .*

Of course you're thinking, *Why didn't they just bin it?* Well, they could have were it not for the fact that

  a. My parents would never ever countenance wasting food.
  b. My parents don't like to opt for an easy solution when a complex deadlock is possible.

So there we were, trapped between the Franco-stein horrors of 1990s artisanal cheese production and the moral rigour of 1950s austerity. Something had to give.

Thankfully we didn't have to keep it for long. Mum and Dad soon devised a cunning plan by which they could smuggle the cheese back to Mick and Eve's. The next time they went round for dinner they took the cheese with them. Bold as brass.

Mick: Oh Jesus, the smell – it's even worse than I remembered.

Eve: [*shrieking*] Get it out of here!

Dad: It's a present. A *present*. You can't return it.

And so it sat in *their* fridge for six weeks.

Next dinner, and it was clear the Flynns were going to have to up their game. They brought the cheese to our house, but instead of openly offering it, they hid it behind the curtains. One–nil. Mum and Dad tracked it down (not hard, for reasons made manifestly clear above) and then returned it and hid it under a floorboard. One–all.

That was in 1991.

It is now 2015, and what you need to know is that the game is *still going on*. Same cheese – different hiding places. So far the cheese has been in flowerpots and hedgerows and under beds and in cupboards. Hell, in one particularly successful gambit, my super-square mum excused herself from dinner, went to the bathroom, pulled out a screwdriver from her purse, unscrewed the bath panel and sneaked the cheese in there. Take THAT, Catwoman.

That particular placement took them six months to find. I distinctly remember the call from Mick several weeks after the dinner.

Mick: Susan, is your mum there?

Me: No, she's out.

Mick: OK. Right. OK. Can you take a message?

Me: Sure.

Mick: Can you . . . I need you to . . . Oh God. Just ask her – have we got the cheese?

Finally they found it, and the game was on again. It travelled back to us in disguise, and last I heard it had gone back to them rammed into the bottom of a bottle of expensive Scotch. Ooops. I've given it away now. First rule of Cheese Swap, you don't talk about Cheese Swap.

As a family we often talk about the cheese, and at the merest mention of its name that smell rises again in our nostrils.

Me: I've never, never to this day smelt anything like it.

Mum: Mmm. Me neither. [*Pause*] Do you think it might have made you gay?

Me: Possibly, Mum. It's possible.

In the spring of 2009 the then controller of BBC2, Janice Hadlow, asked if I'd think about presenting a cake show. By this time I had become the go-to girl for extreme eating for the minimum wage.

I said, 'That sounds like an awful idea. No one is going to watch it, and I can't imagine anything more tedious. It would be like watching paint dry, except worse, because after paint's dry you can at least hang pictures on it and sit back and admire it, whereas with a cake you just eat it and then feel awful about yourself.'

I said no.

But Janice is nothing if not a persistent soul, and when Janice thinks something is a good idea you listen, seeing as she is pretty much the cleverest person in the whole world. In pitching meetings you'd listen in awe as she riffed on Byzantine art and string theory and why the Hanoverians had such dysfunctional families, and then you'd feel bad for pitching her *The House of Hairy Children** or some such piffle.

Still, I said no.

By this point Janice was probably pretty pissed off, but stuck with it using the most effective weapon at her disposal – making me unemployed. Yep, she rather cleverly made sure I had no other work to distract me. Eventually the thought of dicking about with my best mate overcame my reservations about dragging myself and the nation towards morbid obesity and Type 2 diabetes.

From the outset Mary Berry was a dead cert for judge. I'd already had the pleasure of working with her in the 1950s – when she came on *Supersizers* and cooked a horsemeat steak in Stork. Trust me, that's the sort of first meeting you never forget. The male judge, however (as he is now affectionately known), was less set in stone. The first-round casting process failed to turn up a suitable candidate, but then we remembered this bloke on a cable show several years before, all mahogany and burly, pummelling the living shit out of a wannabe cob.

'Yes! He's great – what was his name?'

'Screw his name,' I replied. 'Let's talk about his *hair*.'

Paul Hollywood's barnet is made up of a series of grey vertiginous spikes, which serve not only to repel invaders but also to test the texture of sponges. It's a technique he mastered while working at the Dorchester. Just one simple bend of the waist and he can skewer the cake on his locks. If there is any residue left on his hair, then the cake is underdone. If the hair comes out clean, it's ready to remove from the oven.

So there we were, the four of us – Mary, Paul, myself and

* I believe this is now in production.

Mel – the most ridiculous and over-scrutinized family since the Kardashians. For those who have never seen *The Great British Bake Off*, the show in question, allow me to elaborate. Here's how it works.

I arrive around 8 a.m., impeccably dressed and elegantly coiffured. I then remove these perfect clothes and change into a jam-smeared jacket, ill-fitting low-crotch trousers and muddy brogues while tousling my hair into a wonky cockerel spike – all in an effort to get to the role of 'Sue Perkins'. I have opted to play 'Sue Perkins' as a care-worn scruffy little sugar hog who speaks only in double entendres (see baps, plums, tarts, etc.).

At around 8.30 a.m. my life partner Melanie and I walk into a large tent stationed somewhere in England's green and pleasant land and invite the contestants within to make a perfectly simple, everyday creation. It could be a life-sized statue of Michael Gove in vanilla sponge or a tier of profiteroles that expresses their feelings about nationalism. Simple, everyday stuff. To begin proceedings, I shout the word BAAAAAKE in a strangled and slightly sarcastic manner.

Next it's time for what we have named the Royal Tour, in which either Mel or myself potters around the benches finding out what large-scale adventures in baking the contestants will be attempting. We are joined on this pilgrimage by the show's iconic judging duo, Paul Hollywood and Mary Berry. Their love affair is one of the worst-kept secrets in show business. Paul's job is to listen to the baker's description of the pie / cake / tart in question, leave an ominous pause and then say, 'Mmm. I'll be interested to see if that works,' before walking off, shaking his head. No matter how hard he shakes his head, not a single hair will move. Mary, on the other hand, says very little but sets her eyes to 'Stun'.

My job is to steal and eat as much food as I can. And I can eat *a lot*. My motto: 'If it's at head height or lower I will eat it.' Above head height, I won't touch it. I won't climb for food. I'm not desperate.

For the next four hours I systematically wander round the bakers' work stations, robbing them of ingredients and making them cry because they no longer have enough chocolate to complete their big brown *Schichttorte*. Occasionally I will remove a batter-soaked spoon from my mouth long enough to bellow 'One hour left!' 'Ten minutes!' 'Thirty seconds!' or 'Time's up!' before returning to the bowl like a velociraptor to Bob Peck's face.

After the Royal Tour the other presenter promenades around the benches 'doing emos'. Ostensibly, this is the part where we discover a little more about what makes the contestants tick – their backgrounds, families and personal history. What we're also trying to do, however, is work out how many overwrought puns and how much seaside smuttiness we can squeeze out of the situation. We'll begin with the double entendres: tarts, buns, soggy bottoms, ginger nuts and my own particular favourite, rough puff. Then, when those have been exhausted, we'll move to single entendres – e.g., 'That baguette looks like a penis' and 'Those macaroons resemble tits.'

It's then back to the green room for a couple of tots of rum (medicinal) with Bezza (one of Mary's many nicknames) and a carb-crash in front of the telly. Paul grabs the remote so he can watch a Grand Prix or the Isle of Man TT. We wrest it from his grasp and put on a box set of *Mad Men*. Mary silently endures but secretly wishes for *The Jeremy Kyle Show*, to which she is now addicted. Mel falls asleep, mouth open, within a nanosecond. Mel's capacity for sleep is the stuff of legend.

Several hours later we reappear in the tent. There's the sound of a dozen mixers and the intoxicating smell of lemon zest and caramel. Atoms of icing sugar dance in the air. We sit and wait. Wait for television gold.

And, sure enough, it happens. A baker will drop their bake. That mirror-finish ganache, that tower of biscuits, that scale model of the Parthenon – whatever it might be, crashes to the ground and mingles with a furry floor tile. Suddenly, the entire camera resources of the United Kingdom are on hand to film it. There are more eyes on that spattered sponge than there are trained on the battle-torn streets of Homs in Syria. At some point that baker will do a cry and I will hug him/her until he/she feels uncomfortable and then he/she will do a snot on my blazer. I vow to dry-clean this blazer, but then life gets in the way and I forget. And then the next series comes along; I drag it out of the wardrobe and, hey presto, it takes a small axe to hack off the dried sadness-slime.

Then comes the judging. Paul's judging technique has evolved over the years into the finely honed act it is now. First he embeds his thumb deep into the bake. This thumb is always stained blue, as it has been loitering deep within his jeans pocket for several hours. On removing his thumb, he performs a series of knowing laughs, interspersed with 'underbaked' and 'overproved' barked at random. Mary says very little, but sets her laser eyes to either 'I love you' or 'I'm going to kill you.' When I say Mary says very little, what I mean is that she says very little that is broadcastable on a pre-watershed show. The woman has the face of an angel and the mouth of a docker.

The truth is we're family, with our own unique relationships but united under the banner of love. Paul is Kato to my Clouseau. We constantly try to batter each other with the plastic prop baguettes that litter the tent. He'll sneak up behind me and karate-chop me in the neck with a polymer brioche. I'll clatter him in the knackers with a fake lemon drizzle. It's the love that dare not speak its name. We laugh at his high-performance sports car, which Mel and I attempt either to steal or deface every series. He laughs at my car, but for completely different reasons. He's funny and kind. He's heavy, he's my brother.

Mary is one of the most extraordinary people I've ever had the pleasure of meeting. I love her, and it's a badge of honour that she'd consider me a friend. It's as good as having the Queen as your mate. She is the most unique of souls, walking, as she does, a tightrope between regal dignity and childish mischief. Young at heart and old of soul. In her seventies she went clubbing at Pacha in Ibiza. At the wrap party to series four she downed tequila slammers, forgoing the salt and lemon as a sideshow distraction that needlessly delayed the passage of grog from glass to throat. 'What a palaver,' she said before tossing the fruit over her shoulder and sliding yet another shot down her neck.

And we love the bakers too – we've never had a bad one yet. And by the time we get to meet their families in week ten we feel like we know them because we have spent months listening to their stories and sharing their lives.

Is it strange that the show has been co-opted by the tabloids? Yes. Is that intense ownership of the show sometimes responsible for people saying horribly censorious and humourless things about us? Yes. Is it likely that sections of the above will be taken out of context and printed in a red top in an effort to drum up moral outrage? Of course. You're welcome. Come on, lads. Try proving me wrong.

And yes, sometimes, when the sound is down, the show can look a little like a UKIP recruitment video, with its jingoistic imagery, bunting and green and pleasant landscape. That notwithstanding, I love it. I love the legendary Andy Devonshire, who helms it all so impeccably. I love the production team, the crew, the home economists. It's a treat to come back every year and see the same faces (with ever-bigger waistlines) joining in with us.

Over time it has become the show that it looks like to the general public. But let me tell you, it wasn't always that way.

First series are always hard. And by God this was hard. In its first year *Bake Off* was a touring affair, with the tent dismantled and reassembled in a different part of the UK each week.

For the first weekend we were in beautiful picture-perfect Kingham in Oxfordshire, tent pitched slap bang in the middle of the village green like croissant-obsessed aliens had landed. Roswell-in-the-Wold, as it now resembled, couldn't have been a more perfect spot.

Except.

Except the rain was biblical from the get-go. The heavens opened at 6 a.m. and they stayed open all weekend. The sky moved from black to slate grey to black again. The catering arrived at 7 a.m. in the form of a man called Barry. No gourmand was ever called Barry. There will never be a *Masterchef* champion called Barry. No Barry will accept a Michelin star. That is not the lot of Barrys. Barrys sell cars in Walford, they don't make luncheon.* So, Barry parked up his burger van and all day flipped Shergar steaks on a filthy griddle.

---

* I am now braced for an onslaught of livid, gastronomically blessed Barrys.

There were no takers.

Oftentimes, when you start a big show like this, there is a period of adjustment while the different agencies involved try to rough-hew the production into the shape they want it. Their idea of what the show is might not tally with that of the broadcasters or the presenters. And so it was with *Bake Off*.

The production company was used to making award-winning, intense and provocative documentaries on multiculturalism and poverty, and took this journalistic ethos right into *Bake Off*. Suddenly the bakers were asked rather heavier, personal questions than they had been expecting.

'I just wanted to talk about my tea loaf,' sobbed one of the contestants under his umbrella after a particularly intense interrogation. 'I just want Mary to come and have a look at it . . .'

'Why *Mary*? Do you have issues with your mother?' asked a producer.

'No, I just wanted her to tell me why it's collapsed in the middle.'

A tense pause for effect.

'Have *you* collapsed. Is it you that's collapsed?'

'Please, please just get Mary . . . I need Mary.'

After seeing not one, not two, but *three* of the bakers sobbing, we decided to take a stand. This wasn't the sort of show we were used to presenting, and so, at 9 a.m. on day two we walked out.

Yes, there really is no rule by which you can measure my or Mel's ability to commit career suicide. First we exited *Light Lunch* just at the point it was becoming truly successful. Now we were walking out of a show that was to become almost as powerful as *Top Gear*, only without the casual racism, misogynist 'banter' and punching of co-workers.

There were meetings. Many meetings. We all learned lessons. I learned there's no point getting uppity about things once they've been recorded. It's too late by then. If I want change, I'll effect it on the shop floor. So nowadays, if one of the bakers gets upset or overcome with emotion, I simply start swearing and libelling pharmaceutical companies like there's no tomorrow, and I know that it won't get broadcast. I know they are safe. More and more, that's the nature of our job. Pastoral care. Everyone on the show does their bit to make sure that the stressful, silly hand of television touches the contestants enough to change their lives but not so much it bends them out of shape altogether.

That first series was a slog. Not only did we routinely do fourteen-hour days, but we over-recorded to a ridiculous degree. Remember the historical interviews with a woman dressed as an Anglo Saxon warrior princess? The poetry of the Mayor of Sandwich? The pudding throwers of Yorkshire? Nope. Because none of them made it to screen. It turns out that simply watching nice people make nice cakes is all you need, and everything else is superfluous.

The final of series one took place at Fulham Palace in London. The location scouts had excelled themselves; it looked great, the perfect grandiose backdrop for a season climax, plus it was close to home. There was just one thing they hadn't accounted for:

it was on the Heathrow flight path.

Not just on it. *Right* on it. Every thirty seconds, sometimes less, during daylight hours the belly of a jumbo blocked out the sun above us. Added to which the noise was deafening. There was nothing we could do but soldier on.

Mel/Sue: For the last six weeks Britain's best amateur bakers have been whipping themselves into a frenzy, bashing their dough and caramelizing their nuts in an effort to win the title of –

Sudden roar of a Boeing 747 from Addis Ababa.

Director: CUT! [*Waits for quiet*] Go again!
Mel/Sue: It's the final weekend as we reach the conclusion to our search for Britain's best amateur baker. Inside that tent our plucky threesome have donned their aprons, brandished their whisks –

Airbus A380 from Singapore rumbles across the sky.

Director: CUT! [*Waits for quiet*] Go again!
Mel/Sue: It's the moment they've been waiting for – our final trio of muffin makers are bracing themselves for the biggest weekend of their lives. Grab your *kugelhopfs* and –

Boom of a 777 en route from Beijing.

Director: CUT! [*Waits for quiet*] Quick, there's a lull! Go again!
Mel/Sue   [*gabbling*] IT'S THE FINAL! THERE'S THREE LEFT!
Director: Great! Now let's try that piece to camera about the history of the spotted dick.

In the end the noise proved so disruptive that for the entire finale weekend we were forced to trim all pieces to camera down to a few hasty words. If you watch that show back, you'll see everything delivered in desperate, staccato sound bites –

rushed through before the next plane in the Heathrow queue rumbles into view.

Me: Last challenge. How are you feeling?
Baker: Well –
Me: [*cutting in*] Great. BAKE!

By the time we got to the judging the whole thing was starting to feel more like *They Shoot Horses, Don't They?* than a baking competition. There were now only two bakers in the running, so we reckoned we stood a half-decent chance of leaving before nightfall. We were wrong. Just at the point we could take no more, Paul and Mary opted to get all meta on our arses. This meant that the judging for the final of series one took FOUR AND A HALF HOURS.

Yep. You heard that correctly.

FOUR AND A HALF HOURS.

Here are some things you can do in four and a half hours.

Fly to Moscow.

Complete a marathon.

Begin and end a relationship (if you're me).

Give birth to a child.

What Paul and Mary elected to do in four and a half hours is argue over whether or not a cupcake is a cake. Is it a little cake? Is it a muffin? Is it a light bite? More importantly, what *is* cake? It was exactly the kind of ontological badinage television was invented for.

By the time the show finally ended, I only knew one thing.

I never, *ever* wanted to do it again.

But I did. Something about the combination of people, the allure of a tent in green fields, the flap of bunting, pulled me back. Now, after six series, the show is a finely oiled machine.

Plus, with all the new technology – CGI and green screen – and the judicious placing of mirrors we get the whole thing done in twenty minutes.

BAAAAKE! Overworked! Nice buns! I've still got a taste of plums in my mouth! Halfway through! That looks a little underbaked! Ten minutes left! You've dropped your *croquembouche*! Time's up! Here's Mary and Paul! Soggy bottom! And the winner is . . .

In all seriousness, I often get asked questions about the show, so I thought I'd take an opportunity to answer some of the most regularly posed.

FAQs

Sue, what are you and Mel like behind the scenes of Bake Off?

Well, we're exactly like we are on screen, except instead of puns, we make very nuanced literary allusions to Russian novelists.

Is Mary Berry real?

As real as rum and vodka and wine and whisky. Very real.

What does Paul style his hair with?

Let me answer that with another question. Have you seen *There's Something About Mary*?

Why is there a long-running feud between Dapper Laughs and Mary Berry?

Because he misappropriated her catchphrase, 'proper moist'.

Do you bake?

Not really. Here's why. There are really good shops and some of them serve cake. Added to which, I am mates with Mary Berry, so never go hungry.

Has Bake Off *changed you?*

Yes. I am now made up of 50 per cent carbon and 50 per cent lemon drizzle. I can no longer see my feet when I step on a set of scales. And I cannot go anywhere in the world without someone shouting 'BAAAKE!'

Will we see the series two squirrel again?

No, I'm afraid not. After the tabloid furore, the squirrel was forced to go into hiding. He has now been put into a squirrel protection programme under a different name, for fear of reprisals.

Shame! Will there be any more close-ups of woodland genitals?

There is a sheep's udder in series five. I'm afraid that secondary sexual characteristics are as far as we can go these days without there being a tsunami of manufactured outrage.

Can you remember any of the bakes?

No. I can remember *all* of them.

In my head there's a Rolodex of every single mouthful I've tasted on the show. I'm like a sponge savant, able to recall with breathtaking accuracy the taste of each and every bake: Mary-Anne's Midnight Mocha, Jo Wheatley's Banana Mousse, Ryan's Key Lime Pie – all sorted and available for recall at the flick of a synaptic switch. I am tortured by it.

'My name is Susan and I'm a sugar addict.'

'Hello, Susan . . .'

What will next year's Bake Off *hold? Is there a format change? Could you give us any hints about the first episode?*

OK, but they're going to KILL me for this.

Here's a sneak preview of episode one of series seven.

8.00 p.m. Opening credits. Close-up of tent flaps suggestively swaying in the breeze. Cut away to lambs gambolling in field. Will we see their genitals? Maybe later. For now we move into a kitchen. A child is smearing MARY BERRY in red icing on the walls. The music swells. Suddenly a massive celebratory Hungarian ring swings into view. It covers the child's face. On it we read the legend BAKE OFF.

8.01 Mary and Paul are winched down from the tent ceiling. Collabro sing 'When Will There Be a Harvest for the World'. Mary is rocking a Hillary Clinton-style pantsuit in purple paisley. So is Paul.

8.02 The signature challenge. The bakers are asked to make something that reminds them of childhood. Immediately one of the more senior challengers starts fashioning a representation of the three-day week out of marzipan.

8.07 Sue steals a handful of pistachio nuts from one of the bakers' benches.

8.09 The cry goes up, 'Who has taken my nuts? Who has taken my nuts?' Mel and Sue rush to be first to the double entendre and in doing so Sue is mildly injured by an upturned piping nozzle.

8.12 A twenty-minute VT on the history of the palette knife, voiced by Cherie Lunghi.

8.32 The technical challenge is about to be revealed. Close-up shot of a baker eating his entire hand in fear. A medic is called to attend to the bleeding stump. Mel and Sue fight to make a joke about lending a hand. A deep silence.

8.33 The challenge is announced. The contestants must work together to make a life-sized date and walnut loaf in the shape of Eric Pickles. Time starts now.

8.34 A nine-minute montage of famous spoons.

8.43 The Pickles cake is complete. Mary slowly runs her hand down the soggy sponge seam of Eric's leg. 'What a close texture!' she exclaims. It feels wrong. Very wrong. Time to finally cut away to

8.44 Close-up of lamb's genitals.

8.45 The showstopper challenge. The bakers are tasked with making a batch of biscuits suitable for an up-market wake.

8.46 Staring at ovens.

8.50 Guess the weight of the cake competition.

8.53 Guess the weight of the presenters competition.

8.55 VT insert. Theresa May takes us through her favourite batters.

8.57 Final judging. Who will win star baker? Paul gets into an Aston Martin and handbrake-turns the name of the winner in gravel.

8.59 Collabro sing from their new album, *On all Fours*.

ENJOY.

FIVE

The Rest of the World

The Dalton Highway

In the summer of 2010 I'd just finished recording the first series of *Bake Off*. I was 100 per cent certain it wouldn't be returning* so signed up to do a show called *The World's Most Interesting Roads* instead. Its basic premise was that a couple of telly folk would sit next to one another in a four-by-four, driving across some of the greatest landscapes on the planet, from Nepal to Bolivia to the jungles of Laos. Already I should have been thinking *Why view the brilliance of nature through an insect-splattered windscreen? Why not get out of the car in order to see it in all its glory?* But ours is not to reason why, ours is to do and then get slagged off by A.A. Gill.

I was paired with lovable man-hunk Charlie Boorman, and on first meeting it became clear we were the chalk and cheese of 'Let's do a travelogue.' He liked biking, wearing leather, drinking with the lads and . . . biking. I liked books, puns, 1960s Polish film posters and the odd night at a health spa. I expect the producers thought our differences might lead to some entertaining 'banter' or fighting. But there was no banter or fighting; just a lot of long silences where communication should have been.

We landed at Anchorage, Alaska, late on a gloomy afternoon and headed straight for our beds. Now, when I arrive at a hotel, there are many things I expect to see.

---

* I thank God every day that I am not responsible for my own career.

   a. Bored uniformed staff pretending they are on the phone when you check in so they don't have to talk to you.

   b. Piles of leaflets for the local waxwork museum and log flume.

   c. The mild eye bulge of the concierge when two women request a double room.

What I don't expect to find in reception is a lavishly stuffed and mounted polar bear rearing in my general direction. And that was just the beginning. In every hotel I stayed in in Alaska I'd go to the lobby to make a call and find a mummified musk ox behind me. I'd go get a soda from the machine on the landing, only to find myself in the shadow of a grizzly bear dancing with a couple of Arctic foxes.

If there's one thing I hate more than trophy killing, it's taxidermy. You've killed it. Don't take the piss. Don't fill it with sand and make it play poker with a load of animals that it would have made mincemeat of in the wild, for God's sake.

I was aware that in this state of the Union I was in a minority of one. Saying you don't like slaughtering things in Alaska is like standing up at a UKIP rally and saying you don't think there are enough Polish builders currently working in the South East.

I don't like guns either – they scare the living daylights out of me. I went clay-pigeon shooting once and burst into tears when I hit a target.

Instructor: It's *clay*, Sue – it's not a real pigeon.

Sue: I know. It's just that I've got the idea of a pigeon in my head now . . .

Guns are, however, a part of life in the Last Frontier, so it was inevitable we would film in a gun shop – Jim's Guns, to be precise, one of over thirty licensed firearms warehouses in Anchorage. We walked in. Charlie instantly headed for a high-powered 50 millimetre assault rifle and started talking serial numbers with a man sporting an impressive walrus moustache. I stood there, looking uncomfortable, in the shadow of a rocket launcher.

'Hey there, little lady.'

I immediately froze. I come from a place and time where only serial killers in films say that.

A man in a stained motorcycle singlet and Chris Waddle-inspired mullet stood in front of me. I was distinctly aware that if we had been having this same conversation six feet away, just over the door threshold, I would be speed-dialling the cops around about now.

Ted: My name's Ted. What can I get you? Looking for anything in particular?

Me: No, I'm just . . . browsing. Is that the correct verb? Do you browse through weaponry?

Ted: Sure. Care for a few suggestions?

Me: I dunno. Maybe – what do you have in mind?

Ted: Let me show you something you're going to love.

Unless it's a petition outlawing handguns, Ted, I doubt it.

Ted: OK, so you're out at a swanky party. You're in a little black dress. What do you need?

Me: Spanx? A surgical truss?

Ted: You need . . . this!

Ted brings out a snub-nosed black pistol less than six inches long.

Ted: Smith and Wesson. .38 calibre. Great grip and the recoil won't rip your shoulder out. Pop it in your garter belt and you are ready to go.

Garter belt, Ted? Are we in a fin de siècle *burlesque show?! But Ted is just getting started . . .*

Ted: OK, so . . . aim it at my nuts. Go on!

I really don't want to hold the gun, let alone train it on Ted's little twins.

Ted: Come on, go for the nuts! Come on!

'Come on!' came another voice from the direction of the cash till. I was being heckled by a guy to blow another guy's nuts off.

I'm a sucker for peer pressure so aimed for Ted's groin and pulled the trigger. After it clicked, I realized that I hadn't even bothered to check whether the gun was loaded or not.

Ted: Feels good, huh? Tell you what's better. The great thing about this little baby is that it comes with a laser sight. Depress the trigger a little. See?

I squeeze my forefinger and a red dot appears between Ted's balls.

Me: That's great, Ted. A laser sight. After all, I wouldn't want my ability to kill a stranger to be compromised by being blind drunk.

Charlie saunters over, carrying a bolt-action Remington rifle.

Charlie: Do you know they sell grenades here? It's awesome!

Me: I'll leave you boys to it. Ted, look after those nuts. Charlie, I'll be waiting by that stuffed lynx in reception.

Our next stop was Whittier, a tiny port city on Western Prince William Sound. You go there to watch the orcas, the minke and humpback whales, or to die of hypothermia. Whittier is about an hour's drive from Anchorage, a little more if you get stuck behind a herd of Dall sheep or some rogue moose. It remains one of the weirdest places I've ever visited. It has a total population of around 220, all of whom live in two abandoned army facilities not altogether convincingly converted into condominiums.

Begich Towers, one of these blocks, is a brutalist beige blot on the landscape, looming large over the smattering of thin trees and ramshackle collection of tugboats and pick-up trucks which litters the railway line. Everywhere there is the grey filth of melting snow. The magical freeze was ending when we arrived, and all that remained was the endless drip, drip, drip of the ugly thaw.

'Well, it's certainly living up to its tag line,' said lovely John, our fixer.

'What's that?' I asked.

'Well,' he continued, 'the saying goes, "There's nothing shittier than a day in Whittier."'

That's how legendarily glum it was. It had its own rhyme. I wondered if that sort of thing could catch on back home.

'There's no point in schlepping to crappy old Epping!'

'A smack in the skull is preferable to Hull!'

The first thing the production team decided to do was split us up. Charlie went off to do something – I forget what. Something manly and charismatic, I'll warrant. I was sent off to meet a weather specialist, the legend that is

Brenda T.

Brenda not only ran the local gift shop (specializing in antlers and leather goods – mainly antlers) but supervised the Whittier weather station. Brenda turned out to be as cranky as she was brilliant.

Me: What's the weather doing, Brenda?

Brenda: Shit if I know. Look at the book, dumb-ass. Anyhow, I gotta go feed the reindeer.

I was in clover. Not only was Brenda thrillingly indifferent, bordering on abusive, but she had ANIMALS TO PET.

We headed down the stairs, out of the army condo and into the snow. Over the road there was a pen, inside which were two reindeer which I

INSTANTLY ANTHROPOMORPHIZED.

They're sad in that pen, I thought. *Look at their sad, sad eyes. They want to walk. They want to graze freely. They're telling me that – they're trying to communicate their sadness through the medium of ignoring me.*

Right, I decided. *I'm going to take them for a walk.*

Me: Brenda?

Brenda: [*snarling*] What?

Me: Can I play with the reindeers?

Brenda: Whaddayamean, *play* with them?

Me: I don't know. Maybe . . . walk with them?

Brenda: Jesus Christ, you Europeans . . .

She opens the gate and purposefully grabs one of the reindeer by the rope that hangs from its neck.

Brenda: Take this one. It's less mean.

Me: What?

Brenda: Come on, come on. This one won't kill ya. Now listen, English. Whatever ya do, don't let go.

With that, Brenda shoved the rope into my hand and trudged off into the snow. Suddenly I was left holding my first reindeer. At this point it's fair to say I had certain expectations.

For starters, I expected the reindeer to look at me with gratitude, acknowledging I had liberated her, pupils swelling in adoration, the way they do in Disney films. I expected her to meander towards me, nuzzle at my neck and gently place her antlers either side of my head, cradling me with her horns. I expected to stand there, gently stroking her, breathing in her scent – the smell of Christmas. 'I love you,' I'd whisper. 'Moo,' she would reply – or something close to that. (My reindeer is a little rusty.)

Well, I didn't get any of that. What I did get was a psycho quarter-ton hot-water bottle with attitude. The first thing the reindeer did once my hand hit the rope was roll her eyes in my direction. Then she started moving. I had expected her to be strong, just not that strong. Also, what I hadn't reckoned on was her sheer speed. Reindeer can hit speeds of up to fifty miles an hour when they want to. And this one wanted to. Suddenly I was running through the slush full tilt trying to keep hold of the rope, until the pace became too much and my arm nearly left its socket. I let go of the rope, and off into the distance hurtled Brenda's reindeer.

'There's a moose loose!' I shouted in the heat of the moment. I regret it. It was neither funny nor the correct species of deer. And therefore even less funny.

I trudged up the three flights of stairs to Brenda's flat.

Me: Brenda?
Brenda: What? Tell me you didn't bring a reindeer up a stairwell?
Me: No. I . . . I've lost her.

Brenda rolls her eyes so hard I can actually hear them rotating in her skull. There is much harrumphing. Finally, she puts on her sheepskin coat, moleskin shoes and beaver mittens – then calls someone on her mobile phone, which is the size of a brick. (I guess it has to be if you're dialling wearing beaver mittens.)

Brenda: Mikey, the English has lost the reindeer. Can you get the
        boys on it? [*To me*] Jesus, you . . . I should put a bull's eye
        on you.
Me: Bull's eye? What, like a *target*?

Suddenly I am in an episode of Fargo.
  It is exactly at this moment that Charlie pitches up, looking manly.

Charlie: Hey, I've just been talking with the lads about the head-
         lamp modifications on the Kawasaki Concours.
Me: That's nice. I've been losing livestock.

We got into the Jeeps and drove in circles round the pale streets. I started to get nervous. Brenda's opening gambit had been mild hostility; I didn't want to know what the next level up was like. After two hours of ducking and diving there was still no sign of the reindeer. Nothing. I ended up back at Begich Towers ready for Brenda to run me through with a souvenir antler. As she came out onto the street to meet me, a patrol car pulled up and a policeman yelled, 'Brenda, you lost a reindeer? Only there's one on the railway tracks . . .'

I'd been saved.

I tried really, *really* hard not to give the reindeer a backstory: 'All these years in that pen, no hope of freedom, year after year – I had to come down here and end it once and for all, while I had the chance.' In my head this scene by the railway tracks was an ungulate end game – a suicide bid, years in the making, with me the unwitting accomplice.

I thought about the train coming and wondered how long it would take me, *Railway Children*-style, to strip down salopettes, tracksuit bottoms, woollen thermals and double-sock combo to my pants, in order to wave them – and realized I would freeze to death way before I'd got through the first layer.

I imagined Brenda on the tracks. A locomotive coming. She turns round. The driver catches the look on her face and shits himself. The train comes to a standstill an inch in front of Brenda's nose. Terrified. She has terrified a train. She's like a character from *X-Men*. She can make anything feel mildly, but thrillingly, disciplined.

We arrived at the railroad, where a small crowd of burly men had gathered. The reindeer was busy chewing a tuft of frozen weed poking from the rails. One of the locals stood opposite the reindeer, braced himself and bellowed.

Local: Screw you!

The reindeer pauses for a moment and looks at us.

Local: Yeah, you – ya big bastard. Screw you!

Another joins in.

Local 2:   Screw you!
Me: How is that helping?
Local 2:   Best way to get 'em. Swear at 'em. Always works, no idea
           why.
Me: Oh.

*I make a mental note, in case any of my First Great Western trains back
home ever encounters a Reindeer on the Line.*

Local 3:   Fucker! [*A man in a visor to my left*] You little fucker!
Local 4:   Fucker! [*A woman from behind me*]
Local 5:   Asshole! [*A kid who's just joined the group*]
Me: Any of you been on the *ET* ride at Universal Studios?
           You'd love it!

*By now the reindeer has taken a few tentative steps towards us. The crowd
redoubles its efforts. I join in.*

Crowd: Asshole! Fucker!
Me: You . . . massive dick!

Sure enough, the reindeer increased her speed towards us, crossing the railroad and finally submitting to the tether. Brenda slapped her hard on the butt, emitted a throaty laugh in my general direction and headed off to whittle something horny back at the shop.

Once the reindeer was safely back in her enclosure, I pottered over to say goodbye. I like to think that the look she gave me, right before she stepped on my toe, was one of pure devotion.

'Thank you,' she said. 'Oh, and by the way, I'm a boy. You can tell from the antlers. Fuckwad.'

We resumed our relentless drive northwards, stopping briefly at Wasilla on the way. Lovely John the Fixer had said he could get me an interview with Sarah Palin at her house as he had an in with Todd, her husband.

En route, Charlie asked me, 'Who's Sarah Palin?'

'She's Michael Palin's wife,' I replied, jokingly.

'Oh,' he said, and carried on driving. I still don't know to this day if he was winding me up or if he genuinely believed me. Either way, we travelled the next seventy kilometres in silence.

Once in Wasilla, we parked at the security station at the end of what looked like a very long, posh driveway. I got out.

'What do you want?' said the robotic voice over the intercom.

'I'm here to see Sarah Palin,' I ventured politely.

'Do you have an appointment?'

'No, but I'm with the BBC.'

In retrospect that might not have helped. It was a little like trying to curry favour with Kim Jong-un by telling him about your work experience fortnight with Sony Pictures.

'Wait there,' said the security Dalek as he went off to check my details.

There was a long pause. I could make out John the Fixer in the distance, gesticulating wildly. The more I looked, the more I realized the frantic waving seemed to be for my benefit. I wandered over to find him finishing a phone call.

Me: Hey, John, security is just checking me out. I think I've managed to swing it.

John: I just got off the phone with Todd.

Me: Cool!

John: He said you get the hell off his property or he'll blow you off.

We'd been travelling for hours before the constant bump of hard core gave way to the smooth icy surface of the Dalton Highway. I'd been droning on about early contrapuntal music and Charlie had been telling me what his watch could do at two hundred metres below sea level when we felt the change. Suddenly we were no longer buffeted by loose chippings. We were gliding.

The highway is some 414 miles long, stretching from Livengood, north of Fairbanks, to Deadhorse, near Prudhoe Bay by the Arctic Ocean. It is one of the most remote roads in the world. Sometimes the only thing travelling alongside you is the Trans-Alaska Pipeline. It's grimly ironic that this blot on the landscape – an ugly reminder of our addiction to fossil fuels – is the very thing that created the road and, therefore, the very thing that enables us to experience the pure wonder of this part of the Alaskan landscape.

The moment we hit the ice, I knew we'd hit trouble. The road itself is well maintained and robust – you quietly skate along with no hint of trouble. It's steering that's the issue. It's easy to get in a trance state, overwhelmed by the views, the magnitude of the landscape, the barren beauty of it all, and in doing so let your hands relax a little on the wheel. If you veer, even a tad, that's where they'll get you – those fingers of black ice splayed at the road's edge. Hit one and they'll claw you off track and pull you into a snow-lined gulley with no hope of getting out.

We'd been going an hour or two. I'd been expressing my thoughts on Gothic architecture and Charlie had been telling me how, on an expedition, you can make dirty pants like new by simply reversing them. Occasionally he would pause from his anecdotes to give me helpful pointers on my driving.

'So these bike tours, you get a load of grimy lads, couple of cases of grog, make a fire, get some meat on the go, start telling stories . . .

'WATCH OUT ON THE RIGHT!'

'Sometimes you'll wake and you'll be in the desert with a mouth full of sand and a tent full of empty bottles and you won't ever know how you got there.

'SUE! YOU'RE VEERING TO THE RIGHT!'

It was warm in the car – rhythmic puffs of hot air gusted from the vents, and my belly was full of cheese sandwiches and bad coffee. Visibility was excellent – I could see for miles ahead. Nothing coming. Nothing going. My muscles relaxed. My famously limited attention wavered.

'The local guy will fix us up with a couple of shots of local whisky, then we're back on the bikes. Your arse gets sore after a while, but you can get a half-decent massage from some of the local girls . . .

'WATCH OUT ON THE RIGHT!'

I had gone into a hypnotic state – snow – road – snow – road – snow. The car drifted too far and suddenly hit a talon of black ice. It became impossible to control the steering. It was over in a flash. Our vehicle, now stationary, was at a forty-five-degree angle in a ditch.

Charlie rolled his eyes. Poor guy. Every moment I remained next to him, his masculine credibility plummeted further.

Not knowing anything about cars, I turned the engine on and ceaselessly revved the engine until the smell of burning rubber overwhelmed us.

Charlie: Shit. Axle might be broken.
Me: Is that bad?
Charlie: Yep.
Me: Oh. Sorry. Can we get a new one?

Charlie said nothing and merely turned his attention towards the horizon.

Suddenly, from behind us, a noise like a vast mechanical exhalation. A giant truck hove into view, stopping gracefully just a few inches from our car. The fenders were sparkling and you could smell the heat of the metal.

The cameras turned to the driver, who was stepping down from his cabin. It was an impossibly handsome man in his early thirties – trimmed beard, piercing blue eyes. I felt my personal polarity shift a little, then settle.

Man: You guys in trouble?
Me: No.
Charlie: Yes.
Man: Need a hand?
Charlie: Yes, please.

I stood there, dumbstruck, as thick, sleek cabling was uncoiled, hooks attached, weights and tensions considered.

Throughout, the trucker worked silently. I couldn't help but notice he averted his gaze from the camera. Fascinating, I thought. Perhaps he has escaped to the wild country after a divorce and doesn't want anyone to find him. Perhaps he is on the run. Perhaps he's worried the publicity will alert his pursuers to his location and he'll be caught again.

(I can't emphasize enough how exhausting it is being me.)

Man: What are you guys filming?
Charlie: Oh, just a documentary for the BBC back home.
Me: Is it bothering you? You want us to stop?

I am trying to make maternal concern sound a little sexy, and failing.

Man: No, it's OK.
Me: I can't help noticing you don't like the camera.
Man: Nah. It's just, you know . . .
Me: What?

I am getting close to finding his secret. I lean in.

Man: It's just . . . well . . . I wanted a break from all that stuff.
Me: A break?
Man: Yeah, we just finished season three of *Ice Road Truckers*, and I needed a bit of downtime before the next one. You know.

In the middle of nowhere – *nowhere* – I had managed to crash a car and be rescued by a bone fide global superstar, Jack Jessee. The only thing that could have made the experience weirder was if we'd been hit by Joey Essex, treated on the scene by one of the doctors from *24 Hours in A&E*, then flown home by Jeremy Spake.

Day six. We'd overnighted in Fairbanks, where I'd caroused with a female roller derby team. Boy those girls can party like it's 1958. Sadly, I had to get up and be in the car ready for filming at the crack of dawn.

I was starting to regret the bit in my contract where it said I would be working 'daylight hours'. The closer to the Arctic Circle we got, the more the days lengthened, until we'd only have a few hours of gentle dusk before I'd be back at the wheel.

After I'd finished a fascinating monologue on Dadaism, Charlie took out his earplugs and we stopped for the night. Our pit stop was one of the most magical on earth. Wiseman. I'd call it a village, but the population was fourteen. What does that make it? A grouping? A settlement? Who knows? The moon backlit the pines and the only thing you could hear was the occasional drift of snow in the mountains. A local hunter had told me that I had to be quiet, because the moose were always listening. And so that night I whispered 'Hello' into the depths of the forest, then told them the hunter's exact location – just in case he had been serious about them earwigging.

The next morning I rubbed my nose with the heel of my palm to get the blood flowing again, ate a stack of pancakes, three eggs and a portion of gravy and biscuits. Then we got back in the bloody car.

It was my turn to drive again. By now Charlie was sick of my driving. He was better at the wheel, capable of focusing on the road for more than ninety seconds without getting distracted by a bird or an animal. Plus I think he hated being in the passenger seat because that meant he had to work the CB radio – and this compromised his masculinity. It wasn't right – two grown men, revealing their coordinates to one another. It was just too intimate.

The CB radio is your best friend on the highway. Once your eyes fail in the endless and unrelenting white, you turn to the radio and listen to your salvation – your voice. It is your voice, and the crackling one in the box that comes back at you, that tell you where you are and how you are doing. And whether or not you are still alive.

The temperature was dropping and a vicious wind started to kick around the tyres. As we passed a lone worker at the side of the road, the director, Ian, travelling in the support car behind, radioed through.

'Charlie! Stop! Let's do a piece here, with this guy. This guy spraying the road.'

I was pretty relieved I wasn't involved. It looked like they were going to be talking about technical stuff, plus the wind chill looked like it could turn the tops of your ears into Frazzles.

I watched Charlie chatting away. Poor Ollie, the best sound guy in the business, was standing holding the boom above him, trying not to faint with the cold.

The highway worker was resurfacing the road with a pressure hose. The water started to freeze as soon as it hit the ground. He was motioning forward violently with his hands.

Ten minutes later Charlie bounced back into the car. The ends of his whiskers were crispy.

'Blizzard's coming in,' he said. 'We need to get out now, else we'll get stuck.'

'Right,' I said, trying to pretend this sort of thing happened to me every day. 'I should probably turn the ignition on then.' (I really am very lacking when it comes to initiative.)

'OK!' shouted Ian. (Shouting was Ian's default setting; he really was very commanding.) 'We're breaking for lunch!'

Me: What do you mean? We can't break – we've got to get out of here! There's a storm coming!

Ian: I know. There are some plastic cheese sandwiches and some cold moose cuts. Oh, and Oreos. [*He adds, as if that will somehow sweeten the deal*]

I got out the car and opened my mouth long enough for my taste buds to get anaesthetized by the chill. Then I tucked in. It's amazing how good plastic cheese and moose can taste when you can't taste at all. I plucked up courage to speak to the gaffer.

Me: Hey, Ian, can I have a word?

Ian: Sure. You want to try some of this bear? It's weirdly fishy.

Me: No. Listen, why are we waiting? Isn't that a bit reckless? Can't we have synthetic sandwiches and wild animal meat at our destination?

Ian: Yes, but . . . Well, thing is . . . they've seen the rushes back home . . .

Me: So?

Ian: And they've decided they're not . . . not . . . *dangerous* enough.

There is a slight pause before I respond.

Me: Dangerous?

Ian: Yes. Dangerous. I can see what they mean. There's no point in having 'dangerous' in the title if nothing dangerous happens. You see?

Suddenly everything around me begins moving very slowly.

Me: Why would 'dangerous' be in the title, Ian?

Ian: Because it is. Because that's what this show is – *The World's Most Dangerous Roads.*

Me: No, no, no. The show *I'm* doing is called *The World's Most Interesting Roads.*

Suddenly, I'm thinking, am I on the wrong shoot? Is there a crew somewhere pottering around a creek admiring rare birds and wondering why Bear Grylls is presenting it?

Ian: Well, it was called that originally, Sue, but the title got changed. That was *ages* ago. We did say. Didn't we? Please tell me someone told you.

Suddenly it all made sense – the total lack of tourist traffic on the road, the locals shaking their heads as we chugged out of town. That lone woman crossing herself at the final junction in Fairbanks, the wooden crucifixes that sporadically lined our route. But mainly this – why would you travel on a road made solely of ice WHEN OTHER PERFECTLY SAFE AND SCENIC ROUTES ARE AVAILABLE?

I got back in the car and ingested something that may or may not have been polar bear. Fast.

Me: [*yelling*] Come on, Charlie. We're off!

I reach over and try to pop his seat belt on.

Charlie has difficulty replying, as a clod of indiscriminate meat has attached itself to the roof of his mouth. He has to use the traction of a handful of crisps to dislodge it.

Charlie: [*mumbling*] Hang on. Gimme a second . . .

Me: WE DON'T HAVE A SECOND! [*I scream, channelling Jason Statham again – before putting the car into the wrong gear and revving the engine to fuck*]

Along the side of the entire Dalton Highway there are delineators. These are white and red sticks positioned at regular intervals along the route, giving you some idea as to the visibility. In clear conditions I knew I could see nearly twenty.

Almost as soon as we were under way, I felt a change. Nothing physical. It was instinctive, limbic. Something wicked this way comes – that kind of thing. After a few minutes the steering became a little harder, the tyres a little lazy. The wind started to smack against the window with more of a scream than a whistle. We were now nearing the highest and most exposed point of the route – the Atigun Pass, as it crosses the Brooks Mountain Range, where the ice road snakes violently to the right and up a long and punishing 12 per cent gradient.

Suddenly, from nowhere, the snow started. Not like snow I knew. The snow I'm familiar with has a simple trajectory – falling simply from top to bottom. It comes from up above, it lands at my feet. Simple. This snow was different. It emerged from everywhere – up, down, left and right – and swirled in huge circles around us. Visibility went from fifteen to five delineators in less than ten seconds. The incoming blizzard turned the air white and then the road white until visibility dipped again from five to two to one. Then nothing. Just a wall of white – nothing but white.

A large drift started accumulating on the front right tyre and I tried steering to correct it, but the back kicked out, and suddenly we were – I didn't know – sideways, maybe? All I knew was there was a ravine somewhere to my right and I did *not* want to fall down it.

In a second the vehicle was wedged solid with snow. Suddenly, and rather magnificently, Charlie went into overdrive. I could smell the testosterone coming off him. Every anecdote, every adventure, every cell in his body had been leading him to this. His hero moment. He jumped out of the passenger seat and fiddled with the tyres (to this day I have no idea what he did, but goddam it, it was TECHNICAL) before pulling me out of the driving seat. This was no time for feminist badinage, so I let him. Charlie was the only one of us who was experienced enough to get that car moving again.

And I was the only one experienced enough to get the entire Ice Road community rocking to my CB skills.

It's amazing what you learn about yourself when you come face to face with death. What I learned is that when I confront my own mortality I like to do it in the voice of Fenella Fielding.

For some reason I began to speak like her. I guess I figured that the only people out there listening were men and that in order to get them to save us I'd need to sound really HOT. Is that the action of a feminist? Oh God, I don't know. I really hope so. It was merely self-preservation. I'm sorry.

As Charlie wrestled with the screaming motor, I was pleading down the airwaves in my husky new accent. Most accidents, I remembered from our safety briefing, are caused by eighteen-wheelers ploughing into smaller vehicles. Eighteen-wheelers can't apply their brakes in these conditions – it's just too dangerous. They'd jack-knife on the ice and career to their deaths.

'Northbound four-wheeler stuck at the Atigun Pass,' I pleaded. Although, with that voice, I might as well have been saying, 'Anyone of you big lads fancy a blowie, on the house?'

I kept on going until the radio crackled.

Man: Hello, little lady.

Oh God, not that again. It must be an Alaskan thing.

Man: How can I be of assistance?

Well, hellfire, I just bagged me a mountain man.

I don't remember much about the man who rescued us, other than he was hugely disappointed when he finally made the connection between the sexy voice emanating from his CB and the goofy nerdulant coming towards him, sobbing. He'd expected an incandescent Emily Blunt; he got Gareth Malone. With tits. I also recall that he was wearing a T-shirt in minus thirty degrees. Honestly. How hard can you be? Alaskans.

Our saviour chaperoned us through the blizzard all the way to our final destination – Prudhoe Bay. By that point night had finally fallen and we were so exhausted both Charlie and I fell into our first proper silence together. For the first time in weeks we no longer fought against it, and instead gave in to the blissful quiet.

We parked the four-by-four next to a row of super-trucks shivering in the fierce crosswind. Daisy chains of cabling connected their engines to batteries so they didn't choke in the cold. Stalactites hung from the fenders and slivers of silver ice nestled in the tyre treads.

The complex at Prudhoe was a vast industrial hangar catering for the itinerant thick-necked strongmen who make their living on the oil fields. We entered a voluminous hall – polished floors, hard lines, long empty steel tables. We hadn't eaten for hours and were starving. We could smell food but couldn't see any. We couldn't see a soul. Then, we realized that on each wall sat a giant vending machine. Not the sort of vending machine I grew up with, those derisory affairs in leisure centres which sent a pack of Discos down a steel chute, rendering its contents dust as it smacked down to earth. These were industrial monstrosities, dispensing every food product known to man: Thai green curry, Singapore noodles, burgers, fries, chow mein, pork balls. You name it, the automated metal claws could get it. We jabbed wordlessly at buttons for hours, and pre-prepared international cuisine rained down from the sky.

When I finally got up from the table I remember feeling the twang of muscles I never knew existed, newly warmed sinews spasming from the shock, I guess. I hobbled to my room, which was on the second floor, past a deserted launderette the size of a tennis court. Huge drums spun and stuttered; inside, endless loops of checked shirts and Y-fronts belonging to the myriad men lodging there. I went past a state-of-the-art gymnasium – treadmills beeping, rows of stationary bicycles flashing. No one running. No one cycling. No one.

Everywhere you looked it was like a Stanley Kubrick film – beautiful, chilly vignettes of the automated soulessness of the future.

Where was everyone? Where had they all gone?

'Is there anybody there?' I shouted. Nothing.

For a brief moment I panicked. What if the BBC commissioners had changed their minds again? What if the show had gone from *The World's Most Interesting Roads* to *The World's Most Dangerous Roads* to *The World's Most Sex-Starved Oil Workers*? Or, even worse, *Redneck Psycho-Killers*.

I remember clearly that my door had four locks. I remember I made use of each and every one of them. I remember a perfect silence save the *thrum* of the launderette and the gym and the canteen, and all those other vast, empty mechanized spaces that carried on beating in the absence of human life. I cried. I cried because for a while I had felt truly under threat, lost and insignificant and vulnerable. I cried for my family and friends and my dogs. And I cried because I missed home. Finally at the end of the road I allowed myself the memory of home.

Then I dried my eyes and rehydrated a lasagne using the mini-kettle.

I hope it was dangerous enough for you.

It felt dangerous enough for me.

The Ho Chi Minh Trail

The second time I got into a four-by-four in the name of television I was at least up to speed on the correct title of the show. Forewarned is forearmed. This time my companion was the effortlessly brilliant Dame Liza Tarbuck. Instead of it being a Boorman-esque pairing (me soliloquizing about Bandura's socialization theory and he about the latest tweaks to the BMW series 3 engine), we bonded over the fact we both love Diana Ross and both like behaving like four-year-olds.

I'm pretty sure we are the first women ever to have self-driven the Ho Chi Minh trail. I *know* we are the first women to have done it singing 'Love Hangover' the entire way. When the film was wrapped, I can only imagine the hell endured by the editors, picking their way through endless loops of poorly harmonized 70s disco with inane interjections about the landscape. I imagine the soundtrack in that cutting room went something like this.

Me / Liza: Ah, if there's a cure for this
I don't want it. [Ooh look there's a pig on the back of that motorbike.]
Don't want it.
If there's a remedy
I'll run from it, from it. [Christ, it's hot – got any sun-block?]
Think about it all the time [Mind that water buffalo!]
Never let it out of my mind

'Cause I love you.

I've got the sweetest hangover [If you had to sleep with one of the researchers, which one would it be?]

I don't wanna get over.

Sweetest hangover . . .

As opposed to my trip to Alaska, I couldn't tell you *where* I went. Not a Scooby. It was like a magical mystery tour, but with the word 'magical' replaced with 'breathtakingly unhygienic' and 'morally questionable'. At no point were we shown a map or given directions or provided with any information that could have pinpointed our location. As a result, I can tell you everything that happened, I just can't tell you *where* it happened.

Liza and I would punctuate the tedium of endless driving with games – the finest of which was the Water Buffalo Game. This involved driving into a massive, wet, freshly laid buffalo turd and seeing how heavily you could saturate the driver-side camera in shit.

I told you – four-year-olds.

This meant that when it came to viewing the footage back in London, the editor of the B camera had to listen to us singing 'Love Hangover', punctuated occasionally by a flying wet dung-ball smacking into the camera. I like to think it's the video of the track that Diana always wanted to make but was too creatively blocked to realize.

One day, while travelling through the tiny village of I HAVE NO IDEA, Liza was at the wheel and spotted a ripe bean-bag-shaped pile of fresh manure in the road ahead. This was around the same time I spotted, from the passenger seat, a young schoolboy, in pristine uniform, walking alongside us. Liza steered right, and before I could say anything, she had squarely hit the shit.

Liza: [*roaring with pride*] Bull's eye!
Me: Oh God . . .

In the rear-view mirror we catch sight of the schoolboy, dripping with wet cack.

Liza: [*bellowing*] I am so so sorry!
Me: We're not all like that!

In fact, we are – we are *all like that.*

Though technically a road trip, this adventure turned out to be more of a tour of Asian brothels. Whether the BBC budget was tight, or the production company had spent all the money on GoPros and other camera gadgetry, I don't know. What I do know is that night after night we stayed in rooms that wouldn't have looked out of place in *The Human Centipede 2.*

In the first hotel (definitely a brothel) there was a six-inch gap under my bedroom door. Every hour, on the hour, I'd hear a knock, followed by a thick smoker's cough and a muttering in I DON'T KNOW WHAT LANGUAGE. Each time I would wake up, shout 'No thank you!' in my loudest, poshest voice, then try to bank another sixty-minute kip before it happened all over again.

The room was dank. In the corner, by the open-plan toilet area, stood a black Biffa bin full of stagnant water. Mosquitoes scudded across the surface. I studied it for a while. I was new to Asia and Asian sanitary ware – what on earth was it there for? Eventually I decided it was a kind of makeshift plunge pool, so stripped off, climbed onto a chair and then plopped inside.

Insects nibbled my shoulders. I sluiced then dragged myself out again.

At 5 a.m., after the regular punctuation from wannabe

punters, I woke again – this time to a frenzied squawk, followed by silence, then a pool of blood running under the door towards the bed. It was obviously cock o'clock.

An hour later I got up for breakfast. As always when away from home, I had the vegetarian option – a cloudy soup with morning glory and garlic. Delicious. Delicious right up to the point I drained the bowl and found a chicken's foot bobbing around at the bottom. 'For texture,' said the woman serving.

As we were packing up our things, I muttered over to Liza, who seemed to be trying to get GPS on her phone,

Me: Interesting bathing scenario . . .
Liza: What d'you mean?
Me: Last night. You know – the bath . . .
Liza: What bath?
Me: That massive bin with the scoop in it.
Liza: You mean the toilet water? The water to flush the toilet with?

I swallow very hard.

Me: Yeah. Yeah, that water – the toilet water. Yeah.

You learn fast in Asia.

I have become very familiar with these rooms over recent years – the black mould creeping up the wall, the overhead fan with exposed wiring, the air con that weeps stale water down the walls. The soundtrack is familiar too: the endless scuttle of roaches and geckos. Do you know that big geckos actually *say* 'GECKO'? I didn't, until one spent the entire night doing so right next to my pillow.

'GECKO! GECKO!'

I thought it was Liza taking the piss, but when I turned on

my head torch, I became aware of its enormous dry body scuttling around next to me.

Once we arrived at a hostel (brothel) in I DON'T KNOW WHERE, and the door to my room was locked. Finally a bloke came out, red and sweaty, followed by a young girl. The room smelled of sex and stress. Reception seemed most put out when I asked if they might be able to change the sheets. I didn't sleep. I didn't sleep at all.

At some of the out-of-town places prostitution is a family affair. The mother cooks the dinner, while the daughter stares at the diners and touts for business. It's a dynamic that makes me very queasy, no matter how long I spend in Asia.

I think back on these nights and all I remember is thick heat and the listlessness that comes with it, plastic tables and chairs, the smell of fried garlic, the hum of a fridge full of Lao beer. The sound of men laughing at another table, possibly at you,

very possibly at you.

Several days into the shoot, and after a twelve-hour drive, we arrived at a hostel like the one in *Hostel*. Within minutes there was a power cut. It was the first time I remember being grateful for darkness – just so I wouldn't have to see the inside of my room. As dawn broke, I woke to the sound of Liza knocking at my door. She had the focused mania of the truly sleep-deprived. She hadn't slept a wink and one eye seemed larger than the other.

Liza: Right! We're leaving! We're going home. I've been up all night studying the map and I think I know where we are.

She points to a red squiggle somewhere between Vietnam and Laos.

Liza:	If we get in the car and drive due west, we can get to a checkpoint and get out of here.
Me:	But what will we say?
Liza:	We'll say we've been held prisoner by a documentary crew who won't tell us where we are or what we're doing and that we want to speak to the British embassy.

There's a sudden noise from behind us. It's Ian, the director.

| Ian: | What are you doing, girls? |

. . . he says to the two forty-something women in front of him. We jump.

Liza:	Nothing!
Me:	Nothing!
Ian:	Right, well, let's get on then, shall we?

We hop into the car, ready for the off. The fan blasts hot air into our faces.

| Me/Liza: | 'Don't call a doctor, don't call her momma, don't call her preacher, no I don't need it . . .' |

We set off. The convoy ahead inched forward at a snail's pace, then came to a halt. We craned our necks to see the cause of the delay. There, at the side of the road, was Ian, taking a piss. We stared at him. He carried on pissing, waving us on with his other hand. It really doesn't get more dismissive than that.

From that moment on, the battle lines were drawn. Him versus us. Man versus perimenopause. Whenever he handed us some notes, or moved to direct us, or even give us a friendly pat on the back, the poor guy would hear a chorus of:

Both: Is that your cock hand, Ian?

Because we were following the Ho Chi Minh Trail, the content of the show was naturally very WAR heavy. Everywhere we went, we were encouraged to discuss WAR and all things WAR related. The problem was, whereas the programme-makers might have been keen to talk WAR, the Vietnamese contributors (many of whom had served with the Viet Cong) weren't. It was extraordinary. It was almost as if the conflict had never happened. The locals we met wanted to talk business, the future, the Western world. The Vietnamese were well and truly done with WAR.

But the Americans weren't.

One of the interviews that stays with me most from that trip (sadly heavily edited for transmission) was one we did with a couple of guys who'd been in the Mistys – a US Air Force squadron tasked with disrupting Viet Cong supply lines along the HCM Trail during the war. Flying low, they would identify potential targets, then direct in fighter strikes. These men, now in their sixties, spoke with such emotion and such candour – a world away from the *Top Gun* cocks-out bravado we're used to seeing on our television screens. There was no rootin' or tootin'. No fist pumps. No 'Yee-haw'. They were thoughtful and humble and more than once their eyes filled with tears as they told their story.

Every day these two men would set out in their planes. Their regular tour took them over a particular mountain top and thence down into the valley beyond. Every day, on that mountain top, they would see the same kid, in his teens, rifle in hand, on sentry duty for the Viet Cong. Every day they would look down at the kid, and the kid would look up at them. They saw each other at the beginning of each and every day, these sworn enemies, and yet, for months and months on end, they failed to fire upon each other. They could have blasted that kid off the rock. The kid could have fired a shot that punctured their fuselage and brought them down. They didn't. He didn't. Some telepathic agreement existed from the get-go – that one would not hurt the other. Every other plane, and every other man further down that valley, was fair game. That kid killed other pilots. Those pilots killed many, many other kids.

After the war ended some Mistys returned to Vietnam, not only looking for news of missing comrades but also, in a spirit of reconciliation, to meet those who had once been their targets. In the course of this, the two pilots came face to face with that boy on the hilltop. They learned about his family and about those he had loved who had not been so lucky in the face of the American arsenal. It was an emotional exchange. They still keep in touch.

That conversation brought home to me so clearly how heavily the Vietnam War hangs in the American psyche, and how lightly it is worn by the Vietnamese. For the Americans, I guess, it remains *the* unwinnable war, or at least it was until Afghanistan and Iraq exploded again.

Even though a map was never forthcoming, I do know that we passed from Vietnam into Laos the next day. I didn't need a piece of paper to tell me that – the landscape did it for me. I have never experienced an atmospheric and visual change quite like the one that greeted me at the border – like two different worlds stitched together by nothing more than a makeshift barrier and a security kiosk. In crossing that line, we passed from revving motorcycles, shops and high-pitched chatter into an ancient land of peace and tranquillity. Buffalo wallowed in red mud at the side of the road. Dense forest stretched as far as the eye could see. Even the light was softer, clouded by the breath of the myriad trees beneath.

Laos is a land with a deep contradiction at its heart. Its enduring beauty is forged by horror. The reason the trees have not been felled in their millions, like they have in Vietnam, is that is unsafe to do so, due to the tons of unexploded ordnance that remain in the ground from the WAR. In essence, those exact same bombs are safeguarding the beauty of the natural environment. How screwed up is that?

We were joined at the border checkpoint by five government shadows, representatives of the Lao People's Revolutionary Party, the only legal political party in the country. The head dude looked a little like Fu Manchu, but less jolly. He had grey pegs for teeth and zero laughter lines – I imagine because there had been no laughter in his branch of the LPRP. Ever.

As with their neighbours over the border, the Lao people don't dwell on what has been. They are resilient and resourceful. Every village we visited had houses built on stilts. Those stilts were made from empty shell cases dropped from American war planes. On the roadside small teams of women with wicker baskets picked shrapnel from the bushes. To venture even a metre from the cleared track is to take your life in your hands. Only a week before, a family of four had been blown to smithereens while playing in the land at the back of their house only a stone's throw from where we were passing.

We got out of the car on a whim and went to talk to the women. We wanted to know what that kind of exhausting and hazardous work felt like to do. As we approached, the government officials got out of their vehicles and approached them too. We asked the women a question. They waited for Fu Manchu to answer it. They repeated his answer, which was then translated for us.

They told us just how much they *loved* their work.

Despite constantly being around the props of WAR, none of these experiences had been especially dangerous, so the team decided to up the ante. This was, after all, as I had learned to my cost in Alaska, a show called *The World's Most Dangerous Roads*. The next morning Ian informed us that were heading off to the Sepon Mine, where we'd shadow a private UXO (unexploded ordnance) clearance team.

Liza: What's going on?
Me: Apparently we've got to go and stand on some bombs.
Liza: He's not giving up, is he?
Me: Nope. He won't stop until we're actually dead.
Liza: [*pause*] I don't want to stand on bombs.
Me: Neither do I.
Liza: Well, I'm not doing it. I mean, I'm not Ross Kemp.

So Liza, rather wisely, opted to stay at the base of the mine, whereas Lady Schmuck here crawled up a vast pile of rubble to meet the head of the UXO team.

Me: [*breathless*] So who is this guy anyway?

Ian: He's an ex-special forces Swede called Magnus.

I immediately perked up. Magnus is a name that automatically invokes excitement in me. I have never met an underwhelming Magnus. This Magnus certainly did not disappoint. He was eleven feet tall, cooler than a skinny dip in Naimakka and with a body that looked like a thousand hammers wrapped in velvet.

I noticed that whenever he got close, my skin flushed and my voice shot up an octave. Damn – what is it about us women? The more remote and unreachable a person is, the more we want to save them. And so the more stubborn Magnus was with his answers the more I fell into his sex web.

Me: So, Magnus, where have you worked?

Magnus: Everywhere. Everywhere that is hell. Iran, Iraq, Afghanistan, Sudan, Bosnia, Kosovo. Sudan was the worst . . .

His eyes are trained on the ends of the earth as he speaks.

Me: Do you get to go home much?

Magnus: Home?

Me: Yes.

Magnus: Ha! [*A single, mirthless laugh*] I don't really ever go home.

I bet you don't, you damaged Nordic mega-hunk.

Magnus: I have a cabin in the woods. It is very simple. Sometimes I return there. Alone.

[*Take me there! Take me there, you nomadic, lost soul!*]

Me: Do you . . . do you not have a partner?

Magnus: No. A wife. Once. But there is no room for love when you face death every day.

[*I am in love with you! I am IN LOVE WITH YOU, you remote, disconnected mess of a man.*]

Magnus: But . . .

He holds the pause for what seems like minutes. I lean into him expectantly.

Me: Yes?

Magnus: I do have . . .

Me: Yes . . . [*I whisper breathlessly*]

Magnus: . . . a cat.

And with that our relationship is over.

Now the possibility of a romance had disappeared, I was far more able to focus on the job in hand. Magnus walked me up what appeared to be a mountain of aggregate. We then took a cordoned-off path to the left, overlooking a large depression in the ground.

I stared down.

It is one thing to read that Laos is the most bombed place on the planet (over two million tons of ordnance were dropped on it by the Americans during the Vietnam War); it is quite another to see it with your own eyes.

In the crater down below was one of the most depressing sights I've ever seen.

A small clearance team was painstakingly working, not only horizontally, across the ground, but vertically down to the horrors beneath. The first layer had revealed unexploded phosphorus bombs, pineapple 'bombies' and 250-pounders, the second layer 500-pounders, then, going deeper still, all the way to the vast 3,000-pounders. The scale of the work, and its grindingly slow and meticulous nature, was beyond imagination. Magnus stood at the top of the ridge and calmly informed me that approximately 25 per cent of Laos's villages are still contaminated with unexploded devices from wartime raids, which rained death from the sky, on average, every eight minutes, twenty-four hours a day for nine years.

Ian looked pleased – he had got WAR chat – whereas I felt saddened to my core. For all the team's hard work, it was clear this project was a mere drop in the ocean.

And, then, just at the very point I needed to laugh, I looked back down to see Liza staring up at me, holding a pillowcase she had just personalized with a felt-tip pen. It simply read, 'I AM NOT ROSS KEMP.'

By now, Ian had figured that out of the two evils presenting themselves to him –

- spending another week with us lunatics
- serving time in an Asian prison for our murder

– the latter was preferable. Now that his plan to blow us up had failed, he decided that the next best thing was to drown us in a river. That morning we woke to find an old man in orange robes coughing on the steps of our hostel.

Me: What's he here for?

Ian: A monk's blessing.

Me: Oh. What for?

Ian: It's D-Day.

I had no idea what D-Day involved, but it sounded like something I might want to get blessed for. Liza and I were duly seated on plastic chairs outside our rooms and wrapped casually in thin skeins of cotton by the monk's second in command.

A large bucket of water was placed beside us.

The monk approached, hacking. His skin was like greaseproof paper. There was more muttering. We respectfully bowed our heads in prayer. Now was not the time for 'Love Hangover'.

Suddenly, out of nowhere, the acolyte threw the entire bucket over us. And then, as soon as it had begun, the ceremony was over.

Me: Do you think there was *any* element of the religious about that?

Liza: It was like he was washing a step!

I got up. The water had fairly and squarely sluiced my groin, and nowhere else. I had a blessed vagina. Finally, I had a blessed vagina.

We spent the next hour in damp knickers, driving to the top of a hill. Below, a river raged. We drove down again until we arrived at its banks.

Laos river crossings are often perilous, as the riverbed can be uneven and pocked with bomb craters. Instead of the depth being consistent all the way across, you can find the rock from beneath giving way so you end up totally subsumed by water. The traditional way to undertake a river crossing by car or bike is always to walk it first, bamboo stick in hand, prodding into the murk beneath and gauging the depth. Only this way can you be sure that your car won't sink into a surprise hole.

We stood at the water's edge. It's fair to say neither Liza nor myself was raring keen to take part in what amounted to an Asian wet T-shirt competition. I drew the short straw (again). I slowly waded into the current, stick in hand. To the left of me I could see villagers eviscerating a chicken, and seconds later its alimentary canal floated past me like a bloody question mark. I had barely gone three or four metres when my footing disappeared, and I was plunged in up to my neck. Our guides sat on the bank muttering and shaking their heads. Even Fu Manchu, our communist watchman, seemed keen that we proceed no further – unless the thumbs-down sign means something totally different in that part of the world.

Ian, however, sensed this had the potential to become a properly *Dangerous Road* and excitedly shouted encouragement from the bank. He finally had the chance to *literally* kill two birds with one stone.

I found my footing again, but a mere ten metres in my stick was spirited away by the current. I could feel the rip tugging at my shins. I pressed my toes into the wet rocks underneath to steady myself, but there was simply no way I could carry on without being swept downstream.

'I can't tell how deep it is out here!' I yelled as I inched my way back to the safety of the bank. Ian said nothing, but simply stared at us. It felt a little like a dare. And, as you know, I can't resist a dare.

'Come on, let's do this,' I said in a voice not unlike that of Jason Statham.

Ian carried on staring, before lifting his arm and waving us on.

'Is that your cock hand, Ian?' we chimed in unison.

We slammed the doors shut. The engine purred into life.

'Whatever happens,' said Liza, brightly, 'we laugh. OK? However bad it is, we just laugh and laugh.'

So we did.

Liza put the car into first, hit the biting point and then stepped hard on the accelerator. We launched into the water. First the tyres were slicked, then coated, then submerged. For a while it felt like they had no traction at all, and that we were merely floating. The water came up to the window on one side, but we kept on laughing – my hand on Liza's hand like an aquatic Thelma and Louise. We laughed all the way until the tyres gained purchase again and we were safe on the other side. Fu Manchu's face broke into a smile as he stared across. Thumbs up. Thumbs up. And on we went.

Me/Liza: Ah, if there's a cure for this

I don't want it [Do you think they use pigs as currency here?]

Don't want it.

If there's a remedy

I'll run from it, from it. [I don't know where I've got it from, but I've got a terrible rash on my arse . . .]

Our go-to guy in Laos was a man called Huang, whose main contribution to the project came in the form of an unfeasibly giant tub of cashew nuts (hereafter known as Huang's nuts). When I say giant – I mean, it was a foot-and-a-half Tupperware tube. You could lose your arm in there. After the endless inedible tangle of street noodles, they were a welcome change – although, as the week wore on, and the more nuts were eaten, the harder it was to get those remaining from the bottom. In the end you were mainly dredging up hard commas of other people's skin and bacteria.

As we ventured further into the jungle, approaching I DON'T KNOW WHERE, the roads became skinny. The hills got steeper and the car grumpier. We made it to the outskirts of a tribal village, whereupon we got stuck in a giant pothole. The engine screamed as we tried to rev our way out of it, but the wheels were embedded in thick red clay. We got out and pushed, but our flip-flops sank deep in the goo. The tyre tracks filled with buffalo piss, with mozzies skating on the surface. In the end we had to get the government guys to help us back to some hardcore where the wheels could get purchase.

We puttered past the village – by the wooden stilt houses, a family of pot-bellied pigs, a cluster of chickens. As we left the clearing, the track became treacherous again and we slowed to a near standstill. Suddenly out of the forest came two men, bare-chested, skin gleaming, carrying baskets full of chicken guts. Both had large, sharp machetes in their hands. Liza was driving. They approached my side of the car. One raised his machete.

'Hello, boys!' roared Liza, who had not yet seen the machetes.

'Oh God, help us,' I muttered, because I had.

The men leaned through the open window into the car. I could smell fresh sweat. I could hear my heartbeat. Time to die. And then, suddenly, the atmosphere changed, moving from proper peril to utter calm. The reason? Well, the two tribes-men had just caught sight of Liza's breasts and were now transfixed by them. Why wouldn't they be? They are, after all, the best breasts in show business.

'So, lads . . . Huang's nuts?' she said breezily, proffering the deep tub of cashews.

Fifteen minutes later, after a lot of gawping, nodding and eating, we finally left. At our next pit-stop the producer saun-tered over to us, somewhat surprised.

P: Gosh, they were friendly!
Me: What do you mean?
P: Well when we came for the recce, they came after us with knives! We had to put our foot down and get out of there . . . didn't think we'd make it!

ᴖᴖ

Much to the disappointment of those around us, we completed the Ho Chi Minh Trail safely. We didn't get blown up. We didn't drown. We didn't get macheted by rogue hill-tribe warriors. After another seven hours of driving, we hit a tarmacked road, and from there we cruised to GOD KNOWS WHERE. I do know that by now we were back in Vietnam, propelled by the promise of a final night's sleep in a proper hotel. It had only been a fortnight and yet it seemed like an eternity since I'd slept on something that didn't look like an exhibit in an episode of *CSI Asia*.

The spa hotel was brand new, with polished slate and waterfalls and stuff. I looked around – paranoid – for someone selling their body or their sister's body or their daughter's body. Nothing. I looked for mould on the wall. Nothing. I listened for the sound of blaring transistors or the scream of chickens. Nothing. Just the faint whisper of pan pipes and the light scrape of muslin on toned thigh as a receptionist walked past. If Kelly Hoppen did prisons, this was the sort of place they'd be. Incarcerated. In taupe.

I read through the list of treatments and chose their Vietnamese Massage, which was, apparently, 'famous'. I was led into a cool room, where I peeled off my clothes and lay on a bed, face down, placing my head in what looked like a large cotton polo mint.

Two hands pressed either side of my spine.

Heaven.

Then four hands.

Interesting.

It didn't matter.

Finally, a happy ending.

Epilogue

I am sitting in my parents' garden. The grass is warm. Parker is snuffling beside me, occasionally shooting me a cloudy, sightless glance.

I have returned from months away travelling in Asia. I am a gyroscope of stress, still adjusting to the sheer luxury of my surroundings – the calm, the cool, the peace.

The kitchen door swings open and Dad stands in the doorway. Behind him hangs a grey plastic mask that looks like something out of *Halloween*. It's a relic of his radiotherapy sessions for yet another bout of cancer – this time in the throat, poor sod. He is looking a little worn, and his voice cracks when he speaks, but amid the agony of recuperation there is an unexpected gain – Dad is joyful again. Finally, after endless dances with death, after sixteen years with the black dog, he wants to live.

He wanders out into the sunshine, brandishing a fitness tracker armband.

Dad: Breaking news – I've done my stats for the year. I've walked exactly 1,056 miles.

Me: Not bad!

Mum: [*from within*] Bert! Careful on those steps! You'll fall, and that'll be your hip shattered again.

Dad: I've never shattered my hip!

Mum: Yes, well, you've shattered everything else. It's just a waiting game.

Spectacles

She follows him outside, Marigolds on. They lean against each other. I don't know who is supporting who. Dad continues . . .

Dad: I've walked 2,790,361 steps in total. Do you know what that averages out at?

Me/Mum: No.

Dad: 7,645 steps per day.

Mum: That's very good.

Me: Very good.

Dad: It's amazing to see how far you've gone, isn't it?

I let the weight of that sentence settle a little before answering.

Me: Yes. Yes, it is.

And then it hits me. This travelling, this endless momentum – it's for them – for my mum and dad, who haven't been able to go anywhere for such a very long time. Finally, after years on Pause, they are moving again. Now, finally, maybe I can stay still.

Me: You should put those on your graph, Dad. On the computer. Just think – by the time you've walked into your study, you'll have walked a couple of dozen more steps.

Dad: Good idea. I'll do that.

Mum: I'm coming with you. I don't trust you not to do yourself a mischief.

And off they go, the pair of them. This weird, two-pieced jigsaw that looks like it couldn't possibly fit together as neatly as it does.

I love you, I think as they disappear from view.
  I think it, but I don't say it.
  I love you.

Acknowledgments

There are an awful lot of people to thank. Because I am my parents' daughter, I have catalogued them for easy reference.

Shit-Kickers
Louise Moore, who *made me do this*, Saint Jess of Leeke, who turned patience into an art form, and Jess Jackson, who now understands that my interpretation of 'media ready' is 'I've managed to put my trousers on the right way round'.

My agent and friend, Debi Allen (gives one hundred per cent, only takes fifteen – bargain).

The Fantastic Four – Charlene, Jess, Lucy and Linda at DAA.

Good Samaritans
Joshua Reznak at Mill Lane Vets, and his wonderful nurse Lindsey, for helping me make one of the hardest decisions of my life.

All the brilliant, battle-worn souls who work in the NHS, with particular shout-outs to the doctors and nurses of Mayday, Treliske and West Cornwall hospitals.

Shelley Silas, who once saved me in the rain.

Game Changers
The teachers who inspired me: Lora Sanson, Clare Boyle, Mrs Green, Carol Schroder, Professor Janet Reibstein, Jan and Dennis Cassidy, Neil Cowley and Paul Lewis.

Those at the BBC and beyond who've mentored me and

gifted me inspiring and life-changing adventures, with special thanks to Janice Hadlow and Charlotte Moore.

Rufus Roubicek and Pauline Law, who gave us our first breaks in telly.

Dawn and Jennifer, who gave us our first proper writing gig.

Kith and Kin

My surrogate families: the Giedroycs and the Szilagyis. I make a point of only hanging out with people with unpronounce-able surnames.

Mary Berry, Paul Hollywood, and the entire *Bake Off* team.

My dearest friends; Emma, Nicola, Sarah, Gemma, Neil, Andy and Michele.

Lord Donald and Master Noggin.

Mel, my partner in crime – specifically crimes against comedy.

And lovely Spanner, for not minding me spending hours at my desk in my pants screaming 'WHHHHHYYYYY'.

But most of all, it's for The Family Perkins, whose story this is – even though they might not recognize it.

Permissions

If you enjoyed

SPECTACLES

you might like to read the following
titles by the same author . . .

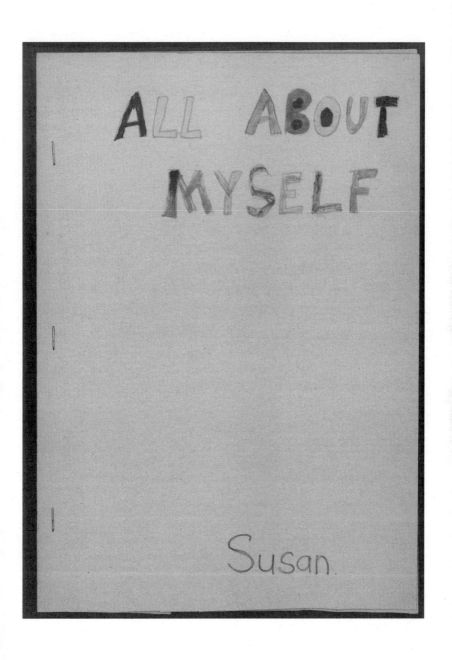

ALL ABOUT
MYSELF

Susan.